BATHING BEAUTY

Royce was nearly as wet as the soggy pile of garments he had thrown on the floor by the time he finished stripping her, and looking down at her, he asked coolly, "Now then, do I have to wash you or are you going to be reasonable about this?"

Scrunched down in the tub, covering her nakedness as best she was able, Pip sent him a murderous look, but common sense told her that she had lost this particular battle. Reluctantly she nodded her wet head and reached for the bar of soap that had fallen into the tub during their struggles.

Not quite trusting her, Royce stared a moment longer, suddenly very conscious of the soft curves she was trying to hide from him. It wasn't his habit to dally with the help, but in this tantalizing and provoking little creature's case, he just might make an exception!

Pip was aware the instant his scrutiny changed and her mouth went dry, the vivid memory of his hard body pressed against hers as they had fought surging through her. She swallowed, suddenly aware of what a very handsome man he was, realizing for the first time how very, very attractive women might find him . . . and how very vulnerable she was.

Also by Shirlee Busbee

SCANDAL BECOMES HER

SURRENDER BECOMES HER

SEDUCTION BECOMES HER

PASSION BECOMES HER

RAPTURE BECOMES HER

Published by Kensington Publishing Corporation

Whisper
To Me
of Love

SHIRLEE BUSBEE

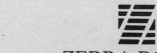

ZEBRA BOOKS
KENSINGTON PUBLISHING CORP.
http://www.kensingtonbooks.com

ZEBRA BOOKS are published by

Kensington Publishing Corp.
119 West 40th Street
New York, NY 10018

All Kensington titles, imprints, and distributed lines are available at
special quantity discounts for bulk purchases for sales promotion,
premiums, fund-raising, educational, or institutional use.

Special book excerpts or customized printings can also be created
to fit specific needs. For details, write or phone the office of the
Kensington Special Sales Manager: Attn. Special Sales Department.
Kensington Publishing Corp., 119 West 40th Street, New York, NY
10018. Phone: 1-800-221-2647.

Zebra and the Z logo Reg. U.S. Pat. & TM Off.

ISBN-13: 978-1-4201-2324-1
ISBN-10: 1-4201-2324-6

First Avon Books Mass-Market Paperback Printing: April 1991
First Zebra Books Mass-Market Paperback Printing: February 2012

10 9 8 7 6 5 4 3 2

Printed in the United States of America

This book is warmly and fondly dedicated to some very nice people who are long overdue for their *book! Here it is, guys, and hope you enjoy it!*

To DON and JOAN BERGER—With this dedication one of Don's greatest fears comes true—he's actually between the pages of one of my books!

To PAUL and PAULA BUSBEE, a pair of my favorite in-laws, as well as just being a sheer delight to me! CHRISTIE, JENNY and TARIN aren't too bad either!

And as always, my really favorite person of all, HOWARD.

PROLOGUE

Villainy at Midnight

ENGLAND, 1796

O villain, villain, smiling, damned villain!
My tables—meet it is I set it down
That one may smile, and smile and be a villain;
At least I'm sure it may be so in Denmark.

SHAKESPEARE, *Hamlet*

Lady Hester Devlin, the Dowager Countess of St. Audries, was dying. Oblivious to the other occupants in the room, she gazed bewilderedly about the sumptuous chamber, the lethargy that was slowly stealing through her slender body making coherent thought difficult. As she lay in solitary splendor in the huge mahogany bed with its silken curtains and fine linen sheets, nothing seemed real to her, not the two men speaking in low tones near the foot of her bed, nor the newborn infant who lay crying softly in the cradle nearby.

Apathetically her eyes continued to scan the spacious room, passing over the delicate chairs in gold velvet, the large mahogany armoire, and the graceful dressing table. It was only when she began to look at the various portraits hanging on the walls that one particular picture caught her interest. A spark suddenly lit her pain-dull green eyes, and a warm smile curved her pale lips as she stared lovingly at the portrait of her late husband, the sixth Earl of St. Audries.

Could it have been only a year ago that he had appeared in her life? Barely eleven months ago that one of the handsomest, most charming lords in all of England had taken her as his bride? Even now it seemed a dream to Hester as she drank in the beloved features of the man in the portrait.

Andrew Devlin, the sixth Earl of St. Audries, had been a particularly handsome man, and the artist had captured his dark, vital looks exactly—the thick, black, curly hair, the proud nose and arrogant chin, as well as the long-lipped, sensuous mouth. All of the Devlins bore a striking and unmistakable resemblance to one another, the exotically almond-shaped gray eyes with their haughtily arched black brows appearing generation after generation without fail. It had been the laughter gleaming in those same gray eyes that had first drawn Hester to the tall, distinguished gentleman the previous spring. She had been just twenty years old, and even though he had been, at forty-five, many years older than she, it had made no difference; she had taken one look at Andrew, Lord Devlin, and fallen deeply in love.

That this handsome, sophisticated member of the aristocracy returned her love seemed almost a dream, and though there were those who said enviously that it was only her great fortune that aroused his interest, when Lord Devlin asked for her hand in marriage, Hester could not bring herself to say no. They had married after an indecently brief courtship, but since Hester had been an orphan and her only guardian had been a fond old uncle, who had been equally bemused by the Earl's desire to marry his niece, no objections had been raised.

Despite the differences in their ages and despite the fact that the Earl of St. Audries's finances had been in desperate straits before his marriage to the Heiress of Bath, as Hester had been called, no one seeing them together could doubt that, incredible though it might seem, theirs was a true love match. That the Earl had lived scandalously, the infuriatingly indifferent object of much shocking gossip and speculation among the rich and powerful, before Hester's advent into his life could not be denied. Nor did he attempt to hide his wild and wicked past from his bride. Perhaps it was his own rueful admission of his less than respectable history that made Hester love him even more.

Hester never doubted his love for her, and that first month of marriage had been thrilling and exciting as she had discovered the erotic pleasures of the flesh in her husband's strong arms. And then there had been *London!* The theater and the balls and the shops had been utterly fascinating to a young woman who had known only the tranquillity of country living and the sedate society of Bath. But Andrew had opened an entire new world for her as he had proudly escorted her about

London, introducing her to the many delights the city had to offer.

But the time she had treasured the most, the time she remembered as being the happiest in her life, was that painfully brief time that they had lived together at St. Audries Hall near the picturesque town of Holford in the lovely Quantock Hills of Somerset. She had enjoyed her honeymoon sojourn in London, but the glorious hills and valleys near her husband's home appealed to something deep inside of her, and she had eagerly looked forward to their life together in this beautiful corner of England.

Those first weeks at St. Audries had been enchanting. During the day, Andrew had acquainted her with the countryside, and together they had made plans for the restorations they would make to the once lovely, but now crumbling, manor home that had housed the Earls of St. Audries for generations. And the nights . . . Even now, months later, her body weakened and racked by pain, a soft smile curved her gentle mouth as she remembered those nights in her husband's arms, not only the passion, but the plans they had made, the children they would have, the improvements to his estate her fortune would allow them to make, the sweet future that awaited them.

A future that had ended with stunning brutality less than six weeks after their marriage. Even now Hester could not believe that Andrew was dead; even now she could not accept the fact that her husband had apparently gone to meet his mistress in a secluded cottage on the estate and that the mistress, furious at his marriage, had driven a knife through his heart before doing the same thing to herself. Hester had been utterly bereft. Not only was the man she had adored and trusted dead, but he had died in such sordid and ugly circumstances. She had not believed his infidelity then, and even now as she lay dying, she still did not believe it.

Andrew had *loved* her! He had admitted to his wicked past and had claimed sincerely that all of his wild living was behind him, and despite overwhelming evidence to the contrary, she still believed that he had spoken sincerely. All through the painful months that had followed his death, Hester had never doubted that there had to be some other explanation for Andrew's having been in that cottage with that woman. There *had* to be! If not, everything Andrew had appeared to be, everything she had loved about him, was a falsehood, and she could not and *would* not accept the knowledge that their entire courtship and marriage had been a sham.

When Andrew's younger brother, Stephen, who had been touring Italy with his wife and young son, hastily returned home to comfort his young, widowed sister-in-law and to inherit the title and estate, Hester had spoken earnestly with him, telling him that she did not believe that Andrew had gone to meet his mistress. Stephen, looking heartbreakingly like Andrew with his black hair and gray eyes, was very kind to her, but Hester could see that he pitied her and believed that his brother had, as the gossips claimed, simply married her for her fortune and had intended to continue with his scandalous life.

Hester had liked Stephen, although she could not say the same for his wife, Lucinda. For some reason, Lucinda greatly resented her and had made no bones about it, making it very clear that *she* was now the Countess of St. Audries and that she could not wait for Hester to remove to the shabby dower house and out of St. Audries Hall. Lucinda had also made it bluntly apparent that she would have preferred that Hester leave St. Audries altogether. "After all," Lucinda had said cruelly, "there is *nothing* here for you, and with your fortune, you can live wherever you choose. *My* husband is now the Earl, and *my* son will one day inherit the title from him." Her hazel eyes full of hostility, she had finished the unpleasant conversation by saying, "And don't be fooled by Stephen's kindness to you. *He* wants you gone from here too—no matter how much he pities you, nor how much he might want to convince you to expend some of your great wealth on this pile of rotten timber and stone he calls home!"

Lucinda's words had cut deeply, but Hester had remained, quietly making plans for the improvements to the dower house and, despite the advice of others, bestowing a large sum of money upon Stephen for the restoration of St. Audries Hall. As she had explained it to him: "It is what your brother would have wanted me to do, and it is in memory of him that I beg you to accept my help."

Reluctantly, for he was a proud young man, Stephen had taken the money, and within days, the work that she and Andrew had dreamed about had begun in earnest. Seeing the many workmen scurrying about what would have been her home had helped her in some indefinable way to get through those first agony-filled weeks after Andrew's sudden death.

The time immediately following her husband's death had passed by in a blur for Hester. Shock upon shock seemed to have been piled onto her slender shoulders and they all contributed to Hester's lack of awareness of the changes within her body. It was not until Andrew had been dead and buried for over a month that Hester concluded that she was pregnant. With a growing sense of awe, she realized that something wonderful would come out of those brief weeks of her marriage—Andrew's child. Possibly his heir.

Needless to say, Lucinda and, to a lesser extent, Stephen were not particularly delighted by the possibility that Hester's child might be a boy. If Andrew's posthumous son was born to Hester, Stephen would lose the title and the ancestral lands and mansion he had assumed were now his. Polite London thought it a delicious situation, and just like Andrew Devlin, even in death, to create a sensation. All through the winter and early spring of 1796, the ton, amidst much malicious speculation (for Lucinda and Stephen were not overly admired), had waited for the birth of Hester's child.

It had not been an easy time for any of the principals. Hester, while delighted with her pregnancy, continued to grieve for her dead husband. Stephen and Lucinda were in a state of great agitation, uncertain whether the home they were living in, a home that was being lavishly and expensively restored to its former grandeur, was actually theirs; and as for the title . . . Were they the Earl and Countess of St. Audries or not?

During these uneasy months, Hester had grown very fond of Stephen. He was unfailingly kind to her and was extremely solicitous of her health and well-being. It was Stephen who undertook on her behalf the overseeing of the complete renovation of the dower house. He had insisted that he be allowed to pay for everything. A wry smile curving his full-lipped mouth, he had said gravely, "It is your money, after all, even if the account has my name on it." But Hester had tossed her blond head and had replied lightly, "Yes, so it is, but if you will remember, I gave it to you . . . to use on the manor house, *not* on your sister-in-law's home!" A twinkle in her green eyes, she had added tartly, "*She* is quite capable of paying her own bills." They had laughed together, and that had been the end of it—the dower house had been as richly and elegantly restored as the main house, and Hester *had* paid her own bills.

As her pregnancy had progressed, Hester had found herself relying more and more on Stephen; he spent a great deal of time with her, willing to run her every errand, and while Hester appreciated this coddling of her, it was also very painful—Stephen looked so very much like Andrew that there were times when he entered a room unexpectedly that her heart would leap in her breast and for one wild moment she would think that miraculously Andrew had come back to her. But then reality would intrude, and the wound of her husband's death would be torn open anew, and she would be dreadfully unhappy for days.

Sometimes Hester fretted that it was Stephen's many kindnesses to her that had aroused Lucinda's antipathy, but when she attempted to discourage his frequent visits, explaining how it might offend his wife, he had merely laughed and brushed her concerns aside, saying negligently, "My wife understands her position well enough. You have nothing to fear from her, and do not distress yourself about her haughty ways—she is merely puffed up with herself for having gone so suddenly and unexpectedly from being the wife of the younger son to possibly being the Countess of St. Audries." If his attitude seemed cold and unfeeling, Hester convinced herself it was only her own imagination, but it still made her wonder about the type of marriage they had.

When Hester was nearly eight months pregnant, it was Stephen who had suggested that she see to the making of her will. Holding her slim hand in his, he had smiled down at her and murmured, "I am certain that you will deliver safely, but should something go wrong . . ." Since she had come to rely on him so heavily these past months, and had never really shaken the apathy that had overtaken her upon Andrew's death, she had obediently followed his instructions and had allowed his attorney to draw up her will. It was an extremely simple document—if she died, her immense fortune passed to her child, and in the tragic event that both she *and* her child should die, the bulk of her wealth would go to "her brother-in-law and *dear* friend, Stephen Devlin."

Her will made, her affairs in the capable hands of her brother-in-law, Hester seemed to lose all interest in life. Her appetite diminished, and day by day she grew paler and weaker. Not even the impending birth of her child aroused her from the debilitating lassitude that had overtaken her. As Stephen had worriedly explained it to the rector, "It is as if her will to live has vanished. All she talks of is Andrew . . . and that soon she hopes they will be together. I am most fearful of her life and that of her child. She is alone in the world, except for me—her uncle died just last month. Poor child! If only there were some way to make her want to live." Stephen had shaken his dark head. "I have done my best, even Lucinda has come to see her, but nothing seems to do any good. If only there was *something* I could do to give her a reason for living. I feel that I have failed her in some way."

The rector, with the familiarity of a long-standing association, had touched him lightly on the arm and murmured soothingly, "Now, now, my son, do not condemn yourself; everyone in the village knows how much you care for your young sister-in-law and how very kind you have been to her during her time of trouble. You have done your best—what happens now is in God's hands."

It had never occurred to Hester that it might be God's will that she would die within weeks of her twenty-first birthday, within hours of giving birth to her daughter. She had only known that in spite of her joy at the prospect of bearing Andrew's child, during these past weeks she had grown weaker and paler with every passing day. She had tried to keep her strength up, eating the nourishing meals prepared by her excellent cook, taking gentle walks in the spring air, and making certain that she got plenty of rest, but still she continued to waste away. And now it appeared that her one great unspoken fear was about to come true—she was dying, leaving her newborn daughter, Morgana, an orphan.

Despairingly she gazed at the small cradle near the side of her bed, wishing desperately that she had the strength to go on living, that this terrible numbness which was spreading inexorably through her body would cease. There was so much love that she would have lavished on her little daughter, so much laughter they would have shared, so much that she wanted to tell Morgana about her father . . . so much that she wanted to protect her small daughter from—especially the lies and gossip about Andrew's death. But there was nothing she could do; she was dying, and she hadn't needed the grave expression on the physician's face, nor the pain in

Stephen's gray eyes, to tell her that the time left to her in this world was to be measured in minutes.

It eased Hester's mind somewhat to know that at least Morgana would be well provided for—Stephen would be her guardian, and Hester had no doubt that he would prove to be a kind and loving one. She worried about Lucinda, though, fearful that Stephen's wife would resent and bully her little daughter and make Morgana's early years unpleasant. But then she reminded herself that Stephen would not allow Lucinda to mistreat Morgana. And as for material things—upon her twenty-first birthday, or upon her marriage, whichever happened first, Morgana would come into the vast fortune that Hester had willed to her, a fortune that Stephen would manage during the years of her minority.

Materially, Morgana would want for nothing, but Hester, having grown up without a mother herself, knew that objects could never take the place of a loving parent, and she was conscious of a great sadness that she would not be there to watch her daughter grow into adulthood.

While Hester did not look forward to dying, if it weren't for Lucinda's unaccountable antipathy toward her, she might have faced her own death more peacefully and with less fear for her infant daughter's future. The situation with Lucinda worried her immensely; she had never quite understood *why* Lucinda had taken such an immediate dislike to her and been unwilling to meet her many overtures of friendship. It had been months before she had learned from the squire's wife that Andrew's name had once been connected with Lucinda's. "It caused quite a bit of talk, I can tell you!" the squire's wife had said forthrightly. "Lucinda had met Stephen first, you see, and they were already engaged when Andrew came on the scene. Andrew seemed quite enchanted with her and paid her marked attention for several weeks before the wedding. She certainly did not discourage his attentions either! I personally think that Lucinda decided she might prefer being a Countess instead of the wife of a penniless younger son—no matter *how* charming and handsome the younger son might be! But nothing came of it, of course." Adding with a kind glance at Hester, "I wouldn't dwell on it, my dear—it happened *years* before the Earl met *you!*"

Even telling herself that Lucinda's dislike might simply be based on the fact that she had been jealous of the woman Andrew had eventually married did not quite explain to Hester why Lucinda acted as she did—after all, she had presumably married the man of her choice, Stephen. So why did she now so obviously resent Andrew's wife? Her open malice had not bothered Hester overmuch in the beginning, and she had assumed that eventually she would be able to dispel Lucinda's animosity and that, in time, they might even become friends. But now that she was dying and the unpleasant realization that Lucinda would be rearing her daughter passed through her brain, Hester was filled with foreboding.

Desperately she tried to rally her fading strength, the driving need to speak to Stephen, to beg him to watch over her daughter, making her more aware of what was happening around her. Rousing herself, she became conscious now of the soft crying of her newborn daughter, and a wave of love flooded through her as she looked at the cradle and caught a glimpse of the infant's surprisingly full head of black hair. Morgana Devlin, her daughter. Andrew's daughter.

Hester's face softened, and it was at that moment that the conversation taking place between the two men at the foot of her bed suddenly impinged upon her brain. Stephen was one of the men, but the other one, she did not recognize, and for the first time, she thought it odd that a stranger should be in her room at all and especially under these circumstances. But it was Stephen's words that made her blood run cold and stilled the urge to call him to her side.

With growing horror and disbelief she listened as Stephen

muttered, "I don't give a damn what you do with the brat—just get rid of it and make certain that she is never found!"

"And how do you intend to explain her disappearance, milord?" the stranger asked. "A great heiress like that doesn't just disappear."

Stephen glanced around the room, mercifully not noticing Hester's increased awareness. "I'll take care of that; don't you worry. No one *needs* to see the infant's body—a pile of rags wrapped in a blanket and placed in the coffin should take care of everything."

"Why don't I just smother the little thing now?" the stranger asked. "It won't be the first time you've called upon me to do murder. . . ."

"Shut up, you fool!" Stephen growled. "I don't have to explain myself to you, but it is simply that even I cavil at infanticide. Just take her away!"

The stranger laughed cynically. "Oh, I understand you very well, indeed. You don't really care if I slay the brat the instant we are out of sight; you are just too squeamish to watch me do it!"

Stephen's face whitened. "I am not paying you a huge sum of gold to listen to your speculations about my motives. Just get rid of the child!"

The man jerked his head in Hester's direction. "And what about her? Are you certain you don't need my help with her?"

For a brief moment, some expression of regret passed across Stephen's handsome face. His voice softer, he murmured, "No. She is dying and there is no reason for anyone to hasten her death. The physician has told me that she will be dead before dawn."

Frighteningly aware that she must act quickly if she was to save her little daughter, Hester gave a small moan as if she were just becoming conscious. When Stephen reached her side, she hid the loathing and fear she felt for him, and said weakly, "Dear Stephen! Are you still keeping watch over me?

How kind of you!" Then, hoping he would detect no change in her voice, she asked, "Is the physician still about? I would like to speak to him."

The two men exchanged glances. "I'm sorry, my dear," Stephen said smoothly, "but he has left. Is there anything that I may do for you?"

Instantly she realized that though they could not be sure that she had overheard them, they were taking no chances. Unless someone entered the room by mistake, Hester knew that she would be allowed to speak to no one. Feverishly she tried to think of some way to outwit them. If not Morgana's life, then Morgana's entire future was at stake, and despite her weakened state, despite the knowledge that she might die at any moment, Hester was determined to find a way to thwart their evil plans.

"My baby!" she cried softly. "Let me hold my baby before I die."

Reluctantly Stephen picked up the infant and placed it in Hester's outstretched arms. Looking at him through tear-filled green eyes, Hester murmured, "Will you give me a few moments alone with her? You will have her a lifetime, while I will have only these precious minutes."

It was apparent that Stephen did not wish to leave her alone, but after a tense moment, he bowed and said quietly, "Of course, my dear. We shall leave you now. I will be in the antechamber—call me if you need me."

Hester nodded weakly, wondering frantically how she could best use the scant time she would have to insure her daughter's safety. Clutching the baby protectively to her breast, she gazed distractedly about the room, seeking some way to save Morgana from the fate the stranger and the man she had thought her dearest friend had planned for the child.

She realized with a sickening lurch of her heart that there was little she could do, but as her gaze fell upon her Bible and the writing paraphernalia that lay on the table next to her bed, a desperate plan occurred to her. Knowing she was helpless to stop them from carrying out their villainous deed unless there was some miraculous interference, she could only hope to leave a record of what she had overheard and some indelible way of identifying the child . . . should Morgana live.

Laying the infant down with almost the last bit of strength she possessed, Hester painfully sat up and reached for the quill and paper. Her movements were clumsy, and she spilled some ink as she laboriously wrote out precisely what she had overheard . . . and what she planned to do. Then, folding the paper, with trembling fingers she quickly hid it in the spine of her Bible.

Nearly exhausted from these efforts, she fell back onto the bed, but driven by the age-old instinct of a mother to protect her young, she gently unwrapped her baby, turning Morgana so that the tiny buttocks were exposed, and reached once again for an object on the table. With a shaking hand, she heated the small seal of the Dowager Countess of St. Audries over the candle flame and then, tears filling her eyes, she murmured, "Dear, *dear* child, forgive me for what I must do to you." And deliberately she branded her daughter on the side of the right buttock.

The baby shrieked, but the distress Morgana suffered in that instant was nothing compared to the agony in her mother's heart for having had to inflict such pain. Tears sliding down her pale cheeks, Hester swiftly examined the brand she had made upon the smooth, tender flesh. Satisfied that it was clearly recognizable as her seal, and fearful that the baby's cry would bring Stephen into the room, she dropped the seal and hastily rewrapped the baby.

She had barely finished when Stephen strode quickly into the room. "What is wrong? I heard the child cry out."

"I think that she is merely hungry and is letting us know

that she wishes to be fed," Hester replied, her voice noticeably weaker than it had been.

Stephen gave Hester a sharp look, his eyes taking in the increased pallor of her skin. "You are worn out!" he scolded, reaching for the baby. "I have already seen to a wet nurse for her. Do not trouble yourself, Hester, I beg you. You will only make yourself worse."

Hating him, yet forced to appear as if all were normal, she smiled faintly, albeit with bitterness, and said cynically, "How can I make myself worse? Dying is the worst that can happen to someone!"

Stephen's eyes closed, and she thought that he might actually be suffering. But then his gray eyes met hers and he said quietly, "No, there are worse things than dying—sometimes *living* is the worst that can happen to you."

Worn out from her exertions, her lifeblood draining away with every second, Hester made no demur as Stephen lifted the baby and placed her in the cradle. Tiredly Hester said, "Will you see to it that my old nanny, Mrs. Gray, is given my Bible? She has been like a mother to me, and I know that she will cherish it and I hope someday give it to Morgana." Her eyes locking with Stephen's, knowing now that everything he said was a lie, she asked softly, "You *do* intend to keep Mrs. Gray on and let her help with Morgana's raising?"

His eyes averted from hers, Stephen said gruffly, "Of course. You know I will do my best by the child."

Wishing she had the strength to call him the liar and villain that he was, Hester glanced away, her eyes widening as they fell upon the stranger who had entered the room behind Stephen. The stranger was about medium height and build, but what caught Hester's gaze was the oddity of his clothes—he was garbed all in black. Even the hat he wore pulled down low over one side of his face was black, and it was only when he turned and the light fell fully upon him that she saw the black patch that covered one eye.

The one-eyed man glanced thoroughly around the room, hardly sparing a look at Hester, who had swiftly closed her eyes as he had moved nearer. A frown marred his forehead when he noticed the spot of freshly spilled ink and saw that the tip of the quill was still damp. Suspicion sharpening his features, he carefully scrutinized every object on the table, his one eye lingering on the small Bible. Almost idly he picked up the Bible and slipped it into the pocket of his shabby greatcoat. "She won't be needing this anymore."

"Will you shut up? She might hear you," Stephen snapped, his eyes on Hester's still form.

The one-eyed man grinned mirthlessly. "She's dead or near enough. She'll never hear anything again. Now let me have the child and I'll be off."

Hester tried frenziedly to rouse herself, tried to rise up and condemn Stephen for what he was about to do, but her body would not obey her; even her eyelids now seemed too heavy to lift. Though she fought gallantly to live, the hemorrhaging that had accompanied Morgana's birth had drained her life away. As the numbing lassitude continued to spread into every part of her body, with death only seconds away, her last thought was of her baby, of the brand she had marked the child with and of the letter she had written. One day, she thought drowsily, one day my baby will regain her rightful place. Morgana *will* survive, and the villainy done this night will not go unpunished!

PART ONE

The Pickpocket

LONDON, ENGLAND
SUMMER, 1815

We know what we are, but know not what we may be.

SHAKESPEARE, *Hamlet*

CHAPTER 1

Newton and Dyot Streets in the Parish of St. Giles were well-known as the headquarters for most of the thieves and pickpockets to be found in London, and so it wasn't surprising that the three inhabitants of a seedy set of rooms in a dilapidated building just a few streets away made their living, such as it was, by thievery. Actually, by the standards of St. Giles Parish, the Fowler siblings lived very well—they had a roof over their heads and seldom went hungry—unlike the majority of those unfortunate wretches who inhabited this part of London. Not for the Fowler family the indignity of sleeping in filthy gutters at the mercy of every cutthroat around—and there were many—nor for them the gin-sodden relief to be found at the various rough taverns that abounded in the area, or the dangers that lurked in every dark alley. Whores, beggars, thieves, and murderers abounded in the narrow, mean streets of St. Giles, but the Fowlers gave it little thought. This was home to them; they knew every twisted street, every squalid gin house, every master criminal in their parish . . . and the ones to avoid.

Which wasn't to say that the Fowlers lived a charmed life; they suffered much of the same misery and had the same fears as most of their fellow miscreants, although there were those envious souls who would swear that Jacko Fowler, at twenty-five, the eldest of the trio, certainly had been smiled upon by Lady Luck. Hadn't he outsmarted and escaped the watch on occasions too numerous to mention? And when finally caught that one disastrous time, hadn't he escaped from the very steps of Newgate? Ah, Jacko was a rum cove, he was! And handsome too, the, er, ladies of the parish agreed, with his brown, wavy hair and dancing blue eyes.

Not that Ben, three years younger than Jacko, was any less clever in his escapades or his attractiveness; it was merely that Jacko was the obvious leader of the trio and possessed a brazen charm that overshadowed Ben's quiet intensity. As for Pip, well, the youngest Fowler, beyond being an outrageous scamp, ever ready with a sharp tongue or an equally keen blade, was considered, at nineteen, too young to have yet made a mark in the world.

The previous summer had been very good for the Fowlers. With the long war with France finally over and Napoleon safely interned on Elba, England had been in a festive mood, and scores of famous visitors had flocked to London—the Czar of Russia and his sister, the Grand Duchess Catherine of Oldenburg, King Frederick of Prussia, and General Blücher, to name just a few of the notables who had graced London that summer of 1814. Not only had London been filled with the victorious heroes of the seemingly interminable war with Napoleon, but there had been a surfeit of fetes and amusements for the public—celebrations had been held in Hyde Park and Green Park with balloon ascents and grand fireworks, amusements that had seen the Fowlers very busy as they had ambled through the excited crowds, their nimble fingers filching a gold pocket watch here, a silken handkerchief there, and whatever other valuable came their way. Oh, it had been a grand summer!

But the year of 1815 was not proving to be as profitable, nor as pleasant, as the past year for the Fowlers. In January they had suffered a most grievous personal tragedy; their mother, Jane Fowler, had died from the consumption that had racked her slender body for as long as her three children could remember. They had been stunned, unable to believe that Jane, who had been the guiding light of their universe, was gone. Gamely, but with far less enthusiasm, they had carried on with their lives, trying to keep the precepts she had drilled into them alive, and coping as best as they were able with the pain of their loss. It wasn't easy, and they viewed the future rather gloomily. Certainly with Napoleon's escape from Elba on the twenty-sixth of February and the reopening of hostilities with France, there was little for anyone to celebrate. The Fowlers' difficulties, however, had nothing to do with Napoleon or the imminent resumption of war on the continent. . . .

"Bloody eyes, Jacko! We're no 'ousebreakers! We do right well enough as it is! Just yesterday, didn't Pip draw a rare thimble from the swell's pit? Why the 'ell do you want to risk our bloody necks this way?" Ben growled, the bright blue eyes that he and Jacko had inherited from their mother snapping with anger.

"Mum wouldn't like it, Jacko," Pip muttered. "You know she wouldn't."

"God strike me blind!" Jacko burst out impatiently. "Do you think Oy'm 'appy about this? Bloody 'ell!"

Pip and Ben exchanged looks, the flickering light from the single candle in the middle of the table at which they sat dancing over their intent faces. Softly Ben spoke the thought uppermost in their minds. "It's the single-peeper, ain't it? 'e's the reason, ain't 'e?"

Jacko looked away, his handsome face tight and strained. "Aye, 'e's the reason," he admitted unhappily. "Told me that if we didn't start bringing 'im more and better goods, we'd 'ave to find ourselves another fencing ken . . . and a different dimber-damber."

A somber silence fell. While the Fowlers operated primarily on their own, they were, as were most of the thieves in St. Giles, part of a larger gang, or knot, as they referred to it, with a definite hierarchy among its members and with certain safe places known only to them where they could secrete their stolen goods. And if their dimber-damber, the leader of their knot, decided he was dissatisfied with them and would no longer allow them to store their ill-gotten gains at the knot's fencing ken, or safe house, they were in desperate straits indeed. No one survived in St. Giles without the help of the other thieves of his particular knot. And the likelihood of finding another knot willing to accept them after they had been cast out of their present gang was not very great.

Moodily Ben said, "May'ap 'tis time we left St. Giles—oy've always fancied being a prigger of prancers, and you're right 'andy with a pair of barking irons—wot say you to being a bloody 'ighwayman? Pip could 'ire on as an ostler at one of the inns and could tip us to the rich 'uns."

Jacko shook his head slowly, but it was Pip who spoke up, saying sharply, "Listen to us! Mother hasn't been dead six months and we're already forgetting the things she taught us. If she could hear the way we're speaking here tonight, she wouldn't hesitate to box all our ears."

Jacko and Ben both looked somewhat shamefaced, and without one hint of his former manner of speech, Jacko said in refined accents that would have done a young lordling proud, "Forgive me! It is just that it is very difficult to live the dual roles that Mother demanded of us. And with her gone . . ." There was a painful silence before Jacko continued, "Without her here to remind us, it is sometimes easier merely to forget all the polite manners she insisted we learn."

Moodily Ben added, "And what good does it do us? Will our fine manners and polite speech get us out of St. Giles? Will it increase our fortunes? Elevate our standing? Does our ability to read and write make life any easier for us? And because we know the proper way to eat and act, do you think it will impress our neighbors?" Ben gave a bitter laugh. "If they could hear us talking now, we would be met with suspicion and mistrust . . . as well as derision for aping the manners of the gentry! Sometimes I wish Mother had forgotten her past and had let us grow up like anyone else in St. Giles!"

Jane Fowler had made no secret of the fact that she had been the illegitimate daughter of an amiable country squire and that she had been raised in the squire's household. She had grown up with all the advantages of a comfortably situated and respectable family. How or why she ended up a whore in one of London's most notorious districts was not a subject she ever discussed with her children. Jacko and Ben could vaguely remember a time when they had lived in a fine house with elegant furnishings and servants, but Pip's earliest memories had been of the grubby little rooms where they now sat.

But despite their sordid circumstances, Jane never let her children forget her early background, insisting upon teaching them to read and write and to speak properly—something they only did in the privacy of their rooms. The rest of the time they adopted the speech and mannerisms of the inhabitants of St. Giles.

While agreeing that their fine manners and speech seemed to gain them little, Pip glanced at Jacko's set features and Ben's unhappy countenance, and said slowly, "It will do us little to complain about something we cannot change. Mother *did* teach us to be different, for whatever reasons, and now that she is no longer here to guide us, I think what we do with our future is up to us."

"Oh, fine words!" Ben said with a sneer. "Our bloody future will be hanging from Tyburn!"

Privately Pip might agree with Ben's assessment of their situation, and the Lord knew it was how many of their associates ended their lives, but unwilling to contemplate that particular fate, the youngest Fowler said in a rush, "What about leaving St. Giles?" Staring earnestly into Jacko's face, Pip added, "You wanted a farm; what is to stop us from pursuing that plan? Instead of becoming housebreakers or

highwaymen, why can't we become farmers, as you originally wanted us to do?"

Jacko closed his eyes in pain and muttered wretchedly,
"Because the dimber-damber won't let me."

An appalled silence met his words. "Won't let you?" Pip
repeated dumbly. "What do you mean?"

Rubbing his hand wearily over his face, Jacko replied dully,
"I thought of us leaving a week after Mother . . ." His throat
closed up painfully, and while he struggled to regain his composure, Pip and Ben both felt the sting of tears at the corners
of their eyes, Jane's death still a distressful subject for her children. Bringing his emotions under control, Jacko finally said
dispiritedly, "I hadn't quite made up my mind how to accomplish our leaving here or where we would go when I accidentally k-k-killed that gentleman. The dimber-damber had been
with me when it happened, and it was just luck that the watch
didn't nab him too; at least I think it was luck. . . . I had talked
to him the previous day about us leaving the knot and St. Giles.
I told him that we wanted to turn respectable." Jacko swallowed painfully, not looking at either of the other two. "He
laughed at me at first. Then when he saw that I was serious,
he grew quite angry and swore that *no one* left his knot alive.
Said we owed him our loyalty, that we owed him for seeing to
it that Mother hadn't had to be a whore up until the day she
died, that we owed him for every piece of bread we ate and
for the very roof over our heads. I thought that he was just
raving and that once he considered it, he wouldn't be so set
against our leaving."

Ben gave a bitter laugh. "Oh, did you? When we are his
best thieves? When we three bring him more fancy trinkets
than just about all the others of the knot combined? You
didn't think he might object? Even *I* know better than that!
Jesus! You should never have told him what you had in mind!
We should have just disappeared."

Miserably Jacko agreed. "I know that now, but I didn't

then! He and Mother seemed to share a special relationship, and I guess that I thought he'd be glad to see her children well out of it. I was wrong." His voice growing thick, Jacko continued, "I saw him a few days after the killing and he told me to put all thoughts of leaving St. Giles out of my mind, that if I tried to leave, he would inform the watch on me and lead them to me. He swore that if I defied him and tried to run, he'd find me, no matter where I went, and set the runners on me. I *cannot* disobey him or my life is forfeit!"

With fear and anger in their eyes, Pip and Ben stared at their oldest brother. Neither doubted the truth of his words, and neither doubted that if the dimber-damber had sworn to find Jacko, that he would. The dimber-damber had tentacles everywhere; there was not one corner of England that escaped his notice, and no matter where Jacko ran to, eventually the dimber-damber would have word of him and his fate would be sealed.

Giving his shoulders a shake, Ben said with forced cheer, "Well, then, I guess we shall become housebreakers, as he wants."

"And bloody damn good ones!" Pip chimed in fiercely.

"Don't be fools!" Jacko said sharply. "He may have me in his grasp, but there is no reason for both of you to sacrifice your lives for me. There is nothing to stop *you* escaping from this miserable existence."

Pip and Ben exchanged glances, then almost in unison they turned to stare at their eldest brother, the stubborn expression on both young faces almost identical. Even before the words were spoken, Jacko knew what they would be. "We're not leaving you!" Ben declared forthrightly. "Do you really think that Pip and me could ever find any peace or happiness knowing you were caught in the toils of the dimber-damber?"

Eyes bright with deep emotion, Pip said vehemently, "We're all in this together and we won't be separated! We'll either flee this ugly hovel together or we'll all dance at the end of a rope!"

Jacko laughed slightly, his set features relaxing. He was sincere in his offer and he would have done everything within his power to help the others escape, but he would not have been honest with himself if he denied the feeling of relief that swept through him at their words. Sitting up straighter in his chair, he sent the two people he loved most in the world a keen glance. "It is decided then? We will become house-breakers?"

Pip and Ben shrugged their shoulders. "We really don't have any other choice, do we?" Ben said.

Flatly, Jacko agreed. "No. The dimber-damber has made sure of that!"

"How soon do you think that he intends for us to start our new endeavor?" Pip asked curiously.

"Within the week, I would suspect. There's that sparring match tomorrow at Fives Court, and we're to work the crowd. . . . I'll probably see him that evening to turn over whatever trinkets we've managed to steal."

Pip stretched and muttered, "I suppose once we get a bit of experience behind us, we'll wonder why we ever had any reservations about becoming housebreakers."

Ben gave the dark, curly head an affectionate caress. "Oh, aye, no doubt you are right. We've become so expert at picking pockets that there is no excitement left—that sparring match to-morrow will probably be rather boring to us, now that we've decided to turn our hands at a different type of crime."

Knowing the daredevil streak in both of his younger siblings, Jacko frowned. "I wouldn't get too cocky if I were you two—we're very good at what we do, but there is also a pos-sibility of a mistake."

Pip hooted with laughter. "A mistake? Me, make a mis-take? And at a sparring match, at that? You know I find them boring, so I'll be much more inclined to concentrate on business—picking pockets for our dear, *dear* dimber-damber. The bloody bastard!"

In one of the grand homes that graced Hanover Square, two gentlemen were enjoying a glass of port, having just finished an excellent meal of spring veal and tender peas. They were sitting in an elegantly appointed room, straw-colored silk-hung walls contrasting nicely with the jewel tones of the ruby- and sapphire-hued Oriental rug that lay upon the floor. Tall, narrow windows that overlooked the square were draped in an exquisite ruby velvet, while overhead the many long tapers of a multifaceted crystal chandelier bathed the spacious room in golden light.

His long legs stretched out comfortably in front of him, Royce Manchester was sprawled in a high-backed chair near the flames that danced on the hearth of a marble-fronted fireplace. Despite the fact that it was early June, the day had been a chilly one, and Royce was glad of the warmth of the fire. Taking a sip of his port, he remarked, "I trust that the weather will be less inclement tomorrow, when we attend that damned sparring match you insisted I *must* see. Since neither of the pugilists are particularly noted for their skill, I suspect that we shall find it rather boring."

Zachary Seymour, Royce's young cousin, merely grinned, knowing full well that Royce *never* allowed himself to become bored. If the match proved to be as dull as Royce feared, Zachary was quite certain that his much-admired cousin would find a way to salvage the afternoon.

It would have been obvious to even the most casual observer that the two men were closely related, in spite of the differences in their ages and coloring. At thirty-three, Royce was at the peak of his physical prowess, his tall body lean and fit, with well-defined, powerful muscles, while Zachary, barely twenty years old, was still a stripling, his shoulders not quite as broad, his movements still sometimes revealing the gawky grace of youth. Zachary might not yet have achieved Royce's powerful build, but he had already surpassed his cousin's six-foot-three-inch height by half an inch—much to his delight and Royce's feigned disgust.

But it wasn't only their tall, broad-shouldered bodies that were similar; each possessed the same compelling topaz-colored eyes and arrogantly slashed black brows. And if Royce's thick, tawny hair was in direct contrast to Zachary's black locks, there were still obvious resemblances in their straight noses and strongly molded chins. In ten years time, except for his black hair, Zachary would look very much like his cousin.

His grin widening just a bit, Zachary murmured, "You're probably right, but since we have nothing else planned, it won't harm us to see how handy they are with their fives." Sending Royce a sly look, he added innocently, "Of course, if the weather remains wet and cold, I could go by myself—I realize that as you grow older, you are more affected by the changes in temperature."

At Royce's startled look of outrage, Zachary burst out laughing, his dark young face alight with mirth at having slipped under his cousin's guard. "Oh, Royce, if you could just see the expression on your face."

"I'm pleased that my advancing years give you such delight. Considering that I am such a doddering old man, I am surprised that you consented to come to England with me!"

"Well, at your age, I couldn't very well let you come alone, could I?"

Royce's shout of laughter greeted Zachary's words. "You ungrateful young devil! I *should* have left you in Louisiana with Dominic and your sister, Melissa! I may be on the brink of my grave when viewed from the eyes of an infant, but at least with me you are spared the billing and cooing of our newlyweds!"

"Infant?" Zachary replied, a little stung, then seeing the teasing glint in Royce's eyes, he grinned a bit shamefacedly. But unwilling to retire from the field defeated, he narrowed his eyes and added dulcetly, "I suppose at your mature age, I do seem an infant."

Royce was not to be drawn, however, and he merely grinned. "Sometimes, my dear cousin, you do indeed!"

Zachary pulled a face, but decided not to pursue this particular line of conversation further. While Royce was never cruel to those he had affection for, he could be quite blunt in his speech. Thinking over several escapades that he had partaken of in the past few weeks since their arrival in the middle of May in England, Zachary wisely changed the subject.

Getting up from his own chair by the fire, Zachary crossed the room to pour himself another glass of port from a crystal decanter. His glass refilled, he turned to his cousin. "Shall I pour you another while I am up?"

"Why not? The night is still young, and it will not shock the servants if their *backwoods* American employer has to be put to bed with his boots on!"

Despite his words, there was nothing "backwoods" about either Royce or Zachary; from the intricate folds of their starched white cravats to the mirror shine of their boots, both men were as elegantly attired as any aristocratic English gentleman. But Zachary was uneasily aware of a caustic note in Royce's voice that should not have been there.

Returning to his seat by the fire after filling Royce's glass, Zachary asked casually, "Have you seen Lord Devlin recently?"

Royce sent him a sardonic glance. "Now, I wonder why you asked that particular question."

"Because the only time you get that particular note in your

voice is when Lord Devlin has said or done something to annoy you."

Royce started to deny it, but then thought better of it. "You're perfectly correct. I was at White's earlier today, and as I was on the point of leaving, Lord Devlin and a few of his cronies arrived. That damned fop wrinkled his haughty nose at me as if he smelled the barnyard and murmured just loud enough so that I could hear, 'I say, it seems as if they let *anyone* join White's these days.' I'll tell you, Zack, I was within ames-ace of calling him out then and there, but George Ponteby was with me and he made certain we left there damned fast."

Zachary grinned at him. "Well, you shouldn't be so surprised—it isn't as if you've gone out of your way to overcome the Earl's dislike of us these past few weeks."

An expression of injured innocence on his handsome face, Royce asked ingenuously, "And what, I ask you, did I ever do to arouse his antipathy in the first place?"

Zachary settled back in his chair, plainly enjoying himself. "Well, in the first place, I don't think that you did anything. Lord Stephen Devlin just doesn't like Americans, especially ones with manners as good or better than his own, and— here's the most telling point—ones who are nearly as wealthy as he is."

"You see! His dislike is entirely irrational!" Royce averred piously, a wicked twinkle in the amber gold eyes at direct variance with his tone of voice.

"Not entirely irrational! The fact that you are an impeccably well-mannered, disgustingly wealthy American with many friends in the best social circles in England may have annoyed him at first, especially since, despite his own aristocratic birth and fortune, he is only tolerated by those same people. But I think that the cause of his *real* animosity toward you may have occurred during your last trip to England, don't you?"

Royce innocently raised his eyebrows. "Why, whatever do you mean? Your new brother-in-law was with me during that trip to England four years ago, and I think if you will ask him, he will tell you that we both behaved with *flawless* decorum."

Zachary nearly choked with laughter at Royce's words. Dominic Slade had not discussed his previous trip to London with Zachary in any great detail, but from the few comments that Dominic *had* dropped, Zachary strongly suspected that there were *several* incidents that were considerably less than decorous! "Of course, you are right," Zachary agreed. "His actions are utterly irrational." Giving his cousin a mocking glance, he murmured, "After all, what did you ever do to him?"

Royce smiled seraphically, staring with great interest at the ruby liquor in his glass.

"I mean, why should the man be upset because four years ago you seduced away his mistress right from under his nose? At least, that's what Dominic intimated one night to me. And of course, no one would be annoyed at losing to you, I believe it was, several thousand pounds playing piquet? *That* happened a scant week after our arrival here, if my memory serves me correctly. Nor would it bother any normal man, after boasting that they owned the finest pair of blooded horses in England, to be soundly bested by you in a race wagered on by half the ton, a race which, let me remind you, occurred just last Wednesday. No. No. You've done nothing to annoy the man at all."

Looking inordinately pleased with himself, Royce said ruminatively, "Well, you know, I would never have singled him out like that if he hadn't annoyed me so much by acting as if I were dirt under his feet, and if he hadn't been so determined to prove that *he* was superior to a mere 'colonial.' Hell, we haven't been an English colony for over forty years! And remember—I wasn't the one who challenged him either to the horse race or that damned tedious game of piquet. He left me no choice each time but to accept the gauntlet he'd thrown down."

"And four years ago, when you stole his mistress?" Zachary inquired with a grin. "Did he challenge you about her, too?"

"Well, no," Royce admitted readily. "But I ask you, could I leave a high-flyer like the lovely Miranda in the care of a skin-fisted old rake like Devlin?"

"Since I have never met the lovely Miranda, I can't answer your question," Zachary replied lightly. "But I think you will agree that the Earl of St. Audries does have *some* foundation for his aversion to your company."

Royce's handsome mouth twisted ruefully. "You know it's the damnedest thing, Zack! I usually don't go out of my way to make enemies, but there is something about Devlin that sets my teeth on edge—and unfortunately, it appears that I have the same effect upon him!"

"Perhaps it's just that the Devlins don't like Americans," Zachary said gloomily, thinking of his own clashes with Julian Devlin, the Earl's heir and only child.

"Could be," Royce agreed quietly. "But in your case and Julian's, I think your disagreements have come about because you both are too much alike!"

"Alike?" Zachary growled with displeasure. "We are nothing alike! How can you possibly compare me with that vain, arrogant puppy?"

Royce smiled at Zachary's words. "Puppy" could very well apply to both Julian Devlin and Zachary Seymour, and while Royce was certain that neither young man was as vain as the other claimed, they were both occasionally arrogant. Despite the animosity between himself and the Earl, Royce actually liked young Devlin, or at least he had seen nothing these past weeks to make him change his initial favorable impression of the young man.

Giving Zachary a lazy smile, Royce said lightly, "Despite

your protests, I'll wager that you and young Devlin will be close cronies once you both realize how much you have in common."

At Zachary's outraged expression, Royce laughed, and rising lithely to his feet, he murmured, "I'll leave you to mull that over while I go in search of far more amiable company— prettier, too!"

A knowing look crossed Zachary's face. "The fair Della?"

"Naturally!"

Driving his pair of high-stepping horses through the London traffic toward the comfortable little house that he had procured for his new mistress, Della Camden, Royce decided that this trip to London was really an excellent experience for his young cousin. Except for a few race meets in Virginia, Zachary hadn't been more than ten miles away from Willowglen, the plantation near Baton Rouge in Louisiana where he and his sister, Melissa, had been born. It was past time that Zachary gained a little "town bronze," and London was certainly the place for *that!*

Royce smiled to himself, thinking of the changes that had occurred in Zachary's life these past months since Dominic Slade had married Melissa. Upon Melissa's marriage to Dominic, who was one of Royce's closest friends, Zachary and Melissa had come into the fortune that had been placed in trust for them by their grandfather. Now, instead of a dilapidated house and overgrown acres, Zachary was the proud possessor of a completely refurbished home, and his lands were thriving under the expert guidance of a competent overseer; for the first time in his life, Zachary had leisure time *and* a sizable fortune resting comfortably in the bank!

Royce almost envied Zachary the early hardships he had endured. Being the oldest child of doting, indulgent, and extremely wealthy parents, Royce had never wanted for anything in his life. When he had reached his majority and might have been expected to strike out on his own, he had been saved, or perhaps cursed, by the providential death of his paternal grandmother, who had left him the bulk of her substantial estate. Yet despite all the good fortune that fate had so generously bestowed upon him, Royce remained curiously indifferent to the fact that he had been blessed with not only a tall, powerful body, handsome face, and an easy charm, but also with wealth and position.

Since he was generally an even-tempered man, some people made the mistake of dismissing him as an indolent dilettante, overlooking the keen intelligence that was constantly at work behind deceptively sleepy tiger eyes. For all his amiability, Royce Manchester could be a dangerous enemy, and if Lord Devlin was not careful, he would discover that not only did Royce possess tiger eyes, but also the tiger's lethal bite. . . .

Narrowly avoiding the overloaded farm cart that suddenly lumbered in his path, Royce smothered a curse, wishing he had recalled the crowded London streets *before* he had suggested this trip to Zachary.

Once word of the Treaty of Ghent, which had ended the War of 1812, had reached Louisiana in the early days of 1815, Royce, bored and restless for a change of scenery, had immediately written to George Ponteby, his third cousin on his father's side, in London. He told him that he would be coming to England just as soon as he could arrange passage, and would George also see about letting a suitable residence for him? The Treaty of Ghent ended the ridiculous war between the United States and England, even though word of its passage had not reached America in time to stop the terrible slaughter of the British by the Americans at the battle of New Orleans in January of 1815. But with the war at last over, the sea lanes between the two countries were now open again, and Royce had been eager to see London and his many friends there.

While it was true that boredom and restlessness had played a large part in his decision to visit England, Dominic's marriage to Melissa had also been a factor in his need to leave Louisiana. Not that Royce begrudged them their connubial bliss; their marriage merely brought home to him the fact that it was time he should think about finding himself a wife and setting up his own nursery.

As with everything, Royce had very definite ideas about what he wanted, and there were several requirements he had in mind when he began his search for a wife: Her family background must be impeccable—no wastrels or unsavory cads would be found lurking in the closet. She would have to be of good character, well mannered and biddable! She must, of course, be attractive, but he didn't care if she was a raving beauty, just as long as she wouldn't frighten the children. He wanted a sensible woman, one who knew what was expected of her and who would be content with keeping his home and bearing his children. A cynical smile curved his mouth. And one who wouldn't interfere in his extremely comfortable life too much!

Having arrived at his destination, Royce immediately left off contemplating the virtues of his as-yet-unknown bride, and with an insistent heat suddenly springing up in his loins, he entered Della's discreet little house. Having heard the front door open and close, Annie, Della's maid, appeared from the back of the house, and crossing the small, tasteful foyer, she took Royce's curly-brimmed beaver hat from him. "Miss Della is still upstairs. Shall I tell her you are here?"

Royce shook his head. "No, that won't be necessary."

He was on the point of going upstairs when Della appeared at the top of the staircase. At the sight of his handsome face and tall, muscular body, a welcoming smile lit her lovely face. "Royce!" she exclaimed gaily. "I didn't expect you this evening."

Della Camden was a tall, voluptuous brunette, and except for the fact that the others had all been blond, she resembled any one of the dozen or so women he'd had in his keeping from time to time since he turned eighteen. Watching her approach, Royce's eyes wandered appreciatively over the lush charms displayed by the low-cut amber satin gown she was wearing. Her full white breasts seemed to spill out of the black-lace-edged bodice, and remembering the taste of that soft flesh in his mouth, Royce felt a tingle of anticipation run through him. Reaching the bottom stair, she put out her hands, and kissing them, Royce murmured, "But where else would I be? Having had the good fortune to snaffle you out from under the noses of several persistent rivals, do you think that now I shall neglect you?"

Her brown eyes twinkled and she answered slyly, "And is *that* the only reason you've come to call? Fear of your former rivals?"

Royce laughed and pulled her into his arms. Staring down into the beautiful face artfully framed by dusky ringlets, Royce brushed his mouth teasingly against her full, pouting mouth and said huskily, "Fear never entered into it—from the moment I laid eyes on you, there was never any doubt in my mind that you would soon be in my keeping! And as for my reasons for calling . . ." He kissed her with sensual expertise, his lips pressing warmly against hers, his tongue seeking and meeting hers in an age-old duel.

Della was pliant and breathless when he finally lifted his mouth from hers. Dropping a tantalizingly brief kiss on her bosom, he lowered his hands to her hips and pulled her firmly against him, making her vividly aware of how very aroused their kiss had made him. Brushing his lips against her ear, he muttered, "Any other questions, sweetheart?"

"God, no!" Della admitted candidly, eagerly pressing her warm body against him. It had been quite a feather in her cap to have caught his interest and she had angled shamelessly for his attention, the other rivals for her charms paling beside Royce's forceful personality and handsome face and form. Fingers tangling in the thick, tawny locks, she looked up into his dark, chiseled features and confessed, "There has never been anyone like you in my bed!"

A frankly carnal cast to his mouth, Royce's hands caressed her buttocks and he murmured, "Well, then, I suppose it is up to me to keep you thinking that way, isn't it?"

Sweeping her up into his arms, he effortlessly carried her swiftly up the stairs to her room. Slamming the door shut with his booted heel, his mouth captured hers, and slowly lowering her, he let her yielding body slide sensually against his.

On fire for him, Della frantically tore at his clothing, fairly purring when her seeking hands touched the warm, hard flesh of his naked chest. But he denied her further exploration. Catching both of her hands, he pulled them behind her back and held them prisoner in one of his hands; with the other, he proceeded to make short work of the frail barrier that kept her sweet breasts from him. One deft tug and the full, pink-tipped mounds were freed for him to touch and taste.

Della groaned with pleasure when his mouth closed over the aching tip and helplessly she pushed herself against him, nearly melting with the hot desire that coursed through her. Her lower body was pressed tightly next to his, and through their clothing she could feel the rigid power of his arousal. With her arms held prisoner behind her and his mouth wreaking passionate havoc on her breasts, she could only twist in erotic abandon in his embrace, the greedy hunger for his possession growing with every passing moment.

As he felt her wild writhing, a tight smile crossed Royce's face. "Easy, easy, sweetheart," he murmured thickly against her breast. "We have the entire night to pleasure each other."

Her eyes glittering with the passion he had aroused, the full mouth red from his kisses, Della shook her head. "No!" she said thickly. "I want you! *Now!*"

The handsome face suddenly hard with desire, Royce muttered, "Very well then—anything to please a lady!"

He released her, his own hands sliding warmly up under

her gown to caress and fondle the waiting warmth he found between her legs. Deliberately he aroused her further, his fingers teasing and preparing her even as she undid his breeches and his swollen manhood sprang free. He allowed her to caress his hard length but for a moment, and then, with a low growl, he lifted her and, with her skirts bunched up around her waist, her legs wrapping hungrily around his hips, in one powerful thrust, he entered her.

Della moaned excitedly as she felt herself impaled upon the magnificent size of him and eagerly she rode him, her head thrown back in mindless rapture. His shoulders braced against the door, his hands cupping her buttocks, Royce joined her in the eager race for ecstasy, his lean body slamming again and again into hers as he drove them both toward the sweet release they sought. Della found it first, a soft scream escaping from her as her body convulsed around him and his mouth crushed against hers, but a moment later Royce, too, reached that scarlet oblivion.

CHAPTER 2

The day of the sparring match dawned clear and sunny and, for London at this time of year, quite pleasant. But for Pip, lying on the thin pallet and staring up at the grubby ceiling overhead, the weather held absolutely no interest whatsoever. The implications of last night's conversation were far more important than whether or not the sun was shining!

Pip wondered grimly what the future would hold for the

Fowlers. They were not yet in utterly desperate straits, but knowing that the dimber-damber held the power of Jacko's life or death in his hands made their situation rather bleak. It was only a matter of time until the dimber-damber demanded something of them that they were not willing to give. . . . Pip swallowed painfully, dismally positive that forcing them to become housebreakers was only the first step in his nasty plans for them and that his ultimate goal was possession of *her!*

Despite the male garb she wore and despite the fact that she had been dressed and had been treated like a boy from the time she had been barely four years old, Pip was actually a girl. In the beginning she had not understood why Jane had insisted she dress as her older brothers did. It was only as she grew older and became aware of what went on about her that she understood the wisdom of her mother's strange decision—the hopeless faces of the pitifully young whores who roamed about the mean streets of St. Giles made appallingly clear to Pip the tawdry future that her mother was trying to help her avoid.

A shiver suddenly shook her slender frame as she imagined what her fate would have been if Jane had not taken steps to postpone it. And unless fate intervened *soon,* she feared that it would not be long before the dimber-damber forced her into becoming a harlot. Just as he had always wanted, she thought grimly, remembering the ugly argument she had overheard a long time ago . . .

She had been almost ten years old and had been sleeping in her mother's bed, recovering from a particularly severe earache, when she had been awakened by loud voices. Confused and still half-asleep, she had listened foggily to the angry words between Jane and the dimber-damber, and only belatedly had she realized that *she* was the bone of contention between them.

"I'll not have it! And before I'll let you set her feet on that path, I'll put myself back on the streets!" Jane's voice had been full of rage and grim determination.

"Don't be more of a fool than you have been all of your life!" the dimber-damber had shot back furiously. "Listen to me, Jane, it'll be a fortune for us! Now, I'm a reasonable man; I understood your feelings when she was younger and why you were against the idea at that time, but she's ten years old now! This nobleman will pay us a princely sum to be the one to take her virginity—nearly as much as he would have when she was five. I tell you that you're daft to say no."

"My God, Rufus! She is a child!" Jane had answered. "Let her be! You don't need another whore—you have a whole stable full of them. Please, if you bear me any affection at all, leave her alone."

"A child?" Rufus had repeated scornfully. "I have several *experienced* little darlings in my string now who are younger than she is! And if she's a child, whose fault is that? I told you when I brought her to you not to get any ideas. She's *mine,* and by God, I'll do with her what I want!"

Until that moment, Pip had never known that the dimber-damber had a real name, but even that knowledge was pushed aside by the horror that coursed through her as she realized precisely what the dimber-damber had in store for her. She didn't understand all of the ramifications of the conversation, but what she had heard was enough to wring a small moan of distress from her.

Jane must have heard the tiny sound she made, because a moment later, Pip heard Jane say, "Hush! She has awakened. We'll talk about it later—but my mind is made up, and it was no idle threat that I made. Unless you want to see me on the streets again, forget about her!"

The dimber-damber and Jane must have discussed the situation further, but though Pip was constantly on the alert, she never again gained any clue from their actions. She was able to surmise, simply by the fact that she had not been forced into prostitution, that Jane must have won the argument—and without having to resort to becoming a streetwalker again.

From that day onward, Pip was more conscious of the sordid ugliness around her than she ever had been before, more aware of the appalling youth of some of the whores and harlots she had formerly ignored, more aware of what a despicable fate lay just in wait for her. But Jane had been there. And now the one person who could protect her from the dimber-damber's monstrous plans was dead!

The future certainly looked bleak to Pip this bright, sunny morning. Instinctively she knew that it would not be much longer before the dimber-damber made his intentions for her clear, and whether he wanted her as his mistress or merely as a new addition to his stable remained to be seen. The end result, however, would be the same—she would be forced to become a whore. Everything inside of her recoiled at that thought. And yet, if she could save Jacko's life . . .

Her fine mouth thinned, and a determined glint entered the heavily lashed gray eyes. She was going to find a way out of their dilemma. She would *not* become *any* man's mistress and suffer her mother's grim fate! Precisely how she was going to accomplish this feat escaped her at the moment, but it was not her nature to meekly accept a fate she found abhorrent.

Jacko came out of the other room just then and grumbled, "Are you two still lying abed? I thought you would have been up by now."

Rubbing his eyes, Ben sat up and retorted, "I don't know why you're so grumpy about it—you just got up yourself!"

Jacko mumbled some reply, and Pip smiled slightly. Neither one of her brothers was particularly amiable first thing in the morning. Jumping lithely to her feet, she ran a hand through her mass of tumbled black curls, and momentarily putting aside her gloomy thoughts, she asked brightly, "Are you through with the washstand? I'd like to use it if you don't mind."

Jacko waved his hand, indicating his permission, and Pip scampered through the doorway into what had been Jane's room. It was almost like entering a different world. The delicately carved mahogany bed was a massive thing, nearly filling the entire little room, the bed curtains a billowy mass of expensive green silk—Jane's favorite color. Upon the floor lay an Oriental carpet that looked as if it belonged in the home of some nobleman. There was also a tiny satinwood dressing table with a matching mirror above it, and crammed into a corner was a green-marble-topped washing stand. A fine bone china pitcher and bowl sat on it, and Pip felt a pang, as she always did whenever she entered this room. This room held the remnants of Jane's other life, the elegant life she had lived before her rich lovers had deserted her for younger women, and it was a constant, pitiful reminder of how far Jane had fallen, how very drab and dreary the life of her children was.

The life she lived never bothered Pip, except when she entered this one room; then for a moment she was struck by a sense of sadness, almost despair, wondering if it were her fate to live the rest of her life in squalor with the threat of danger always hanging over her head. But then, realizing that at present there was no chance of changing things, she would carelessly shrug her slim shoulders and go about her way, just as she did this morning.

Walking to the washstand, she poured some of the tepid water from the pitcher into the bowl and gave her face and hands a quick wash. Then, stopping in front of the satinwood dressing table, she picked up a beautiful tortoiseshell brush and dragged it through her short curls. She seldom glanced into the mirror, but this morning, perhaps wondering why the dimber-damber wanted her, she was curious about her charms or lack of them.

Her face was heart-shaped, with a determined chin and delicately molded, high cheekbones, but as far as Pip was concerned, it was nothing out of the ordinary. Neither were her mouth and eyes particularly noteworthy, Pip's critical gaze completely missing the full, almost sultry beauty of her lips and the impact her smoky gray eyes, with their long, thick lashes and strikingly arched black eyebrows, had on people. The deliberately cut short, black, curly hair rioted over her small head in untidy ringlets that barely brushed the nape of her neck, the blue-blackness of her hair intensifying the almost alabaster hue of her fair skin. To Pip, everything looked completely wrong, her mouth too large, her eyebrows too marked, her hair too dark with her pale skin, and the smoky gray color of her eyes rather dull. Only her nose found favor with her—it was straight and delicately formed, with just the slightest tilt at the end. And as for her body . . . Pip grimaced. She was small, scrawny as a starved chicken, Jacko said, and whatever feminine curves she may have possessed were easily hidden beneath the bulky boy's clothing she wore. She imagined trying to hide Molly, the barmaid's quivering mounds of plump flesh beneath her own clothes and smiled at the picture that presented itself, the cheeky grin revealing even white teeth. No. She was much better off with the small, firm bosom she did possess than to lay claim to Molly's obvious charms.

Annoyed by her introspection this morning, she stuck out her tongue at her image and left the room to join her brothers at the table. Breakfast was a hurried affair, the three Fowlers falling upon the stale bread and cheese like starving animals and washing it down with the dark, bitter ale they had brought home with them the previous evening.

There was little conversation between them, each one busy with his or her own thoughts, and though nothing was said, Pip knew that her brothers were thinking about last night and how they could escape from the dimber-damber's control.

Having swallowed the last of the bread, Pip inelegantly and in a fashion that would have gained her an instant reprimand from Jane, wiped her mouth on her sleeve and asked suddenly, "Jacko, if England is not safe for us, couldn't we go to America? Surely the dimber-damber's arm is not *that* long! I've heard tell that there is a good life for the common man there—if you're willing to work, and God knows we are. We might even be able to buy a farm, like you wanted."

Jacko and Ben both looked up at her words, and for the first time in many a day, there was a sudden gleam of hope in Jacko's blue eyes. "By God! Why didn't I think of that! We could leave all of this behind us . . . even take on different names and start a new life entirely."

Ben appeared as excited by the prospect as Jacko, but a bit more cautious than his older brother. "Getting passage without the dimber-damber finding out about it will be damned tricky."

"And we'd have to leave behind all of Mother's things—the instant we tried to move anything from here, he would know," Pip added with a frown.

"I don't think that Mum would want us to risk our lives merely to keep her treasures," Jacko said. "There are a few of her trinkets that we could put in our pockets, but we would have to leave with just the clothes on our backs—and with what gold we have hidden in our shoes."

All three nodded solemnly, each one aware that without further discussion, a decision had been made. Her face alight with enthusiasm, Pip leaned forward eagerly. "How soon can we leave?"

Running his hand over the stubble on his chin, Jacko said slowly, "First we'll have to find out when the next ship is leaving . . . and then somehow we'll have to secure passage without the dimber-damber discovering what we are about. It'll be risky. . . ." He cast a questioning look at the other two. "If we fail . . . we'll be done for; you know that—the dimber-damber will make certain we die or go to Newgate."

"We know," Pip said firmly, "but I'd rather try to escape from him than to remain here at his mercy."

Jacko gave her a keen glance. A dangerous note in his voice, he asked, "He hasn't tried anything with you, has he?" Before Pip could answer, he reached across the battered table and touched her gently on the hand. "I'd kill him, Pip, before I'd let him make you work in his stable."

"Aye," Ben chimed in grimly. "We've been anxious about you since Mum died, but you don't have to worry that he'll get his filthy paws on you—me and Jacko will take care of him if he dares try to put you on the street."

Her voice thick with emotion, Pip said hesitantly, "I didn't know if you were . . ."

"Aware of his plans for you?" Jacko inserted grimly. "Darling, just because you dress and act like a boy doesn't mean that Ben or I have *ever* forgotten that you are our little sister."

"Mum explained it to us a long time ago," Ben chimed in softly. "And while you might have thought you were turned loose on the streets by yourself, we always kept an eye on you."

"Aye! And we'll not *ever* allow the dimber-damber to hurt you in any way—we'd kill him first and take our chances on riding the three-legged mare," Jacko finished harshly.

Jacko's reference to hanging made Pip shiver with fear for them, even as a wash of relief sped through her. Just knowing they were there, knowing that she was no longer alone with her fears, gave her a sense of comfort. Feeling the unaccustomed sting of tears in her eyes, she sent her two brothers a tremulous smile. Her heart full of love for them, she tried to interject a lighter note. "Well, you see, that settles it! We have to go to America now—I can't have you two risking your lives for me!"

They all three smiled at one another, the bond between them very strong, and almost as one, three pairs of hands met in the middle of that scarred table and clasped one another tightly. "We'll find a way out of this dilemma somehow," Jacko swore.

Pip shot him a cheeky grin. "Bloody right we will! But until then, I guess we had better content ourselves with plucking some ripe pigeons today at the sparring match."

Ben was on the point of making a teasing comment when there was a sharp rap on the door. Instantly, whatever lightness there had been about them vanished, each one instinctively reaching for the knives they always carried. Swiftly they spread out in the room, Jacko silently approaching nearer the door.

"Who is it?" Jacko demanded gruffly.

"Now, who do you think it is?" came back from the other side of the door, the irritation in the cultured voice obvious.

There was only one person who talked that way in St. Giles, and all three Fowlers stiffened.

"The *dimber-damber!*" Pip whispered urgently. "What can he want? We have our plans for the day."

Jacko shrugged and opened the door.

It was indeed the dimber-damber, and without a word, he stalked through the opened doorway, taking in with a single glance the aggressive stances of Pip and her brothers. A humorless smile curved his thin mouth and he shook his head slightly as if he was amused by their actions.

The dimber-damber was a well-made man and there was such an air of malevolent power about him that he appeared to dominate the room, dwarfing everybody and everything in it. Today, as usual, he was dressed all in black, from the black hat pulled low to the swirling black velvet cape and the gleaming black boots upon his feet. He carried a long black cane with a silver top, a cane that Pip knew concealed a sword in its slim length, and black leather gloves were on his slender hands. Even his skin was swarthy, and the few strands of hair that showed from beneath his hat were dark. The one eye he still possessed was black, and where the other should have been, he wore a black silk patch, which gave his already sinister appearance an even greater impact.

An aura of darkness surrounded him, something cold and evil entering the room when he did. He was the uncrowned king of St. Giles, his tentacles everywhere, his wishes carried out instantly and without question. . . . To disobey was certain death. It was whispered that even various members of the aristocracy feared him, that the dark deeds he committed for those unwise lords and ladies who were desperate enough to request his help became shackles that bound them to him.

He was a villainous, mysterious figure. Not the members of the aristocracy whom he held in his power, nor the minions of St. Giles who dared not thwart him, knew much about him. Not his past, nor his name, not where he lived, nor where he had come from, nor where or how he had come to lose his eye . . . There were ancient thieves and worn-out old harlots who told tales about him stretching back for over thirty years, and yet he did not look to be more than forty-five years of age. Some claimed that he had made a pact with the devil. Because he was fastidious in his dress and manner and his speech was impeccable, even among the members of the knot, there was speculation that he was the bastard child of a great lord but had been raised as befitted the son of a member of the aristocracy. Gossip claimed that, using intricate disguises, he moved freely from the houses of the well-born and wealthy to the hovels of the wretched and poor. As many people as there were in London, so were there as many stories about the dimber-damber.

Ignoring the not-precisely-welcoming air of the three inhabitants of the room, the dimber-damber commandeered Jane's chair, and seating himself, he remarked idly, "Expecting someone else, my dear children?"

Ben hunched a shoulder and reseated himself at the table. "It's a dangerous world we live in— how could we know it was only you?"

"Only me! You know, I almost think that I am insulted," the dimber-damber remarked cuttingly as he ran his fingers up and down the long, black cane.

Used to his acerbic manner, the Fowlers were not dismayed by his words; Jacko and Pip slowly seated themselves, side by side, at the table.

There was an awkward silence as the dimber-damber's black eye slowly traveled over the three young faces. "Hmm. I can see that Jacko has told you about my plans for you all," the dimber-damber finally remarked. "And I can see for myself that you are as enthusiastic as your brother."

Ben sent him a sullen look. "Don't tell me you expected us to be *pleased?*" he said sarcastically.

The dimber-damber frowned at Ben's tone of voice and said icily, "It really doesn't matter to me whether you are pleased or not! What matters is that you do as I say! Is that understood?"

Three heads nodded resentfully, and the one-eyed man smiled nastily. "Well, I'm glad that we understand each other." His one eye moved to Pip's face and wandered over her features. An odd note in his voice, he murmured, "Of course, there is perhaps another way that you could satisfy me. . . ."

Everyone knew exactly what he was referring to, and Pip felt her heart skip a beat in her breast. She had known this might happen, but she had not expected it to occur this soon. Her face white, she lifted her chin proudly, and coolly met the stare of that one black eye, silently daring him to make his despicable proposal plain. "I think not!" Jacko growled. "We'll hang first!"

"You probably will," the dimber-damber replied in a bored tone, and then, as if losing interest in that particular subject, went on, "And since you're not of mind to accommodate me, I suppose we'll have to talk about today's plan."

"What about it?" Jacko asked a little uneasily. "I thought it was all settled."

"Hmm, yes, I suppose you did, my dear boy, but there is one little thing that I want you to do for me. There will be several members of the ton attending the match, and it should prove to be a rich day for us, but there is one gentleman in particular that I want to make certain you rob."

"Why?" Pip asked, astonished. This was a most unusual request, unless it was well-known that the singled-out individual was carrying something of great worth on his person.

The dimber-damber smiled coldly. "Let us just say that the gentleman has annoyed me by winning a horse race in which I had wagered against him. As you well know, I dislike losing excessively, and I wish to create a bit of discomfort for him."

It didn't matter to the Fowlers who they robbed or why, and so, after shrugging their shoulders, it was Jacko who asked, "Who is it? How shall we know him?"

"The gentleman's name is Royce Manchester. He is a wealthy American and you will be able to identify him both by his accent, which is quite pronounced, and also by his size and coloring. He is a tall man, well over six feet, and quite strongly built. His hair is almost fair, not brown, not blond. He will be accompanied, no doubt, by his cousin, Zachary Seymour, a youth of about twenty, who is just slightly taller than Manchester. Seymour has black hair." The dimber-damber stopped speaking and cast them a sardonic glance. "Knowing your expertise, I have complete trust that you will find Manchester for me and lift anything of value he may have on him."

"And that will satisfy you?" Pip asked dryly.

The dimber-damber fixed her with a hard stare. "No, my dear, it will not—but it will afford me a little amusement until something else catches my attention. . . ."

Pip looked away, her mouth dry. She'd rob the King himself if it meant escaping from the dimber-damber's bed, and as for robbing Royce Manchester, what did she care? One plumb pigeon was the same as another as far as she was concerned.

CHAPTER 3

S killfully driving his pair of chestnut geldings through the thronged streets of London, Royce Manchester was struck by a sudden longing for the peace and tranquillity of a backcountry lane—Lord knew that only madmen deliberately subjected themselves to this type of punishment. Having narrowly escaped a collision with a speeding mail coach and a farm wagon filled with vegetables, it was with relief that Royce guided his pair down St. Martin's Street.

It soon became apparent from the many horses and vehicles which lined the cobblestone street that the fight was going to be well attended, and after securing the dubious services of one of the several street urchins who vociferously promised to watch the horses and gig for him, Royce strolled with Zachary in the direction of Fives Court. Nodding to several acquaintances, they slowly made their way through the boisterous crowd to join a group of friends gathered near one corner of the ring where the fight would take place.

"Oh, I say! It's about time you arrived—the match is about to begin," exclaimed George Ponteby, the nondescript features above his intricately tied and starched white cravat slightly flushed with excitement. Though Ponteby was distantly related to Royce, there was little resemblance between them.

George was just about medium height, rather slender in build, and while his face was considered handsome enough, there was nothing particularly remarkable or memorable about him. Yet Ponteby was extremely well liked, his easygoing nature and amiable personality making him a welcome addition to any gathering. Being a member of a reputable family as well as having his own respectable fortune gave Ponteby entrée anywhere.

Royce greeted him affably and was instantly absorbed into the group of fashionably attired gentlemen. Zachary hung about for a few moments, speaking politely to several of Royce's friends before spotting a few cronies of his own. Taking leave of the older group, Zachary quickly made his way through the restlessly surging crowd to join his friends.

The fight area was outside, and the cobblestone street around the ring was thronged with people from all walks of life. There were, to be sure, members of the ton, like Ponteby and Royce, attending, but there were also a number of lesser folk, businessmen, bankers, and merchants, as well as street vendors, butchers, and fishmongers . . . and thieves and pickpockets. The group was predominantly male, although a few tawdry-dressed streetwalkers in stained silks of scarlet and purple flittered hopefully throughout the multitude. Dogs and young boys ran excitedly in and out of the crowd, and snatches of laughter and conversation floated in the warm June air.

From the sidelines, where she leaned idly against the wall of a brick building, Pip watched the comings and goings, keeping an eye out for the tall American whom she was to rob. She spotted Royce and Zachary the instant they appeared, their height making them immediately noticeable. Squashing a particularly insistent flea between her dirty nails, she pushed herself away from the wall and unobtrusively tagged after the pair. While she was fairly certain that the tall, broad-shouldered gentleman in the expertly cut tobacco brown jacket was her prey, experience had taught her not to make assumptions, and so she sidled nearer, waiting for the gentleman in the curly-brimmed beaver hat to speak. Hearing the easy drawl when he spoke to his acquaintances clinched it for her and she glanced around, looking for either Ben or Jacko to let them know that she had marked the swell. Her diminutive height made it nearly impossible for her to find either one of her brothers in the constantly shifting mass, and eventually she was forced to leave Royce's vicinity and go in search of them.

Fortunately, she did not have to go far, and she had just reached the fringe of the crowd when she spotted Ben at his post on the other side of the street. Putting two fingers in her mouth, she gave an earsplitting whistle that was instantly recognizable to Ben. He glanced up, and when his eyes lighted on her, Pip sent him a wide grin and jerked her head toward the ring.

Correctly interpreting her signal, Ben idly moved away from his position and wandered off to find Jacko to let him know that all was well—so far. Now that their prey had been found, they could go about their business of working the crowd. Passing a plump banker who had unwisely worn a tempting watch on a gold chain, Ben deftly lifted it from the unsuspecting man and continued on his way.

Pip, too, was busy as she slowly worked her way back to Royce's proximity. The press and jostle of the crowd made her task easy, and by the time she found Royce again, she had managed to steal two very fine silk handkerchiefs, a silver snuffbox, and a jeweled stickpin. Her small size made her efforts ludicrously easy, few people paying any attention to the grubby little street urchin garbed in a shabby, ill-fitting green jacket and worn gray pantaloons. The small black cloth cap with its concealing visor was pulled low, almost onto the bridge of her nose, and it effectively hid most of her face, but allowed her to scan the crowd unobtrusively.

Since Pip was the smallest of the Fowlers, able to move with eel-like ease through the milling throng, and the one with the cleverest fingers, it had been decided among them that she would be the one to rob Manchester. Having positioned herself near the tall American, she watched him for several moments, sizing him up and making a mental inventory of his belongings, selecting which objects would be the most expensive and easily stolen.

If Royce noticed the small, poorly dressed figure lurking near his particular group, he gave no sign. In fact, Royce was too busy watching Zachary and Julian Devlin stiffly greeting each other to pay any attention to the little fellow in the green jacket.

Julian Devlin was nearly as tall as Zachary, with black hair and the well-known striking brows and gray eyes of all the Devlins. He was, at just twenty-two, whipcord-lean and arrogantly handsome. An utterly charming young rogue, he carried himself proudly, as befitted the heir and only child of the Earl of St. Audries.

Royce found it extremely enlightening that neither Julian nor Zachary had attempted to make the many friends they had in common choose between them. And while it was obvious that there was some constraint between the two young men, Royce was rather pleased at the way they each attempted to act with civility around the other.

As he was about to turn away, Royce's attention was caught by the sudden scowl that lit young Devlin's chiseled features, and looking to see what had caused such displeasure, he was not exactly surprised to see the Earl himself and a coterie of friends leisurely making their way through the crowd, stopping to greet this one and that as they edged nearer the ring. So the gossip is true, Royce thought. The Earl and his son *are* estranged. At least it shows the boy has excellent taste, Royce reflected grimly as he recognized several of the men in the group around the Earl.

Stephen Devlin, the Earl of St. Audries, for reasons not exactly clear, was not universally liked by the various members of the ton. There was certainly no fault to be found with either his elegantly handsome features or his polished manners. Because of his birth and breeding, as well as the fortune he had inherited from his sister-in-law upon her tragic death nearly twenty years ago, he had entrée everywhere, but this did not insure that he was equally respected and esteemed. For the most part, he and his wife, Lucinda, were merely tolerated by the leaders of society, the gossips whispering that they were a little too proud of themselves, a bit too smugly delighted with their unexpected ascension to the title and wealth. Consequently the people who did find their company enjoyable were not of the highest standing. And that definitely applies to those two fellows, Royce decided caustically as his gaze fell upon Martin Wetherly and Rufe Stafford, who were part of the circle around the Earl.

The two men who had found such disfavor with Royce were both gentlemen from the country who had managed to secure respectable fortunes. As with the Earl, there was no obvious reason for them to be held in contempt, and yet there was something about the pair of them that made them not exactly welcome additions to the homes and soirees of the more discerning members of London society. Like the Earl, they could not claim admittance to the inner ranks of the arbitrators of fashion, and unlike the Earl, they had no claim to the nobility and thus were treated with even less tolerance than was shown Lord Devlin and his wife.

Feeling as he did about Lord Devlin, Royce found nothing strange in the fact that the Earl's two boon companions were a pair of obvious toadeaters with a particularly grating unctuous manner about them. Watching as they fawned all over the Earl, Royce curled his fine lips in disdain.

"A bit too conspicuous in their eagerness to please m'lord, aren't they?" inquired a smooth voice to Royce's left.

Turning slightly, Royce met the cynical gaze of Allan Newell, an elegantly attired gentleman who did his tailor proud. His coat of blue superfine fit superbly across his shoulders, and his fawn breeches clung snugly to his muscled thighs. Somewhere between the age of forty-five and fifty, Newell was a familiar figure on the London scene. Not precisely a handsome man, yet one with a great deal of charm and presence, he was reputed to be quite wealthy, and though his family had no claim to either title or fame, most hostesses were not displeased to have his name on their invitation lists. Yet, like Wetherly and Stafford, Newell was considered not quite up to snuff by certain high sticklers. Though he was more eminently regarded than the others—not only because of his polished manners but also because his lack of social standing appeared not to bother him—there were certain doors that were closed to him also.

Since Allan was a sporting crony of George's, it was only natural that Royce should have met him, and while Royce could find nothing wrong with the man's behavior, there was something about him that Royce found faintly offensive. Newell seemed to take unnecessary pleasure in ridiculing the foibles of others, and there was a certain deliberate cruelty in some of his comments about the actions of members of the ton. Allan Newell was not someone Royce would have suspected George to befriend, but as it was not any of his business who George had as friends, Royce kept his feelings to himself and treated Newell politely.

Preferring to keep his opinion of the Earl's companions to himself, Royce merely shrugged at Newell's comment and, turning away, said to George, "I thought you said the match was about to begin."

"Oh, it is! It is, my dear fellow. See, the bruisers are entering the ring now."

And so it was; the two brawny men, stripped to their breeches, were indeed clambering into the roped-off ring. A murmur of excitement swept through the crowd as the two pugilists met in the center of the ring and curled their ham-like hands into rock-hard fists.

Pip had taken advantage of the crowd's focusing on the inhabitants in the ring to edge even nearer to Manchester, but the gentlemen who made up the circle around him were pressed too closely together for her to get into the position she needed in order to carry out her task. Frustrated and annoyed, she waited impatiently for a shift in the crowd, hoping she would be able to sidle right up to the tall American's side. Deciding that she could do nothing about robbing Manchester for a while, she let her gaze idly skim those nearby. Always looking for the unwary pigeon to pluck, she noticed a fashionably attired gentleman to her right whose attention was fixed intently on the two half-naked figures bobbing and weaving in the ring. A gold seal hung from one of his fobs, and almost effortlessly Pip's nimble fingers skillfully relieved him of the adornment. Rather pleased with herself, she carefully scanned the individuals in her area for another likely target.

In the press of the crowd, it was difficult to move about freely, and not seeing any other easy mark within her range, Pip sighed and tried to pretend that she was interested in the match. Her lack of inches made it rather difficult for her to see the ring clearly, and she spent several irritating moments dancing about on her toes, craning her neck, trying to pretend she was avidly interested in what held the other spectators spellbound. Conveniently, before she became too bored, there appeared unexpectedly, and to her delight, a little gap in the men around the American, and Pip wiggled instantly into the space. Unfortunately, though closer to her prey, she was still not in a position to lift any valuables from him, and she gloomily resigned herself to waiting until after the match, when the crowd began to disperse, before putting her clever fingers to work emptying Mr. Manchester's pockets. Whistling soundlessly, she fidgeted from foot to foot and gazed leisurely about her, wondering where Ben and Jacko were and if the match had proved as profitable for them. Sparring matches usually were, the shoving and pushing of the tightly packed crowd making their work easier. And the fact that everyone's attention was usually on the ring only aided them in their thievery. Except, Pip thought darkly, they're so bloody *boring!*

Politely stifling a huge yawn of utter boredom, Royce began to glance around the crowd. Directly across from him, on the other side of the ring, he saw Zachary and his group of nattily dressed friends, their jubilant cheers when the big bruiser in the dark breeches landed a solid hit on the chin of the other pugilist making it evident on whom they had wagered *their* money.

His topaz gaze moving on, Royce happened to meet the unfriendly dark-eyed stare of Martin Wetherly, who was standing next to the Earl and his group near the edge of the ring. For a split second their eyes held, only cool disinterest evident in Royce's steady gaze, but inwardly he was wondering what he had done to arouse the hostility that Wetherly made no attempt to conceal. Was it simply because Wetherly was a close friend of the Earl's and he was merely reflecting the Earl's oft-professed dislike of him? Or was it something else?

Wetherly broke eye contact first, his gaze slowly moving a scant second later back to the inhabitants of the ring, making Royce wonder if he had mistaken the ugly look in the dark eyes. Deciding that he was letting the unfortunate antagonism that existed between himself and the Earl color his thoughts, Royce gave himself a mental shaking. There was probably nothing in Wetherly's stare to give him pause—he really must make an effort to stop reading sinister motives in simple actions.

Royce forced himself to concentrate on the activity in the ring and for the next hour or so managed to appear enthralled by the two bruisers. Fortunately, before he became too bored again, the match ended, the fellow in the black breeches knocking his opponent down with a furious blow to the jaw. But for Royce, escape was not immediate—he had to wait for Zachary to re-join him, and Zachary, of course, full of excitement about the fight, was in no hurry to join in the mass exodus that was taking place. Royce listened patiently to Zachary's colorful descriptions of the fight they had both just watched, but when he finally thought he had Zachary slowly moving in the direction of their gig, George and several of his friends chimed in and proceeded to go over all the various highlights of the match, no one except Royce, apparently, willing to move a foot until the subject was satisfactorily exhausted.

The crowd was rapidly dispersing by now, and Royce was on the point of bodily picking up Zachary and carrying him to the gig when Zachary looked at him and grinned. "I suppose," Zachary said sheepishly, "you are ready to leave now."

His face wearing an expression of long-suffering boredom, Royce answered dulcetly, "It would be pleasant."

"Oh, I say!" exclaimed George. "We can't have the afternoon end yet! Shall we all retire to one of the clubs for a game or two of hazard or faro?"

Royce demurred, the vision of lovely Della waiting for him on the soft feather bed in the discreet little house he had obtained for her making him distinctly disinclined for more masculine company. His hand firmly on Zachary's upper arm as he edged away from George and his friends, Royce said smoothly, "Some other time for me. I'm afraid I have other plans."

There were murmurs of regret from the others, but Royce did not allow himself to be swayed and doggedly kept Zachary moving along with the remnants of the crowd. At this point the majority of the throng had thinned out and disappeared, and although there were still groups of stragglers here and there,

Royce and the others were able to move more freely in the direction they wanted.

Royce's group had passed several men on horseback and had dodged between a few carts and curricles when at last Royce saw his pair and gig. Concentrating on reaching his horses, he was not consciously aware of the small figure in the green jacket and gray pantaloons who had been dogging his heels for quite some time. It was only when the boy appeared to stumble and fell against him that Royce's sharp senses took over and he realized in an instant what was happening.

Pip had grown almost desperate while waiting to snatch Manchester's valuables, and if it hadn't been for the one-eyed man's express wish that Manchester be robbed, she would have given up on him long ago. Though she had found him early on and had remained as close to him as possible, there had never been just the right opportunity to pick his pockets. Someone was always right by his side, and instead of mingling with the crowd as it gradually dispersed, Manchester and his friends had lingered, talking, until Pip had feared someone would notice her lurking about and comment on it. No one had, and just when she thought she was going to have to risk being spotted, Manchester and his chatty friends had *finally* started to move. But the crowd that she had relied upon to cover her movements had disappeared, and while there were still many people about, they were too widely scattered to give her much protection.

She glanced around, hoping to see Ben or Jacko. Maybe between the three of them, they could maneuver Manchester into an alley and rob him before he reached his vehicle and anyone knew what was happening. As she caught sight of her brothers where they lounged near several gigs and curricles, a feeling of relief swept over her. Good. Once they saw her, they would realize that she needed help.

But Jacko and Ben were not looking in her direction, and

Pip's heart sank when the American suddenly swerved and began walking purposefully toward a pair of chestnut horses which were harnessed to a stylish gig. Once Manchester climbed into the gig, the chance was lost; shuddering at the thought of facing the one-eyed man's wrath if she failed to carry out his command, Pip gamely attempted to do what she had been trained to do all her life—pick a pocket.

Pip's stumble as she fell against the tall American was a thing of grace and skill. So were the nimble fingers that deftly lifted his golden seal and the heavy gold watch from his vest pocket. The watch and seal slipped instantly into the capricious pockets of her own coat, and Pip was almost on the point of congratulating herself for accomplishing such a risky venture when an iron-fingered hand suddenly clamped itself around her slender wrist.

Not aware of her danger yet, appearing to have regained her balance, Pip grinned saucily in the direction of the American and said cheekily, "Thanks, mister! Oy would have fallen 'cept for you."

"I don't think so," said a cold voice. "And I would appreciate it if you handed back the watch and seal you have just stolen. Then we shall see how you like a trip to Newgate!"

Her heart thumping frantically in her breast, Pip made a valiant attempt to brazen her way out of this disastrous situation. "Blimey, mister! Oy don't know wot you're talkin' about!"

"Oh, I think you do; in fact, I think you know *exactly* 'wot' I'm talking about! Now, hand over my watch!"

It was by far the most dangerous predicament Pip had ever been in, and her blood ran cold when several of the gentlemen who had been with the American at the sparring match formed a small, curious group around them. Reminding herself not to panic, to remain calm, no matter how bad it looked, Pip glanced quickly around to see if Jacko and Ben had noticed her difficulty.

They had. Even as Pip twisted uneasily in the grasp of the well-dressed gentleman, Jacko and Ben were walking rapidly in her direction, the carefully bland expression on their faces letting her know that they had something planned to extricate her from this unpleasant situation.

Relaxing slightly, knowing that her brothers wouldn't allow her to be carried off to Newgate without a fight, Pip put on her most innocent expression and, not looking at her captor, glanced hopefully around at the other gentlemen. "Lord luv us! Now, Oy ask you fine gentlemen—do Oy look like a bloody thief?"

Pip did appear beguilingly innocent as she stood there, an appealing smile on her soft lips, her small body half-hidden by the ill-fitting clothes, the visor of her black cap pulled low on her forehead, hiding the too old gray eyes. She had the look of a little lost waif, and as the seconds spun out, a flicker of doubt was seen in some of the eyes that stared at her.

But Royce wasn't the least bit fooled, and seeing that his friends were wavering, he snorted and, in one swift movement, reached into Pip's pocket and withdrew his watch and the seal as well as a silk handkerchief, which George fumingly identified as his own. Whatever doubt may have been engendered by Pip's innocent air was immediately banished.

But Pip was not without resources, and pushing back the cap with her free hand, she opened her eyes very wide and said in tones of amazement, "Well, bugger me blind! Where the 'ell did those come from?"

Torn between the desire to laugh at this outrageous scamp's antics and a strong desire to box his ears, Royce transferred his hold to the collar of the green jacket and contented himself with giving the little devil a brief shake. "And that will be enough out of you!" he said with just a suspicion of a laugh in his voice.

Pip heard the note of laughter and wiggled around to stare up in astonishment at the tall, tawny-haired gentleman. It had been her observation that *most* people would have been furious in this situation, but the American seemed, for some incomprehensible reason, to have found something amusing about being robbed!

For as long as she lived, Pip would never forget the sudden leap her heart gave the instant her eyes fell upon Royce Manchester's hard, handsome face. He was not the handsomest man she had ever seen before, his features too broadly defined to be considered classically handsome, and yet there was something so commanding, so striking, about that lean-planed face, the high cheekbones and unyielding jaw, that Pip was conscious of a shiver of excitement sliding down her spine. For the first time in her entire life, she was suddenly aware of a man in a way that startled and confused her. The full mouth above that very formidable chin was elegantly chiseled, and the arrogant nose with the slightly flaring nostrils only added to the powerful impact his features made upon her. But it was his eyes, those thickly lashed, compelling topaz eyes and their heavy black brows, that made her breath catch in her throat. Tiger eyes, she thought half-hysterically, and steeled herself to stand as unflinching as possible beneath their bright examining gaze.

Staring down into the upturned face of his little thief, Royce suddenly frowned, realizing that there was something *very* familiar about the boy. And yet . . . Almost absently, Royce pushed the cloth cap farther off the boy's face. A wealth of grimy black, curly hair was exposed to his contemplative stare, and for the first time he got a clear view of those distinctively arched black brows and unforgettable gray eyes. Now, where, Royce wondered scowlingly, have I seen a face like this before?

"Having trouble, are we, Manchester?" inquired a hatefully silky voice.

Lifting his gaze from the boy's face, Royce looked at the speaker, who had just strolled up. It was the Earl of St. Audries, and he was flanked by his two cronies, Stafford and Wetherly. It was obvious that they had come not to help but to gloat, and Royce felt a stab of irritation. Not now, he thought irascibly; I am in no mood to fence with you, you sarcastic bastard! But then, as he stared into the Earl's cat-shaped gray eyes, he sucked in his breath as realization dawned. I know *precisely* where I've seen this boy's features before, he admitted grimly to himself, and I'm staring at them right this very moment!

Ever eager to seize any opportunity that might arise, Pip twisted around in the direction of the new voice, hoping that she might be able to take advantage of this unexpected encounter. But her heart sank as her eyes fell upon the trio of elegantly attired gentlemen who had just walked up. Despite the slight hint of animosity that she had detected in the speaker's voice, it was apparent that they were not going to help *her!* Her agile brain busy with seeking a way, *any* way, out of her current dilemma, after the first cursory glance at the three gentlemen, she started to look away when something about the taller of the three men caught her attention.

The Earl of St. Audries was a tall, slender man nearing fifty years of age. Like Newell, he was undeniably a credit to his tailor, his form-fitting coat of maroon cloth clinging lovingly to his shoulders, and his buff-colored breeches displaying admirably the muscled length of his long legs. He carried a slim walking stick and, unlike most of the others, was hatless.

Perhaps it was the lack of a hat that caused Pip to take a second, longer look at the Earl, and when she did, she gasped and stiffened. In stunned disbelief she stared openmouthed at the Earl's carefully arranged black curls—curls very like her own—but it was the strikingly arrogant arch of the black eyebrows above his exotically shaped smoky gray eyes that held her frozen with shock.

Pip had often wondered what her father had looked like,

had often wondered if she resembled him at all, for her features bore no similarity to Jane's. And now, when she least expected it, she discovered that the features she stared at every morning were merely a younger, softer near mirror image of the slim, elegant gentleman standing in front of her!

CHAPTER 4

P ip's soft gasp had not gone unnoticed by Royce, nor the stiffening in the small body, and almost the instant he realized that his young thief could be none other than a bastard child of the Earl of St. Audries, he also understood the significance of the child's reaction. Until this precise moment, the boy had never known that his father had to have been this man standing in front of him—how else could one explain the little street rat possessing those unmistakable Devlin eyes?

Not quite able to believe what she was seeing, hungrily Pip cataloged every feature of the Earl's dark, haughty face. The shapes of their faces were not exactly alike, nor were their mouths and noses literally duplicated, but those brows and eyes . . . Those brows and eyes marked her as having this man's blood in her veins, and there was no doubt in Pip's mind that this man was her father. Giddy as she was with that knowledge, for an instant the gravity of her situation disappeared and she choked back a half-hysterical giggle as she envisioned the gentleman's reaction if she were to suddenly fling herself onto his chest and exclaim, *"Father!* I have searched everywhere for you! Don't you recognize me? I am your *daughter!*"

Staring at the aloof, disdainful features, she got the decided impression that the gentleman would *not* be pleased! In fact, as the first shock wore off and she began to study him more objectively, noting the sulky mouth and chilly expression in the gray eyes, she came to the conclusion that she didn't think she would care to know the man any better than she did at this moment. He looked to be an arrogant, cold-blooded fellow, and almost unconsciously she pressed nearer to Royce, as if seeking to repudiate any connection between them.

The Earl, intent upon baiting the American, had not paid the least heed to the grubby street urchin in Royce's grasp, and when Royce had remained silent, the Earl murmured, "Have you decided to consort with the lower orders? Perhaps you feel more comfortable in their company?"

Royce smiled, not a very nice smile. "Well, their manners are certainly better than some I could name."

The Earl's face darkened and he stepped forward aggressively, but George Ponteby, ever the peacemaker, spoke up quickly. "It is the most amazing thing, Stephen—Royce here caught this little beggar stealing from us. Imagine that!"

The small pickpocket held captive by Royce's firm hold on the collar of the green jacket suddenly became the focus of all eyes. Ever after, Royce wondered precisely what prompted him to casually pull the black cap down low on the boy's face, effectively concealing his resemblance to the Earl before anyone else could notice it. Had he been trying to avoid an embarrassing scene? Or . . . or had he known instinctively that the boy needed protection . . . that the child's life might very well be in grave danger if his relationship to the Earl was perceived by others?

"A thief, eh?" said Wetherly, his dark eyes sweeping over Pip's small figure. "What do you intend to do with him?"

It was a question that only moments before Royce could

have answered without hesitation; but now, in light of what he suspected, he found himself reluctant to simply turn the boy over to the watch. Yet what else was he to do? He could hardly shove the boy at the Earl and say, "Don't you think *you* ought to do something?" Somehow he didn't think that the Earl would appreciate having a bastard child suddenly thrust upon him. So what was he to do? Turn the wretched little devil loose to rob again?

As Royce hesitated, one of the two tough-looking young men who had approached about the same time as the Earl and his companions spoke up. "We'd be 'appy to 'elp you, sir. We can turn the bloody little bloke over to the watch for you. Be 'appy too! Save you the trouble, it would."

Royce glanced at the two young men, noting their hard young faces and the odd eagerness of their manner. It was their very eagerness that aroused his suspicion—they were just a little *too* keen in their professed desire to help. Both men looked to be in their early twenties, although it was difficult to tell; the rough life they lived had left its inevitable mark on their faces and they could have been much younger than they appeared. No fool, Royce guessed immediately that they were probably the pickpocket's companions, and the wary stillness, the almost bated breath of his captive, gave the game away. Smiling grimly, Royce replied, "Thank you very kindly for your generous offer, but I'll see to it myself."

Pip's heart sank and surreptitiously she sent Jacko a look of half bravado, half fright. It seemed that, unless Jacko and Ben acted fast, she would find herself in Newgate very soon.

"Seems a pity to turn over such a young creature to the mercy of the watch," drawled a new voice, and undaunted, Pip glanced around hopefully.

It had been the Earl's other companion, Rufe Stafford, who had spoken. "Being an American, you wouldn't know the fate that will probably await our young thief here. More than likely the boy will hang. And all because he dared to steal a few trinkets from you." His gaze lifting to meet Royce's eyes, he added with a note of censure, "It seems rather unfair—the boy was probably only stealing to put food in his belly, while you would never miss the items he had taken, and yet he will very likely lose his life over the incident."

"Perhaps you would like to see to the boy's welfare?" Royce asked sarcastically. "Since you seem to have his best interests at heart, am I to understand that you wish to take responsibility for him?"

Stafford's eyes narrowed. "That wasn't what I meant, and you know it! I was merely pointing out what his fate might be."

Newell, who had been standing next to Royce, entered the conversation at that point. "It *does* seem a shame that the boy should hang for such a minor offense. After all, you *did* get your belongings back."

There were some murmurs of assent from the various other gentlemen gathered around, and George Ponteby said uncertainly, "Er, it *does* seem a bit extreme for the little fellow to suffer such a grievous fate. He's a mere child."

Speculation gleaming in her gray eyes, Pip looked optimistically from one well-dressed gentleman to another, hardly able to believe what she was hearing. Who could understand the gentry? She had been caught red-handed, yet these wealthy, aristocratic gentlemen actually seemed to care about what happened to her, and if she was lucky, she might yet escape a trip to Newgate. Unconsciously the beginnings of a cocky little grin twitched at the corner of her mouth.

"I see," Royce said slowly. "It is the consensus that I should let the boy go?"

Pip was very nearly openly grinning at this point, and she stood a little straighter, certain that she would go free.

"Hmm, I don't know about that," George admitted unhappily. "If you let him go, he'll just rob someone else."

Royce had found this sudden concern over the fate of one small London thief amusing up to this point, but his patience was wearing thin, and with more than a little exasperation evident in his voice, he demanded, "Then what in God's name do you suggest I do? Adopt him and introduce him into my household? Remove him from the temptation of evil?"

George brightened. "Oh, I say, Royce, what a splendid idea!"

Pip didn't think it was a splendid idea at all and sent a black look in George's direction. Why couldn't he keep his bloody mouth shut?

But the idea, once proposed, seemed to catch the fancy of several of the other gentlemen. Even Francis Atwater, another of George's friends, who had remained silent up until now, spoke up. "You know, that is not such a ridiculous idea. Perhaps if you were to find him honest employment, it would be the making of him."

In growing disbelief Royce stared at his friends. They couldn't really expect him to take this filthy little devil into his household, could they? From the encouraging expressions on several of the faces, it was obvious that his companions expected him to do precisely that! Feeling decidedly beleaguered, Royce glanced around, hoping to find an avenue of escape from what was rapidly becoming an extremely sticky situation. He certainly didn't want to see the boy hanged, but on the other hand, he was *not,* he thought grimly, about to have the thieving bastard son of the Earl of St. Audries foisted off on him!

"Of course," Martin Wetherly said suddenly, "if you don't want to see the boy hanged and you don't want to take on the responsibility for him yourself, you *could* simply let him go. As someone pointed out—you have retrieved your belongings. You could just cry quits."

But George was having none of this. His blue eyes very earnest, he said quickly, "Oh, no. That would never do! The little fellow would probably continue to thieve and would end up in Newgate anyway. No. No. We must think of something else." George was an extremely amiable gentleman, but until this moment, Royce had forgotten one particularly irritating trait of George's—once he got an idea into his head, there was no swaying him from it. And George, it appeared, had decided to embark on a crusade, the hapless pickpocket inadvertently becoming the object of his good intentions.

The light of a social redeemer glinting in his eyes, George said firmly, "You *should* take him home, Royce. Find something for him to do in your household. See to it that the boy is removed from his usual criminal haunts. Train him to be a footman or the like. You are such a clever fellow, I'm sure you could think of something."

Royce was rather fond of George in a vague fashion, but at this very moment his thoughts about his cousin were definitely *not* affectionate and he nearly groaned out loud when, once again, several of the other gentlemen joined in, seconding George's suggestion. But worse was to come. Zachary, of all people, suddenly said warmly, "You know, Royce, George is right. You can't want the boy to hang, and you can't just let him go on thieving either. Why not see if the butler or the cook can't make use of him?"

Royce made a face, and sending Zachary a dark look, he growled, "Et tu, Brute?"

Zachary smiled sunnily at him. "Yes, I'm afraid that I side with George in this matter. Think of it as a good deed."

Royce still might have found a way to escape being saddled with a "good deed" that he certainly didn't want if the Earl hadn't spoken up just then. A sneer in his voice, the Earl remarked to no one in particular, "Oh, my! How very droll! Our visiting American is going to take it upon himself to teach the little guttersnipe some manners. This should prove most amusing! Rather like the kettle calling the pot black, don't you think?"

Apparently only Stafford and Wetherly found the snide comment amusing, the other gentlemen, George and his friends, closing ranks behind Royce, the expressions on their faces revealing their distaste for the Earl's words. Fighting to keep a grip on his temper, Royce narrowed his eyes, and his hand tightened on Pip's collar. For one long, dangerous moment, he seriously considered calling out the Earl. He would have liked nothing better than to meet the Earl on the dueling field, and if the man persisted in baiting him this way, sooner or later they *would* end up settling their differences in the time-honored way—pistols at twenty paces!

Fortunately, before Royce's temper got the better of him and he challenged the Earl to a duel, George gave a nervous laugh and defused the increasingly tense situation by saying lightly, "Hmm, yes, that might be true, except my cousin is more of a *silver*-plated kettle, wouldn't you say?"

Francis Atwater instantly followed his lead, and looking at the Earl, he said with a titter, "Oh, my, yes! Especially since he won that enormous wager from you, I would most definitely say silver-plated!"

For a moment it looked as if the Earl would continue with his offensive behavior, but seeing that Royce's friends were determined to deflect his malevolent remarks, he gave it up for the time being. Smiling nastily, he bowed and murmured, "As you say. But luck will not always be on his side."

Royce would have liked to mention that it was *talent,* not luck, that had enabled him to best the Earl so far, but George must have read the intent in his eyes, for he promptly and very painfully trod on Royce's booted foot. Royce muffled a yelp and glared at George. But George was too busy speeding the Earl and his friends on their way to pay Royce any further heed. Smiling sweetly at the Earl, George murmured, "Yes. Yes. You are entirely right. If you will excuse me now, we must be on our way."

"What about the boy?" asked Wetherly.

"Oh, my, yes, the boy!" exclaimed George fussily. "Don't give him another thought!" Smiling angelically at Royce, he said happily, "Royce will see to him."

Recognizing defeat when it faced him, Royce put on a very good face of it. "Yes, I intend to take the boy home with me and see if we can't convince him that honesty and hard work are far more profitable than thievery," he said blandly. He glanced down at the filthy little creature in his hold and muttered, "I'm sure that after a bath and a change of clothes, one would not recognize him." He added dryly, "Whether he can be convinced not to rob me blind as I sleep helplessly in my bed remains to be seen!"

Pip was aghast at his words and helplessly she looked across at Jacko and Ben where they stood just beyond the gentlemen. This was terrible! Newgate would be *greatly* preferred!

"Do you think it wise to introduce such a creature into your own home?" Newell asked curiously.

Royce looked down at Pip, who scowled up at him, the gray eyes promising all sorts of vengeance. Sighing, Royce admitted, "Probably not! But at the moment I see no help for it."

When it had become apparent that there would be no further opportunity to vent his spleen against the American, the Earl had lost interest in the affair and was already strolling away with his two unpleasant cronies at his heels. George, too, having blithely consigned Pip's welfare to Royce, had now, for the time being, put the affair from his mind, and placing his arm through Newell's, suggested to the others that they toddle on over to St. James to see if any amusement could be found there. "And Manchester?" inquired Newell gently. "What is he to do?"

George looked pained. "My cousin will be occupied this afternoon seeing to the welfare of his little thief!"

A faint smile on his lips, Royce watched as George and the others wandered on their way, leaving only himself, the pickpocket, and Zachary. Even the two young men who had offered to turn the boy over to the watch had disappeared.

Pip couldn't believe it when, with a sly wink and a nod of the head, Jacko and Ben had faded away. They had deserted her! Up to this point she had waited almost passively to see what would transpire, but now that Jacko and Ben had left her to her own devices, she realized that if she was to escape, she would have to do it on her own. *All* on her own! With that in mind, she aimed a vicious kick in the direction of the American's shin and began to struggle violently to free herself.

Her foot connected painfully with Royce's shin, and as he had been caught off guard due to the boy's quiet manner until now, the suddenness of the unexpected attack almost loosened his hold on the thief's jacket. Ignoring the explosive pain below his knee, Royce cursed furiously, and grimly set about keeping hold of the biting, kicking, scratching little hellhound who had tried to rob him.

It was an uneven contest, and though Pip did her best and managed to inflict a certain amount of damage before Royce finally had her forcibly subdued, there had never been any doubt about the outcome. Snatching a lap rug from his gig and throwing it over the squirming, astonishingly bloodthirsty creature his pickpocket had suddenly turned into, Royce quickly and efficiently trapped the thrashing little body in its heavy folds. Breathing heavily from his exertions, for Pip, driven by an almost blind panic, had fought with every bit of strength and cunning that she possessed, Royce nursed his bloody hand, which now bore a perfect imprint of the thief's teeth, and with a decidedly less than gentle movement, picked up the wiggling, rug-shrouded figure and tossed it roughly into the gig.

Turning to Zachary, who had stood there watching the proceedings with a huge grin on his face, Royce snarled, "If you are through gaping like a country bumpkin at the fair and unless you want me to drive off and leave you stranded here, I recommend that you get into the vehicle at once!"

Meekly Zachary did as he was ordered, and wisely he kept his mouth shut during the wild ride that followed through

London's streets. Royce was a notable whip, which was fortunate—only an expert could have driven those hot-blooded, high-strung horses at that speed along the crowded, twisting streets without coming to grief. It was only when they pulled up in front of the elegant house on Hanover Square that Zachary realized that he had been holding his breath practically from the moment Royce had set the horses in motion.

As for the rug-covered object pressed between them, it had continued to thrash about with alarming savagery, and the fluency and originality of the muttered curses that had come from beneath the heavy folds had even caused Royce's eyebrows to raise. His normally unruffled manner reasserting itself, Royce suddenly grinned at a particularly gruesome fate promised by his captive and shook his head. Alighting gracefully from the gig, Royce said with a hint of laughter in his voice, "Yes, I am quite certain that you would indeed enjoy slicing off my, er, privates and stuffing them in my bone box—but fortunately for me, I shall take *great* care that you have neither the means nor the opportunity!"

Trapped beneath the folds of the rug, Pip heard the amused note in his voice and went silent with shock. What sort of depraved monster had captured her? Any man worth his salt would have taken grave offense at the various insults she had hurled at him, but this bloody American seemed to find the entire situation something to laugh about! Blast his eyes!

But Pip had no time for further reflection. Feeling those strong hands fastening about her, she began to struggle more fiercely, and though she managed to inflict the occasional blow, the big American carried her effortlessly into the house. It was only after she had been dumped unceremoniously onto the floor that she was able to fight clear of the enveloping folds of the rug and face her captor once again.

Like a spitting, clawing pantheress, she came up off the

floor, the gray eyes nearly black with fury and the ebony curls almost bristling with defiance. Breathing heavily, as much from her exertions as from the anger, mingled with fear, that was pumping through her veins, Pip wasted not a moment before launching herself at Royce. She had paid no heed to her surroundings beyond ascertaining that the American stood between her and a pair of heavily carved doors, which she assumed led to freedom, and her one thought, much like a cornered animal, was escape.

If Royce found the boy's fierce and persistent attempts to escape surprising, his handsome features gave no clue as he easily blocked the frenzied attack. Catching the boy by the shoulders, with humiliating ease he lifted his attacker off the floor and with no discernible effort held him at a distance, the vicious kicks and blows aimed at him barely making contact.

Infuriated, as well as chagrined by her situation, Pip completely lost her head, and forgetting for a moment her dual language, through gritted teeth she snarled, "If I ever get free of you, I will indeed slice up your liver and bit by bit make you eat it!"

"Will you indeed, my little tiger cub? But aren't you mistaken? . . . Wasn't it my, er, privates you wanted under the knife?" Royce asked lightly, one haughty eyebrow cocked at the beautifully accented English that came from the boy's mouth. Interesting. Not only did the child bear remarkable resemblance to the Earl of St. Audries, but it appeared he spoke, in addition to the rough language of the slums, also the King's English. How very bizarre! Scenting a mystery, Royce felt his curiosity about the boy intensify, and whatever half-formed plans he may have had for him changed in that instant. It wasn't just a matter anymore of redeeming the boy from a life of misery and crime; there was a puzzle to be solved. . . .

Pip realized her mistake at once, and her eyes widened

with dismay. Desperately trying to undo the damage, she began to struggle wildly again and muttered, "Aye, Oy will! Oy'll dice it up fine afor Oy stuff it down your bloody throat, Oy will."

"Oh, I'm quite certain that given half the chance, you would not hesitate to dismember me, but I'm afraid that as I have grown rather attached to my body, I cannot allow you to take that sort of liberty," Royce remarked with a faint smile. A black look was the only answer to his words, and realizing from the way the boy's struggles had weakened that the child was worn out, Royce stopped teasing. "If I set you down, have I your word that you will not attack me or the members of my household again?"

More exhausted than she had realized, Pip longed to accept this unexpected offer, but fear and the overwhelming need to escape still dominated her. Again she began to wiggle in his grasp.

While Royce might admire the child's spirit, he was also growing short-tempered, and giving the boy a brief and less than gentle shake, he said bluntly, "You have nothing to fear from me or my household. We mean you no harm, although I'm sure that you would disagree on that particular subject. You cannot escape, and since I am much bigger and stronger than you are, we can remain here in this position until you pass out or you can accept my offer. Whether you continue this uneven struggle or not, the results will still be the same—you *will* remain under my control. Now, have I your word?"

Reluctantly Pip nodded her curly, dark head. But defeat left a bitter taste in her mouth, and the gray eyes were angrily defiant and the slender body stiff with resentment as Royce slowly lowered her until her feet touched the floor and then released her. A surly cast to the delicately curved mouth, she stood there glaring at her captor, wondering what he intended to do with her next.

Unhappily surveying his unwilling dependent, Royce was

wondering much the same thing. The Lord knew that benevolence was not one of his more developed qualities, and if it were not for the mystery the boy represented, Royce was uneasily aware that he would have cravenly let the boy go. Immediately and with no further thought on the subject! Since by his own choice, that was an option no longer open to him, Royce continued to study the scrawny boy, considering precisely how the child could be made to fit into his already well-run and more than adequately staffed household.

"What's your name, boy?" Royce asked abruptly. He wasn't the least surprised when the boy shot him a dark look and lifted his chin haughtily. It seemed the Devlins were arrogant from birth! Holding on to his temper, Royce tried again. "What about your parents? Won't they be worried about you? Won't you tell me anything about yourself?"

A hostile stare was his only answer, and sighing, Royce let his gaze travel over the glowering, unimposing figure cluttering up his usually immaculate foyer. The boy looked to be far too small and delicate for his age, but Royce assumed that several weeks of decent food and sleep would help alleviate that fact. Having felt the force of the boy's teeth, fist, and feet, he knew, despite the puny size, that the child was strong and healthy—if undernourished. Food, clothing, and quarters were no problem, but what the hell was he to *do* with the vicious little monster once it had been fed, bathed, and put to bed?

Oblivious to Zachary standing to his left and his butler staring with astonishment from him to the boy, half-angrily, half-ruefully, Royce stared back at the dirty, shabby figure before him. His gaze eventually alighted on the boy's sullen face, and he was suddenly conscious of what a *very* pretty boy he had captured. Almost an exotically beautiful boy, he thought to himself, his eyes slowly moving over the startling aristocratic features. Those damned Devlin eyes, he mused silently, they are unmistakable! And yet it wasn't just the memorable gray eyes that bespoke good breeding; it was also glaringly apparent in the haughtily tilted little nose, the sculpted cheeks, and the full, enchantingly curved mouth. Aware his thoughts were wandering, he snapped to no one in particular, "Well, what the hell are we going to do with this surprising addition to our household? Make him my damned page?"

There was a choking sound from the direction of his butler, and since Zachary, a grin upon his mouth, remained mute, Royce rounded on that poor individual. "Ah, Chambers, you have a suggestion?"

Chambers, like all of the other servants, had not been in Royce's employment long—just as George Ponteby had procured the house for his cousin, so had he seen to the hiring of an exemplary staff.

The sight of his employer dumping a dirty little street boy onto the gleaming floor of the foyer had given Chambers pause, but rising to the occasion, he said calmly, "Perhaps, after the boy has been, er, cleaned and fed, you shall have come up with a better idea, sir."

"Don't like that one?" Royce asked, a grin tugging at the corners of his mouth.

Chambers bowed slightly. "I believe, sir, that after you have enjoyed the light luncheon that is waiting for you in the sunroom and have had some time for reflection, you will be thinking more clearly. In the meantime, if I have your permission, I shall take the boy away and see to it that he is fed and garbed more appropriately for a gentleman's household."

Relieved that for the moment, the boy's welfare was being taken care of, Royce nodded and said happily, "Very good, Chambers. I shall leave the boy in your capable hands." Royce started to turn away, but conscious that his unwanted dependent might make a break for it, he looked back at Chambers. "See to it that someone is with the little beggar at all times, and take precautions that he can't escape—I have no doubt that if you turn your back on him, he will be out the door before you can say, Jack be quick!"

Royce clapped a hand on Zachary's shoulder. "Shall we eat? This morning's events have left me, for one, famished."

Zachary agreed with alacrity, and leaving Pip staring with mistrustful eyes at Chambers, Royce and Zachary disappeared in the direction of the sun-room.

CHAPTER 5

Upon entering the sun-room, Royce and Zachary discovered a delicious repast laid out on the long buffet that graced one windowed wall. Within moments they had heaped their plates high and were sitting at a filigreed black iron table enjoying the mouth-watering efforts of Ivy Chambers.

It was some time later, as Royce was leaning back in his chair, having just finished eating a particularly tasty bit of lemon tart, that a harried and disheveled Chambers entered the room. Replete and feeling much more in charity with the world, visions of Della's opulent charms beginning to swirl through his brain, Royce glanced inquiringly at Chambers. The anguished expression on Chambers's usually good-humored features, as well as his bedraggled appearance, banished Royce's feeling of contentment.

Half rising from his chair, Royce demanded, "What is it? The boy? He hasn't escaped?"

Wringing his hands, Chambers said unhappily, "Sir, I have tried my best, we *all* have tried to carry out your orders regarding the, er, child, but . . ." Indignation got the better of him and he burst out resentfully, "Sir, it is impossible! The dirty little beast has a knife and will not let us near him! I barely escaped with my life!"

His golden eyes flashing with irritation, Royce flung down his napkin. "I see I'll have to settle this matter myself—and in a manner I'm certain won't please our unwilling guest! Take me to him!"

The kitchen, which also served as the servants' hall, was a large, cheerful room; a huge black iron stove dominated the area, and an enormous open fireplace, originally used for the majority of the cooking, took up nearly an entire wall. The floor was brick, and from a few of the heavy, smoke-blackened beams of the ceiling hung bunches of onions, garlic, and various pungently scented herbs. The air was filled with the pleasant aroma of roasting meat and baking pies, but Royce wasn't aware of it, his whole attention focused on the grim-faced little creature half-crouched in the far corner, a wicked-looking knife held in one grubby hand.

It was obvious from the condition of the room—overturned stools and buckets, broken crockery, and a great deal of spilled water—that a mighty battle had taken place. Chambers's appearance had prepared Royce for what he would find, so the damp, disheveled state of the women—wet aprons twisted and rumpled, and their normally neat white caps decidedly askew—came as no surprise to him. I knew that blasted imp was going to be trouble the moment I laid eyes on him! he thought angrily as he strode into the center of the kitchen.

The maids nervously moved away as Royce approached, and surveying the pugnacious tilt to the boy's chin, the feral glitter in the gray eyes, and the decidedly competent way the boy held the knife, Royce sighed impatiently. It was obvious that getting the boy into the copper tub, which had been filled with steaming water and placed in front of the fireplace, was not going to be an easy task, but irritated as he was, Royce almost looked forward to the tussle that was going to take place.

Curtly he ordered everyone from the kitchen. "And don't come back in here until I call for you—no matter how much noise you hear!"

Pip stiffened at his words, a wary expression leaping in her eyes, her heart banging painfully in her chest. Dirty street fighting was nothing new to her, and once she'd gotten her hands on the knife, defending herself from the combined staff had been relatively easy. A cocky little smile suddenly flashed across her face. The knife had scared them all to death, and they had scattered squawking like chickens before a hawk!

Watching the servants hurry from the kitchen, Pip carefully eyed the tall man who dominated the room. She should have been relieved that there was now only one person to face, but there was something about the aggressive stance of the big American that made her *very* uneasy. He took a step forward, and her hand tightened on the knife.

"Stay away!" she snarled. "Stay right there or Oy'll split your gullet, Oy will!"

His mouth tightened, and holding on to his temper with an effort, Royce said more amiably than he felt, "We can do this two ways—easily and with a minimum of exertion on both our parts or . . ."

Pip glared into his handsome face and sniffed contemptuously. "Or wot?" she sneered. "You'll send me to Newgate? Wot will your fancy friends think of that, after your fine words about takin' care of me, Oy'd like to know?"

Why she was goading him, she didn't know, but there was something about him that made her skin prickle and aroused some demon of mischief within her. With bated breath she watched a muscle jump in his hard cheek, and at the angry glitter that blazed in his golden eyes, she suddenly wished she hadn't been quite so brazen.

"All right, that does it!" Royce exclaimed explosively, his temper getting the best of him. "I gave you a chance, but I'm through humoring you!"

Uneasily she stared at him as he whipped off his fine jacket and began to wrap it around his arm, but that same demon that had prompted her before took control again, and to her horror, she heard herself saying, "'umoring me! Wot a bloody jest!"

The words had barely left her mouth before Royce lunged at her, leading with the coat-wrapped arm. He came at her fast and furious, and Pip barely had time to take a vicious swipe at him before he crowded her back into the corner with his big body, giving her little room to maneuver. But Pip had been in tight quarters before, and wiggling like an eel, she eluded his grasp; swiftly bringing up her knee, she deliberately struck him in the groin.

Pain exploded through Royce as her knee slammed into that most vulnerable part of his body, and for one breathless moment he was certain that he was going to pass out. Despite the agonizing blow, he recovered himself quickly, but not quite quickly enough, and Pip darted out from the corner, her knife flashing as she wildly struck at his upper arm, the blade slicing through the fabric to cut the firm flesh underneath.

Royce winced, hardly able to believe that the little devil had actually wounded him. Half-furious, half-impressed with the wretched creature's fighting spirit, he lunged after him, his hand catching hold of the boy's coat. His fingers tightly grasping the material, Royce gave a powerful jerk that brought the boy hurtling back toward him. The instant his chest made contact with his opponent's back, Royce snaked one arm around the boy's neck and, despite the twisting gyrations of his prey, held the boy prisoner against him. Moving swiftly, with his other hand he reached around and, avoiding the flailing knife, finally managed to grab the slender wrist that held the weapon.

Fright such as she had never known coursed through Pip, and cursing venomously, she struggled to break away from him. It was no use. The arm around her neck was nearly choking her, and a yelp of sheer pain escaped her as the fingers of his other hand tightened with punishing strength around the wrist that held the knife.

His breath was warm in her ear as he said savagely, "Drop it! Drop it or I'll break your damn wrist."

Not doubting it for a second, Pip let the knife fall to the floor and she breathed a faint sigh of relief when his brutal hold on her wrist lightened. But her ordeal was not over, as she well knew, and she was already gathering her forces to continue the fight when he spun her around and began with swift, furious actions to strip off her clothing.

Ignoring the throbbing pain between his legs and suppressing the urge to half throttle the little bastard, Royce concentrated sourly on his task. The sooner the boy was stripped and in the bath, the sooner he could escape to more pleasant surroundings!

There was such violence in his actions that Pip was momentarily stunned. The worn outer coat took but a second for him to discard, and with one brutal movement, he ripped her shirt open. Suddenly galvanized by a primitive fear, not thinking about the consequences, she leaped at him, her fingers outstretched to claw his face. Her tormentor narrowly avoided the attack, and cursing under his breath, he grabbed Pip's arms and brutally pinioned them behind her back.

They were both breathing heavily, their flushed faces inches from each other, their bodies pressed intimately together as they glared at each other. Pip was conscious of an odd tingle traveling through her body as they remained there locked together, her breasts crushed against his wide chest, her slender legs closely pressed to his muscled thighs, and it frightened her . . . as did the dawning truth in his golden eyes.

"Let me go!" she spat furiously, beginning again to struggle violently.

"Oh, no you don't!" Royce growled, not quite able to believe the evidence revealed by their intimate stance. But it was true. Through his shirt, he could feel her firm breasts pushing against his chest, and the fluid softness of the thighs locked against his was decidedly feminine! To his astonishment, he felt desire stir—as well as angry frustration. If a mere boy had been a problem, a girl was certainly going to create even more turmoil in his household!

In spite of Pip's frantic struggles, he held her from him, staring first down into the upturned features, wondering how he could have been so blind. The delicate bone structure, the heavily lashed gray eyes, and the sinfully erotic curve to the full mouth so near his own were glaringly obvious now that he knew the truth. His eyes dropped, and a warm gleam entered their golden depths as his gaze traveled over her rose-tipped, impudent breasts. No. This was no boy.

The look in his eyes both frightened and elated Pip, and confused by her reaction to him, she took refuge in bravado. Ignoring her embarrassment, a pugnacious set to her chin, she glared at him and hissed, "Blimey! Wot're you staring at? Ain't you ever seen a female afor?"

His anger fading a trifle, and choosing to be amused by her insolence, he grinned down at her and murmured, "Well, yes, but never one who passes herself off as a boy. Would you care to explain yourself to me?"

"Oy don't 'ave to tell you nothin'!" Pip replied, wishing herself ten thousand miles away, vividly aware of her naked breasts and the way his eyes strayed in that direction. "You've no right to do anythin' to me!"

"True," he answered dryly. "I suppose I could have just called the watch and let them take you to Newgate." At the look of pure fright that suddenly crossed her gamin little face, Royce cursed and, spinning her around, marched her over to the copper tub. Speaking to the back of her head, he said grimly, "I'm going to give you a choice—you can undress and get in that tub by yourself, or I shall do it for you. Which is it to be?"

Even knowing she was beaten, something rebelled within Pip and she made one last desperate bid to escape. Nimbly twisting out of his slackened grasp, she darted toward what she fervently hoped was an outside door, but she hadn't taken two steps before she felt the American's strong hands close around her. If she had thought he had been angry before, there was no doubt that he was furious now!

Easily subduing her wriggling little form, he slung her over his shoulder and grimly made for the tub. Not bothering to treat her gently, he snarled, "I've never been an admirer of men who beat women, but you've made me see the distinct possibilities of its usefulness!"

Pip opened her mouth to fire back a retort, but she suddenly found herself being flung through the air and landing with a huge splash in the copper tub. Coughing and gulping, she struggled in the water, but he held her fast and, with frighteningly savage movements, made astonishingly short work of her clothing.

Royce was nearly as wet as the soggy pile of garments he had thrown on the floor by the time he finished stripping her, and looking down at her, he asked coolly, "Now then, do I have to wash you or are you going to be reasonable about this?"

Scrunched down in the tub, covering her nakedness as best she was able, Pip sent him a murderous look, but common sense told her that she had lost this particular battle. Reluctantly she nodded her wet head and reached for the bar of soap that had fallen into the tub during their struggles.

Not quite trusting her, Royce stared a moment longer, suddenly very conscious of the soft curves she was trying to hide from him. It wasn't his habit to dally with the help, but in this tantalizing and provoking little creature's case, he just might make an exception!

Pip was aware the instant his scrutiny changed and her mouth went dry, the vivid memory of his hard body pressed against hers as they had fought surging through her. She swallowed, suddenly aware of what a very handsome man he was, realizing for the first time how very, very attractive women might find him . . . and how very vulnerable she was.

A sound from the doorway distracted him, and glancing over his shoulder, Royce wasn't surprised to see Zachary and the servants peering around the doorframe. He cocked an eyebrow and murmured, "Yes, it's safe to enter now. We haven't killed each other"—he shot Pip a considering look—"yet!"

Mistrustfully watching the others file into the room, Pip muttered, "Oy don't want them touchin' me! Oy can wash meself."

Thinking how *very* much, under different circumstances, he would enjoying bathing her himself, Royce regretfully pushed that alluring vision away and sternly asked, "Have I your word that you will not attempt to escape?"

Vigorously Pip nodded her dark head.

"Very well, then," he replied levelly. "I'll leave you for the present, but I'll want a word with you in the morning." He shot her a hard look. "Be aware that someone will still be watching you and that all doors leading from this house are locked against you."

Pip shrugged; let him think *that* would stop her! After dark, when all the servants had gone to bed, would be soon enough to effect her escape, she thought smugly, and in the meantime . . . in the meantime, she'd enjoy this new adventure—especially since he'd seen to it that she didn't have any other choice! Flashing him a disarming smile, she quipped saucily, "Werry well, guvnor. Werry well, indeed!"

Royce almost blinked at the blinding change of expression on her face, and nodding his head, he forced himself to walk away from her. Giving himself a mental shake, he turned away. "I think everything is settled for the moment," he remarked, facing the others. Then, acting as if he found himself in this sort of situation every day, he added, "Chambers, I shall expect you to see to it that our, er, guest does not escape. *Do* check all the doors."

Ignoring the grin on Zachary's face, Royce bowed slightly in Ivy Chambers's direction and murmured, "Madame, forgive me for creating more problems for you, but I know that for the moment I can leave the care of the young lady in your capable hands."

Flustered, her pretty face flushed from her exertions, Ivy bobbed a quick curtsy and mumbled, "Oh, sir! I will do my very best."

Giving her an attractive smile, Royce nodded, and eager to escape from the increasingly troublesome dilemma created by the simple act of preventing himself from being robbed, he attempted to retreat rather rapidly from the kitchen. A thought struck him, and stopping at the doorway, he glanced back. Cocking an eyebrow at the woman in the tub, he asked, "Are you ever going to tell me your name?"

Having momentarily resigned herself to enjoying this interlude among the gentry, Pip shot him a cheeky grin. "Pip! 'at's me name. And yours, guvnor?" she inquired boldly.

With an effort, Royce held back the urge to laugh at her audacity, but unable to resist her, he bowed slightly and murmured, "Royce Manchester, at your service."

"Coo! And a right polite cove you can be, Royce Manchester," Pip replied brashly.

His eyes locked intimately with hers. "I can be many things . . . if it suits me."

Pip's breath caught in her throat and with widened eyes she stared at him, unable to move until he smiled enigmatically and left the room. Heart beating fast, she continued to gaze, as if mesmerized, at the doorway through which he had vanished, Zachary close on his heels.

There was a small silence when the two men had left, and then, somewhat uneasily, Ivy Chambers said, "Now then, Pip, you gave the master your word and we're going to trust you to keep it. Wash yourself, and when you are done, I shall have another bucket of water warmed to rinse your hair."

Having decided that no harm had been meant by their ministrations, Pip nodded and, after Ivy had handed her a rag, began to bathe. Once the other women had discreetly turned away and Chambers had left the room and she was allowed a bit of privacy, Pip discovered that a bath wasn't such a terrible thing, after all. The water felt warm and soothing against her skin, and the soap, while harsh and smelling slightly of lye, did a miraculous job of removing all signs of dirt from her body. Her hair washed and rinsed by Alice, one of the younger housemaids, Pip felt so clean, she was certain she would squeak when she walked.

Clothing proved to be a bit of a problem, but the ever resourceful Ivy finally produced a blue gingham gown that she had worn several years ago. Glancing from Ivy's attractively plump figure to the gown, Pip looked dubious.

Not the least offended, Ivy said easily, "Oh, yes, I was able to wear such a garment . . . *many* years ago!"

The gown, as well as the meager undergarments Ivy was able to provide, was something of a novelty to Pip, and at first she was somewhat hesitant in her movements as she wandered around the big kitchen. She was watched with varying degrees of wariness and curiosity by the other women, but from the pleasant expressions on their faces and the one or two friendly smiles that had been sent her way, Pip was confident that they had no hostile intentions toward her.

Ivy's actions a few moments later confirmed Pip's reading of the situation. Putting a plate of bread, cheese, and ham on the table, Ivy said in a motherly tone, "It will be hours before dinner; you might as well eat this now."

It had been hours since Pip had eaten that skimpy meal with her brothers, and flashing a grateful smile at Ivy, she sat down and delved into the food. Thoughtfully chewing a piece of excellently cured ham, she glanced surreptitiously around the kitchen, already beginning to plan her escape. An escape that, considering the unnerving effect Royce Manchester had upon her, had become imperative.

While Pip was finishing her meal in the kitchen and scheming to escape, Royce was fending off Zachary's teasing comments in the front salon. Fixing his young relative with a stern look that was at variance with the laughter in his eyes, Royce said grandly, "Yes, yes, it does complicate matters, but just think how very worthy her redemption shall make us feel! Why, we may have saved her from a life of harlotry and salacious behavior."

Zachary, who, like his cousin, was also very astute, looked exceedingly innocent as he murmured, "Now, why did I have the distinct impression that you planned *precisely* that sort of life for her?"

Zachary's estimation of the situation cut a little too close to the bone for Royce, but he couldn't deny he'd found the little pickpocket . . . *interesting!* "You should watch that tongue of yours, young man," Royce said irritably. "It is going to get you into trouble."

"Yes, and something else of yours is likely to get *you* into trouble!"

Zachary's teasing remark was unanswerable, and beyond smiling ruefully at his cousin, Royce said nothing more on the subject of Pip. Reaching for his York tan gloves where they lay on a nearby table, Royce merely said, "If you are not to dine here, inform Chambers, will you? I am going out now and don't know when I shall return."

"Della?" Zachary asked.

"Exactly," Royce replied, and strode from the room, eager to escape from further questions . . . and the unwanted, surprisingly erotic images of a certain cheeky little wench that drifted through his mind.

Royce's visit to Della was quite the pleasurable experience he had hoped it would be, and if a fleeting thought of Pip as his mistress crossed his mind, he exasperatedly pushed it aside. The very idea was ridiculous! Not returning to the house on Hanover Square, after leaving a smilingly satisfied Della, Royce went in search of further amusement at one of the many gambling clubs that he patronized. Unfortunately, the news of the events at Fives Court had spread throughout the ton, and everywhere he went, he found that this morning's occurrence was the main topic of conversation. Displeased with the notoriety the pickpocket's advent into his life had created, he returned home and somewhat bad-temperedly retired for the night.

In spite of the drama of the day, Pip, unlike Royce, had fallen instantly asleep in the small, cramped room to which she had been assigned by Chambers. But then, Pip knew she was going to escape, and instead of fighting against her current situation, she embraced it with enthusiasm, looking upon this sure-to-be-brief time in the house of a wealthy man as a grand adventure, and she determinedly pushed all thoughts of Royce Manchester aside.

It was not too difficult a task, considering the life she had led, and while never being allowed beyond the kitchen and servants' quarters, Pip marveled at the fine and pampered life the servants of the rich lived. Seeing the clean and neat clothing of the others made her uncomfortably conscious of the pile of filthy rags that she had worn upon her arrival. A pile of filthy rags that Ivy had thrown away with an exclamation of disgust. Slightly ashamed of her background for the first time in her life, almost reverently Pip had smoothed out the faint creases in the blue and white gingham gown. The gown had never been an expensive one, nor had it ever been in the height of fashion, but to a young woman who had never owned such a garment before, the faded gown was the loveliest item she had ever worn, and she took a child's uncritical pleasure in it.

Even the meal they ate that night aroused her admiration, food such as she had never dreamed of—tender roast lamb, the meat nearly melting in her mouth, delicately flavored peas, and deliciously creamed potatoes, as well as a variety of side dishes, but it was the sweets, the creams and tarts, that caused her eyes to nearly start from her head. And taste! Oh, Lord, she thought pleasurably as she finished her third strawberry cream, wait until I tell Jacko and Ben!

Royce's servants were kind to her once they realized that she was going to behave, and though conversation among them all was a bit stilted and guarded, Pip lost some of her inbred hostility and contempt for them. She had always assumed that she lived the best possible life—the freedom of the streets, the lack of responsibilities—and not unnaturally, being raised as she had, she had looked down upon those who took honest employment as staid and spiritless fools. But her belief in the superiority of her life-style was being quickly eroded with every hour that she spent in Royce's house. It was as if an entirely new world had opened up for her, and she could not quite take in the enormity of it.

As the hour had grown later, though, and it became apparent that the day's labors were done, Pip could feel herself growing edgy. Soon she would leave this place, and as Ivy escorted her from the kitchen to the cramped room where she would sleep that night, Pip could not help one last backward glance at the kitchen. She told herself it was to memorize her escape route, but a tiny part of her acknowledged that she wanted that big, friendly room and what had happened within it imprinted on her memory.

Pip was given a room all to herself at the back of the house, just down the small hall from where Chambers and Ivy slept, and while it was hardly larger than a closet, the simple fact of never having had a room of her own made her inordinately pleased with it. As did the entirely new experience of actually sleeping in a bed—granted, the old mattress was lumpy and thin and the bed narrow, but since she had only known a blanket upon the floor, the accommodations seemed almost luxurious to her.

Worn out from the happenings of the day, unable to even spare a moment to speculate about the man she had identified as her father or the odd impact Royce Manchester had upon her emotions, Pip fell asleep the moment her head hit the thin little pillow that had been provided. She had not been fearful that she would sleep through the night— from childhood, she had trained herself to awake at any given time, and it was after three o'clock in the morning when she suddenly awoke, almost as if someone had touched her.

For just a few moments, she lay there in the silence of the night, savoring these last precious seconds in her own room and bed. Then, with a faint regret at leaving such comfort, yet eager to escape to the world she knew, she slipped from the bed. She dressed swiftly and silently in the darkness, a feeling of guilt sweeping through her at the knowledge that she would be absconding with Ivy's dress. It struck her as very strange that mere hours ago, she would have thought nothing of stealing Ivy's belongings, but now . . .

Uneasy at the state of her mind, she stealthily left her room and crept down the narrow hallway. Her descent to the kitchen was without incident, and she had just carefully advanced halfway across the big room toward the bolted and barred door that led to the outside before she became aware that she was not alone.

Stiffening in alarm, she froze, all of her senses alert as she sought to discover the position of the other person in the room with her. There was a moment of tense silence as she stood there listening intently before she heard the faintest little noise to her left. Carefully she swiveled her head in that direction, her eyes trying to pierce the concealing blackness, and it was in that instant that she became chillingly conscious of the presence of the *second* person in the room. She had only a moment to comprehend this startling fact when suddenly she felt a sharp blow to the head.

The blow was not hard enough to knock her out, though it stunned her, and reacting immediately, even as she stumbled, she rammed her elbow viciously in the stomach of her attacker. The muffled curse that greeted her actions filled her with a fierce satisfaction in that split second before she recognized the voice.

Ignoring her throbbing head, she spun around. "*Jacko!* Is that you?"

"Bloody eyes! Who the hell else would it be?" Jacko growled back at her. "Jesus, Pip, I swear you've put a hole in my belly."

"Well, next time, don't come creeping up behind me in the dark," she replied tartly, one hand gingerly rubbing the sore spot on her head. "Besides, what are you complaining about? I'm the one who got hit on the head."

"Hush!" Ben whispered as he came up to stand by Pip. "Have you forgotten where we are?"

Both Pip and Jacko subsided, nursing their respective hurts, and after a second, Pip said softly, "Shall we go now?"

There was an odd little silence and then Jacko said quietly, "We have to talk to you first, Pip. Ben and I have a plan."

Uneasy and not knowing why, Pip fidgeted, asking almost petulantly, "Can't we wait until we are out of here to talk about it?"

Again there was that odd little silence, and Pip's uneasiness grew. There was something her brothers weren't telling her, something that she wasn't going to like when she heard it.

A soft scraping sound broke the silence as Ben deftly lit the small candle he carried in his pocket. In the faint light of the wavering flame, the three siblings stared at one another.

Pip had forgotten her appearance, but the admiring expressions on her brothers' faces reminded her instantly.

"Coo!" Ben said proudly. "Don't you look like a right prime article!"

Jacko echoed his brother. "Pip! Who would have guessed that a mere gown would make you look so devilish fine!"

Pip smiled, basking in her brothers' warm compliments. Forgetting the need to escape, almost coquettishly she spread her skirts and twirled slightly. "Really?" she asked shyly, her face full of innocent pride.

Her brothers nodded enthusiastically. Then, almost as one, their smiles faded and Jacko sighed. "How are you . . . I mean, you are not hurt, are you? No one has been cruel to you, have they?"

Pip shook her head. "No," she answered honestly. "Nearly everyone has been most kind to me. The servants are a bit uncertain of me, but they have treated me well." A scowl marred her face. "Except for the bloody American! He damned near drowned me, and I didn't appreciate his arrogant manner or his methods!" She dwelt blackly on Royce's high-handed actions for a moment before admitting fairly, "But he is not necessarily cruel." Pushing aside her grudge against the master of the house, she excitedly informed them, "I was given a room all by myself! Imagine—a bed of my very own!"

Her brothers looked suitably impressed. But it was Ben who asked intently, "Then you wouldn't mind staying here for a while?"

"*Stay* here?" Pip repeated in a shocked voice. "Why should I stay here?" Alarm flooded through her. "I want to go home!"

Looking extremely uncomfortable in the flickering light,

Jacko said gruffly, "Pip, Ben and I have been thinking—being here might be the safest place for you."

"Safe? What do you mean? Why won't I be safe with you?"

Jacko and Ben exchanged glances. Gently Ben said, "Pip, we were coming after you anyway, but before we left our rooms, the dimber-damber came to see us, raging at us that we had allowed you to be captured. He was furious about what happened this morning—more furious than I have ever seen him." Ben shuddered. "I actually thought for a moment that he would do us a violence." His voice lowered and he said grimly, "But, Pip, it wasn't our failure to rob the American that aroused his fury, it was *your being beyond his power!*"

As Pip continued to look uncomprehendingly from face to face, Jacko said urgently, "Don't you see, Pip! *Here* you are safe! He cannot touch you here." Jacko hesitated a moment before adding reluctantly, "Pip, he was so angry, he wasn't watching what he said to us, and he made it very clear that he has plans for you—has had plans for you for a long time." Jacko frowned. "He muttered wild things, things that don't really make any sense, things about how *you* were going to be his way of gaining revenge for all the slights and sneers he's suffered over the years. But he did make it very clear that he's not waiting any longer to have you in his bed. If you come back with us tonight," Jacko said bluntly, "by this time tomorrow you will be his mistress—willing or not!"

Pip swallowed back the sudden surge of bile that rose in her throat. *Never!* she thought fiercely. Fate might eventually cast her in an unpleasant role—that of a kept woman—but *not* the one-eyed man's! And as for staying here . . . Royce Manchester's lean, handsome face leaped before her eyes and she was conscious of a great rush of mingled resentment and uneasiness. The big American disturbed her in ways that no one ever had, and she wasn't so certain that she wanted to remain in his vicinity.

"We can find someplace else for me to hide," she offered desperately.

"Can *you* think of any other place that will be safe from the dimber-damber? As safe as this one?" Jacko asked harshly.

Reluctantly Pip shook her head and said dully, "Very well, I'll stay." Her eyes full of anguish, she asked fearfully, "But what of you? What will you tell him?"

It was obvious that it had been her reaction that had been their greatest concern, because both her brothers seemed to relax and Ben actually grinned as he said, "We'll simply tell him that the house was too big for us to search through every room for you and that before we could finish looking for you, one of the servants awoke and we had to escape."

"But he'll send you back again."

"Oh, yes, he bloody will do that, but at least for a few days, we'll keep him off the scent."

Ben's words did not offer much comfort to Pip. "I don't like it! He'll have you killed if he thinks you have disobeyed him."

"No, he won't," Jacko said calmly. "First of all, it would never occur to him that we are not telling him the truth. We have always obeyed him in the past—why should he think any differently now?" Not expecting an answer, he went on, "Anyway, after a few days, we will tell him that we finally managed to find you alone, but that you swore you'd scream the house down if we attempted to take you from it. In the meantime, you make certain whatever room you sleep in is secured against someone sneaking in on you." His face grim, he added, "Ben and I can keep him at bay for a while, but sooner or later, more likely sooner, he is going to grow impatient with our excuses and send someone else after you— someone who won't disobey him! We'll do what we can to make things difficult for them, but you'll have to be on your guard also."

Pip stared at them in the fitful light for a long moment. Her expression a mixture of worry and resignation, she finally nodded and threw herself against Jacko's chest, hugging him fiercely. "Be careful," she said vehemently. Then, after doing the same to Ben, as if not giving herself time to think, she fled in the darkness.

CHAPTER 6

Royce woke with a start, not certain what had roused him from his fitful slumber. He lay there in the darkness for several moments listening intently, but heard nothing out of the ordinary. From the street below came the creak of a passing carriage, the horses' hooves rattling noisily on the cobblestone street, and in the distance he heard the night watchman call the hour of three o'clock.

There was no sound within the house, yet *something* had awakened him. A sixth sense? Or instinct? Or, he thought with a wry smile, sheer cussedness?

As the minutes passed and he still did not hear anything that could have brought him so suddenly and alertly awake, Royce rose from the bed and reached for his night robe, which he knew lay on the chair near the bed. Shrugging into the handsome garment of black silk, he found his slippers beneath the bed and, after putting them on, crossed to the long mahogany bureau that stood against one wall. In the darkness he scrabbled about until he found candle and flint. A second later, the candle lit, he glanced around his room.

Nothing there to have awakened him. But something had. And instinct told him it had nothing to do with sheer cussedness. Royce was a man who relied heavily on his instincts, and just as those same instincts had kept him from trouble in the past, they now prompted him to satisfy his curiosity about why he had come so suddenly awake.

After pocketing the small pistol he frequently carried concealed on his person, he blew out the candle and put it and the flint in his other pocket before slowly opening the door. The hallway stretched black and silent before him, and moving noiselessly, he carefully made his way downstairs, all his senses alert for the first sign of danger.

Pausing in the big entry hall, he stood there listening, still trying to figure out what had caused him to awaken. He heard no sounds except what would be normal—the clock ticking on the marble mantel, and the faint hiss and pop of the nearly dead fire in the main salon. Yet the feeling that someone had entered the house, the strong feeling that his defenses had been breached, would not go away. As the moments passed, however, and he neither heard nor saw anything to arouse his suspicions, he began to feel a bit silly standing there in the darkness, one hand wrapped tightly about the small pistol. He was about to turn away and go back to his bed when the tiniest sound, the faintest whisper of noise, had him spinning around and staring intently through the blackness in the direction of the kitchen.

There had been a muffled noise, almost of pain, and it had been that soft, instantly smothered sound that had caught his attention. Moving carefully, he glided through the dining room and butler's pantry to stand motionless on the other side of the green baize door that led to the kitchen. From underneath the door, the faint flicker of candlelight confirmed the presence of someone else moving furtively through the house. . . .

Edging closer, his ear pressed to the thin material of the door, Royce was startled to hear Pip say urgently, "But he'll send you back again."

A man's voice, one he didn't recognize, spoke up, saying

quietly, "Oh, yes, he bloody will do that, but at least for a few days, we'll keep him off the scent."

It was obvious that Pip knew the gentleman, and Royce was on the point of making his presence known when a third voice entered the conversation in the kitchen. Royce found the conversation most interesting, and having a fair guess as to the identity of the two men in his kitchen with Pip, he stood there listening attentively to the words that flew between the three of them.

Royce sensed rather than heard Pip's departure, and deciding that there was no time to lose, in one swift motion he pushed open the baize door and entered the kitchen. The two intruders were clearly silhouetted in the flickering light of the candle, and as their attention had been on Pip and her exit from the kitchen, Royce's entrance went unnoticed until he said mildly, "A rather late hour to come calling, gentlemen, wouldn't you say?"

Almost as one, Jacko and Ben spun around, their faces paling when they saw the small pistol Royce held menacingly in his hand. Jacko made a sudden movement to douse the candle, but the deadly promise in Royce's voice as he said, "I wouldn't if I were you—a bullet between the eyes will definitely not add to your attractiveness with the ladies," made Jacko think better of the notion. Shrugging his shoulders, Jacko let his hands fall helplessly to his sides and warily he eyed Royce.

Royce was pleased that his surmise about the identity of the two intruders had been correct. "We weren't formally introduced this afternoon, when you so, er, kindly offered to take the little pickpocket off my hands, so I'll have your names now, if you don't mind."

Jacko and Ben stood staring at him mutely, their sullen expressions making it clear that they had no intention of cooperating with him. "You know," Royce said, "you have nothing to fear from me. I mean you no harm and I have no intention of turning you over to the watch. Since Pip's well-being apparently rests in my hands at present, don't you think it would be a good idea if we three came to some sort of understanding?"

Uneasily Jacko and Ben continued to eye him, but after several seconds had passed, Jacko asked bluntly, "Why?"

Royce sighed and admitted unabashedly, "I really have no idea. Let us just say that I am curious about your presence in my kitchen at this hour of the morning and even more intrigued by the portion of your conversation with Pip that I overheard." When the two young men still displayed no signs of dropping their hostile suspicion, Royce sighed again. In a bored tone of voice he finally said, "We can stand here for what is left of the night, gentlemen . . . or we can adjourn to the front salon and have a polite discussion between ourselves—it all depends on what you want to do."

Confused by his lack of anger and his polite manner with them, Jacko and Ben glanced at each other, Jacko finally asking cautiously, "Wot do you 'ave in mind us talkin' about, guvnor?"

Royce grimaced. "Well, first of all, you can drop that deplorable accent of yours—remember, I overheard you speaking to Pip, so I am aware that you can speak the King's English—when you want to."

Still suspicious of his motives and not dropping their guard one bit, Ben asked, "Wot do you want to know?"

"A number of things," Royce admitted, "but let us find a more comfortable place in which to talk. If you will carry the candle and walk in front of me, I shall direct you to the salon." Approaching the table, Royce lit his own candle and his smile faded slightly as he added quietly, "And don't think of trying anything silly—I'm certain I should have no trouble shooting at least one of you if you try to escape."

They made it to the front salon without incident, and after quickly lighting several of the wall sconces that graced the room, Royce blew out his own candle and indicated that Ben should do the same. Walking over to the Boulle cabinet that sat against one wall, Royce asked conversationally, "Would you like a brandy or perhaps some cognac?"

Looking more confused and uncertain by the moment, Jacko muttered nervously, "Whatever, it doesn't matter."

Smiling to himself at their obvious unease, Royce deftly poured three brandies. "Please, seat yourselves. There will be no formality between us."

After flashing an increasingly anxious glance around the elegant, richly furnished room, Ben said gruffly, "Don't think we ought to—might get your fine furniture dirty."

"Well then, I shall just have to purchase some more, won't I?" Royce said gently, adding with quiet authority, "Don't be foolish; sit."

Mindful of their shabby, filthy clothes, Jacko and Ben gingerly sat on the damask-covered sofa, the expensive crystal brandy snifters Royce handed them looking incongruous in their dirt-stained fingers. Wanting to alleviate some of their uneasiness and finding himself inexplicably touched by them, Royce said in a kind voice, "You really do have nothing to fear from me. I was sincere when I said I mean you no harm."

Like animals that have only known cruelty from men of his station, Jacko and Ben stared at Royce, mistrust warring with the urge to believe what he said. There was silence in the room while several long minutes passed, the Fowlers watching Royce intently, trying to gauge whether he was telling them the truth or not. They must have come to some conclusion, because Ben suddenly asked, "What is it that you want from us?"

Relieved that they appeared willing to talk, Royce settled himself in a sapphire velvet chair across from them and said mildly, "Well, to begin with, I think we should introduce ourselves. . . . I am Royce Manchester, an American from Louisiana presently visiting London, and you are . . . ?"

Still not entirely won over, Jacko took a cautious sip of his brandy before saying unenthusiastically, "I'm Jacko Fowler and this is my brother, Ben."

It was a start, and realizing that he was not going to be able to overcome their not-unexpected suspicions without difficulty, Royce set about putting them at their ease. Charming them with his smile and polite and encouraging manner, bit by bit, word by word, he was able to learn a great deal about them. The brandy certainly helped, and by the time Ben had finished his second snifter and Jacko was halfway through his third, they had decided that Manchester was not such a bad cove after all—even if he was gentry.

Royce found their conversation fascinating and he had listened with rapt attention as they had spoken of their mother, of her insistence that they speak properly and that they learn to read and write. It came as no surprise to Royce to discover that Jane had been a high-flyer and that her three children were the bastards by a trio of her wealthy protectors. Of their life in St. Giles, they were a little less forthcoming, but eventually Royce was able to piece it together rather accurately from what they did let drop.

As the hour grew later and the brandy continued to work its wiles, they talked almost freely about their dimber-damber, repeating all the speculation and legend about him, making no attempt to hide their loathing and terror of him or the fact that he held their lives in the palm of his hand. Precisely what this greatly-to-be-feared one-eyed man held over them, they did not disclose—the brandy and Royce's manner may have loosened their tongues to an extraordinary degree, but not for anything would they have admitted to a stranger, albeit a sympathetic stranger, that Jacko was a murderer.

Dawn was less than an hour away when Royce said sardonically, "And to think that I was on the verge of growing bored! In less than twenty-four hours, I have been set upon by a pickpocket, a pickpocket, I might add, that I am coerced by motives I do not understand myself into taking into my household. A pickpocket, mind you, who turns out to be female! If that is not enough, my house is broken into by her brothers, and I discover that somehow I have aroused the enmity of a legendary master criminal who has one eye and who, as the leader of a horde of unprincipled and murderous rogues, will stop at nothing to gain the possession of this same pickpocket that I have reluctantly taken under my protection!" His expression half-angry, half-amused, Royce looked at the two young men who now sprawled comfortably on his elegant sofa and asked dryly, "Would you say that I have just rendered a correct reading of the situation?"

Jacko and Ben amiably nodded their heads in unison. "That's right, guvnor," Jacko said admiringly. "You didn't forget a thing . . . except that you agreed to let Pip stay here for the time being and that you would see to it that a lock was put on the door to her room."

Torn between amusement and annoyance, Royce took a sip of his own brandy. If it weren't for Pip's amazing resemblance to the Earl of St. Audries, he'd call the watch and have the whole trio of Fowlers carted away and be done with this ridiculous farce! But if Pip was, as he suspected, the bastard child of the Earl, then he sure as hell didn't want her falling into the hands of this mysterious dimber-damber! She deserved a better fate than that!

Rising to his feet, Royce said, "The servants will be stirring soon, and if you are to leave here undetected, we had better see about it now."

Their movements less than steady, Jacko and Ben stood up. "We'll have to tell the dimber-damber that we couldn't find Pip and found your brandy bottle instead!" Ben muttered, a silly smile upon his face. "He'll cuff our ears and be furious, but I think he will believe us."

"We had better be certain," Royce said slowly. Glancing purposefully around the room, he walked over and picked up a lovely silver candelabra and also a silver tray and bowl. Stuffing everything inside an astonished Jacko's jacket, he handed an ivory toothpick case and an enamel and gold snuffbox to Ben. "I don't suspect your dimber-damber would be happy if you didn't have something to show for your efforts."

Amusement dancing in his topaz eyes at their bemused expressions, he urged them in the direction of the kitchen. Catching a whiff of Ben's brandy-laden breath, Royce murmured, "On second thought, I think he would have believed you anyway. Trust me."

Oddly enough, Ben and Jacko did trust Royce. There had been something about him that had overcome their ingrained prejudice against members of the gentry. They had liked him immensely once he had banished their initial suspicion, and as they staggered away from the house on Hanover Square, they were both satisfied that for the moment, Pip was safe . . . at least from the one-eyed man.

In spite of their liking him, neither brother believed that Royce was motivated by strictly altruistic concerns—they had lived too long in St. Giles to think that Royce was doing them a favor simply from the goodness of his heart! Even though they did not speak of it, Pip's brothers were fairly certain that Royce had definite plans for Pip and that those plans were not very different from what the dimber-damber had in mind. But, of course the American was the lesser of two evils, and they hoped to be able to bring Pip safely home somehow before Manchester made any demands on her.

This evening's events had been riveting, and while Royce had learned far more about London's murky underworld than he had ever wanted to know, he had found the tale of Pip and her brothers and the one-eyed man undeniably engrossing.

Thinking of the one-eyed man as he slowly shed his robe and slipped into bed made him frown. How in the hell had he managed to arouse the ire of such a man? Royce wondered, deeply perplexed. *He* had no dealings with such men. So what had he done to come to the attention of this dreaded master criminal? Jesus! First St. Audries and now this sinister creature! Suppressing a yawn, he decided that it must be the devil's own luck that all he seemed to do since he had arrived in London this time was make enemies! Not a pleasant thought on which to go to sleep!

Despite his long night and the occasional yawn, Royce discovered himself strangely awake. Dawn could not be far away, and he thought he heard the servants beginning to move about downstairs as they performed their various tasks. Which made him think of Pip and wonder what the hell he was going to do with her.

Getting a lock put on her door was simple. So was seeing to it that more intricate and substantial locks were placed on all the doors leading to the outside—but that did not solve the problem of second-guessing a group of thugs who would no doubt be seeking to gain entrance to his house. Royce reflected, not for the first time since Pip had come into his life, that perhaps he was letting his curiosity about her marked resemblance to the Earl of St. Audries override his common sense. But he *was* curious about her, extremely so—she represented a mystery, and he damn well wanted to get to the bottom of it. He smiled grimly. And if, in getting to the bottom of it, he could cause the haughty Earl some discomfort—so much the better! Since his conversation with her brothers, Royce had already figured out the circumstances of Pip's birth. It was obvious that at some point in time, the Earl had been Jane Fowler's protector and that Pip was the result of that liaison. Yet it didn't explain everything. St. Audries was a wealthy man, and having a bastard child was not unusual for many of the male members of the peerage—so why had the Earl simply abandoned his child? Why had he made no provisions at all for her upbringing? The Lord knew he could afford it! The same questions might also apply to Pip's brothers, but while Royce didn't doubt that they too had aristocratic blood in their veins, he didn't know the circumstances of their fathers' finances, and he did in regards to Pip. The boys' fathers might have been younger sons with no fortunes of their own, or it was even possible that Jane had never told their fathers of their impending birth. Which could also explain why the Earl had not taken steps to insure some sort of future for his bastard daughter . . .

Somehow Royce didn't believe that the answer was as simple as that, and as he lay there in his bed considering various situations that would explain everything to his satisfaction, the feeling grew that there was more to Pip's heritage than he had discovered so far. It was a ridiculous notion, even he would allow that, but still he could not shake the idea that there was a mystery here, that there was more to Pip's history than met the eye.

Rising from his bed the next morning, he instantly rang the velvet bell rope that hung nearby and waited impatiently for Chambers to appear. He had barely had time to put on his robe and throw some water onto his face from the dark blue china pitcher that sat upon the large, marble-topped washstand in his dressing room when Chambers knocked on the door.

Entering on Royce's command, Chambers came into the room carrying a large silver tray which contained a coffeepot, a china creamer, a cup, and some freshly toasted slices of bread, as well as some fresh strawberry jam. Sitting the tray down on a table, Chambers said pleasantly, "Good morning, sir. I trust you slept well?"

Royce murmured some polite reply and for the next few moments contented himself with conversing idly with his butler. Sipping the coffee that Chambers handed to him, Royce finally asked the question that was uppermost in his mind. "Our, er, guest, she has caused no difficulties today?"

Chambers smiled, his blue eyes dancing. "Oh, no, sir. She has been most . . ." He stopped his smile from deepening. "It has been most *interesting*."

Cocking an eyebrow, Royce murmured, "Oh, has it? Perhaps you would care to elaborate upon that statement."

"Well, she does have a rather strange way of talking, doesn't she, sir? And you would be amazed at how nimble her fingers are! Why, she lifted my watch and fob just as prettily as you please . . . and with the most beguiling smile imaginable, handed them right back to me! She has kept us all captivated with her many tricks, I can tell you. Even Mr. Zachary is quite fascinated—he and his friends have been in the kitchen this past hour playing cards with her. She is very good, I gather, from the comments that I have heard."

Not precisely pleased with the report given to him by Chambers, Royce dismissed his butler and, dispensing with the services of his valet, dressed rather swiftly. Even without the help of his valet, it was not very many minutes later that Royce, looking every bit as elegant as he normally did, strolled casually into the kitchen. The sight that met his eyes made his lips twitch with cynical amusement—the little pickpocket was sitting comfortably on the kitchen table playing cards with a trio of young bloods! His presence as yet undetected, he stood there for several moments watching the scene unfolding before his eyes.

Pip was indeed sitting cross-legged upon the scrubbed oak table, her skirts ruched up about her shapely calves. For a long moment, Royce's eyes rested upon her bare feet, the restless wiggling of her toes plainly revealing her excitement. Her head was bent, her eyes fixed on the cards she held in her hands, and intently Royce's gaze traveled over the shiny, curly black head down to the pert bosom that was plainly revealed by the simple cut of the gingham gown. Well, she cleaned up fairly decently, he thought sourly, but he could see that she was going to be a nuisance—especially if she was going to corrupt his household this way!

Despite his irritation and to his utter astonishment, he found his gaze going back to the soft curve of her tempting breasts, wondering idly about their shape and texture . . . and how they would feel in his hands. Royce stiffened. Good God! What the hell was he thinking of! With an effort, he tore his gaze away from Pip and forced himself to concentrate on the others seated around the table. Zachary, of course, he had no trouble recognizing, nor did he have trouble placing the other two young bucks—Jeremy Shackelford and Leland Merryfield, two of Zachary's closest cronies. In the background he could see Ivy Chambers busy at the huge black stove, and there were two young housemaids attempting to wash dishes when their attention was not distracted by the laughter and ribald comments coming from the group at the table. Chambers, too, had found a reason to remain in the kitchen, and he was earnestly instructing the footman in the art of polishing silver—when his attention was not drawn to the cardplayers. It was obvious that Pip's presence was going to play havoc with his household, Royce thought sardonically, especially if the kitchen became the most sought-after room in the house!

Not quite certain whether he was irritated or amused by the scene before him, Royce was on the point of announcing himself when, in reaction to a card thrown down by Leland, Pip said gleefully, "Blimey, guvnor! Oy think Oy win this game!" And flashing her own cards, which brought forth groans from the other two players, she scooped up the small pile of silver coins that had been resting in the center of the table.

Royce stepped further into the room. "Am I now running a gambling establishment? Strange, I can't remember doing so."

A guilty expression on his handsome face, Zachary leaped to his feet. "Royce!" he said unnecessarily. "What are *you* doing here?"

Dryly Royce answered, "Well, it *is* my kitchen, you understand."

Zachary flushed. "I know that!" he said exasperatedly. "But what brings you down here? You *never* come here!"

"I would have said the same of you, and yet here I find you. I wonder why that is."

His initial embarrassment fading, Zachary grinned. "Jeremy and Leland didn't believe me when I told them that the pickpocket was really a girl . . . and so we came down here to see Pip and . . ."

"And I think I can figure out the rest for myself." Glancing at the two red-faced young men, Royce nodded to them and remarked, "I trust, having seen for yourselves the newest addition to my household, that your doubts about her sex have been laid to rest?"

Grinning sheepishly, both young men muttered some reply and rose hastily to their feet. "We should be going," Jeremy said. "We had only planned to stay for a few minutes."

Looking at Zachary, Leland asked, "Are you coming to Tattersall's with us? I understand that Lord Marchmount is going to be selling that bruising bay stallion of his."

There was no disguising Zachary's eagerness to join them, and after bidding Royce good-bye, the trio were on the point of leaving the kitchen when, almost as one, they turned in Pip's direction. "You will give us a chance to win back our money, won't you?" Zachary asked.

Pip grinned. "It would be me pleasure, guvnors!"

Their laughter lingering in the air, the three young men disappeared through the green baize door, leaving Pip face-to-face with Royce. She hadn't been nervous about seeing him again until the very moment she had glanced up and found those tiger eyes upon her. Even then, ignoring the sudden thump of her heart, she had pretended a nonchalance that she did not feel, certain she would not allow Royce Manchester to rattle her. Bravado was second nature to her, but when a swift, surreptitious peek around the kitchen revealed that everyone else had suddenly found other jobs to do in other rooms in the house, some of her jaunty confidence slipped. But Pip was spunky, and with a deliberately carefree sparkle in her eyes, she lifted her chin proudly. "Afternoon, guvnor! 'ave a nice sleep?"

Royce sat on the edge of the table. "Yes, I did, as a matter of fact. And you? Did you sleep nicely?"

Pushing aside the memory of the meeting with Jacko and Ben in the kitchen, Pip answered quickly, "Oh, yes. Oy 'ad me a foine sleep."

Pip was seated mere inches from where Royce lounged against the table, and she was unbearably conscious of his long, lean, muscular length so near her. She had never been this aware of a man in her life, and his close proximity, particularly after the way he had handled her yesterday, made her wary. Afraid her eyes would reveal her uneasiness, she looked down at her toes, suddenly mortified that he had discovered her in this position.

While they were alone in the kitchen at the moment, Royce didn't think that they would be able to talk without interruption for very long. Standing up, he said abruptly, "I want to talk to you in private. Come along with me to the library."

Pip looked mutinous and she was thinking about defying him when his hand suddenly closed tightly around her upper arm and, half dragging her with him, he strode rapidly from the kitchen. Glancing down at her, he remarked coolly, "It wasn't a request. I'm used to being obeyed, and as long as you are under my roof, you will do as I say—without, I might add, argument!"

Seething, her eyes dark with anger and resentment, Pip stumbled along at his side. Arrogant bastard! she thought savagely.

Her face was very expressive, and Royce grinned. "Yes, I am," he said softly as he opened the paneled door to the library and shoved her ungently inside.

His words gave her a shock, and warily she eyed him. Blimey! Did he read minds, too?

She jumped when he drawled near her ear, "Upon occasion I've been known to do that also."

Suspicious that she had fallen into the hands of a practitioner of the black arts, she backed away from him when he finally released her arm, and watched him mistrustfully. Steadily he met her gaze, and staring up into that hard, handsome face, in spite of her uneasiness and dislike of his overbearing manner, she was uncomfortably conscious of the dynamic appeal of those arrogantly sculpted features . . . that and the sleek power of his long-limbed body. Confused by her very awareness of him as a *man,* Pip took refuge in anger, and with her mouth set rebelliously, she demanded, "Well, guvnor? Wot now?"

Settling himself easily against the corner of a large walnut desk, Royce folded his arms across his chest and said dryly, "Now, infant, you and I come to an understanding about your role in my household and what I will and will not tolerate— and we'll begin with gambling in the kitchen. *That* little pastime will cease!"

Gambling wasn't a particular passion of hers, but his words and manner stung. "Bloody eyes!" she drawled insultingly. "'ow else am Oy to amuse meself?"

His eyes narrowed. "You can *amuse* yourself by learning the habits and demeanor of my excellent servants! Ivy and the other girls will teach you what you need to know. . . . And I would suggest that unless you *really* want to leave my household, you earnestly apply yourself!"

"Suppose Oy don't want to be a bloody servant? Suppose Oy want to go 'ome?" Pip demanded, hands on her hips.

A cynical smile curved his mouth. "Do you?" Royce asked deliberately. "The, er, attentions of the one-eyed man don't bother you?"

Pip blanched, her eyes widening. Forgetting her role for a moment, she stepped closer to him. "What do you know of the one-eyed man?"

"Merely what your brothers were kind enough to tell me last night."

Pip gasped. "My brothers? You saw them last night?" Fear shot through her, and forgetting her own peril, she demanded urgently, "Where are they? Did you hurt them?" A horrible thought struck her. "N-N-Not Newgate?"

Unaccountably moved by her obvious distress, Royce was quick to reassure her. "No, they're not in Newgate—they are unharmed and left here unmolested . . . after we had a most enlightening conversation."

Pip regarded him warily, trying to get her jumbled thoughts in order. Could she trust his word? And how much had her brothers told him? Obviously he knew something of the one-eyed man. . . . Giving herself a shake and hoping he had not caught her slip in speech, she stuck out her chin and asked sharply, "And 'ow do Oy know you're tellin' the truth?"

Her lightning change of personality fascinated Royce—one moment that gamin face had been full of fear, the gray eyes dark with anxiety, and the next . . . He smiled faintly, studying the pugnacious tilt to her chin, the mutinous cast to the generous mouth. A soft-spoken lady one moment and a tart-tongued street urchin the next!

His golden eyes meeting hers, Royce admitted candidly, "I can offer you no proof of what happened, nor do I intend to—you'll just have to take my word for it! Suffice it to say, though, I awoke and found your brothers in the kitchen shortly after your conversation with them. I, ah, persuaded them to confide in me, which they did. As for proof—your brothers must have trusted me or I wouldn't have known about your one-eyed dimber-damber, nor the fact that you can speak the King's English when it suits you. I doubt that they would have revealed so much if I'd had them arrested and carted off to Newgate."

Pip stared at him, slowly digesting what he had revealed. There was the ring of truth about what he said, but . . . "You could 'ave tortured them, made them tell you wot you wanted to know."

Not used to having his word doubted, especially not by someone like this small, irritating creature before him, Royce snarled softly, "I don't torture people as a rule, although in your case I just might make an exception, and I'm certainly not going to waste any more of my time trying to convince you that I'm telling the truth!" He shot her a look almost of dislike. "I told your brothers that in order to keep you safe from the one-eyed man, you could stay here for the time being, but if I'm to provide you with *temporary* asylum, you are going to have to live by my rules. Is that understood?"

Her black curls fairly bristling with rage, Pip glared at him. "Of course, m'lord! Anything you say, m'lord!" she snapped angrily. "Shall I kiss your feet in gratitude?"

"Why, you ungrateful—!" Royce lunged for her, and grasping her shoulders, he shook her. "If you don't learn to keep a proper tongue in your mouth, I may indeed resort to torture!" He smiled tauntingly. "And *enjoy* it!"

Pip aimed a furious kick at him, but deftly Royce avoided the blow. "Oh, no you don't, my little guttersnipe! I suffered enough of that kind of punishment from you yesterday!" His hands slid down her arms, and capturing her wrists, he jerked them behind her back. "And now what are you going to do?" he asked as she struggled helplessly in his grasp. "Bite me?"

"It's a thought!" Pip spat, her head flung back as she stared up at his mocking features, her gray eyes almost black with fury, her breasts heaving from her wild exertions to escape his hold.

Royce held her squirming body easily against his, and as he looked down into her upturned face, the impact of her loveliness suddenly hit him. Almost incredulously his gaze traveled over her features, the clear alabaster skin which was in such charming contrast to the ebony blackness of her curls, the haughty little nose, and the clarity and depth of those thickly lashed, smoky gray eyes. Still marveling, he let his eyes wander down the haughty little nose to the tempting lushness of her voluptuous mouth. An odd note in his voice, he muttered, "Who would have dreamed that such loveliness lay beneath all that grime?"

Pip's heart seemed to leap within her breast and she was assailed by a strange breathlessness. Her body suddenly felt as if it were on fire wherever it touched his tall, powerful form, and it frightened and pleasured her at the same time. Not understanding what was happening between them, but unbearably conscious that some new, dangerous emotion had leapt up between them, she renewed her struggles to escape from him.

To her astonishment, Royce let her go, and stumbling away from him, she only stopped when her back was against the door. Wordlessly they stared at each other across the room, and then, almost as if the odd awareness had never been, Royce's mouth compressed grimly and he said roughly, "Unless you want a well-deserved beating, I would suggest that you get back to the kitchens and apply yourself most earnestly to making yourself useful!"

Fighting down the urge to hurl an angry reply at his arrogant head, Pip forced herself to remain calm. Taking a deep breath, determined to pretend that he didn't arouse all sorts of conflicting emotions within her, she asked the question uppermost in her mind. "Why?" At his look of irritation that she was continuing to defy him, she quickly amended her question. "I mean why are you doing this? Letting my brothers go. Providing me a place to stay. Why don't you just toss me out in the streets to take my chances?"

Royce sent her an enigmatic look. He had indulged her far more than a mere guttersnipe deserved, and he saw no reason to explain that her resemblance to the Earl of St. Audries interested him. Obliquely he answered, "Let's just say that it pleases me and that I might find you useful in more ways than one, shall we?"

It was an unsatisfactory reply, but from the closed expression on his face, she suspected that she wasn't going to learn anything more from him. Forcing a cheeky grin to her lips, she quipped, "Well, then, guvnor, is that all? Oy'm to learn to be a bloody good 'ittle servant?"

Amusement gleaming in his golden eyes, Royce said softly, "I think that you can drop the accent, brat! We both know you can speak properly. Do so!"

Driven by some demon of mischief, Pip retorted, "Wot if Oy don't want to?"

There was a charged silence. Then, all amusement gone, Royce said in a dangerous tone, "I think that you would be wise not to fight me on this, infant. . . . We both know which of us is the stronger, and in case you've forgotten, I'll be happy to refresh your memory."

Suddenly terrified at the thought of being at his mercy, of being brought up next to that hard, powerful body, Pip was out of the room almost before the words had left his mouth, vanishing as if the hounds of hell were at her heels. For a long time after she had gone, Royce stared at the shut door, still half-stunned by her unexpected loveliness. The tempting softness of her mouth flashed across his mind and he could remember vividly the sensation of that slim body crushed against his. "No wonder the one-eyed man has plans for her," he muttered to himself. And as for keeping her safe from the one-eyed man . . . There was a sudden flare of heat between his thighs, and under his breath, he growled, "From him certainly, but will she be safe from *me?*"

PART TWO

Dangerous Refuge

A rosebud set with little willful thorns,
And sweet as English air could make
her, she.

ALFRED, LORD TENNYSON, *The Princess*

CHAPTER 7

Disturbed and flustered from her meeting with Royce, Pip fled back to the kitchen, trying to regain some of her shattered composure. I hate him! she thought fiercely as she hurried down the long hallway. He's an arrogant beast! An overbearing monster! But then, remembering her body's odd reaction to him, she was painfully conscious of a wild flutter in her stomach. It's nothing, she told herself stoutly. Nothing at all! And if it weren't for the one-eyed man, she wouldn't stay one minute longer in his house!

It was an odd day for Pip. Accustomed as she was to roaming freely about the streets of London, it seemed very strange to remain in the house all day. And of course, since she had never been anywhere remotely resembling her present whereabouts, she was innocently fascinated by everything that went on around her and more than willing to try her hand at whatever chore was assigned to her—whether she knew what she was doing or not!

She had tackled her first task, making piecrusts, with great exuberance, but had been promptly informed by Ivy in a gently chiding tone that perhaps she had better attempt something that required a little less skill. Despite Pip's enthusiastic efforts, the resulting piecrusts had been a disaster; not only was the final product unrecognizable, but Pip had been covered with flour from head to toe and had, to her amazement, managed to spread flour from one end of the kitchen to the other!

It had taken some time to clean up Pip and restore the area to its usual immaculate state, and Ivy, still not aware of the potential for calamity, had then set the girl to cracking eggs for a custard—another mistake, as Ivy soon learned. Not knowing how else to accomplish it, for culinary skill was *not* Pip's forte, after some careful thought, she had taken to crushing the eggs on the table, picking out the shell, and then scraping the remaining glop into a bowl!

She sincerely tried her best to be useful and to follow instructions, but everything was so very peculiar to her—not only the surroundings, and the people, but the entire situation was foreign to her. She wasn't stupid; it was merely that while other females may have been learning the mysteries of various womanly chores and the like from their mothers, Pip had been on the streets deftly lifting the valuables of unwary toffs and swells!

Understandably exasperated with her, Ivy had finally thrust a broom into her hand and had asked, with a not-surprising hint of sarcasm in her voice, if Pip thought she could sweep the floor without coming to grief. Humbly Pip had nodded her head and had scrupulously swept up every scrap and crumb she could find.

Despite the bustle of the other servants about her and the novelty of her situation, Pip could not stop herself from thinking about her conversation with her brothers last night *and* Royce's talk with them! How would the one-eyed man take the news that Jacko and Ben had not been able to find her? Would he believe them? Would he harm them? And how soon before he grew tired of excuses from her brothers and set someone else the task of wresting her from this place of refuge? And then there was Royce. . . . How much did he know? And what had he done to convince her brothers to confide in him?

As she worked, Pip had deliberately kept her thoughts from straying to Royce. She didn't like thinking about him, didn't like remembering the strange emotions and sensations he aroused within her. She tried to tell herself that she should be grateful to him, but gratitude was not an emotion that Royce Manchester raised in her breast. No, he had stirred other emotions, and they unsettled her, made her aware of her body in ways that filled her with agitation. Forcing herself to concentrate on the task in front of her, she was inordinately thankful that the chores assigned her kept her out of his path. Until she understood what was happening within herself, she wanted no more confrontations with the arrogant, vastly disturbing Mr. Manchester!

Perplexed and anxious, Pip managed to get through the first day in Royce's house. She missed her brothers immensely in spite of the kindliness and friendliness of the other servants and the constant activity going on around her. The kitchen was the hub of the household; not only were meals prepared here, but anything pertaining to the running of the house was planned and discussed here, and it was the place where all the servants ate and congregated.

Pip gathered from the comments she heard and from the satisfied attitudes of the others that Royce Manchester was an excellent man to work for—more than once that day, Ivy Chambers had said, "If all Americans were as nice as Mr. Manchester and Mr. Zachary, I'd emigrate to America, I would indeed!" Chambers himself seemed to echo this statement, nodding his head in agreement with Ivy's statement.

In addition to Ivy and Robert Chambers, there was Royce's valet, Edward Spurling, a small, precise, quiet man; Mr. Zachary's valet, William Smedley; and three maids varying in age from Alice, the youngest at sixteen, to Sarah, the oldest at twenty-seven, Hazel being in the middle at twenty years of age. Having associated, except for her mother, exclusively with men all of her life, Pip had been a bit uncertain about the other women, but they had proved to be an unusually friendly lot, teasing her not ungently about her mistakes and doing their best to make her feel welcome.

The footman, Tom Cooper, while pleasant enough and a

handsome young man, with wavy brown hair and limpid blue eyes, was very aware that he had all three of the housemaids half in love with him, and consequently, his manner was a trifle smug. Pip didn't exactly *dis*like him, but she thought him a bit too taken with himself.

Young Matt Hatton was another story, though. Barely thirteen, he had the lowest position on the staff and was at the beck and call of everyone else. Pip had been drawn to him on sight. It might have been the laughing sparkle in his hazel eyes or the impudent grin he flashed her now and then, or even his shock of red hair and freckled face that aroused her liking, but Pip suspected it had to do with the jaunty little air that clung to him. He might be the lowest member of the staff, but from his cocky manner, no one would have guessed it!

During the daylight hours, Pip was able to keep thoughts of the one-eyed man at bay, but as the day ended and darkness fell, she caught herself glancing nervously around, almost as if she expected to look up and see the one-eyed man standing in the room with her. Whether by accident or design, she had not been left alone for one moment during the day, and most of her chores had been centered in the kitchen, where there was always someone nearby. The few times that she had left the kitchen, one of the other servants had been with her. Even when Alice and Matt had been sent on some errands in the afternoon and actually could have used Pip's help in carrying their various burdens back to the house, Ivy had kept Pip near her side, and Pip had been secretly relieved—the one-eyed man was as perfectly capable of having her snatched from the street in broad daylight as he was of having someone creep into the house at night to whisk her away.

She didn't actually expect an attack tonight; if an assault was made on the house again this soon, it would more than likely be her brothers doing the housebreaking, and she had nothing to fear from them, but who knew what the one-eyed man had planned? Perhaps he had not believed Jacko and

Ben and was even now ordering her kidnapping by someone else . . . someone else who would not fail. She shuddered, and casting an uneasy glance at the heavy wooden back door as she helped Alice wash dishes in the scullery, she was surprised to see a shiny new lock and bolt had been added to the door. A lock and bolt that had not been there earlier in the day.

With a nonchalance she did not feel, she remarked, "Oh, is that a *new* lock on the door?"

Alice looked at the door and said, "Indeed it is! The master instructed the locksmith to put it on this afternoon while you were helping Hazel in the linen closet. Said he'd heard that there had been thieves about lately and didn't want to take any chances."

Pip smiled weakly and bent her head to hide the flush of pleasure that dyed her cheeks. It was possible that the reason stated by Alice was the correct one, but Pip could not help feeling that the new lock had been installed to make the one-eyed man's task more difficult.

And the truth of that feeling was proven later that night when she finally went to her room after Ivy had dismissed her. Pip had entered her tiny quarters. Turning to shut the door, she froze, her stunned gaze encountering the obviously new sturdy brackets and the heavy wooden bar leaning nearby. Almost dazedly she picked up the bar and slid it into place, her thoughts torn between astonishment and thankfulness.

It seemed that the American had been serious about keeping her safe from the one-eyed man. But why? she couldn't help asking herself a few seconds later as she absently lit her stub of a candle and prepared for bed. Sitting on her bed, her chin propped on her knees, in the flickering light of her little candle, she stared at the securely bolted door. No one would be able to enter her room now without her assent, and even though she knew that not the stoutest bar nor the cleverest lock could keep out a determined thief forever, the sight of that hefty wooden bar gave her much comfort. At least tonight she had no fears of being snatched from her bed and taken to the one-eyed man!

But if she had no fears about the one-eyed man tonight, her thoughts about the big American were still muddled. Why *was* he providing her a place of safety? He'd said she could be useful to him in more ways than one. . . . How? Even she could see that he didn't really need an extra servant. So what possible use could he have in mind?

Dressing that evening for the Mortimers' ball, Royce was wondering acidly if any usefulness that Pip's startling resemblance to the Earl of St. Audries might serve would be worth the notoriety her presence in his life was causing. The day had not been a pleasant one for him. Scowling as he stood before a cheval glass expertly tying his cravat, he decided that he was heartily sick of turning aside avid and downright impertinent questions about Pip and what he planned to do with her . . . and hearing how bloody lucky he was!

Zachary's two friends had not been loath to spread the further interesting news that the pickpocket had turned out to be a girl! "Devilish fine-looking article! Reminds me of someone, though—think I've seen her somewhere before!" Jeremy had told his friends when he had met them at Tattersall's. Leland had chimed in with "A damned fine piece, to be sure! Jeremy's right—looks familiar." And while Zachary had not added much to the conversation, in no time at all the males of polite London were aware of the fact that Royce Manchester had a beautiful young woman he had caught picking his pocket installed in his house on Hanover Square. Once he had seen Jeremy and Leland in the kitchen, Royce had known that it would be impossible to keep Pip's sex a secret, but he had hoped that word would not spread quite as fast as it had, or that it would not arouse much curiosity on the part of his acquaintances and friends. His hopes were naive and ill founded, as he soon discovered.

Royce had barely entered White's Club that afternoon when he was accosted by none other than Francis Atwater. His rakishly handsome face alight with speculation, Francis had said, "Well done, Manchester! I hear that your little pickpocket is definitely a lovely bit of baggage." Smirking, he had added, "I just wish that it had been *my* pocket she had been picking!" Since George had already made a similar comment, Royce had been halfway prepared, and instead of glaring as he had at George, he had simply smiled and continued on his way. What Royce had not been prepared for was to find himself and the little pickpocket the topic of conversation among his acquaintances wherever he went that day! To his dismay, he discovered that he had only to enter his usual, exclusively male, haunts for conversation to falter a second and then to take off more loudly as someone would cry out jovially, "Here he is now, the lucky rogue! Tell us, is she as beautiful as that young cub Leland says?"

And while, for the most part, Royce was able to take the teasing in good stead, he wasn't thrilled when Rufe Stafford and Martin Wetherly accosted him later that afternoon and, with salacious curiosity evident in their expressions, proceeded to bait him unmercifully. His dark eyes full of malice, Rufe Stafford drawled, "And to think I was of the opinion that you were actually doing a *good* deed!" Martin Wetherly, standing by his side, smirked and added snidely, "Oh, he was, my good man, he was—a good deed for *himself!*" Wetherly was plainly enjoying himself, in spite of the ill-disguised animosity in his brown eyes. Deciding he would gain nothing by trying to defend himself to the Earl's bosom friends, Royce merely smiled tightly and went on his way.

If one more person commented one more time about his good *luck,* Royce thought grimly as his valet helped him into his formfitting coat, he feared he'd throttle him! It was damned *bad* luck, as far as he was concerned! Taking one last look as he prepared to leave his room, Royce wondered sourly if his male friends would think him quite so lucky if they knew about the mysterious one-eyed man and if it were *their* houses that would be under attack by God knew what sort of murderous rogues! Ha!

In some respects Royce had not been overly surprised at how swiftly the news of Pip's sex had traveled through the circles of the male members of the ton, and he had been partially prepared to endure a few days of being the butt of sly jesting before interest waned and some other new bit of gossip or scandal caught their attention. He had known that the ladies would learn soon enough all the facts pertaining to the little pickpocket—after all, husbands *did* talk to wives and, of course, between lovers—but Royce had figured that he would have at least one day of grace before enduring another wave of sly questioning and speculative glances.

However, he was proven wrong on this surmise also. No sooner had he paid his respects to Lord and Lady Mortimer and was on the point of joining the other guests than Lady Mortimer, a matron of some fifty years, tapped him lightly on the arm and said in her blunt manner, "Heard about the little gel you've got in your house, Manchester." Her wise blue eyes boring into his, she added, "Hope you mean well by her."

Since most of the advice he had received this day had been to the contrary, Royce smothered a grin and murmured some polite reply before joining the other guests. Hoping that it was merely a fluke that Lady Mortimer had already learned about Pip, he made his way through the silk- and satin-garbed crowd, stopping to chat with first this person and then that. He was quite a popular fellow, and from his previous trips to London and his relationship, however distant, to the Pontebys, Royce was very familiar with numerous members of the ton. But as he continued on his way and met the raised eyebrows and unusually cool manner of some of the more formidable matrons, as well as the arch looks and knowing smiles of some of the less circumspect ladies, Royce's heart sank. Good Lord! Was there no one in polite London who hadn't heard of yesterday's exploits and the surprising aftermath?

The Mortimer ball was not the sort of social event that Royce looked forward to, and up until Pip's unexpected advent into his life, he had been on the point of crying off and finding a livelier way to spend the evening. It had been a desire to escape for a while the nudges and sly smiles of his friends at the various clubs and gaming hells he frequented that had prompted him to attend the Mortimer ball after all— that and a strong desire to put the problems associated with Pip from his mind. He had thought, mistakenly as it turned out, that an evening mingling in mixed society, with the more rakish element *not* in attendance, would allow him to postpone thinking further about Pip and would also allow him some breathing space.

Meeting the condemning stare of yet another socially rigid matron, and guessing correctly the reason for it, Royce sighed. All of London, it seemed, was positive he had procured the little pickpocket for his own salacious and vile purposes, and one half congratulated him for it, while the other half condemned him! He was being seen as either a clever knave or an iniquitous seducer of innocents. Neither reputation found any favor with him, and determined to put it all behind him, with a decisive stride he sought out Julia Summerfield, the tall, cool beauty who was also one of the two women he had concluded might make a suitable bride for him. A short while later, as he whirled the statuesque young lady about the ballroom floor, Royce was able to push Pip from his mind, his gaze resting appreciatively on Julia's lovely face. They were waltzing, Royce's hand at her waist firmly guiding Julia as they skimmed elegantly across the floor, her blue, gauzy gown billowing out around her.

At twenty-two, Julia was a very self-possessed young lady, and it was the calm, unruffled air about her as much as her lovely features—hair as fair as summer wheat; large, intelligent, thickly lashed eyes; and queenly grace and build—that had first aroused Royce's interest. She was tall, without the coltish gawkiness of so many tall women, and there were no simpering, missish mannerisms about her—something Royce found very refreshing, having had to endure the mawkish antics of several young ladies over the years.

Smiling into her china blue eyes, Royce remarked lightly, "You are a delightful partner; I have seldom waltzed with anyone as graceful."

Julia smiled serenely and replied courteously, "You are very polite."

At her words, unexpectedly the picture of Pip sitting in the tub, the damp, black curls framing her animated face, and her gray eyes filled with impudence as she had said, "Coo! And a right polite cove you can be, Royce Manchester!" flashed through his brain. It was an unsettling occurrence, all the more so when he realized disturbingly that Pip's comment held more meaning for him. More than a little irritated at his wayward thoughts, Royce frowned slightly.

Seeing his frown, Julia asked, "Is something wrong?"

Instantly composing his features into a pleasant mask, Royce answered easily, "Of course not. Why do you ask?"

Effortlessly following his lead around the crowded floor, Julia said, "You were frowning . . . and I wondered if perhaps something was troubling you."

There was a note in her voice that made him look at her more closely, and when she flushed under his intent gaze, he said resignedly, "You've heard about the pickpocket, haven't you?"

Her eyes not meeting his, she said stiffly, "I believe it is common knowledge." Then, in a rush, she added, "Everyone is talking about it."

"And what is your opinion on the matter?" Royce asked curiously as the waltz ended and he escorted her from the floor.

"It isn't my place to have an opinion about your private life," Julia answered modestly.

Suppressing the unkind thought that she sounded priggish, and pursuing this conversation for reasons unclear to himself, Royce inquired slowly, "But suppose you did have the right to make judgments about me—what would be your opinion then?"

They had almost reached the area where Julia's chaperon, a maiden aunt, sat, and Julia stopped and stared searchingly into Royce's dark, handsome face, his amber gold eyes very bright beneath the arching black brows. Her expression calm, she said deliberately, "I'm certain you had your reasons for acting as you did . . . and as long as you do not flaunt the relationship, I feel it is no one's business."

His eyes hard, Royce asked bluntly, "Not even a wife's?"

Steadily meeting his gaze, she said quietly, "Not even a wife's."

Oddly dissatisfied with her answer, Royce left Julia in the care of her aunt and wandered into the punch room. He had not precisely planned to remain faithful when he married—who did?—but he found it strangely distasteful that Julia was prepared to overlook his peccadillos. Again his thoughts turned to Pip. He had no way of knowing, but he suspected that she would not be so sanguine about the situation. And to his intense annoyance, he found himself wondering *exactly* what Pip's answer would have been to the same question. Growing increasingly angry at the way Pip seemed to have invaded his every thought, after enjoying several cups of the strong drink and enduring more sly comments from the gentlemen gathered around the punch bowl, Royce decided to go in search of more convivial company. He was looking through the colorful, constantly shifting throng for his hosts, intending to take his leave, when someone to his left murmured, "Ah, there you are! I wondered if you would tear yourself away from the charms of the little pickpocket and join us this evening." When Royce spun around, Allan Newell raised his quizzing glass and added, "I hear that she is really quite a fetching little thing beneath all that grime. Who would have guessed it?"

Garbed in a dove gray coat and black evening breeches, Allan Newell looked very elegant. His crisp sable hair framed an almost handsome face and brought attention to the lustrous darkness of his eyes. His pleasing looks, coupled with his fine manners and reputed wealth, made his appearance here tonight *not* surprising.

Not bothering to hide his irritation, Royce gave Newell a curt bow and said grimly, "You know, the next person who makes mention of yesterday's events or the titillating fact that the pickpocket is a female, I think I shall do him a violence." Giving Newell a hard look, he ended bluntly, "I trust you understand me?"

A superior smile on his mouth, Newell tilted his head slightly. "Oh, my! You really are annoyed about all this, aren't you?"

"Wouldn't you be?" Royce asked levelly.

Newell shrugged. "No doubt. It must be devilish uncomfortable finding oneself the object of so much libidinous speculation."

"Devilish, indeed!" Royce admitted with a grin, suddenly finding the situation humorous. If utter strangers wished to waste their time pondering his designs on one particularly saucy little pickpocket, who was he to deny them their pleasure? In a much better frame of mind, he continued his search for Lord and Lady Mortimer, still intent on leaving.

He had just spied Lady Mortimer talking to Lady Jersey when a voluptuous young woman with guinea gold hair stepped into his path. A warm smile upon her full, red mouth and invitation in the big, green eyes, Heather Cresswell asked flirtatiously, "Have you been looking for me?"

Of the two women he was considering as possible brides, Royce found himself most drawn to Heather's blatant sensuality. He admired Julia and usually found her to be charming company, but there was something about Heather that appealed to his deeply carnal nature. Not quite as tall as Julia, she was still a trifle above average height, and despite her patrician features, there was something about Heather that made most men think the most deliciously lewd thoughts. It may have been the slight sway in her walk, or the lush ripeness of her figure—which she had no qualms about displaying freely—or even the pouting lure of her full lips that attracted a man's attention, but whatever it was, Royce found himself suddenly in not such a hurry to leave the ball. Since she was a widow and, at twenty-six, able to handle her own affairs, Heather was allowed far more license than someone like Julia, and Royce saw no harm in paying outrageous court to the widow Cresswell.

Heather's blatant attempts to fix his interest with her amused Royce, but since he wasn't against an enjoyable dalliance with such an attractive woman, he made no attempt to free himself from her clinging presence. In fact, as he smiled mockingly down into Heather's darkly lashed green eyes, he decided sardonically that an undeniably public flirtation with her might go a long way in settling all the wagging tongues Pip's advent into his life had caused.

"Have I been looking for you?" Royce repeated teasingly. "But of course I have. . . . Why else would I be here?"

Heather laughed, and tapping his arm with her fan, she said lightly, "What an absolute bouncer!" One slim eyebrow arched. "I suppose that is why you have been part of the Summerfield chit's court—pining for me?"

Royce lifted her hand to his lips; his golden eyes dancing, he murmured, "Naturally."

"La! What a rake you are. . . . And if you were not the most fascinating man here tonight, I wouldn't allow you to charm me this way." Heather wasn't lying. As far as she was concerned, he was quite fascinating, and she was determined to have him—with or without the benefit of a wedding ring! Almost avariciously her eyes scanned his tall, powerful form, lingering on the broad shoulders covered by the expertly tailored plum coat, and the long, elegantly muscular legs clothed in well-fitting kerseymere pantaloons. Thinking of that magnificent body naked and locked passionately to hers brought a flush to her cheeks, and speculatively she raised her eyes to his, not bothering to hide the fact that she found him attractive. Very!

The expression in her green eyes was not hard to decipher, and Royce almost smiled at her obvious lures. Seduction of the widow Cresswell had not been on his mind, but if the lady had different ideas . . . A warm gleam entered his golden eyes. If the lady had different ideas, who was he to dissuade her? Bending his tawny head, he asked softly, "And do I? Charm you?"

Heather's breath quickened at his warm breath on her ear. She glanced enticingly over her shoulder, the mocking retort dying on her lips at the sudden sensual glitter in his eyes. Hot, wild hunger shafted through her body. She wanted him! Wanted to know if that hard, mobile mouth was as exciting as it looked . . . was desperate to let that powerful body possess hers. Aware that she might be throwing away a chance of marriage, but too mesmerized by him to care at the moment, recklessly she admitted, "You know you do." Oblivious to whoever might be watching them, she ran a caressing finger down his sleeve and added huskily, "If we were alone, I might be able to show you how very much you *do* charm me."

The invitation was implicit. A boldly carnal curve to his lower lip, Royce murmured, "I think we've done our duty to the Mortimers' ball, don't you? May I escort you home?"

Heather didn't hesitate, her nipples instantly swelling beneath her silken gown. "I would be delighted to have your company."

They bid their adieux, and a scant while later, Royce was sprawled easily on the plump velvet cushions of Heather's town coach, Heather half sitting, half leaning against him. The interior of the coach was in darkness except for the occasional dull gleam as they passed one of the gaslit lamps that dotted the cobblestone streets, the sound of the horses' hooves rhythmically echoing in the stillness of the night.

There was a warm intimacy between them, and the coach had not traveled half a block before Royce lazily pulled an eager Heather into his arms, his mouth coming down passionately on hers. Heather groaned at the force of the hungry desire that flooded through her at his touch, and the fleeting thought occurred to her that his kiss was even more exciting than she had imagined. Shamelessly she pressed nearer, frankly offering herself to him, and when his devastating mouth left hers and traveled lower, she arched up frantically against him, her fingers clenching his thick, tawny hair.

He freed her breasts, and his lips on her naked flesh was an exquisite torment that had Heather twisting wildly in his embrace. Hungry for him, she boldly caressed the thick bulge in his pantaloons, and his growl of pleasure excited her immensely. It took but a moment to release him from the pantaloons, and she was trembling with anticipation as her hand closed around the hard, heated power of him.

Nearly melting with desire, she sank back against the velvet cushions, the sway of the coach adding to her pleasure as Royce's hands unerringly probed beneath her silken skirts. Deliberately he brought her to the brink with his caresses, and just when she was certain she would die of longing, his forceful body joined with hers. She splintered into a million sparks of ecstasy, her scream of delight caught in his hard kiss. In the hours that followed Royce proved to Heather again and again that not even her most erotic dreams could have prepared her for the reality of his powerful lovemaking.

Entering the house on Hanover Square shortly before dawn, Royce greeted Chambers somewhat absently, his thoughts still on the beauteous charms of the lovely widow. It was only when Chambers rather noisily shot the bolt of the newly installed lock that Royce was jolted back to his present circumstances. Memories of the previous hours vanished, to be replaced by the unpleasant knowledge that his home was probably under siege by some malevolent villain, and almost irritably, Royce said, "I see that the locksmith has been here as I requested."

"Oh, yes, sir. He came late this afternoon and took care of everything." Keeping his face carefully expressionless, Chambers added, "Including the new bolt on the, er, young lady's door."

A cynical smile crossed Royce's face. Everyone was so certain that he had Pip's seduction in mind, and he wondered sardonically what the gossips would say if they knew about the locks on her door! Locks that would keep her as safe and chaste as a novice in a nunnery!

CHAPTER 8

Pip found the kitchen in a nervous flutter the next morning when she ventured downstairs. Ivy Chambers had been awakened during the night by a terrible toothache and had been hurried off to have the offending tooth drawn. Hazel had been hastily drafted to temporarily fill Ivy's position, and she was not handling the sudden promotion well. "I'm no cook!" she had muttered under her breath as she haphazardly took over the running of the kitchen. Pip made herself useful, and things might have evened themselves out if Chambers, perhaps distracted by worry about his wife, hadn't slipped and fallen in the pantry.

His injuries were not severe—a bump on the head and a slightly sprained wrist—but it threw the entire staff off balance. With both the cook and the butler indisposed, the kitchen was still in an upheaval when Royce rang down for his morning coffee a few hours later.

Normally Pip would not have been pressed into delivering the master's tray, but a flustered Hazel, agonizing over whether to fix the veal or a leg of lamb for supper, agitatedly pushed the big silver tray in her hands and muttered, "There! I hope I haven't forgotten anything. Take it right up to him—second floor, third door to the right."

With a sinking heart, Pip slowly made her way upstairs, hoping fervently that Royce had gone back to sleep and that she could deliver the tray and depart without any confrontation with him. Luck seemed to be with her. Her soft tap on the oak door elicited no response, and gingerly she opened the door and peeked inside.

The huge room was gorgeous in a decidedly masculine way. Elegantly fashioned walnut and rosewood furniture was scattered tastefully about the area, and upon the floor lay a vivid Turkey red carpet, sapphire, emerald, and gold tones rioting across it in a bold design. But it was the man apparently asleep in the amber-brocade-draped bed who riveted her attention.

Against her will she was drawn farther into the room, crossing it silently, and absently placing the tray on a walnut drum table near the bed, her eyes never leaving the striking features of the tousled, tawny-haired man in the bed.

He looks so different, she thought, astonished, as she hovered nervously a few feet from the bed, her gaze wandering over the long, thick, black lashes that lay against his proudly molded cheekbones. Without the brilliance of those golden eyes to mock and distract her, Pip studied him, focusing on his arrogant nose and the chiseled perfection of his mouth. He *is* handsome, she decided reluctantly, wishing it weren't so. But handsome is as handsome does, she concluded with a saucy toss of her head, fighting against the urge to continue looking at him.

His chest was bare, one muscled arm outflung, the other lying next to him; the fine linen sheets were ruched down to below his navel, and giving in to the nearly uncontrollable urge, she lingered and let her eyes continue their discovery of him. The thick mat of tawny curls that covered his broad chest fascinated her, and she was conscious of a tingling in her fingers, as if they wanted to touch him, to feel the warm flesh beneath the whorls of hair.

She swallowed uneasily, suddenly frightened of the direction of her wayward thoughts. But she was mesmerized by the indolent length of him and helplessly she stood rooted to the spot, wanting to turn away, and yet . . . Her gaze dropped to the flat stomach and the arrow of golden brown hair that disappeared beneath the linen sheets, all sorts of strange new sensations springing to life within her.

Genuinely appalled by her actions, she gave a little gasp and, with an effort, tore her gaze away and turned her back on him. Pip had only taken two steps away from the bed when Royce's voice stopped her in her tracks.

"Leaving so soon?" he drawled mockingly from behind her. "Didn't you like what you saw?"

Mortified and furious at the same time, she spun around. The sight of Royce half sitting up in the bed, a lock of tawny hair tumbling endearingly across his brow, the golden eyes full of mockery, made her heart thump painfully in her chest. Marshaling her forces against the sheer power of his attractiveness, she snapped, "You should have told me you were awake! It wasn't very polite to pretend to be asleep!"

Oblivious to his partially uncovered state, he sat up and stretched, the muscles bunching and flexing in his body. "And your staring at me wasn't impolite?" he asked dryly.

"I wasn't *staring!*" she ground out, knowing very well that she had been—avidly! "I merely wanted to see if you were asleep!"

Royce snorted. "I had to have been awake—how else could I have rung the kitchen?"

"You looked asleep!" Pip insisted tightly, her hands clenched at her sides, wishing she dared strike that taunting mouth.

She was very, *very* pretty when she was angry, Royce decided thoughtfully, his eyes on her angry face. To his surprise, he was discovering that he took a perverse enjoyment in rousing her wrath, taking pleasure in watching her eyes change to a dark, stormy gray, and the rosy flush that rushed into her cheeks at his provoking words and behavior. Insolently his gaze slid over her, noting the agitated rise and fall of the firmly rounded breasts beneath the blue and white gingham gown. The little pickpocket had distinct possibilities, he mused cynically, his eyes roving with increasingly sensual speculation over her delicate features and slim body. If her resemblance to St. Audries proved to be profitless, he considered slowly, a blatantly carnal smile curving his full mouth, perhaps he would . . .

Startled and angry at the direction of his thoughts—seducing housemaids was *not* his style!—Royce said abruptly, "Since you brought the tray, pour me a cup of coffee, will you?"

Pip glared at him, but relieved that he was dropping the embarrassing subject, she stalked over to the tray and, with angry motions, did as he requested. Her mouth set, she sharply demanded, "How do you like it? Black?"

Royce nodded, and when she handed him the china cup and saucer, he asked idly, "How are you settling in? Everyone treating you well?"

Before she could stop herself, she retorted tartly, "There is only *one* person in this house whose treatment I find offensive!"

Over the rim of his cup, he regarded her unblinkingly, something in the depths of that golden gaze making Pip's heartbeat increase. Warily she eyed him, stoutly telling herself that she had nothing to fear, but prudently she took a step backward.

"A wise move," Royce murmured softly, something about him reminding Pip unnervingly of a big cat calculating the precise moment for a lethal attack.

Deciding the sooner she was away from his disruptive presence, the better, Pip took a deep breath and asked, "Shall I leave now or is there anything else you want from me?"

Inexplicably her words conjured up all manner of erotic acts he could demand of her, and to his angry consternation, he felt himself hardening under the concealing folds of the linen sheet. At least he fervently hoped they were concealing! Annoyed by his unexpected intense reaction to her, he scowled. "You may leave. *You* can do nothing for me!"

There was something so insulting about his tone and words that Pip felt her temper soar uncontrollably. Arrogant bastard! Staring furiously at him, she was conscious that beneath her anger, some other emotion was struggling to spring forth, that it was this other emotion that prompted her to defy and provoke him. She ignored the wisdom that urged her to leave now, before there was further trouble, her eyes narrowing as they rested on the pitcher of freshly squeezed, *cold* orange juice that Hazel had placed on the tray. M'lord needed some of his imperiousness dashed! Suddenly smiling sweetly, she inquired dulcetly, "Perhaps some juice before I leave?" Not waiting for his consent, she picked up the crystal pitcher and audaciously emptied the contents into his lap.

Torn between delight and horror, Pip watched the incredulous disbelief surge across his handsome features in that split second before the icy impact of the liquid hit him. Not waiting a moment longer, a nervous giggle escaping from her at the look on his face, she bolted from the room, his muffled bellow following her down the stairs.

Undecided whether to laugh or rage at her impudent actions, Royce gingerly got up from his wet bed. Little devil! he thought half-angrily, half-admiringly. Just you wait, you wretched imp of Satan, he swore to himself as he proceeded to wash at the marble-topped stand, a recently filled pitcher of water and a china bowl resting on it for his use. The next time we meet, he promised tersely, you're not going to get away so easily!

Royce had just finished washing and had pulled on a pair of buckskin breeches when he heard the door to his sitting room opening. Unexpectedly his pulses leaped. Had his small tormentor returned?

He was astonished at the depth of his disappointment when his visitor turned out to be Zachary. Pushing decidedly wicked thoughts of the continuing war with the saucy little pickpocket from his mind, Royce greeted his cousin and swiftly ushered him out of his bedchamber. He was offering no explanations about that juice-stained bed!

Except for a few events, like the sparring match and the occasional ride in Hyde Park, Royce's and Zachary's paths seldom crossed these days. Zachary was busy with his own friends and spent little time at home. Though they shared a meal now and then, they were seldom in each other's company, and Royce was almost glad of Zachary's visit this morning—it provided him with an opportunity to inform him of his meeting with Pip's brothers and all that he had learned from them. He had debated the wisdom of telling Zachary what was going on, not wishing to involve him in any unnecessary danger, but he had concluded that there was more danger in Zachary's ignorance of the one-eyed man than his knowledge, and so as soon as Zachary had been seated in his sitting room, Royce revealed to him all that he knew about Pip, her brothers, and the mysterious one-eyed man.

Zachary was agog with delight, his topaz eyes glittering with excitement. "By Jove, Royce! Why, this is the most capital thing that has happened since we came to London! I'll tell you the truth, I've been getting a bit bored here in the city, but *now!*" Leaning forward enthusiastically, he asked, "Do you want me to patrol the house at night? I have that dandy pair of pistols I just purchased last week—they'd stop any housebreaker, I can tell you!" Becoming even more excited at the intrepid prospects appearing before him, he added zealously, "Or if you're already doing that, I could guard the door to Pip's room. By God! I would certainly like to lay hands on this damned one-eyed man!"

Since this had been the exact reaction Royce had feared, he tried to dampen Zachary's enthusiasm. "Zack! If Pip's brothers are to be believed, the one-eyed man is not, I repeat, *not* to be treated as if he were some form of new entertainment I have procured for you! The man is deadly and he apparently has tentacles everywhere—even within the ton. *Any*one could be helping him."

"Oh, come now," Zachary said uneasily. "It can't be that bad. I mean, I know these brothers of Pip's told you some very unsettling tales of this one-eyed creature's power, but you don't *really* believe that he has dominion over the members of the ton, do you? How could he?"

"Very simply," Royce replied heavily. "I'll give you a few examples—suppose impoverished Lord X and Lady Y wish to marry; the only problem is that Lady Y already has a husband, a very *rich* husband. . . . The one-eyed man, for a price, disposes of Lady Y's husband in a way in which no suspicion falls upon the two principles. After a reasonable time, the lovers are married and, one presumes, live happily ever after—on the murdered Lord Y's fortune. Or suppose young Lord Z is waiting impatiently for his rich old uncle to die; he makes a bargain with the one-eyed man, and before too long, the rich old uncle suffers a stroke and dies. Everyone is happy, Lord Z inherits the fortune he coveted, and the one-eyed man is richly paid for his efforts. Or suppose that the Duke of A's youngest daughter suddenly finds herself in an embarrassing way—the one-eyed man sees to it that 'the embarrassment' is taken care of and disappears." His face and voice grim, Royce ended with, "Everyone is satisfied with the situation—particularly the one-eyed man. Not only has he been exorbitantly rewarded for his efforts, but now he holds all of his former employers in the palm of his hand. If they wish their ugly secrets to remain hidden, they will do *whatever* he requires of them!"

"Good Lord!" Zachary exclaimed, aghast. "When you put it that way, it sounds so very reasonable."

"And now you understand why what I have said must remain between ourselves?"

Zachary nodded glumly. "Don't worry about me! I shan't breathe a word to anyone—not even to Jeremy and Leland!"

Thinking of those two young rattles and how swiftly they had spread the word of Pip's sex through the ton, Royce said fervently, "Especially *not* Jeremy and Leland!"

Smiling slightly, Zachary stood up and said, "Have no fear! I know that they are two of the biggest gossips in London."

Walking with Zachary to the door, Royce asked, "Are you seeing them this morning?"

"Oh, yes! We are going for a ride in Hyde Park." Zachary added casually, "Perhaps one day next week you and some of your friends would care to come riding with us?"

"Excellent idea!" Royce agreed cordially. "I'll speak to George and some of the others about it."

They parted amicably, each going his separate way. Royce returned to his bedroom to finish dressing, and catching sight of the juice-stained bed, an odd smile curved his mouth. He would say one thing for the advent of the little pickpocket into his household—he wasn't bored!

During the next few days, there were no more confrontations between Royce and Pip, although he saw her now and then as she flitted busily about the house doing various chores. On more than one occasion, to his growing irritation, he found his gaze drawn irresistibly in her direction. Through half-shuttered eyes, he would watch as she worked, and he would marvel again at the smooth alabaster skin and the strikingly lovely features. To his annoyance, inevitably his gaze would slide consideringly over the gentle thrust of her bosom and the slimness of her waist and hips under the old gingham gown, and the indecent thoughts that filled his mind during those times disturbed him and made his lips twist with derision. It wasn't, he reminded himself sardonically, as if his carnal needs were not being taken care of frequently and most enjoyably! But despite Della's opulent charms and Heather's bold pursuit of him, and his own best intentions, whenever Pip was in his vicinity, invariably he was conscious of decidedly *dis*honorable speculation about her.

If it weren't for her amazing resemblance to the Earl (he hadn't quite decided how he was going to make use of *that!*) and the promise he'd made that she could remain here in order to escape the one-eyed man, he mused savagely one morning as he was preparing to join some friends at Manton's Shooting Gallery, he'd toss her out into the streets on that delectable little derriere of hers and put an end to this increasing fascination she seemed to hold for him! Angrily pulling on his fastidiously polished black boots, ignoring the outraged shriek from his valet, Spurling, he was beginning to wonder if this damned one-eyed man even existed. Certainly there had been no sign of him! Not that he gave a bloody hell about that supposedly villainous creature—the way he was feeling right now, he'd welcome the chance to vent some of his frustration, and a bruising fight with a master criminal would be just the thing!

To his utter fury, Pip entered his bedchamber just then, a freshly ironed stack of cravats over her arm, and Royce swore softly at the sudden leap of his pulse. Cursing his earlier concurrence with Chambers's suggestion that because Pip was so inept in the kitchen, she be assigned to Hazel to help with the cleaning and running of various errands throughout the house, Royce glared at her. If she'd just stay out of his sight!

Oblivious to his valet's openmouthed stare, antagonism fairly radiating from him, he said rather harshly, "I ordered those cloths twenty minutes ago. What the devil took you so long?"

Pip had done her best to keep out of his way these past few days—his powerful presence unsettled her and roused emotions that made her toss and turn restlessly at night on her narrow little bed. Unfortunately it *was* his house, and some contact with him had been unavoidable, but those moments when she had to be in the same room with him were fraught with a prickly awareness of that long, lean body and the bright, hooded gaze that followed her every movement. No words would pass between them, and she would keep her features deliberately expressionless as she worked swiftly, wanting desperately to get away from him, the knowledge that he watched her making her resentful and yet tremble and feel strangely breathless.

She had tried very hard to keep a civil tongue lately, and though she was embarrassed at Spurling's presence, Royce's unfair attitude weakened her restraint. "Well, *excuuuse* me, guvnor!" she drawled brashly. "If you bloody well wanted them in such a hurry, perhaps your lordship could have stirred himself to come and get them!"

Royce's mouth tightened, but as he stared down into her flushed, angry features, the expressive gray eyes and the haughty tilt to the little nose, he felt his fury ebb and laughter rise up inside of him. As a servant, she was proving to be singularly impertinent! But there was something about her that, in spite of himself, he found vastly appealing. She needed to be taught a lesson, though, he decided with a glint in his eyes, one he was eventually going to enjoy teaching her, about the foolhardiness of sassing one's employer! But willing to let her escape unscathed this time, he took the cravats from her arm. "Remind me," he murmured dryly as he turned away, "to beat you someday, will you? Now, please leave; you've annoyed me enough for one day."

Not certain whether she was relieved or angry at his dismissal, Pip glared at his broad back and, to poor Spurling's utter shock, stuck out her tongue at Royce. What she wouldn't give to yank that tawny hair from his arrogant head!

Royce smiled when he heard the door slam forcefully behind her. Little termagant! It might be a pleasure to tame her to his hand.

He frowned at that thought and deliberately dismissed her from his mind. The morning at Manton's Shooting Gallery passed pleasantly, and Royce was pleased to see that the idle weeks in London had done nothing to interfere with his unerring aim. He parted from his friends a few hours later and was strolling toward the house on Hanover Square when Heather Cresswell accosted him.

She was driving a high-perch phaeton pulled by a pair of magnificent high-stepping black geldings. Smiling up at her, Royce admitted that she made an attractive sight with her guinea gold curls peeking out from under the rakishly tilted dark green hat, and her lush figure well displayed in a form-fitting black riding habit trimmed in the same green color as her hat. He had sent her an enormous basket of fragrant yellow roses and a polite note the morning after they had made love, but he had not seen her since that night.

Holding the reins easily in her black-gloved hands, she asked archly, "Would you like a ride? Or are you one of those men who don't trust women to drive as well as they do?"

Grinning, Royce shook his head and lithely swung up into the place beside her. "When they are as beautiful as you, I find that it really doesn't matter," he murmured lightly.

She tipped her head at his compliment and set her horses in motion. They drove in silence for a moment and then Heather shot him an avid glance and, forgetting all her plans to lure him further into her web, admitted petulantly, "I expected to see you before this—didn't the night we shared mean anything to you? Where have you been?"

Royce looked at her thoughtfully. While he had been paying lazy court to her, her reputation was not unknown to him—the widow Cresswell was discreet with her lovers, but she had by no means remained chaste since her husband's untimely death. They had made each other no promises, and her sudden possessiveness grated on him. Picking his words with care, he replied, "I apologize if you feel neglected, but I wasn't aware that the night we spent together constituted more than it was—a very pleasurable interlude for both of us."

Suddenly aware that shrewishness would gain her nothing, Heather cunningly changed her tactics. Royce Manchester was everything she had ever wanted in a man, and she was determined to be his wife. Her green eyes narrowed calculatingly as she stared ahead. He had wanted her that night they had made love, she thought slowly, and never doubting her allure, she was positive that she could make him want her again. . . . If she could arrange for them to be caught in a compromising position . . . As she deliberately let one of her hands slide down to his muscled thigh, a sensual smile curved her full mouth. Boldly she explored the hard flesh beneath her fingers, and glancing over at him, she said breathlessly, "I've missed you, darling. I had hoped that you would come to me again."

"I think," Royce drawled coolly as he politely removed her fingers from his thigh, "that you would do well to keep your hands on the reins."

"Oh, pooh," she protested with a pout, "never tell me that you are a prude."

Royce almost smiled. Prudishness was not one of his failings! But Heather's actions faintly repelled him, and he was startled to find himself thinking of Pip and her audacious behavior. At least, he admitted cynically to himself, Pip's outrageous manner toward him was refreshing—if infuriating.

With an effort, he switched his wayward attention back to the woman at his side, and sending Heather a mocking glance, he murmured, "Far be it for me to tell a beautiful female anything!"

Wanting to end the conversation, Royce fortuitously caught sight of one of the most notorious gossips in London and swiftly seized the opportunity. Smiling down at Heather, he said, "But I would suggest that you acknowledge Lady Belmont's wave, unless you want tongues to wag faster than they are already."

Heather's mouth tightened at the sight of the dowdy female who was waving at them. Cutting Lady Belmont was not to be condoned, and sighing for the lost opportunity, Heather pulled her horses over and smiled sunnily at the older woman. Quite how it happened, she was never certain, but in the course of the next few moments, Royce vacated the vehicle and she found herself driving off with Lady Belmont at her side!

Having escaped Heather's clutches, Royce wandered home in search of solitude. He met Zachary in the hallway, just as his cousin was on his way out again. Recalling their earlier conversation, he said, "I spoke with George at Manton's this morning, and if it is convenient with you, we shall go riding on Tuesday in Hyde Park."

Zachary readily agreed to the date and disappeared out the front door. Feeling strangely out of sorts, Royce walked into the library, thinking that he might while away a few hours examining some of the fine books that lined the walls.

Unenthusiastically his gaze wandered around the pleasant

room, stopping abruptly when he caught sight of a black, curly head peeking above the back of one of the red leather chairs that were scattered about the long room. Having a fair idea of who those curls belonged to, Royce walked over to the secluded corner where Pip sat reading.

Totally absorbed in a novel, Pip didn't hear his soft-footed approach. It was apparent she had been sent in here to dust. A feather duster lay forlornly against the chair in which she sat; several dust rags and a container of lemon-scented beeswax were scattered along the shelf near her head.

She had no idea that he was in the room until Royce suddenly reached across and plucked the book from her hands. She gasped in surprise, then, seeing who it was, she scrambled to her feet. Her face a picture of vexation and guilt, she muttered, "Bloody eyes! I thought you had left the house! You're not supposed to be here!"

Tamping down an urge to laugh, Royce drawled mockingly, "I wasn't aware that you were in charge of my social calendar." Not giving her a chance to answer, he looked at the book in his hand. "Is this some new duty that has been assigned to you? Reading Jane Austen?"

Pip flushed, wishing that it had been anyone else who had caught her and that the sight of him didn't cause her pulse to leap in the most peculiar manner. "You know very well it isn't!" she said defiantly.

Royce stared at her, one hawkish brow rising at her tone of voice. Cursing her unruly tongue, Pip looked away, uneasily conscious that she was in the wrong. She owed him a great deal, and he had been *extremely* forbearing, she admitted grudgingly. Grimly Pip brought her volatile emotions under control. "Chambers sent me in here to dust and . . ." A look of wonder crossed her expressive face. "I've never seen so many books, and I just . . ." She shrugged. "I got to looking at them and before I knew it, I was thoroughly engrossed." She flashed him a look from beneath her lashes, and despite her best intentions, asked impudently, "Are you going to beat me?"

Her sheer bravado dragged a reluctant laugh from Royce, and shaking his tawny head, he admitted, "I probably should, but I won't . . . this time!" A glint entered his golden eyes and he added dryly, "When you do finally make me lose my temper, I suspect the beating I shall give you will ensure that you don't sit for a week!"

The gray eyes flashing dangerously, she replied tightly, "And do you think that you shall escape unscathed if you lay a hand on me?"

Royce looked at her, at the tempting rosy mouth and the bosom heaving beneath her gown, and something powerful and elemental surged fiercely through him. Incredulously he realized that he would very much like to lay his hands on her, but not in anger. . . . A sensual smile curved his mouth. No. Not in anger. Displeased with the direction of his thoughts, he sought a way to diffuse the situation, and glancing down at the book in his hands, he asked lightly, "Do you like to read?"

Not quite trusting the expression in his golden eyes, Pip answered cautiously, "I don't know—a pickpocket usually doesn't have time for such entertainments."

"But then, how many pickpockets do you know who know how to read?" Royce asked teasingly. "I doubt reading is a requirement for deft little fingers!"

Brusquely motioning her to the chair in which she had been sitting, Royce lounged on the black damask sofa across from her. Somewhat gingerly Pip obeyed him, a wary cast to her face.

Royce grimaced at her stiff posture, her hands folded demurely in her lap, but he couldn't help noticing what a very pretty picture she made, her black hair and clear skin contrasting attractively with the red leather of the chair, the gray eyes clear and direct beneath their long, spiky lashes. Consideringly his gaze slid over the slim figure, and he frowned. He really was getting tired of that blue and white gingham gown. She needed more clothes. . . .

Jerking his thoughts away from the disturbing images that flitted through his mind, he inquired softly, "Are you a good pickpocket?"

Still cautious, but relaxing slightly, Pip couldn't help crowing, "Guvnor—I'm one of the best!" She shot him a dark look. "You were just lucky when you caught me!"

Lazily Royce retorted, "Lucky is not precisely the word I would use to characterize myself these past days."

Pip grinned, but for once, wisely kept her mouth shut. She didn't want to argue with him, and to her astonishment, she didn't want this conversation to end. Greedily she was storing up every moment of it, memorizing his handsome features, the way his eyes crinkled at the corners when he smiled, the way his beautifully sculpted mouth twitched with suppressed amusement when she said something particularly outrageous. Against her will, covertly her eyes traveled over the grace and suppleness of that tall, muscular body as he reclined indolently on the sofa across from her, and she was aware of an odd warmth seeping languidly through her slender body.

To their utter astonishment, they talked easily for several more moments, Royce encouraging Pip to tell him of her life in St. Giles, Pip convincing Royce to detail some of the differences he found between England and America. It was an odd moment in time, and Royce found himself rather annoyed when Chambers entered the room and disturbed the strange intimacy between them.

"Oh, sir!" he exclaimed, embarrassed. "I didn't realize that young Pip was here with you!" He glanced curiously at them and then asked uneasily, "Er, is there anything I can get you?"

The moment was shattered, and rising to his feet, Royce shook his head and summarily dismissed the butler. Annoyed with himself for allowing the little pickpocket to intrude further into his life, Royce glanced sourly at Pip, who had also risen upon Chambers's entrance. A sardonic twist to his mouth, he said cynically, "You had better report to Chambers immediately—your advent into my life has caused enough gossip as it is, and I don't need to find myself the object of my own servants' tittle-tattle!"

Stung at his abrupt change, Pip retorted sharply, "You were the one who ordered me to sit down!"

"And it's probably the first damned order I've given you that you've obeyed!" Feeling the need to enrage her, to put some distance between them and the odd little intimate interlude they had shared so briefly, Royce added icily, "Before you cause me more trouble, please follow Chambers, and take your bloody dust rags with you!"

Pip was surprised at the shaft of pain that went through her at his cold words. "*You're* the one who caused all the trouble!" she retorted, trying to hide her bewilderment. "My life was just fine until you appeared in it!"

"Oh?" he asked derisively. "You're eager for the life the one-eyed man has planned for you?"

Infuriated at the way he turned her words on her, she said rashly, "At least with him I wouldn't have to put up with the likes of you!"

Something snapped inside of Royce at her words, and stunning both of them, he caught her wrists in his hands and pulled her next to him. "Are you saying you *want* to become his mistress?" he asked, his voice thick with some savage emotion he could feel but not understand.

Frightened of the sleeping tiger she had roused, confused by the elation his reaction made her feel, Pip glanced away from the glittering golden eyes and almost whispered, "No. No. I don't want to be his mistress!"

That tempting mouth of hers was mere inches from his, and Royce felt his body stirring. His gaze locked on her rosy lips, he lowered his head to kiss her when Pip said in a very small voice, "I don't want to be *your* mistress either."

Royce let go of her, his face an icy mask. Pip didn't dally. In less than a second, she was out the door like a doe escaping from a tiger, a large, very hungry tiger. . . .

CHAPTER 9

The ride through Hyde Park proved to be enjoyable, although Royce was not precisely pleased when the Earl of St. Audries's friends, Rufe Stafford and Martin Wetherly, invited themselves to join them. He was even less pleased when the two men clung like leeches to the group and politeness forced him to invite them back to the house to partake of the light repast that Ivy Chambers had prepared in anticipation of several of the gentlemen accompanying Royce and Zachary home.

The group consisted of perhaps fifteen gentlemen, including George Ponteby, Allan Newell, Francis Atwater, Stafford, and Wetherly, as well as several of Zachary's friends. Leland and Jeremy were naturally part of the group, but Royce was plainly astonished to see that young Julian Devlin had also been included. While all the others were busy serving themselves from the lavish buffet set out in the dining room, Royce cocked an eyebrow in Julian's direction and glanced questioningly at Zachary.

Almost shamefacedly Zachary murmured quietly, "He's not really a bad sort, you know. He can't help it if the Earl is his father!" Looking slightly apologetic, Zachary added, "You don't mind that he is here, do you?"

"Good Lord, no!" Royce said with a laugh. "I am just surprised, since when you last spoke of him, it was with great dislike." A teasing glint in his eyes, he added, "And that must have been, oh, let me see, all of four days ago."

Zachary grinned briefly. "The thing is, Royce, I thought he was a haughty bastard like his father, but he isn't." Glancing around to see that the others were still preoccupied with the tempting delicacies spread out before them, his young face intent, Zachary said soberly, "Last night a group of us were carousing in Covent Garden when we accidentally crossed the Earl's path. St. Audries was extremely drunk and spoke very sneeringly to Julian. By God, I'll tell you true, *I* wouldn't have been able to prevent myself from striking out if *any*one, much less my father, had spoken to me in that insulting manner, but Julian behaved most admirably. When St. Audries could not provoke Julian to action, I guess he wanted to find someone else to annoy." Zachary's mouth twisted wryly. "Unfortunately, he spotted me and launched into a vitriolic attack on Americans—you and me in particular. It was all very ugly and embarrassing, but in a flash Julian interrupted his father and *defended* me! I was astounded, I can tell you, even more so later in the evening when he came up to me and apologized for his father's behavior."

Thoughtfully Royce glanced across at the subject of their conversation. Julian Devlin was a son any man would have been proud to claim—tall, handsome, a charming manner about him, and from everything that Royce had heard, universally well liked by both the younger and older members of the ton. So what had this exemplary young man done to arouse his father's ire? Was it simply sheer cussedness on the Earl's part? Could the Earl possibly be jealous that his son enjoyed the admiration and acceptance that was denied to him? Or was it merely the differences of opinion and life-style that differentiate one generation from another? Somehow Royce didn't think it was as simple as that, and he found himself, as the afternoon progressed, speculatively glancing now and again at young Julian Devlin.

The group had long ago finished eating and had left the dining room and were at present scattered about the front salon, discussing what little news there was concerning Napoleon and the pitched battle that was certain to take place soon in Belgium. Since Napoleon's escape from Elba in late February, all of Europe had been closely monitoring the former French Emperor's movements. The representatives of the victorious allies, Russia, Britain, Prussia, and Austria, as well as members of a French delegation, had been attending the Congress of Vienna, where they had been trying to divide Napoleon's Empire amongst themselves; however, Napoleon's escape had vanquished all of their petty squabbling and they had been galvanized into action as they had been forced to hastily reassemble their armies to meet this new threat to peace.

By June, Napoleon's troops were already marshaled along the Belgian frontier awaiting his imminent arrival from Paris. The Prussian army, under Marshal Blücher, was poised on the lower Rhine, and the Duke of Wellington's headquarters were at Brussels. Since Wellington had no definite intelligence regarding Napoleon's movements, he was keeping various divisions of his army within easy distance of that capital. The stage was set for a great struggle; all that was needed was the appearance of the great man himself, Napoleon. . . .

"Just think," Francis Atwater said slowly, "while we are here calmly discussing the situation, Blücher and Wellington may be at this very moment fighting for their very lives against Napoleon."

"Or," Royce commented dryly, "Napoleon may have suffered his final defeat."

A small silence fell over the room as the gentlemen considered both statements, then George Ponteby suddenly raised his glass of hock and said loudly, "To Wellington, may he thoroughly trounce the Corsican monster!"

There were murmurs of agreement from everyone, and each man drank to the impromptu toast. The conversation became less serious after that, some gentlemen proceeding to lay wagers on when the battle would take place, others putting aside talk of Napoleon and discussing the attributes of their tailors, their horses, or their mistresses, depending on who was talking.

Standing a little apart from the others, Royce idly studied the various men in his salon, his gaze pausing for a moment on the animated features of Julian Devlin as that young man argued with undisguised enthusiasm the merits of a particular horse he had just purchased at Tattersall's. Royce couldn't hear what he said, but it was obvious from the expression on the faces of Jeremy and Leland that they disagreed, while Zachary appeared to be seconding every word Julian uttered. Smiling faintly, Royce took a sip of hock, watching the play of emotions that crossed Julian's handsome face.

Royce was situated not far from the group containing Julian, and as he continued to watch him, Royce was struck again at how unmistakable were the Devlin features. Except for the obvious male and female differences, Julian and Pip bore an undeniably striking resemblance to each other. As they should, Royce thought wryly, considering that the Earl no doubt had sired them both. Yet there were subtle differences; the shape of Pip's face was entirely different, even though she shared with Julian the haughtily arched black brows and exotically shaped gray eyes, as well as the black, curly hair and the determined chin. Royce had first thought that he had overestimated Pip's resemblance to the St. Audries family, but having grown used to her face these past few days and now astutely observing Julian's corresponding features, he acknowledged that, if anything, he had *under*estimated their similarity. He hadn't yet decided how to use Pip's resemblance, but he was confident the answer would come to him when necessary.

It was by now early evening, and Royce wandered over to his guests who were beginning to take their leave. Half an hour later, nearly everyone, including Zachary and his friends, had departed in search of other amusement. Only Ponteby, Newell, Atwater, and Wetherly remained in the salon, and it suddenly dawned on Royce that Stafford, who had been there not a second ago, was missing.

Instantly suspicious, albeit for no good cause—Stafford *could* have left without taking his leave—Royce excused himself for a moment and stepped out of the salon into the main entrance hall. If Stafford was, as he suspected, still in the house, where would the man have gone? Royce glanced up the stairs, but then dismissed that idea—it was unlikely that even Stafford could think of an excuse to seek out the upper portions of the house. Of course, the man may have left the room for no more mysterious reason than he needed to use the water closet, but Royce, his unease growing with every moment, doubted it. Deciding to take a quick look into the dining room on the slight chance that Stafford had merely gone in search of a bit more food, Royce crossed the hall and was on the point of opening the double doors that led to the dining room when he heard Pip's outraged voice on the other side. Immediately throwing wide the doors, Royce charged angrily into the room only to be brought up sharply by the scene that rapidly unfolded before his eyes.

It might have been an accident that Stafford had returned to the dining room just in time to discover Pip clearing away the used dishes, or there may have been a more sinister motive behind his actions. At any rate, he *had* found Pip, looking very pretty in her blue and white gingham gown, a half-full tureen of carp soup in her hands. Apparently, after catching her arm, Stafford had proceeded, as best Royce was able to ascertain, to make her a most improper offer. Pip had reacted with characteristic aplomb.

The carp soup sloshing dangerously, Pip's cheeks stained rosy with temper, her gray eyes flashing like summer lightning, she jerked her arm out of Stafford's grasp. "Why, you bloody bugger! Get your filthy hands off me! And I'd sooner lie in the gutter with a swineherder than to suffer *your* touch!"

Even as Royce crossed the dining room, Stafford made the mistake of grabbing hold of Pip's shoulders and shaking her. "We'll just see about that, you haughty little bitch!" And oblivious of the soup tureen between their bodies, he crushed Pip's body next to his and brutally kissed her.

Royce had only covered half the distance of the room before Pip yanked her mouth away from Stafford's and, managing to escape his hold, proceeded to empty the contents of the tureen over his head. Stafford yelped and leaped back a step as the fine china tureen shattered when it hit the floor. Pip, however, wasn't finished with him yet. Taking vicious aim, she brought her knee up savagely between his legs, making him nearly double over with pain. "And *that*," she snarled, "is to make certain that you don't make the mistake again of pressing your attentions where they most definitely are *not* wanted!"

"And if you don't understand precisely what she means," Royce added silkily, "I shall be happy to explain it further to you—after I rip out your liver and have it for dinner!"

Both Pip and Stafford spun around at Royce's voice, but while Pip's face revealed her delight at his appearance, Stafford went pale and nervously mopped the remains of the carp soup from his face with a linen handkerchief. Hastily he said, "Nothing to get upset about, old fellow. Just a serving wench."

Royce's eyes narrowed and he took a threatening step nearer to Stafford. "But you see, she is *my* serving wench! And I object strenuously to my servants having to put up with the likes of you!"

"Oh, come now!" Stafford muttered. "Less than a week ago she was just some little pickpocket from one of the worst rookeries in London. But just so you don't misunderstand me, I am willing to pay you for her." Smiling unctuously, he said, "Name your price and I'll take her away and you won't be bothered with her again."

Royce's hands closed roughly about Stafford's starched cravat. "She isn't for sale! And if I ever catch you within a mile of her, I shall take great pleasure in personally severing every limb from your body." Giving Stafford a powerful shake, he asked dangerously, "Have I made myself clear?"

"My dear boy," drawled Ponteby from the doorway, "you have made yourself clear to *all* of us! Now, do please unhand the poor creature—I'm certain you have frightened him near to death with your crude American manners."

Glancing over his shoulder, Royce was annoyed to see that the others were coming into the room. His temper abating a trifle, he loosened his hold on Stafford and, as if not trusting himself, moved slightly away from him. He looked at Pip, who had watched the scene with wide gray eyes, and motioned for her to leave. With a swirl of blue and white skirts, she disappeared instantly.

George raised his quizzing glass in the direction she had disappeared and murmured, "The little pickpocket?"

Royce nodded curtly, his fists clenched menacingly at his sides.

Clutching his ruined cravat, Stafford took comfort from the presence of the others and in a voice filled with outrage said, "The man attacked me! He physically assaulted me!" Gaining courage with every passing second, he drew himself up and uttered portentously, "I shall have to call him out!"

"Oh, no, that would never do!" said George. "Can't fight a duel over a mere pickpocket! No matter how lovely she is!"

"I have no intention of fighting a duel with Stafford," Royce said coolly, advancing determinedly in Stafford's direction. "I do, however, have every intention of throwing him out of my house!"

Stafford took one look at the grim expression on Royce's face and decided that retreat was the better part of valor. He hurried toward his friend, Wetherly. "*Well!* 'pon my word, Martin, let us leave here immediately!"

Precisely how much he had seen or what Wetherly thought of the unpleasant scene that had just taken place was difficult to ascertain. His swarthy face was expressionless, and the dark eyes revealed no emotion whatsoever. His voice prosaic, he said, "As you wish." Wetherly bowed slightly in Royce's direction, saying politely, "Good day to you, Manchester. Delightful time."

Chambers appeared at the doorway suddenly, obviously, from the wary look on his face, having learned from Pip what had transpired. Royce glanced at his butler and then, looking at Wetherly, said levelly, "I'm pleased you enjoyed yourself. Chambers will show you the way out."

There was a peculiar silence after Chambers had escorted Wetherly and Stafford from the dining room. George broke it by murmuring, "A deucedly nasty pair of fellows. Can't think why you invited 'em to the house."

Dryly Royce commented, "I didn't—they just sort of came along, and at the time it seemed less trouble to have them underfoot than to shake free of them."

George nodded slowly. Looking across at Atwater, his usually sleepy expression replaced by anxiety, he asked, "Think there will be a lot of talk? Wouldn't want Royce to be troubled by a lot of nonsense."

Atwater shrugged. "I'm sure they will waste no time telling the Earl what happened, and if he can twist the story to make Royce appear in a bad light, I'm positive that he will. However, I believe the entire sordid incident will blow over."

"Perhaps," said Newell, his dark eyes thoughtful. "I

wonder, though, if there is any real danger that Stafford will carry out his threat and challenge Royce to a duel."

Royce snorted. "Gentlemen! I appreciate your concern, but I'm not worried about the likes of Rufe Stafford! If he wants to spread this tawdry little tale from one end of London to the other, it doesn't bother me—after all, *he* was the one caught making advances to my servant! And as for meeting him in a duel, it is out of the question."

"Why?" George asked interestedly.

"Is Stafford particularly noted for his skill with either the sword or the pistol?" Royce asked patiently.

George shook his head, and Royce smiled. "And would you characterize my expertise with both weapons as trifling?"

As George remembered how many wafers Royce had effortlessly notched one morning last week at Manton's Shooting Gallery, as well as his deadly grace with the rapier, his anxious expression vanished and he smiled sheepishly. "Forgot!" he said unabashedly. "You're right—wouldn't be fair for you to meet him."

The four gentlemen continued talking for a few minutes longer, and then Ponteby, Atwater, and Newell took their leave of Royce and headed to their various establishments to change for whatever evening's amusements they had planned. Shutting the door firmly behind them, Royce hesitated for a long moment in the elegant foyer, thinking over the scene with Pip.

Had it been just coincidence, he wondered uneasily, that Wetherly and Stafford had attached themselves to himself and his friends this afternoon? Or had it been deliberate? And was it just an accident that Stafford had found Pip alone in the dining room, or had Stafford been purposely searching for her? His face grim, Royce stared unseeingly up the winding staircase. Had the one-eyed man decided to take a different tack? Could Stafford have been working at his direction? Stafford *had* attempted to get Pip out of the house—first with his improper suggestion and then by offering to buy her. . . . It wasn't only thieves in the night who constituted a threat to Pip's safety. Wanting to reassure himself that she had suffered no harm from Stafford's handling, he went in search of her.

When Pip had escaped from the ugly scene in the dining room, she had been too angry at Stafford and too relieved by Royce's timely interference to think very clearly. Furiously scrubbing her mouth with the back of her hand as if to wipe away the foul taste of Stafford's kiss, she had dashed into the kitchen and, ignoring the interested stares of the other servants, had spoken quietly to Chambers, giving him a brief report of what had just transpired. Chambers's shocked exclamation and his speedy exit from the kitchen had caused a raised eyebrow or two, but when it became apparent that Pip was not going to tell the others what she had told him, they turned their attentions to whatever tasks they had been doing before her sudden entrance in their midst.

Ivy, however, gave her an inquiring look, and Pip walked over to her side near the big, black stove, where she was busy cooking a lemon-brandy sauce for tomorrow's custard. In a low undertone, Pip quickly related all that she had told Chambers. When she finished speaking, Ivy looked at her closely and asked with concern, "Are you all right? The gentleman didn't hurt you?"

Pip flashed her a brief smile. "I think your sympathy should be with him—he's the one who had a tureen of hot soup dumped on his head!"

Ivy frowned. "I just hope that you are not blamed for what happened. The gentry can be such fools at times!"

Pip was on the verge of asking her what she meant when Ivy dismissed her by saying briskly, "Well, there is no help for it, and for the time being, I think I'll keep you busy in the kitchen. Go help Alice in the scullery."

It was only then, as she helped Alice wash and scour the

dirty dishes and pots, that Pip had time to actually think about what had happened in the dining room.

She hadn't been frightened when she saw one of the gentlemen coming into the room, although she had been a little nervous. She hadn't been a servant for very long, and this would be the first time all the lessons that had been drilled into her the past few days by the other servants would be put to the test. But there had been something about the gentleman, something about the furtive way that he had entered the room and the pleased expression that had suddenly flashed across his face when he had seen her, that had made her uneasy. Telling herself she had lived among thieves too long, she had smiled brightly and asked, "May I help you, sir? Is there something I can get for you?"

The gentleman was expensively dressed, his cravat as white and rigidly starched as the ones worn by Royce and Zachary, and the cut of his coat bespoke fine tailoring, yet there was something about him that continued to make Pip edgy. His smile was a little too oily, the gleam in the brown eyes a bit too pronounced, and his tone of voice . . . There had been *such* satisfaction in his voice, such sordid meaning in his tone, when he had said, "Oh, I'm quite certain that there are several ways that you could help me, my dear." Pip had been instantly on her guard.

When he had propositioned her, when the import of his vulgar offer had sunk into her brain, Pip's first reaction had been astonishment. In fact, she had been so astonished by the notion that this utter stranger seemed to be laboring under the assumption that she might *like* his attentions that she had very nearly giggled. But when he had taken hold of her arm and had repeated his suggestion, any desire to giggle had been instantly banished. And she certainly had not felt like giggling when he had put his wet mouth against hers!

Even now, thinking of it made her stomach lurch. Not even recalling the look on his face when she had dumped the tureen of soup over his head and had used her knee to further emphasize her displeasure with his actions could dispel her feeling of having been sullied in some indefinable way. His kiss had been horrible, and she shuddered slightly. To think that he had actually thought she would be flattered by his attentions!

Putting the plate down on a nearby counter, she picked up another, her thoughts automatically flying to Royce and the odd excitement she had felt when she had heard his voice and had looked around to see him rushing into the room. A dreamy little smile curved her mouth. He had been magnificent! Those tiger eyes full of fury, the lean, hard face angry and intent, and the aura of danger that had radiated from his tall, powerful body had taken Pip's breath away. Now, if *he* had been the one to kiss her . . . A flush seared its way up across her cheeks, and almost angrily she wiped the plate in her hand. What a fool she was! It was thoughts like those that would put her feet irrevocably on the path her mother had trod, and Pip found the idea of selling herself to whichever gentleman took her fancy utterly distasteful.

Not that she condemned her mother! Lord, no! Jane had lived her life as she had seen fit, and Pip would have been the last one to sit judgment on her, but even if Pip had long ago come to grips with her mother's way of life, that didn't mean she wanted to live the same way. Her lips curved ruefully. It was rather strange, actually, that none of Jane's children were particularly interested in pursuing the life their mother had shown them. Jacko wanted to be a farmer, and Ben, well, Ben had always been fascinated with horses, and Pip suspected that given half a chance, he would be blissfully content doing anything that allowed him to move among the glossy-coated four-legged creatures he so admired.

And as for herself . . . She frowned. What *did* she want out of life? Her mouth twisted. For the present she would settle for escaping permanently from the one-eyed man! And after that? Her little face thoughtful, she absently reached for another plate. St. Giles didn't encourage dreams, but if there was a dream that Pip cherished, it was one of respectability. She didn't know how she was to obtain it, but if there was ever a chance to leave behind her squalid past, to live like *normal* people, she knew she would leap at it. Deep in her heart she hungered for the conventional life that Chambers and Ivy led, almost envied them their stolid respectability. Since she had been too busy living by her wits, thoughts of love and marriage had never entered her head, but she suddenly found herself wishing desperately that somewhere there were a man—a *good* man, a respectable man—who wouldn't care a fig about whether her parents had been married or about what she had done before she met him. She wanted a man who would love her for what she *could* be, one who would sanctify their union by marriage and allow her to experience all the placid domesticity that had escaped her so far. A grin flitted across her face. Well, perhaps, not *too* placid! She sobered, realizing the futility of her dreams. She'd just have to content herself with Jacko's dream of going to America. But if they achieved the impossible and managed to reach America, would she really be happy working on a farm with her brothers for the rest of her life?

If they owned a farm, *Jacko* would be happy, and if the farm had horses on it, then *Ben* would be happy, but what about her? Would that sort of life make her happy? Yes, she admitted helplessly, *if* that life had a man like Royce Manchester in it! The thought had slid so slyly into her mind that she had been unable to suppress it, and she gasped at her own audacity. Who was she to think that someone as wealthy and respectably connected, someone as sophisticated as Royce Manchester, would ever be willing to offer someone like her more than the occasional sharing of his bed?

Pip had no illusions. Men like Royce really only had one use for women like her, and that was as their mistresses. Was that how it had been for her mother? she wondered sickly. Had her mother met a man whom she had wanted under any circumstances, and when that man was finished with her, had she been so heartbroken, so devastated, that it hadn't mattered what happened to her after that? It frightened Pip and made her angry to think that her infatuation with Royce Manchester might lead her to fall into the same trap her mother had, fall into it and end her days in the same pitiful way. She took a deep breath. She wasn't going to let *that* happen! No more silly fancies, she vowed grimly. None!

It was most unfortunate for her peace of mind that Chambers came to the doorway of the scullery just then and said quietly, "Pip, the master would like to see you in the library."

CHAPTER 10

Pip's eyes were huge as she stared at him. "Why?" she asked breathlessly. Something Ivy had said earlier suddenly assumed great significance and she blurted out, "He isn't angry with me, is he? He doesn't think it was my fault, does he?"

Chambers could only shrug his shoulders. "I really can't say, my dear. He merely requested your presence."

"Oh," she said blankly, certain that she was going to be met by a very angry man. Leaving the safety of the kitchen, she grimaced. What did it matter? Every time she was in his vicinity, all her good intentions to keep a civil tongue in her mouth vanished. If he wasn't angry, she thought mournfully, he certainly would be by the time she opened her mouth a few times and spoke without thinking. It shouldn't have mattered to her that he might be angry with her, but it did—quite a bit—and she sighed. If only he were not so very intriguing, or so very handsome, she thought bleakly. And if only just the mere idea of seeing him didn't make her heart beat in the most alarming manner!

Angry at herself and just a little resentful at the power Royce seemed to wield over her wayward emotions, with a decided lack of enthusiasm, Pip made her way to the library. Reminding herself again of her mother's fate, her soft mouth set in a determined line, she knocked on the double doors and, at Royce's command, entered the room.

Of all the rooms of the house, this one was Pip's favorite. It was a long, narrow room, with a wide fireplace at one end. The walls were lined from floor to ceiling with leather-bound books of various hues, and a row of tall windows looked out over the tiny rose garden at the rear of the house. A softly colored Axminster carpet covered a portion of the gleaming wooden floors in front of the fireplace, and several comfortable red leather chairs, a black damask sofa, and a few satinwood tables were scattered across the carpeted area.

Today, however, Pip's delight in the room was subdued, and deliberately keeping her eyes downcast, unwilling to let herself even look at Royce, she quickly crossed the room to stand in front of him as he lounged near the fireplace. "You wanted to see me, sir?" she asked stiffly.

Royce let his gaze travel slowly over her slender form, thinking, not for the first time, that she really needed some other piece of attire than his cook's castoff garment. Not that she didn't look charming in the faded blue and white gingham, it was just that Royce wondered what she would look like in fine muslins and gossamer silks or . . . wearing nothing at all. . . .

Startled by the positively indecent pictures that flashed through his brain, he forcibly brought himself back to the matter at hand and his stunning reaction to the tableau that had met his eyes in the dining room such a short time ago.

Royce had never experienced the savage emotions that had exploded through him at the sight of Pip in Stafford's embrace. He had been furious, outraged that another man had dared to touch her—touch her in ways he had only dreamed of. And he had been shocked to realize that mixed in with this fury and rage had been a powerful sensation of possession— Pip was *his,* and only *he* should have the right to taste that provocatively shaped mouth! It had only been by the greatest exertion of effort that he had been able to keep his hands off Stafford, and not even Pip's obvious dislike of the situation and her subsequent retaliations against Stafford had stilled Royce's strong desire to inflict grievous punishment upon the other man. Just remembering Stafford's hands on Pip made his temper rise, and his voice harsher than he meant it to be, he said, "I wanted to talk to you about this evening. Explain to me, please, what occurred before I entered the room."

Reacting to his tone of voice, Pip stiffened angrily, and Ivy's words ringing unpleasantly in her mind, she answered tersely, "There is nothing to explain—I was clearing the buffet when that creature came in and grabbed me. You saw the rest." Her eyes locked on Royce's brilliantly shined Hessian boots. "May I leave now? There are things that I have to do in the kitchen."

"No, goddammit, you may not leave!" Royce said explosively, both her words and her manner unexpectedly infuriating him. "What the hell is the matter with you? *I'm* not the one who assaulted you!"

Guiltily conscious of the truth of his words, Pip smothered the heartfelt apology that hovered on her lips. Grimly she reminded herself that it was far better that he think her an ungrateful, sullen little wretch than to have him being *nice* to her. Angry, she could keep him at a distance, but otherwise . . . Otherwise, she admitted miserably, she found him far too attractive. Taking a deep breath, she asked stonily, "Is that all, sir?"

Resisting the urge to shake her silly, Royce fought his

temper under control and forced himself to act with his usual calm. Yet unable to keep himself from touching her, he reached out with one hand and gently tipped up her face. His compelling eyes stared down into hers. "Are you all right?" he asked softly. "He didn't hurt you in any way, did he?"

At his touch, light though it was, Pip felt a funny little quiver in the pit of her stomach, and helplessly she looked up at him. "I'm fine; he didn't hurt me."

His fingers unconsciously caressing the smooth skin of her jaw, Royce's gaze roamed with blatant pleasure over her features, missing nothing, from the curly, black hair that framed her face to the heavily fringed smoky gray eyes and the almost pouting fullness of her rosy mouth. His eyes locked on her lower lip, he admitted in a low voice, "It's as well for him that you say so. . . . Otherwise, I think I might be driven to kill him."

Pip wanted to move away—he was standing much too close for her peace of mind, his big body nearly touching hers—but she could not seem to force herself to move. She was unbearably conscious of his hard, muscled length scant inches from her, painfully conscious of the strange drumming in her blood as each second passed and he continued to stare at her. Mesmerized by the rhythmic motion of his fingers on her skin, she watched him wordlessly, aware of the danger of this sudden intimacy, but unable to break away from him. As the moments spun by, feeling some comment was required of her, she said huskily, "Then I'm glad I can set your mind at ease—I would not want his death on my conscience."

Royce, too, was aware of the inherent risks of their situation, but like Pip, he could not seem to bring himself to shatter the moment. Beneath his fingers, her skin was warm and soft, and that sweet mouth, that sweet mouth which had haunted his dreams unceasingly these past days, was so temptingly near. Warning himself that it would be both dishonorable and cavalier to give in to the growing desire to taste that mouth, to crush that slender body against his own,

Royce nobly tried to focus his thoughts on something else other than Pip's tantalizing charms, and almost desperately he seized upon another subject. He did not, however, move away from her, nor did he stop the gentle, feather-light movements of his fingers along her cheek as he murmured, "Have you heard from your brothers?"

Pip blinked, so lost in the sweet beguilement of his softly stroking fingers that it took a second for his words to register. Gathering her scattered thoughts about her, she answered, "No, I haven't." A thought occurred to her and she asked, "Have you seen them again?"

Royce frowned slightly. "No, I haven't, but I don't believe it is cause for alarm, do you?"

Pip shook her head. "They know I'm safe, and they wouldn't want the one-eyed man to learn that they have been loitering in this vicinity. I suspect that I will hear something from them soon, though." She grinned. "Even if they have to rob you to get a message to me!"

Royce smiled at her words. There was no need to prolong the conversation between them, yet he found himself reluctant to end it. Seizing on the first thing that crossed his mind, he asked lightly, "And how are you doing under Chambers's tutelage?"

"Well, I haven't broken anything yet, and he says that I am a quick learner," she answered dryly.

Royce grinned. "I must tell you that Chambers is positively astonished at how quickly you have managed to rid yourself of your, er, colorful way of talking. He tells me every day how much you have improved."

Pip laughed, a sparkle in the gray eyes. "Well, you *did* tell me to drop the accent," she replied demurely.

His smile gone, his voice suddenly husky, he muttered, "And will you always obey me so readily?"

Pip's mouth was suddenly dry, her heart hammering in her breast, as the earlier dangerously seductive quality to their situation returned without warning. Her gray eyes locked with his and she found herself saying breathlessly, "I-I-I don't kn-kn-know; I think it would depend upon what y-y-you asked of me."

Neither seemed capable of breaking the sensual spell that was weaving itself so insidiously around them. His voice deepening, Royce murmured, "I wonder what you would do if I made the sort of offer that Stafford presented to you." One hand still caressing her face, the other moved to where it gently cradled her dark head, his fingers moving seductively through her black curls. "Would you, I wonder, react the same way?"

Her heart nearly stood still at his words, and a slow, treacherous excitement slid deliciously through her slender body. This was madness, she thought wildly with one part of her brain, I must escape, and yet . . . and yet there was a part of her that found this moment too intriguing, too hypnotizing, to break away. Her eyes huge in her small face, her lips unconsciously inviting, Pip stared mesmerized up at his dark features. In a throaty voice that sounded nothing like her own, she asked recklessly, "Are you saying you want me for your mistress?"

"I'm saying," Royce admitted bluntly, "that you are driving me half-mad and that if I don't kiss you, I think I shall very definitely go *completely* mad!"

Giving her no chance to reply, as if he could stand it no longer, Royce crushed her slim shape against him, his lips hungrily finding hers. His mouth was hard and seeking against hers, his kiss both demanding and coaxing as his lips moved with a carnal explicitness on hers. This was no innocent kiss of first love, this was a man's kiss, a man whose desires had been kept too long in check, and Pip's fervently virginal response was not what he was seeking. Against her stunned mouth, he muttered thickly, "Sweet Jesus, open your mouth to me! Let me . . . I must . . ."

But Royce was too driven by the almost frantic desire to kiss her fully, to take possession of her mouth, that he could not wait for her to obey. He had hardly uttered the words before his fingers caught her chin and gently pulled downward, forcing her lips to open slightly. It was all he needed, and with a half groan, half sigh, he boldly took what was so helplessly offered, his tongue plunging deeply into her mouth.

For one mad moment Pip reveled in his kiss, and then the terrifying knowledge of where this could take them flooded icily through her. From here it would be a simple step to become his lover, his plaything, and she retained just enough sanity to resist. Frantically pushing against his shoulders, she twisted her mouth away from the intoxicating pleasure of his kiss. "Don't!"

Gripped by the most intense desire he had ever felt in his life, Royce murmured dazedly, "What? Don't kiss you? Don't hold you in my arms like this? You ask the impossible of me, sweetheart."

His lips gently caressed her temple and cheek, his breath warm and exciting on her flesh, and Pip felt her resistance crumbling. It was only a kiss, she told herself fiercely. Surely she could allow herself the pleasure of his kiss without losing her head completely . . . just this once!

She looked up at him, her pulse thudding wildly through her body at the expression in his eyes, and then his mouth touched hers and she was lost. Drowning in the explicitly hungry demand, Pip could deny him nothing, her mouth accommodating the searching thrust of his tongue, her arms coming up to hold him nearer, her fingers unconsciously clenching against his broad back as her young, aroused body pressed eagerly into him. Totally oblivious to anything but Royce's big body and the mindless pleasure of being in his arms and experiencing the uncompromising passion of his kiss, Pip could not even think, she could only feel. Feel the smooth fabric of his jacket beneath her fingers, feel the strength and warmth of his body as it pressed against her, and feel the erotic abrasion of his tongue as he thoroughly and passionately explored the sweet confines of her mouth.

As Royce continued to kiss her so hungrily, his one hand

holding her head captive, the other sliding determinedly down her back to cup her buttocks and draw her even nearer, Pip was dimly aware that her body was reacting with a mind of its own and she swayed in his embrace, unconsciously rubbing against him. Her breasts were straining beneath the soft fabric of her gown, and she knew a mad desire to bare them to his gaze . . . and touch. A shudder went through her at the image of Royce touching her naked breasts and she suddenly became achingly aware of the insistent throb between her legs. The sweet sensation of Royce's hand fondling her hips was undeniably arousing, but no more arousing than the aggressive thrust of his rigid shaft between their locked bodies. Even through their clothing she could feel his violent arousal, the heat and size of him, exciting her further as he held her still and deliberately urged her against him.

But kissing soon wasn't enough, and impatiently Royce lifted the skirts of her gown and eagerly slid his hand beneath her drawers to caress and explore the soft skin of her buttocks, gently squeezing and kneading the firm flesh he found there. Pip gasped at the sensation of his hand against her naked skin, a bolt of undisguised pleasure shooting through her. She was on fire, her body tingling and aching for fulfillment, and she moaned with helpless pleasure when his caressing hand left her buttock and slowly crept between their twisting bodies.

Royce's hand trembled as he explored her soft belly, his fingers aching to plunge lower, to sink deep within her heated flesh, to tease her, to ready her for his possession. He was painfully aroused, so swollen and ready to take her that it was all he could do not to throw her on the floor and satisfy himself this very instant. He had never felt anything like the driving, blind desire that consumed him at this moment. Her mouth was so sweet, her uninhibited response as intoxicating as rare wine, and Royce knew that he was very close to losing complete control over himself.

The intimate touch of his hand on her belly brought Pip

crashing painfully back to reality, and gallingly aware of how very close she was to forgetting Jane's pitiful life, and her own avowal to escape that same fate, she began to struggle in his arms. She must have been mad to let events get to this point, mad to have thought that one kiss would satisfy a man like Royce Manchester!

Royce did not immediately release her; he was still too deeply aroused to even realize that she was no longer sharing this sweet ecstasy. When Pip wrenched her mouth away from his, and her fingers tightly grasped his exploring hand to still its wandering movements, he raised his head and glanced down at her incredulously.

Angry with him for being so damnably attractive, furious with herself for not being able to resist his allure, Pip glared at him. "Stop it! Take your hands off me! My mother may have been a whore, but I am not!" Rage was driving her, fear compelling her to put as much distance between them as possible. "I may be your servant and you may have offered me refuge from the one-eyed man, but I have no intention of exchanging one whoremaster for another!"

Her words were ugly, but there was some truth in them, and Royce's chiseled features froze. A woman had never made him lose control like this—*ever*—and certainly he had never before been consumed with desire for his own servant! He was appalled at his own actions, and Pip's words bit deep, flaying him unmercifully. But infuriated by his response to her, almost hating her for the unsatisfied aching desire that still burned within him, he growled, "Since you've made your feelings insultingly clear, I suggest that you leave! Go back to the kitchen, where you belong." Throwing her a black look, he added, "For your sanity, as well as mine, for God's sake, *stay there!*"

Pip bolted from the room. Certain the other servants would take one look at her face and know what had just transpired, with a low sob, she half ran, half walked to the servant's staircase and hurried to her room.

Thankful that she had met no one on her way, she stumbled into her room and flung herself onto the bed. Her body ached with unfulfilled passion, her breasts still swollen, the sweet throbbing between her legs unabated. Horrified at how near she had come to giving herself to Royce, she stared numbly at the ceiling, tears of shame and despair trickling from her eyes.

I would have given myself to him, she thought sickly. I would have let him have me there on the floor and I would not have made one move to stop him. . . .

Angry and frightened by her behavior, she rolled onto her stomach and buried her face in the small pillow. She was a fool! Did she think so little of herself that she would allow herself to become his plaything? Did she really want to follow in her mother's footsteps? A shudder went through her. No! But could she trust herself to remain immune to his charm? Would she be able to continue to resist him if he persisted in his sensual attack on her emotions?

For one wild moment she considered fleeing. Running as far and as fast as she could to escape him. But then a bitter laugh came from her throat. And run right into the hands of the one-eyed man! She had no escape. Drearily she realized that if she left the relative sanctuary of Royce's house, she would be forsaking all safety. Royce was the only one capable of standing between her and the one-eyed man's despicable plans for her. Her brothers would try to protect her, but what could they do against the one-eyed man? Jacko was already firmly caught in his toils, and it was Jacko's very plight that gave the one-eyed man such a tremendous weapon against her. It was not a pleasant thought. But then, neither was becoming Royce's mistress. . . .

Would it be so very awful? she wondered unhappily. So very awful to have him care for her, to allow him to set her up in a fine house, and to have him buy her lovely clothes, but most of all, to have him in her arms and bed? Would it *really* be a fate worse than death? Not if he cared for me and it wasn't *just* my body that he wanted, she acknowledged honestly. If he cared deeply for me, I would be able to deny him nothing. Angry at the train of her thoughts, she grimaced at her own silliness, and some of her embarrassment fading, she sat up and looked morosely about her tiny room. Life had been so simple less than a week ago. Well, not exactly simple, she confessed fairly as she recalled her fears of the one-eyed man. But at least it had been familiar! At least then she had recognized her enemy, but now . . .

Now I am my own enemy, she thought dryly. My own enemy and so much like my mother that it frightens me. Gloomily she considered the possibility that all-unknowingly she had somehow prompted the ugly incident in the dining room. Why else had an utter stranger come bang-up to her and suggested she might like to be his mistress?

For a long time she thought about that incident, and the more she thought about it, the more positive she became that the man's offer had not been prompted by anything that she had done. He had been looking for me, she concluded suddenly. Looking for me. And the offer, if I had accepted it, was merely an excuse to get me out of the house! He had even, she remembered uneasily, offered to *buy* me from Royce! A chill splintered down her spine. The one-eyed man! *He* had to have been behind it!

Royce had already come to the same conclusions, but at the moment he was too busy to speculate about the schemes of the one-eyed man, cursing himself for being an unprincipled rutting boar, unfit and untrustworthy to associate with any women other than whores and light-skirts. He was appalled by what had nearly happened between Pip and himself in the library, and infuriated by the knowledge that, given the same circumstances, the same thing could happen again. *Would* happen again! And the next time, he thought grimly, I damn well might not be able to stop!

What the hell was there about young Pip that made him nearly abandon a lifetime of principle? He was supposed to be *protecting* her, not seducing her, he reminded himself furiously. And if that was not reason enough, he would do well to remember that, temporarily at least, she was his servant, and he *never* dallied with servants—his own or anybody else's! His actions with Pip had left him genuinely horrified. Horrified, but unfortunately, not repentant. Even while vilifying and cursing himself, he still could not get the sweet taste of Pip's mouth out of his mind, nor the exciting softness of her skin, the tantalizing silkiness of the firmly rounded flesh of her buttocks. As he stood there in the library, memory washed warmly over him and he could still almost feel her yielding body in his arms, still feel her moving sensually against him, still feel the exquisitely soft texture of her mouth and tongue as he had kissed her. . . .

Thoroughly disgusted with himself, he frowned blackly as he gazed unseeingly down the long room. And what disgusted him most of all was the unpleasant knowledge that what had happened would be repeated. . . . Having held her in his arms once, he knew himself too well to delude himself in thinking that he would now, with righteous morality, put her from him. He wouldn't, and he knew it. He wanted Pip, and he regretfully, but bluntly, admitted that he was going to have her. . . .

CHAPTER 11

G rimly refusing to dwell further on the vexing problem of Pip, Royce deliberately switched his thoughts to something that had been niggling at the back of his mind. It seemed odd that there had been no further word from the Fowler brothers, and while he wasn't precisely worried, he wondered if all was well with them. Belatedly he realized that he should have made arrangements for them to keep in touch with him—even if only in a dire emergency. Royce's mouth thinned. Pip was not only turning his world upside-down, she was also, it appeared, addling his wits!

Wanting some distance between himself and Pip, and deciding he might make some *very* discreet inquiries about the Fowlers, with no certain destination in mind, after speaking briefly with Chambers, he left the house.

Since strolling alone through London after dark was a dangerous proposition at best, Royce had not gone very far before he realized his own folly. Irritated by this further proof that he was not thinking very clearly these days, he stopped abruptly a few feet from the murky light shed by one of the gas-fueled streetlights. On the point of turning on his heel and returning home, he froze as he heard a furtive sound issuing from the shadowy darkness of a narrow alley to his left. Certain it was a thief looking to rob him, he cursed himself again and one hand tightened on the fashionable walking stick he was carrying as he carefully reached for the small pistol he automatically always kept with him. Hoping he could avoid bloodshed, he called sharply, "Who's there?"

"Damn your bloody eyes! Shut your bone box!" Jacko hissed from his concealment in the alley. "Do you want to let everyone know that we're here?"

Royce's relief was immediate. A crooked smile on his mouth, he kept his eyes on the dim gleam of the streetlight and murmured, "You may choose the most unorthodox methods of meeting, but allow me to say that I am most gratified to hear from you. You *are* all right? Both of you?"

Ben chuckled softly. "Oh, aye, guvnor—except for a few cuts and bruises, we're right and tight." He paused, then added with a hint of censure, "You're a right hard one to catch alone. We've been watching the house these past five days hoping that sooner or later you would venture out alone and we could talk. Couldn't believe our luck when you walked out the door tonight."

Royce knew he could not dally here long without arousing suspicion. "Is there some place that we can meet safely?" he asked quietly.

"Now, I was hoping that *you'd* come up with some place," Jacko replied frankly.

Still betraying no clue of the conversation that was taking place, idly tapping his walking stick on the tip of his boots, Royce frowned for a second, then an idea came to him. "I have a mistress kept in a snug little house three doors down from Serjeants' Inn on Chancery Lane. We could repair there."

"The mort won't cackle?" Ben asked cautiously, in the tenseness of the moment reverting to the language of thieves.

"Er, if you mean she won't tell, I think I can make certain of that," Royce answered lightly. He glanced up and down the street before adding, "And I think we should bring this conversation to an end. I shall meet you there in an hour. That will give me time enough to see that Della is either safely out of the house or knows to keep her mouth shut."

"An hour," Jacko echoed before he and Ben disappeared.

Royce instantly returned home, and ordering his rig brought around, a few minutes later was driving smartly toward the house of his mistress. He had no qualms about using Della's house to meet with Jacko and Ben—after all, he was paying for it, and Della had struck him as a singularly *un*curious and complacent young woman. As long as she was comfortable, she betrayed little interest beyond what affected her. And if he was being watched, it would not arouse suspicion if he chose to call upon his mistress, no matter what the hour.

He quickly mounted the two steps that led to the house. Irritated and just a bit resentful about the way one small woman named Pip was wreaking havoc in his well-ordered life, Royce entered the house. He was not surprised to find Della home—after all, she *was* being kept for his enjoyment!

Though the hour was not late, Della had retired to her bed, and after leaving his hat and walking stick with the maid, Royce mounted the stairs to her room. Entering the expensively furnished bedchamber, Royce found Della lying on the wide bed, several plumb black satin pillows arranged around her shoulders, as she idly leafed through a book of various fashion plates. She was clothed, barely, in a diaphanous negligee of emerald green silk, which gave enticing glimpses of her generous curves. Della was undoubtedly a beautiful young woman, and her heavy, dark brown hair emphasized her almost handsome features and delicate, creamy complexion.

Delighted to see him, her big, brown eyes full of sensual anticipation as he approached the bed, she flung herself at him, sinuously winding her arms about him, and offered her full mouth to his kiss. Not inclined to resist such a blatant invitation, and perhaps trying to prove to himself that he was *not* as enamored of Pip as he feared, Royce kissed Della, albeit with far less passion than she had expected. A tiny frown pleating her forehead, she ran her fingers through his tawny hair and asked huskily, "I've displeased you?"

Feeling distinctly uneasy, Royce put her slightly from him and murmured, "No, my dear, of course not. I have other things on my mind tonight."

Raising one perfectly sculpted brow, Della asked blankly, "Then why are you here?"

Royce grinned. One of the things that had struck him about Della almost from the moment he had met her was that she seldom minced words—and that she knew precisely her place in his life. There was nothing coy or guileful about Della. She was an expensive high-flyer and she made no bones about it. As long as her current protector kept her in a style she enjoyed and did not mistreat her, she was willing to give him both her body and, oddly enough, her loyalty, and it had been that much-touted last trait which had drawn Royce to her as much as her voluptuous body.

Somewhat ruefully Royce admitted, "Actually, I didn't come to see you. . . . I merely wanted a private place to meet with a few friends."

Losing interest immediately, she said, "Oh!" and sank back against her satin pillows. Picking up the fashion plates, she murmured, "You can tell Annie to serve you refreshments in the front salon."

Bending over, Royce dropped an affectionate kiss on her cheek. "I think I shall have to buy you that diamond necklace, after all."

She smiled with pleasure at the promised treat and, after blowing him a kiss, became absorbed once more in the pictures of the latest gowns.

Whistling softly, Royce walked back downstairs, and entering the salon, he rang for the chambermaid, Annie. Upon Annie's prompt arrival, he told her to bring in a bottle of brandy and some glasses and that she could then retire for the night. For a moment he frowned. Annie might be a problem, but then he remembered that Annie had come with Della, and he didn't believe that Della would keep a tongue-flapping maid. Still, he was just as happy that Annie's quarters were in the attics on the fourth floor and that it was unlikely she would notice anything amiss. Reasonably satisfied that everything was going well, he settled back in a green velvet chair to await the arrival of Ben and Jacko.

He hadn't long to wait. Annie had not been gone more than ten minutes when the door to the parlor cautiously opened and Ben and Jacko slid silently into the room. "No one saw us," Jacko commented as he took a seat at one end of a long, damask-covered sofa which was placed directly across from Royce. "We came in the back way, through the alley."

Selecting a channel-backed chair that matched the one in

which Royce sat, Ben advised, "I'd get a different lock for the back entrance—it didn't take me two seconds to have it open."

Almost idly Royce noticed that both young men had chosen to sit in the shadows, far from the flickering light of the single candelabra that had been lit earlier, but refraining from bringing attention to their actions, he replied lightly, "Thank you." A faint grin curving his chiseled mouth, he added, "You have both been so generous in showing me the error of my ways. It wasn't until you Fowlers came into my life that I became aware that a whole new world was unexplored by me."

Both young men laughed. "And I'll wager you rue the day you ever met us!" Jacko retorted wryly.

"Er, not yet," Royce admitted dryly. "Although there are some days that I wonder if my wits have gone wandering!"

Rising to his feet, Royce walked over to the mahogany table where Annie had left the tray of refreshments. Without asking, he poured three very large brandies and was on the point of handing one to Ben when he got a fairly clear look at Ben's face.

"Good Lord!" Royce exclaimed in shocked accents. "What the hell happened to you?"

Suddenly suspicious, he strode over and grabbed the candelabra, holding it high so that the light fell fully upon the two men's faces. And seeing the damage that had been done to them, he caught his breath sharply.

Wearily Jacko said, "Put that bloody thing down! We'll tell you what happened."

His mouth compressed angrily, Royce replied tartly, "I can see for myself what happened!" But he did as Jacko requested, and without another word, finished serving the brandies he had poured.

It was obvious that someone had administered a severe and vicious beating to both young men sometime in the past few days, and Royce had a very good idea who it had been. Seated once more, he demanded harshly, "Was it the one-eyed man? Didn't he believe you?"

Ben gave an ugly laugh. "Oh, he believed us, all right. What you see is the result of the lesson he gave us *not* to fail the next time he sends us to do a task for him!"

Royce winced. He didn't need to look at their battered faces again to remember the sight of their swollen, bruised features—they were indelibly printed on his brain. Feeling responsible for what had happened to them, Royce was aware of a huge, billowing rage building within him, and unconsciously his hands curled into fists. Just five minutes, he thought savagely, five minutes alone with this one-eyed man, and I'll teach him not to vent his petty rage on those weaker than himself!

Knowing any offer of sympathy would be rejected out of hand, Royce took a sip of his brandy. Selecting his words with care, he asked, "Is it safe for you to remain in association with him?"

Again Ben laughed bitterly. "If you will remember, we don't have much choice!"

"Very well," Royce said quietly, putting down his snifter of brandy. "Let me tell you what I have been busy about since we last talked."

Briefly Royce told them everything that had transpired since their first meeting, ending with this evening's curious event involving Stafford. The two Fowlers had remained silent until Royce finished speaking; then, after taking a long pull on his brandy, Jacko said, "I had wondered what he planned when he told us that he would take care of it himself." A wolfish grin suddenly slashed Jacko's cheeks. "Seems the one-eyed man was no more successful than we were!"

Royce frowned slightly. "You're certain that what happened wasn't just a coincidence?"

His blue eyes very bright and direct, Ben entered the

conversation; looking at Royce, he asked dryly, "You *don't* think it was the one-eyed man?"

"Oh, I'm positive it was; I just don't want us starting at every shadow and becoming convinced that *any*thing out of the ordinary is always caused by the one-eyed man. And by the way," he asked wryly, "does our nemesis have a name? Other than dimber-damber or the one-eyed man?"

"None that I ever heard," Jacko replied. "Even Mum never referred to him as anything but the dimber-damber or the one-eyed man. Why?"

"I was just hoping that perhaps we might gain a clue to his identity if he had a name—even a first name might give us a clue."

"You could ask Pip," Ben interjected. "She might have heard something that we didn't. She was at home more than we were and with Mum a lot more. Mum might have let something drop."

From all that he had heard of Jane Fowler, Royce doubted that she would have ever just "let something drop." In his opinion, she seemed to have been a very closemouthed, secretive woman. She had been, on the surface, very open about her proclivities and life-style, yet he found it particularly revealing that none of her children had any clue as to their parentage, nor, when questioned, did they have any real knowledge of her life before she came to London. While she had told them the bare facts of her upbringing, she had neglected to tell them *precisely* where she had been born, neither the county nor the village . . . or the name of her father. The whole story might have been the most outrageous fiction, all of it a lie. Except that at some time in her life, Royce concluded thoughtfully, she *had* learned the ways of the wellborn—her children's speech and manners were proof of that! Perhaps she had merely mimicked her lovers? It was a possibility. Switching his mind back to the matter at hand, Royce nodded his head slightly and said, "I will talk to Pip, but I doubt that she will have anything to add to what you have already told me about the man."

"So what do we do now?" Jacko asked.

Royce hesitated, then slowly inquired, "How dangerous would it be for you to attempt to follow the one-eyed man? To find out where he goes when he is not busy with your, er, knot. He has to have some other life beyond what you know of him. And if we could discover what that life is, we would be in a better position to strike back at him, or at least protect ourselves from him."

Both young men seemed startled at the idea of taking aggressive action against the dimber-damber, Jacko's blue eyes widening in shock and Ben's young face going blank with astonishment. All of their lives the one-eyed man had been the power that controlled their every waking hour, and even while they had considered ways to escape from that power and had defied him about whisking Pip out of Royce's house, the idea of taking direct action against him had never occurred to them.

"You mean *spy* on him?" Jacko demanded incredulously.

"Why not?" Royce returned imperturbably. "Unless we learn more about him, we are fighting with a blindfold over our eyes. He can strike at will, and at present, we have no way of either anticipating his moves or even of taking preventive action." Leaning forward in his chair, his topaz eyes intent, he added vehemently, "Don't you see! Knowing nothing about him, we are as vulnerable as a staked lamb to a tiger! We are forced into the position of taking evasive action only after he attacks, and we are forced to simply wait for him to strike at us, whenever *he* chooses—as it is now, he has all the cards." Royce grimaced. "Not all of them—our only ace is the fact that he still believes that you two are loyal to him."

Rubbing his chin reflectively, Ben murmured, "I don't know . . . I *think* he believed us, but it worries me just a little that he didn't order us to make another attempt. It was almost as if he *didn't* trust us anymore."

Jacko nodded, but presented another point of view. "It might be that it is *only* in connection with *Pip* that he mistrusts us. I can't believe that he wouldn't have killed us outright if he had thought that we were actively working against him in everything."

"So?" Royce asked. "How dangerous is it, and can you do it . . . without putting yourselves at further risk?"

Ben took a deep breath, expelling the air slowly. "It'll be dangerous, there is no doubt of that . . . but I think we can do it."

"Think?" Royce repeated dryly. "In dealing with this man, I don't believe that mere thinking will suffice. You have to *know* you can do it!"

His bruised face grim, Jacko said harshly, "We can do it. We have the element of surprise on our side—even if he mistrusts us about Pip, he won't be expecting rebellion behind his back." A cocky grin suddenly split his mouth. "And me and Ben are as soft-footed as cats—we should have no trouble following him."

Uneasy about the plan, but seeing no other way, Royce stared at them, wondering if he wasn't putting their lives in grave danger. Not used to asking others to risk their necks while he remained safely in the background, Royce was again conscious of that feeling of billowing rage deep within himself. He was helpless to aid the Fowlers beyond what he had done so far, and he detested his current position. If only there were some other way . . .

As a thought suddenly struck him, he jerked up in his chair and remarked to the room at large, "What a fool I am!" Looking at the two surprised young men, he said eagerly, "I can arrange passage for all of you to America—you'll be safe there!"

Ordinarily pride would have caused the Fowlers to reject the offer out of hand, but Pip's situation and the vicious beating they had taken had given them pause. A glimmer of excitement growing in their eyes, the two men stared at each other. What each saw in the other's eyes must have convinced them, because as one, they said, "How soon?"

Not giving himself time to think, pushing aside thoughts of making Pip his mistress with puritanical zeal, Royce said, "I can see my businessman tomorrow and he can take care of everything for me. Once we have assured ourselves of your passage on the first ship leaving port for American waters, all we have to do is keep Pip safe and you two out of trouble until the ship sails. The riskiest part of our venture will be getting you all on board without arousing the suspicions of the one-eyed man."

"If you can get Pip there, don't worry about us! Just tell us the name of the ship and when she sails, and we'll be there!" Jacko answered almost merrily.

Royce smiled faintly. If only, he thought cynically, everything goes as easily as planned. Rising to his feet, he said, "Before we say good night, I suggest we come up with some way to contact each other if need be. We can use this house to meet in, and I believe that my mistress can be trusted, but even if we decide upon certain times and dates to meet, we will still need some sort of a signal to alert each other in case of an emergency. Do you have any ideas?"

Ben and Jacko glanced at each other, shaking their heads. There was brief silence, then Royce snapped his fingers. "Curtains," he said succinctly.

At their expression of puzzlement, he added, "We could position a certain way the curtains of one particular window in the house. Halfway open or completely shut or whatever. Then all we need to do is to decide which position is the alarm signal. That position will mean that we must meet here at once."

Embellishing on his plan, Royce added, "Since the third floor is largely unused, I suggest we select the third window from the right on the third floor. The regular position will be half-open. All the way open will mean we should meet that night at, say, ten o'clock, and all the way shut will mean we must see each other immediately."

The plan was agreed upon, and on that note, they parted, all three of them feeling inordinately pleased with the situation. Well, not exactly pleased, in Royce's case. Driving his curricle at a smart pace through the shadowy London streets, he could not help but wonder what had possessed him to act in a manner so against his own interests. Sending Jacko and Ben to America bothered him not a bit; it was the idea of parting with Pip that aroused an odd little ache in the region of his chest. To his utter astonishment, he realized that, inexplicably, he had grown rather used to knowing that she was nearby. By sending her to America, he was, at least for the near future, putting her beyond his reach and denying himself the pleasure of making her his mistress. But it *had* to be, he thought almost savagely. Here she would constantly be in danger from the one-eyed man, but in America she should be safe, and he would just have to console himself by telling himself that he was acting most nobly. The thought offered little comfort, and his mouth twisted. Why was it that the noblest action always seemed to provide the least amount of enjoyment?

Entering the house moments later, Royce found himself strangely restless yet with no real desire to seek entertainment elsewhere. After dismissing Chambers for the night, he wandered about the lower floor of the house, unable to settle comfortably in any one room. By London standards, the evening was still young, not much past ten o'clock, and there was any one of a dozen places he could go to seek fellowship or amusement, but for some reason, they held no interest for him. He gave a twisted smile. The only place he really wanted to be was in Pip's bed, and since he *hoped* he still had too many scruples to seek her out, he deliberately kept a firm rein on the primitive urgings of his body and attempted to keep his mind on other things.

The problem was that not only did he not wish for the company of others, he was also not sleepy. If anything, the evening's occurrences had left him agreeably stimulated—it was Royce's nature to take action, not languish awaiting the outcome of events, as he had these last few days, and he was reasonably satisfied with the plans he had made with the Fowlers . . . except for the depressing knowledge that shortly, Pip would be sailing out of his life. But at least she will be *safe* from the one-eyed man, he reminded himself harshly time and again. She will be safe from *both* of us, he added with blunt honesty, well aware that for his peace of mind, Pip could not leave London too soon.

Yet Wednesday morning, seated in his agent's well-appointed office, after their initial greetings, when it was finally time to discuss his reasons for calling upon the man, Royce was strangely reluctant to voice his actual request. He spun out their desultory conversation as long as he could, and he knew that Roger Steadham must be wondering at his actions. Growing more furious with himself by the moment, Royce finally leaned back in the brass and leather chair and murmured, "You must be curious why I am here this morning."

Roger Steadham was a young man not quite thirty-five years of age, with medium height and build, and he had come highly recommended by George Ponteby. "Extremely capable and discreet fellow" was precisely what George had said, and Roger was exactly that. His hazel eyes meeting Royce's gaze openly, he smiled politely and replied, "I'm certain you will tell me the reason for this visit when it suits you."

Royce laughed grimly. "Well, what I am about to ask you doesn't suit me at all, but I see no other course. I wish to arrange for passage to America for four people. Leaving on the first ship sailing there from London."

If Steadham was surprised by Royce's request, he gave no clue, saying merely, "Oh, I'm sorry to hear that you are cutting your stay here in England short."

Royce was on the point of correcting him when he stopped himself. He had decided to ask for four passages simply to cloud the issue, and if Steadham wanted to think they were for his party, well, so much the better.

Royce made a noncommittal reply and, after a few more minutes of conversation, rose to his feet and prepared to depart. "Well, then," he said amiably, "I will leave matters in your hands. Please advise me of the ship and sailing dates just as soon as possible."

Steadham eagerly assured him that he would, and diffidently escorted him from the office. While deeply regretting the necessity for Pip's imminent, abrupt departure from his life, as he sauntered away from Steadham's offices, Royce was rather pleased and satisfied with the morning's work, and went in search of other amusements.

Royce might not have been so sanguine if he had realized that his visit to Steadham's office had been observed and that as he walked away, a dark figure lurked in the shadows of the tall buildings, the man's malevolent gaze locked on his retreating form.

For several minutes longer, the shabbily garbed man stared in the direction in which the long-legged American had disappeared, and then, after one last ugly look, the man slid around the side of the building and entered the back way. Stealthily he climbed the staircase until he reached the floor he wanted. Betraying his familiarity with the area, he silently bypassed the rooms full of busy clerks to gain direct entrance to Steadham's private office. Like a shadow, he drifted into the room, startling Roger Steadham.

That the man was no stranger to Roger was evident from the way his eyes widened apprehensively and he exclaimed, "Good Lord! What are you doing here? You promised you would never contact me again."

The man smiled thinly, his one eye impaling Roger where he sat. "You'll forgive me," he drawled sarcastically, "but sometimes I find that there are certain promises I cannot keep—just as you cannot seem able to avoid the gaming hells. Pity you don't have another wealthy aunt, isn't it?"

Roger went white at his words and looked away. Knowing there was no escape, he eventually asked in a dead tone of voice, "What do you want from me?"

"Oh, nothing very much," the one-eyed man replied pleasantly. "I merely want to know what business you just transacted with Royce Manchester. . . ."

CHAPTER 12

As if unable to believe his ears, Steadham stared across the width of his huge mahogany desk at the one-eyed man. "That's all?" he finally asked incredulously.

The one-eyed man sent him another of those cold, thin smiles. "Yes, "he answered soothingly, "that's all."

Relieved that nothing more ominous was being asked of him, Roger shrugged his shoulders and related Royce's request. The one-eyed man was thoughtful for several moments, speculation gleaming in that one cold, dark eye. "Hmm. so Mr. Manchester has grown tired of London, has he? Now, I wonder why I have difficulty believing that?" As if coming to some decision, he stood up slowly and said, "Very well, go ahead and make Manchester's arrangements . . . but see to it that there is nothing suitable for him until, say, oh, the first of August."

"But that's well over a month away! I'm certain that I could find him passage before that," Roger protested.

The one-eyed man smiled. "I know," he said coolly. "But you *will* do as I say, won't you?"

Frighteningly aware of how easily the one-eyed man could destroy him if he wished, Roger shrugged helplessly. "If that is what you wish."

Flashing Roger a smile full of malice, the one-eyed man glided to the door. "You are always *so* reasonable! So pleasant to do business with you, my dear fellow."

The one-eyed man unobtrusively made his way to one of several places he kept in various locations all over the city. It had not taken him very long after he had embarked upon his present career for him to see the wisdom of having more than one place in which to seek asylum . . . or transact business. A grim smile curved his mouth. How many desperate souls at one time or another had followed him, hoping to catch him out, to set a trap, never realizing that he seldom used the same place two times running and that he deliberately had no clear pattern in either the routes he followed or the locations he used?

Reaching his destination, a small, fairly elegant set of rooms not many blocks away from Steadham's suite of offices, after a careful examination of the area, and seeing nothing to arouse his suspicions, he slipped inside, using the back entrance. He *never* kept any place for his own use that did not have more than one entrance—several if he could arrange it.

Swiftly entering the rooms, he automatically threw the latch and the bolt on the door. Satisfied now that no one would enter behind him, he turned away and in one easy movement removed first his concealing black, slouch-crowned, broad-brimmed hat, then the black patch that covered his eye. Running a hand through his hair, he walked over to a small marquetry wardrobe. Swiftly divesting himself of the shabby clothes he had worn to call upon Steadham, he hung them neatly in the wardrobe and took out a different set of clothes. Laying the garments on the bed, he then poured himself some water from a china pitcher that sat on a wash-stand nearby and proceeded to cleanse himself.

Refreshed, he dressed in his normal garb for this time of day—starched linen cravat, superbly cut jacket of expensive material, finely made breeches, and boots as highly shined and elegantly fashioned as any to be found in London. Brushing his dark hair with a pair of silver-backed brushes, he glanced at himself in the mirror. Although there were obvious signs of dissipation on the regular features, a self-indulgent curve to the mouth, and a calculating glitter in the dark eyes, it was not an *un*handsome face that stared back at him. The plentiful dark hair still showed no hint of gray even though he was less than a year away from having lived five decades. Pleased with the image that was reflected back at him, he walked into a somewhat larger sitting room.

From a mother-of-pearl-inlaid box, he selected a thin, black cheroot, and after lighting it and pouring himself a glass of wine from one of the various crystal decanters that sat upon a long walnut table, he wandered over to a comfortable green leather chair. Alternately sipping his wine and smoking his cheroot, he thoughtfully considered this morning's events.

So Manchester was considering leaving London, hmm? Not for a moment did he believe it. Manchester had only arrived less than a month ago for an extended stay—why would the man now suddenly change his mind? So what was the damned American up to?

A ploy? he wondered. Perhaps. But then, Manchester had had no way of knowing that his plans would be discovered so soon. He smiled. How very wise it had been of him to place a spy within the Manchester household. And how wise of him to have decided to be the one to shadow Manchester's movements this morning, once his spy had alerted him to the fact Manchester was seeing Roger Steadham. There were others he could have assigned to such a menial task, but his instincts had prompted him to do it himself.

His dark eyes narrowed. The American was proving to be quite a nuisance, always underfoot, always, it seemed, disrupting his well-laid plans. He had been growing very annoyed with him even before the incident involving Pip, but now . . .

An ugly expression twisted his face. He was not used to being thwarted. For over twenty years, ever since he had first donned the disguise of the original one-eyed man, he had been all-powerful and he was conscious of a great anger inside him at the ease with which Manchester had been disrupting his life of late. First that damned horse race, he thought furiously, that damned horse race which had cost him an enormous sum of money. Then Della . . . And now *Pip!*

His fingers tightened about the slender stem of his wineglass. It had annoyed him more than a little when Manchester had mounted Della as his mistress. For some time he'd had his eye on her; her reputation of being singularly loyal to her protector and the fact that she knew how to keep her mouth shut had made him decide that she would be a very valuable tool. The American's advent into the picture had momentarily changed his plans, but there was little doubt in his mind that eventually, once he applied the appropriate pressure, Della would see things his way, even if, as a last resort, he had to break her spirit to obtain her compliance. A cruel smile crossed his face as he envisioned, not without pleasure, the ways in which a recalcitrant woman could be made to obey his slightest command. Manchester's protection was making his task more difficult, and the thought of having the American murdered briefly crossed his mind. It would solve several problems for him. Certainly the American's death would catapult Pip back onto the streets again and into his hands. And once Pip was in his power . . .

He had such wonderful plans for Pip . . . grandiose

schemes for Morgana Devlin—and they did *not* include
having her become the plaything of Royce Manchester! His
knuckles suddenly showed whitely around the stem of his
wineglass. Those blasted Fowler louts! To fail him now when
he had relied most on them! For a moment the nearly maniacal fury that had erupted through him when Jacko and Ben
had told him that they could not find Pip in Manchester's
house almost got the better of him, but he managed with a
tremendous effort to master his rage. Very well, they had
failed, and grudgingly he conceded that there may have been
some excuse for their failure, but he was still angry about it.
He was also very angry that his second attempt had been no
more successful than the first, although he had not held high
hopes of it succeeding. But it rankled nonetheless. How dare
Manchester refuse to sell her! he thought furiously. How
dare Manchester, inadvertently or not, come between him
and what he wanted!

No one ever stood in his way for very long. *No one!* And
he certainly wasn't going to allow some colonial upstart to
ruin all his plans—plans he had nurtured for almost half his
life. Well, that wasn't quite true—in the beginning he hadn't
really known what to do with the infant Morgana and had
very nearly simply disposed of her, as that fool Devlin
seemed to think he would. He laughed cynically. What absolute agonies Devlin would suffer if he knew that Morgana
was still alive . . . and that there was proof of her identity. He
laughed again as he pictured the horror that would appear
on the Earl's handsome face at learning such shattering news.
If he didn't have his own schemes to further, it would be utterly delightful to let Devlin know immediately that his niece
was still alive. Regretfully he pushed the idea away. No. The
time was not yet ripe. Morgana's ultimate place was at his
side, and until he was ready, Devlin was the *last* person he
wanted to learn of Morgana's presence in this world. Smiling
slightly, he consoled himself with the thought that he was

merely *postponing* the delight of teasing Devlin and Lucinda with the knowledge that Morgana was alive. In time, he thought, his smile widening, in time he would destroy the Earl, and take a great deal of pleasure in doing it—it would certainly take the sting out of every slight, every snub, the Earl had sent his way over the years.

His good humor momentarily restored, he took another sip of his wine. Well, since he couldn't bait the Earl with knowledge about Morgana, at least not yet, he was going to have to concentrate his energies on extracting a suitable punishment from Royce Manchester for interfering with his plans, and also, more important to him at present, on wresting Pip away from the American. Again the thought of having Royce murdered crossed his mind, and he supposed that if Manchester continued to be such a thorn in his side, he really would be forced to have the man killed. Arranging the American's death would be childishly easy, and he spent several moments considering various assassins who would carry out his wishes if the need became imperative. Pip, however, was a different matter.

She was proving to be most annoyingly stubborn, he concluded slowly as he sipped his wine and smoked his cheroot. Pip's open aversion to him presented quite a problem, not that her aversion bothered him—at the first opportunity, he would take a great deal of enjoyment in breaking her to his will, but in the meantime, he had to think of a way to get her out of the American's clutches. Short of ordering Manchester's death, that was turning out to be far more difficult than he had originally envisioned. He had been almost certain that Manchester would leap at the opportunity to be rid of Pip, considering all the gossip and malicious speculation going around London. But such had proved not to be the case. Manchester had been furious about what had happened—*that* had been patently obvious from the scene in the dining room! The man had been enraged, almost to the point of violence, which seemed to indicate some sort of attachment between him and Pip.

Taking another sip of his wine, he frowned darkly. When the time was right, and that time was rapidly approaching, forcing Pip to accept him as her husband was going to be difficult enough without her having conceived some silly passion for the American. A thought struck him. Perhaps, he decided slowly, it wouldn't be such a bad idea, after all. . . . If Pip really was enamored of Manchester, he might be able to turn her emotional involvement to his advantage. Besotted women were notorious for sacrificing themselves for the ones they loved, and if he could convince her that by marrying him, she would be saving Manchester's life . . . He smiled. Mayhap he wouldn't have Manchester killed—at least not immediately. If he could use the man as a weapon against Pip . . . use the continuation of Manchester's life to control her . . . Of course.

Pleased with a possible solution to one of his problems, he considered it further. *If* Pip was halfway in love with Manchester, it gave him a very powerful weapon. He didn't even have to scheme to get her out of the house—she would come to him on her own . . . to save Manchester! Smiling broadly, he took another sip of his wine. There were still some obstacles to be removed, but overall, he was very pleased with his deductions. He was a little concerned, though, that he might have misread the situation between Pip and Manchester, and concluded that it might be wise to observe them more closely a bit longer before he made definite plans. Now, it occurred to him, might be the time to speak with the spy he had placed in the Manchester household and see if the man had observed anything useful.

He sat there for several more minutes mulling over his conclusions, going back over everything that had happened lately, carefully making certain that he had not overlooked any clue that might point to danger for him, or might reveal that he had drastically misread the situation. While he was generally quite satisfied with his speculations, Jacko and

Ben's failure nagged at him. They *should* have been able to find Pip that night and ferret her away! He believed their explanations, but the suspicion that they might be lying to him had returned more than once the past few days to irritate him. That was something else he could discuss with his tool so snugly encased in the Manchester household. Carelessly flicking the ash from his black cheroot, he stared unseeingly at the curling blue smoke that wafted in the air. If Jacko and Ben were lying . . .

If Jacko and Ben were lying, it was going to make the next few weeks extremely unpleasant, he thought slowly. And possibly dangerous for him. He had little doubt that he could outwit them, but they were clever—he would grant them that—and they could prove to be annoying, if unworthy, opponents.

But if they were lying, *why* were they lying? Because they didn't want to see Pip in his possession? Or was there some other, more sinister, reason behind their lies . . . *if* they lied? Did Manchester have anything to do with their failure to bring Pip to him? It was nearly inconceivable to him, but briefly he considered the disturbing possibility that Manchester and the Fowlers might have joined forces. Now, *that* alliance would be exceptionally dangerous, and while he didn't seriously believe such a thing had happened, on more than one occasion, his very survival had hinged on his habit of speculating on the wildest and most improbable situations.

He held Jacko's life in his hands, so he didn't really fear Pip's oldest brother, but it might behoove him to gain some hold over Ben—besides his brother's life, of course. Yes, it would be wise to bring young Ben to heel—nothing as spectacular as the murder he had arranged for Jacko's benefit, but something that would strongly remind Ben where his loyalties lay. . . .

Jane's two sons had never interested him overmuch, and a bored yawn escaped him. Deliberately he turned his thoughts to other things, such as his proposed removal from the city. London was beginning to get a little thin of company, and he was almost looking forward to a change of scenery—about this time of year, most of polite London deserted the city for the delights to be found at the seashore or, in some cases, at various country estates. He hadn't quite made up his mind yet whether he would follow the Regent's lead and stay at Brighton, or accept one of the many invitations he had received to stay at one of the more palatial country places. Inhaling again on his cheroot, he thought about it awhile, briefly even considering a stay at his own sumptuous estate in the country. It all, he finally decided, depended on the situation with Pip. . . .

Coincidentally, he was not the only one that day speculating on plans for the removal from London. Royce and Zachary, just rising from an excellent repast prepared by Ivy Chambers, were discussing the very same topic.

"You're going to be staying with Julian Devlin?" Royce asked in some surprise. "I realize that you two have settled whatever differences lay between you, but are you certain you want to spend several weeks in the country with him?"

Zachary smiled sheepishly. "I know it seems odd, but once we put aside our posturing and stopped trying to get the better of each other, we discovered that we have many interests in common." His eyes lit up with enthusiasm. "Julian says that there is great fishing at St. Audries and that we can do some *real* riding and driving, not just those tame gambols in Hyde Park that pass for riding in London. It seems *forever* since I have had a bruising good ride! Everything is so restrained here. I am most eager to leave the city, I can tell you!"

Zachary's statements were not great revelations to Royce. He had been fairly confident that at first Zachary would be utterly fascinated by what a wicked city like London had to offer an enterprising youth, especially an enterprising youth who had never been to a city larger than the sleepy little town of Baton Rouge on the Mississippi River in Louisiana, and he had been prepared for his young cousin's interest to wane once the initial impact of London had faded. Aware, too, of the dearth of company to be found in London as the summer progressed, Royce had been considering several invitations they had received to visit various relatives and friends in the country. He had made no definite commitments as yet, and Zachary was old enough to make his own plans, so Royce had no real objections to his young cousin's proposed stay with Julian Devlin . . . except the Earl would no doubt be in residence, and Royce was concerned that Devlin might make Zachary's visit extremely uncomfortable.

Glancing across at Zachary as they entered the salon, Royce asked thoughtfully, "And the Earl? Have you forgotten him?"

Zachary shook his head. "That was my first question to Julian, but he says his father seldom stays at St. Audries Hall. Says it has too many painful memories for him."

Royce's left eyebrow rose skeptically. "Painful memories? The Earl?"

"Hmm," replied Zachary as he threw himself down on the sofa. "Julian says the Earl was very devoted to his sister-in-law, and when she died, he discovered he couldn't bear to remain in a place that reminded him so much of her tragic death."

His face wearing an expression of sardonic disbelief, Royce retorted, "We *are* talking about the same man, aren't we? The seventh Earl of St. Audries, Stephen Devlin? A more haughty, arrogant bastard I have never met! And you are trying to tell me that he actually suffers from tender sensibilities? Now, I can't imagine why I have trouble believing that!"

Grinning, Zachary said, "Well, according to his son, it's the *only* tender emotion the Earl has ever expended on anyone other than himself! Supposedly it is the Earl's excessive attachment to his deceased sister-in-law that caused the final rift between the Earl and his Countess." Zachary's grin faded just a little as he added, "I understand that the Dowager wasn't your usual old dragon—she was reputed to be charming, very young, and *very* lovely—and Lucinda apparently made it abundantly clear that she was not the least bit unhappy when the other woman died in childbirth. Of course," he added bluntly, "*she* wouldn't be—the Devlin fortune of which Lady Lucinda is so quick to mention came from the Dowager Countess. If the poor little thing hadn't left all of her worldly goods to the Earl, the Devlins would be poor as church mice!"

Interested in spite of himself, but unable to suppress the teasing comment, Royce drawled, "My, but you and Julian really seemed to have covered a great deal of family history in a very short time!"

Flushing slightly, Zachary answered quickly, "Oh, it's not Julian who told me everything. Leland's mama and Lady Lucinda are bosom friends, and it is Leland and Jeremy who explained everything to me when I commented once on the coldness between Julian's parents—it is very obvious, even to a stranger like me, that there is no love lost between them. Leland swears it is because the Earl had fallen in love with his brother's widow and that Lucinda could never forgive him for it. According to Leland, Lady Lucinda has an exceptional memory, and even after nearly twenty years, she is still full of envy and hatred for her dead sister-in-law. Leland's mama claims it is because Lucinda really wanted to marry the Earl's older brother, the sixth Earl, and that Lady Lucinda hated his young widow simply because he chose to marry her over Lady Lucinda. *He* evidently was *nothing* like Julian's father! Leland says that everyone thought that the present Earl's brother was a smashing fellow. They called him the 'Dashing Earl,' and he was very well liked amongst the ton. From what I've seen, I'll wager that Julian is more like his uncle than his father!"

A fascinated eye on Zachary's face, Royce replied faintly, "How, er, enlightening. I cannot tell you how . . . *overcome*

I am to hear all this positively riveting information about the Earl and his family."

Zachary shot him a suspicious look, and seeing the amusement twinkling in the topaz eyes, he laughed. "Leland is a good gun, but he *will* go on and on!"

"Yes," returned Royce dulcetly, "and you seem to have picked up the same habit!"

Zachary smiled ruefully. "Well, you can't deny that it really is an absorbing story. I mean, the dashing Earl marrying a great heiress half his age, and then, just when everyone expected him to settle down into obscurity in the country with his young and beautiful bride, he was murdered! And then the bereft young widow was consoled by his brother, who inherited the title and who, incidentally, was known to hate him, and then *she* dies, and her baby daughter with her—it's like something Shakespeare would have written!"

"And since when," Royce asked dryly, "have you become such an ardent admirer of the bard? If I remember correctly, you flatly refused to accompany me to the theater a few weeks ago to see *Othello* performed."

Zachary pulled a face. "Oh, that! It's not the same," he said in a dismissing tone.

They conversed idly for a few moments longer, and then, as usual, Zachary disappeared, intent upon his own pursuits. Royce was thoughtful after his cousin's departure, and wandering about the elegant salon, he considered the information that Zachary had just imparted to him. It was history, many of the main characters dead for over twenty years, and yet Royce found it strangely riveting. Was it because Stephen Devlin had inherited a fortune from his brother's widow that he was so quick to resent others who had acquired wealth in more traditional manners? Could these long-ago events explain the Earl's aversion to him? He doubted it, but Zachary's words kept spinning through his mind . . . especially that part about the infant daughter who had died at birth. . . .

If Royce found the Earl's history interesting, Pip would have been fascinated by it. After all, Zachary had been talking about *her* family, even if her relationship was on the wrong side of the blanket!

In the days since she had come to the house on Hanover Square, she had almost managed to push aside the knowledge that she had actually seen the man who had fathered her. Jacko and Ben didn't even know that she had discovered her father, and while errant thoughts of the tall, haughty gentleman she had seen that fateful day flitted through her mind, there was little she could do to find out more about him. From his clothing and bearing, she knew him to be a gentleman, but beyond that, she knew absolutely nothing about him. She didn't even know his name, and though she was certain Royce would tell her if she asked him, she was oddly reluctant to do so. It wasn't that she wasn't curious—she was, almost insatiably so, and she would have hung on every word that Zachary had uttered about the dead Earl and his wife— but there was something about the man she believed to have fathered her that made her distinctly uneasy. Something in the cold gray eyes and the forbidding set of his mouth that made Pip not precisely enthusiastic about furthering her acquaintance with him. And being of a somewhat practical mind, she didn't think that knowing more about him would change her life in any appreciable manner. He had obviously put Jane from his mind a long time ago, and his only emotion upon learning that a daughter had resulted from his liaison with a high-flyer he had once kept would probably be annoyance.

In spite of being the newest and lowliest servant in the household, her days spent rushing about from one task to the other, constantly at the beck and call of all the other servants, Pip did have moments of quiet in which, when images of Royce did not dominate her brain, she had thought about the gentleman whose features were so like her own. It was true she was not particularly eager to get to know the man she believed to be her father, but it was also true that she could not help the occasional little fantasy in which, upon learning of her existence, her father swept her away to a marvelous life of ease and luxury where she was his much-doted-upon daughter.

Far too often for her liking or peace of mind, however, she had other, more vivid, fantasies, and these were invariably centered about her large, handsome employer. As in the daydream involving her father, Royce, too, swept her away to a life of ease and luxury, but there was *nothing* paternal in the way Royce treated her! Nearly every night, in the privacy of her cramped room as she lay on her hard little bed, memories of the way Royce had kissed her would insidiously invade her mind no matter how hard she fought against them. Just remembering how it felt to have his strong arms around her, his mouth hard and seeking on hers, would cause her body to react wildly, and in mere seconds she would be moaning with frustration as wave after wave of intense desire would sweep over her.

Pip tried desperately not to dwell on what had happened that evening in the library when Royce had taken her in his arms and kissed her, but in spite of all her good resolutions to the contrary, the memory would not go away. If anything, it became more powerful and more insistent, until her young body was almost constantly in a state of yearning arousal, burning with the need to have Royce's muscled length pressed against her, to feel again the savage possession of his mouth on hers.

She had not slept well since that evening, her nights spent in restless tossing on her bed, and her sleeplessness was beginning to be noticed by the others. By Tuesday she was pale and wan, the purple shadows under her eyes giving her the appearance of a starving waif. That morning, as the servants were hastily eating breakfast in the big kitchen, Ivy worriedly expressed the concern that they were giving her too much to do. Afraid that someone would realize that it was sleepless nights spent longing for their employer's embrace that caused her wan look, Pip had felt her face flame with embarrassment, and she had quickly assured Ivy that such was not the case. To prove her point, she worked tirelessly that day, hoping that perhaps she could exhaust her slender body so that when night fell, she would not once again be tormented with images of Royce making love to her.

Unfortunately, no matter what she did, she was still beset with the most erotic thoughts and fantasies imaginable and she tossed fitfully on her bed, her body aching for the touch of one man. This must have been how my mother felt that first time, she thought miserably as she stared unseeingly at the ceiling overhead. Had Jane lain awake night after night so bedeviled by the longings of her flesh that finally she could bear it no longer and had given in to the urgings of her body? Had the hunger for one particular man been her mother's downfall? And was she on the point of making the same mistake?

CHAPTER 13

Preoccupied with her own thoughts, Pip moved about the house in an unhappy daze. She was faced with a dilemma that was becoming more and more painful with every passing day. Even the fear of the one-eyed man had momentarily vanished from her mind, and though she was conscious of missing her brothers, of longing to see and talk to them, the majority of her thoughts were centered on how she was going

to resolve the powerful attraction that existed between herself—
a guttersnipe, bastard, and thief—and the wealthy, wellborn
master of the house. To make matters worse, her problem was
tangled up not only with the nearly irresistible magnetism that
existed between them, but also with the changes that living in
his house had made within her.

In St. Giles, she had accepted life as she had found it, and
if, occasionally, she had wondered if there was some other
future for her, she had been too busy thieving, and lately worrying about being forced to whore for the one-eyed man, to
spend much time on speculation about her destiny.

But living in Royce's house had opened her eyes to an entirely new world. It wasn't just that the house was richly furnished with all manner of elegant objects that she had never
dreamed of, let alone touched or seen; nor was it the enjoyable, regular meals; it wasn't even the pleasure of having her
own little room with its hard, narrow bed, or of wearing a
dress nor the joy of discovering what it meant to be *really*
clean, that was making a radical impact on her. What affected
Pip the most, aside from her preoccupation with the master
of the house, was the notion that she was doing *honest* work,
that she did not have to constantly be sizing up the person
next to her with an eye to picking a pocket, that she needn't
fear she would suddenly feel a rough hand on her shoulder
and be instantly carted off to Newgate. No, here in Royce's
house she was at ease with herself for the first time in her life,
and she found that she delighted in the orderly routine that
ruled the lives of his servants. She *liked* rising every day at
dawn to join the others in the kitchen for a hasty meal before
they went about their appointed tasks; she liked knowing that
on Mondays and Fridays she and Hazel would be thoroughly
cleaning the upper rooms; she liked knowing that on Tuesday
she would be helping Ivy in the kitchen and that on Wednesday she would work with Sarah as the older woman patiently
attempted to teach her how to mend linen and sew a fine

seam; and she even liked knowing that every evening she would be helping Alice wash and dry the mountain of dirty dishes, the completion of that task signaled the end of her chores for the day.

As a matter of fact, she thought half-forlornly, half-blissfully, as she absently dusted the mantel in Royce's study, there was little about living in Royce's house that she *didn't* like, aside from his unsettling presence and the disturbing sensations he made her feel. And while she knew that someday she would have to leave the sanctuary of this house, the things she had learned while living here would remain with her forever. Never again, she vowed with a little scowl, would she be a thief! *Never!* She was not going to live the rest of her life in fear of being transported to some godforsaken penal colony or hanged on Tyburn! And since at the moment the chance of sailing for America seemed extremely slim at best, she was going to have to consider precisely how she intended to make her living once she left Royce's house. Which brought her back to her very painful dilemma. Was she, in spite of her best intentions, going to become a whore like her mother?

Until she had met Royce Manchester, she would have sworn vehemently that she would rather die than allow herself to become a rich man's plaything, but that was before her young body had been assailed by the heady desire that one man's kiss could arouse. Now she wasn't so certain.

Frowning blackly at an unoffending silver candelabra as she briskly whisked her dustrag over it, she asked herself for perhaps the hundredth time—would it really be so very awful if they became lovers and she let him buy her fine clothes and install her in a snug little house? Her lip curled. Every instinct cried out against what she was considering, yet . . .

Moodily she walked about the room, dusting and cleaning, her thoughts dark and brooding. *What else is there for me to do?* she asked herself viciously. *Of course, I could aspire to be a servant in someone else's house,* she reminded herself uncertainly, but recalling the shocking tales from the other servants, horrifying tales of rape and sadistic beatings, Pip doubted that she would tamely bear any such abuse by brutal and disagreeable employers.

So what was she to do? she wondered exasperatedly. Hope that miraculously she and her brothers would gain passage to America? Hope that the one-eyed man would abandon his ugly plans for her? She snorted. That bloody well wasn't likely to happen! And while she was safe now, what would happen when either Royce grew tired of protecting her or he returned to America? She couldn't count on him standing between her and the one-eyed man forever, could she?

Furious with herself, she narrowed her eyes and stared grimly at the lovely carpet that lay on the floor. If she couldn't sink what pride she possessed and simply live to be at his command, she had better think of something else! Pacing the floor with restless energy, she considered the options available to a woman in her position and came to the conclusion that unless she wished to be a servant all her life, or intended to return to thieving, she had only one other way of gaining some sort of life for herself—selling her body—and that if she didn't want to end up like her mother, she was going to have to put a very high price on herself. Her small chin took on a stubborn tilt. If Royce Manchester wanted her badly enough, he should be willing to pay a high price, a *very* high price. . . . It was a repugnant thought, one that horrified her, and yet the St. Giles part of her, the part that had seen accomplished harlots of nine or ten hawking their pitifully young bodies to passersby, the part of her that acknowledged that her own mother had been a high-priced whore, commended her hardheaded practicality.

The whole business was too ugly, too sordid, to contemplate! But despairingly she reminded herself that women in her position had no business being squeamish or even hesitating when a toff like Royce Manchester expressed an interest in them. He'd already asked her what she would do if he made her an offer, and she'd be a fool if she let him off too cheaply. There were her brothers to think of, too! If she could bring herself to the sticking point, she stood an excellent chance of gaining what would be, for them, a small fortune, fortune enough to even buy a farm in the new land and to enable her brothers to fulfill their dreams. And if she had to sell herself to gain them all that—at least *she* would have chosen the man she wished to take her virginity, and *not* the one-eyed man!

Defiantly Pip tossed her black, curly head, deliberately ignoring the feeling of shame that curled in her stomach at the knowledge of what she was seriously considering doing. Quashing her reservations, ignoring the feelings of degradation and regret that hammered in her brain, she set her soft mouth in a grim line. The next time Royce Manchester decided to kiss and caress her, she thought obstinately, she'd make it very clear that while she had no objections to his touch—he was going to have to make it worth her while!

Her decision made, she should have felt relieved, but she was conscious of only a black emptiness within herself, and listlessly she continued to move about the room, not even aware of what she did. She was so lost in her unhappy speculations that she did not hear the door open and shut behind her, and the first indication she had that she was not alone was when Royce murmured with amusement, "I believe that you have dusted that particular picture quite enough."

Startled, she whirled around, her heart slamming into her chest at the sight of the object of her thoughts standing a scant few feet behind her. He was garbed quite casually for this time of day, especially in London. He wore a white linen shirt, the sleeves rolled up to his elbows, and the open neck giving a tantalizing glimpse of curling, tawny hair at the base of his throat; formfitting russet breeches hugged his muscular thighs, making Pip intensely aware of his potent masculinity. A crooked smile curved his mouth, and the thick, tawny hair on his head was tousled as if he had run his fingers through it several times. There was a teasing glint in the depths of those tiger's eyes, and Pip was almost breathless simply staring at him.

Embarrassed by her reaction to him, she ducked her head and muttered some inane reply. Intending to put as much distance as possible between them, she hurried toward the door, but she had not taken more than a few steps before Royce reached out and caught her arm.

"Don't go rushing off so quickly," he said easily. "I have been looking for you. I want to talk to you about some plans I have made for you."

Her mouth suddenly dry, she glanced up at him. Was he going to ask her to become his mistress? Oh, Lord, she hoped not! Despite all her good intentions, she dreaded the idea of following in her mother's footsteps and compromising herself before sheer necessity *demanded* it.

It had taken Royce a great deal of steely determination to go in search of Pip with the set intention of telling her what was being planned, and he had sworn savagely to himself that not by so much as a blink of an eyelash would he betray how very much the thought of her leaving his house, of her leaving England, filled him with an odd feeling of despair. It should be easy enough to do, he had told himself repeatedly; after all, she meant nothing to him—even if he did find her devilishly enchanting! There would be other women—her intrusion into his well-ordered life and everything connected with her had been merely a fascinating little diversion. A few weeks from now he would be hard-pressed to remember her name, let alone what she looked like. Unfortunately, when he came upon her in his office and had barely begun his prepared little speech, Pip looked up at him, those fascinating gray eyes with their long, black lashes fixed earnestly on his face, and to his intense annoyance, he felt all his good intentions fading. All of them.

Cursing himself for being a lustful bastard and hoping that

she had not noticed that there was now a prominent bulge in the front of his breeches where there had not been one before, Royce continued rather irritably, "I saw your brothers, and it was decided that the most practical manner of eluding the one-eyed man would be for all of you to sail to America. I've already seen my agent about arranging passage, and in not too many days you all should be on your way to an American port."

Stunned by his words, Pip stared up at his lean, dark face, her eyes widening and her lips unconsciously parting. Leave him? she thought with a queer pang. Leave him and never see him again? She shook her head dazedly, as if unable to believe what he had said. America. He was sending her away to America. Was it only a short time ago that her one wish in life was to escape to America with her brothers? She fought down a wild desire to laugh and cry at the same time. How ironic— now that her dearest wish seemed to be on the verge of coming true, all she felt was a dull ache in the region of her heart.

She took a step nearer to him, one small, slim hand resting lightly on his chest. Her head tipped back, her eyes dark as the clouds heralding a thunderstorm, she asked recklessly, "Is that what you want? For me to leave?"

Royce might have been able to suppress his baser instincts if she had simply accepted his word without question, if only she had not touched him. . . . Through the fine material of his shirt he could feel the heat of her hand, and his body responded violently to her nearness, the ache between his legs becoming nearly unbearable, the hungry desire coiling even tighter in his belly, increasing his already rampant arousal. Did he want her to leave? A bitter smile curved his chiseled mouth. Oh, yes, he wanted her to leave . . . as much as he wanted the sun to stop shining, the moon to stop rising, and his heart to cease beating. . . .

In spite of all his good intentions, the proximity of Pip's warm body proved too great a temptation; his desire for her *and* the fact that he was seldom denied something he wanted combined together to override everything but the growing need to have her in his arms again. Unwisely Royce ignored any lingering doubts he may have had and let the passion that was within him dictate his actions. A frankly sensuous smile curving his lips, he brushed her mouth with his and murmured, "No, I don't want you to leave. . . . At this very moment, all I really want is to carry you over to that very comfortable sofa against the wall. . . ." His lips slid along her jaw, his teeth gently nipping the soft skin as into her ear he whispered, "I want to lay you there and strip every single piece of clothing from your body until you are naked in my arms . . . and then I want to make love to you. *That's* what I want!"

Pip's breath caught in her throat, the blood thundering so loudly in her head that she could not think, could not concentrate on anything but the turbulent emotions Royce's words evoked within her. Dazedly she shook her head, trying frantically to clear her mind of the blatant erotic images that were insidiously filling it. This was wrong! She mustn't let this happen! And yet . . . and yet, Royce's mouth was warm and caressing against the curve of her ear, the gentle bite of his teeth exciting, and a treacherous wave of desire curled in her belly.

Sanity not yet entirely clouded by the powerfully fundamental sensations Royce was so easily conjuring, once again Pip shook her head, trying frantically to remind herself of all the reasons why she should fight against him. "No," she muttered thickly, painfully, "Don't do this to me. Let me go."

"Let you go?" Royce repeated huskily. "You can ask that of me?" Intoxicatingly his mouth touched hers, and against her lips, and as if the words were torn from him, he groaned tautly, "I cannot!"

Sweeping her into his arms, he kissed her with all the pent-up passion within him, and mesmerized by the fierce delight of his embrace, Pip felt her desperate clutch on reality shatter. In a part of her mind, she knew she was going to regret this, knew that her life and the path she was following were going to change irrevocably, and yet she was powerless against the elemental forces that rejoiced at his touch, helpless against the primitive needs that clamored within her slender body.

Oblivious to their surroundings, conscious only of the sweet yielding form in his arms, Royce kissed her urgently, his mouth hard and demanding against hers, his hands roaming feverishly over her slimness. He wanted to touch her everywhere at once, his fingers skimming down her taut back, his hands fondling her firm buttocks, urging her against his arousal before sliding swiftly upward to caress the gentle swell of her breasts. There was a desperation about his movements, as if he were obsessed by an uncontrollable fever that could only be assuaged by the possession of Pip's slender body.

Always in full command of his emotions, never had Royce been so aroused, so driven by desire that he could think of little else but how frantically he wanted her, how very much he *needed* to bury his aching flesh deep within hers. A sophisticated man to whom lovemaking was a finely honed art, Royce suddenly found himself gripped by such a consuming passion that the only real thing in the world for him at the moment was Pip's soft, clinging body. Drowning in a whirlpool of desire, a fierce desire that would not brook any denial, Royce groaned softly as his tongue plunged deeply into the honied warmth of Pip's mouth. A tremor of sweet delight wound its way through his big body as he thoroughly searched her mouth, his hands dropping to her buttocks again to lift and crush her against him.

Lost in a world of heady sensations, very aware of his powerful arousal, of his hands tightly cupping her bottom, Pip felt her entire body respond to his nearness. His kiss was devastating, the bold, piercing exploration of his tongue making her heart pound, making her slender body ache and throb with a strange yearning. She could not get close enough to him, compulsively arching herself up against him, trying to ease the aching demand that had hardened her nipples and had the area between her thighs pulsating with a liquid warmth. The sheer size and heat of him pressing so intimately against the juncture of her legs excited her further, and she knew that she would die of wanting if he did not also fill her body as completely as his tongue filled her mouth. Instinctively Pip met the increasingly urgent thrust of his tongue with her own, a jolt of pleasure streaking through her when he muttered, "Yes, kiss me back . . . oh, *yes,* sweetheart, taste me as I taste you. . . ."

Helplessly Pip complied, her small, warm tongue flicking into his mouth, nearly driving Royce to his knees with the flood of intense pleasure that raced through his body. Restraining his baser instincts, he encouraged her to explore his mouth as he had done hers, his tongue gently gliding against hers, urging her to kiss him as deeply as he had her. It was a sweet torment as he held his own passions in check and let her learn the taste and contour of him. A groan broke from him and he said thickly, "Oh, Jesus! I cannot bear it any longer, I must, I must . . ."

Pip was only dimly aware of what he was doing; she felt herself shifted slightly, heard the sound of ripping cloth, and then, to her fervent gratification, felt the warmth of his hand on her naked breast. The insistent tug of his fingers on her nipples had her twisting wildly in his grasp, the driving urge for something more not giving her any respite, the sharp ache between her thighs growing more pronounced as the seconds passed.

The weight and texture of those hard little breasts was nearly Royce's undoing, and with a muttered oath, he lifted her slightly and almost ravenously began to suckle on the naked flesh he had exposed. Pip's gown was hanging in tatters at her waist, but unaware or uncaring, she pushed herself up frantically to his searching mouth, the scrape and bite of his teeth on her swollen nipples wringing a small moan of helpless delight from her.

She was on fire, beset by emotions so fundamental, so basic to life itself, that she could not control the primitive commands of her body. Desperately her fingers clawed at his shoulders, the desire to touch his naked skin nearly overpowering, and to her satisfaction, she suddenly felt the material of his shirt give way and she purred with pleasure when her fingers encountered the warmth of his bare skin.

Incapable of concentrating on anything but the merciless desire that gripped him, Royce was ignorant of the fact that Pip had managed to divest him of his shirt, but he groaned deep in his throat when he felt the touch of her hands on his naked chest. Her fingers seared his flesh wherever they touched, and when she instinctively caressed his own rigidly erect nipples, Royce thought he would disgrace himself.

His mouth found hers in a rough kiss and effortlessly he carried her over to the sofa, his lips never leaving hers as he gently lowered her to the soft cushions. Kneeling beside the indigo velvet sofa, Royce made short work of Pip's dress, swiftly stripping it from her body, leaving her lying naked before him.

The touch of the sofa against her back slightly roused Pip from the trancelike state she was in, and feeling the last remnant of her clothing being relentlessly removed—suddenly alarmed her. Passion fading a little, her eyes widening with stunned comprehension of what was happening, she stuttered foolishly, "M-my d-d-dress! W-w-what did you d-d-do to my d-d-dress?"

Smiling tenderly down at her, Royce ran a finger along the top of her breasts and murmured, "Don't worry about it—I'll buy you another. A dozen, dozens, if you wish." He gave a husky laugh, and his eyes glittering with a golden fire, he added, "I'll clothe you in silks and satins and then give us both pleasure when I tear them off of you."

Pip swallowed with difficulty, her gaze mesmerized by the activity of his busy fingers as, with a ruthless economy of movement, he stripped away his own clothing until he was standing before her in naked splendor. Oh, and he *was* splendid, Pip admitted giddily, her eyes sliding with shy appreciation over his tall, muscular body, the strong arms and the powerful thighs. Whorls of thick, tawny hair covered his wide chest, the hair arrowing downward as it reached his hard waist before widening into a mass of dark gold curls at his groin. Pip had never seen a naked man before, certainly never a rampantly *aroused* male, and in dazed bemusement she stared at the sheer rigid bulk of his manhood as it sprang brazenly and unashamedly from the dark gold curls. A stallion, she thought half-hysterically, half-blissfully. A beautiful tawny stallion and he wants me . . . as I want him, she conceded with a small quiver deep within her body, her nipples tightening painfully as she gazed at his magnificent form, a pool of liquid fire flaming between her legs.

Looking down at her, seeing for the first time the naked feminine charms that had haunted his dreams, Royce drew his breath in sharply. Pip made an undoubtedly sensuously appealing picture as she lay there on the indigo velvet sofa, her pale skin gleaming like alabaster against the blue-blackness of the material. Her dark, curly hair was tousled, her lips were crimson and swollen from Royce's kisses, and her eyes were a smoky purple from the desire that he had aroused within her. With an effort, he restrained himself from falling upon her like a ravening beast, taking instead an erotic pleasure in the rise and fall of her small, impudently tilted breasts, the nipples as red and sweet as berries, the taste of them still lingering on his tongue. She was finely made, her waist slim; the flare of her slender hips and the surprising length of her delicately formed legs were exquisite. My pocket Venus, Royce mused. And she will be *mine,* he admitted with an undeniably possessive curve to his handsome mouth.

Unwilling to deny himself a moment longer, Royce dropped to his knees, his hands unerringly reaching for Pip. With a muffled cry he pulled her against him, his lips finding hers in a hungry, probing kiss, his tongue invading and thrusting into her mouth with an almost brutal urgency. But kissing her soon wasn't enough, and his mouth reluctantly left hers to travel hotly down her chest to her breasts, where his tongue curled tightly around the throbbing nipples, the avid touch of his lips as he pulled and tugged at her breasts, making Pip arch helplessly up against his mouth.

Nearly shaking from the force of the potent emotions that commanded her, Pip moved her hands restlessly over him, taking simple pleasure in the hard, warm flesh beneath her fingers. Yearningly she stroked him, his shoulders, the sleekly muscled arms, the taut, broad back, wanting the sweet torture of his mouth against her breasts to continue, marveling that he found her desirable, and when his big body slid up onto the sofa beside her, it seemed the most natural thing in the world to cling to him, to press herself invitingly against him.

Royce growled softly at the touch of Pip's body against his own, the need to take her, to find the ecstasy he knew awaited them, inflaming him even further. She was so sweet, so responsive, under his mouth and touch that he hungered to taste every inch of her, to take hours leisurely exploring her soft, white body, but he very much feared that if he did not have relief soon from the savage, pulsating ache that filled his body, he would quietly go insane.

His mouth sought hers, the blunt demand of his lips and tongue revealing the depth of the passion that consumed him. With a swift, sure movement, his thigh slid between hers, and Pip gasped at the intimate gesture, wild new sensations flooding through her as gently, teasingly, he moved his thigh against her. Racked by the same passion, Pip was helpless in his arms, unable to deny him anything, and when his hand slid between her legs, his seeking fingers parting and deeply caressing the silken heat he found there, she surged violently upward, her body eagerly meeting this new invasion. Her blood thudding in her veins, her heart beating furiously, Pip writhed beneath his touch, her body reacting with a mind of its own, and she reached for him, wanting to give him as much pleasure as he was giving her.

But Royce captured her searching hands, and holding them above her head in one of his, he muttered thickly into her mouth, "No. Not this time. This time I could not bear it if you touched me."

Keeping her hands captive in one hand, he continued to kiss her fiercely as he settled his big body between her legs, his intention clear. Pip knew a moment of panic, but then it was too late, his fingers parting the way for him as inexorably his swollen shaft began to sink deep within her. The feeling that exploded through her slender body was indescribable, part wonder, part pain, as he sank deeper and deeper into her welcoming flesh, her virginity proving a frail barrier against his total possession.

But it *was* a barrier, and as he felt it, Royce's eyes flew open in shocked comprehension; he was unable to believe that she was still a virgin. It didn't matter, he told himself dazedly—it was too late, the damage done before he realized it, and he was too aroused to stop now, the taut, silken heat of her body so seductive that he could not think of anything but how she made him feel at this very moment. Groaning aloud his intense pleasure, he moved on her, urgently thrusting himself again and again into the sweet depths of her, his movements helplessly wild and compulsive as he felt her respond, felt her body rise up uncontrollably to meet the downward thrust of his.

Lost in a welter of violent emotions, Pip matched his frantic movements as she desperately sought some guessed-at heaven, her hands twisting in his grasp, her mind and body utterly at Royce's command. Again and again he thrust into her, each powerful thrust making Pip greedy for the next. Suddenly she stiffened, a wave of such intense rapture, such shameless gratification, surging through her that her body shook from it and she cried aloud.

His features strained from the effort of holding back his own ecstasy, a glitter of satisfaction flamed momentarily in his amber gold eyes at her cry, and almost with a sigh Royce felt himself explode with pleasure. The fierce motions of his body slowed as passion ebbed from him, but he continued to kiss Pip with lazy contentment, unable to bring himself to part from her.

Finally, though, he had to move, and levering himself slightly away from her, he looked down into her passion-flushed face and said aloud the thought that had been in his mind from the instant he had kissed her today. "I can't let you go," he said harshly. "Not now. Now you are mine and I will not let you go."

CHAPTER 14

Stunned by what had just occurred, her body still tingling from Royce's fierce possession, Pip stared up into his dark face in dazed incomprehension. Disconcertingly aware of their nakedness, of the frank intimacy of their positions as they lay there together on the sofa, Royce's big body half-covering hers, one muscular thigh boldly thrust between her legs, Pip was too confused by the turbulent emotions coursing through her body to understand what he was saying.

Had it only been moments ago, she wondered bewilderedly, that she had ranged aimlessly around this room, lost in her own unhappy thoughts? And now . . . and now she knew the power of his body moving on hers, now she *knew* the ecstasy that could be shared between two lovers, and now, she thought miserably, now her feet were firmly set on the path her mother had followed.

Oh, she might not have put a price on her favors this first time, but the instant Royce had taken her into his arms and kissed her, kissed her so passionately that coherent thought had fled, the decision about her future had been made and there was no going back. She had let him make love to her, had gladly given him her virginity, had reveled in the power and strength of his beautiful body as he had possessed her, but now she must face cold reality. And cold reality was that men like Royce Manchester had only one use for women like her. They didn't fall in love with them, nor did they ever consider marriage with them—they enjoyed their bodies, and when the initial passion had fled, they discarded them and went on to the next woman who caught their fancy. It had always been that way and would always be that way, and yet Pip couldn't help wishing desperately that events had worked out differently.

Regretfully her clear gray eyes slowly moved over Royce's dark, intent features, from the rebellious lock of golden brown hair that fell across the broad forehead, down to the thick, arching, black brows, her gaze deliberately avoiding meeting the deep-set amber gold eyes before traveling on to the handsome nose and finally lingering on the full, mobile mouth. Unable to tear her eyes away, she stared at those chiseled lips, those lips, she thought suddenly with a shiver, those lips that give me so much pleasure, that do such wickedly wonderful things to my body, that sinfully appealing mouth that I . . . She stopped and swallowed with difficulty. She would want her husband to possess the same features, the same qualities, and she realized painfully that she wanted her husband to be very much like Royce Manchester.

It was an appalling admission, one that filled her with angry despair. Women like her could not afford to aspire to marriage with men like Royce Manchester. Bitterly she railed at herself for being a fool, for being so stupid to let her dreams center on someone like him, a man who, except for a trick of fate, might never have crossed her path, a man who might enjoy her body, but who would never consider her more than an object of his desire. A knife twisted viciously in her chest, and for the first time in her life, she longed to have been born someone else, to have been born a lady of fortune and birth, a woman who might have been able to command marriage with Royce Manchester. . . .

Royce's lazily caressing hand at her throat brought Pip shatteringly back to the present, and helplessly she met the glitter of those topaz eyes. He was looking at her keenly, the expression in those tiger's eyes hard to define, not quite satisfaction, not quite possession, but something in that golden stare made her shiver. And whether it was with anticipation or fear, she could not say.

He seemed fascinated with her body, his gaze finally leaving her face to slide slowly down the length of her slender body, her flesh flaming wherever his eyes touched, her nipples tightening, her breathing quickening, and incredibly, her loins suddenly aching to have him bury himself within her again. When his hand left her throat and wandered to her breast, her fingers dug into the softness of the velvet cushion as she frantically willed herself not to betray just how deeply his mere touch affected her.

Not content to just look, Royce swiftly bent his head and captured one impudent nipple between his teeth. "God!" he muttered against her warm skin, "I never want to move from here, I just want to lie here and make love to you again and again . . . and again." He gave her nipple one last gently teasing bite and then, with an obvious reluctance, rolled away from her and sat up.

One arm resting on the back of the sofa, he leaned forward, a rueful expression on his handsome face as he glanced down at her and admitted, "This wasn't very wise, was it? I never meant to fall upon you that way, and if I had known it was your first time . . ." His eyes darkened and his voice was thick as he said, "If I had known you were a virgin, I would have wanted everything to be perfect for you—certainly I would have chosen a better time and a better setting to make you mine!" Almost as if he could not help himself, his free hand closed around her breast; the fingers rhythmically kneading the soft flesh, and the tiger's eyes filled with an oddly tender light, he demanded huskily, "I didn't hurt you very badly, did I?"

Shaken by the husky tenderness in his voice, Pip could only stare up at him mutely, her eyes full of smoky secrets. She was unbearably conscious of his naked form almost touching her, of his muscular thigh resting only inches from her torso, and of the spiraling need his insistent fondling of her breast was arousing within her. How could she have been such an utter slut? How could she continue to lie here so passively, letting him caress her at will, making no attempt to break away from him? Ashamed of herself, alarmed by the wanton sensations that were building within her with every passing moment, with every stroke of his fingers on her breast, Pip angrily forced herself to act.

Swiftly brushing aside his hand, she jerked upright in one quick movement. Her back against the arm of the sofa, she drew her legs defensively to her chest and wrapped her arms tightly around them. Longingly she glanced at her torn gown where it lay just a few feet from the sofa, where Royce had tossed it, but feeling that she was now at least partially shielded from his blatant appraisal of her naked body, Pip shot Royce a speculative look from beneath her lashes.

He didn't seem at all perturbed by what had happened as he just sat there calmly, mere inches from her, his nakedness apparently not bothering him one whit, and she was suddenly struck by what a ludicrous picture they must present, both of them stark naked in the middle of the afternoon in his office, where anyone could walk in on them. She was unable to prevent the tiny grin that tugged at the corners of her mouth as she pictured the expression on the face of Royce's *very* proper Mr. Spurling, should the valet come in search of his master and discover them in this position.

Tiny though the grin was, Royce caught it, and a smile on his own mouth, he murmured, "You haven't answered my question, but since you can smile about it, I must not have caused you too much pain."

The art of dissembling was something that Pip had never learned, and to her utter horror, she found herself saying earnestly, "Oh, no! You didn't hurt me hardly at all—just a very little in the beginning." Shyly she confessed, "I never knew it would feel so wonderful."

His eyes darkened passionately and one hand reached out to cup her chin. Without her knowing it, he had moved closer, and his mouth just above hers, he said softly, "I don't think that it is a good idea for me to hear such things—I want to make love to you again, right *now,* and if it weren't for the fact that I know you must have suffered some pain, I'm very much afraid you would already be beneath me!" He dropped a hard kiss on her startled mouth and muttered, "Don't tempt me, or the extremely recent loss of your virginity won't stop me from taking you a second time within a very *few* moments!"

As if only becoming aware of their surroundings at that instant, he grinned at her and said mockingly, "Besides, I am very much afraid that we would not be so lucky a second time and I think it would behoove us to get dressed before we are found in this rather, ah, compromising situation."

Standing up in a single catlike movement, Royce casually reached for his scattered garments and, with unhurried, economical movements, put on his clothes, evidently not suffering from the same modesty that beset Pip. Her cheeks flaming scarlet, she glanced away from his magnificent form, willing herself not to stare at the tall, muscled body that had just given her such unforgettable pleasure.

He was nearly dressed before she began to scramble around, gathering up her pitifully few pieces of clothing, and it was only when she hastily pulled the old gingham gown over her head that the full extent of the damage Royce had done to the garment was apparent. The gown was irreparably ripped from the neck to the waist, and there was no way of fastening it—or of hiding the havoc his seeking hands had caused to the worn material. Dismayed by the destruction of the gown, with trembling fingers, Pip tried again and again to fasten and hide the torn material. It was useless, and her eyes full of anxiety, she glanced across at Royce.

"Ivy's gown is ruined! She only lent it to me; how can I repay her? I can't fasten it . . . and I have nothing else to wear." Shame evident in her voice, she added helplessly, "What am I to do? I can't go back to the kitchen this way."

An enigmatic expression in his topaz eyes, Royce murmured, "No, of course you can't go back to the kitchen . . . but then, I never intended that you would stay there forever."

Something in his voice made Pip's heart beat alarmingly fast. "What do you mean by that?" she demanded sharply.

"I mean," Royce said slowly as he walked over to her and captured her chin between his strong fingers, "that it is time for you and I to stop playing games with each other. After this afternoon, do you really think that I shall let you return to the kitchen? That I shall let you be treated like a servant?"

Pip swallowed painfully. Guessing what Royce was about to suggest and needing, for her own pride, to be the one to set the terms of their arrangement, she heard herself saying coolly, "I think we should discuss the price of our relationship, before this goes any further."

Royce wasn't quite certain what role Pip would play in his life after today, but he was fiercely positive that what he felt for her was far different from the businesslike arrangement he had with Della, and he was enraged that she was so willing to put a price on the powerful emotions that lay between them. The warm expression in his eyes faded and his fingers tightened on her chin. "And precisely what do you mean by that?" he demanded.

Amazed at herself and ignoring the quaking in the pit of her stomach, Pip met his gaze squarely and said bluntly, "If I am to be your mistress, it is going to cost you a great deal . . . a *very* great deal of money."

"I see," he bit out furiously, a cold, golden light glowing in the depths of his eyes. "And just what are your terms, my dear?"

Not hesitating, disregarding the pain in her heart, Pip replied stoutly, "A house. I want a house in the country that will be mine alone. And money."

Royce was astounded at the feeling of disappointment that slashed through him at her words. What he had expected from her, he didn't know, but he had believed what they had shared had been priceless, a moment that he would never forget . . . that he never wanted to forget. It was obvious, however, that he had misjudged the situation completely, that she was nothing but a mercenary little bitch! Furious for allowing himself to be utterly beguiled by that lovely face and yielding body, he barely restrained the savage urge to shake her senseless, to make her admit that what they had shared had been precious. But then, what could he expect from a little tart plucked from the gutter? He should have known better!

Eyes narrowed dangerously, he finally asked in a sneering voice, "What, no jewels? No gowns? No expensive carriage and fine horses to take you all over town? Or am I to understand that those things are just automatically part of the payment?"

Pip had been concentrating so hard on forcing herself to act with hardheaded practicality, concentrating grimly on the future she must secure for her brothers and herself, that she had not thought beyond the most important items. As she heard the scorn in his voice, her heart twisted, and wishing dully that this ugly scene were over, she almost retreated from her stance. But what else could she do? she wondered miserably, especially *now!* If she didn't want to be passed from protector to protector until she ended up like her mother, it was vital that she lay down the most advantageous terms for herself and her brothers.

Mortified by what she was doing, yet unable to see any other way out of her predicament, she jerked her head away and muttered in a small voice, "Yes, all those things too."

Royce took a deep, angry breath, but his voice was cool as he said, "Very well. I shall see to it."

Startled, Pip glanced at him, unable to believe that he was giving in so tamely. "Y-Y-You're not going t-t-to a-a-argue with me about it?" she stammered uneasily, her thickly lashed gray eyes very big in her small face.

Royce smiled grimly. "Of course not! I'm a rich man," he snarled softly, "and I've always been willing to pay for my pleasures . . . no matter what the price." He pulled her to him and kissed her cruelly, showing none of the tenderness he had earlier. Lifting his mouth from her bruised lips, he said savagely, "And believe me, you will *earn* every penny I expend on you, sweetheart!"

Pride stiffened her spine, and her chin held high in the air, she said in a gritty little voice, "I intend to!"

"Very well," he snapped, "we understand each other." He cast a disparaging glance at her torn gown and said coolly, "And I think the first order of business ought to be some new clothing for you."

Before Pip could protest, he strode over to the velvet bell rope that hung just behind his desk, and giving it a vicious yank, he turned back to face her. It was an uncomfortable few minutes as they stood there silently glaring at each other, neither one willing or able to think of anything to say that would bridge the chasm that had suddenly sprung open between them.

It was with relief that Pip heard the tap on the door and watched Royce cross the room and fling it open. Chambers waited on the other side of the door, his polite expression fading just a bit when he caught sight of Royce's face, and his eyes widening in shocked dismay when he glimpsed Pip's forlorn features over Royce's shoulder. Fortunately, before he noticed the torn gown, in a tone of voice Chambers had never heard from him, Royce said bluntly, "Find Spurling and tell him to bring me a cloak. *Immediately!*"

Ever the polite butler, Chambers bowed slightly and said with stiff punctiliousness, "Of course, sir. I shall see to it this very instant." Chambers hesitated a moment, then added, "I was on my way to find you when you rang, sir—Lady Whitlock and Lady Devlin have just come to call." Shooting his employer a nervous glance, Chambers continued, "I placed them in the blue salon—they indicated that they had come to call on a matter of some importance."

A black frown darkened Royce's already angry face and he cursed under his breath. Lady Whitlock was a meddling old busybody who was noted for pouncing upon the unwary and lecturing them *incessantly* on whatever charity had lately caught her fancy, and if she was not lecturing, she was soliciting funds for one worthy cause or another. To save the downtrodden was her mission in life, and she carried it to the extreme, most members of the ton avoiding her like the plague. Unfortunately Lady Whitlock went *everywhere,* and she seized every occasion to expound upon whatever happened to be her pet project at the time. Her only redeeming feature, and opinion was divided about it, was the fact that she spent a great deal of the huge fortune she had inherited from her husband on these same good works. Only last week she had trapped Royce as he had strolled toward White's and he had not been able to escape from her clutches until he had promised to contribute an enormous sum of money to a fund to provide food for the hundreds of stray and homeless mongrels that roamed London's streets. Since he had seen his banker that same afternoon and had seen to it that Lady Whitlock received the funds she had requested, he was puzzled by her presence here at his house this afternoon. And as for her companion, Lady Devlin . . . His frown grew even blacker. What the devil could she want?

Glancing down at his casual attire, he pulled a rueful face. Lord, he couldn't meet them this way. Looking at Chambers, he smiled wryly and murmured, "Better have Spurling bring me a waistcoat and jacket while he's about it."

Silence descended in the room again once Chambers departed, and it was only broken when Spurling arrived with the requested items. Taking them from the obviously curious valet, Royce thanked him and added, "Tell Chambers that I shall want my curricle brought round. Just as soon as I finish with the ladies, I shall be leaving the house for a while."

After Spurling had left, Royce threw the cloak in Pip's direction and hastily donned the waistcoat and jacket. His voice cool, he said, "I shall not be very long. Wait here until I return, and then we shall see about procuring some other garments for you." His mouth twisted and he added dryly, "After all, you *did* earn them, didn't you?"

Pip hated him in that moment, but before she could hurl a scathing reply at him, he was gone, the door shutting with unnecessary force behind him.

Entering the blue salon, Royce found that Chambers had served the women some lemonade and cream cakes, and smiling politely, he commented, "I'm sorry to have kept you waiting, ladies, but I'm happy to see that my servant has already seen to your comforts."

The two women were sitting on a long Sheraton sofa covered in a blue tapestry material, their full skirts artfully arranged about their ankles. Already familiar with Lady Whitlock, Royce nodded politely in her direction before fixing his gaze on the wife of the Earl of St. Audries. He knew Lucinda Devlin by sight, but he had never been formally introduced to her. Lady Whitlock, with a great deal of fluttering lashes and arch looks, rectified this omission.

At forty-two years of age, Lucinda Devlin was still a striking woman. Her dark, lustrous hair, cleverly arranged in a chignon with a few tendrils of hair curving at her temples and cheeks, was as yet untouched by any sign of gray. And while there were some signs of aging on her face, an occasional faint crease near the long-lashed hazel eyes and a line or two at the corners of her voluptuously curved mouth, her body was that of a woman half her age, her bosom high and firm, her waist slim, and her hips slender. It was obvious from the sexually appreciative look she slanted up at Royce as he bowed over her extended hand that she enjoyed masculine company, but Royce could not for the life of him figure out why she was here with a silly, frumpish old creature like Lady Whitlock.

The contrast between the two women as they sat on the sofa was quite conspicuous. Lady Whitlock would not see sixty again, and it showed, her wispy, flyaway white hair framing a deeply seamed face that had not been attractive even when young; her ill-fitting, hideous gown of puce silk clashed violently with Lucinda's expertly styled frock of apricot muslin. Lucinda was noted for her various lovers, while Lady Whitlock was equally noted for her sincere dedication to those less fortunate than she. They were an odd pair, to be sure, and as the three of them continued to make polite conversation, Royce could not help wondering what brought them to his house together—especially in view of the fact that it was well-known that he was not on the best of terms with Lucinda's husband.

As if in answer to his unspoken question, Lucinda put down her glass of lemonade and said casually, "You are being very kind to see us, but I am certain that you are wondering why we are here." At Royce's nod, she continued, "My cousin and I are here on a . . . a mission of mercy, you might say."

Cousins! Royce thought in astonishment. Who would have believed it, looking at the much older, frumpish Lady Whitlock and the lovely, stylishly attired Lucinda? Certainly not he, but at least it seemed he now knew why they were together. And as for a "mission of mercy" . . . He cocked an eyebrow. "Yes?" he asked interestedly. "What can I do for you?"

Lucinda appeared slightly embarrassed, and with a pretty show of deference, she turned to her cousin. "Letty, this was your idea; perhaps *you* had better explain it." Giving Royce a limpid look, Lucinda added, "Letty simply begged me to come along with her this morning, and while I don't usually allow her to embroil me in her schemes, I thought it would be an excellent opportunity to finally meet you—I have heard a great deal about you."

Not certain whether to be flattered or not, Royce merely smiled and fixed his attention on Lady Whitlock. After several false starts, Lady Whitlock finally said in a rush, "It is about that pickpocket person that you have here in the house."

Royce couldn't have been more astounded if she had suddenly blurted out that she was here to steal the family silver! Good God! What the devil did Pip have to do with this shatter-brained old woman?

"Pickpocket person?" he asked in a neutral tone. "What about her?"

Her faded blue eyes locked anxiously on his, Lady Whitlock murmured nervously, "Well, as you are no doubt aware, there has been a great deal of talk about her presence in your house—you being a bachelor and all—and I thought that it might be better if she were to come live with me."

Lucinda laughed coquettishly. "I told her that it was all nonsense! But once dear Letty gets an idea into her head, there is no swaying her. She is quite convinced that this poor young thing would be much happier in a house with a woman in it."

His brain very busy behind his polite expression, Royce answered dryly, "But there already is a woman in this household—several, in fact."

Lady Whitlock appeared flustered, and for several seconds she fiddled uneasily with one of the expensive India scarves that she had draped about her person before she ventured helplessly, "Oh, you mean servants! But that is not the same; servants can only teach her so much, but as a lady of birth and breeding, I can instruct her more fully in the proper way to comport herself." A note of almost pleading in her voice, her blue eyes fixed appealingly on his, she added in a low voice, "It is very important to me that she come to my home. I promise that I will treat her well, and you can be quite satisfied that you have done the right thing."

It was apparent that Lady Whitlock was attaching much more importance to what should have been a simple request than necessary, and Royce had a very good idea why. I wonder, he thought idly, precisely what the one-eyed man holds over your poor head. Even Lucinda seemed astonished at her cousin's actions, saying bluntly, "Why, Letty, I have never seen you this way! How can a little guttersnipe that you have never laid eyes on before mean so much to you?"

And deciding to test his surmise that the one-eyed man had something to do with Lady Whitlock's visit today, Royce added smoothly, "Yes, exactly why are you so determined that your home will provide her with better advantages than mine? Or perhaps, it is someone *else* who wants her out of my house and into yours? Someone who suggested it would be to your benefit to approach me?"

Thoroughly routed, a flicker of stark terror in the depths of the faded blue eyes, Lady Whitlock surged to her feet, silken skirts rustling. Attempting to bluff her way clear, Lady Whitlock said agitatedly, "Well! I have no idea what you are talking about! From the goodness of my heart, I merely wanted to offer you a solution to a situation that might be proving embarrassing. As for someone *else* having anything to do with my being here—why, the whole idea is utterly preposterous! If you don't want me to take the child, simply say so!"

"I don't want you to take the pickpocket, who, by the way, is *not* a child!" Royce answered coolly, her reaction confirming his suspicion.

Looking completely mystified by her cousin's erratic behavior, Lucinda also rose to her feet, albeit far more gracefully. Smiling up into Royce's face, she murmured, "I'm afraid that dear Letty is not feeling quite herself today. Please accept my apologies for any inconvenience our visit may have caused you."

"No inconvenience at all," Royce replied gallantly. "It was my pleasure to meet you, and of course"—he bowed diffidently in Lady Whitlock's direction—"I am always happy to see you, Lady Whitlock."

Staring at him as if he were a deadly cobra, Lady Whitlock sniffed disdainfully and, gathering her puce skirts around her, sailed from the room, Lucinda following hurriedly in her wake. Royce followed them, signaling Chambers, who was waiting in the main hallway to open the door for them. The door had hardly shut behind the ladies before Royce demanded, "The curricle—you ordered it?"

"Yes, sir. I believe it is already in the street waiting for you."

"Fine! I shall get Pip, and then we will be gone for several hours." Royce hesitated only a second, then added bluntly, "As you may have gathered, she will not be returning to her usual duties, nor will her quarters be the same. Please have the master suite prepared, and have my things moved to it."

A glitter in the golden brown eyes that brooked no arguments, even if Chambers had been so inclined, Royce continued curtly, "She will be sharing the adjoining room with me until I can find her more suitable lodgings. In the meantime, I want her treated with courtesy and respect."

If Chambers was surprised, not only by what Royce had told him, but by the mere fact that he had explained *anything* at all to him, his features did not betray it. His voice toneless, he bowed and said, "Of course, sir. I shall see to it at once."

Hoping that Pip would prove as amenable, Royce strode quickly down the hall to his office. Finding Pip standing in the middle of the room, the too large cloak completely obscuring her slender form, Royce muttered, "Good! You are ready. Come, let us leave." He smiled thinly. "I always believe in paying my debts immediately, and while it may take me a bit to find you your house, I *can* see to it that you have some clothes and jewels before this day is much older."

Eyes downcast, her head bent, Pip slid past him, the cold, hard lump of despair in her breast nearly making her cry out from the pain of it. She had done it! She had sold herself to Royce Manchester, and the knowledge brought her nothing but a feeling of bitterness and regret. Not even the realization that she would gain a fortune, a future for herself and her brothers, could console her for what she had done. Wretchedly she wished she could call back the words, could relive those moments before her wicked tongue had placed her in this invidious situation. Her body still ached from Royce's lovemaking, and she knew that it would fade rapidly, but the ache in her heart, the ache in her heart was forever. . . .

Silently she let Royce guide her into the hall and out the door and down the broad steps to the street. She looked neither left nor right, but pride eventually came to her rescue, and straightening her slim shoulders, she lifted her head proudly. So what if she was going to be a rich man's mistress? It had been good enough for her mother; why should she cavil?

She wasn't even aware of the two other women just

preparing to enter their carriage until Royce tipped his head and said coolly, "Ladies."

Curiosity caused her to glance momentarily in that direction, but she was so lost in her own misery that beyond recognizing them as ladies of fashion, they held little interest for her and she turned to gaze listlessly ahead. Pip may not have found them particularly interesting, but one of them at least found her *extremely* interesting. Her face white, the hazel eyes dilated with stunned fury, Lucinda Devlin stared in shocked disbelief at the lovely features of the young woman being helped into the curricle by Manchester.

"My God, I don't believe it! Hester's brat!" she hissed viciously. "She's *alive!*" Grasping Lady Whitlock's arm painfully, Lucinda watched intently as the curricle was driven smartly away. Her voluptuous mouth thinned angrily, Lucinda turned to glare wrathfully at a suddenly very frightened Lady Whitlock and said grimly, "I think, dear Letty, that it is time that you tell me *exactly* why you wanted to house that young woman . . . and who put you up to it."

Unaware of Lucinda Devlin's reactions, Royce and Pip rode swiftly through the crowded London streets toward the establishment of a modiste who was well-known to Royce. There was no conversation between them, and it was only when they had pulled up in front of a modest-looking little building near Bond Street that Royce spoke. He gave Pip a hard look and asked, "Do you have any name other than 'Pip'?" His eyes bitter, a scornful bite to his words, he added harshly, "Somehow it doesn't quite have the ring necessary for the career you have chosen. Surely your mother didn't name you 'Pip.'"

Pip heard his voice as if from a long distance, an icy depression quelling any desire to fire up at his deliberately provoking manner. She thought for a long moment, then answered dully, "Morgana. My name is Morgana."

PART THREE

Morgana

Demoniac frenzy, moping melancholy,
And moon-struck madness.

JOHN MILTON, *Paradise Lost*

CHAPTER 15

Madame Duchand was a tall, handsome Frenchwoman who claimed to have several years ago escaped from the guillotine. Whether she did indeed have aristocratic antecedents was questionable, but no one questioned the skilled workmanship and stylish cut of the gowns she fashioned. Royce was known to her, and as he and Morgana entered the elegantly appointed shop, Madame Duchand, her dark eyes moving assessingly from one set face to another, exclaimed warmly, "Ah, Monsieur Manchester! It is good to see you again. How may I serve you today?"

Royce smiled thinly, and giving Morgana a contemptuous push forward, he said bluntly, "I want you to dress her—everything from the skin out and from the soles of her feet to the top of her head."

Madame Duchand studied Morgana's angry features. Not certain of the situation and not wishing to annoy a wealthy patron, she inquired smoothly, "It will be my pleasure, monsieur . . . but perhaps you have some ideas about the colors and style of the garments?"

Wrapped in her own icy despair, Morgana was only vaguely aware of the comments being made. In a matter of hours, the entire fabric of her life had changed, and she was still trying to grapple with its enormous significance. If only she had never laid eyes on Royce Manchester! Because of the tall, powerful man at her side and her own treacherous body, any hope of ever gaining respectability was destroyed, and whatever dreams she may have harbored about her future were completely annihilated. She might have seriously considered becoming his mistress, even have convinced herself that it was the wise thing to do, and yet she knew that in the end she would have found it impossible to propose such a relationship if this afternoon's events hadn't forced it upon her. If only she had merely accepted the knowledge that he was sending her away to America instead of . . . Her eyes bleak with anger and hopelessness, she stared blindly at the rich blues, greens, and russet hues of the Axminster carpet at her feet, cursing the unruly tongue that had precipitated the devastating scene in Royce's study. If only she hadn't asked just those questions at just that time, and had been able to fight free of the dark spell he had wound around her, she might be, at this very moment, happily discussing the desperately longed-for trip to America. Her soft mouth twisted. But no, instead, she was a rich man's whore, soon to be bought and paid for!

An anguished sob welled up inside her, but ruthlessly she quelled it. No! She would not cry, and she was *not* going to end up like her mother! For an outrageous sum, she had agreed to be the mistress of a man who fascinated and infuriated her, one who beguiled and enraged her at the same time, but she could not imagine, at any price, sharing the stunning intimacies that Royce demanded with another man! When this humiliating arrangement ended, she would make good use of what she had earned in such a degrading manner and flee to America and join her brothers. In the New World, with her squalid past behind her, she'd fashion a new life for herself and her brothers, one that would hold all the respectability she craved.

Her shoulders straightened and her chin lifted. Someday all this would be in the past, and she wasn't about to let the ugly situation defeat her! In the unpleasant moments that followed, she tried to cling to that small, comforting thought, but Royce's manner with her, the angry contempt with which he seemed to regard her, sent a wave of furious indignation surging to the fore. What did *he* have to be angry about? Why was he looking at her as if she had taken advantage of *him?*

Madame had divested her of Royce's cloak and had for several moments been turning Morgana this way and that, examining the slender form with an expert eye. What Madame thought of the torn blue and white gingham gown was anyone's guess, but being a sophisticated woman and knowing the ways of the world, she allowed no expression of either condemnation or pity to cross her face. Glancing across at Royce for direction, Madame finally asked, *"Un jeune fille,* perhaps? Or did you want something more, ah, what is the word? Dashing?"

A hard expression in his golden eyes, Royce said grimly, "Since there is nothing innocent about her, I think the word 'dashing' would definitely apply!"

"Oh, la la!" Madame replied teasingly, discreetly ignoring the tension building between the two. "A dashing young lady about town, perhaps?"

Deliberately goading Morgana, Royce shot her a challenging look. *"Lady* isn't precisely the word I would use to describe her!"

His words stung, and deciding to beat him at his own game, Morgana asked sweetly, "Whore, perhaps?" Ignoring Madame's shocked gasp, she looked at the modiste and inquired demurely, "Yes, let us choose something appropriate for a whore!"

Royce swore furiously, and taking violent hold of Morgana's arm, he demanded of Madame, "Is there a place we may talk alone?"

Her black eyes snapping with avid curiosity, Madame nodded and murmured, "Over there, monsieur—the second door to the left . . . Other of my patrons often wish to confer in private. You will be quite alone there."

The room was small, but tastefully furnished—a pair of

channel-back chairs of straw-colored silk were at one end, a satinwood table placed between them, and a pale blue brocaded sofa sat against one wall. But Royce had no time to appreciate the decor, and standing in the middle of the room, he glared at Morgana and shook her fiercely. "What the hell are you playing at? Calling yourself a whore?"

There was something extremely satisfying about rousing his fury, and defiantly she returned, "But isn't that what I am now? A whore?"

"Goddamit!" Royce snarled softly, his golden eyes glittering with suppressed violence. "You might be grasping and greedy, but since you were a virgin mere hours ago, I hardly think the word 'whore' applies to you! You're going to go back out there and behave yourself. I'll allow you a certain amount of choice, but just to thwart me, you're not going to deck yourself out like a cheap slut! You *will* obey me or . . ."

Her cheeks flushed, temper, resentment, and anger driving her, she said rashly, "Or what? You'll beat me?"

Royce's eyes narrowed, and at the look in them, Morgana took a step backward. "By God!" he swore tautly. "You've been asking for this for a long time!"

"Don't you dare!" she hissed, realizing belatedly that she had pushed him too far. She made a frantic leap for the door, but Royce caught her before she had taken two steps. Ignoring her thrashing legs and arms, he swept her up in his arms and carried her to the sofa. Sitting down, oblivious to the curses she hurled at his head and the heaving and squirming of her body, he ruthlessly dragged her wildly struggling form across his knees.

Morgana fought fiercely with all the strength within her slender body, but all too soon, she found herself in the ignominious position of having her chest and abdomen pressed roughly against the hard muscles of his thighs, her vulnerable buttocks exposed to him. Her skirts tossed over her shoulders, she cursed malevolently and increased her violent attempts to escape from him. "You bloody bastard! You lay a hand on me and I'll skewer your liver! See if I don't!"

Once, her threats might have made him laugh, but having thoroughly lost his own formidable temper for the first time in his life, Royce found nothing humorous about the situation. What was even worse, the violent thrashing of her body was arousing him, and that, perhaps more than anything, utterly enraged him. She had defied, taunted, and bedeviled him with impunity for the last time! Blind fury consuming him, his broad hand landed with an eminently satisfying slap against her firm flesh.

There was a stunned silence in the room for one startled moment, and then, at Morgana's outraged scream, Royce was suddenly plunged into the shocking realization of what he was doing. He had never laid a violent hand on a woman in his life, never before so totally lost his temper, and that he should be so overcome with fury as to strike the one woman who fascinated him above all others appalled him as nothing ever had. Shaken by what he had done, furious that she had the power to bring him to this point, he slackened his hold as he sought desperately to regain his senses. Morgana promptly bit him.

Her sharp little teeth sunk deeply into the flesh of his thigh, Royce manfully suppressed a pained howl as he jumped to his feet. Dumped unceremoniously onto the floor by his abrupt action, Morgana scrambled upright, her eyes flashing dangerously, fists knotted, ready to do battle.

Looking first at the rigid, enraged little figure across from him and then down to the noticeable tear in his breeches, he recognized the ridiculousness of the situation. Amusement instantly replacing his fury, Royce held up a hand placatingly and drawled softly, "Pax, you bloodthirsty little she-devil! Shall we cry quits? If I promise not to beat you, will you swear not to bite me?"

Her own anger faded almost as quickly as his, and feeling

suddenly drained, she muttered, "Just don't ever try to strike me again!"

An odd light in his eyes, Royce stepped nearer to her, and running a caressing finger down her cheek, he murmured, "Will you accept my apology? I did not mean to treat you in such a fashion." He laughed ruefully. "I'm certain we can deal better than this. Shall we try?"

Mutely Morgana nodded her dark, curly head, wishing her heart would not convulse so wildly every time he touched her.

They did try to maintain some sort of peace, and for the next several hours an uneasy cooperation existed between them, and yet neither could forget their reasons for being at Madame Duchand's. Morgana would not have been human if she had failed to be enchanted by the array of fabrics and style plates Madame placed before her, and at first she took great enjoyment in the process of selecting a wardrobe far beyond even her most extravagant dreams. But the peace between Morgana and Royce could not last, and as the time passed, as each garment was discussed, the style, fabrics, and trims decided on, there was increasing constraint between them. Morgana became quieter and quieter and more withdrawn; Royce's features became more and more harsh, a hard edge creeping into his voice.

Ironically, it was a gown that ended any semblance of cooperation between them. It had been ordered by a young woman known to be in the keeping of a notoriously decadent Marquis, but never paid for, and Morgana had been transfixed by the iridescent glow of the rich ruby silk. Madame had hesitated to show it, but since Monsieur seemed in such a generous mood, she had shrugged and hustled Morgana into it. When Morgana walked out of the dressing room, Royce's breath caught sharply in his throat and the desire he'd been certain had been tamed came surging fiercely through him.

Standing uncertainly in the center of the room, Morgana was a sight to arouse even the most jaded appetite. The gleaming ruby gown was cut low across the bosom and trimmed lavishly with black lace, and it clung lovingly to her body. Its provocative style was such that Morgana's breasts seemed ready to spill out from the top, the black lace contrasting erotically with her soft, white bosom. It was narrowly fitted, and although Morgana was more slender than the woman it had originally been constructed for, the gown clearly revealed all of her gentle curves, the rich ruby silk material striking against her clear, pale skin, smoky gray eyes, and black, curly hair.

Unaware of its effect on Royce, Morgana was only conscious of the way it made her feel—like a woman of the world, assured and confident of her own allure. Caught up in her own enjoyment of the garment, she was startled to hear Royce say thickly, "No! We don't want this one —it is not her style!"

Not understanding the powerful emotions clamoring within Royce, she glanced over at him and blurted out, "Oh, but I do like this one! Couldn't we discard one of the others instead?"

"No!" Royce replied coldly. A strong sensation of possessiveness had joined with his feverish desire, and he was furiously aware that he was acting like a jealous fool . . . and yet he could not stop himself. She was his, and he would not garb her for other men's delectation!

Stubbornly Morgana dug in her heels. "Why?" she demanded, half-confused, half-angered by his stance.

"Because," he replied imperiously, "I do not wish it! Now, take that damned gown off before I tear it off you!"

Swallowing back an angry retort, Morgana spun on her heels and ran to the dressing room. Chin set stubbornly, she said to the unruffled Madame Duchand, "I want this dress. See that it is included when you send the others."

Hiding an amused smile, Madame answered softly, "But of course, mademoiselle! The gown, it is you, *oui?*"

Feeling as if she had won some sort of battle, Morgana let Madame dress her in another gown. Since all of Madame's clothes were made on request, there had only been a few garments that could be readied immediately. Fortunately there were two that Royce had found suitable—the one Morgana was currently wearing, a delightful confection of Brussels lace and green-sprigged muslin, and another of rose satin, shot with white and ornamented with a rich white silk trimming.

Coldly ignoring Royce, Morgana stood stiffly at his side as the rose satin gown was wrapped and boxed, the air between them nearly vibrating with all the emotions each was trying to control. Promising to have several of the garments they had selected this afternoon readied as soon as possible, Madame was escorting them to the door when it suddenly flew open and a flushed-faced boy cried, "Have you heard the news? *Bony's been beaten at Waterloo!*"

Little else could be learned from their excited informant, but from the furious ringing of the cathedral bells throughout London and the laughing and crying mobs they passed as they rode back to Hanover Square, it was apparent the news had been correct. Napoleon had been defeated! The Corsican monster had been finally beaten, this time for good! Briefly the joyful news of Napoleon's loss at Waterloo lightened the tension between Morgana and Royce, but by the time they had reached the house, there was again a decided air of tension between them.

Chambers met them at the door, his face beaming with pleasure. "Have you heard the news, sir! Bonaparte has been thoroughly trounced. Oh, but this is a great day for England!"

Briefly a smile flitted across Royce's face, and seemingly indifferent to Morgana standing mutely at his side, he conversed with the butler for a few moments longer. Then, as if suddenly remembering her presence, he inquired of Chambers, "Have you prepared the rooms as I asked?"

Darting an unhappy look at Morgana, Chambers nodded his head. "Yes, sir! They are ready, just as you requested."

Royce's grip on Morgana's arm was painful, almost as if he expected her to bolt as he hurried her up the stairs. Once they entered the suite, he slammed the door forcefully behind them and instantly snatched his hand away from her as if contact with her were distasteful.

She had not known what to expect once they had reached the house, and uneasily her gaze slid around the spacious, richly furnished room, her breath catching audibly in her throat when, through a wide archway framed by a pair of carved double doors, she caught sight of the huge, silken-hung bed. Her face paled, and from the wide-eyed stare she flashed his way, it was obvious that she was fearful he was about to throw her on the bed and seal their infamous bargain. Royce smiled nastily. "You needn't fear that I intend to avail myself of your . . . *services* tonight! You have made your demands quite, *quite* clear!" Raking her with a blatantly insulting look, he added tautly, "Until I can meet your price, I don't plan on enjoying that perfect little body of yours. In the meantime, you may amuse yourself here, counting your gains as they arrive and dwelling upon how much pleasure you will give me once I have found a suitable residence for you!"

He stalked furiously from the room, anger and distaste evident in the rigid set of his broad shoulders and the violent bang of the door as he wrathfully slammed it shut behind him. For a long, painful moment, Morgana stared at the shut door, a cold, miserable numbness growing within her. Oh, my God! What have I done!

Royce was thinking much the same thing as he barged into his study and headed immediately for the tray of liquors that were kept in a walnut cabinet near his desk. God! He must be mad to have let some little thieving pickpocket get under his skin this way! Pouring himself a generous amount of fine French brandy, fine *smuggled* French brandy, he immediately tossed it down and poured himself another. Flinging himself down in a nearby chair, he stared moodily around the room, avoiding looking at the sofa where he had made love to Morgana just hours ago.

The brandy was beginning to warm him, and he was beginning to feel that perhaps events were not quite as bad as he envisioned, when the door to the study suddenly burst open and Zachary, an expression of utter outrage on his face, loomed in the doorway. "Is it true?" he demanded, his fists clenched dangerously at his sides.

Having a fair idea what Zachary was talking about and wishing to avoid the confrontation that his young cousin obviously hoped for, Royce tried to divert him. His features perfectly bland, he remarked imperturbably, "Yes, it's true—Napoleon has been defeated at Waterloo."

Zachary's eyes narrowed, and slamming the door shut behind him, he came over to stand aggressively in front of Royce. "That's *not* what I was referring to," he ground out. "And you damn well know it! Have you seduced Pip?"

Royce winced at the ugly words, but unwilling to excuse his actions, he replied levelly, "Yes, I have—only, she goes by the name of Morgana now." His mouth twisted. "Pip is no more—only Morgana, my mistress, resides here now."

The expression of shocked disillusionment and contempt that crossed Zachary's face hurt Royce deeply. Zachary had always followed his lead and had from early childhood viewed him as an infallible, heroic being. It was painfully clear that with this one rash act, he had destroyed his young cousin's good opinion of him.

Zachary took an agitated step about the study, his fists clenching and unclenching spasmodically. "I could not believe it when I asked Chambers where you had gone with Pip and why he was preparing that suite of rooms for occupancy." Zachary laughed bitterly. "He is loyal to you, do you know that? It took every ounce of charm I possess and a downright threat of force to get the truth out of him." He threw Royce a look of utter loathing. "I thought better of you! She was here under your protection! You were supposed to protect her from the one-eyed man, and instead, you bloody well seduced her yourself!" Almost despairingly he demanded, "How could you do such a thing?"

There was no easy explanation, nor was Royce used to explaining himself. Staring broodingly at the amber liquor in his glass, he muttered, "It happened! Let it go at that!"

Zachary swore softly under his breath and, without another look at Royce, flung himself out of the room.

Pouring himself another snifter of brandy, Royce glanced at the nearly empty decanter and grimaced. A caustic smile curved his mouth. He wondered grimly if he was drinking to obliterate the harsh reality of Morgana's words or to keep himself from mounting the stairs and taking what was rightfully his—after all, he was *paying* for her, wasn't he? Royce couldn't tell.

The next morning he went to see George Ponteby, and upon George's recommendation, Royce hired a respectable estate agent to procure a tidy little house for him. A house, he admitted cynically, that he intended to turn over to the delectable little slut upstairs who occupied a damnably inordinate portion of his thoughts, and *that* situation did not change as the days passed.

Telling her brothers that she would not be joining them when they left for America had not been pleasant. Royce had not spared himself anything and had quite bluntly explained the circumstances to them. He was surprised and yet not surprised when Jacko and Ben seemed to be not unduly concerned with what had happened, and the repulsive suspicion that he had been deliberately set up by the three Fowlers had taken firm root in his brain. Oh, perhaps they had not hit upon their despicable scheme at that very first meeting when he had caught her picking his pocket, but he was not entirely convinced that they had not immediately seized the opportunity to leave temptation in his path. Perhaps, Royce considered blackly, the one-eyed man didn't even exist. It was possible all the incidents blamed on the one-eyed man— Stafford's actions and Lady Whitlock's offer—were genuine. Even the beating given the Fowlers could have been administered by someone else. Perhaps the one-eyed man was simply a fantasy they had concocted for his benefit. A compelling reason to keep their sister in his house. He had believed in the one-eyed man implicitly in the beginning, but now . . . now that Pi—no, *Morgana,* had shown her true colors, he wondered bitterly if he hadn't been spun a Canterbury story.

If telling the Fowlers that he had seduced their sister and intended, with her approval, to set her up as his mistress had been unpleasant, having to face his own servants with what he had done, even if he didn't offer any excuses or explanation for his actions to them, had been even more distasteful. Though they were extremely well trained, Royce was sourly aware of a strong feeling of disapproval emanating from several of them these past days, and he was resentfully conscious that they viewed Morgana with a great deal of sympathy, laying all the blame for the current situation squarely at his feet. They would not dare voice their disapproval, and while they still gave him excellent service, some of the obvious admiration and affectionate esteem with which they had previously regarded him was missing. He didn't really blame them in the least for feeling as they did—he *had* committed a black sin indeed, and no one was more gallingly aware of it than he!

Finishing off another brandy some ten days later, Royce was prowling restlessly around his study, cursing the day Morgana had entered his life, cursing his own folly for not instantly having turned her over to the Watch for incarceration in Newgate, and cursing himself for being such an immoral, lascivious bastard that he could not keep his hands off her! He was also paying a bitter price for his folly—these past ten days, he and Zachary had barely spoken to each other, and Zachary had taken to staying away from the house on Hanover Square as much as possible, his displeasure with the situation clear.

Moodily finishing off the last of the brandy, Royce wandered about the room, studiously keeping his gaze from the sofa where he and Morgana had made love. One thing was positive, he thought dismally—mounting Morgana as his mistress was certainly causing him far more pain and frustration than pleasure! He laughed harshly to himself. He was indeed frustrated, and Zachary's defection as well as his servants' ill-disguised disapproval had brought him pain, but—and this was most bitter of all—he knew in his heart that he would not undo what he had done. He wanted Morgana, and he wanted her at any price, even if it meant losing the esteem of everybody around him. She was *his,* and in his darkest moments he suspected that he would do just about anything, short of murder—and he wasn't even certain about *that*—to keep her in his possession.

It was a painful admission. Until her advent into his life, Royce had always considered himself an honorable, fair-minded, level-headed man. He was not given to fits and starts; he lived his life in a sedate manner and could be counted on to be the clear-thinking one in a crisis. In the past he had laughed at the follies committed by other men while under the spell of an innocent miss or in the throes of a mad infatuation with some clever harlot, and had always considered himself aloof from such antics. Such was not the case any longer. He *was* infatuated with Morgana, he admitted sourly; nothing else could explain his uncharacteristic actions over these past several days.

Tossing ceaselessly in his bed at night, remembering

vividly Morgana's soft form thrashing beneath him, he was burningly aware that he had merely to walk through the adjoining sitting rooms that separated their bedchambers to find the source of all his discomforts. Find the source of discomfort and sweet oblivion, too. Night after night, his body tight and aching for release, he had fantasized about taking that short walk, about entering her bedchamber and climbing into that big bed of hers and seeking the sheer carnal pleasure he knew he would find in her soft, corrupt flesh. Only pride and a stubborn determination not to let her know how completely she had enslaved him kept him from doing just that. But oh, how he was tempted . . .

It wouldn't be long now, he reminded himself tautly, not long at all, until he could bury himself once more in the scalding warmth of her slender body. Not long until he could take his fill of her, slake this uncontrollable passion she had aroused within him. Thomas Grimsly, the estate agent he had hired, had called on him that very afternoon and had discussed a few of the houses that might meet Morgana's demands. Royce was certain that in a *very* short time, perhaps only mere days, he would have fulfilled the last of her damned requirements. Soon she would have her bloody house, and if Grimsly thought him extravagant for *buying* his mistress a house of her own, so what? It was his money, and if he wanted to squander it on a greedy little strumpet, that was his business!

A mirthless smile curved his mobile mouth. He had already spent a fortune on the scheming baggage. Buying things for her gave him a curious pleasure—pain: He wanted her to have everything a woman could desire, even if she *was* a conniving little slut willing to sell herself to him, and he could not seem to stop himself from purchasing for her whatever caught his eye. But while the thought of her wearing and using all the items he had purchased for her delighted him, his delight was also mixed with a strong feeling of regret.

Precisely what he regretted, he couldn't say, but he could not dispel the odd feeling of pain that knotted in his chest whenever he thought of the cold, hard fact that Morgana was *selling* herself to him—that all of the objects he had purchased for her were simply part of the price he was paying to enjoy that supple little body of hers.

The arrangement with Morgana shouldn't have bothered him at all—he had been keeping a mistress off and on since he was seventeen years old, and it had never before given him a moment's qualm that he was *paying* for the woman's time and the use of her body. Granted the women had not been virgins, nor had he ever expended the excessive amount on them that he would on Morgana by the time he bought her the house she wanted, but . . .

Scowling furiously, he tossed off the last of his brandy, determined to waste no more time thinking about the wretched, grasping little hussy, no doubt sleeping soundly upstairs, happily dreaming of the fortune he was spending on her. Consoling himself with the knowledge that soon enough, her nights would not be given to *sleep,* he left the room.

Departing the house in search of entertainment that would keep his thoughts off Morgana, a short while later, he wandered into White's. The club was crowded at this time of night, and spying George and several of his cronies indifferently playing cards in one of the rooms set aside for such purposes, Royce joined them.

Curiously, after all the interest his first encounter with Morgana had caused, no one in the ton seemed the least surprised that he had made his little pickpocket his mistress. Oh, there were a few matrons who looked at him askance, and of course, there was the occasional congratulatory remark made by some of the more *un*gentlemanly gentlemen, but for the most part, society was indifferent. After all, these things *happen,* m'dear!

But if most of society appeared indifferent, there was one

household in polite London in which the news of Morgana's very *existence,* let alone the fact that she had become the mistress of a certain wealthy visiting American, aroused both abject fear and utter fury. The Earl of St. Audries may have originally taken an irrational dislike to Royce Manchester, but the news his wife poured with furious agitation into his ear when he arrived home at her urgent request from a stay in Brighton crystallized the irrational dislike into sheer hatred.

His gray eyes blazing with disbelief, he had at first angrily dismissed her words as the height of folly. They were alone in the handsome library at St. Audries house on Brook Street, the Earl looking tall and elegant in his gray breeches and dark blue, formfitting coat of superfine. Irritably pulling off his gloves after having listened in growing incredulity to his wife's story, he replied peevishly, "Oh, don't be more stupid than you already are, you silly slut! The child is *dead!* And has been dead for these past twenty years!" Throwing his fulminating wife an exasperated glance, he added grimly, "Good God! I was there when the bloody little thief tried to rob him. I saw the filthy creature then and I can tell you it wasn't *Morgana!* "

"That may well be—but at that time it wasn't even known that she was female!" Forcing her lips into the semblance of a smile, Lucinda asked with cutting sweetness, "So if you didn't know the child was female, pray tell me how you knew it wasn't Hester's brat? Did you even *look* at her?"

The Earl shot his wife a glance of dislike. "All right! I didn't pay any attention to the creature, I'll admit that, but I still say that you are hallucinating if you think you saw Morgana Devlin at Royce Manchester's! Morgana Devlin *died* nearly twenty years ago! Can't you get that through your skull? Perhaps a stay at Bedlam would clear your mind!"

"Oh, you'd like that, wouldn't you? You'd do just about anything to rid yourself of me, wouldn't you?"

He nodded amiably. "Provided no blame fell on me, of course . . . But then, you've always known that, my dear." His eyes darkened, the hatred in them obvious. "You've known that ever since you had the bad taste to prefer my brother over *me!*"

"Oh, for God's sake," Lucinda burst out irritably, "don't tell me you're still harping on that! It was over and done with years ago, and you know it—besides, you never made your intentions clear until after Andrew started courting me."

"Courting? Is that what you have deluded yourself into thinking it was?" the Earl asked sarcastically. "From my observation, it appeared more like a sow in heat displaying herself for a notoriously well-known rutting boar!"

Lucinda's hands clenched into fists and her eyes narrowed with loathing. It was obvious from her stance that she would have enjoyed nothing more than actually physically attacking him, but as the moments passed, she visibly brought herself under control. Giving him a thin-lipped smile, she finally said, "You have your opinion of that time and I have mine. . . . That incident *is* in the past, but if something else from the past is not to destroy us, you *must* believe me when I say that the young woman in Manchester's house has to be Morgana!"

If Lucinda had continued to rail at him and had even, as she had all during their stormy marriage, flung herself at him, clawing and kicking, Stephen would have easily dismissed her words and actions as sheer spite, but the fact that she had deliberately brought her formidable temper under control gave him pause. Only something of great importance could have caused her to forgo the pleasure of continuing this ugly confrontation. A slight frown marred his forehead. "What makes you so certain?"

"I *saw* her, I tell you! There is no mistaking those features."

Stephen shrugged. "So. Even if she is the very image of her mother—it proves nothing."

"She is not the *very* image of her mother—she is obviously a Devlin, too, but a Devlin whose features clearly bear Hester's stamp. And *that's* what has me worried."

"Oh, come now, if she looks like a Devlin, she is probably one of Drew's by-blows and nothing for you to get in a snit about," the Earl said dismissingly. "As for looking like Hester, I think you are imagining things."

Lucinda, her bronze-green silken skirts rustling, crossed the room to stand next to her husband. Her lovely face was filled with anxiety and frustration as she laid her hand on his arm and said urgently, "Stephen, you *must* listen to me! I am not simply trying to vex you. That young woman is real, and while at first one notices only the Devlin features—they are unmistakable—if one knew Hester, it would be equally obvious that she is her daughter. It is true she has the Devlin eyes and the well-known look of the Devlins, but there is something about the shape of her face, her nose and mouth, that brings Hester forcibly to mind. If it weren't for the dark hair and those scowling brows and gray eyes, she would be the very picture of Hester."

Lucinda's grave manner as well as the urgency in her tone caused him to take a long, considering look at his wife. What he saw in her eyes and face caused a ripple of disquietude through his entire body. Whether it was true or not, Lucinda obviously believed that she had seen Hester's daughter. He still did not credit it, but a note of nervousness in his voice for the first time, he said, "It can't be—the one-eyed man *promised* me he'd take care of the brat. Why would he lie when he has everything to lose by not fulfilling his part of the bargain? No one would ever trust him again! He would be ruined!"

"I can't believe he did it deliberately," Lucinda muttered despairingly. "But something obviously went wrong. I don't know what happened—mayhap he couldn't bring himself to kill an infant and pawned the child off on someone, never dreaming that she would ever be catapulted into our midst this way."

"My God!" Stephen cried hoarsely. "If the creature really *is* Morgana . . . and it could be proven . . ." A shudder went through him. Everything, he would lose everything—he might even hang if the entire truth of the matter came out. Once someone started looking into the events of nearly twenty years ago, who knew where it would stop . . . what would be uncovered?

"Now do you see why I wrote to you so frantically?" Lucinda asked quietly. "Something must be done before others notice the resemblance."

"I know! I know!" he muttered, agitatedly pacing the confines of the library, forcing himself to banish his fear and to concentrate on the most immediate danger. "It might not be quite as bad as we think." At Lucinda's look of incredulity, he added quickly, "No one really knew Hester as we did. Who is likely to remember her or even what she looked like? That old uncle of hers was her only living relative and he died years ago." He frowned slightly. "I vaguely remember a miniature of her that had been painted for Andrew, but over the years, Lord knows what happened to it—I haven't seen it in ages, at any rate. At present I believe there is only one portrait of her, and that is at St. Audries—it can be hidden in the attics and another portrait of some other ancestor substituted. No one is likely to notice the substitution, and besides, we are seldom there." His face darkened and he shot her a venomous glance. "Only your bloody son enjoys staying there, and it is highly unlikely that he or any of his friends would even spare a look at the portrait gallery, much less realize that something was different. We have nothing to fear from that end."

Straightening his shoulders, a confident expression now replacing his earlier nervousness, he added, "And if, by chance, this creature really is Morgana and her identity is discovered before we can settle the matter, no one can connect *us* to her disappearance—we can be as shocked and distressed as anybody. *We* had nothing to do with any of it! It was a dreadful time for us, losing first our dear sister-in-law and then her baby, too. We were simply too overcome with grief to know what was going on then. We were told the child died—why should we have believed any different? We shall loudly and vehemently proclaim our outrage that our sweet niece had been taken away in such a dastardly manner . . . and we will let everyone know how overjoyed we are that the truth has finally come out and she has been returned to us."

Reluctantly Lucinda nodded her head. "It will serve if the worst happens," she agreed thoughtfully. They exchanged looks. "But we don't intend for the worst to happen, do we?" she asked coolly.

Stephen appeared to study the mirror shine of his black Hessian boots. "No," he finally said in a careful tone. "We don't intend to let it happen."

A bit uncertainly Lucinda inquired, "Should we arrange to meet with the one-eyed man? If he is unaware of what has happened, perhaps he can settle the problem for us— especially since he was supposed to have taken care of everything years ago!"

"And if he is very well aware of what has happened? What if he deliberately kept Morgana alive and she is some part of his nefarious plans? Have you thought of that?" Stephen asked bluntly.

Lucinda drew in her breath in a frightened gasp. She hated the one-eyed man, feared him, too, but it had never occurred to her that he might be working against her. The one-eyed man was a tool; granted, he was a dangerous one, one who had the nasty habit of occasionally returning to demand more money to keep his mouth shut about what he knew, but all in all, he was useful—if terrifying. "Do you honestly think that he would . . ." she began, but the thought was too terrible to contemplate.

Throwing her an impatient look, Stephen snapped, "I have no idea what the hell he would do! But until I am certain that this creature really is Morgana and that it is just sheer bloody bad luck that she has appeared practically under our very noses, I don't intend to trust anyone. Certainly not the one-eyed man!"

"And the girl? What about her?" she asked urgently.

Stephen fiddled with his meticulously arranged cravat. "I think," he said slowly, "that Manchester's new mistress, whether she is Morgana or not, is about to have a dreadful accident." He smiled coldly at his wife. "A *fatal* accident!"

CHAPTER 16

As previously arranged, Thomas Grimsly came to call on Royce the next afternoon and the two men settled down in Royce's office to discuss the various residences that Mr. Grimsly had already inspected and thought might be suitable. Laying down a sketch of a small, but very fine, Queen Anne manor house situated on the outskirts of London, in Hampstead, Grimsly nervously cleared his throat and muttered, "Um, this has been a most difficult task for me . . . and while I know of several excellent properties that could be purchased . . . um, the present owners are rather, ah, *particular* about *who* would be living in their house."

Thomas Grimsly was a small, neat man, his stiffly starched linen cravat arranged in precise, if uninspired folds, his brown coat and fawn breeches expertly cut and fitting his slender frame to perfection. He was in his middle years; his once brown hair was liberally sprinkled with gray, and his time-worn features were plain if pleasant. There was an air of deference about him that bespoke his many years of dealing successfully with haughty aristocrats. From his uneasy manner, Royce suspected that Grimsly was searching for a tactful way of telling him that not everyone wanted his previous home turned into a love nest for a rich man's mistress! Grimsly shot Royce a considering glance, and seeing nothing but polite attention in Royce's handsome face, he continued cautiously, "Um, most owners assume that their properties are going to be lived in by respectable, wealthy people like themselves . . . and, um, not everyone would be *pleased* to have a um . . . um . . ."

As Grimsly sought anxiously for a polite way of saying it, Royce took pity on his obvious discomfort and smiled faintly. "A soiled dove living in the neighborhood? A high-flyer taking her ease in what had been their home?"

It was apparent from Royce's expression and tone that he understood Grimsly's dilemma, and inordinately relieved that the gentleman was not going to cut up rough about the situation, Grimsly nodded his head eagerly. "Exactly! And because of that fact, it limits the houses and properties that I have available to show you." He added hastily, in case his client thought that he would be incapable of filling his requirements, "However, I *do* have a few very nice places that you might like to look at, after I have shown you the sketches and explained their locations and sizes and whatnot."

Together they reviewed the material that Grimsly had brought with him, and from the half dozen or so properties offered, Royce selected three to view himself. It was decided that the house in Hampstead could be seen tomorrow morning and that another likely property, this one situated in Kew, could be examined in the afternoon. If neither of these two places suited Royce, on Thursday they would ride out to Tunbridge Wells and view another prospect.

Under different circumstances, Royce would have found both of the residences he inspected the next day utterly charming, but while he had almost completely convinced himself that Jacko and Ben had conjured up the one-eyed man for their own purposes, there was a part of him that wasn't quite ready to dismiss the existence of the villain entirely, and consequently he viewed the properties differently than he would have normally. The elegant little Queen Anne manor house in Hampstead would have been idyllic except for the fact that it sat quite some distance back from a main road in solitary splendor, an overgrown, winding carriageway eventually leading to the house. Glancing around at the shaggy shrubs and trees that seemed almost to hover over the house—making ideal hiding places for someone intent on gaining entrance undetected—Royce immediately discarded any notion of buying *this* house! The house in Kew was actually one of the newer villas that had been built by the wealthy, but again, Royce didn't like its situation—it sat at the end of a long, narrow lane, and its nearest neighbor was nearly two miles away. Again, he found himself considering how very easy it would be for anyone to gain entrance to the grounds, and from there, the house itself. Both places were hardly more than an hour's ride from London, and that, too, made him a trifle uneasy. *If* the one-eyed man was intent on kidnapping Pi—*Morgana* for his own black purposes, Royce damn well wasn't going to make it easy for the bloody bastard! Morgana would have her blasted house, but he was going to make certain that she'd be safe in it!

And so it was that the first Thursday in July found Royce near Tunbridge Wells, and he liked what he saw immediately. The house, actually a *cottage ornée* designed by John Nash before he had become the Regent's protégé, was absolutely charming, but it was the setting that appealed to Royce. The building sat in the middle of nearly a hundred acres of rolling woodland, *but*—and this is what Royce found most attractive—the entire parcel was surrounded by an ancient, thick, impenetrable yew hedge. And there was a gatekeeper's cottage at the beginning of the only road to the house. Two stout iron gates guarded the entrance, and it was obvious that not just anybody could come wandering onto the property. The road that led to the house was wide and ambled pleasantly along a clear, shallow creek, and Royce was further pleased to discover that the house, built on the site of an old keep, long since torn down, was situated in the center of a walled courtyard.

An earlier owner had expanded the original walled courtyard, and the immediate grounds within the stone walls, liberally interspersed with several pairs of filigreed iron gates, which gave views of the areas beyond the walls, now consisted of nearly ten acres of manicured lawns, tall oaks, and lime trees; several stone-paved paths, delightfully bordered with wallflowers, roses, lavender, and peonies, wandered here and there. A short distance outside the walled courtyard, at the rear of the house, there was even a small lake, in its center a man-made island with an airy white gazebo. While Royce would have found the whole setting absolutely beguiling under any circumstances, what truly impressed him was the fact that anyone attempting to gain entrance to the house had to first get past the yew hedge and/or the gatekeeper; and once those obstacles were surmounted, there was still the walled courtyard to contend with. Taking another long look at the ten-foot-high wall and even considering all the gates that would require locks, he decided that of the properties he had seen so far, this one most suited his needs. The fact that there were some neighbors less than a mile down the road also pleased him, as did the knowledge that the house was situated several hours ride from London . . . and the one-eyed man.

The house itself was of stone, six large dormers jutting out from the sloping, thatched roof. Tall, wide French doors lined the long wing of the L-shaped building, and they opened onto stone-paved areas bordered with all manner of blooming flowers and shrubs. Called a "cottage," it had been built when the desire of the aristocracy and wealthy for the simple life, the bucolic life, had just become fashionable, and it was like no cottage that Royce had ever seen in his life—there was a long library, a drawing room, a huge dining room, a morning room, the kitchen with its attendant rooms, several other elegant rooms with no particular designation, and ten bedrooms, plus a servants' wing! Quite the *cottage,* indeed!

Since most of the morning had been spent traveling down from London, it was late by the time Royce and Grimsly finished their inspection of the premises, and they spent the night at an extremely pleasant inn in Tunbridge Wells. The next morning, in no real hurry to return to London, Royce, with Grimsly at his side, wandered about Tunbridge Wells, finding it an attractive town. Though Brighton was considered the most fashionable of the summer towns, Tunbridge Wells was still sought out by many of those in the ton, and while the number of visitors coming to the town to take the waters had dwindled, it still had a thriving population.

Royce had known yesterday that he was going to buy Lime Tree Cottage, as it was called, but it was not until they were halfway back to London that he informed Grimsly of his decision. A delighted smile on his mouth, Grimsly murmured, "I am very happy that I could be of service to you, sir, and I am certain that you will find the cottage to be everything that you desire. Shall I have the proper deeds and such drawn up after we reach London this evening? I can meet with my principal before dinner and have him sign everything that is necessary—I know he will be quite pleased to learn that his difficulties are at an end." He pulled a disapproving face. "Gambling debts, you know."

Royce wasn't surprised—entire fortunes were known to have turned on the roll of the dice, and there were many among the ton who were wealthy one day and ruined the next. He nodded his tawny head in tacit understanding and answered Grimsly's question. "Yes, I should like the papers drawn up as soon as possible, if it is not too much trouble. I shall see my banker first thing tomorrow morning and shall make all the arrangements necessary for the transfer of funds." Royce hesitated a moment, appearing to concentrate on keeping his lively pair of shining chestnut geldings trotting at a spanking pace. There was silence for a few moments as the curricle bowled along the main road to London, and then Royce said abruptly, "I know that I told you that the house would be in the woman's name alone, but I have changed my mind and I want my name on the deed too."

Mr. Grimsly nodded slightly and said agreeably, "Of course, sir—it will be no problem at all."

Extremely satisfied with his activities over the past twenty-four hours, Royce was whistling merrily as he bounded up the steps to the house on Hanover Square a few hours later. If all went well, by this time next week, he and Morgana would be comfortably installed in Lime Tree Cottage, and he was conscious of a leap in his blood when he realized precisely what that meant. . . . No more lonely nights . . . no more violent tossing about, thinking of her sweet charms. In less than seven days, if he could arrange it, he would be sampling the delights of Morgana's body to his heart's content.

Not even Chambers's stiff greeting could dampen his mood, and smiling lightly, he handed his butler his hat and gloves and asked, "Everything go well while I was gone?"

A slight frown marring his forehead, Chambers replied, "Well, not exactly, sir." At Royce's suddenly grim expression, he hurried into speech. "It is nothing very bad—it was just that I noticed that several of the locks had been tampered with during the night. No one heard anything out of the ordinary, but it was obvious this morning when I went about unlocking that the locks on the doors were scratched and scuffed, as if someone had attempted to pry them open."

Conscious of a chill sliding down his back, his belief in the one-eyed man instantly restored, Royce stared thoughtfully at his butler for several moments. Of course, it *could* have been merely housebreakers—thieves with no connection at all to the one-eyed man—but he didn't think such was the case, and he consoled himself with the knowledge that no harm had been done . . . yet. Not allowing himself to think how he would have felt to learn that Morgana had been snatched away from him while he had been gone, Royce kept his unpleasant speculations to himself, and not wanting to cause any undue alarm, he remarked easily, "I suppose this is one of the hazards of living in London, but since they didn't get into the house, I shouldn't worry." On the surface appearing to treat the matter lightly, Royce smiled and asked, "Anything else?"

Chambers shook his head and said dryly, "No, sir. Everything is just as you would want it."

There was a note in Chambers's voice that Royce didn't like; he realized that the last comment was as close to sarcasm as someone in his butler's position could come, and was uncomfortably aware of the reason behind it, causing whatever had remained of his good humor to vanish. Striving to keep an even temper, Royce asked lightly, "Is Zachary in?" At Chambers's curt nod, he added, "Please tell him to meet me in my office, will you? Oh, and would you bring us something to drink? Thank you."

Hanging on to his determinedly pleasant mood at the sight of Zachary's scowling features when that young man joined him in his office a few minutes later, Royce inquired politely, "And how have you been these past few days? Still enjoying London?"

Zachary shrugged indifferently and threw himself down into one of the leather chairs. "What did you want to see me about?"

Before Royce could reply, there was a brief rap on the door and Chambers entered with a heavily laden silver tray. There were several bottles of various wines on it, glasses, and some plates piled high with cold roast beef, cheese, and freshly baked sliced bread; with pleasure, Royce spied a large platter of the lemon tarts he enjoyed so much. Having a good idea who had so thoughtfully added food to his original request, Royce smiled faintly. At least *Ivy* didn't still consider him a monster of depravity, he thought wryly.

But his smile faded after Chambers left and he turned to look at his sullen-faced cousin. Sighing, Royce sat down behind the large mahogany desk in front of Zachary, and crossing his booted feet, he carefully placed them on one corner. Leaning back comfortably in the high-backed chair, he said resignedly, "Go ahead. Vent your spleen. We might as well get all the unpleasantness over with at once."

Zachary shot him an unfriendly look. "Is that all this is to you? *Unpleasant?* You cravenly seduce a young woman who looked to you for protection! How can you excuse that?"

Just about anyone else, Royce would have floored with a powerful right fist, but Zachary was his favorite cousin and he cared deeply about the boy. Controlling his rising temper with an effort, Royce said quietly, "It is a long time since I have made excuses for myself, and I'm not about to start now . . . not even for *you!* I know you are unhappy about the current situation, but giving me killing looks and treating me as if I were a leper is not going to undo what happened."

Zachary continued to look at him in that unfriendly manner, a contemptuous snort his only answer to Royce's even words.

Royce completely understood Zachary's displeasure—hell, he wasn't proud of what had happened himself!—but there were limits to how much disapproval he was willing to take, and he had just about had enough! His face grim, he said levelly, "I think instead of continuing to cast me in the role of blackest villainy, you need to remind yourself of a few things— such as the fact that I didn't force her. You didn't hear her come running or screaming from my embrace, did you? Nor did I set the price or even suggest she become my mistress." Some of his old hurt and anger at Morgana's actions came flooding back and he snarled softly, "No, my young man, *that* was all her connivance! I was just the poor besotted fool who couldn't keep his hands off of what was offered me!"

Furious for saying far more than he had meant to, Royce sat up violently, the legs of his chair hitting the carpeted floor with a loud thud. "Jesus! Believe me, I wish to hell I had never laid eyes on her!" Standing up, he walked over to where Chambers had set the tray and poured himself a generous glass of wine. His back to Zachary, he muttered, "Get out of here. We obviously have nothing to say."

While angry and distressed about Morgana's seduction by Royce, Zachary was finding it hard going to maintain his distance from his cousin. Not only were there years of affection and admiration between them, but London had opened Zachary's eyes to many things that once would have shocked and repelled him. He had been astonished to discover that very few members of the ton thought that there was anything out of the ordinary about Royce's actions. Many applauded him, for as his friend Jeremy had said reasonably just the other evening, "What else is a man to do with a lovely wench like that? Waste of fine feminine flesh to keep her as a *servant!* Besides, if not your cousin, then some other lucky fellow would do the same thing—and he might not be as generous!" Warming to his theme, Jeremy had leaned forward and continued earnestly, "Thing is, delectable little creatures like her either find themselves a protector or they end up in a bordello or on the streets. Think your cousin did her a favor!"

Zachary hadn't reached that conclusion, but during his time in London, he had become sophisticated enough to recognize that there was a great deal of truth in Jeremy's statement—no matter *how* cold and unfeeling it might sound. It was apparent, too, from the steady stream of boxes and packages arriving at the house daily, that Morgana was benefiting greatly from the arrangement, and it hadn't escaped Zachary's notice that she had made no attempt to enlist help to escape from Royce, nor had she refused any of the expensive objects that came her way.

Prompted as much by a desire to heal the breach with his cousin as the knowledge, distasteful though it might be, that Royce had acted no differently than would have the overwhelming majority of men placed in his position, Zachary muttered, "Royce, we can't go on this way. . . . I-I-I don't like being at daggers drawn with you." Taking a deep breath, he added magnanimously, "Perhaps I was too hasty in my condemnation of you—it was none of my business. It is just that I *like* Pi—*Morgana,* and I overreacted to what happened between you. It was not my place to pass judgment on you. I'm sorry."

It was an exceedingly handsome apology, and while Royce was enormously relieved to hear Zachary's words, they also shamed him—he should never have allowed a situation that put Zachary in this position to arise. Turning to face his cousin, he smiled crookedly and said, "There is no need for you to apologize—I think it is I who owe you an apology for creating this damnable situation!"

A weight lifted from Zachary's shoulders, and grinning a bit shamefacedly, he admitted, "I've been acting very starchy, haven't I?"

"Very!" Royce said with a laugh.

Harmony restored between them, they conversed for several more minutes, and at first it was rather awkward until they firmly reestablished their affectionate rapport. As the moments passed and they brought each other up-to-date with their various activities, the unpleasantness of the past several days was forgotten as if it had never occurred.

It was only after they demolished the tray of food and had finished off one of the bottles of wine that Royce brought up the subject of the locks. His face serious, he asked, "Did

Chambers tell you about the locks being tampered with last night?"

Zachary nodded, his own face concerned. "Yes, he did first thing this morning. I looked at all of them, and it is apparent that someone made a rather amateur go at attempting to force their way into the house."

"Amateur?" Royce asked, one black brow raised skeptically. "The one-eyed man is no amateur, nor, if I am to believe Jacko and Ben, does he consort with amateurs."

Zachary shrugged his shoulders. "Perhaps I'm wrong—you'll just have to see them yourself and see if you don't agree with me."

An hour later, just having completed his own inspection of the doors and their various locks, Royce agreed that Zachary's assessment had been correct. The attempted break-in had been an unmistakably amateur attempt, the scratches and marks on the doors clearly revealing that someone had ineptly tried to either force the locks or pry open the doors. But the attempt itself puzzled Royce, and after a great deal of thought, he came to the unsettling conclusion that last night's occurrence could not have been the work of the one-eyed man or his minions—the attempt was too, well, *amateur*. Royce kept coming back to that one thought. An amateur. Someone who was not familiar with the tools of housebreaking. Someone, he was fairly confident, who was not connected with the one-eyed man. . . . But if not the one-eyed one . . . then who? And why?

All through the next few days, that particular line of thought kept swirling around at the back of his brain, even as he went about various tasks. The transactions involving the purchase of Lime Tree Cottage went very smoothly, and shortly, Royce found his bank account hugely depleted; but in exchange, he held the deed to the property. He and Morgana. It gave him a peculiar feeling to see her name on the deed next to his—almost as if she were his wife and they had bought the property together. . . .

Infuriated with himself for even allowing such a nonsensical idea to cross his mind, he pushed the silly notion aside and concentrated determinedly on other things. Such as why he had heard nothing from Roger Steadham, his business agent, about a sailing date for the Fowler brothers. Now that Morgana had become his mistress, there was no question of her going to America without *him,* and he decided that he might as well see Mr. Steadham; in the course of discovering why he had heard nothing from him, he could also relay the information that the number of passages had changed from four to two.

Consequently, at two o'clock on Monday afternoon, Royce was seated comfortably in Mr. Steadham's office exchanging polite banter with him before they settled down to discuss business. If he thought Mr. Steadham seemed a trifle nervous, he told himself idly that it was because the man must have other pressures on his mind, and he didn't immediately connect Steadham's odd behavior with *his* business.

At the first mention of the passages, however, Steadham's face paled, his eyes dilated, and he stammered, "The p-p-passages you requested? Oh, I'm sorry, but it seems that there are none available until late summer. Possibly August or early September."

Steadham's reaction would have alerted even someone far less astute than Royce Manchester, and Royce was instantly suspicious. His polite smile fading and the golden eyes narrowed, Royce asked quietly, "Are you telling me that there is *nothing* sailing from England to America until then?"

Steadham smiled sickly. "Nothing that would be suitable for you," he offered weakly.

Royce sent him a long, thoughtful look. There could be all manner of reasons to explain Steadham's behavior, and under different circumstances, Royce might have accepted Steadham's actions and words at face value. But that was before he had learned of the mysterious one-eyed one, and Royce could be forgiven for wondering sourly if Steadham wasn't just another poor devil caught in the toils of the one-eyed man. Or was Steadham telling the truth? It would be no problem to double-check the accuracy of the information Steadham had given him, but with a sinking sensation in the pit of his stomach, Royce was certain he would discover that Steadham was lying to him and that the one-eyed man was behind his odd behavior. That particular conclusion was inescapable and . . . chilling. But was it coincidence or design that the one-eyed man had learned of his visit to Steadham? Or had he been warned by someone of what had been planned?

Royce didn't like the direction of his thoughts. Even if he could dismiss it as pure accident that his business agent was someone who, for whatever reasons, owed the one-eyed man alliance, and further convince himself that it was sheer coincidence that the one-eyed man had learned of his desire to purchase the four passages to America, the fact that the one-eyed man had obviously ordered Steadham to lie about the availability of those passages was definitely ominous. But was the one-eyed man simply being inordinately cautious or had he known that those passages to America were for the Fowlers?

Aware that he would learn nothing further from Steadham and not wishing to betray the tenor of his thoughts, Royce finally said easily, "Very well. If there is nothing before that time, I shall simply have to settle for what you can find for me." Sending Steadham a charming smile, he added, "Perhaps it is just as well—my plans have changed slightly since I last spoke with you, and I now just require two passages." Only polite inquiry on his face, he asked guilelessly, "Do you think that would make any difference on securing an earlier departure date?"

Steadham moved restlessly in his chair, and not meeting Royce's gaze, he muttered, "I'll look into it, but I believe that I will have to stick to my previous estimate."

Steadham's reply didn't surprise Royce, especially if the one-eyed man didn't want those passages secured in the near future, and rising lightly to his feet, Royce took his leave as speedily as possible. His thoughts were very busy and *very* dark as he walked away from Steadham's office, and he wasted little time in checking out the truth of Steadham's story, stopping at the first shipping office he came to and inquiring into possible dates for sailing to America. What he learned confirmed his suspicion that Steadham had been lying to him—there were two ships sailing within the week, and both still had passages available. . . .

So. Steadham had lied. Royce supposed that if he wanted to waste time in idle speculation, he could come up with several possible reasons for the business agent to act as he had, but there was only *one* reason as far as Royce was concerned—that bloody damned one-eyed man!

Returning to Hanover Square, he was scowling blackly as he entered the house, knowing that it was imperative that he meet with the Fowler brothers, and knowing that in order to do so, he was going to have to go to Della's. . . . Retreating to his study, he paced back and forth, cursing the day he had ever laid eyes on Morgana Fowler!

Unfortunately, his mood was not any better some time later when Chambers knocked timidly on the door (the master's moods these days was extremely volatile!) and informed Royce that dinner was being served. He was expecting to dine alone—Zachary was dining with friends and there were no invited guests. His features moody, he stalked to the dining room only to be brought up short by the sight of Morgana confidently sitting at the head of the table and *wearing the ruby gown!*

Suddenly Royce had a very good idea of what it felt like to be apoplectic with rage. "What the hell are you doing here? And where in the *bloody* hell did you get that blasted gown?"

Despite the quaking in her limbs, Morgana's chin lifted. It had been quite brave of her to coolly inform Chambers that she would be dining downstairs tonight, and, she realized nervously, unaccountably foolish to wear the ruby gown. Since the afternoon at Madame Duchand's, she had been immured in the elegant suite of rooms upstairs; except for Hazel, who had been hastily assigned as her maid, and Chambers, who served her meals, she had seen no one, and quite frankly, while being both remorseful and angry, she was tired of being treated like a leper. She bitterly regretted her hasty bargain, and the long, penitent, solitary hours she had spent these past days had left her with a great deal of time to reflect upon just how very, *very* repulsive her position was . . . and how much more so it was going to be once Royce had procured the house she had so rashly demanded. The arrival of each new purchase—luxurious, brightly colored muslin, silk, and satin gowns, delicate chemises, lovely petticoats, shoes, hats, as well as several bottles of exotically scented perfumes, soaps, and powders—was a silent reproach, and she viewed each new item with horrified revulsion.

The notion of throwing herself on Royce's mercy and begging him to forgo their ugly bargain and send her to America with her brothers had crossed her mind frequently. But the painfully vivid memory of the expression on his face when he had stated that she would *earn* every penny he spent on her had Morgana grimly convinced that begging Royce Manchester for *any*thing would only bring her further humiliation, and her already battered pride quailed at being forced to grovel before him—and to no avail! Since she couldn't grovel, there was only one thing left to do—please herself as much as she dared, and that included wearing the contested ruby gown and making her presence felt within the household. It had seemed a very good idea several hours ago when it had first occurred to her, but seeing the thunderous expression on Royce's face, she wished that she had thought things a little further and had considered his probable reaction!

But she hadn't, and not about to let him intimidate her further, she summoned all her failing courage to reply sweetly,

"I'm intending to eat my dinner, and as for the gown—you know very well that it was purchased from Madame Duchand!"

Throwing himself down in a chair at the other end of the long, damask-covered table, Royce contented himself with sending her a look filled with loathing. Upstart little baggage! he thought irascibly. And encroaching, too—pushing her way into his dining room this way! Who did she think she was? And yet even as he stared at her in the flickering light of the silver candelabras that graced the table, he was aware of his desire stirring.

She was undeniably ravishingly lovely as she sat so regally down the table from him, her smooth, white skin rising temptingly above the silk and lace of the gleaming ruby and black gown. His eyes dropped to the surprising fullness of her breasts, the gown cut so low that it stopped just shy of revealing her nipples. He was painfully erect in an instant, and inordinately thankful that she could not see the noticeable effect she had upon him, he took refuge in anger and said in a surly tone, "I don't remember inviting you to share my meal—but I do remember distinctly refusing to buy you that damn gown!"

Pasting an angelic smile on her mouth, she murmured, "Since I live here in this house, I don't believe that I *have* to wait for you to invite me anywhere!"

He let her comment pass, and a sardonic expression crossed his face. "And the gown?" he inquired. "Would you care to explain how it got in your wardrobe?"

Not liking the look in his eyes at all, she was cravenly grateful when Chambers entered just then with the first course of the meal. For the present, the subject was dropped.

Dinner was not pleasant. Morgana had to force down each sip of soup, each bite of meat, fighting to keep her composure in the face of Royce's ill-concealed antipathy and her own treacherous senses. Certain she hated him, convinced she was furious with him, she still could not control the sudden wild beating of her heart when she glanced up and caught his gaze locked on her bosom. To her mortification, her nipples tightened and a rush of dizzying excitement hurtled through her. Looking at his down-bent tawny head as he cut a piece of the excellent roast beef Ivy had prepared tonight, Morgana was conscious of a longing for things to be different between them, for them to share a far different relationship from the one in which they found themselves.

The presence of the other servants as they served the meal made conversation difficult, and Royce and Morgana were barely polite to each other. The last course was finally presented, and Morgana's heart sank when she heard Royce say to Chambers, "That will be all for now. I'll let you know when we are through in here."

Risking a glance at Royce, despite her uncomfortable situation, Morgana was unbearably conscious of just what a handsome, vital man he was as he lounged there, one long-fingered hand idly twirling his wineglass, the other resting casually on the table. His face was very dark above the pristine whiteness of his cravat, and the dark blue coat, with its gilt buttons shining brightly in the candlelight, fit his broad shoulders and muscled arms to perfection. Without volition, she remembered the strength of that lean body, the warmth of his flesh against hers, and she was suddenly breathless. Desperate to get away from him before she did something even more foolish than she already had, she leaped to her feet and, tossing down her napkin, remarked, "I shall leave you to your brandy now."

Royce sent her a heavy-lidded stare and murmured softly, "Not yet, sweetheart! You still haven't explained about the gown. . . ." Insultingly he let his gaze roam over her body. "Of course, now that I have seen it again, I can't remember why I objected in the first place." His gaze blatantly stripping her, he added in a goading tone, "It displays your wares very nicely. . . . Reminds me of just what I am paying for!"

Morgana blanched, her fingers closing into white-knuckled

fists. Pain knifed through her at his words, and forgetting whatever good resolutions she may have made, she tossed her dark, curly head and snapped, "Just remember that until you have purchased my house, by your own words, you only get to *look!*"

Royce lunged for her, but Morgana's courage had failed and she was already dashing for the door. Fingers frantically scrabbling against the crystal knob, she flung the door open and bolted into the hall and up the stairs. In the asylum of her room, her back resting against the door, she waited with thumping heart for the sound of his pursuit, but there was nothing. She had bearded the tiger and escaped once again . . . but for how long? she wondered uneasily. For how long?

CHAPTER 17

Undecided whether to charge after her or vent his fury by smashing his fist into the wall, Royce frowned darkly at the doorway through which she had disappeared. Oh, the hell with her! he thought angrily. She was nothing but a conniving little bitch anyway! Why let her upset him? Cursing under his breath, he realized that his reaction to Morgana tonight made it clear that he had to see Della, *should* have explained events to her long before this! Morgana's presence in his house was creating more than one set of problems— how did one graciously inform the first mistress of her ouster by the presence of a *second* mistress?

It was a problem that Royce had never faced before in his

life and had never *expected* to face, and he had grappled with it off and on ever since the afternoon he had made love to Morgana. To his credit, he did not want to cause Della any more pain or humiliation than necessary, and he had racked his brain these past several days trying to come up with an honorable solution. Except to drive by Della's house to check on the signal, he had avoided the area. However, to soothe his guilty conscience, and it had not soothed it *very* much, Royce had made arrangements before his trip to Tunbridge Wells for his jeweler to have delivered to Della an exorbitantly expensive diamond necklace and matching earrings.

Angry with himself for letting the situation even arise in the first place, it was with a determined set to his broad shoulders that he walked up the few steps to Della's house and entered. Della, wearing an extremely lovely gown of bronze-shot silk, was waiting for him in the attractive salon where he had met with the Fowler brothers. It was evident by the reproachfulness in her brown eyes that the news of Morgana's place in his life had already reached her, and Royce felt like a complete cad.

Flashing her that particularly attractive crooked grin of his, he bent his tawny head and kissed the slim, white hand that she extended. Not wishing to prolong the unpleasantness longer than necessary, after seating himself on the sofa next to her, he asked quietly, "I assume that you have heard about Morgana?"

Della nodded. "Yes, several gentlemen were very quick to tell me that you had taken another mistress. . . . I think I would have preferred to hear it from you."

Royce winced and took her hands in his. "There is nothing I can say that will excuse my actions. I can only apologize to you and hope that in time you will forgive my very bad manners." The topaz eyes searched hers intently. "Della, if there is anything I can do to make this easier for you . . ."

She smiled faintly, one of her hands coming up to lightly

caress his lean cheek. "Short of having you throw your new mistress out in the streets, I can think of nothing." Despite himself, Royce wore an expression betraying the unlikeliness of *that* occurring, and Della laughed, albeit a trifle wryly. "I didn't really expect that you would, but I thought it was worth a try." Laying her hand in her lap, she added, "Don't feel too remorseful—you have been a very generous lover, both with your pocketbook and your body. . . ." She sent him a long, sensually appreciative look, her gaze lingering on his wide chest and hard thighs. "I think I shall miss you in my bed almost as much as I shall miss your generosity. But women in my profession are aware of the transient nature of our liaisons, and I knew it would come to an end one day—perhaps not as swiftly as it has!" She shot him a careful glance from beneath her lashes. "I hope that you do not want me to leave this house immediately. . . ." And at Royce's confirmation that she could stay for several more weeks if she wished, she smiled. "Oh, it wouldn't be that long. You see, I have not been idle either—my new protector will have me housed at a new address in Tunbridge Wells before the week is ended!"

There was a startled silence, then Royce grinned ruefully and murmured, "I suppose I deserved that!"

Della could be forgiven for the satisfied smile that curved her mouth. "Yes, you did, you handsome bastard!" she said without heat. "You've used me most dreadfully."

"My conduct has been deplorable," Royce agreed readily, noting with relief the faint glimmer of laughter that lurked in her wide, brown eyes.

"Abominable!" she said.

"Reprehensible!" he conceded.

Della laughed. "Shall we cry quits? Or shall we continue?"

Royce smiled wryly. "I think we should cry quits and admit that my conduct was indeed dreadful, deplorable, abominable, and reprehensible!"

Della's fingers reached out again to touch his face. A warm

expression in her eyes, she murmured, "I shall miss you, Royce Manchester."

Royce captured her hand, and pressing a kiss into the palm, he muttered, "Thank you, Della. You have treated me most handsomely in spite of my shabby behavior."

"Ah, but it will cost you, Royce," Della said with a twinkle in her eyes. "I think you owe me that pair of chestnuts you ... and a high-perch phaeton to go with them." "I will have the

drive ... answered without hesitation. ... morning and shall put ... sheepishly, "Would ... telling me the name of the gentleman who replaced me so speedily in your affections?"

For a moment, he thought she was going to refuse, and he would not have blamed her, but with a shrug of her slender shoulders, she answered calmly, "Of course not. He is one of several gentlemen who had been paying court to me before you arrived on the London scene. I had just about made up my mind to accept his offer when you appeared." She added bluntly, "And quite frankly, I now wish I had not let your handsome face turn my head and had become his mistress in the first place."

Royce looked suitably chastened, although there was a mocking glint in the depths of those amber gold eyes. "Yes, I know," he admitted meekly, "that there were several friends of mine in the running to gain your favors—Newell and Atwater make no bones about it that I stole you right out from under their noses."

"As well as those of Devlin, Wetherly, and Stafford!" Della couldn't help bragging.

Telling himself it was no longer any of his business, but disliking on principle the idea that it might be Devlin who was now keeping Della, he inquired bluntly, "And is it the Earl?"

"No," Della replied, "it is a very wealthy gentleman named Jasper Simonds."

Royce frowned. "Jasper Simonds? I don't believe that I have heard his name before."

"Probably not," Della replied. "He is somewhat reticent and he does not talk a great deal about his background... know that he is *very* wealthy and that while ... with the highest in the land, he is ... members of the aristo... dries and his ...

...plished so easily, Royce spent the next several moments chatting quite amiably with his former mistress. Prior to his taking his leave of her, he elicited the information that she would be staying the night with Simonds, since her new protector objected to bedding her in a house being paid for by her former lover.

Curious about the man who had so opportunely replaced him in Della's life, Royce immediately went in search of his cousin, George. He found him at White's, surrounded by his usual coterie of friends, Atwater and Newell among them, and it was some time before Royce was able to have a private word with him. Eventually he cut his gregarious cousin out from the pack, and finding a quiet corner in the club, he was finally able to ask George about Jasper Simonds.

"Jasper Simonds, hmm?" George said thoughtfully. "Tall, black-eyed, slender fellow? Keeps to himself? Might have the smell of the shop about him, but full of brass?"

Royce looked impatient. "George, if I don't know the fellow, how the devil would I know if he was short or tall, fat or skinny? Do you know him, and what do you know about him?"

George shrugged. "Think you do know 'im. Met him already. Know I introduced you to him when you first arrived."

"George!" Royce began in exasperation. "You introduced me to half of London when I first arrived! How am I to remember everyone? Now, quit teasing me and tell me what you know about him."

"Not much to tell," George offered with sleepy amiability. "He don't run in our crowd very often—sticks more with the Devlin bunch. Very wealthy, but no one knows where his blunt came from. Haven't heard anything about his family. Might be shopkeepers and he don't want it known. Why d'you want to know?"

Smiling ruefully, Royce returned, "He's Della's new protector."

"Oh!" George replied, a knowing twinkle in his eyes. "Feel like he set a pair of horns on your head, hey?"

"Not precisely, and Lord knows I deserve them after the trick I played on Della with Morgana, but I was just curious about him. I feel, well, sort of a sense of responsibility toward her, considering the way our relationship ended."

"Shouldn't worry," George murmured. "Women like Della—like cats—always end on their feet . . . or backs, as the case may be!"

They spoke for a few moments more, then just as they were about to end their conversation, Royce asked slowly, "George, have you ever heard anything about a . . . a one-eyed man?"

The effect on his unflappable, convivial cousin was startling. George stiffened as if shot, and his normally ruddy complexion became pasty. "And what do you know about *him?*" George demanded in a hoarse voice.

"I think I asked the question first," Royce returned quietly, George's reaction filling him with an odd anxiety. Good Lord! His cousin couldn't possibly have had dealings with such a creature. Not *George!*

And almost as if he could read his mind, George said hastily, "Don't know 'im myself." He shuddered and glanced nervously around the room before adding, "He's a bad 'un—had a good friend, a dear friend who got caught in his toils. Killed himself. Messy affair." Dread evident in his blue eyes,

George clutched Royce's arm and demanded apprehensively, "You ain't met him yourself? You're not, er, having him *do* things for you, are you? Not wise, Royce. If you need help, come to me—I'll sport the blunt. Don't go to that one-eyed devil. Be the end of you! Like my friend!"

Soothing his cousin's fears that he had not employed the dubious services of the one-eyed man took some time, but eventually Royce was able to deftly segue the conversation around to the more pleasant topic of his impending removal to Tunbridge Wells. George immediately brightened, and in the course of their conversation, somehow—and he was never certain how it happened, which was the way it always was with George—Royce found himself inviting his cousin to come and stay at Lime Tree Cottage. Shaking his head at his own folly, he strolled back to the house on Hanover Square, rather than riding on such a fine day, enjoying the late afternoon sunshine.

Royce had not spoken to Morgana about either the purchase of the house or their imminent removal to Tunbridge Wells—he had not even mentioned it to the servants. Deciding that it was past time to do so, upon his arrival home, he called Chambers into his office and explained everything to him.

Chambers did not so much as blink an eye at the stunning news that in less than six days they would all be leaving London and taking up residence in Tunbridge Wells. His voice colorless, Chambers replied, "Of course, sir. I shall see to everything."

Smiling faintly, Royce said apologetically, "I should have said something to you sooner, but I have had other things on my mind. Will it be terribly inconvenient for all of you?"

Chambers thawed just a bit. "Oh, no, sir. Since you leased this house furnished, there will only be our personal effects to pack and transport." A question in his eyes, he asked carefully, "And is, the, er, cottage furnished?"

"Yes—very tastefully," Royce answered with a gleam of mockery in his topaz eyes. "I may be using it for iniquitous purposes, but the previous owner had exquisite taste and he sold the cottage to me with all its contents."

Chambers did not take the bait, and bowing low, he left the room. Royce wandered about his office for several more seconds before deciding that he could not put off telling Morgana about Lime Tree Cottage any longer. Precisely why he was reluctant to tell her, he couldn't have explained himself, but he suspected it had a great deal to do with his violent distaste for the whole idea of *buying* his way into her bed. Which was most peculiar considering that he had not thought twice about the expense of keeping Della or the cost of the prized chestnuts and phaeton that were his parting gift to her! Something inside him rebelled at placing Morgana in the same category as Della, and perhaps *that* more than any one thing infuriated him.

His handsome face set and grim, he stalked from his office and swiftly mounted the stairs in search of the most baffling, beguiling little witch whom it had ever been his misfortune to meet! Entering the luxurious ivory and blue sitting room that separated his suite from hers, Royce found the object of his thoughts seated demurely on a long, low sofa covered in ivory brocade.

The now fashionably cut black curls framing her beautiful face, Morgana was wearing an enchanting gown of lavender muslin, a copy of Lord Bryon's *The Corsair,* which had been published the previous year, lying open on her lap.

To his great irritation, Royce was uneasily aware of the sudden leap in his pulse that the mere sight of her caused, and his voice and words were harsher than he intended as he said without preamble, "I've found you your bloody house! It is located in Tunbridge Wells, and if all goes well, we shall remove there on Friday." A dangerous glitter in the golden brown eyes, he smiled insultingly as his gaze raked her up and down. "And after our arrival, I trust that before too many hours pass, I'll be able to judge for myself if you're worth the fortune you're costing me!"

In stunned silence, Morgana stared up into his dark face, a myriad of confused thoughts tumbling through her brain. She had seen so little of him since that afternoon in his office that just his presence here in her rooms was startling. Both longing and dreading for him to come to her, she hungrily drank in the sight of his tall, lean body, his arrogant face, dark and forbidding against the white cravat at his throat. As she watched him stride confidently across the room toward her, her gaze paused obsessively on the full bottom lip of that wickedly attractive mouth, and a flutter, part fright, part delight, in the pit of her stomach reminded her forcibly that this man held her fate in his hands . . . because she loved him! And because she loved him, he all-unknowingly wielded great power over her—power that she would never admit to him, power that she hated. She had barely grappled with the conflicting turmoil of emotion his appearance created within her when he had hurled those ugly words at her. Pride coming to her rescue, she tilted her chin haughtily and, determined to meet his cool arrogance with some of her own, said brashly, "Perhaps you should worry first that I approve of my bloody house! I am, after all, the one who must be satisfied!"

To say which of them was the most astonished by her words would have been impossible. Royce's face tightened, and appalled with herself, Morgana could not quite believe that she had actually said such an outrageous thing. It ranked right up there with the hasty demands that had gotten her in this position in the first place, and she cursed her unruly tongue. But she wouldn't back down; she had gone too far along this path she unwillingly trod to retreat now, and with a stubborn look on her features, she faced him defiantly.

Royce took a deep breath and regarded her hostilely. "Oh, I don't think there will be any doubt of your liking it," he sneered. "Although there is a possibility that you may find it a bit too elegant and refined for your liking—it is, for your information, one of the former properties of a Duke. And even if he is a gambler and fool enough to sell it to finance his losses at the faro table, he is a man of excellent birth and breeding—something that can't be said about a little gutter-snipe like you!"

There was a wealth of insult in his last words, and infuri-ated by both his manner and his remarks, Morgana sprang to her feet, her hand flashing to strike his dark face before either of them knew what was happening. The ringing sound of her palm connecting solidly with his cheek seemed to echo in the dangerous stillness that suddenly filled the room.

His eyes glittering with a golden fire, Royce caught her shoulders in an iron grasp and jerked her up next to him. "By God, it only needed *that!*" His mouth came down punish-ingly on hers and there was no gentleness in him as he forced her lips apart, compelling her to accept the hungry ravish-ment of his tongue. He meant to hurt her, meant to punish her for not only the violent turmoil she created within him, but also for possessing the rapacious greed of a whore, but . . . ah, Jesus, it was sweet to have her in his arms again, so incredi-bly gratifying to feel her slim body next to his, to fully taste the honied warmth of her mouth once more. Compulsively he kissed her, wanting desperately to make her suffer for what she was doing to him, for turning his life upside-down, for evoking confusing emotions he did *not* want to feel, but against his will, the fury eased, only to be instantly replaced with a powerful, implacable desire.

The moment Royce had laid hands on her, Morgana had stiffened, and she had begun to struggle to escape even before his mouth came down so brutally on hers. Equally enraged, she had fought him, wanting to hurt him as he was hurting her, her fists striking viciously about his broad shoulders and tawny head as she had tried furiously to escape from his in-tentionally bruising kiss. But it was to no avail as ruthlessly he took what he wanted, her lips parting helplessly beneath the fierce onslaught of his. The blood thudding violently in her temples, she battled to break away from him, to escape

from the insulting heartlessness of his kiss, but he easily captured her flailing arms and crushed her even closer to the hard
wall of his body.

Blind fury at her helplessness burst through her, and in that
moment, she actually hated him. How *dare* he treat her this
way! And yet, even as that thought flashed through her mind,
she was dimly aware of a subtle change within him. There was
still no escape, he still held her clamped tightly against him,
and his lips and tongue still ravaged her mouth, but there was
something different in the way he embraced her. . . . The
sudden swell of his manhood against her belly was stunning,
and a new, wildly potent emotion, still fierce but having *nothing* to do with anger, erupted between them. Locked relentlessly in his hungry embrace, his urgent arousal boldly
evident, it wasn't surprising that the memory of his naked
body thrusting deeply into hers washed over Morgana, making
her cling where once she had fought so wildly to escape. Instinctively she responded to the difference in him, her body
pressing against his, her lips softening, almost hesitantly seeking the further plunder of his tongue.

A primitive desire, not untouched by the fury that had racked
Royce and Morgana both only a second before, swept them relentlessly onward as Royce's hands impatiently found her soft
breast, his fingers cupping and teasing their slight shape, creating a savage flood of wanting within Morgana. She trembled,
her breasts tight and throbbing under his touch, her loins con-
tracting almost painfully with the blunt force of the hunger
that knotted and clawed in her belly. He had awakened her to
passion, and her slim body now knew the meaning of that frantic, pulsating ache that grew deep within her, knew that the ache
would only grow until it overshadowed everything but the
wholly elemental need to have him possess her.

Consumed by the same inexorable emotions that gripped
Morgana, Royce lost control, and with a muffled oath, he
swung her up in his arms and blindly found his way to her
bedchamber. Following her body down onto the silken cover-

let, he hurriedly swept her clothing aside, his fingers feverishly seeking the sweet heat between her pale thighs, his own body aching and eager to take hers.

At his probing touch, Morgana moaned, her hips surging upward against his hands, clearly revealing her own helpless arousal. His heart pounding wildly, barely aware of his actions, Royce tore open his breeches and, with an animalistic exclamation of pleasure, in one frenzied movement buried himself deeply within her. Passionately he kissed her, his big body driving urgently time and again into the eagerly receptive heat of hers, the intensely erotic sensation of flesh sliding silkily against flesh hurtling them both almost instantly into rampant ecstasy.

For a long time afterward, they lay locked together on the crumpled coverlet, Morgana stunned and ashamed that such a wantonly violent act could have given her such undreamed-of pleasure. Could that wild creature thrashing and moaning beneath Royce have been herself? Could one go from such intense anger and rage to such intoxicating oblivion so swiftly? Her body ached and tingled from his ungentle taking, and to her everlasting mortification, she could not deny that she had actually taken pleasure in their fierce lovemaking.

With a start, she felt Royce move away from her, and highly embarrassed and shocked by not only what had just transpired between them but also the licentious picture she must make with her skirts tossed up about her shoulders, her thighs still half-splayed from locking him to her, she sat up quickly. A hot flush stained her face and there was a distinct tremble to her hands as she hastily arranged her rumpled skirts into some semblance of order. Unable to meet his gaze, she kept her face averted from him, her eyes fixed dully on the satin coverlet of the bed.

Silently Royce regarded her delicate profile, the haughty little nose and stubborn chin, for once at an utter loss for words. Nothing like this had ever happened to him before, and he was staggered and unnerved by his almost savage actions, by the uncontrollable passion that had obliterated every thought from his mind, but the compelling need to possess her. He had never treated a woman as he had just treated her—there had always been a lazy sensuality about his lovemaking, an unhurried appreciation of the love act, not this, this wild, almost frenzied compulsion to brand her with his body. It was as if, by possessing her, he could lose the demons that rode him, that in those moments of burning ecstasy, when his body merged with hers, he could forget what lay between them, purge from his mind the knowledge that it was only greed that gave him command over her body. . . .

His mouth tightened. And what the bloody hell was it he wanted from her? he wondered acidly. Love? A bitter smile twisted his mouth. Jesus! She must have bewitched him entirely if he could think something like that! Disgusted with himself, furious and confused by his own emotions, Royce glanced at her almost with hatred and said coldly, "I suppose that this little incident is going to cost me something more than just a mere trinket to show my appreciation of that lovely little body of yours."

There were many things that Morgana could have expected him to say, but that hadn't been one of them. She was so enraged by his words that momentarily she forgot the role she had chosen. A wrathful glitter in the stormy gray eyes, her breasts swelling angrily beneath the lavender muslin, Morgana glared at him. "Get the hell out of my room, you cold-blooded bastard! Haven't you humiliated me enough? Must you add to it?"

For a long moment he stared at her, taking in the bright, furious eyes and the angry flush on her cheeks. She looked magnificent, her mouth still rosy and slightly swollen from his kisses, the silky black locks disarrayed by his lovemaking curling in wild disorder about her face, reminding him forcibly of the little street urchin he had first brought home. His chest tightened uncomfortably, a powerful emotion knifing sharply through him. A pang of regret? Or something else? Some deeper emotion? Whatever it was, he knew he didn't want to leave her like this, and almost without volition, his fingers touched her cheek gently. "I apologize," he said softly, his eyes searching hers intently as if the answer to some great puzzle could be found in their clear gray depths.

His apology astonished her, and dumbly she stared back at him, not certain what to say or do, her eyes meeting his with the same intensity with which he gazed into hers. She could tell nothing from those tiger's eyes, their expression shuttered and hidden from her, and she wondered resentfully how she could have been such a fool to fall in love with him—more important, how she could have been such a blind, *bloody* fool to let herself become his mistress. Hadn't her mother's bitterly sad ending taught her anything? Anything at all? Angry with herself, bewildered and ashamed by her uninhibited response to him, Morgana tore her gaze away from his. "It doesn't matter—*that's* why I'm here, isn't it?" There was the furious glitter of tears in her eyes as she swung back to stare at him. A brittle smile on her soft mouth, she added, "What does anything matter? I was born a pawn! First the one-eyed man's thief and now your whore!"

Her statement hit him with the force of a blow, and a queer combination of rage and pain balled in his chest. There was nothing he could say; he could not refute what she said, there was too much truth in it, and yet . . . and yet he was almost sick with rage to hear her say those ugly words. His fingers dropped from her cheek, and his eyes cold and bleak, he said harshly, "At least I will not keep you in some damned hovel living like a half-wild animal, or put you in danger of Newgate and a hanging on Tyburn . . . nor," he added with a steely thread in his voice, "will I *ever* allow you to escape me."

There were no other words between them, both of them prey to so many violently conflicting emotions that it was almost with relief that they parted. Morgana threw herself facedown on the satin coverlet the instant he disappeared from view. There were no tears from her, though; she was too confused, too angry, to cry. She could only lie there and curse with great facility a fate that had allowed her to ever cross his path.

Royce did a great deal of cursing at fate also, and it can't be said that his swearing was any less colorful or imaginative than Morgana's—he just did it longer. Even that night as he lay wide-awake in his bed, he was still cursing himself, Morgana, fate—any disagreeable thing he could conjure up. It didn't help, as he had known it wouldn't, and as the hours passed, he finally admitted that whatever he felt for Morgana Fowler—and he wasn't about to put a name on it—that emotion was so deeply embedded within him that he doubted he'd ever be able to tear it from him.

In the distance Royce heard a clock strike four, and sleep was finally beginning to steal over him when there was a sound nearby that had him stiffening in his bed, every nerve in his body suddenly alert. Vainly his gaze tried to pierce the darkness, and not moving a muscle, he listened carefully, attempting to find the source of the sound that had disturbed him. It came again, a faint click and the soft hush of his bedroom door shutting. But had someone entered or left? Instinct told him that someone had entered the room, was in fact *still in the room,* and every nerve in his big body told him that whoever it was, whoever stood there hidden in darkness, had not come here for any good deed.

The bedroom was almost in total blackness, but a tiny shaft of moonlight from a partially opened drape at one of the windows allowed him to barely make out the faint shapes of furniture near him, and carefully his gaze moved from one object to the other, searching for something out of the ordinary, something that would pinpoint the danger. And there was danger; Royce could feel it emanating from the as yet unidentified person lurking in the darkness, and his muscles tensed for action.

Concentrating intently on the menace-filled silence, straining to hear any betraying sound, Royce did not call out, did not demand identification of the person he was positive had just so stealthily entered his room. He had an extremely strong premonition that he would get no reply anyway, but would instead give away the fact that he was awake . . . and therefore not the easy target his intruder might have expected to find.

It was a deadly little game they played, Royce alert and ready to fight, yet unwilling to move, afraid of betraying his only advantage, his wakefulness, while his opponent skulked in the darkness, choosing his moment to strike. And the creature would strike; Royce never doubted it for a moment. And he cursed himself, knowing the dangers as he did, for not having taken precautions—even if nothing more than sleeping with his pistol or knife beneath his pillow. But was his intruder, he wondered tensely, a mere housebreaker, or an assassin sent by the one-eyed man?

He didn't have long to speculate; almost immediately he heard the whispering glide of feet across the carpet heading directly toward his bed, and his heart pounded heavily, his body preparing itself to fight. His eyes half-slitted to give the impression of sleep, Royce lay there frozen, waiting impatiently for his intruder to come closer.

The intruder made an unexpected, swift rush to the side of the bed, and it was that tiny bit of moonlight that saved Royce's life, the silver shaft of light gleaming ever so faintly on the long-bladed knife that was suddenly poised over him. With explosive, lightning speed, he surged upward, his fingers closing brutally around the wrist of the hand that held the knife.

There was a male's snarl of enraged shock and then the intruder began to fight with a maniacal strength, nearly tearing his wrist free from Royce's powerful hold. They fought savagely in the darkness of the room, the man viciously trying to escape and yet at the same time plunge that deadly blade into Royce. As their bodies twisted together, the knife between them, their breathing was harsh and loud, and the occasional scrape and crash of furniture added to the increasing sound of the violent battle as they stumbled and careened around the room.

Royce guessed they were fairly matched in size and condition, but as they continued to fight, he became unpleasantly aware of the inherent dangers in fighting a clothed opponent when one is stark naked. The blade painfully nicked and sliced his bare flesh here and there in those desperate moments when he could not quite avoid or control the man's wild slashings. Once, his toes were cruelly smashed beneath the booted foot of the other, and only by sheer willpower was he able to ignore the burst of pain and keep his attention focused entirely on the constantly seeking knife. Aware that he was bleeding from a half dozen cuts, grimly, methodically, he grappled with his assailant, knowing that unless he did something immediately, soon that wicked blade would inflict grievous damage.

Suddenly several things happened at once. The door that separated his rooms from Morgana's flew open. "Royce, are you safe? What is happening?" Morgana called anxiously, a candle flickering in her hand. At the same time she appeared on the scene, at the hall entrance to his room, Mr. Spurling, the valet, stammered nervously, "S-S-Sir? I-I-Is everything a-a-all right?" And in that instant the ferocious battle between the two men brought them into the tiny ray of moonlight that beamed into the room, and Royce caught a fleeting glimpse of his opponent. *The one-eyed man!*

There was no mistaking the black patch at the eye, but the majority of the man's features were obscured by the slouch brim of his hat, which was pulled low across part of his face. Those portions of his face that could be seen in the faint moonlight were so contorted by hatred and fury that they were nearly unrecognizable as human. Royce had halfway been prepared for some sort of attack, but he had never really believed that it would be directed against him personally, that someone would actually try to kill him, nor had he ever considered that the one-eyed man himself would be the attacker, and for just a split second, sheer astonishment loosened his grasp on his assailant.

With a surprised grunt, the one-eyed man tore free and, like a striking snake, made a reckless thrust with the knife in Royce's direction. Royce, leaping backward to avoid the vicious lunge, stumbled into one of the overturned chairs and went down with a heavy thud. The one-eyed man wasted no time with him, but hurtled toward Morgana, his intention, whether to hurt her or to take her with him, unclear.

She had no time to think, only to react, and with action born of desperation, she boldly jabbed the candle into his good eye. Screaming with anguish, the one-eyed man dropped his knife, his hands ripping the candle from hers, before spinning around and racing to the opened doorway, where Spurling stood there frozen. Knocking the poor valet aside, he disappeared into the darkness.

CHAPTER 18

Pandemonium reigned for several wild seconds, Morgana's frantic exclamation hanging in the air as she flew across the darkness to kneel beside Royce's struggling form where he fought furiously to disentangle his lower limbs from the wooden arms of the chair. Clucking fearfully to himself, Mr. Spurling finally recovered sufficiently enough from his fright and the force of the one-eyed man's impact to scrabble around and hastily find a candelabra and light it. Almost immediately, with an angry curse, Royce kicked free of the chair and bounded to his feet, Morgana hovering anxiously at his side. Adding to the confusion, Zachary, roused by the racket, suddenly loomed up behind Mr. Spurling, a cocked pistol in his hand as he demanded grimly, "What the bloody hell is going on?"

Somehow, Morgana was in Royce's arms, her hands moving urgently over him, as if reassuring herself that he was not greatly harmed, her voice full of concern as she asked huskily, "You're not hurt? He did not stab you?"

Oblivious to his nakedness, to the blood that trickled down his body from the half dozen or so cuts that the one-eyed man had inflicted during their violent struggle, barely aware of his arm protectively around Morgana's slender shoulders, he dragged her willy-nilly along with him as he strode over to where Zachary and Mr. Spurling crowded in the doorway. The expression on his face must have been fierce, because Zachary and Mr. Spurling instantly gave way before him, and stepping into the hallway, he glanced disgustedly up and down, his gaze meeting silent darkness.

"The bastard got away!" he muttered viciously under his breath as he swung around and reentered the room.

"The one-eyed man!" Zachary said excitedly. "He sent an assailant after you?"

Ignoring Mr. Spurling's fluttering attempts to clothe him in a flamboyant dressing robe of black silk heavily embroidered with gold and crimson thread, Royce glanced at Zachary and smiled—trust his cousin, with youth's eager seeking of adventure, to be thrilled about tonight's events! Amusement dancing in the golden eyes, Royce murmured, "Ah, better than that! The one-eyed man himself paid me a visit!"

Mr. Spurling had by now managed to get Royce into the robe, and almost absently Royce's arm once more went around Morgana's shoulders, unconsciously holding her next to his side as if he were reassuring himself that she was unhurt. Morgana unashamedly clung to him, still not quite able to convince herself that the one-eyed man had not harmed him, and her eyes darkened with alarm when, through a gape in the dressing robe, she caught sight of the blood on his chest.

"You're bleeding!" she cried softly.

Zachary and Mr. Spurling exclaimed anxiously, converging on Royce, but he waved them away. "It is nothing—mere scratches, although I'm sure that the one-eyed man wishes they were far more serious." He glanced at Morgana, his arm tightening slightly about her. "*You* are not hurt? He did not touch you?"

She shook her head. "No. Everything happened so fast that he didn't have time to harm me."

It wasn't to be expected that the noise of the fight could go unnoticed by the rest of the household, and Chambers, a lighted candle in his hand, suddenly appeared in the doorway, a concerned expression on his features; just beyond him, Ivy hovered, her eyes big and alarmed in her pleasant face. Explanations were swiftly given, and though Royce continued to protest that he was not seriously hurt, no one paid him any heed. While Chambers disappeared to the kitchen for hot water and bandages, as well as some whiskey and brandy, Zachary, a nervous Mr. Spurling at his heels, conducted a thorough search of the downstairs. There was no sign of the one-eyed man, but they did discover the servants' entrance door at the rear of the house standing wide open. Further examination revealed that there was no new damage done to the lock, and the conclusion was inescapable that someone in the house must have opened the door to let him in. . . .

Royce didn't seem surprised when Zachary reported what he had found; in fact, it was almost as if Royce had expected it. By this time, Chambers had returned with the supplies needed, and in a remarkably short period of time, Ivy and Morgana were busy cleaning and examining Royce's cuts and scrapes. As he had said, the wounds were not grave, and once the two women had seen for themselves the truth of this and had the ugly gashes dressed to their satisfaction, everyone began to relax and discuss the attack. Royce remained silent through most of the animated discourse, and it was only when

they had begun to speak of more mundane things—the earliness of the hour, the daily routine that would soon begin—
that he entered the conversation.

His room had been hurriedly put to rights and he was
lounging in a chair covered in a deep ruby velvet, the richness
of his vividly embroidered black silk robe intensified against
the fabric of the chair. Aching just a little from his many cuts
and bruises, Royce looked steadily at Mr. Spurling and asked
softly, "And how was it that you were so providentially nearby
tonight, Mr. Spurling?"

Every eye was suddenly on him, and Mr. Spurling started,
his neat features congealing into an expression of alarm.
"M-M-Me? N-N-Nearby?" he stammered uneasily, his pale
blue eyes darting from one face to the other. "I-I-I'm not certain w-w-what you m-m-mean, sir."

"Oh, I think you do," Royce replied slowly, his gaze boring
unwaveringly into the other man. "Surely it is not your
normal practice to roam about the house at night. Why
weren't you upstairs in your quarters like all the others?"

Mr. Spurling swallowed convulsively, his agitation and distress clearly evident to everyone else. Suspiciously, he was still
garbed in day wear, the dark, discreet clothes—breeches,
white shirt, modestly tied cravat, and nicely fitting jacket—
that plainly betrayed his profession. He was a small man, with
thinning brown hair, which he kept neatly groomed, and his
features were quite unremarkable. He easily blended into the
background—an often necessary attribute for a valet. Watching him closely as he stood there nearly wringing his hands in
distress, Royce wondered idly if some of his nervousness
might not be the result of suddenly finding himself the cyno-
sure of everyone's interest, or was it something else . . . ?

"No reply?" Royce asked with deceptive gentleness.

Mr. Spurling drew himself up as tall as his diminutive
height would allow, and taking a deep breath, he said weakly,
"I could not sleep, sir, and d-d-decided that since Mr. Cham-

bers had informed me of our unexpected r-r-removal to the country on Friday, I would s-s-start packing some of your clothes." Anxiety clouding his features, he added passionately, "Sir! You cannot believe that I had anything to do with that creature's attack on you! I swear to you that I am telling the truth!"

Aware of the earliness of the hour and that it was highly unlikely he would gain anything from further questioning of Mr. Spurling, Royce made some noncommittal reply and dismissed his valet, along with Ivy and Chambers. When they had left, Zachary moved from his position where he had been leaning against one of the bedposts of Royce's bed and demanded, "Do you think that poor old Spurling is in league with the one-eyed man?"

The bitter discord between Morgana and Royce momentarily forgotten, she sat on the floor near his chair, one hand resting absently on his knee, her demure cambric and lace nightgown reposing in a cream and rose froth about her legs. Her dark, curly head had been bent as she seemed to study the intricate pattern in the jeweled tones of the Aubusson carpet that lay upon the floor, but at Zachary's words, she jerked upright, her eyes widening with consternation. "A spy?" she said in horrified accents. "Someone within your very household?"

Royce cocked an eyebrow at her. "Why not? The one-eyed man may seem omnipotent, but I assure you that he is not—I suspect that he merely has many tools in many different places. And I wouldn't be surprised to find, if we cared to investigate more thoroughly, that our Mr. Spurling either has had the one-eyed man do him a . . . *favor* sometime in the past . . . or someone whom Mr. Spurling holds dear has had dealings with the one-eyed man, and in order to protect them, he is doing the one-eyed man's bidding."

A frown marring his handsome face, Zachary inquired darkly, "What are you going to do about Spurling? If he let the one-eyed man into the house tonight, he can do it again. We can't just let him spy on us!"

Royce smiled faintly, one hand gently caressing Morgana's shoulder. "Unfortunately, I'm afraid we have no other choice," he said lightly.

"What?" Zachary ejaculated angrily. "You're going to let that mouse-faced little bastard run tame through the house? You're not going to let him go?"

A thoughtful expression on his face, Royce answered slowly, "If I let him go, the one-eyed man will only replace him with someone else—someone else I *don't* know is spying on me. By keeping Spurling in my employment, at least I have some control over what he learns and when he learns it. Knowing he is the one-eyed man's tool gives us a small advantage."

Dawning admiration spreading across his features, Zachary grinned at him. "Oh, I say, Royce, that is clever!" An eager gleam suddenly leaped into his eyes and he added excitedly, "We might even use Spurling to lead us to the one-eyed man!"

"For the moment," Royce answered crushingly, visions of Zachary following Spurling into Lord knew what kind of danger flitting through his brain, "we will do no such thing! Morgana's brothers are already trying to track him to his hiding place."

Morgana gave a small, frightened gasp, and Royce cursed his unwary tongue. "They will take every care," he consoled her quickly. "They know the dangers and they are almost as crafty and shrewd as he is—more importantly, he won't be expecting trouble from them."

She drew in a deep, shaky breath. "I know," she said simply, "it is just that he is so evil, and if he even just suspected that they were not loyal to him, he would kill them."

There was nothing Royce could say that would calm her fears, but attempting to focus her thoughts on something else, he said, "At least we foiled his plans tonight—I am still alive, and you are still unhurt and under my protection."

It was an unfortunate choice of words, for it reminded her forcibly of her invidious position, and she stiffened, drawing away instantly from him. Not meeting his eye, she stood up swiftly, and glancing across at Zachary, she smiled faintly and murmured, "If you'll excuse me, I think I shall seek out my bed for the short time that is left us. Good night."

Very aware of the air of constraint that had so abruptly entered the room, and seeking to lighten it, Zachary smiled at her and, walking nearer, picked up her hand and pressed a gallant kiss to the soft flesh. His gaze fixed on her lovely face. "It was brilliant of you to poke him in the eye with that candle—maybe he won't even have one eye to see out of now!"

Glad to forget for a moment the situation between herself and Royce, she grinned impishly up at Zachary. "Being raised in St. Giles *does* have its advantages, and having to think quickly and act immediately upon it is one of the first things you learn."

Zachary was only half listening to her, his gaze roaming appreciatively across her face, when something he should have noticed before hit him like a thunderbolt. Perhaps the fact that he had only seen her briefly a few times and had only very recently spent any amount of time in Julian's company excused his lack of recognition, but tonight, staring keenly into her lovely little features as he was, the conclusion was inescapable—Morgana Fowler resembled, to an astounding degree, Julian Devlin! Gazing intently now into Morgana's upturned face, he recognized that though there were obvious differences between them, even beyond those of male and female, they still bore a marked likeness to each other. Why, he thought dazedly, they could be brother and sister!

Unconsciously his grasp upon her hand tightened and she glanced up at him in surprise, her eyes widening when she caught the stunned expression in his gaze. "What is it?" she asked urgently. "Why are you looking at me that way?"

"Um, um, it's just that," Zachary began uncomfortably, "that you remind me of someone."

Before Morgana could question him further, Royce drawled languidly, "Yes, of course, probably that little ballet dancer you have been dangling after this past month." Glancing at Morgana, he said dismissingly, "Didn't I hear you say that you were going to bed?"

Morgana flushed, her hand tingling to connect with his arrogant face, and after a hurried but very sweet good night to Zachary, ignoring Royce entirely, she swept from the room. There was an odd silence after she had departed, Zachary staring for several seconds in the direction in which she had disappeared. Slowly turning around, he looked at his cousin. "How long have you known that she's Julian's sister?" he asked quietly, his young face grave and troubled.

Royce sighed, knowing that the next few moments were not going to be pleasant. Walking over to a long mahogany bureau, to the tray of decanters filled with whiskey and brandy that Chambers had brought up, Royce poured himself a glass of whiskey and, glancing over his shoulder at Zachary, lifted a heavy black brow in question. Zachary shook his head vehemently and muttered, "It is damn near daylight!"

Royce grimaced and took a large swallow. "I know," he replied levelly, "but from that outraged look upon your face and the crusading set of your jaw, I have the lowering opinion that I am going to need some, er, reinforcements."

"You knew who she was right from the beginning, didn't you?" Zachary demanded hotly.

"Well, let's just say that I had a strong suspicion she was a byblow of the Earl's," Royce admitted easily, but there was a watchful expression in his eyes.

"And it doesn't bother you," Zachary asked explosively, an

indignant look on his handsome face, "that you have taken as your mistress a young woman who is the daughter of an Earl?"

"*Bastard* daughter," Royce said thoughtfully, his eyes fixed on the amber liquid in the bottom of his glass.

"What difference does *that* make?" Zachary nearly howled with outrage. "It's obvious she's a St. Audries—even if she was born on the wrong side of the blanket."

"Yes, she is the Earl's daughter—and what a wonderful way of living he gave to her, condemning her to life in the gutter with thieves, murderers, and whores as her nearest companions, letting her have to steal and thieve for the very bread she ate." Royce gave an ugly laugh. "Oh, yes, her fine father did nobly by her, didn't he?" He swallowed another drink of whiskey. Defiance clear in the arrogant set of his tawny head, Royce growled, "At least with me, I know that she is reasonably safe from hanging at Tyburn, and I know that she sleeps in comfort and not in some filthy, vermin-infested hovel! I know that she is clothed and fed, and"—his mouth twisted—"except for my presence in her bed, she is not in constant danger of being raped or savaged by any brute who might cross her path!" Daring Zachary to contradict him, he glared at his cousin and said fiercely, "At least I keep her *safe*—something that bastard father of hers never did!"

There was such deep emotion, such passionate feeling, in Royce's voice that Zachary stared at him, an arrested expression on his face, as the most amazing thought flitted through his brain. The answer to Royce's out-of-character behavior these past weeks had been there right in front of him the entire time and he hadn't even seen it, Zachary thought, amazed. He gave his older cousin another considering glance, wondering how long it would be before the truth became obvious even to someone as stubborn and blind as Royce. A funny little smile suddenly tugged at the corners of his mouth, and in a surprisingly meek tone of voice, Zachary said, "Yes, of course. You're absolutely right. I don't know why I didn't look at it in that particular light until now."

Suspiciously, Royce regarded him. "You're not going to lecture me? No comment about how morally wrong it is?"

Zachary shook his head. "Not my place," he said firmly. "I should never have brought the subject up in the first place."

"Well, thank God for that!" Royce said ungraciously, and tossed off the remainder of his whiskey. Under his breath he muttered, "Don't you think it bothers me, too? . . . Under different circumstances, if she had been his legitimate child, instead of being at daggers drawn with St. Audries, I might be suing for the hand of his daughter in marriage!"

"Ah, so the wind *is* blowing in that direction," Zachary said with a great deal of satisfaction.

Royce gritted his teeth and flung him a furious look. "No, the wind doesn't blow in *that* direction!" he snarled, plainly affronted by Zachary's comment. "Marriage with her doesn't even enter the question, and don't be filling your head with some nonsensical romantic notion that hasn't a cat's chance in hell of coming true—she is my *mistress,* and that is all she'll ever be'"

"If you say so," Zachary murmured dulcetly, and yawning hugely, cutting off Royce's vehement rejoinder, he said sleepily, "I think that I shall follow Morgana's lead and seek out my own bed. It has been a very long night."

It *had* been a very long night, but after Zachary departed from his room, Royce had no desire to return to his bed. Scowling, he poured himself another glass of whiskey and, sipping it more sedately this time, wandered aimlessly around his elegantly appointed bedchamber, deliberately keeping his thoughts away from the subject of Morgana Fowler. Fortunately the one-eyed man's attack on him made that a relatively easy task and he found himself reliving those violent moments in the darkness.

Despite everything he had learned about the one-eyed man, even George's confirmation of his actual existence, there had been a tiny part of Royce that had been just a little skeptical about the extent of the one-eyed man's powers. He wasn't skeptical anymore; Steadham was obviously in the man's clutches, and George had definitely substantiated that the creature did, in fact, exist. But tonight . . . A shiver went down Royce's spine. Tonight the one-eyed man himself had deliberately tried to kill him. It was a highly unsettling thought.

Not that he had not faced the possibility of death before— the dueling field was not foreign to him; he had fought several duels and won, his marksmanship and expert swordplay well known—but this was different. There was something twisted and ugly about it, something dark and treacherous, something that had nothing to do with saving one's honor or reacting to an insufferable insult. Tonight had been an attempt at cold-blooded murder, and if he had not been awake, if he had been sleeping soundly . . . He took another long swallow of his whiskey. If fate had not been on his side tonight, he would be dead.

It was interesting, though, he mused slowly, that the one-eyed man himself had come to kill him and had not sent one of his minions. Why? From what little he knew of the man, it was not his habit to do the nasty work himself—he had all manner of desperate men to do his bidding . . . and take the risks—so why had he deviated from his normal procedure? That question bothered Royce quite a bit. It indicated that the one-eyed man was taking a *very* personal interest in this situation, that Royce Manchester had become something more than just a nuisance or an easy mark to be robbed or used in some nefarious manner. No. The one-eyed man wanted him dead. Wanted him dead so strongly that he was willing to do the deed himself, and it was *that* knowledge which Royce found so unsettling.

Of course, it all came back to Morgana. Royce smiled bitterly. Of course. But *why?* he wondered with a frown. Beyond her undoubted loveliness and charm, what made her so important to the one-eyed man? He knew that the one-eyed man had wanted Morgana for his mistress, but that wasn't sufficient reason to run the risks that the man had run tonight. Or was it?

His face tightened and he angrily confronted something that he had never wanted to—if positions were reversed and it was the one-eyed man who held Morgana, Royce grimly acknowledged that he would dare *anything* to get her back. He would tear London apart, brick by brick, until he found her, and he would not hesitate to kill anyone who stood between him and the woman he lov—the woman he *wanted!*

Tonight's event made the move to Tunbridge Wells imperative! He must make sure Morgana was safe! After dressing hastily, Royce jerked the velvet bell rope by his bed to summon Chambers.

Chambers appeared at his door almost immediately, a silver tray bearing a silver coffeepot, various oddments, and a china cup in his hands. In the time since he had vacated Royce's rooms, he had dressed for the day and was again his usual correct, impassive self, although there was a warmer look in his gaze when it rested upon his employer. Apparently, Royce thought with amusement, his near brush with death had redeemed him in the butler's eyes.

Sipping appreciatively the hot black coffee Chambers had poured for him, Royce said bluntly, "I'm afraid that last night has changed our plans. We shall begin removal to Tunbridge Wells immediately."

Chambers nodded his brown head. "Yes, sir. I assumed that such would be the case, and the servants are already packing those things that we will take with us. I spoke with the coachman and he is busy preparing the horses and seeing about any extra vehicles and horses we may need."

Royce grinned at him over the rim of his gold-trimmed cup. "Chambers, have I told you that you are an inordinately exceptional fellow? I am very glad that my cousin George recommended you and your estimable wife to me!"

A faint pleased blush briefly appeared on the butler's

cheek. He bowed low and murmured, "And we, sir, are very happy to serve you."

Amusement openly glinting in the topaz eyes, Royce couldn't resist teasing. "Even if you disapprove of my relationship with a certain young lady?"

Recovering some of his punctilious manner, Chambers replied loftily, "Sir, it is not for me to question your activities."

Still smiling, Royce dismissed him, and walking over to a cherry-wood writing table which sat in front of one of the windows, he sat down and began to write a few notes to certain people, informing them of his sudden decision to leave London. He did not tell them why.

It wasn't to be expected that the household could be moved within twenty-four hours, but by that evening, more than half the household staff had already departed for Lime Tree Cottage, and the few who remained were scheduled to depart by no later than noon the next day. Royce had been undecided about sending Spurling down with the first group, and he had finally concluded that he would rather have the man here, where he could keep an eye on him—no use letting him spy out the land any sooner than was necessary! Zachary, Royce, and Morgana would be driving down in Royce's curricle, leaving at first light in the morning.

It had been a very busy day for everyone, and though Morgana, Royce, and Zachary were tense, half-ready for another attack by the one-eyed man, things went smoothly. Royce had remained at home most of the day, mainly because he could not bring himself to entrust Morgana's safety solely to Zachary—much to Zachary's disgust! But it was essential that Royce meet again with Morgana's brothers, and so he had reluctantly torn himself away in the very late afternoon long enough to arrange the signal. As the hour had grown later and the time for the meeting approached, the expression on his handsome face had become darker and more scowling. If he had disliked leaving Morgana alone with only Zachary to guard her during daylight, he disliked it even more once darkness had fallen. He had no choice but to leave her, and after pressing a hard kiss on her mouth and exhorting Zachary for perhaps the hundredth time to keep her safe and to take no chances, he swiftly departed for the meeting with the Fowlers.

Since Della was out for the evening with her new protector, Jacko and Ben were already in the house, comfortably seated in the salon in which they usually met, when he arrived, and wasting little time, Royce instantly brought them up-to-date. The stunned astonishment on both faces and Jacko's disbelieving question, "*Himself?* Are you positive it was the one-eyed man himself?" only confirmed Royce's opinion that the one-eyed man's interest in him was something out of the ordinary. It did not reassure him.

A worried expression in the blue eyes, Ben said slowly, "It's a good thing that you're leaving London in the morning. If he wants you dead bad enough to do it himself, the sooner you are away from here, the better." Giving Royce a hard look, he asked, "I don't suppose you could leave tonight?"

Royce shook his head decisively. "No. I have no intention of driving on an unfamiliar road in the dark—certainly not a road where an ambush could lurk upon every curve! In the house, at least, I can take precautions, but in the open countryside at night . . ."

Jacko nodded his head in agreement. "He's right, Ben. Tomorrow will be soon enough. Now, where exactly is this Lime Tree Cottage? We'll want to see Pip before we sail."

His expression thoughtful, Royce regarded them for a long moment. At their last meeting together, on the day Della had explained to Royce that Jasper Simonds was now her new protector, Royce had told the Fowler brothers all about Steadham and also informed them that he had made arrangements for them to sail for America on the seventeenth of July. He had also made it abundantly clear that Morgana would be staying with him in England, which had provoked quite an argument between the three men. Jacko and Ben might have accepted him as their sister's lover and protector, and they might have been grateful for what he was doing for them, but they were uneasy about leaving her behind, and it was only when Royce had finally convinced them that he sincerely intended to bring her to America with him when he set sail in the fall that they fell in with his plans. They still were not happy with the fact that Morgana was to remain behind, but they had become resigned to it. Or had they? Royce wondered as he continued to study them.

Jacko must have suspected what he was thinking, because he suddenly grinned and murmured, "Guvnor, if we wanted to snatch her from you, there would be nothing you could do to stop us—we know every precaution you have taken. And don't forget she's our sister; she would help us rather than fight against us as she would the one-eyed man." Sobering, he added more seriously, "We settled things between us last week when we agreed to leave her in your care. . . . All we want is a chance to say good-bye to her before we sail. You wouldn't deny us that, would you?"

Royce believed him, and his moment of wariness gone, concisely he gave them directions. Fixing them with a level stare, he finished with "Be especially careful when you come to Lime Tree Cottage. I'm certain the one-eyed man will discover soon enough where we have gone—particularly since he has his own spy within my household—but we don't want him knowing that *we* are working together!"

Nodding his head, Ben said sharply, "We ain't fools exactly, you know!"

"No, I'm aware of that—I am being overly cautious." Glancing questioningly at them, he asked, "I don't suppose you have learned anything new about him?"

Jacko looked very sly. "Well, you're wrong, guvnor! He has been a crafty old fox, and we've lost him as often as we've been able to follow him, but we've learned a few things. Such as he has more than one hiding place—probably dozens of 'em scattered all over London; we've followed him to three of them already. But this is what's interesting—we ain't sure, but we think that the one-eyed man ain't really one-eyed and that he's a member of the gentry!" Having delivered his astonishing news, Jacko watched Royce expectantly.

"Good God!" Royce exclaimed in tones of angry exasperation. "If that is the case, I probably have been rubbing shoulders with the bloody bastard all this time and didn't even know it!"

"Our thoughts exactly," Ben said softly. "He could be anyone, someone you know, even a friend of yours. . . ."

CHAPTER 19

Wednesday morning dawned bright and sunny, and Royce, Zachary, and Morgana were able to leave the house on Hanover Square as scheduled. Pulling smartly away from the house less than an hour after dawn, Royce breathed a faint sigh of relief, eager to put London and the one-eyed man behind him, but Ben's words of last night were still uncomfortably swirling around in his brain.

His thoughts only half on the horses he was driving, Royce kept going over last night's conversation with Jacko and Ben again and again, wishing he could dismiss entirely all that they had said. Reviewing their words, he admitted that they had told him very little; they *suspected* a great deal, but they had proof of nothing! And while he might want to simply dismiss their suspicions, instinct told him that Jacko and Ben had stumbled onto the truth. It would explain one thing about the one-eyed man, Royce admitted unwillingly as his curricle left the gray pall of London behind and the long-legged strides of the horses began to rapidly diminish the distance to Tunbridge Wells—such as how the one-eyed man managed to learn that various members of the aristocracy had need of his services. . . . He was one of them!

Concentrating grimly on the ugly implications of what he had learned last night from Morgana's brothers, Royce scowled, unaware of the passing countryside or even the presence of the other two occupants of the curricle. It was Morgana's gasp of pleasure that roused him from his black thoughts and caused him to glance at her.

Dressed in the height of fashion in a rose-colored pelisse with cherry red braid at the collar and cuffs and a wide-brim chip-straw hat with ribbons that matched the braid on her pelisse, Morgana looked especially fetching this morning. From between the openings at the bottom of the pelisse, there was a glimpse of the apple green muslin gown she wore underneath, and the cherry red ribbons of the hat were tied in a saucy bow beneath one ear. But it wasn't just her stylish clothing that made her so rivetingly attractive this morning—her mouth was curved in an enchanting smile and her gray eyes sparkled with enthusiasm.

Watching the expression of delighted awe on her lovely face, the sheer untrammeled pleasure she took in the wooded little valleys and open, undulating grassy pastures that flew by as the horses continued to trot down the road at a spanking pace, Royce felt something tighten in his chest. If only, he thought fiercely, I could keep her looking like that—eager, happy, and without a care in the world! If only there were no one-eyed man for her to fear, and if only she weren't a grasping little harlot! He frowned at the unpleasant direction of his thoughts, but not at all inclined to dampen her obviously high spirits, Royce refused to dwell on all the disagreeable aspects of their relationship. Morgana was safe and happy for the moment, and he found that knowledge oddly satisfying.

A half-tender, half-amused smile twitched at the corner of his mouth when her eyes widened and a wondering smile lit up her animated face at the sight of a dainty spotted deer darting across the road. Turning to him, she asked excitedly, "Wasn't it simply beautiful?"

His eyes roaming appreciatively over her countenance, her bright eyes and flushed cheeks, Royce said with a strange note in his voice, "Yes. Quite the most beautiful thing I have ever seen in my life."

Morgana glanced uncertainly up at him, her face becomingly framed by the chip-straw with its big, cherry red bow. A question in the huge gray eyes, she stared at him, her heart suddenly beating rather erratically in her breast at the expression in Royce's tiger eyes. For a long moment they looked at each other, their gazes locked and intent, until Zachary broke the queer little silence by asking dryly, "We are talking about the deer, aren't we?"

Tearing his gaze away and blindly focusing on the horses, Royce answered automatically, "Of course. What else could I have been referring to?"

Looking at the two instantly shuttered faces, Zachary laughed and murmured, "Of course! It couldn't have been anything else."

The journey to Tunbridge Wells was largely uneventful. Since the hour was early, once they had left London a few miles behind them, they had the road almost to themselves, the only other travelers being the occasional coach or a farmer's cart loaded with produce on its way to market. It was a leisurely trip. They stopped about ten o'clock at a posting inn that George had recommended to rest and water the horses and to stretch their legs. They had eaten a scant breakfast hours ago, so they also partook of a tastily prepared meal before continuing their travels.

Since Morgana had never been away from the smoke-filled skies of industrial London, had never known anything but the constant noise, the stench, the sheer multitude of people, and the oppressive gloom of building pressing upon building, the open countryside was a wondrous place to her. She had never seen wild deer before, nor glimpsed a little brown rabbit scuttling along the edge of the road, and had, quite frankly, never noticed the intense blue of the sky—the sky in London often blotted out by the gray smudge of smoke and fog that frequently shrouded the city. Each bright patch of wildflowers, each copse of willowy green trees, became an enchanted oasis to her, and she could not help exclaiming aloud with pleasure. To someone raised in a place filled with vermin and grime, to someone at home with narrow, twisting alleys clogged with filth, almost literally entombed by the dark, shabby buildings that stood slumped together, the sheer *openness* of the landscape was a breathtaking experience.

The curricle crested a slight rise, and seeing the land falling away in gently undulating swells of small, tree-dotted valleys, with cottages, farms, and orchards scattered here and there, Morgana could not help exclaiming ecstatically, "Oh! It is *so* lovely! I never dreamed it could be so very beautiful." A small red fox unexpectedly loped across the road in front of the curricle and she sighed blissfully, "A *fox!* Oh, did you see it?"

Royce and Zachary glanced curiously at her. They took for granted the solitude of the verdant and tangled growth of their homeland, Louisiana, as well as the multitude of animals that roamed that lush wilderness, and equally at ease in England's more-populated, less-forested meadows and rolling hills, neither one had given any thought to the fact that Morgana had never been out of the crowded, building-smothered streets and alleys of London in her life, that she had always lived in a narrow, mean little world surrounded by buildings of rotting lumber and crumbling stone. Her utter fascination with the widening expanse and the animals that inhabited it seemed to be extreme, and just a bit bored by her naive wonder,

Zachary yawned and murmured, "It's only a damned fox, Morgana. Nothing to get all cock-a-hoop about!"

Morgana's face fell, and Royce was aware of a strong desire to box Zachary's ears. He was hurriedly searching for some way to restore her happy mood when she said innocently, "But you don't understand, Zachary—I have never seen a *real* live fox before . . . or a rabbit . . . or a deer, or even a meadow, and so to me, it is all very exciting." She smiled impishly and added, "You have to remember—*this* is only the third time I have ever ridden in a vehicle! And the other two times were that day I picked Royce's pocket and then when he took me to the dressmaker's. *Everything* is new and thrilling to me—even 'only a damned fox'!"

Royce was taken aback, the enormity of the simple things that had been denied her hitting him like a blow. Looking distressed, Zachary apologized profusely, "Oh, Jesus, Morgana! I never thought! Please forgive me! Of course you find it exciting—as well you should! I am an insensitive bumpkin not to have realized it."

Desperately seeking to retrieve himself, Zachary spied three deer grazing peacefully nearby in a grassy paddock. "Look!" he said excitedly, "See those deer over there?"

And though he knew he was acting the fool, Royce chimed in eagerly with "And over there near that hedge—there is a rabbit! See it?"

The polite world of London would have been agape at the wild enthusiasm two of its members suddenly displayed for avidly spotting and pointing out such bucolic pleasures as a hare nibbling a patch of clover, a newborn calf struggling to stand, and a small hedgehog lazily meandering down the middle of the road. The miles flew by as Zachary and Royce fell over themselves to bring to Morgana's rapt attention all the glories to be found in the English countryside; not one rabbit, one deer, nor one wildflower was allowed to pass without their zealous comment. By the time the gig passed the gatekeeper's cottage and the horses swung down the road to Lime Tree Cottage, Morgana was far more conversant with the flora and fauna of England than she had ever thought possible!

The gray eyes sparkling brightly, an excited flush on her cheeks and a beguiling smile curving her mouth, she exclaimed blissfully, "How exciting this has been! I feared that we would be dreadfully bored, but the time has passed so swiftly that I cannot believe that we are actually here already!"

Smiling warmly down at her, the difficulties that lay between them momentarily forgotten, Royce said lightly, "Dare I hope that it has been our company that made the journey seem so short?"

She giggled delightfully and said saucily, "The company was most enjoyable, but the scenery . . . and the animals; *that's* what made the time pass!"

"A hit!" Zachary shouted with glee. "A palpable hit, Royce!"

"Well, it certainly puts me in my place, doesn't it?" Royce replied easily, not a whit abashed by her comment. He was, he admitted uneasily to himself, thoroughly under her spell, and it mattered naught to him that she came from the gutter or that it was only his money that kept her by his side. She had only to sigh for him to crave to kill dragons in her behalf, and the sight of a frown on those lovely features could smite him like a blow. And as for a smile . . . he grinned idiotically— for one of her smiles, he would willingly act the fool!

Unfortunately Royce's lightheartedness could not last. He was, though he tried to pretend otherwise, painfully conscious, if not *furiously* conscious, that Morgana *should* represent nothing more to him than a pleasant interlude. Her only purpose was to slake his passion, passion that she seemed capable of igniting without effort; but mysteriously and, Royce would have said, unfairly, her presence in his life had become vital to his happiness—at least for the present, he amended grimly. And so as the horses turned a broad curve and Lime Tree Cottage came into view, he was mistrustful and angry at the effortless way she had snarled his normally serene and unruffled composure into a mass of seething contradictions, and utterly baffled at how handily she had aroused emotions, such as jealousy and possessiveness, that he had never guessed he could feel.

Royce found himself slowing the horses as they approached Lime Tree Cottage, a prime example of the lengths a besotted fool would go to please a woman. He waited expectantly for Morgana's reaction to her first sight of the house that he had bought for her. When it came, it was everything that he could have hoped for—she paled, her eyes widened, her fingers clutched his arm, and a gasp of sheer wonderment escaped from her.

There was no denying that the house made a charming sight, sitting, as it did, on a slight hill, and at this distance, the stone walls that surrounded it did not conceal any of its elegance. Sunlight glinted on the many tall, arched windows of the gracefully sprawling building, and the thatched roof with its many dormers gave it, despite its grand size, a quaint air. Roses, larkspur, daisies, and tall wallflowers grew in seemingly wild profusion near the windows and doors, and an emerald, tree-dotted lawn surrounded the two-story building, with several flower-lined paths leading here and there in a beguilingly aimless fashion. Various necessary outbuildings could be glimpsed beyond the house, but it was the cottage, actually more of a mansion, that held the eye and excited the admiration. In spite of its impressive grandeur, there was something exceedingly welcoming and cozy about it, and Morgana was spellbound as the curricle passed through the pair of filigreed iron gates and the horses finally stopped in front of the building.

She could say nothing, she could only stare with something between astonishment and terror at the magnificent "cottage" that Royce had supposedly purchased for her. When he had first mentioned the place to her, she had quite literally expected some snug little farmer's cottage where she and her brothers would eventually live quite happily, but *this* . . . Her mind boggled at the knowledge that in order to share her bed, Royce had gone out and secured a damned bloody mansion!

It didn't matter that he had done so at her express wish—she had writhed with shame more than one night since she had stated her outrageous demands, but she had also tried to console herself with the intelligence that she was doing this for her own future, as well as that of her brothers, and that Manchester was reputed to be quite wealthy and could very well afford to be generous to his mistress. But even so, she had never expected the "cottage" to resemble the elegant and gracious structure before her, nor had she ever dreamed to own such a magnificent house herself.

For Morgana, raised as she had been in one of the worst overcrowded slums in London, the idea of calling Lime Tree Cottage home or claiming to own it was incomprehensible. Accustomed as she was to the cramped and tawdry furnishings of her own tiny two-room home in St. Giles, the house on Hanover Square had been almost intimidatingly spacious and extravagantly furnished, and viewing the building before her, she was conscious of a hollow feeling in her chest as she strongly suspected that the house on Hanover Square would fit inside it twice! Royce *couldn't* have purchased this property for her!

Grabbing hold of her soaring imagination, she finally, thankfully, decided that she had leaped to conclusions—this was not *her* cottage, this belonged to some wealthy acquaintance of Royce's. Satisfied that she had discovered the truth, she smiled uncertainly up at him and asked, "Are we going to be stopping here long?"

If he was puzzled by her question, he gave no sign other than a quizzical lift of one heavy black brow. Those tiger's eyes gleaming like molten gold between his thick, dark lashes, Royce murmured, "I suppose that all depends upon you. If you don't like it, we shall see if there is something else that does catch your fancy in the neighborhood."

Morgana swallowed. She glanced at the majestic house and then back at Royce. After clearing her throat nervously, she asked in a small voice, "Is this Lime Tree Cottage?"

Smiling sardonically, Royce nodded his head. "Yes. Do you like it?"

"Well, I jolly well like it, I can tell you!" Zachary exclaimed as he leaped nimbly down from the curricle. "This is a splendid place, Royce." Looking very boyish, he added with a grin, "P'haps I'll stay with you and Morgana and give Julian's place the go-by this summer."

"I think you should address that comment to Morgana, since it is *her* house." Oblivious to the frozen little figure by his side, Royce tossed the reins to young Matt, who had just run up, and climbing down from the vehicle, he said tartly to Zachary, "She might not care for your company, you know." Turning to Matt, he greeted him pleasantly. "Good day, young man. I see that you all must have arrived here safely. How do you like your new quarters?"

His red hair blazing in the sun, his freckled face full of pleasure, Matt replied eagerly, "It's a bang-up place, guvnor! I've even got me own room over the stables and won't 'ave to put up with Tom's boasting of 'is 'andsome face when 'e arrives!" Reverently holding the reins that Royce had tossed him, he added, "And coachman says that if I pay attention and work very 'ard and you agree to it, he may allow me to train as a groom."

Royce laughed and said, "Well, perhaps I shall speak with him today and make it official!"

Matt beamed up at him, and it was clear that young Matt was completely and utterly Royce's slave. The wide double doors of the house swung open just then, and Chambers, regal and correct as always, appeared in the doorway. For the next several moments, there was a small flurry of movement and noise as greetings were exchanged and Morgana was helped from the curricle and escorted into the house.

In the very short time that Chambers and the other servants had been at Lime Tree Cottage, they had been busy preparing for the master's arrival; the most obvious sign was the huge, fresh floral bouquets everywhere one looked. After seeing to it that Royce, Morgana, and Zachary were made comfortable in the spacious and exquisitely furnished drawing room and that they had been served with appropriate refreshments, Chambers said quietly to Royce, "Everything is unpacked and your rooms are ready whenever you wish to see them. We have seen to it that the larder has been stocked, and unless you object, Cook will have dinner ready at seven o'clock. However, sir, when you have a moment, I should like to discuss with you the additions that I have seen necessary to add to the staff."

Lounging carelessly in a comfortable high-back chair of green leather, Royce took a sip of his wine and replied, "Tell Cook that I see no reason to change her plans, and as for the other, I see nothing wrong with right now."

Chambers bowed slightly and admitted hesitantly, "I have taken the liberty of hiring a few young farm girls to help in the house itself, and after making inquiries hereabouts, I have also hired some gardeners to keep the grounds in order." Royce nodded, and seeing that his actions provoked no reprimand, Chambers went on smoothly, "Coachman, too, has found it necessary to hire several young men to work in the stables." He ended uneasily with "I'm afraid, sir, that between us, we have more than doubled your staff."

"It doesn't matter," Royce said mildly. "I was aware that the move to the country would entail more staff—I'm gratified that you lifted that particular burden from my shoulders." An attractive grin tugging at his chiseled mouth, he added, "I trust your judgment, so have no fear you'll find complaints from *me!*"

Obviously pleased, Chambers answered warmly, "Thank you, sir. I have done what I could, and once the others arrive from London, we should be able to provide you with a modicum of comfort. Will there be anything else?"

Royce shook his head. "Not for the moment." He glanced around at the others and added, "Unless, of course, Morgana or Zachary require your services."

Zachary shook his dark head, but Morgana, who had been oddly silent from the instant of arrival, spoke up and said in a small voice, "I should like to be shown to my room. I am very tired."

Royce gave her a thoughtful look, then shrugged. "Whatever you wish, my dear," he said dryly. "Chambers will be happy to show you the way . . . and should you dislike the room chosen for you, you can, of course, change it."

Morgana was still in such a state of shock at the magnificence and size of the "cottage" that it wouldn't have mattered which of the ten bedrooms available Chambers denoted as hers. She was vaguely aware that it was a large, lovely suite of rooms—a bedchamber, sitting room, and dressing room, much like those she had used in London, although these were far larger and in some ways more charmingly furnished, with less formal arrangements and a delightfully airy feeling about the furniture. Her rooms were tastefully decorated in pastel shades of lavender, rose, and cream, but she paid her surroundings little heed as she wandered unhappily about the gracious bedchamber, not even sparing a glance out any of the tall windows on two sides of the room which revealed enchanting views of the parklike grounds that encircled the house.

Not conscious of her actions, she finally stopped pacing restlessly about the room at a pair of French doors that opened out onto an enticing little balcony, and flinging wide the doors, she stepped outside. Though it was late afternoon, the day was still sunny and quite warm, and spying an elegant Louis Quinze chaise positioned invitingly near the wide wooden railing of the balcony, she walked over and lay down on it.

Staring blankly at the blue sky overhead, she wondered dully how she had gotten herself into this position. She would freely acknowledge that she had not been thinking very clearly when she had put a price on her favors, but that aside, she had certainly never expected that Royce would even contemplate, much less buy, a place like Lime Tree Cottage for her. She might have been able to still the pangs of her conscience and to rationalize any qualms she might have had about what she was doing if the house had turned out to be what she expected—a pleasant little property, perhaps an acre or two, with a cozy three- or four-room cottage—but *this!* She swallowed. This was obscene—utter insanity for a man like Royce Manchester to throw away a fortune on a mansion like this simply to obtain entrance to a woman's bed . . . even *her* bed!

She sighed unhappily, feeling rather confused and angry at the same time. Her life of late seemed to have spun off on a wild tangent, and *nothing* seemed to be going as planned—she could not even embark on the only sensible course for a woman in her position without it evolving into something far more perplexing and complicated than she had ever dreamed! Morgana scowled. If only she hadn't botched the simple picking of a pocket! From that moment on, she had been swept up into a treacherous whirlwind that showed no signs of freeing her from its wild and erratic gyrations, and she cursed a fate that had hurled her willy-nilly into Royce Manchester's life.

If she was being fair, some of the events that had happened to her since she had first looked up into Royce's lean, dark face would never be forgotten or regretted. It would be hypocritical to pretend that she had not thoroughly enjoyed her stay in the house on Hanover Square, had not reveled in the novelty of her own bed or a myriad of other simple things that had been denied her until she had met Royce Manchester. Nor, though she tried very hard to act otherwise, was she completely indifferent to her elegant surroundings or the many lovely clothes and objects that Royce had bought for her. And most important of all—she could *never* regret having discovered the utter rapture of being possessed by the man she loved. . . .

And if she loved him, she thought painfully, was it right to put a price on the unadulterated joy his lovemaking gave her? She could reconcile with her conscience what he had done for her so far, albeit with difficulty, but if she accepted this house, then she sullied and made ugly every moment she had ever spent in his arms. Feeling exceedingly wretched, she finally admitted something that she had been trying very hard to ignore—she already *had* sullied the love she felt for him simply by allowing him to buy for her the things that he had these past few weeks.

Her eyes filled with tears, but angrily she forced them back. She would *not* cry! She might be a greedy, grasping harpy, but she was not a sniveling, whining baby! She had gotten herself into this situation, and somehow she was going to bloody well get herself out of it!

As she jerked upright on the chaise, her mouth took on a stubborn slant. She would renounce everything that he had given her! She would ask, no, *demand* that she be put to work with the other servants, she would insist that she be treated no differently from anyone else who worked for him! And as for the powerful current of emotion that surged between herself and Royce . . . She swallowed with difficulty. Somehow, and she didn't delude herself that it would be easy or painless, she would have to overcome this unwanted love she had for him, force herself to forget the rapture of his embrace. After all, she reminded herself bitterly, I am nothing but a thieving pickpocket he plucked from the gutter, and there is absolutely no future for me in his life!

At present, Royce Manchester wanted her in his bed—but for how long? And loving him as she did, was she willing simply to allow him to use her and then, when she bored him, toss her aside? Morgana knew the answer to that question; she only wished she had thought more deeply about what she had been doing when she had so rashly plunged willy-nilly into this position. For the sake of the love she felt for him and her own decidedly battered self-respect, she came to the unhappy conclusion that it would be far better to be his servant scrubbing the floors of his kitchen than to humiliate herself night after night by sharing his bed.

Unfortunately, in all her thoughts, Morgana had neglected to consider several aspects of her current situation. With the one-eyed man lurking around every corner, it seemed, ready to snatch her for his own nefarious purposes, she was not precisely in a position to merely walk away if the relationship with Royce rapidly deteriorated. Nor had she even considered what Royce's reaction to her decision might be. . . .

An hour later, she faced him in the lovely, pastel-hued bedchamber. Royce had barely entered the room when, not giving herself a chance to retreat, she said jerkily, "I must talk to you! This state of affairs cannot continue!"

"And what particular state of affairs is that?" he replied with an indulgent smile on his mouth. "The long nights in your chaste, lonely bed perhaps?" A glitter in the golden eyes, his gaze traveled hungrily over her slim form, fully appreciating the expensive simplicity of the apple green muslin gown. "I can assure you that with the purchase of this house, those nights have come to an end!"

He reached for her, but Morgana eluded his outstretched hands, dancing nervously away from him, and she uttered despairingly, "I cannot accept this house! I do not want it! It is obscene!"

Royce stiffened as if he had been poleaxed, and risking a wary glance at his frozen features, she muttered, "I think it would be best for all of us if you simply let me go back to the kitchen and if we forgot that there was ever anything between us but the relationship of master and servant!"

The tiger eyes narrowed dangerously, and in a menacingly silky voice, he asked, "Thinking to cheat me, my dear? It damn well won't wash—I've paid for you and you're *mine!*"

CHAPTER 20

Her heart thudding painfully, Morgana stared dumbly at him. She could not believe that he had so stupidly misinterpreted her words. She had no intention of *cheating* him, the bloody fool! She was trying, and rather handsomely at that, she thought angrily, to do the honorable thing! Hanging on to her temper with an effort and still hoping to try to explain her feelings to him, she closed her mouth with a snap when Royce said cynically, "Sweetheart, if you're attempting to raise your price, it's a little late for that! You've made your damned bargain and now you will have to, er, figuratively, sleep in the bed of your own making."

The gray eyes darkening like storm clouds, Morgana gritted her teeth and spat, "I'm not trying to *cheat* you out of anything! I am," she said loftily, "merely trying to tell you that I cannot—"

"That you cannot go to bed with me?" he interrupted her dryly. "Don't you think it's rather late to start adding further demands?"

While she stood there fulminating with wrath, he walked over to her, and tipping up her face, he looked down into her stormy features and murmured, "It's far, *far* too late, my dear, for any more protestations. You agreed to become my mistress—you named your price and you made the bargain." A steely glint in his topaz eyes, he added, "I have no intention of allowing you to change your mind, and nothing you can say will stop me from claiming what is already mine!" Insolently his gaze roamed over her body. "For the moment, I *own* you—you set the terms of our agreement, and by God, you're going to live up to your promise!"

Her eyes blazing, she jerked her chin out of his hold. "You don't own me! No one does—not even the one-eyed man!" She laughed bitterly. "I stayed with you in London of *my own free will,* you buffle-headed lobcock! Do you honestly think you could have kept me a prisoner if I'd *really* wanted to escape? Don't delude yourself—I stayed under your"—she spat the word out insultingly—"*protection* because it was safer to put up with your demands than to risk the fate planned for me by the one-eyed man!"

Royce's face paled at her words and he said bitterly, "And to think that while I was cursing myself for taking advantage of you and suffering pangs of conscience for my treatment of you, you were merely using *me* for your own ends! How utterly foolish of me to have wasted one moment of regret on you." He smiled caustically into her stunned face. "Forgive me! I'll not make *that* mistake again!"

Catching her up in his arms before she had a chance to react, he crushed her mouth beneath his in a contemptuously brutal kiss. There was such fury behind that kiss, such anger, that Morgana was helpless, and there was nothing for her to do but suffer the barely controlled savagery of his embrace. Her lips stung from the pressure of his and she struggled violently to escape his brutal kiss, moaning softly in protest against the plundering invasion of his tongue.

At that sound, low though it had been, Royce seemed to come to his senses, and with a muffled oath, he flung her from him. She half stumbled, half fell against the bed, and eyes wide with apprehension, she looked back at him, almost expecting him to fall upon her like a ravening beast. She had never actually feared Royce before, but she did this time, and it was evident in the depths of those clear gray eyes as she stared at him, her body tensed as if for a blow.

The expression in her eyes, the almost cowering posture of her slender body, struck him like a sword in the heart, and in a shaken voice, he muttered, "Oh Jesus! I never meant to frighten you. I only . . . I only want to lov—" The anguish in his voice touched her deeply, and she realized instinctively that Royce could never hurt her, would *never* hurt her. But even if he would not physically harm her, her love for him gave him the power to wound her in ways he could not even guess. He would never know how difficult it was for her to remain where she was by the bed and not fly across the room to him, to wind her arms about him and offer him comfort.

For an endless moment they stared silently at each other, then Royce smiled sourly. "I had such visions of pleasure about tonight, but I find that my appetite for you has been effectively killed." She blanched and he said cruelly, "Oh, you needn't fear that it has been stilled for all time; it is just that for the present, I find the idea of sharing your bed rather distasteful." In a dangerously silky tone he continued, "Actually, you are to be congratulated! You have managed to milk a small fortune from me and you have cleverly managed to keep me from enjoying what I have paid handsomely for—no mean feat, my dear."

Rosy flags of temper flying in her cheeks, she spat angrily, "You bloody *fool!* How dare you insinuate such ugly things about me! If anyone should feel put-upon, it is me!"

"Oh, and why is that, my dear?" he asked coldly. "Are you

disappointed in my generosity so far? Or perhaps you are displeased with my lack of ardor?" His mouth tightened. "Believe me, we can remedy *that* fact immediately, if you like!"

The expression in his eyes and the set of his mouth suddenly reminded Morgana of a stalking tiger, and she shook her head, no, and stepped hastily away from him, almost as if she feared he would pounce upon her.

He smiled, not a very nice smile. "You are wise—my temper where you are concerned does not seem to be very stable. But don't worry, sweetheart, I have no intention of making you pay your debts—at least not tonight. . . ."

Morgana stared numbly up at his dark face, wondering desperately how things had gone so terribly awry. Gathering her shattered courage around her, she tried one last time to explain and said urgently, "You don't understand—it's not what you—"

"No," he interrupted in that same silky, dangerous tone he'd used a moment before, "it is you who do not understand. You've gained yourself some time, my dear, but that's all you've gained. No one makes a fool of me, and certainly not a little slip of a woman like you. You *will* share that bed behind you with me, and you will be my mistress for as long as I want you." He smiled, but it didn't reach his topaz eyes. "You may try to escape if you wish; I won't even try to stop you. Just remember that unlike the one-eyed man's efforts to date, I wouldn't allow you to run very far, and when I found you . . ." His smile was suddenly very cold. "When I found you, let's just say that when I was finished with you, you wouldn't want to run away from me again."

Royce glanced at the bed sardonically before he murmured, "Enjoy your solitary slumbers, sweetheart—they won't be for long, I promise you!"

He walked arrogantly from the room while Morgana remained frozen by the bed for several seconds after he had left. Finally, letting her breath out in a shaken gasp, she sank down on the soft, feather-filled mattress, her thoughts whirling chaotically through her mind.

Royce had said cruel things to her—as she had to him, she admitted guiltily. But he had threatened her, insulted her, and treated her shamefully, she thought angrily as she remembered that ruthless kiss, but . . . Her face softened. He had also said that his treatment of her had not set easily with his conscience, and from his words, it was obvious that he had not merely slaked his passion with her body and then dismissed her from his mind. Her mouth drooped. He had also stated that he regretted his actions. . . .

Sighing, she got up and wandered unhappily around the room. What a devil of a fix! She was in love with a man with whom there was no hope of any future, helplessly enamored of a man who *regretted,* by his own words, making love to her!

Lifting her chin proudly, she looked blankly around the lovely room. He may have regretted those times she had spent in his arms, but *she* did not, and she was not going to let his cruel words tarnish her cherished memories of being possessed by the man she loved. Let *him* regret their lovemaking—she did *not!*

It wouldn't have occurred to Royce to regret making love to Morgana—what he regretted, and regretted fiercely, was the circumstances surrounding those wondrous moments when he had lost himself in the sweetness of her body. However, at this moment, he did indeed regret *everything* to do with Morgana; a black scowl darkening his handsome face, he virulently cursed the day he had ever laid eyes on her! Too lost in the welter of confusion within his own emotions, he never even considered that he might have misunderstood the situation with Morgana, might have leaped to some very wrong conclusions!

Deciding that he was not fit company for man or beast, he strode angrily away from the house, needing to put as much distance as possible between himself and the source of his troubles. Goddamn her! he thought furiously. How dare she throw his gift in his face! How dare she try to squeeze further recompense out of him! He should not have let her feelings deter him from taking what he had already purchased! He should have ignored that little moan of pain when he kissed her—he should have thrown her on the bed and taken her then and there! So what if he caused her pain? Hadn't she caused him pain? Pain such as he had never thought possible when he had realized that she was indifferent to the beauties of Lime Tree Cottage, that she hadn't realized that it was not the sort of place that men usually bought for their mistresses. He gritted his teeth with rage when he remembered how very much he had looked forward to her enjoyment of the house . . . how much he had looked forward to showing her around, to sharing with her the unexpected delight he felt for the property, and how very much he had looked forward to having her in his arms again.

Well, the greedy little bitch wasn't screwing one more guinea out of him! Not, he admitted with a dangerous smile, until she had paid her present debt!

Royce walked for quite some time, not really noticing the attractively landscaped park in which the house sat, heedless of the flower-lined brick footpaths that wandered with a delightful aimlessness here and there. He did a lot of thinking during his distracted ramblings, but he settled nothing in his mind, his thoughts and emotions still as tangled and confused as they had been when he had flung himself out of Morgana's presence.

At least, he admitted wryly as he finally made his way back to the house, he had gotten his temper under control and would be able to look at Morgana without being torn between the desire to break her lovely neck and an equally strong desire to kiss her senseless!

Indeed, he and Morgana both behaved themselves admirably when they met for dinner in the gracious dining room with its several pairs of French doors open to the still-sun-warmed air of early evening. Few people would have thought that there was anything amiss, from the polite conversation they exchanged and the quiet enjoyment they seemed to take from the deliciously prepared meal that Chambers set before them. Only Zachary was aware of the constraint between them, and he frowned as he looked from one face to the other.

I wonder, he thought uneasily, what the hell has happened between them now to make them act so scrupulously polite to one another? After Morgana had departed for the evening and he and Royce sat at the long, white-linen-covered table drinking from a bottle of excellent brandy that Chambers had found in the wine cellar, Zachary seriously considered asking Royce point-blank that very question, but one look at his cousin's dark, dangerous face and he hastily abandoned that idea!

The next morning, the situation between Morgana and Royce seemed to have resolved itself slightly—they acted far more natural in each other's company, although Zachary, who was watching them closely, sensed that there was still some constraint between them. But that aside, it proved a most pleasant day, the three of them acquainting themselves with all the delights of Lime Tree Cottage, Royce proudly showing them around the various rooms of the house, including the big glass conservatory at the rear of the house, filled with every kind of exotic plant and flower imaginable. Since the fine weather held, they toured several of the outbuildings and the extensive grounds within the stone walls, Morgana sighing with pleasure as each turn of the various pathways revealed some enchantingly landscaped little oasis—a stone bench framed by a rose-covered arch, or a miniature pool with water lilies and a small waterfall, and of course, there were flowers and trees everywhere.

It wasn't until Friday that Royce showed Morgana and Zachary the actual perimeters of the land, and later they shared a picnic on the island in the middle of the small lake. Royce and Zachary had rowed them out there in a small boat, and amidst much laughter and teasing, they had unloaded the bulging wicker basket that Ivy had stuffed with all manner of delicacies. The gleaming white gazebo proved to be quite commodious and comfortable—a round iron table stood in the middle of the building, and wide wooden benches, heaped with huge, gaily colored pillows, had been built next to the walls.

Returning to the house later that afternoon, Royce and Zachary decided to drive into Tunbridge Wells for some further exploration, while Morgana opted to remain at the house. Royce hesitated at leaving her alone with only the servants, the specter of the one-eyed man rising up to worry him, but he stilled his fears with the knowledge that Morgana was far safer here than she had been in London. After all, they were miles from London, and a presumably trustworthy gatekeeper had already been installed at the only entrance to the property and would, one hoped, keep out any unwanted visitors—Royce had personally selected the man and had given him very explicit instructions.

The hiring of new servants had given Royce some concern—how could he be certain that he was not employing another minion of the one-eyed man? But he had reluctantly convinced himself that it was unlikely that the one-eyed man's grasp was as strong here as it was in London, and even if there were some poor fools in the area who owed the one-eyed man their allegiance, it was unlikely that they would happen to be the very people hired to work at Lime Tree Cottage.

Eyeing with satisfaction the impenetrable yew hedge that surrounded the property as they drove away, Royce told himself again that Morgana would be perfectly safe. But telling himself she would be safe and actually believing it were two different things, and though he enjoyed the tour of Tunbridge Wells, his thoughts were constantly on Morgana. He and Zachary were on the point of leaving when Royce caught sight of a tall, well-dressed figure walking in their direction, and as he recognized the fellow, his attention became totally focused on that particular individual.

There was no mistaking the dark, handsome features of the

Earl of St. Audries, and considering how the Earl usually acted in his presence, Royce was quite prepared for Stephen Devlin to make some sneering remark as they met. To his astonishment and no little suspicion, Stephen Devlin smiled warmly, and after greeting Royce and Zachary politely, he said jovially, "I see that the charms of the town have drawn you here, too."

Keeping his features bland, Royce smiled, too, and murmured, "Yes, we have found it quite fascinating, in spite of it not being considered as fashionable as it once was." Though he gave no sign of it, Royce couldn't help leaping to the conclusion that the Earl's unexpected appearance in Tunbridge Wells, as well as his astonishing friendliness, was in some way connected to Morgana . . . or the one-eyed man. Extremely wary about the situation, but deciding to see just how far the Earl's seeming affability went, Royce asked innocently, "Have you been here long yourself?"

Stephen answered easily, "Oh, no, I just arrived a few days ago—Tuesday afternoon, to be exact. The Countess and I came down with Stafford. Martin Wetherly is here too, but he came down alone earlier that day. Wetherly owns a rather pleasant villa just beyond town, and we are all staying with him."

The Earl was volunteering far too much information, and Royce felt a shiver of unease slide down his spine. Stephen's unusual friendliness and volubility had him distinctly worried, and the knowledge that Stafford and Wetherly were also about did not soothe his growing anxiety in the least. "How long do you intend to stay?" Royce asked bluntly.

"Oh, I expect all summer," Stephen replied promptly. "Wetherly is having an extended house party, and several of us decided to give Brighton the go-by this year." Some of the Earl's normal haughtiness returned as his smile faded and he said scathingly, "Since the Regent has become so enamored of the place, all manner of riffraff flock there along with the ton, and quite frankly, it is not all to my taste. I do not like rubbing shoulders with a bunch of commoners!" Apparently realizing that he was not endearing himself to the two American "commoners," he recovered himself instantly and smiled once more. "After the crush of the London Season, the idea of summer in the country sounded vastly appealing."

Royce and Zachary made some polite reply, Zachary adding shyly, "I am looking forward to visiting your son at St. Audries Hall next week—he said that I will find it a welcome change from the city."

Stephen's eyes hardened for a moment. "I'm sure that you will enjoy your visit there, and I must confess that several of my friends will be better off out of the city. The evening before we left, Wetherly, Stafford, and Newell had a night of deep drinking—Newell is so under the weather that he will not arrive until next week, and Wetherly has not ventured from his room since he arrived!" The Earl laughed, inviting Royce and Zachary to join him. Shaking his dark head, he added, "No one has seen Newell since that night, so we can only guess at its effect upon *him!* What Wetherly looks like, I can only imagine—I have not even laid eyes on him since my arrival. If they are as knocked about as Stafford, I don't blame them for hiding away—poor Stafford fell down a flight of stairs on his way home and gave himself the most hideously bruised eye."

Royce froze, and he was very conscious of Zachary's gasp of surprise. To prevent Zachary from blurting out some unwise comment, Royce said swiftly, "I'm sorry to hear that they are all indisposed. You must be finding it a bit dull on your own."

The Earl smiled thinly. "Oh, I have been keeping myself amused—I have several friends who own property in the vicinity. I admit that it is a rather hasty and impromptu house party that Wetherly has put together—some of the others won't be arriving until late next week, but there are enough of us already here to keep things lively." Something sly entered Stephen's gray eyes. "Wetherly convinced some old aunt of his to act as his hostess and chaperon, and the dashing widow Cresswell, along with her married sister, are part of the house party." Something that almost resembled a smirk curved his thin lips and he continued, "I believe that Julia Summerfield and her father are joining the party also—you were very assiduous in your attentions to those young ladies, were you not?" When Royce remained silent, Stephen shrugged and murmured snidely, "I understand that they are not precisely happy with you at the moment. . . . The latest on-dit is that they are distressed at the cavalier way in which you have abandoned them these past weeks." Either forgetting his amiable role or deliberately abandoning it, Stephen turned the smirk into an ugly smile as he drawled, "You don't seem to be very consistent in your affections, do you? First Cresswell, then Summerfield . . . but I understand that the lovely Della threw *you* over!"

Smiling imperturbably, Royce murmured, "You certainly seem to have made yourself familiar with all the aspects of my amorous pursuits. I wonder why. Envy, perhaps?"

Zachary choked back a laugh, but the Earl found nothing amusing in Royce's remarks, and he let his hatred of Royce peek through his once amiable facade. Ignoring Royce's taunt, his words dripping with venom, Stephen said, "I had the pleasure of speaking with the fair Della only yesterday on this very street, and she seems quite pleased with her new protector. She is a beautiful woman; too bad she lost interest in you! I wouldn't repine, however; Jasper Simonds appears to be giving her a great deal of pleasure, both in bed and out of it, something that you apparently didn't!"

Royce regarded Stephen for a long, thoughtful moment, almost glad that the Earl's friendly manner had slipped. Suddenly bored by the confrontation and furious with this icy-hearted bastard who had fathered a child and cruelly deserted her, leaving her without a backward glance to grow up in one of the most dangerous slums in all of London, Royce was aware of a savage need to hit back—even if Stephen would not fully understand his remarks . . . unless, of course, Morgana's identity was already known to him. . . . Smiling mockingly, Royce shrugged his broad shoulders and said carelessly, "It doesn't matter. . . . My new mistress satisfies *me!* There is something about her . . . an *aristocratic* manner that I find quite enchanting." His topaz eyes glittering with golden lights, he added silkily, "She may have come from the gutter, but I would suspect that her blood is as blue as yours."

Royce's remarks hit deeper than he knew. Their effect on Stephen, however, was gratifying, and the Earl's reaction to his barb confirmed something that Royce had begun to suspect from the moment Stephen had approached them—the Earl *knew* the identity of his new mistress. Stephen's gray eyes darkened with naked fury and his face had gone white at Royce's mocking words. Lips curled back in a snarl of rage, his hand tightened noticeably on the fashionable ebony walking stick he carried. For one second Royce thought the Earl would actually strike him, but hatred twisting the handsome features, Stephen replied, "You could be mistaken, you know—after all, what does someone like you know about aristocrats!"

Royce merely smiled, an infuriatingly cool smile, and with a smothered curse, Stephen spun around and stalked away at a rapid pace.

"Well!" Zachary said in astonishment. "It's obvious he knows Morgana is your mistress and is not very happy about it! Your comments certainly put the wind up him!"

Royce was silent for a moment, staring grimly after Devlin's departing figure. What the devil! The Earl's reaction seemed extreme considering the situation, and Royce frowned. "I know he bears me no love," he said slowly, "and it can't have pleased him to learn that his bastard daughter is my mistress, and I'd like to know exactly how he discovered *that* interesting fact, but damn it all—he callously abandoned her years ago, so why should he fly off in a rage like that now? And why in the hell was he so bloody friendly? And informative!"

A frown still on his face, Royce suggested that they leave for Lime Tree Cottage immediately, and as Zachary agreed, moments later they departed from Tunbridge Wells. The meeting with the Earl disturbed him, and even though he and Zachary continued to discuss the strange meeting and the Earl's even stranger behavior during the short ride home, Royce was very conscious of a strong urge to see for himself that Morgana was safe—with Wetherly and Stafford in the same area, *anything* could happen!

For Morgana, though she was conscious of the day suddenly going flat when Royce drove away, the time had passed most pleasantly while the two men had been gone. She had wandered around the house doing some quiet exploring on her own, and while she was exceedingly enchanted by the house and its furnishings, she still could not comprehend that Royce had actually bought this magnificent place with her in mind. It was inconceivable, and the stubborn determination to make him understand that she did not want it hardened in her mind. Not that she was not utterly beguiled by the house and its grounds. It was the most wondrous place she had ever seen in her life, but . . . Her lovely little face twisted. If I allow him to give it to me, it would make my love for him a tawdry thing, something ugly and sordid.

Quelling the miserable thoughts that threatened to disrupt her hard-won tranquillity, she went in search of companionship, and scant moments later, she was seated happily in the big, sunny kitchen, laughing and talking with Ivy and Alice. It was *not* the normally accepted place for a woman in her position, but then, it had not been so very many days ago that Morgana had been a servant herself, and not such a long time before *that* that she had been roaming the streets of London like a hungry little cat, sometimes finding dinner in scrap heaps!

Ivy had poured her a glass of still warm milk from the evening's milking of the estate's cow and had pushed a plate of freshly baked shortbread in front of her, and like the street urchin she had been such a short time ago, Morgana ate with open relish as they talked. There had been a bit of stiffness between them, and Ivy had tried to shoo her out of the kitchen, but Morgana's sweet smile and confiding ways had put Ivy's feelings of impropriety to rest, and as the minutes passed, the three of them were all talking quite easily.

Spying the huge black and white cat that sat serenely in the middle of the open-beamed room, Morgana excitedly left her seat at the scrubbed oak table and, expensive muslin skirts billowing about her, sank slowly to the floor. Picking up the purring animal, she reverently stroked its fur and said in a low voice, "Oh, what a beauty! Does it live here?"

Ivy snorted. "It's a he, and he wasn't such a beauty when we arrived here and I found him squalling at the back door, I can tell you! Filthy thing, but I like a cat about, and so we bathed him and fed him and he hasn't left yet."

Alice giggled. "Chambers found him wandering upstairs and he's been in a fine fit worrying that the master will be angry at the animal's presence in the house."

Deciding that as she hadn't yet been allowed to renounce all interest in the house, she could therefore have some say on what transpired within its walls, Morgana stood up, holding the cat and rubbing her cheek against the soft fur, and said coolly, "Well, I don't mind if he's in the house—in fact, I shall take him upstairs with me and he can sleep on the foot of my bed!" And *the master,* she thought darkly, can make what he wants of that!

Cradling the purring cat in her arms, she left the kitchen and was on the point of going upstairs when there was the sound of a vehicle driving up to the front entrance. Her cheeks suddenly flushed, a breathless excitement unexpectedly flooding through her slender body, she spun around to stare as Royce entered the house a moment later.

To his intense annoyance, Royce's heartbeat quickened, the blood suddenly leaping in his veins, and he was irritatingly conscious of an inexplicable lifting of his spirits at the sight of Morgana standing at the base of the curving staircase, a huge black and white cat clasped in her arms. She was wearing a beguiling gown of periwinkle blue, the short puff sleeves and modest neckline trimmed in a blond lace, and the silky black curls, worn a trifle longer than when she had first come under his care, framed her charming features. A wide blue satin ribbon had been artfully threaded through her black hair, and her soft, rosy lips were half-parted as her gaze remained locked with his. The almond-shaped gray eyes were almost blue, the color of the gown reflecting in them, and Royce knew a nearly irresistible impulse to cross the brief distance that separated them and taste for himself the sweetness of that full, tempting mouth.

Wordlessly they stared at each other until Zachary, entering just behind Royce, exclaimed, "Good God! Where did you find that monster?"

Wrenching her gaze away from the bold appraisal of Royce's golden-eyed stare, Morgana sent Zachary a blinding smile and said with a certain amount of defiance, "In the kitchen! Ivy says she likes a cat about the place, and I am going to have him sleep on my bed!"

Zachary snickered and murmured, "I imagine that Royce will have something to say about that!"

Ignoring Zachary, an urbane smile curving his handsome mouth, Royce walked with that lazy, predatory stride of his over to where Morgana stood. Tipping up her face, his eyes once more on her soft mouth, he asked gently, "Do you really prefer the company of a cat in your bed to mine?"

Nearly mesmerized by his powerful presence, Morgana stared up into his dark, lean features, absently noting the tawny lock of hair that persisted in falling across his forehead before her eyes dropped and lingered on the audaciously passionate curve of his bottom lip. Remembering the feel of those hard lips crushed against hers, remembering the heat of his mouth and tongue on her breast, she was aware of a languorous warmth spreading through her body and she swayed helplessly toward him. Unknowingly, desire glowed in the depths of her eyes and she asked huskily, "Do I have a choice?"

One big hand gently cradling her flushed cheek, Royce smiled and shook his head slowly. The topaz eyes warm with a frankly sensual light, he said thickly, "Not really—but then, neither have I, sweetheart, since the moment I laid eyes on you. . . ."

As if having said more than he'd meant to, Royce turned away, and leaving her standing there openmouthed in astonishment, he said lightly to Zachary, "Shall we see if Chambers can find another bottle of that excellent brandy for us to sample after dinner? Or would you prefer some of that devilish fine hock we had last night?"

"Oh, the brandy!" Zachary replied without hesitation. Royce was already walking away, and Zachary stepped nearer to Morgana. He winked at her and murmured, "He's right, y'know—he hasn't had a choice, you've got him tangled in knots—and if you play your cards right, you'll win this game! My money's on you, brat, so don't let me down!" He laughed aloud at her expression of utter bewilderment, and then, whistling merrily to himself, he strolled after Royce.

CHAPTER 21

Dinner that evening was uneventful, and as she had done since their arrival, Morgana excused herself after they'd finished eating and returned upstairs to her room, leaving the men to enjoy their brandy. Normally she was alone, but tonight the black and white cat kept her company, and since

Ivy had told her that he was a good ratter, she named him, rather unimaginatively, "Ratter." He ended up as Morgana had planned, sleeping on the bed with her, and even managed to convince her to share in a saucer some of the warm milk she drank each night before retiring. More than satisfied with her new friend and cowardly refusing to even speculate about Zachary's teasing remarks, she fell asleep, with Ratter sprawled comfortably across her stomach.

Once Morgana had departed from the dining room, the conversation between the two men turned immediately to the meeting with the Earl of St. Audries that afternoon. Sipping the brandy that Chambers had unearthed from the former owner's expertly stocked wine cellar, Royce mused aloud, "I wonder how he found out that Morgana, or rather, his bastard daughter, is my new mistress. The only other people who have seen her besides ourselves have been the servants. . . ." He paused before saying slowly, "Of course, Stafford could have said something—I don't think any of the others paid her any heed that day, and he is the Earl's good friend."

Zachary frowned. "What about Spurling? If he spies for the one-eyed man, why not someone else as well?"

It was Royce's turn to frown. "I wonder if Spurling really is in the one-eyed man's pocket. He seems such an unlikely tool." Royce sighed moodily before adding, "Whatever the case, I have been having the devil's own time trying to fit together all the pieces of that particular puzzle!" Looking at Zachary over the rim of his brandy snifter, he suggested idly, "It's possible that Devlin bribed someone in the household to tell him about her, although *why* my new mistress would be of interest to him, I cannot think! His informant would be bound to have noticed the resemblance and more than likely would have mentioned it to the Earl. Devlin's not stupid, and he would have immediately realized who she must be. . . ." Royce grimaced. "It would explain him knowing who she is, but Devlin has never shown the least interest in my doings before, so why would he now?" Taking another swallow of the dark amber liquid in his snifter, he said thoughtfully, "No, it's far more likely that Stafford or Wetherly told him of the resemblance." Royce's gaze narrowed. "I'd forgotten that Lady Devlin had come to call with that flighty cousin of hers, Lady Whitlock. I wonder . . ."

"But they didn't actually *meet* Morgana, did they?" Zachary asked.

"Mmm, no, but they were just getting into their carriage when Morgana and I were leaving to go to the dressmaker's— they could have seen her then. It would have been only a brief glimpse, but it might have been enough."

Looking puzzled, Zachary questioned, "But would she say something?" He coughed delicately. "Bastards are not something a woman discusses with her husband—especially not *his* bastards! And why would she care anyway?"

"Why would the Earl care? He obviously abandoned Morgana without a care years ago," Royce said exasperatedly.

They speculated several moments longer, even touching briefly on the subject of Stafford's bruised face and the curious fact that no one had seen either Wetherly or Newell since the night of the one-eyed man's attack on Royce. It seemed somewhat sinister, particularly in view of the fact that the one-eyed man could very well be anyone of the gentlemen mentioned. . . . "Hell!" Royce growled irritably. "There are any number of gentlemen that he could be—all we know for sure is that he is fairly tall and that he is dark-eyed! Without a great deal of effort, I can name a dozen or so members of the ton who fit that description! As an example—look at George's friend Atwater. . . . He is moderately tall and he has dark eyes. And then there is that fellow Jasper Simonds—I've never met him, but George mentioned his black eyes and height. And then there's Newell, Wetherly, Stafford, Barrows, Eden, and St. John—they all have dark eyes and are fairly tall. Hell, that description could fit nearly half of the male population from Cornwall! As far as clues are concerned, we have devilish damn little!"

As the hour grew late, though they continued to discuss and explore many different avenues of conjecture about the one-eyed man, the Earl of St. Audries, and Morgana's connection with both of those gentlemen, eventually they had to abandon the subject, having reached no especially satisfying conclusions. Stifling a huge yawn, Royce finally rose from the table and said mockingly, "It is all your fault you know."

"What?" Zachary yelped with astonishment. "How can you blame this situation on me?"

Royce smiled sweetly. "Very easily—it was *your* idea to attend that blasted sparring match!"

Zachary was still heatedly expostulating how utterly unfair Royce's thinking was when they parted at their bedroom doors upstairs.

Since the rest of the servants from London had arrived and settled in, by Saturday a normal routine had been established in the household. Morgana, Royce, and Zachary continued to become more familiar with the house and grounds, and the day passed quite enjoyably. After dinner that evening, Morgana again politely excused herself and was on the point of leaving when Royce said abruptly, "I shall see you later— there are a few things that I wish to discuss with you."

Morgana shot him a wary glance. Despite their disagreement, he had been most kind to her since the night of their arrival, very nearly disarming her by treating her in a teasing, friendly manner. She had wondered during the past few days precisely how long a respite he would allow her before forcing a confrontation, and the answer was suddenly there before her—not very long at all. Giving a quick nod of her black, curly head, she practically bolted from the room.

A brooding expression on his handsome face, Royce stared at the door she had shut behind her. Looking over at Zachary, he pulled a wry face and admitted, "I've got to tell her about Jacko and Ben's departure on Monday, and I'm not looking forward to it!"

"You haven't told her yet?" Zachary asked in surprise.

"No. I'd thought to wait a few days, to let her get used to the house before springing it on her, and I'd hoped . . ." He stopped, deciding that he wasn't about to tell his cousin that he'd hoped to be able to tell her one night as she lay locked in his arms, their bodies relaxed and satiated from lovemaking. His mouth twisted. He was beginning to doubt that she would ever willingly let him touch her again—not only was she likely to be distressed to learn that her brothers were leaving her behind in England, trusting in his promise to bring her to America, but considering that she had attempted to extort more money from him for the pleasure of sharing her bed, she was no doubt going to be furious once he confessed that Lime Tree Cottage was only *half* hers! He took a long swallow of brandy. What a damnable coil he'd gotten himself into! And the really hellish part of it was—he wouldn't extricate himself from Morgana's little claws even if he could. His face hardened. But there were some things she had to learn, and tonight, agreeable or not, she was going to learn that promises were made to be kept. Especially, he thought harshly, promises made to *him!*

It was after midnight when Royce finally found himself standing before the door that separated Morgana's sitting room from his. He and Zachary had finished another bottle of brandy before parting for the night, but the amount of liquor consumed had nothing to do with the sudden increased beat of his heart, or the fierce clenching in his loins whenever he considered the outcome of the impending confrontation with Morgana. Even as he had impatiently stripped out of his evening clothes and, after washing lightly, had shrugged into his black silk robe with its rich embroidery of gold and crimson, he had argued with himself about the wisdom of what he was doing. It was not the morality of it that bothered him— as far as he was concerned, righteousness was on his side; Morgana *owed* him!—but there was something inside him that regretted bitterly that it had come to this, that the powerful, inexplicable emotions she aroused so easily within him had been reduced to nothing more than a mere business transaction! He smiled grimly. Well, it had been her choice, and by God, she was going to live up to it!

He entered without knocking, and swiftly crossing the darkened sitting room, he stopped in the doorway of her bedchamber, admiring the pretty picture revealed by the glowing light of the silver candelabra near the bed.

The heavy satin cream-colored bed curtains were tied back at the four corners of the huge bed with bands of rose-hued velvet, giving Royce an unobstructed view of the two occupants. Morgana was half sitting, half lying in the middle of the bed, several silk pillows in shades of rose, cream, and lavender piled behind her, and curled comfortably by her side was Ratter. The tall candelabra was on a marble-topped mahogany stand that had been placed next to the bed, and its flickering golden light seemed to caress Morgana's intent features and slender form as she lay reading, one slim hand absently stroking Ratter's black and white fur.

She looked incredibly lovely, Royce thought, his gaze traveling from the top of her bent curly head, down to the soft alabaster shoulders bared by the daring cut of her silken nightgown. He remembered selecting this particular gown, thinking at the time that its pale amethyst color would enhance the clarity of her skin, and he was pleased to see that he had been right, his eyes lingering at the top of the gown, where just a hint of her entrancing bosom could be seen. A possessive light entered the golden eyes as he continued to stare at her slender shape, the filmy gown hiding very little from his hungry stare.

He must have made a sound, for suddenly she glanced up, and across the width of the big room, their eyes met. Morgana felt her heart slam painfully in her chest as she spied him lounging there in the doorway, darkness yawning behind him.

With an effort, she tore her gaze from his mesmerizing stare and shyly her eyes wandered over him, unconsciously noticing the way the black silk of his robe clung lovingly to his broad shoulders, trying very hard not to let her eyes linger on the strands of tawny hair that curled at the open throat of the robe. She knew what he looked like and felt like beneath that robe, the memory of his hard-muscled chest brushing against her breasts as he had made love to her that first time exploding through her mind. A sensual warmth unexpectedly suffused her entire body and she was humiliatingly aware of warm, treacherous languor creeping into her limbs the longer she stared at his tall, powerful form.

She was suddenly, wildly, burning to have him touch her, to have him take her into his arms and, for those mindless moments that she was in his embrace, banish all the confusion and uncertainty that lay in her heart. She *loved* him! Loved him and wanted him with every fiber and sinew of her being! Helpless to stop herself, she lifted her eyes to his face, and her breath caught in her chest at the frankly carnal expression on his handsome features.

Unaware of his impact on her, Royce pushed lazily away from the doorjamb where he had been lounging, and walking over to her, he murmured, "I'm glad that you have not yet gone to sleep."

Trying to ignore the pounding of her heart, trying to pretend that she wasn't unbearably conscious of him and the blatantly erotic appraisal of his golden eyes, she put her book aside, and as Ratter jumped from the bed and stalked majestically out of the room, she said primly, "I have been waiting up for you—you said you wanted to talk to me."

He smiled faintly and, without invitation, sat down on the bed beside her. Lifting up one of her limp hands, he pressed a warm kiss to the soft flesh and asked, "And is that the *only* reason you allow me in your bedchamber this hour of the night?"

She unsuccessfully attempted to retrieve her hand. "Of course! Why else would you be here?"

Royce gave a husky laugh and tugged her easily into his arms. His mouth drifting warmly across hers, he breathed,

"Oh, sweetheart, I can think of dozens of reasons . . . but there is only one that matters to me at this moment!"

In the split second before his lips settled with undisguised enjoyment on hers, Morgana thought of resisting him, of trying to fight free from his embrace, but then his mouth caught hers, and with a soft sigh, she forgot everything but the expert seduction of his kiss. She let him pull her closer to him, her own slender arms clutching at his broad back as he lazily deepened the kiss, his tongue unhurriedly exploring the shape and texture of her lips before sliding effortlessly into the warm intimacy of her mouth. His tongue teased and plainly wooed as leisurely, thoroughly, he explored the sweet confines of her mouth, his pleasure evident in the low groan he gave when Morgana's tongue slid warmly against his, meeting each gentle thrust with one of her own.

Breathless and slightly wary at her welcome response, he slowly lifted his tawny head to look intently into her flushed features. She was lovely beyond words, the black, curly hair seeming to heighten the alabaster clarity of her skin, the amethyst glow of her gown giving her cat-slanted gray eyes a purple hue, his kiss having deepened the rosy color of her temptingly full mouth. Staring at her with growing perplexity, Royce was uncomfortably aware of something tightening deep within him, something that had less to do with the heavy throb of his undeniably swollen manhood than with the pure delight he took in simply having her in his arms. That he wanted her, that he wanted to slake the fierce desire she aroused so easily within him, he understood, but his sheer *need* of her, his need to be with her, to have the right to take care of her, utterly bewildered him.

Some of his bewilderment showed in the golden eyes that stared so fixedly into hers, and making a halfhearted attempt to rouse herself from his dark spell, Morgana asked nervously, "Have you changed your mind? Don't you want me?"

Royce closed his eyes as if in pain, exclaiming passionately, "Not want you! *Dear God!*" Opening his eyes, his gaze wandering possessively over her, he muttered angrily, "I dream of little else! You have bewitched me—stolen my wits until all I can think of is the sweetness of your kiss, the rapture your soft body gives me, and the indescribable pleasure I find in your simplest act!" He laughed, but there was a bitter edge to it, and staring at her almost as if he disliked her, he demanded harshly, "Does *this* feel as if I don't want you?" And he grabbed one of her hands and shoved it roughly against his rigid member.

Morgana's face flamed at his blunt action, but she did not withdraw her hand, his tortured words sending a wild surge of almost savage delight shooting through her body. He cared *something* for her! It was plain that he desired her, plain, too, that he was fighting against feeling anything other than lust, but it was also wondrously apparent, she thought happily, that it was not *just* her body that commanded his attention. Nothing had changed between them and yet . . . and yet it seemed as if *everything* had changed between them. Made bold by his words, her fingers gently caressing the hard flesh that he had shoved her hand against, she surprised them both by saying almost in a purr, "Perhaps you should *show* me. . . ."

Astonishment held him motionless for a heartbeat and then desire suffused his face, making his eyes glitter like molten gold as he growled softly, "Perhaps I should, and if you are going to continue to touch me that way—the sooner, the better!"

Despite his words, he took his time with her, pressing her down gently into the mattress, his lips and hands taking the most shocking liberties as he began to unerringly remove her garment. Morgana trembled as his hands slid up her thighs, pushing the amethyst gown out of his way, his warm mouth following the same path as his hands, even brushing tantalizingly over the black, tightly curled hair at the juncture of her legs. She gasped as he seemed inclined to linger there, his thumb moving rhythmically over the soft flesh, his lips pressing tender kisses on that same achingly sensitive area, kisses that terrified and excited her unbearably.

Breathless and almost frightened by the dizzying excitement that shot up through her body as he remained there between her slim thighs, nuzzling and lightly exploring, Morgana reached for him, her fingers tangling in the thick, tawny hair, urging him upward, Lifting his head, he glanced up questioningly, his golden eyes bright and burning with desire. Shy suddenly and, with her gown ruched up about her waist, embarrassed by her near nakedness, she flushed and stammered, "S-S-Stop! What are you doing to m-m-me?"

Smiling crookedly, he dropped a brief kiss where the curly hair met her lower abdomen. "I hoped I was giving you pleasure . . . wasn't I?"

She swallowed with difficulty, her eyes very big in her delicate face. "Yes," she admitted huskily, "b-b-but it feels so . . . so . . . it frightens me—as if my body isn't my own, as if some depraved creature has entered me."

His smile grew very wicked. "A creature that is also wildly abandoned in my arms, I should hope," he teased lightly, and levering himself up slightly, he kissed her softly on the mouth. "Don't be afraid. I won't let anything happen to you. . . ." Glancing at her slender, half-naked body, his gaze traveling inch by inch over her long, slim legs upward until he was looking down into her lovely features, his eyes darkened and he said thickly, "Oh, but, sweetheart, there are so many ways to make love, so many ways to give each other pleasure. . . ."

Her mouth tingling from his kiss, his hand scorching her flesh where it rested lightly on her belly, she could only stare up at his lean features, wanting precisely the same thing that he did, but too uncertain of herself, too new to his lovemaking, to baldly admit it. Instead, her arms crept around his neck, and burying her face between the lapels of his robe, she kissed him sensually at the base of his neck, where his pulse beat strongly.

Royce groaned, feeling her sweet kiss burning through his big body like wildfire, and his fingers clenched urgently against her belly. His lazy manner gone, with far more haste than he had shown so far, he divested her of her gown, tossing it violently away. With fingers that shook, he tore open the belted knot at his waist and in a feverish haste, whipped out of his robe, mad to be rid of his own clothing, wanting no barriers to separate his body from hers.

Hungrily his mouth fastened on hers, and kissing Morgana with all the unbridled passion within him, he jerked her to him, molding her slender curves next to his hard, muscled length. His hands urgently cupped her buttocks, holding her firmly against the throbbing force of his achingly full member. The touch of her warm, yielding flesh pressed eagerly next to his filled him with such fierce desire, such overwhelming tenderness, that he shuddered with the powerful emotions that twined and twisted within him. Again and again he kissed her, his probing tongue delving deeper and deeper into her mouth, utterly permeating the dark confines of her mouth with the taste and texture of him. Kissing soon wasn't enough to appease the increasingly frantic hunger that raged through him, and driven by the demands of his body, he rubbed sinuously against her, pleasuring and exciting both of them by his blatantly erotic movements.

Wildly adrift in a rising sea of primitive sensation, Morgana clung to him, kissing him back with wanton shamelessness, and as she arched her slim body into his, blind, elemental desire, as potent and intoxicating as wine, trapped her and made her a willing captive to his demands. Her breasts, crushed into the thick hair of his chest, ached, and her nipples had grown tight and swollen, the sweet friction of her body sliding against his making her almost giddy from the emotions that spiraled with growing urgency through her. She wanted him, wanted the fierce pleasure of his mouth and hands everywhere on her body, desperately craved the touch of his lips and tongue at her breast, the feel of his warm hands exploring her intimately.

Royce shifted slightly, one heavy thigh slipping between hers, and his knee bumping gently, deliberately, against the highly sensitized flesh at the juncture of her legs, he drove her half-wild with his teasing motions. She knew he was aroused, she could feel the swollen length of him crushed between their twisting bodies, and yet beyond the mind-drugging kisses he gave her and the restless movements of his hands across her back and buttocks, he made no attempt to explore further. Her body stingingly alive, the pulsating ache in her loins nearly intolerable, she caught his encroaching thigh between her legs and pushed down frantically, seeking release from the passionate demands that held her in thrall.

Groaning his delight at her actions, Royce's mouth left hers and sought the aching tips of her breasts. She tasted like nectar, and like a starving man, he suckled and pulled at her hard little nipples, his teeth lightly scraping against the responsive skin.

She was already totally aroused, and the touch of his lips and teeth on her breasts was nearly her undoing as she arched up wildly into his mouth, offering herself freely, her body trembling as pleasure flooded through her. His arm slid under her, and for mindless moments he held her to him, his mouth sweetly ravaging the tender flesh of her breasts, taking sensual gratification in the taste of her and the feverish twisting of her body. Unable to help herself, wanting to give him pleasure too, she reached for him, her small hand closing clumsily around him, marveling at her own wantonness and the size and heat of him.

He stiffened at her first tentative caress, and his mouth against her ear, he put his hand over hers and muttered, "No, sweetheart, this way . . ." and he taught her the motion and way of it. His breathing ragged, his body responded with obvious enthusiasm to her touch.

Feeling his reaction, feeling the swell and pulsation of his flesh as she caressed him, Morgana was fascinated and excited at the same time. So fascinated, in fact, that when he reached for her once more, she gently pushed him away, wanted to concentrate fully on the havoc she was so fervently wreaking upon him. Royce let her have her way for the moment, and his face tight with desire, the golden eyes glittering with promises of sweet vengeance, he lay back against the mattress and let her do what she willed.

It was a tender torment he did not think that he could endure for very long, her slightest caress making him grit his teeth to keep from disgracing himself—something that she found highly diverting. Wondering if she realized how utterly seductive she was as she lounged there half sitting, half lying beside him, her intent gaze locked on a certain part of his anatomy as she explored the length and breadth of him, Royce tried desperately not to explode into a million shards of ecstasy. It was almost useless; her eager ministrations alone would have been sufficient to break the iron control he had of his body, but the sight of her jutting breasts, the nipples still swollen and rosy from his mouth, made him groan and reach for her again.

Startled when she felt his hands upon her, Morgana looked up, and the expression in his eyes stilled the protest on her lips. Her heart began to beat in thick, heavy strokes, and her body was suddenly awash with an intense eagerness to experience what she saw in his gaze. She met the hard crush of his mouth with her own, her mouth opening to accept the hungry thrust of his tongue. It was clear his indulgence was at an end as he rained passionately savage kisses on first her mouth and then her breasts. She was aching from the force of the desire he had incited within her when his lips deserted her nipples and began to travel slowly, inexorably, downward across her waist and belly to the black triangle of curls at the top of her thighs. Morgana could hardly breathe; her skin felt as if it were on fire, the blood thrumming so violently through her veins that the world receded completely when his open mouth found her. A soft, keening cry, half protest, half delight, broke from her as he parted her flesh and his tongue probed and brushed against the sweetness he found there. She burned from his touch, the thrusting caresses of his tongue inflaming her until she writhed like a wild thing on the bed, her head twisting from side to side.

Royce held her fast, deliberately allowing her no succor from the rapid stroke of his tongue. He could feel the tension growing within her slender body, and the demanding ache within his own grew until it was nearly unbearable. He wanted to seek relief, wanted to bury himself fully within the soft, silken sheath of her, but more, he first wanted her to have the exquisite pleasure he sensed was only seconds away for her.

Morgana could not bear it any longer; the sheer carnal pleasure Royce was evoking from her frightened her, and she was even more frightened by the abandoned creature she had become, an abandoned creature who eagerly allowed him to do this wonderfully decadent act. Anxiety in her voice, she tugged frantically at his hair and cried, "Stop! Oh, please stop!"

His eyes glazed with passion, Royce gazed uncomprehendingly at her for a moment; then, realizing that she was frightened and suspecting that he was pushing her too far, too fast, he smiled twistedly and murmured ruefully, "Virgins! I've never had one before, sweetheart, so you'll have to make allowances for me!" Moving up beside her, he pulled her into his arms; kissing her mouth and then her ear, he whispered, "I shall try not to shock you too much by the things that I want to do to you, but you are so damned delectable that I don't know if I can help myself."

He kissed her again, his hands curving possessively around her breasts, his thumbs teasing her nipples, effortlessly bringing her once more to the edge of ecstasy, and this time he did not hesitate—he could not; he had reached his own limits. Parting her thighs with his knees, he gently stroked her with his fingers, and then, with an exultant groan, he thrust into the tight heat of her.

Buried deeply within her, he felt Morgana wrap her arms fervently around him, her nipples pushing impudently against his chest. Royce kissed her passionately, the satiny clasp of her body around his rigid manhood hurling him instantly into a dark whirlpool of erotic delight. He had meant to savor this moment, had meant to make love to her slowly, lazily, but he could not, Morgana's hips already moving in an anciently seductive motion that banished rational thought.

Ecstasy already spiraling up through her body from the moment he entered her, Morgana moved wildly beneath him, wanting him to drive into her, wanting his fiercest possession. Her mouth against his, she pleaded huskily, "Oh, please . . . please love me!" She heard his guttural exclamation, almost a growl of assent, then nothing as his big body slammed into hers again and again, sending such an inferno of dazzling ecstasy exploding through her that she thought she would faint from the joy of it.

With savage satisfaction, Royce felt the pulsations that racked her, and freed now to find his own pleasure, in a frenzy to reach that desperately longed-for peak, he plunged more frantically into the velvety heat of her body. A second later, making no effort to hide the delight her body gave him, he shuddered violently and moaned softly as he found his own delirious release.

At peace for the moment from the demons that had driven them, they lay together, their bodies touching, Royce dropping butterfly-light kisses on her brow and the corner of her mouth, Morgana gently caressing his arm and thigh. Sleep came to Morgana first, but for a long time afterward, Royce simply held her slender body next to his, shaken by the emotions she made him feel.

Still greatly bewildered, but filled also with a powerful tenderness that he could not deny, he stared down at her sleeping body, marveling at her slender beauty as the candlelight played gently over her smooth, unmarked flesh. . . . He frowned suddenly, seeing for the first time the small, round scar on her hip. Rising up, he bent over and examined it more closely, his frown increasing as he realized it was a very old scar and clearly represented a crest of some sort. Now, why, he wondered darkly, would anyone have branded her in such a barbaric manner?

He was on the point of waking her to ask when there was

suddenly a loud ruckus at the front of the house. Morgana jerked upright, sleep gone, even as Royce was leaping from the bed and flinging on his robe. Fearing another attack from the one-eyed man, he raced to his own room and snatched up the loaded pistol he now kept handy. Returning to Morgana's room, he lit another candle, and motioning her to remain where she was, he stepped into the wide hall.

Zachary, armed with pistol and candle as he was, met him, and as the noise continued unabated and was obviously coming from the front door of the house, they leaped down the long, winding staircase. Chambers, his nightcap askew, a stout poker in one hand, was already at the front door demanding identification from the shouting people on the other side.

Royce recognized one of the voices, Jacko's, and threw wide the door; Morgana's oldest brother and a vociferously protesting gatekeeper immediately stumbled into the black-and-white-tiled foyer. It took a moment for Royce to reassure the burly gatekeeper that Jacko was an acquaintance, and then, turning to Jacko, he demanded, "What is it? What is wrong?"

His face strained, the blue eyes dark with fear, Jacko gasped, "It's the one-eyed man! He betrayed us! *Ben's in Newgate!*"

PART FOUR

Nemesis

Though the mills of God grind slowly,
yet they grind exceedingly small.

F. VON LOGAU, "Retribution"

CHAPTER 22

There was a brief, electric silence, and then it seemed as if everyone spoke at once, an urgent, wild babble suddenly filling the hall until Royce's authoritative voice rose above it. *"Quiet! And I mean quiet immediately!"* he commanded, and silence fell. Looking at his butler, he said a trifle more calmly, "Chambers, go get some brandy and some glasses and bring them to the front salon. You did an excellent job," Royce said to the gatekeeper, a muscular young fellow named Bullard. "I should have warned you about Morgana's brothers. You can go now, and with my thanks for fulfilling your duties so commendably." Looking across at Zachary, Royce added, "You will come with me and Jacko."

Royce had been so intent upon calming the babble that he had forgotten Morgana—she'd had no intention of remaining meekly in the bedchamber while he went to confront possible danger, but she had been forced to waste precious seconds searching for the gown that Royce had carelessly tossed away earlier. Since the garment was almost transparent, and not knowing what she would face downstairs, she'd had to waste more time scrambling around for a robe.

It had taken her only moments, but heedless of Royce's order to stay where she was, she had rushed to the top of the stairs and then stopped abruptly when she caught sight of Jacko. The fact that Jacko was alone didn't actually impinge upon her consciousness; all she saw was that her brother was there and that Royce had events well in hand. "Oh, Jacko! It's *you!*" she cried gladly, hurtling down the stairs like a small whirlwind, throwing herself into her brother's arms.

Chambers and Bullard had barely turned away when Morgana appeared, and they both halted and glanced back in time to see Jacko sweep her into a hearty embrace. A hint of a smile on his face, Chambers continued on his way, but Bullard hesitated, his gaze fixed unwaveringly on Morgana's flushed, up-turned face as she stared happily at Jacko. Clearing his throat nervously, Bullard finally dragged his blue eyes away from Morgana's face, and looking at Royce, he said bluntly, "Sir. Think you should know that there was a fine gentleman just this afternoon nosing around the entrance." An apologetic expression on his earnest features, he muttered, "He was real polite, but he asked a lot of questions, but being as how you had warned me to be careful of strangers, I didn't answer him. I'm sorry to say that when he departed, I dismissed him from my mind—you *are* new to the area, and a lot of folk are just plain curious about the new owner."

Royce's face was grim as he listened to John Bullard's words, but he wasn't surprised. He had been expecting something like this to happen, but he was puzzled why young Bullard had chosen this moment to tell him about the incident.

Bullard enlightened him almost immediately. "He was an older man, but think you should know that he looked uncommonly like that young lady over there."

Zachary, an almost avuncular grin on his handsome face, had been too busy watching Morgana and Jacko's embrace to pay much attention to what Bullard had been saying to Royce, but he caught Bullard's last words, and his grin vanished. Worry evident in his topaz eyes, his gaze met Royce's. "Devlin! It had to have been him!"

Royce shot him a black look, making it clear he didn't want Zachary saying any more on the subject. Realizing his mistake and embarrassed by it, Zachary beat a hasty retreat, and turning to the oblivious Morgana and Jacko, he said quickly, "Let us go to the salon—Chambers will be back soon with the brandy, and if I know him, or rather, Ivy, probably some food to sustain us at this hour of the morning."

After the trio had disappeared, Royce said to Bullard, "What's done is done . . . but in the future, I want to know *instantly* when *anyone,* man or woman, child or stripling, approaches you and begins to ask questions—no matter how unimportant their questions may seem. Now, precisely what did the gentleman ask you?"

A crestfallen expression on his face, Bullard replied instantly, "I can't remember exactly, sir, but I recall that he wanted to know how many people were in the household, if you'd hired any local people, and did I know any of them. He was very friendly, and when he asked if I knew how long you would be staying here, I just guessed it was because he was curious about a newcomer—people in the country *are* interested in such things." Shamefacedly he admitted, "I should have been more suspicious, especially after you warned us about strangers, but I just dismissed the gent as being nosy." He frowned. "Now that I think of it, he did seem overly curious to know if there was a young lady staying with you, and he seemed to take quite an interest in the fact that the property was completely surrounded by the yew hedge. Seem to remember him asking me if the gateway was the only way into the property and if someone actually lived in the cottage there." Bullard suddenly grinned. "It's a good thing I hadn't seen the young lady before or I might have given something away—they look so very alike."

"Well, that's something I'd prefer you keep to yourself," Royce said bluntly.

Bullard glanced at him keenly, and then, nodding his blond head, he said fervently, "You can trust me, sir! I wasn't rude, but I didn't tell him anything. He didn't seem to like it when I told him that the master didn't encourage his servants to gossip! Drove off in a bit of a temper, I can tell you."

Royce smiled faintly, amused at the idea of the haughty Earl being reprimanded by a mere servant for gossiping. Clapping Bullard on the shoulder, Royce urged him toward the door. "No harm's been done, so don't dwell on it. Do, however, warn me the very instant anyone questions you, and tell your brothers the same." Smiling easily, Royce opened the front door and asked lightly, "Have you all settled comfortably in the cottage?"

Bullard nodded eagerly. "Oh, yes, sir. It's a good thing that there are three of us living there and taking turns at the gate, otherwise I might have missed that young man tonight." And thinking that Royce might have thought he had committed further dereliction in his duties, he said quickly, "Before me and the young man came to the house, I woke Elmer and Harry, and they are standing guard until I get back."

"Very good. I will rest easier for what is left of the night, knowing that I am in the competent hands of the Bullard brothers."

Beaming proudly, Bullard departed, and after shutting the door behind him, Royce stared at the carved wood for a moment, a faint smile curving his mobile mouth. It seemed that he had chosen his gatekeepers well, if tonight's actions were anything to go by. Then his smile faded as he considered what John Bullard had told him. So the Earl was asking questions, was he? Why? Royce wondered. Was it simply the embarrassment of having such an obvious byblow of his embarking upon an undeniably scandalous career? Or was there another reason?

When Royce entered the salon, he found Morgana and Jacko sitting side by side on one of the low, tapestry-covered sofas in the large, elegant room. Zachary, in his night robe, was lounging in a channel-back chair of straw-colored satin, and it was apparent from the tense expression on all three young faces that they had been discussing Ben's incarceration in Newgate. Strolling over to stand in front of the handsome fireplace with its classically designed mantel of gray marble, Royce said quietly, "I think that we should postpone any further talk about Ben until after Chambers has served us and departed."

Since that topic was uppermost in everyone's minds, it was an oddly quiet room that Chambers entered a few moments later. Aware that he was preventing conversation, and not unnaturally consumed by great curiosity, Chambers tried to go about his duties quickly, longing to stay and listen and yet knowing that nothing of interest would be said as long as he remained in the room. Setting down a huge tray which held a variety of liquid refreshments, brandy, whiskey, even a pot of tea, as well as several plates heaped with cheeses, breads, cold ham, and thinly sliced roast beef, he bowed in Royce's direction and said evenly, "Will that be all, sir?"

Royce nodded, and eyeing the plates of food, smiled. "I see that Ivy must have been aroused by our little contretemps also."

Glad of an excuse to linger, Chambers nodded. "Oh, yes, sir! The pounding on the front door woke several of us, but"—he sent a meaningful look at Royce—"while Ivy was determined to follow me, I insisted she remain in the kitchen as I thought it best if I saw to any trouble by myself. I ordered the others to go back to bed—told them that it was probably nothing and that Ivy and I would take care of everything." His expression becoming even more eloquent, he added pithily, "The less people involved, the better, don't you think, sir?"

Amusement twinkled in Royce's eyes; he knew very well that Chambers would like to be invited to remain, but indicating that the butler was no longer needed, he walked with him to the door. "You handled the situation most admirably . . . and I shall not force you to languish too long before I satisfy all of your curiosity about tonight's events." He hesitated a moment, the twinkle dying from his eyes, and said seriously, "For now, you will have to be content to learn that our unexpected visitor is Morgana's brother, Jacko Fowler, and that he has brought us important news about her other brother,

Ben. I would prefer you keep that information between yourself and Ivy."

Immensely pleased that the master had enlightened him somewhat, Chambers bowed low, and sedately left the room, his neatly tied flannel robe flapping softly around his bony ankles. Turning back to the other three, Royce pushed his hands in the pockets of his own night robe and said quietly, "I think we can talk freely now. Tell us what happened, Jacko."

Morgana poured her brother a glass of whiskey and pressed it into his hand as Jacko began speaking. "Since our ship sails on Monday, me and Ben were planning on coming down here tonight to see Pip." He took a big gulp of the whiskey and, sending Royce a defiant look, went on doggedly, "We figured you wouldn't mind if we stayed overnight—we wanted to see for ourselves that all was well with Pip and to make certain that you were going to keep your word about bringing her with you when you sail in the fall. Besides, being as how it would be our last chance to see our sister for several months, we didn't think you'd—"

"What the devil are you talking about?" Morgana demanded sharply, an accusatory glance moving back and forth between Royce's inscrutable features and Jacko's stubbornly truculent ones.

"You haven't told her?" Jacko asked in astonishment. "She doesn't know that we were to sail to America on Monday?"

"Ah, no, as a matter of fact," Royce answered easily, ignoring Morgana's gasp of stunned outrage. "I had intended to tell her long before now, but the time never seemed right." He glanced at Morgana, his golden gaze moving with unmistakable appreciation over her lovely features. She looked very small and appealing in a robe of purple velvet, her curly black hair rioting in wild disorder over her head as she sat there beside her brother, but the furious expression in those slanted gray eyes . . . Royce sighed. She was angry, and a part of him didn't blame her for feeling as she did. He *should* have told her. His eyes meeting hers steadily, he admitted bluntly, "I wanted you settled in before I embarked upon an explanation that you weren't going to like. You were going to be upset to learn that your brothers were leaving you here in my care while they sailed to America, and I wanted to postpone distressing you as long as I could—at least until you felt more comfortable here at Lime Tree Cottage."

Ben forgotten at the moment, oblivious to Zachary and Jacko's utterly rapt interest, Morgana glared at Royce, the gray eyes dark as storm clouds. "Distress me?" she demanded. "When has *that* ever stopped you?" Springing up angrily from the sofa, she stalked across the room and stood militantly in front of Royce. "Is that what tonight was all about? Is that why you came to my bed?" Her voice rising scornfully, she added, "To make me more *comfortable?*"

"An unfortunate choice of words on my part," Royce answered coolly, the topaz eyes watching her narrowly. "As for tonight and what happened between us, I don't intend to discuss it in front of an audience!"

Suddenly becoming aware of Jacko and Zachary and their undisguised fascination with what was being said, Morgana blushed becomingly. Her fight disappearing in an instant, her mouth set in a mutinous line, she flounced down on the sofa next to Jacko, contenting herself with throwing Royce a look full of daggers.

With great aplomb, Royce poured himself a snifter of brandy and stood once more before the fireplace. "Now, where were we?" And glancing at Jacko, he continued with unruffled composure, "I believe you were saying something about coming down to see your sister before you sailed on Monday?"

"Er, yes," Jacko muttered, still caught up in the revealing exchange between Morgana and Royce. The changes in his sister in the weeks since he had last seen her were enormous. She was no longer a grimy little street urchin of indeterminate sex; instead, he had been confronted by a beautiful, *clean* young lady in costly clothes—granted, the clothes consisted of little more than a nightgown and robe, but Jacko could recognize quality when he saw it. Where once dirty, unkempt hair had framed an unwashed face that habitually wore a pinched, almost crafty expression, he now found silky, artfully cut curls, and the features he now stared at were softer and more lovely than he had ever imagined. There was a bloom about Morgana that was unmistakable, a sparkle in the gray eyes that had never been there before, her clear skin glowing with health and vitality, and even the way she moved was different, flowing and feminine where before she had been forced to hide behind a boyish disguise. The changes pleased Jacko, and yet they made him feel slightly awkward, almost as if he didn't know this beguiling, sweetly scented little creature who had flung herself into his arms and whose fingers even now clung tightly to his dirty hand. He had been self-conscious, uncomfortably aware of his filthy body, greasy, disheveled hair, and equally filthy, foul-smelling, stained clothing, but the sharp exchange between Pip and Royce had somehow reassured him. She might be wearing fancy clothes and look like a lady, but Pip was still Pip! Gathering up his straying thoughts, Jacko pressed Pip's hand more warmly and said, "We had planned to be here before dark. We figured we would stay here until it was time to leave for the docks in London." He shot Royce a dulcet look. "Thought you wouldn't mind providing us transportation back to London, and we didn't think that if the one-eyed man noticed we were missing, he would look for us here."

"But something went wrong?" Royce interjected when Jacko stopped to grab a bite of the bread and meat that Morgana had fixed for him. From the way he wolfed the food down, it was obvious that he had not eaten in a long time. Royce gave him a moment, then repeated, "But something went wrong . . . ?"

The blue eyes full of anxiety, Jacko nodded swiftly. "Bad wrong!" he said in a low, tormented voice. "The one-eyed man showed up at our rooms night before last, said he had a small job he wanted us to do for him. It didn't seem to be too difficult, and since we didn't want to arouse his suspicions, we didn't try to wiggle out of it."

"I take it the 'small job' turned out to be a trap?" Royce asked quietly, setting down his empty snifter on the mantel and helping himself to a slice of bread and cheese.

"Yes, it was! And it's the devil's own luck that I am not in Newgate with Ben this very moment," Jacko said roughly. "There was this gentleman the one-eyed man wanted us to rob, said the gentry cove always wore a fine ruby that he had a fancy to own. Told us where the fellow would be this morning, or rather yesterday morning. Said the fellow would be driving up from the country to put his affairs in order before leaving the city for the summer. Said it would be our only chance to bite the blow for a long time." Jacko rubbed the back of his neck. "It seemed simple enough and it was something we've done time and again, so we weren't looking for trouble."

"But you found it," Royce commented dryly.

"Oh, yes, we found it!" Jacko replied bitterly. His forehead wrinkled in memory, Jacko said slowly, "The fellow had to have been warned, because he was ready for us—the instant we neared him, before we had even touched him, he struck Ben a mighty blow to the head with his fist, nearly knocking Ben to the ground with the force of it. And then quick as a flash the bloody bastard whipped out a sword stick and came right at me! Ben was groggy, stumbling about while I was trying to keep the fellow's attention on me to give Ben time to recover and avoid being stabbed at the same time, when all of a sudden out of nowhere four members of the watch are there, swinging their cudgels." Shame and despair in his voice, Jacko confessed, "All I could think of was getting out of there—I thought Ben was behind me, and I dodged through the alleys and streets until I knew I had lost any pursuers. Ben wasn't with me when I stopped running, but I wasn't worried—we've often had to split up to escape, and I just figured he'd be waiting for me back at our rooms." Bleakly he said, "He wasn't, but someone else was—the watch! I almost walked slap into their arms before I noticed them lurking about where we live, and that's when I knew for certain that the one-eyed man had betrayed us." Tossing down some more whiskey that Morgana had just poured for him, Jacko continued, "I hung around awhile, thinking that maybe I had gotten there before Ben, but after a while, I knew that things were very bad for us. I had to keep hidden, but I also had to know what had happened to Ben. I did some damn cautious snooping, not knowing who I could trust anymore, and discovered that he had been taken away to Newgate. As soon as I learned that, I started out for here." He sighed tiredly. "I walked when I had to, but I was able to cadge a ride with a farm cart every now and then."

"I wonder," Royce began slowly, "if the one-eyed man's betrayal is because he realized that you had been following him, or if he has somehow learned of your imminent departure from England."

Jacko shrugged listlessly. "What does it matter? Ben's in Newgate, and until he is freed, we're not going anywhere!"

"My point exactly!" Royce said bluntly. "By having Ben in Newgate, he has to know that none of you will be leaving the country . . . which gives him time to concoct further plots to kidnap Morgana!"

Silence fell in the room, no one having anything to add to the conversation. Several seconds passed, all lost in their own thoughts, before Zachary asked softly, "How are we going to get Ben out of Newgate?"

After tossing down the last of his brandy, Royce replied

crisply, "Without a great deal of trouble, I should hope! I shall leave at first light and return to London. George will know which magistrate or judge I should see, and if all goes well, Ben will be sitting here with us by tomorrow evening!"

"And if it doesn't?" Morgana asked anxiously.

Royce smiled gently at her. "Sweetheart, please have a little faith in my persuasive powers!" Attempting to interject a lighter note into the proceedings, he grinned. "If I cannot convince the authorities that Ben must be released in my care, I'm quite positive that I shall be able to find someone who, for a handsome consideration, will be quite willing to look the other way and allow Ben to escape." His teasing mood disappearing, Royce looked at Morgana and promised grimly, "Believe me, one way or another, I will free your brother for you. It may take longer than we want, but Ben *will* be free— I swear it!"

"I shall go with you!" Zachary said grimly, leaning forward intently.

"And me!" Jacko said promptly.

Morgana opened her mouth to state her intention of being included, but Royce slanted her a fierce glance and snarled softly, "Don't even *think* of offering to accompany me!" Her mouth shut with a snap and her chin lifted belligerently.

Looking at the two younger men, Royce said forcefully, "No one is coming with me—I'll need you here to guard Morgana, and I see no reason for us to split up our pitifully few forces any more than necessary."

Both Zachary and Jacko were much inclined to argue with this line of reasoning, but eventually Royce made them see the sense of what he proposed. "Don't you see! He may very well have arranged Ben's capture for just this reason—to divide us, and in our desire to free Ben, momentarily let ourselves be distracted from his main purpose . . . the possession of Morgana! If we all go hying off to London, we may be playing right into his hands!"

Royce's words were irrefutable, and the subject was closed. Walking over and putting his empty snifter on the tray, he said levelly, "I think for now we should all seek our beds for what is left of the night. Jacko, there are any number of guest bedrooms for you to choose from, so let's find you one and let you get some sleep."

Jacko grimaced and looked down at his soiled and tattered garments. "I think I should find a hayloft—there is no telling what lives on my body and in these clothes."

Royce smiled slightly. "I'm certain that our inimitable Chambers has already seen to it that there is some warm water and soap in one of the bedchambers, and he will have no doubt made arrangements to burn your clothing as soon as you are out of them! I suspect that he is patiently waiting outside this door to inform us of his actions. Would you like to place a wager on it?"

A huge yawn suddenly overtook Jacko, and covering his mouth hurriedly, he shook his head. "I'm not used to manners of the gentry—you would be sure to win."

The four of them walked out of the salon, and as Royce had predicted, Chambers was waiting for them in the entryway. Bowing and looking not the least incongruous in his flannel night robe, Chambers intoned quietly, "Sir, I took the liberty of having some water heated and placed in the green bedroom, next to Master Zachary's room. After he has washed, if the young man would put his, er, *soiled* garments outside the door, I shall see to their disposal. I'm certain by tomorrow morning we will have found him something more appropriate to wear."

"Did I not tell you that Chambers would see to everything?" Royce asked, smiling broadly.

Taking Jacko by the arm, in a friendly manner Zachary

said, "Come with me; I shall show you to your room, and I think that as far as clothing is concerned, I have several garments that, with very little altering, would probably fit you. By tomorrow, we'll have you looking like a swell!"

It was as well that they all parted on that light note, because Royce's expression was decidedly grim as he restlessly paced the confines of his room just a few minutes later. He was far more worried than he had let on, and while he was positive that he could make arrangements for Ben's freedom, he rather doubted that it could be done in a relatively brief time. Which means, he thought darkly, Ben must remain in Newgate, where the one-eyed man's minions could reach him at any time . . . and there was no longer any question of being able to get the Fowler brothers out of the country any time soon.

But it was Morgana's place in all of this that had him the most alarmed, and he cursed himself roundly for not having put her on the first ship leaving England weeks ago. If he hadn't allowed his own selfish desires to rule his head, she and her brothers would be safe now, somewhere on the high seas, halfway to America. Instead, he admitted with a fierce scowl, Ben is in Newgate and she is in increasingly more danger—and will be as long as she is within striking range of the one-eyed man . . . or until the one-eyed man is dead!

Royce smiled, a tiger's smile, and there was a distinctly feral gleam in his tiger eyes as he considered the pleasure it would give him to kill the one-eyed man. If only, he thought savagely, there were some way to force the one-eyed man to break cover . . . to have him strike at me, instead of Morgana and her brothers. A mirthless smile curved his handsome mouth. How foolish of him—the one-eyed man had already attacked him once, and he *still* didn't know what had provoked it . . . or why the man had set Morgana and her brothers on him in the first place. . . .

It was obvious that the one-eyed man had to be someone

he knew, someone whom, in the beginning, he had inadvertently annoyed—that would explain the order to have Morgana pick his pocket. But that plan had gone wrong, and worse, from the other man's point of view, Royce realized even more clearly, Morgana had fallen into his hands and was no longer in the power of the one-eyed man. It was glaringly apparent, too, that Morgana was not just a minor member of his knot of thieves—Royce was certain that if it had been any other female member who had been caught by him, the one-eyed man would not have made any effort to free her, certainly would not have gone to the lengths to which he had so far. No. The sequence of events seemed to revolve around Morgana herself. Why? Because the one-eyed man had planned to make her his mistress? Or was it somehow connected to the fact that she was the bastard daughter of the Earl of St. Audries?

Lost in his own thoughts, Royce didn't hear Morgana enter the room until she was beside him and touched him on the arm. He spun around, catching her arm in a bruising grip, the expression on his face so dangerous that Morgana gasped and stepped back slightly.

Seeing who it was, he softened his expression and instantly let go of her arm. A crooked smile on his face, he muttered, "I'm sorry, I didn't realize that it was you."

Smiling uncertainly up at him, she said thankfully, "I'm only glad that I am *not* the person you thought I was!"

Royce made some light reply, and then, the topaz eyes wary, he asked, "What are you doing here? I assumed that you would be in bed."

Morgana's eyes gravely searched his features. When she had first learned of the planned departure of her brothers, she had been enraged—thoroughly enraged that Royce had not told her and just a little hurt that Jacko and Ben would abandon her so cavalierly. But she'd had time to think about it, and reluctantly she admitted that Royce's reasons made a great deal of sense. She hadn't totally forgiven him his deceit, but she was willing to listen to his explanation. Her face somber, she asked quietly, "When were you going to tell me about their sailing?"

Royce made a face, and aware that she was not overtly hostile, he risked putting his arms around her and pulling her next to him. Her slender body pressing confidingly against his, his chin resting on her curly black hair, he murmured, "Tonight. I came to your room with the intention of telling you. . . ." A husky note entered his voice. "But I'm afraid that I got, ah, distracted."

Her cheek pressed warmly against his heart, Morgana tried to ignore the sudden heat that flooded her body and asked in a very small voice, "Royce, will you really be able to free Ben?"

He tipped up her chin, and his mouth teasingly brushed against hers. "Yes, I'll get him out. It's not difficult if you have money and position—which I do, so don't worry about it. I can't promise that I'll be able to free him tomorrow, but soon we'll have him here with us."

Momentarily reassured, worry of the one-eyed man forgotten for now, she smiled mistily up at him, her gray eyes soft and unknowingly inviting.

With her breasts burning into his chest, her lips only inches from his, Royce instantly lost the train of his thought, and when she moved with unconscious seduction against him, Ben, the one-eyed man, flew from his mind, leaving only a blind, hungry desire to take her again. His arms convulsively tightened around her, and he crushed her next to him, deliberately making her aware of his suddenly rigid manhood. Thickly he said, "You're distracting me again."

Caught in the same sensual trap that held Royce, Morgana smiled demurely, and as her lips touched his, she murmured, "Oh, I hope so. . . ."

CHAPTER 23

Royce was extremely tired and irritable when he arrived in London the next morning, and while he didn't begrudge one moment of the time he had spent in Morgana's arms when he should have been sleeping, he was very much aware that making love to her through the rest of the night hadn't been the wisest thing he had ever done in his life. A sensual smile suddenly curved his full bottom lip. Not the wisest, but definitely the most memorable, he admitted candidly to himself as certain blatantly erotic images flitted across his brain.

Rousing himself from his decidedly lascivious musings, he stopped his horses in front of George's set of rooms on Little Argyll Street, and turning to an extremely proud Matt Hatton, who had accompanied him as his groom, Royce said, "Go to their heads. If all goes well, I shan't be gone long."

Fortunately George was at home, and while he was still garbed in a fine silk robe lavishly embellished with a paisley design, he seemed quite happy to see Royce . . . happy, but a bit mystified. Greetings had been exchanged and they were comfortably seated in a small but tastefully decorated room that served as George's salon. George's valet, Thompson, a tall, somber-faced individual, had served them cups of hot, black coffee and had departed, leaving the two men to talk privately.

"What the devil are you doing back in town?" George demanded. "Thought you were settled in the country. Thought I was to come down and visit you there this week. Something happen?"

Briefly Royce explained the reason for his sudden trip to town.

George's blue eyes grew very wide. "Want me to find you a magistrate? A judge?"

"Well, I had hoped that you would know of someone I could approach."

George pursed his lips, frowning slightly as he stared across at his tall, muscular cousin. "I think you should put it from your mind," he said at last. "Think you should dump the gel on the streets and wash your hands of the brothers. Think you're going to get in a lot of trouble if you don't. That one-eyed fellow ain't to be trifled with. I warned you."

Looking apologetic, Royce nodded his tawny head. "I agree with you, but unfortunately, I'm afraid that I cannot. You see, I'm rather uncommonly fascinated at the moment by the, er, gel, and I can't just turn my back on her."

"Fascinated! Bewitched is more like it!" George exclaimed acidly. "Hardly more than a fortnight ago, the on-dit was that you were hanging out for a wife to take back to America with you! Had the females all in a twitter." Sending him a sharp glance, George demanded with stubborn persistence, "What about the widow Cresswell and that Summerfield chit? I thought you were dangling after one of them." Almost accusatively he added, "You told me you were considering them!"

"Well, yes, I was—and while I admit to being fascinated, I didn't say that I planned to *marry* this particular little baggage," Royce replied lightly, a glimmer of amusement dancing in the depths of his golden eyes.

That seemed to reassure George somewhat, for he relaxed back into his chair and took a restoring sip of his coffee. "Thank heavens for that! Can't have you marrying a little nobody plucked out of the gutter! Can't have you marrying a little nobody period! It ain't done by people like us! You need to choose a wife carefully—you have the family and future generations to consider!"

There was a time, and not in the too distant past, when Royce would have instantly echoed George's words, but this morning, for some reason, he found his cousin's attitude more than a little annoying.

Uneasy with the topic of conversation, Royce said bleakly, "Naturally. To do otherwise would be unthinkable!"

George beamed at him. "My sentiments exactly! Now, let's put all this nonsense about seeing a magistrate behind us and enjoy the day." Struck by a sudden thought, George looked extraordinarily pleased with himself as he said, "London has been so thin of company this past week, think I shall ride down to Tunbridge Wells with you when you leave. Thompson could pack my things and I could be ready to leave this afternoon, if you like."

Royce was very aware that George was trying to distract him and get him safely out of London and away from further confrontations with the one-eyed man. He had never really appreciated George's loyalties to his friends and family until this moment, and gently Royce murmured, "George, I haven't given up wanting to see a magistrate, and I'm not leaving London until I make some sort of arrangements to get Ben out of Newgate."

Dismay evident on his pleasant features, George blustered, "But, but you said . . . !"

"I said," Royce interrupted mildly, "that I wasn't going to marry her—I didn't say that anything else had changed. Now, are you going to help me or not?"

"Don't want to see you get hurt," George said anxiously. "Favorite relative! Don't like the way that one-eyed man keeps interfering in your life—he's dangerous, Royce."

"But you *will* help me?"

George sighed heavily. "Naturally."

Smiling slightly, Royce asked, "Then you are acquainted with a judge or a magistrate who will help us?"

"Acquainted with everyone!" George said in an affronted tone.

"Yes, I'm sure you are," Royce said quickly, "but all we care about at the moment is someone to help us with Ben."

George pursed his lips thoughtfully and said, "Let me get dressed and then we can go round to the house of a fellow I know. Splendid fellow! Certain he can help us—and if he can't, he'll know who can!"

Royce hesitated. "I want to go to Newgate and see Ben first. After I've seen Ben, then I shall return here for you and we can go see your magistrate at that time."

George didn't like that idea at all, but eventually he was forced to agree. "Don't," George said heavily as Royce prepared to leave, "do anything foolish!"

The idea of doing anything foolish was the furthest thought from Royce's mind when he finally stood before the gray bulk of Newgate. Even the warmth of the July sun did not chase away the chill that seemed to seep into his very bones as he stared at the solid stone structure before him. Grim, dark, and dank were words that rose to his mind to describe it, and he was conscious of a strong desire to have this meeting over with in the shortest possible time. To his relief, he discovered that there was nothing to prevent him from seeing Ben—visitors seemed to come and go at will, with very little done to prevent the criminals outside of prison from mingling with those held in Newgate. Having left a wide-eyed, nervous Matt with his curricle and horses, Royce was briefly scrutinized by a turnkey at the lodge, who immediately recognized him as being a wealthy member of the upper classes, and thereby did not subject him to the humiliation of a strip search, which sometimes happened if it was suspected the visitor was attempting to smuggle in a means of escape for a prisoner.

Since Ben had not yet stood trial for his offense, he was being held in the chapel-yard, and the turnkey, a hulking, sour-faced individual who had not been in close proximity to water or soap in quite some time, was on the point of showing Royce there when Royce stopped him by saying, "Is there any place for my friend and I to talk privately?"

"For a price," the man said slyly. "For a price, you can have anything you want."

Without further words, Royce passed him a coin, and a few moments later, he was shown to a small, bare cubicle. The turnkey disappeared, and in a mercifully short time, Ben walked listlessly into the room, his head bent, the irons on his wrists clanking unpleasantly, his entire presence revealing bleak despair and utter defeat.

Ben looked very young . . . and very scared, but the sight of Royce's tall, powerful form transformed him, and an eager light suddenly gleamed in the blue eyes. "Thank God it is *you* and not the one-eyed man! I was afraid that he had gotten Jacko, too—that Jacko might even be dead."

Ben's words were spoken in a low voice, both he and Royce extremely conscious of the turnkey who lurked just outside the opened doorway. Royce motioned Ben to come farther into the room, and they positioned themselves as far away from the door as they could; the entire conversation was conducted in tones barely above a whisper, with the occasional wary eye cast over their shoulders in the turnkey's direction.

"No, your brother is fine and safely at Lime Tree Cottage with your sister—and if all goes well, you shall join them shortly," Royce murmured lightly. "I shall be seeing a magistrate after I leave you here today, and I hope that we shall effect a speedy release for you."

They spoke softly for several minutes, Royce relating all that had happened and questioning Ben's side of things. Basically Ben repeated the same tale that Jacko had told, able to add little to what Royce already knew. Ben seemed well enough, but there was an ugly bruise on his forehead, and it was obvious that he was frightened. "Do you really think that you can get me released?" Ben asked.

Royce smiled encouragingly. "Never doubt it, my young friend! If I have to come back and dismantle this prison stone by stone, I shall have you free! But until that time, what can I do to make your stay here more bearable?"

Ben hesitated, frowning in thought. "It's going to cost you," he said slowly. "But if you are willing to spend the blunt, I could be transferred to the state side, where the quarters are less crowded and generally there is a better class of criminal kept there—provided they can pay."

"Somehow that doesn't surprise me," Royce said dryly. "And I suppose I should also make some arrangements to have food, bedding, and clothing supplied to you while you remain here?"

A little of his spirit returning, Ben flashed him a brief grin. "Appreciate it if you would, guvnor! The food, what there is of it, is bloody awful, and as far as a bed or bedding . . ." Ben snorted. "That's something to be dreamed about!"

Smiling slightly, Royce murmured, "Very well, then. I shall see to it." His smile fading, he bent a somber look upon Ben. "I think that we can assume that the one-eyed man now knows of your association with me, if he didn't know it already—Jacko's precipitous rush to Lime Tree Cottage has most certainly alerted him, and my sudden return to town and visit to you will have confirmed the fact that you are no longer loyal to him. You are in a very dangerous position, Ben. I can only do so much to protect you while you remain within these walls—and I cannot guarantee how soon I can have you free. I can have you transferred as you suggested, and I can have several luxuries supplied to you, but you will have to watch your back and be on the lookout for the one-eyed man to try to strike at you here."

Ben nodded his head. "I know that—but I think if he wanted me dead, you wouldn't be talking to me right now! I think he merely wanted me, maybe Jacko, too, confined in a place where we couldn't get out." His eyes meeting Royce's, he muttered unhappily, "I think he knew that Jacko and me were sailing tomorrow and I think this is his way of making sure that we don't!"

"I wouldn't be at all surprised if you aren't right," Royce agreed grimly. "By having you in Newgate, he has certainly put paid to *that* little plan!"

They spoke quietly for a few moments longer, Royce reassuring Ben that all that could be done, would be done, to get him free. Forcing a cheerful smile on his handsome face, Royce finally said, "Don't be alarmed if events do not move as swiftly as we want them to, and don't become anxious if you do not see me for a few days. I shall try to keep you abreast of what is happening, and if I cannot come to see you, I will send someone else." He frowned. "But I think we should have some sign to let you know that the person or note really is from me. . . ." As he looked at the gold signet ring on his finger, his face instantly cleared, and after a quick glance at the doorway to make certain the turnkey was not watching them, he showed it to Ben, commanding softly, "Look at this ring carefully; it has my initials in the center, and the person who comes from me will show you this ring. Any note from me will be sealed by the stamp of this ring—otherwise, assume that it is a trap!"

The turnkey, his expression even more sullen and surly than when Royce had first seen him, appeared instantly when Royce called for him. Ordering Royce to remain in the cubicle while he returned Ben to the chapel-yard, the turnkey disappeared with Ben, leaving Royce to restlessly pace until the turnkey returned. Satisfied with his meeting with Ben, before leaving Newgate, Royce saw the governor of the prison and made the necessary arrangements to have Ben moved. He also paid what seemed like an exorbitant garnish to insure that Ben was given clean clothing, bedding, and decent food.

It was with a hearty sigh of relief that he and Matt quickly drove away from the depressing sight of the infamous New- gate. Frowning blackly, Royce slowly drove his horses toward George's rooms, chastising himself yet again for not having adequately protected Morgana and her brothers from the one- eyed man from the very beginning. His face resembled a thundercloud by the time he drew up his horses in front of George's rooms.

George took one look at his expression and asked fearfully, "Never tell me that you could not see the boy?"

Royce shook his tawny head. "I saw Ben with no difficulty at all—I was just angry at my own stupidity in not sending the woman away the moment I learned about the one-eyed man and his foul plans for her."

His blue eyes very innocent, George asked slyly, "Were his plans so very different than yours for her?"

"Dammit, there's no comparison!" Royce said explosively. "I had no intention of *forcing* the woman—nor did I intend to put her on the streets to whore!" Yet even as he said the words, with a sinking feeling in his gut, Royce realized that there really wasn't a great deal of difference between his ac- tions and what the one-eyed man had planned for Morgana. She had been a virgin until that day in his study, and now, by the very act of making her his mistress, he had put her on the same path that the one-eyed man intended for her. Angry with himself all over again, Royce growled, "Oh, have done with it! You're right, of course. I think I must have gone a little mad these past weeks." His face grim, he added, "But I have every intention of setting things right just as soon as I can! And seeing your magistrate will be the first step in that direction. Shall we leave?"

Upon their arrival, they had been shown immediately by an ever-so-correct butler into the liberally stocked library of the magistrate's elegant home just off Berkeley Square. The man they had come to see, Mr. Blackwell, had been a well-known barrister within polite society before he had become a magistrate, and he looked every bit the representative of the King's justice, being a tall man with a leonine head full of silvery hair, and brilliant hazel eyes which were filled with a keen intelligence.

Royce had been a bit wary—with George, one never quite knew what to expect—and he was relieved to discover that Mr. Blackwell seemed to be exactly the sort of man he needed.

Succinctly Royce explained the situation, leaving out everything that he thought irrelevant, concentrating just on the event that had put Ben in Newgate, making no mention of the one-eyed man or of Ben's other siblings. Mr. Blackwell listened gravely, nodding his handsome head now and then. When Royce had finished speaking, he said slowly, "Between your arrival here this afternoon and my receipt of the note that George had sent to me this morning, I took the liberty of doing some checking on Ben Fowler." Bending a particularly severe look at Royce, he asked heavily, "Are you aware that Fowler has two brothers and that all three of them are closely associated with one of the most dangerous master criminals London has ever known? They are part of a vicious gang run by an individual known only as the 'one-eyed man.' Did you know that Bow Street has long been aware of this connection and of the many unlawful activities of your young friend and his siblings?"

Royce kept his face perfectly blank, although he deliberately allowed a faint expression of shock to cross it before he said, "No, I wasn't. I assumed that Ben sailed rather close to the wind, but I had no idea he was as steeped in crime as you indicate." Leaning forward in his chair, his eyes fixed intently on Blackwell's, Royce said persuasively, "But despite all that, the young man has many good qualities, and I believe that if I can remove him from this criminal environment, get him a new start in America, he will do very well. He is an intelligent youth, a clever youth, quick to learn and not *un*educated. I would very much like to help him. I have the means to do so and would be willing to expend whatever is necessary to free him. Will you help me?"

There was a long, thoughtful silence as Blackwell stared consideringly at Royce. Looking down at some papers on the desk in front of him, he asked almost idly, "Do you know the gentleman that he attempted to rob? A Mr. Martin Wetherly, I believe."

"Wetherly!" George said with shocked surprise, entering the conversation for the first time. "It was Wetherly the little whelp was trying to rob?"

Hiding his own shock at the identity of the man, Royce was inordinately grateful for George's timely interruption, since it momentarily focused Blackwell's attention on his cousin. His mind racing, Royce only half listened to Blackwell's reply to George's question, but when the magistrate turned back to him, he left off his wild speculations and admitted readily, "Yes, I am acquainted with Mr. Wetherly. But I do not see what bearing that has on the situation. . . ."

"Perhaps none," Blackwell replied easily. "I was merely wondering if you knew him, and if you did, do you think you could convince him to drop his complaint against Ben Fowler?"

Confident that it was no coincidence that Ben and Jacko had been sent to rob Wetherly and that Wetherly was somehow connected with the one-eyed man, Royce shook his head decisively. "No. I don't think that, under *any* circumstances Wetherly could be made to drop his complaint. Is that the only way that Ben can be set free? If there is any other way that I can gain his release, I swear to you that he will leave the country immediately! Wouldn't that be satisfactory? . . .That and a generous donation to whatever charity you think appropriate?"

It was a delicate moment, and there was another long, pregnant pause before Blackwell finally nodded slowly and murmured, "I think that we can arrange his release . . .

especially since you are willing to vouch for the young man and intend to wean him from his deplorable ways." Giving Royce a hard look, he said bluntly, "After I have secured his release, I will indeed want him *immediately* escorted to a ship by a pair of Bow Street runners, who will remain on the docks until the ship actually sails and can confirm that he did leave the country."

"The ship is due to sail tomorrow morning," Royce told him, meeting the eaglelike gaze.

Mr. Blackwell shook his head. "Unfortunately, that is too soon. Even though this is all highly irregular, there are still proper channels that must be followed, and I am afraid that it will be at least a week, if not two, before your young friend can be freed." When Royce would have objected, he held up a warning finger and said crisply, "And even when I have secured his release, he remains in Newgate until he is escorted to the ship. I would suggest that you see a shipping agent tomorrow and see what vessels are sailing for America at the beginning of August. Get his passage secured on the first ship sailing around that date and I shall do the rest."

Royce considered arguing with the man, desperately hoping that there was still some way that he could get at least Ben on the ship sailing tomorrow, but the granite expression on Mr. Blackwell's face made him realize that further discussion was useless. Grateful that *some* progress had been made and that he could tell Morgana and Jacko that Ben would be free, although not as speedily as they had hoped, Royce smiled charmingly and graciously expressed his profound thanks for Mr. Blackwell's intercession.

After leaving Blackwell's house, Royce declined George's invitation to join him in a visit to White's, and yawning hugely, he murmured, "What I'd like to do is sleep for several hours—you forget that I have been up and about since before dawn this morning, and it is already nearly five o'clock in the afternoon."

A place to sleep presented a slight problem—the house on

Hanover Square had been closed up and the linens stripped, and Royce was considering staying at an inn when George spoke up, saying thoughtfully, "Sleep at my place. Have an extra room with a bed."

It was nearly eight o'clock in the evening by the time he sank blissfully into the softness of the feather bed mattress in George's spare room, and he was sleepily aware of one vital thing missing that would have made the prospect of the next several hours spent in bed even more appealing . . . Morgana in his arms. It was his last conscious thought for some time as sleep caught and held him deeply in its toils.

He had assumed that he would probably sleep the entire night away, but after only five or six hours of rest, he woke, his mind instantly filled with the problems that faced him. Fragments of thoughts about Morgana, Wetherly, the one-eyed man, and Ben all swirled through his brain, and realizing that further sleep was impossible for now, he put his arms behind his head and lay there thinking about the best way to keep Morgana safe. The best way, he decided grimly, would be to get her out of England, but now, with Ben in Newgate, that particular option was no longer available to them. He had suggested it to her last night and she had adamantly refused! Lime Tree Cottage could only provide so much protection, and he was beginning to fear that nothing less than a contingent of heavily armed guards would stop the one-eyed man from getting his hands on Morgana. And the more people I introduce to the household, he concluded grimly, the more likely it is that one or several will be placed there by the one-eyed man.

So how do I protect her? he wondered. She won't leave England without her brother, so until then, how am I to keep her safe? Lock her in a nunnery? A faint smile crossed his face. Hardly. Appeal to the Earl to put her under his protection as his bastard daughter? Would that halt the one-eyed man? Royce didn't think so, and he was conscious of a disagreeable chill sliding down his spine at the idea of

Morgana being placed in the care of the Earl. Might as well give her to the one-eyed man!

So. Beyond doing what he had, until Ben was free and the three Fowlers were on a ship sailing for America, how could he *insure* Morgana's safety? The one-eyed man had power, but there were places where his power did not extend. . . . If she will not leave England; if a nunnery is out; if armed guards are not practical and the one-eyed man is as determined to possess her as it seems he is . . . how can I put her in a position where the one-eyed man *dare* not touch her?

The answer, when it came to him, hit him like a lightning bolt, and with a half-cynical, half-wry smile, he admitted that it was the perfect solution—he would get precisely what he wanted, and Morgana *should* be safe from the one-eyed man! Respectability provided its own impenetrable barrier against the likes of the one-eyed man!

Easy within himself, a sense of rightness seeping through his big body, Royce gradually let himself be lulled to sleep again. Thank God, he thought drowsily in those last waking seconds, George knows a bishop!

CHAPTER 24

Royce had hit upon the solution to his most immediate problem, and coincidentally, so had the Earl of St. Audries. But while, in London, Royce fell back to sleep, sleep was the last thing on Stephen Devlin's mind! Nearly floating with euphoria at his own clevernesses, he excitedly paced the elegant confines of his room in Martin Wetherly's home near Tunbridge Wells, a pleased smile on his handsome features.

Stephen was not alone; Lucinda sat tensely in a blue velvet Hepplewhite chair and watched her husband's movements with a slight frown. "But are you sure that it will work?" she demanded for perhaps the tenth time since she had entered his room over an hour ago.

Stephen threw her an impatient look. "Of course it will work! All I need now is to see that she swallows it and all our troubles will be over, my dear."

It was an odd hour for them to be meeting, but the day had been a busy one, with several new guests arriving in the afternoon, and in the evening, Wetherly had arranged a dinner party, inviting several local people to swell the ranks of the guests already staying at his home. It was only after everyone had retired that Lucinda, following Stephen's whispered command, had been able to leave her room, just across the hall from his, and meet with her husband.

Lucinda's frown increased. "But how will you do that? *You* can't simply walk into the house and hand it to her!"

"Of course not!" Stephen said indignantly. Smiling smugly, he added, "I made it a point to chat up one of the new kitchen maids at Lime Tree Cottage this afternoon—told her a most affecting story."

"Stephen, you bloody *fool!* Don't you realize that when the chit dies, there are going to be questions asked? How do you know that you can trust whoever supplied you with the poison to keep their mouth shut? And how can you be sure your little kitchen maid won't realize precisely who you are?"

Looking highly affronted, Stephen demanded angrily, "Do you take me for an utter idiot? I secured the poison—and *very* discreetly, I might add—in London, before we even came down here. Do you really think that the local authorities are going to trace a poison bought by a mysterious stranger several days ago from an, ah . . . accommodating physician in London to the sudden death of a little doxy in Tunbridge Wells?" Not expecting an answer, he sent her a scathing glance before continuing harshly, "As for the kitchen maid, I didn't just drive up to her and introduce myself! I took the precaution of wearing a disguise—a very handsome pair of mustaches and a rather dapper beard which I obtained from a theatrical company in London. In *disguise,* I rented a gig and a horse from one of the local stables in order to dazzle my innocent little dupe!"

Lucinda was impressed in spite of herself; her frown vanished and she regarded him more favorably. "At least this sounds far more sensible than your ridiculous attempt to break into Manchester's London house and stab her in her sleep. Do you think your amateurish effort was noticed?"

A spot of red burned high on each cheekbone as he said coldly, "It doesn't matter! This idea will work!"

Reluctantly she admitted, "You've obviously thought it all out and planned well."

"Naturally!" he retorted sharply. "I don't intend to hang! I've been very clever in my activities, and I doubt that there is anyone who can connect the Earl of St. Audries with anything that I have done so far."

"But getting the poison to her . . . How will you do that?" Lucinda asked worriedly.

Stephen smiled. "The little kitchen maid, of course! I told her the most affecting tale this afternoon, swearing her to silence." Contemptuously he said, "She is a simple creature who believed every silly word that fell from my lips. I told her that Manchester had wickedly stolen Morgana away from me, that he had cast a spell over my beloved and that he was cruelly keeping us apart, plying Morgana with evil drugs so that she did not remember me and had eyes only for him!"

Lucinda looked incredulous. "And she actually believed this Canterbury tale of yours?"

"Lapped it up like a cat at a cream bowl!" Stephen said

with a pleased chuckle. "I *told* you—she is nothing but a thick-witted country simpleton! I could have told her I was Father Christmas and she would have believed me! I have her thoroughly convinced that behind Manchester's handsome face and charm lies a villain with an evil heart! She thought my story the most touching." He laughed. "Do you know the stupid cow actually cried when I told her of my anguish when Manchester cruelly tore Morgana away from me and would not let me see her?"

Since Lucinda had no very high regard for those of a lesser degree than herself, she found it easy to believe Stephen's words, but she still wasn't totally convinced that Stephen's plan would work. "Well, you may have told her a most convincing and affecting tale, but how does that get the poison to Morgana?"

He smiled. "I am meeting Clara—that's our simple-minded dupe's name—tomorrow . . . to give her a 'love potion' to administer to my beloved. A love potion that will instantly counteract the evil poisons that Manchester has fed my darling and will allow her to remember me and the love we share. Clever, don't you think?"

On the surface, Lucinda could find no fault with his plan. Her paramount concern, however, was that their part in it, hers particularly, remain undetected no matter what the outcome, and she questioned sharply, "You're positive that no one can connect you to the deed?"

"How can they? Once Morgana is dead, they will be searching for the mythical stranger who accosted Clara—not the Earl of St. Audries! Believe me, I have covered my tracks well!"

Slowly Lucinda nodded. "You *have* been rather clever about it. I'll just be glad when it is over and done with—as it should have been years ago! I still can hardly credit that she is alive!"

His face dark and grim, Stephen said viciously, "Rest easy,

my dear, in the certain knowledge that by this time tomorrow, Morgana Devlin *will* be dead!"

Rather pleased overall by Stephen's plan, Lucinda left shortly and crossed the wide hall to her own room. The room was in darkness except for the small pool of light coming from a candle that she had left burning near the bed when she had gone to see her husband. Her thoughts were still on the recent conversation with Stephen, and so it was that as she walked to her bed and tossed aside the silk robe she had donned over her nightgown, she didn't notice the sinister outline of the man hidden in the shadows.

Oblivious to anything but her own musings, she blew out the candle and got into bed. A catlike smile on her face, she lay there a moment savoring the knowledge that soon, a deed that they had thought safely accomplished long ago would in fact be done. And *my* child will be the lord of St. Audries Hall, with *no one* to gainsay him! Hester's brat will finally be dead and done with!

She was so lost in her own thoughts that she wasn't aware of the man's stealthy approach to the bed until it was too late. Her first indication that she was not alone was the feel of his hand clamping down brutally across her mouth and his voice in her ear whispering threateningly, "One sound. One little sound, my sweet, and it will be the last one you ever make."

The scream died in her throat, and with wide, frightened eyes she peered fearfully through the darkness, her heart thumping madly in her breast. Dear God! What did he want? Who was he?

She didn't have long to wait for answers. There was a slight movement and then suddenly the candle flared into light, and to her horror, she found herself staring up into the face of the one-eyed man!

He enjoyed her shock and fright, noting with pleasure the way her eyes dilated in sheer terror when she recognized him. Smiling faintly, he nodded his head, his face half-shielded by the low brim of his slouch hat. "Yes, my dear, after all these years, it is I."

There was a soft, strangled croak from her, and he smiled even more widely. "Now, let me see, didn't I ask you not to do something?" His other hand closing menacingly around her slim throat, he purred, "Didn't I warn you not to make a sound?"

The powerful fingers tightened and Lucinda blanched, nodding her head in desperate haste. Merciful heavens! He was going to kill her!

As if reading her thoughts, he shook his head and said softly, "No, my dear, I have no intention of killing you. I'm going to let you speak, but don't even let the idea of screaming cross your mind, hmmm? Because if it does . . ."

The threat was unspoken, but Lucinda was aware that it was very real nonetheless, and she breathed only slightly more easily when the brutal pressure of his hand was removed from her mouth. With terror-filled eyes, she stared at his half-hidden dark, intimidating features, wishing frantically that she were a thousand miles away and that she had never, *ever* sought his particular help. . . .

She swallowed painfully and asked huskily, "What do you want? I-I-I didn't s-s-send for you."

An unpleasant smile curved his lips. "The days when you and your likes send for me are nearly over, my dear. I'm not here at your bidding this time; this time I have business of my own. Suppose you tell me precisely what it was that your charming husband needed to discuss with you at this hour of the night."

Startled, she looked at him, her mouth half-open. "How did . . . how did you know?"

"There are not many things that escape me—especially not things concerning the handsome Earl of St. Audries and his beautiful Countess. After all, we go back such a *long* way, don't we?"

"Do you really want to know what I was doing in my husband's room at this time of night? Surely you can guess?" She stretched languidly, like a woman whose body has been well loved.

His one eye fixed appreciatively on her voluptuous curves clearly defined under the light blanket that lay across her, he gave a low bark of sneering laughter. "Never tell me you were in the Earl's bed?"

"Why not? Is it so very hard to believe?"

With a careless flick of the wrist, he flipped aside the blanket and took a long, humiliatingly thorough survey of her body, the finely spun silk of her nightgown nearly transparent and hiding nothing from his scrutiny. When he was finished, his eye wandered up to her lovely face and he shrugged. "It wouldn't be if I didn't happen to know that he hasn't shared your bed since he made the distasteful discovery that he had married his brother's leavings."

Her hand flew with the speed of a striking snake, but his was faster and his fingers tightened brutally around her slender wrist as he said cruelly, "Did you think I didn't know?" He laughed cynically. "You forget Stephen's association with me goes back even further than ours, sweet, sweet Lucinda. He was very bitter about the trick you played upon him—I think he really did love you in the beginning, and he was quite shattered when he discovered that there had been an extremely compelling reason for you to give off your pursuit of Andrew and finally accept his proposal of marriage."

"I don't know what you're talking about!" Lucinda snapped, her lovely eyes glittering angrily.

He only smiled. "Oh, yes, you do, my sweet! And you might have gotten away with it if it hadn't been for the unfortunate fact that when he was eighteen, your dear husband came down with a particularly virulent case of a childish complaint—mumps!" He ignored her half-frightened, half-furious gasp. "Did you know he nearly died of them? He hours of calmly and concisely explaining his reasoning and making it clear that he was not going to change his mind, he wore George down. It was apparent that George was of the mind that his cousin was half-mad! It was as plain as the nose on your face that Royce was blithely determined to commit social suicide and that he would eventually come to bitterly regret this rash act and perhaps even blame *him* someday. But even though George was unhappy with the situation, he helped Royce obtain the special license, albeit reluctantly.

It was late afternoon when they returned to George's rooms, the special license resting snugly in Royce's pocket. Letting George down from the gig, Royce then departed immediately for the shipping office where he had first obtained passage for Jacko and Ben.

On his way to the shipping office, Royce came to another important conclusion—there was no *real* reason for him to remain in England. He had come to London in search of an antidote for the vague restlessness and boredom that had plagued him of late and with the half-formed intention of seeking a bride—he had, to his dismay and profound astonishment, found both in the small, slender shape of Morgana Fowler! He smiled faintly. From the instant Morgana had pitchforked into his life, he could readily attest to having not suffered a moment of boredom—quite the opposite in fact! By this time tomorrow, he would have his bride, which had been his second reason for coming to England, and since he would feel a lot safer the farther away Morgana was from the arms of the one-eyed man, there was no logical reason why he shouldn't arrange passage back to America for all of them. Marrying her was certainly going to give the one-eyed man pause, but putting an ocean between Morgana and the one-eyed man seemed even wiser! Which, he admitted with a wry grimace, is what I should have done in the beginning, if my brain hadn't been so addled!

His mind made up, after conferring with the shipping agent, a Mr. Samuelson, and discovering that there was a ship which suited his needs sailing for New Orleans on August the fourth, he promptly purchased several passages.

Very pleased with his afternoon's accomplishments, Royce returned to George's rooms. Since Royce's business with Mr. Samuelson had not taken long, George was still there, having not yet departed for his usual haunts, and in spite of his earlier unhappiness with Royce's plans, he seemed quite glad to see him. Glad, that was, until Royce indicated that he would be leaving within the hour for Lime Tree Cottage. A crestfallen expression on his pleasant features, he stared despondently at Royce. "Thought you'd stay another night," he protested feebly. "Thought we might dine together and discuss, er, wedding plans."

Feeling sorry for his cousin's dilemma, Royce flashed him a disarming smile. Clapping him affectionately on the shoulder, Royce murmured lightly, "What you mean is you want more time in which to try to talk me out of it."

George had the grace to flush and mutter, "Honorable thing to do! What friends are for—help each other avoid mistakes!"

"Contrary to what you think, my friend, I am not making a mistake," Royce replied easily. An odd note in his voice, he admitted, "I really do want to marry her, and if I don't marry her, I doubt that I shall marry at all."

Incredulous, George regarded him. Misgiving evident in his voice, he said, "Think she's put a spell on you! Dangerous creatures, women! Avoid 'em myself!"

"Perhaps she has put a spell on me, but if she has, it is one that I am thoroughly enjoying. Come now, wipe that unhappy look from your face and tell me that you are going to accompany me back to Tunbridge Wells. I shall want a friendly face at my wedding tomorrow."

George was thoroughly rattled, but despite Royce's warm entreaties, his firm belief that Royce was making a disastrous mistake, one he could make without *him,* remained unchanged. Shaking his head decisively, he said, "Come down didn't, though, but the disease left him unable to father a child. . . . Now, isn't *that* interesting?"

"How do you know all this?" she demanded furiously, glaring at him like a cornered cat.

Having seated himself comfortably on the bed beside her, he laughed. "It wasn't all that hard to find out over twenty years ago—about the mumps, I mean. The other was only known by the physician and perhaps one or two others, but it was your handsome husband who explained it all to me. . . ."

Fear and rage contorted her beautiful face and she hissed, "You're lying! You're making this up! Why would Stephen tell *you?*"

He looked surprised. "Why should I lie? What would it gain me? But Stephen did tell me—it was at our very first meeting and he was rather drunk. He spent a great deal of time explaining to me why he wanted me to, er, take care of a problem for him . . . why it was so vital to him."

"I don't believe you! You can't prove it!" she said with furious desperation.

"Probably not . . . unless, of course, Stephen wanted to come forth and announce to the world that his son is really his dead brother's bastard!"

"Stop it! Stop it!" she cried. Fighting to control herself, she took a deep, shuddering breath, frantically thinking of some way to refute his words.

He watched her with interest, cynical amusement glittering in that one dark eye. It was such a pleasure to watch her squirm. To finally be able to extract a little bit of revenge for all those snubs and slights she and others like her had given him over the years. For a moment he gazed at the lush curves of her body, remembering nearly ten years ago when he had amorously pursued her, thinking to make her his mistress. His face hardened. She had refused him, making it brutally clear that while she enjoyed his company and the expensive trinkets he had bestowed upon her, she wasn't about to become the mistress of a mere nobody!

Rage against her and the others of her ilk, the titled members of the aristocracy, those haughty members who formed the exclusive inner circle of the ton, rose up to nearly choke him. Ah, yes, most of them were perfectly willing to enjoy his money and hospitality, content for the males to be closely associated with him, even condescending to invite him to their homes, but let his gaze stray to one of their daughters or sisters and he suddenly found doors slamming in his face! He might be wealthy, he might have learned the manners and style of a gentleman, but when it came to marriage, as far as the more powerful members of the ton were concerned, he was *still* the younger son of some obscure country squire and *not* quite good enough for them! An ugly expression on his face, he stared at Lucinda. Not even good enough to be the lover of one of the most notorious sluts in London!

The look on his face frightened her, and Lucinda asked fearfully, "What are you thinking? What are you going to do?"

Her words brought him back to the present. "But I told you, my dear—I'm extremely curious about what you were doing in your husband's rooms tonight."

"And I told you! Would you like for me to explain the act to you?"

For a long, thoughtful pause, he considered her. It was clear that she was going to stick to her story. She really needed to be taught a lesson. A smile lifted one corner of his mouth and he reached out to trail a finger suggestively between her breasts. "Why not? I might find it instructive."

Lucinda's breath caught sharply in her throat. "Don't!" she said thickly, trying not to show her fear.

Ignoring her, with a sudden, vicious movement, his fingers crushed the delicate material and he ripped open her gown to the waist, her full, rosy-tipped breasts spilling free. The dark eye glistened with pleasure at the sight of her lying there helpless before him, the charms that had been denied him now his for the taking. He sensed her fear and revulsion, and it excited him almost as much as the lush, inviting flesh before him. For too long he had been forced to let creatures like Lucinda and her husband treat him with disdain and arrogance; for too long, as the one-eyed man, he had merely been a tool paid to do their bidding, but that time was nearly over. . . . How often, he wondered idly, his fingers boldly caressing Lucinda's warm flesh, had he let these wealthy, well-born fools think that they had command over him as he had gently, inexorably, drawn them into his web, until, too late, they discovered that *they* were the ones being commanded?

Soon he would have no more need of the one-eyed man—and he wouldn't need to be careful around people like Lucinda any longer. She and her ilk had served his purpose, and he was free now to treat them as he wished. He had fortune enough, and once he married Morgana and she had taken her rightful place, he would have his longed-for position amongst the most powerful in the land—they would be forced to accept him into their ranks for his wife's sake. A black scowl crossed his features. Of course, Manchester had to be dealt with. . . .

A painful groan from Lucinda as his fingers tightened savagely around her breast brought him back from his wandering thoughts. She was frightened and he enjoyed that, and deliberately he tore the rest of her gown wide open, staring with lustful appreciation at her voluptuous charms. Though she stiffened with outrage and her eyes were full of fury, he didn't fear that she would cry out—she had too much to lose, and he knew he could do whatever he willed with her and she would keep her mouth shut. So many secrets, he thought smugly. So many secrets, and I know them all!

Seeking to extract the greatest amount of pleasure from this confrontation, he intentionally baited her. "Tell me," he asked in a purring tone, "does Stephen know the part you played in the death of his beloved Hester? I know that when she first fell ill, you and he had already decided that if she were to die, I was to get rid of the child, but did he know that you made *certain* she died? Let me see . . . wasn't it arsenic that I arranged for you to have? Arsenic that you so assiduously plied sweet Hester with all the weeks and months before she gave birth! My, but you must have been furious when she simply wouldn't die!" He smiled unkindly at her. "You really should have increased the dosage sooner, my dear, then she never would have lived long enough to give birth, but I expect you were too frightened of being found out to finish the deed before then."

Her body naked to his gaze and touch, Lucinda had never been so vulnerable in her life. It was terrorizing enough that she had lived for nearly twenty years with the knowledge that he could expose her, albeit not without implicating himself . . . but he was a criminal able to lose himself amongst the slums and dregs of London, while she . . . she was the Countess of St. Audries. None knew better than she how easy it would be to drop a word here, a whisper there, and even if it could not be proven, she would be ruined, shunned and ostracized by everyone who knew her.

And Stephen, she thought with a shiver, Stephen would murder her if he ever guessed or even suspected that Hester's death had not been from natural causes. He had adored that mewling little bitch, and Lucinda never doubted that if Hester had lived, Stephen would have wasted little time in putting himself in the position of being able to marry his brother's widow! Whether he would have divorced her or seen the one-eyed man about ridding him of a wife he detested, Lucinda had never been able to decide, but over the years she had gleefully hugged to herself the sweet knowledge that it was *Hester* who lay in the grave and *she* who was the Countess of St. Audries and that it was *her* child who would inherit St. Audries Hall and its broad acres!

All her schemes had been for that one goal, and frightened though she was, she wasn't about to let this one-eyed piece of offal destroy everything.

Her lovely hazel eyes full of hatred, she spat, "You can prove nothing! And if memory serves me correctly, Hester died of a hemorrhage!"

He nodded his head amiably in agreement. "Probably. But it was the poison that *you* gave her over the months that wore her down, that wasted her flesh and put her in such a weakened condition that she could not recover." Since he no longer cared what Lucinda knew, he added slyly, "It's a wonder the child survived. . . ."

All the frightened fury she had experienced upon learning that Hester's child still lived, that she and Stephen had paid this wretched creature a fortune over the years to dispose of Morgana and that he had cheated them, suddenly exploded through her. Heedless of her nakedness, forgetful of the power he held over her, Lucinda surged up from the bed, her hands curved in claws as she struck for his face. "You *bastard!*" she snarled. "You *lied* to us when you said you had taken care of her! You lied! You lied! You *lied!*"

She was nearly hysterical with rage, but even though she had moved swiftly, he was swifter and easily captured her flailing arms. Effortlessly quelling her wild struggles, he asked sharply, "And how did you know that?"

Realizing she could not beat him, she stopped fighting and said sullenly, "I saw her once in London! She is Manchester's latest mistress!"

Lucinda didn't know it, but her words had given the one-eyed man a definite shock. He had only been taunting Lucinda with mention of the child and he had not admitted that Morgana was still alive, but it appeared that the Devlins had been a jump ahead of him this time—not only did they know, along with half of London, about Manchester's new mistress, but they knew it was *Morgana!* And if they knew it, how many others had seen her and guessed something of the truth? It would be natural for everyone to suppose at first that she was Stephen's byblow . . . until someone remembered that Stephen had been out of the country for nearly two years prior to Morgana's birth. The gossips would then name Andrew as her father, and there would be a great deal of idle and malicious speculation about the future of this presumed illegitimate daughter of the dead Earl . . . until some old cat realized that Morgana was exactly the same age as the Earl's heir would have been had she lived. . . . He bit back a curse. Fool that he was, he had told Jane Morgana's actual date of birth, and it wouldn't take much checking for anyone to discover that it was precisely the same as the little heiress's who had died at birth. Their given names were the same too. . . .

Nothing could be proved, of course, he reassured himself uneasily, but he wanted Morgana in his power and at his side as his wife before the storm of curiosity about her raged through polite society. As Morgana's husband, *he* would be the one to reveal the truth!

Suddenly losing interest in tormenting Lucinda any longer, the one-eyed man released her abruptly and stood up. He needed to think, to consider this new turn of events, but first there was Lucinda. . . .

He eyed her as she lay sullenly on the bed. He had to silence her before he could safely leave the room, not because he feared she would call out the alarm, but because he didn't trust her not to try to spy on him and see where he went. Softly he said, "I'm afraid, my dear, that I really must treat you in a most ungentlemanly way."

Wondering angrily what new sort of torture he had decided upon, she turned to stare at him resentfully. He was smiling at her, which made her extremely uneasy, and she was on the point of demanding what he intended to do when he struck her a brutally powerful blow on her chin and blackness thundered down around her.

After making certain that she was truly unconscious, the one-eyed man blew out the candle and, in the darkness, slipped from her room. Ever watchful, he swiftly hurried down the hall to the suite of rooms that had been assigned to him.

Moments later, he was safely in his own rooms, the one-eyed man's disguise dispensed with and carefully hidden in his valise. Garbed now in an elegant dark blue dressing gown, he relaxed in a high-backed chair of russet leather, enjoying a snifter of brandy from the tray of refreshments Wetherly had ordered placed in all his guests' rooms.

He took another sip of his brandy and turned his mind to tonight's events. So Stephen and Lucinda knew that Morgana was alive and was Manchester's mistress. . . .

His face twisted with fury and he swallowed the remainder of his brandy in one huge gulp. *Manchester!* I should have killed him weeks ago, he admitted with impotent rage. That or have stormed the house and forcibly removed Morgana and *damn* the public outcry that would have resulted from such a violent act taking place in the very bosom of the ton!

Even now he could hardly contain the bitter rage that filled him whenever he thought of Morgana lying in Manchester's arms . . . whenever he thought of her lost virginity . . . virginity that was to have been his! How many nights had he lain awake visualizing the moment when he would finally make Morgana his, when she would finally realize that he was her fate, that she would belong to no one but *him!*

But all *that* has changed, he thought viciously. There was nothing that he could do about his failed attempt in London to kill the American, nor could he change the fact that Morgana was no longer a virgin and that when she came to his bed, it would be with the memory of Manchester's kisses upon her lips!

With an oath, he violently threw his snifter against the wall, uncaring when it shattered, uncaring if anyone heard the noise. He was going to kill Manchester, and take great delight in doing so, and then he was going to erase virtually every vestige of the memory of the American from Morgana's mind. It would be only *his* kisses she remembered, only *his* lovemaking that she hungered for, and this time spent with Manchester would be utterly wiped from her memory!

But first, he thought with a sudden, sobering return to cold sanity, first there was Jacko and Ben, who badly needed to be taught a lesson, and Newgate was only the start of it. And then, he mused slowly, an ugly smile on his mouth, and then there is the lovely Countess and her charming husband. . . .

CHAPTER 25

The one-eyed man was not at *all* pleased with the current state of affairs. Lucinda and Stephen should never have learned that Morgana was still alive . . . not until he had decided that the time was right for them to learn of that fascinating little snippet. He had anticipated for months the exquisite enjoyment he would take in taunting them with the news that she still lived.

Thoughtfully he stroked his chin, staring blankly at the rich ruby color of the carpet. It would appear, he concluded acidly, that the source of his current troubles, troubles such as he had not encountered in all his years of being the one-eyed man, could be laid squarely at the feet of that upstart American, Royce Manchester!

Until Manchester's appearance on the London scene, he'd

had events well in hand, and in the years since he had first donned the disguise of the original one-eyed man, he'd grown very used to feeling all-powerful. Until Manchester, he thought angrily, remembering the race when Manchester's horses had run Devlin's animals into the ground. *That,* he admitted viciously, had cost him a grand sum and had been the beginning of his present unhappiness.

Because of Morgana and his obsession with her, he had made many mistakes, mistakes that had proven costly and would prove even more costly if he wasn't careful and didn't start using that icily analytical brain of his instead of letting his emotions rule him.

The Earl and his wife were definitely a problem for him, now that they knew about Morgana. Originally a nuisance, the Devlins were now dangerous—they knew he had betrayed them, and they had nothing to lose and everything to gain by arranging Morgana's death!

He frowned as another problem occurred to him. Morgana's resemblance to the St. Audries was striking, and if Lucinda, with only one glimpse, had recognized her instantly, then as she was introduced to more and more members of society—which would happen, even if her introduction was only to certain *male* acquaintances of Manchester's—someone would be bound to realize that she had to be Andrew's daughter, and it wouldn't be long after that before the coincidence of names and birth dates would be discovered. He had slipped up rather badly in telling Jane of Morgana's real name and date of birth!

Springing up from his chair, he began to pace aimlessly around the room, his hands loosely clasped behind his back. At least I didn't slip up with young Ben, he thought with a malevolent smile. But his smile faded as he remembered that Jacko shouldn't have escaped his net—Jacko, as well as Ben, should have been currently residing in Newgate! And yet . . . and yet he wasn't so very sorry that Jacko had escaped—at least he knew without a doubt that Jane's brats were no longer loyal to him, that they had been working hand in glove with Manchester these past weeks.

Jacko may have eluded his net in London, but it had been easy enough to follow his panicked trail to Lime Tree Cottage, just as it had been easy enough to learn of Manchester's frantic dash to London and his meeting with Ben.

Originally, having the brothers thrown into Newgate had been planned only as a safeguard, merely a ploy to make certain that Morgana remained in England. With her brothers locked in prison, Morgana would never go off to America and he would then have had plenty of time to make plans of his own.

The unpleasant discovery that all this time, Jane's brats had been in Manchester's pocket had enraged him, but it had also explained a few things that had puzzled him of late. Their failure to effect Morgana's escape from Manchester, for one, and for another, the uneasy sensation he'd had recently that someone had been following him—knowing what he did now, he was positive that Jacko and Ben, no doubt at Manchester's orders, had been stalking him all over London with an eye to his death or capture.

Deceitful, ungrateful little bastards, he thought furiously, betraying me the moment my back was turned! Once I've taken care of Manchester, I'll teach those two a long overdue lesson! First, however, he concluded grimly, plans must be made to thwart any arrangements made by the Earl for Morgana's death! When that problem was solved, he'd not waste any more time removing Morgana from Manchester's hands! A thin smile crossed his mouth. Once Morgana is in my power, all of them—Manchester, Jane's brats, and the Devlins—will learn how unwise it was, how *very* unwise it was, to meddle in his affairs!

His brain busy with schemes and visions of the various methods of revenge he would employ against Manchester and the others, he finally sought out his bed. Devlin, he decided

on Wednesday—after you've done the deed!" He thought a moment, then added with paralyzing honesty, "Don't want the family blaming *me!*"

Royce laughed. "Very well. I shall look forward to your arrival then." A teasing gleam in his golden eyes, Royce said dulcetly, "My bride and I will be waiting eagerly to see you."

Looking very like he had just discovered a bug in his porridge, George eventually forced a smile and nodded his head. Royce took his leave and, with mounting excitement, urged his horses away from London and headed them in the direction of Tunbridge Wells.

Since he had gotten such a late start from the city, it was well after dark before he and Matt finally stopped the tired and sweat-flecked horses at the gateway guarded by the Bullard brothers. The oldest of the Bullard brothers, Harry, was at his post, and slowing his horses, Royce waited patiently until Harry realized that the visitor was his employer and then hurriedly unlocked and opened the stout iron gates.

His open countenance revealed by the light of the lantern he carried, Harry smiled widely and said easily, "Good evening, sir! Sorry for the delay in opening the gate—didn't expect you this late at night."

Royce made some polite reply and then asked, "Everything is well at the house? No strangers or troubles while I've been gone?"

Frowning slightly, Harry answered slowly, "It's been right quiet these past two days, but the thing is—John said you wanted to know about *any*thing that didn't seem normal— think you ought to know that one of the new housemaids, Clara is her name, if I remember rightly, came back from town this afternoon in a rig driven by a fellow of the type that don't usually take to little country misses, if you understand me?"

Royce stiffened and asked tautly, "A gentleman? Tall, handsome man with dark hair and gray eyes?"

"Can't tell you that—he let Clara down before they actually

got here, just down the lane a bit, and all I could see was that he wasn't dressed like a farmer or such and that he was heavily bearded."

"I see," Royce said slowly. "Thank you for the information— continue to keep your eyes and ears open."

Driving away, Royce felt his light mood vanish and he was aware of sudden, insistent urgency to see Morgana. The incident with the housemaid could be innocent, and just because the man had not appeared to be a local farmer didn't mean that his interest in Clara wasn't perfectly understandable. And yet . . . and yet Bullard's simple words filled Royce with an inexplicable sense of danger, and while he would have normally pushed away any such nonsensical ideas about premonition, he could not shake the increasingly unpleasant sensation that it was paramount that he see Morgana at once, that to delay could be fatal!

Suddenly frightened and not quite knowing why, he urged his tired horses into a dead run, the need to reach the house in the shortest possible time taking precedence over everything. In spite of their obvious exhaustion, his horses obeyed instantly, racing down the dark lane with long-legged strides, and moments later, they swept around the long, curving driveway in front of the house. Royce barely jerked them to a snorting, heaving stop before he was springing down from the gig and flinging the reins to Matt. Almost running up the path that led to the house, Royce shouted over his shoulder to Matt, "Treat them well! They deserve an extra ration of grain tonight!"

Driven by his irrational fear, he leaped up the steps and flung himself inside the house, only to be brought up short by the sheer normalcy of everything. A crystal chandelier cast the soft glow of candlelight over the wide entry hall, and Chambers had been just crossing it, a tray of liquor and glasses in his hands, when Royce made his hasty entrance. Startled at his master's abrupt entrance into the house, Chambers gave an exclamation of surprise and said, a trifle embarrassed, "Good heavens, sir! What a start you gave me, charging into the house that way!" Recovering himself, he bowed briefly and said politely, "I am just on my way to take the young gentlemen some refreshment in the billiard room, but after that, if you like, I shall have Cook prepare a tray of food for you." He coughed slightly and murmured, "Miss Fowler went up to her rooms not long ago. I saw one of the housemaids taking up her nightly drink of milk just a moment ago, so I expect that she had not yet retired for the night."

It was obvious that nothing untoward had occurred—the house seemed quiet and normal for this time of night—and suddenly feeling ridiculous for getting the wind up over such a silly thing as the fact that a man had given one of the housemaids a ride home, Royce shrugged ruefully. A charming smile on his mouth, he murmured, "Something to eat would be splendid—it is a long drive from London, and I did not want to waste time at any of the posting houses. I shall be in Miss Fowler's rooms, so you may serve me there when the food is ready. Oh, and send along a bottle of brandy, too, please."

Chambers nodded and was on the point of leaving when Zachary and Jacko came strolling out from the billiard room. Grinning, Zachary said, "Thought I heard your voice out here." Then, as he noticed that Royce was alone, the grin faded and he asked quickly, "What happened with Ben? He is not with you?"

Royce shook his head, only half listening to what Zachary was saying, his eyes riveted on the handsome young man standing beside Zachary. He knew the man garbed in the stylish dark blue jacket and buff breeches was Jacko, yet he was having trouble reconciling this very fashionable gentleman with Morgana's rather disreputable and grubby brother. From his attractively cropped chestnut hair and starched white cravat to his gleaming black Hessian boots, Jacko looked to be the very epitome of an English gentleman of leisure. He was a very handsome youth, his shoulders broad and square, and though only of average height, his body was lean and compact, while his very blue eyes were clear and direct, the nose nobly proportioned and his mouth surprisingly sensitive.

Reaching out his hand, Royce smiled and murmured, "And do I have the honor of addressing Mr. Jacko Fowler?"

Jacko grinned. "Aye, guvnor, you do! Bloody eyes! Who'd 'uv thought it when last we met?"

Royce laughed. "Well, I'm certainly pleased that you were able to find something suitable to wear. I must say that I am impressed with the changes!" Teasingly he added, "Dare I hope that Ben will clean up as well once we get him here?"

His grin gone, Jacko asked anxiously, "Did you see him? Will you be able to free him? Is he all right?"

Royce held up a hand placatingly, and glancing around and catching Chambers's avidly interested gaze, he turned back to Jacko and Zachary and murmured, "I want to see Morgana before she goes to sleep, but I will tell you this much—I saw Ben, and all will be well. I'll explain more in just a little while. Excuse me, if you will?"

Despite being obviously eaten alive with curiosity, both young men had to be content with what little information Royce had given them, and reluctantly they nodded and turned back to the billiard room. Royce, the special license suddenly burning against his breast, bounded up the stairs in search of Morgana.

He stopped at his own room just long enough to toss aside the caped driving coat he was wearing, and then, after a quick and, oddly enough, nervous glance at his reflection in the mirror, he quickly crossed the sitting room that separated their suites. Standing outside the entrance to Morgana's bedchamber, on the point of pushing open the door, he was conscious of the heightened beat of his heart and an inexplicable feeling that the entire course of his life was about to change. My God! he thought with a sickening lurch in the pit of his stomach. What if she refuses me? And something that should have been glaringly apparent to him before now exploded with vivid clarity through his mind. *I love her!* he admitted with astonishment. I'm not marrying her to protect her from the one-eyed man—I'm marrying her because I love her and want more than anything else in the world for her to be my wife!

It was a stunning discovery, and dazedly he shook his head, marveling at his own stupidity. No wonder he had suddenly lost interest in the widow Cresswell and young Julia Summerfield! Since the evening of the Mortimer ball, he had not given either woman a second thought—all his attention had been on the beguiling creature who had tried to pick his pocket! A soft smile curved his usually hard mouth, and he admitted wryly that at first, as Pip, with her saucy tongue and gamin grin, she had amused him; and then, as Morgana, whose soft body and sweet kisses inflamed him, she had utterly captivated him. There was no denying it—from the instant Morgana entered his life, she had fascinated him, and fool that he was, he had dismissed the powerful emotions she aroused so easily within him as mere lust! It wasn't as his mistress that he wanted her to grace his home, but as his wife!

He stood there silently for several seconds, trying to come to grips with the astounding knowledge that an emotion he had once scornfully dismissed as having no place in his life now had him firmly snared in its tenacious coil. And that it was a pocket-sized, saucy-tongued minx whose only claim to good breeding was the fact that she was the bastard daughter of a man he heartily disliked who had brought him to this pass was the most amazing part of it! Still shaking his head at his own folly, he pushed open the door and walked into Morgana's bedchamber.

She was not alone; the housemaid who had brought up her warm milk was still in the room. Royce vaguely recognized the young woman as one of the new servants they had hired from the area and then dismissed her from his mind, all his attention on Morgana.

The maid was standing in the opened doorway that led to the main hall and was obviously on the point of departure when he entered the room. Morgana, wearing a gauzy pale lavender robe over her demure white lawn nightgown, had her back to Royce, and she was busily pouring Ratter a saucer of milk from her glass.

A tender smile curving his mouth, Royce strolled a few steps farther into the room, admiring the enticing shape of Morgana's buttocks when she bent down to give Ratter the saucer of milk. It was only when the cat began to hungrily lap up the milk that she straightened, and turning around, she spied Royce halfway across the room from her.

A breathtakingly sweet smile lit her lovely features, and with something perilously close to a squeak, she sped over the distance that divided them and hurled her slender body into his waiting arms. "Oh, but I have missed you!" she exclaimed guilelessly, her arms wrapping tightly around his neck. "Even with Jacko and Zachary in the house, it was very lonely without you."

His blood racing, Royce stared down into her upturned features, the sheer force of his so-newly-discovered love momentarily robbing him of rational speech. His mouth brushing hers, his arms holding her crushed against him, he muttered, "Sweet! So very sweet!"

Oblivious to the maid gawking at them in the doorway, Royce kissed Morgana, the uninhibited eagerness of her response making her kiss everything a returning lover could have wished for, and Royce thoroughly enjoyed her ardent welcome. He kissed her for a long, long time, savoring the sweetness that was Morgana's alone, his heart nearly bursting with the love he felt for her. It was only when they breathlessly parted that they became aware of the maid staring at them. Royce's eyebrow lifted at the expression of horrified outrage on her young face, but before he could say anything, Morgana gently untangled herself from his embrace and said crisply, "Thank you, Clara, that will be all."

Clara took one last clearly disapproving look and then shut the door firmly behind her. The name made Royce frown, and pulling Morgana back into his arms, he asked, "What do you know about her? Has she given you any trouble?"

Morgana glanced at him in surprise. "Clara? No, she is actually very pleasant to me. I have no complaints about her at all. Why do you ask?"

"Mmm, no particular reason," he replied slowly, deciding that there was no reason to unduly alarm her—especially since there was probably nothing to be alarmed about! "Now, I believe that you were telling me, and very nicely too, how very much you missed me. . . ."

Morgana blushed, suddenly embarrassed at her shameless greeting to him, but Royce only laughed and kissed her again. Sitting down in a large, overstuffed chair, he pulled her onto his lap, and settling her comfortably in his arms, he nuzzled her ear and murmured, "I think if you give me a kiss or two, I might be able to remember why it was that I had to go to London."

Morgana's innocent joy in his return vanished, and feeling like the greatest beast in nature that she had forgotten even for a moment her brother's plight, she questioned fearfully, "Ben? You were not able to free him?"

Holding her closer to him, he dropped a kiss on her head and said cheerfully, "Not as soon as I would have liked, but don't worry, sweetheart; I've seen a magistrate, and he has assured me that he can arrange Ben's release—provided Ben goes directly from Newgate to a ship sailing for America! In the meantime, I've made arrangements to make his stay in prison as pleasant as possible."

They spoke for quite some time about Royce's trip to London and his visit to Ben, Royce telling her all he had done, but deliberately making no mention of the special license and his plan for all of them to sail to America. Curled confidingly against him, Morgana watched his face with huge, anxious eyes, listening intently to every detail. When he finished speaking, her usually vivid little face sad, she said dolefully, "I know sending Jacko and Ben to America is the wisest course, but oh, I shall miss them so very much—even if you have promised to take me to them when you leave England."

Royce took a deep breath and said carefully, "Well, that's something that I'd like to talk to you about, my dear. . . ."

Morgana was only half listening to him, her thoughts on the dreaded departure of her brothers, and listlessly she got up from his lap and wandered over to where her glass of milk reposed on a small rosewood table. Picking up the glass, she was on the point of drinking it when there was a harsh exclamation from Royce, and the next thing she knew, he was flying across the room and, in one frighteningly violent motion, knocked the glass from her hand. Astonished, she stared at his white, grim features and demanded half-angrily, half-worriedly, "What is it? Why did you act so?"

He didn't answer her, only grasped her arm fiercely and pointed. She gazed in the direction he indicated, and with dawning horror, she stared at Ratter, the cat's lifeless body frozen in the last act of an agonized writhe, the partially finished saucer of milk inches from his horribly contorted body. Milk that she had been about to drink . . .

CHAPTER 26

There was a tense silence as they stared in growing horror at the cat's still form, and then, with a sob, Morgana buried her head in Royce's chest. His face grim, he held her protectively next to him as he murmured soothingly in her ear, meaningless phrases that were, oddly enough, comforting.

Eventually her shock and fright lessened somewhat, and pulling slightly away from him, she gave one last watery hiccup; looking up into his set features, she asked disbelievingly, "Someone just tried to kill me, didn't they?"

Royce would have liked to deny her simple question, and for one instant he seriously considered trying to cloud the truth, to console her with empty words, but she deserved better than that, and if, as it appeared, someone was trying to kill her, she needed to be alert and watchful for danger. His arm tightened around her shoulders and bleakly he said, "It would appear so—and I would very much like to have a conversation with young Clara."

"Clara?" Morgana uttered dumbfoundedly. "Why would she want to kill me?" Her face clouded. "Why would anyone want to kill me?"

Royce had no answers for her. This unexpected attack on Morgana momentarily had him baffled. There were only two people who could have more than a passing interest in Morgana—the one-eyed man and the Earl of St. Audries. The one-eyed man was capable of anything, even cold-blooded murder, but Royce had difficulty believing that the one-eyed man, having failed to kidnap her, now wanted her dead. And the Earl? What possible reason could he have? Granted Devlin might find it distressingly repugnant to discover his bastard daughter had become the mistress of a man he had made abundantly clear he disliked intensely, but murder? It didn't make any sense! Someone, however, obviously wanted her dead! But who? And more important, why?

Settling Morgana gently in a chair, Royce mercifully covered Ratter's pitifully twisted body with a pillowcase he snatched off the bed, and then, walking to the bell rope, he gave it a peremptory yank. Glancing across at her, he said harshly, "The next few moments may be exceedingly unpleasant. Do you wish to remain here?"

She nodded, keeping her gaze averted from Ratter's body.

"You seriously believe that Clara knows something about what happened?" she asked quietly, incredulity apparent in her cat-shaped gray eyes.

"It seems a logical point to start. After all, she was the one who brought you the milk this evening, and Harry Bullard saw her dismount from a vehicle this afternoon driven by a stranger—a stranger who seemed to be taking pains *not* to be seen!" Royce would not tell her any more. Under the present circumstances, he certainly wasn't about to blurt out the fact that her father, the man who had callously abandoned her at birth, was lurking in the neighborhood and had been nosing around trying to elicit information about her! There was also no point in mentioning that Stephen Devlin was very high on his list of suspected poisoners—and he couldn't bring up one fact without the other!

Sooner or later she would have to know that the Earl of St. Audries was her father, but as she had just survived an ugly brush with death, Royce didn't feel that it was imperative she know that her father might have just tried to kill her! Let her concentrate on the stranger for the present, he thought reluctantly, but very soon, for her own safety, I *must* explain to her about Devlin.

Chambers answered his ring, a question in his blue eyes. "You rang, sir? Cook will have your tray ready in just a few moments."

Royce nodded. "I'm not worried about *that!*" he said roughly. "What I would like to know is everything that you can tell me about one of the local housemaids who was hired recently. Clara is her name, and she just brought up Miss Fowler's usual glass of warm milk."

Looking slightly flustered and just a little anxious, Chambers answered readily, "You must mean Clara Holbrook. Her family is a local one, farmers, I believe, and when I first inquired about additional servants, her name was mentioned to me by several people as an honest, hardworking young woman—and so she has proven to be. Has she done something wrong?"

"That remains to be seen," Royce replied austerely. "Have her sent up here, will you?"

Chambers left immediately, his features betraying little of the rampant curiosity that roiled in his breast. A few minutes later, there was a timid knock on the door, and at Royce's command, it opened and Clara Holbrook entered the room.

Clara was not a prepossessing young woman. Just twenty years old, she was not very tall and was inclined to plumpness; her hair, which was a mousy brown, was stuffed untidily under a white frilled cap, and her large, faintly vacant blue eyes were the best features in a plain, moon-shaped face. Casting an avid glance around the room, an expression of excitement mingled with apprehension flickering across her features, she gave a brief curtsy. Since Ratter's body was hidden from her, she saw nothing strange in the room and recited woodenly, "Chambers said that you wanted to see me, sir?"

"Yes, I did," Royce said neutrally. "I'd like you to tell me about the gentleman who was so very kind to give you a ride back to the cottage this afternoon."

The slightly vacuous expression that she habitually wore instantly vanished, and Clara paled noticeably. "I-I-I don't k-k-know what you m-m-mean, sir!" she stammered, nervously twisting the corner of her white apron.

"I think you do!" Royce stated bluntly. "And if you are wise, young woman, you will tell me immediately what I want to know—if you don't, I shall have no recourse but to send for the magistrate and have you detained for questioning in the attempted murder of Miss Fowler!"

"I never!" Clara burst out indignantly. "Why, I wouldn't hurt a hair on Miss Fowler's head!" Throwing Royce a hostile look, she muttered sullenly, "Which is more than can be said for some folk around here!"

Royce lifted one thick black brow and murmured sardonically, "I'm sure that you know what you mean by that comment, but before you regale us with what is sure to be a fascinating explanation, perhaps you would like to tell us how the milk you brought up for Miss Fowler this evening came to be poisoned!"

"You're daft!" she protested vehemently. "It wasn't no poison that I put into Miss Fowler's milk!"

"Ah, so you admit that you *did* put something into her milk tonight," Royce pounced immediately.

Clara glanced over at Morgana, who had been intently watching the swift exchange. Reassured by the encouraging smile that Morgana sent her way and feeling decidedly righteous, she answered boldly, "And what if I did?"

Royce contemplated her for a long moment, puzzled by her defiant air and the hostility with which she regarded him. Deciding that since she held him in such unaccountable antipathy, there was only one way to get to the bottom of this in a hurry, he commanded softly, "Come over here; I'd like to show you something."

Mistrust evident in her face, she cautiously approached him. As she came nearer to him, the pillowcase that covered Ratter's body came into her view for the first time. Perplexity obvious, she glanced from Royce to the patch of white on the floor.

"Go ahead," Royce said quietly. "Lift it up and look underneath."

Some of the tenseness that gripped the other two occupants transmitted itself to her, and after darting an uncertain look at each of them, she took a deep breath and swept aside the pillowcase. In horror she staggered backward, her gaze fixed on the cat's grotesquely positioned body, the half-finished saucer of milk inches from the lifeless form. It would have been apparent to someone far less astute than Clara what had transpired, and her eyes nearly started from her head at the ugly sight; she gulped noisily and then, promptly burying her face in her apron, burst into tears.

Morgana rushed from the chair and put her arms around Clara's plump shoulders. "Please don't cry," she begged gently. "Just tell us who gave you whatever it was you put into my milk this evening."

Royce twitched the pillowcase from Clara's nerveless fingers and once again covered Ratter's body. "We don't believe that you meant your mistress any harm . . . but someone did, and you can tell us who it was."

It took a great deal of coaxing, but in between fits and starts and bouts of profuse tears, seated next to Morgana on the sofa in the sitting room, to which they had adjourned, Clara managed eventually to tell her story. In growing amazement Royce and Morgana listened to the preposterous tale that Clara had been told.

"But, Clara, it is all *untrue!*" Morgana said fiercely. "Mr. Manchester has not drugged me!" A lovely flush staining her cheeks, she added passionately, "And you must believe me when I say that I have no other lover! Whoever this man is, he is *not* my lover and he has lied to you! *He* is the villain, not Mr. Manchester!"

Clara cast a nervous glance over at Royce where he sat in a chair across from them. His position and expression must have satisfied her, because looking back at Morgana, she said earnestly, "But don't you see, miss, if you were drugged, that's what you *would* say!"

"You're forgetting one thing, Clara," Royce interjected reasonably, despite having a strong urge to throttle the silly twit. "Whatever he gave you to put into her milk tonight, it wasn't something to counteract the drug I have supposedly been giving her, *it would have killed her!*" His face exceedingly grim, he concluded harshly, "If my arrival hadn't delayed her drinking the milk long enough for the poison to kill Ratter, there would have been two dead bodies lying on the floor in the other room, and one of them would have been the young lady who is sitting next to you!"

This induced another bout of noisy sobbing and tears from Clara. Morgana threw Royce a mitigating look, and Royce grimaced disgustedly. It took Morgana a while, but once again she had Clara soothed and willing to tell them what she knew. But even though they questioned her closely, there was precious little else to be learned. She didn't know the man—he was a stranger to her. No, she had never seen him around the area, and he had made no plans to meet with her again. Beyond describing him as heavily bearded, a tall man, she thought, but she didn't know for sure since she had only seen him in the gig, she couldn't tell them much more about him. He did have ever-so-nice manners, she confessed unhappily, and a proper way of speaking, and he dressed far more nattily than any of the local men she knew, almost as fine as a gentleman, but that was all she could tell them.

Smothering back a frustrated curse, Royce eventually dismissed her, speeding her on her way with the command "And tell Chambers to come up here to dispose of the cat!"

As could be expected, Chambers was aghast at what had happened, and once he had removed Ratter's body and restored the bedchamber to a pristine neatness, he told Royce somberly, "I will take special care in getting rid of the milk so that it is not allowed to cause any further harm." His face very worried, he asked quietly, "How is Miss Morgana feeling? What a terrible thing for her to experience! Who could have done such a viciously cruel act?"

"Morgana is just fine, although she is understandably shaken by what happened," Royce answered candidly. "But as for who tried to murder her, I have no idea." A steely glint in his golden eyes, Royce looked at Chambers and said bluntly, "I want Clara Holbrook out of this house at first light—and from now on, either you or Ivy are the only ones to touch *any* food or drink that is to be served to Morgana, and you alone are to bring it to her."

Fear evident in his eyes, Chambers replied in appalled tones, "Sir! You do not think that someone will try to poison her again!"

"I don't know," Royce retorted sharply, "but I am unwilling to run the risk! It was pure luck that I arrived when I did, and

I'm not willing to wager that luck will always be on our side." His features hard and dangerous, Royce added grimly, "Keep your eyes and ears open, and watch everyone—someone tried to kill your mistress tonight, and if we don't want them succeeding, we will have to take better precautions than we have so far." He frowned and said, "I don't know if there will be any way of stopping Clara from spreading the real story, but I want you to give out that the cat died naturally—which, of course, upset Morgana since everyone knew how fond she was of the animal. I believe that Clara will probably go along with what you say, since this situation does not present her in a very good light—and even if her tongue wags from here to London, I still want her out of here as soon as possible! And keep a sharp eye on her until then!"

After Chambers had departed, Royce returned immediately to the sitting room, where he had left Morgana. Determinedly casual, he smiled tenderly at Morgana and asked lightly, "Would you mind waiting here for me while I go talk to your brother and Zachary and let them know what has transpired?"

Despite herself, Morgana yawned, and trying to match his mood, gave him a sleepy smile as she replied, "No, but don't be surprised if I am asleep when you return."

He laughed and, dropping a faint kiss on her upturned lips, went in search of Zachary and Jacko. He found them in the billiard room, and from their absorption in the game they were playing, it was obvious they were unaware of what had taken place upstairs only moments previously.

As concisely as he could, over snifters of brandy, Royce brought them up-to-date, deliberately telling them about his trip to London and the arrangements he had made to secure Ben's release from Newgate before introducing the ugly subject of the murder attempt on Morgana. If both young men had been reasonably satisfied with the outcome of the trip to London, they were horrified at the attempt on Morgana's life.

Royce was able to calm their most immediate fears about Morgana's safety, but not unnaturally, it was some time before he could leave them and return to Morgana.

When Royce entered the sitting room, he discovered Morgana drowsing, curled like a kitten, in one corner of the sofa, and reaching down for her, he murmured, "Come along, sleepyhead, I think it is well past your bedtime."

Before she knew what he was about, he had scooped her up into his arms and was striding rapidly into his bedchamber. Misty-eyed, she stared up at his dark face, admiring the firm jut of his jaw and the chiseled perfection of his long, mobile mouth. He had saved her life, and if she hadn't already been in love with him, his actions tonight would have sent her tumbling head over heels into that state. As it was, she was feeling something dangerously close to adoration, and only by focusing on him and the emotions he aroused within her was she able to conquer the suffocating fear that welled up inside her every time she thought of Ratter's lifeless body. . . .

It was obvious that he was treating her like fragile porcelain, and she was grateful for the way he was trying to keep what had happened in perspective—not lightly brushing it aside, yet not unduly dwelling on the subject either. She *knew* someone had tried to kill her tonight, and that awful knowledge filled her with terror, but she was strong and she was resilient and she wasn't about to simply give in to the icy fear that lurked at the edges of her subconsciousness—a fact that Royce seemed not to know, if his indulgent actions were anything to go by. When he had deposited her gently on his bed and, with all the care and cosseting of a nanny, had removed her lavender robe and placed her under the covers, a pile of soft pillows at her back, she muttered half-teasingly, half-seriously, "Royce, I really am all right. I was frightened at first and I am saddened by what happened to Ratter, but I am not about to go into a decline! Remember I grew up in St. Giles, and I am not so delicate that I cannot bear to ever sleep in that room again! I'm fine, really!"

Undoing his cravat and tossing aside his jacket, still deliberately playing it with a light hand, Royce grinned at her. "Ah, but you have misconstrued my motives, sweetheart! It is *I* who cannot bear to have you sleep in that room! I want you right here beside me, so that I can sleep soundly knowing you are close at hand." His eyes were full of mocking laughter, but there was a deceptive blitheness to his tone that belied how very serious he was—after what had nearly happened tonight, he could not tolerate the notion of not having her safely within touching distance!

Blowing out the candle that flickered on the marble-topped table beside his bed, Royce hurriedly finished undressing. A moment later, he slid into bed, his arms instantly reaching to pull Morgana's small body next to his. With her protectively enveloped in his strong embrace, her slender body resting confidingly against him, some of the fear and tension that he had kept rigidly under control all evening lessened. But, he thought with a sigh, they couldn't just pretend the murder attempt had not taken place—they were going to have to discuss it more thoroughly.

Dropping a brief kiss on her temple, he tightened his arms a little and he said huskily, "I don't want to distress you, sweetheart, but we have to talk a bit more about what happened tonight."

He felt her nod her head and he asked gently, "I know we haven't talked a great deal about your life in St. Giles, but beyond the one-eyed man, and I don't know that he was behind tonight's attack, is there anyone who, for *any* reason, would want to harm you?"

Morgana stirred uneasily. While Royce had been closeted with Jacko and Zachary, she'd had time to think a great deal about what had happened, and it still had her completely baffled . . . and scared. It was terrifying to think that she had an unknown enemy, someone who wanted her dead and who had gone to considerable trouble to arrange for her to die—a rather gruesome death, if Ratter's pitiful body was any indication!

Royce's question was a logical one, and she had already asked it of herself—and had found no answers. Her fingers idly toying with the hair on his chest, she said miserably, "While you were talking to Jacko and Zachary, I thought and thought about who could possibly hate me so much that they would try to murder me, and I can think of no one!" She swallowed convulsively. "Royce, in the city, we kept to ourselves—partly because of my deception. Believe me, we didn't want anyone taking a second look at Jacko and Ben's little *brother!* And partly because of the way Mum raised us—we were always aware of the double role we played, not only because I was a girl disguised as a boy, but because we didn't really fit in with the others." She sighed and said unhappily, "It was difficult speaking and acting one way with Mum and then another with everyone else, and it just seemed safer to keep to ourselves. Besides, Mum made it plain she didn't really want us mingling with the usual inhabitants of St. Giles. When we weren't out pilfering for the one-eyed man, we were usually with Mum. Oh, it's true that Jacko and Ben roamed about more than I did—because of my deception, I stayed close to our rooms." Despair evident in her words, she cried, "I didn't *know* anyone, so how could they hate me?"

Royce couldn't think of an answer to her pitiful question, and he spent the next several moments comforting and calming her. When he thought she could handle further probing, he asked quietly, "What about the one-eyed man? Would the fact that he had not been able to get his hands on you make him want you dead?"

Morgana gave a heavy sigh. "I don't know. I don't think so, but then, I never thought that *any*one would try to kill me!"

Kissing her softly on the cheek and brushing the springy curls back from her forehead, knowing he could not put off the question that had haunted him from the instant he had realized that someone had tried to poison her, Royce asked carefully, "What about your father?"

Morgana stiffened, the picture of that coldly elegant face suddenly flashing through her mind, the slightly slanted gray eyes, gray eyes that she had inherited, hard and icy. She had been instinctively aware from the moment she had seen him on the fateful day when Royce had come into her life that the tall, disdainful gentleman represented some sort of danger to her, but she had pushed the unpleasant idea aside. And perhaps it had been instinct, too, that had quelled any further desire to find out more about him. Beyond that first rush of excitement in seeing him, she had not given him much thought, all her emotions and feelings taken up with what had been happening between herself and Royce. . . .

But, she mused slowly, recalling her first sight of the man who had fathered her, Royce, too, must have felt something menacing, for he had kept her face hidden from the man's view. He obviously knew her father, and had not thought it wise that he recognize her. She sighed unhappily. She had often wondered about the man who had fathered her, and there were dozens of things that she wanted to know about him, but oddly enough, now that the subject had been broached, especially since it had been under these sinister circumstances, she found herself reluctant to ask too much about him.

"You know who he is, don't you? You saw him that day—and didn't want him to see me. Why?" she finally asked.

In the darkness Royce grimaced. "Yes, I know him. And yes, I saw him the day you tried to pick my pocket, but as to why I didn't want him to recognize you—and you have to remember that I was still under the impression that you were a boy!—I can't tell you. With everything else that was happening at that moment, it just didn't seem like the proper time for him to acknowledge you, if you understand what I mean."

Royce felt her nod and he found himself tensing for her

next question—he didn't relish talking about Stephen Devlin, and the fact that the Earl was her father made him even less inclined to talk about the man. If Morgana had pushed curiosity about him aside, Royce had been perfectly happy to let sleeping dogs lie, and he had hoped that she wouldn't ask too many questions about her father until some of the current animosity that existed between him and Devlin had lessened—especially now since he wanted to make her his wife! He didn't think that being a hairsbreadth away from challenging your prospective wife's father to a duel was a particularly auspicious start to a marriage!

But tonight's events had forced his hand. In view of what little they knew, it would have been foolhardy on his part *not* to have introduced the subject of her father. Now that he had, however, he was extremely reluctant to pursue it beyond his initial question.

It wasn't likely that Morgana was going to change the topic, and with a sinking heart, he heard her say uncertainly, "He looked, um, rather haughty and forbidding to me that day, but perhaps I was wrong in my impression of him. Is he a nice man?"

Now, how in the hell did he answer *that?* Royce inquired savagely of himself. *Nice* was not a word he had ever heard applied to Stephen Devlin. Cold, arrogant, disdainful . . . those were words that had been frequently ascribed to the current Earl of St. Audries, as a matter of fact, his own dislike of the man aside, Royce couldn't recall anything pleasant ever being said about Stephen Devlin—or his wife, for that matter! Which was not something he particularly wanted to tell the man's daughter! Frantically Royce groped for some way to explain to Morgana about her father without letting his own antagonism for the man color his speech.

Royce hesitated so long that Morgana grew apprehensive. She had asked a simple question; why couldn't he give her a simple answer? Was her father a monster? Perhaps he knew some terrible scandal about the man and didn't want to tell her, she speculated uneasily. It was only hours later that she would wonder if Royce had purposely kept the truth from her, but in light of what had happened this evening, suddenly anxious not to plunge into what might very well be another unpleasant and distressing scene, she said quickly, "Never mind! I don't know him—nor do I care to! And since he never paid me any mind in the first nineteen years of my life, why, now, should he not only be interested in me, but want to kill me?"

Inordinately relieved that she had saved him from a nasty explanation, Royce instantly seized on the escape she presented him and said hastily, "I don't know that he *is* behind what happened tonight! And you are probably right—if he abandoned you at birth and didn't care enough to find out what happened to you, he can't have any reason to want to kill you."

There was an uneasy silence between them, then Morgana snuggled closer to him and asked in a small voice, "What are we going to do, Royce? I-I-I don't want to die."

Her fear was evident, and his heart clenched in anguish for her. Desperate to distract her from such horrifying thoughts, he did the only thing he could—he crushed her next to his big body and kissed her with all the love and passion that was in him. "You're not going to die!" he said fiercely a few moments later, still holding her tightly to him, his mouth exploring her cheek and ear. "What you're going to do," he declared vehemently, "is marry me!"

Morgana froze, hardly able to believe her ears. "Marry you?" she finally got out in a dazed tone. "But you don't want to marry me!"

He kissed her very thoroughly, and when he lifted his head, a hint of laughter in his voice, he murmured, "Oh, but I do, sweetheart! I find that I want to marry you more than anything else in the world."

Her lips stinging from the passionate force of his kisses, her body shamefully tingling with anticipation of his lovemaking,

Morgana could hardly make sense of what was happening. Feeling as if she had wandered into a world comprised of frightening nightmares and blissful dreams, she tried to make out his beloved features in the darkness. Royce must be suffering from shock, she finally decided. Scant hours ago, someone had tried to murder her, and now he was saying that he wanted to marry her!

Morgana loved him with all the passion of her young heart and body, and if she had been asked what she wanted most in life, she would have answered without hesitation—to spend the rest of her days with Royce Manchester! But *marriage!* It was a state she had never conceived to share with the man at her side—she was his mistress, a bastard who, until a very short while ago, had earned her living picking pockets! She had no fine relations; one of her brothers was currently in Newgate, for heaven's sake! She had no powerful connections and no money, her only asset her slender young body, which was already his for the taking, and yet this rich, wellborn American appeared to want to marry her! It was incomprehensible!

She shook her head as if trying to clear it and muttered gruffly, "I think that you must have had one brandy too many when you talked to Jacko and Zachary!"

Her reply wasn't precisely what Royce wanted to hear, and he was a little shaken that his first, and he hoped only, proposal of marriage was being met with such an unflattering degree of skepticism! A trifle hurt, he demanded half-angrily, half-laughingly, "Morgana, don't you *want* to marry me?"

"Oh, but I do!" she averred helplessly, her soft hands unconsciously caressing the hard planes of his face. "I *do* want to marry you . . . but you can't possibly want to marry someone like me!"

"Oh, but I do!" he mimicked her softly, his lips brushing tantalizingly across hers. "I very much want to marry you, and I intend to marry you without further delay! I obtained in

London a special license, and it is resting at this moment ever so securely in the pocket of my coat . . . and with your consent, I have every intention of putting it to excellent use tomorrow!" He kissed her again, a sweetly tender kiss, and asked huskily, "Are you going to marry me tomorrow, sweetheart?"

"Oh, yes!" she answered giddily, fearful that this was a wondrous dream and that all too soon she would wake.

He kissed her again, this time more hungrily, his hand going to her breast, to cup and fondle the warm flesh. "By this time tomorrow," he said thickly when he finally lifted his plundering mouth from hers, "you will be my wife, and then *no one* will be able to take you away from me . . . *ever!*"

His words thrilled her, and they more than fulfilled every fantasy she had ever had about Royce Manchester, but she was painfully aware of words that he had not said—three extremely simple words that every woman wants to hear . . . *I love you!* She told herself that she was being greedy, that Royce had offered her far more than she had ever dreamed or had any right to hope for, and yet . . . and yet there was a little ache in the region of her heart, a tiny pain that would not quite go away.

Telling herself angrily that she was being greedy and ridiculous to wish for more, she clung to him, planting small, unknowingly provocative kisses at the corner of his mouth, trying to convince herself that it was enough that he wanted to marry her, trying desperately to push away the uneasy questions that kept tumbling through her brain.

She should be ecstatic, she thought unhappily, delighted that she would join the ranks of respectability—that she no longer had to fear that one day she would end up as her mother. She should be overjoyed that the man she loved wished to make her his wife, and yet she could not help wondering *why,* out of all the women he could have married, women far more his equal, he had chosen to marry her, a bastard child with no fame or fortune, a little pickpocket from the notorious precincts of St. Giles. . . .

CHAPTER 27

The marriage of Royce Manchester and Morgana Fowler was, by necessity, a small, very private affair. It took place in the parlor of a local justice of the peace, and despite being rather hastily put together, it went off surprisingly well.

When apprised early that next morning of the approaching nuptials, Zachary and Jacko, after excitedly and happily congratulating the principals, immediately threw themselves wholeheartedly into seeing that it was no shoddy event. In this endeavor they were ably assisted by Chambers and the staff from London. Chambers and his wife, Ivy, were especially pleased at this very satisfactory outcome to a situation that had caused them much heartburnings—they could once again hold their heads up high, confident in the knowledge that they were working in a *respectable* household!

With the wildly enthusiastic, if inept, help of Zachary and Jacko, the staff was able to insure that the soon-to-be Mrs. Manchester had a memorable wedding. The small parlor where the event took place was overflowing with several tubs and urns of flowers—tall, delicately hued gladiolus, airy sprays of baby's breath, and huge yellow lilies—and the bride herself wore a wreath of delicate white rosebuds on her black, curly head in place of the traditional orange blossoms.

Morgana made a lovely bride, her cheeks flushed rosily with excitement, the gray eyes clear and sparkling, and wearing a rose-sprigged white muslin gown, she looked almost ethereal as she stood in stunned elation at Royce's side before the justice of the peace. Royce's appearance complemented

Morgana's, garbed as he was in a formfitting coat of dark blue superfine with gold buttons, his snowy white cravat starched and intricately arranged, the tawny locks glinting with golden lights from the sunshine that poured into the room. They were without a doubt a handsome couple, and with Zachary, Jacko, and a beaming Chambers and tearful Ivy looking on, Morgana and Royce were wed at two o'clock on July 18, 1815, precisely one month after Napoleon's devastating defeat at Waterloo.

Afterward they retired instantly to Lime Tree Cottage, where the remainder of the servants had been busy preparing the house to receive its new mistress. Because she had once been one of them, even if only briefly, the London servants took a particular pride and interest in the proceedings, and for the afternoon, Royce had banished the lines that separated master from servant. Alice, Hazel, Matt, and the others were eagerly waiting for the wedding party in the main salon, bouquets of flowers everywhere. In a daze, Morgana surveyed their smiling faces as they shyly came forth to offer good wishes for her marriage, still not quite able to fully comprehend that she was indeed Royce's wife. Time and again she would glance at him and then at the wide gold band Royce had purchased in London yesterday, the gold band that he had put on her finger less than an hour ago, and then she would shake her head in amazement. Neither Zachary's exuberant embrace and muttered "I knew that Royce would do the right thing! Isn't he a great gun?" nor Jacko's bearlike hug when he lifted her from the ground and swung her around the room as he bestowed his most hearty congratulations, seemed to make it any more real. She was convinced that she must be dreaming, but then she would look over at Royce and her heart would melt with love for him. Dream or not, it didn't matter. She loved him!

The day proved to be an extremely happy one for Morgana, the only sad note the fact that her mother, Jane, had not lived long enough to see her so wondrously established and that Ben could not have been here to witness the wedding. She had not entirely forgotten the horrors of last night either, and every now and then, when she least expected it, the knowledge that someone had tried to kill her would slide unpleasantly across her thoughts.

Royce had not forgotten last night either, and he was never very far away from his bride, those golden eyes watchful and alert, despite feeling there was nothing to fear from anyone in the room. But if he felt fairly comfortable in trusting Chambers and Ivy and the majority of the London servants, he was not entirely easy in the matter either. More than once his gaze rested upon his valet, Mr. Spurling, as he wondered again whether the precise little man had told the truth that night the one-eyed man had attacked him; and if Spurling *had* told the truth, it still meant that someone here was a spy for the one-eyed man! Not the most reassuring idea, Royce concluded derisively, as he continued to study the various servants, his speculative glance stopping for quite some time on handsome young Tom Cooper. Now, *that's* who I would use, Royce decided sourly as he took note of the crafty intelligence in the limpid blue eyes and the man's easy charm with the servant girls.

Just then Morgana gave a delightful gurgle of laughter at a lighthearted quip from Zachary, and Royce's interest in Mr. Cooper vanished, his gaze coming back to warmly caress his wife's lovely features. It gave him a surprising amount of pleasure to call her "wife," and that reminded him that he had not yet written the announcement of their marriage for publication in the London papers—and the sooner that was done, the safer she would be, he thought grimly. Unwilling to simply abandon her in the middle of the festivities, Royce held off disappearing into his study for another hour, and by that time, the small gathering was beginning to dissipate and the household members were returning to their traditional roles.

A short time later, Morgana retired upstairs to change her gown, and Royce signaled Zachary and Jacko to follow him into his study. Seating himself behind an elegant kneehole desk, he smiled at the other occupants and waved them to a pair of barrel chairs covered in fine Spanish leather. Reaching for several pieces of vellum and lifting a black-feathered quill from its Boulle inkstand, he remarked, "I just want to write out the notice for the *Times,* and then I want to discuss your plans for this evening—I have a few things I'd like you to do for me, if you don't mind."

A trifle surprised, Zachary and Jacko glanced at each other and then shrugged. There were a few moments of silence broken only by the scratch of the quill against paper, and then, his missives completed to his satisfaction, Royce folded the papers and, placing each one inside an envelope, sealed them.

His task finished, he laid the envelopes aside and explained, "I shall have Matt leave early tomorrow and take those up to London—the sooner news of my marriage to Morgana becomes public, the easier I shall rest! Which brings me to my reason for calling you in here." Looking hard at Zachary, his attractive features taking on a grim cast that was becoming almost habitual of late, he said bluntly, "I want you to be highly visible tonight—go everywhere you think that you will meet members of the ton and any other acquaintances of ours from London who might be visiting in the Tunbridge Wells area. And even if you have to crudely finagle your way into Wetherly's house party, I particularly want you to find members of that group and talk loudly and at great length about the wedding today. Tell as many people as you can, as often and as soon as you can, but make certain you find at least some of the people who are staying at Wetherly's house and tell them. I want *everyone* to learn of Morgana's marriage to me within the shortest possible time. . . . Perhaps then the one-eyed man will think twice about continuing with his attempts to regain Morgana, and even more importantly now, it's possible that whoever tried to kill her last night will think better of it."

"Do you honestly believe that?" Jacko asked quietly, his face grave and his blue eyes fixed anxiously on Royce's face.

Royce uneasily rubbed the back of his neck. "I don't know, but for the moment, it's the only thing that I can do. Until we know either who is trying to kill her or why, we are rather at a loss, but hopefully the marriage today has strengthened our position somewhat." He grimaced wryly and confessed frankly, "Not to wrap it in clean linen—by marrying your sister, I have lifted her out of the ranks of obscurity and into the very bosom of the ton! When someone strikes at her now, they are no longer dealing with a little waif I found in the gutter, they are dealing with the wife of a wealthy, well-connected member of society—even if I am an American!"

Zachary nodded his dark head, saying dryly, "I suppose that having a great-grandfather who was a Viscount is something that we can be grateful for!"

Jacko cleared his throat uncomfortably and muttered, "I wonder if it wouldn't be better if Zachary went alone tonight." He smiled faintly. "I'm afraid that you will find no Viscounts or even a mere lord in the background of the Fowler family."

His features inscrutable, Royce glanced over Jacko, taking in the neatly tied cravat, the expert fit of the bottle green jacket and thigh-hugging buff breeches that he wore. It was obvious that Zachary's overflowing wardrobe had been raided to good effect and that there were some notable needlewomen in the house to have so quickly made the necessary alterations needed to accommodate Jacko's sturdier build. Anyone meeting him for the first time would promptly take him for a member of the leisured class, and Royce had no doubt that Jacko could hold up his end in any conversation that might be instituted. Meeting Jacko's worried gaze, Royce said silkily, "Since you and Morgana have no idea who your fathers were,

I wouldn't be so quick to state that there are no members of the aristocracy in your heredity—you might be surprised!"

Jacko grinned slightly and nodded. "But I still don't think it's a good idea to foist myself onto your friends."

Royce suddenly looked very haughty, his nostrils flaring a little. "Why?" he asked coolly. "Aren't you my wife's brother? Am I not to acknowledge her relatives?"

Knowing when he was beaten, Jacko spread his hands deprecatingly, his eyes twinkling, and he laughed. "Very well, kind sir. On your head be it! And don't say I didn't try to warn you if I make a cake of myself!"

"Oh, but you have nothing to fear, my young friend," Royce drawled, with a mocking glint in his topaz eyes. "I'm sure that you will meet several members of the ton tonight whose manners and morals will make yours seem rather genteel and sophisticated! However, there is one thing I do think that we should definitely change. . . . *Jack* has a much more, er, respectable sound than Jacko, don't you think?"

"Of course!" Zachary agreed excitedly. "Jack Fowler; that shall be your name!"

Shrugging his shoulders, the newly renamed young man obligingly allowed, "Jack it shall be!"

The three men spoke briefly, again speculating on the reasons behind the attack on Morgana and discussing plans to keep her safe. Eventually, though, the topic was exhausted, and since there was not any reason for them to remain at the house, and with Royce's strictures in mind, it was not too many minutes later before Zachary and Jack departed for Tunbridge Wells in Royce's gig.

The house seemed very quiet after Zachary and Jack had left; the initial excitement surrounding the wedding had faded, and the servants had returned to their usual duties. Alone in his study, Royce glanced around the pleasant room, thinking that under different circumstances, he would have been very satisfied living here—but knowing that someone wanted to kill his very new bride made him anxious to be gone from this place, eager for the date of sailing to arrive. Realizing with a start that in all the furor last night and then the commotion in arranging the wedding today, he had not yet mentioned the fact that they would be sailing for New Orleans in just a little over two weeks, Royce hurried from his study, eager to see his bride, and *not* just because he wished to tell her about their impending departure from England!

He found Morgana coming down the stairs; in place of the rosebud wreath, a spangled pink silk ribbon had been wound through her black curls, and she had changed into a simple muslin frock with puffed sleeves in a charming shade of rose. Watching her graceful progress, realizing that this utterly beguiling young woman with those delicately lovely features and smiling gray eyes was actually his *wife,* Royce was conscious of a powerful surge, a nearly overwhelming sensation of love and pride flooding through him.

Meeting her at the base of the stairs, he flashed her a charming smile, one that made Morgana's heart beat erratically in her breast, and kissing her hand, he murmured, "And do I have the honor of addressing *Mrs.* Manchester?"

She dimpled enchantingly, laughter gleaming in the depths of her clear gray eyes, and dropping him a saucy curtsy, she replied impudently, "Well, bugger me blind if you ain't!"

Royce threw back his tawny head and laughed; then, uncaring where they were or who saw them, he swept her up into his arms and kissed her soundly. They parted breathlessly from the embrace, the sweet, heady knowledge that their relationship had changed irrevocably flaring between them. No longer were they merely mistress and protector, no longer just man and woman slaking each other's passion; now they were man and wife, their lives unalterably linked forever.

Wordlessly they stared at each other, Royce feeling his heart swelling uncontrollably with love for her; Morgana shaken by how very fortunate she had been to have this man who she unashamedly adored want her for his wife . . . and it *almost* didn't matter that he had never said that he loved her—she had, she was quite positive, love enough for both of them!

They might have stood there indefinitely staring besottedly at each other if Chambers, a broad smile on his face, hadn't coughed discreetly and murmured, "Sir, madam, since it is very fine, I have taken the liberty of having Cook prepare a picnic supper for you." Not quite looking at them, apparently fascinated by the architecture of the staircase behind them, a staircase he had seen *numerous* times before, he added casually, "I believe that the lake is quite pleasant this time of day."

Royce couldn't help laughing at such overt manipulation, and turning to look at his butler's now carefully bland face, he said jestingly, "If Wellington had men of your caliber with him at Waterloo, it is no wonder that Napoleon was defeated! Such expert maneuvering, I have never before encountered!"

Chambers's lips twitched, but he bowed and asked, "Would you like me to bring you the basket?"

Glancing at Morgana and seeing her pleased expression, Royce nodded. "An excellent idea!" he replied instantly, wanting very much to keep his bride happy.

Carrying a large wicker basket and some blankets and soft pillows, Morgana and Royce left the house a short time later, sped on their way by a beatifically smiling Chambers. Leisurely they strolled down one of the many flower-lined, winding paths that crisscrossed the property, enjoying the sweet scent of violets and roses that drifted in the warm summer air. They wandered aimlessly, having no particular destination in mind, stopping every now and then to admire an especially pretty view or an eye-catching blossom or bush.

Eventually they settled on a spot, out of sight of the house, near the shore of the lake, and they spread their blankets and scattered the pillows under the wide, spreading arms of a magnificent English oak tree. The light meal that Ivy had prepared had been delicious—crusty meat-filled tarts, an artichoke pie, mild yellow cheese, a loaf of bread still warm from the oven, and for dessert, juicy purple grapes and plump red strawberries glistening from their dusting with sugar. Royce detected Chambers's fine hand in the three bottles of superb hock they found in the hamper, and having done a fairly decent job of demolishing the repast, Morgana popped one last sweet strawberry in her mouth and declared blissfully that she had never eaten a meal that tasted so good.

Together they repacked the basket, Royce keeping out the half-full bottle of hock which was all that remained of the wine, and then they settled themselves comfortably on the blanket, content just to enjoy the solitude and tranquillity of the waning afternoon. Morgana, a soft pillow behind her shoulders, rested against the trunk of the oak tree, Royce's head in her lap, and her fingers toyed gently with his thick, tawny hair. Dreamily she stared down into his relaxed features, almost painfully conscious that she had never been so happy in her entire life. She wanted to hug this moment to her, to capture it, to always be able, no matter what the future might hold, to live again this time of sweet contentment.

Royce suddenly caught her straying fingers and, bringing her palm to his mouth, pressed a decidedly erotic kiss against the soft flesh, shattering the tranquil spell that had overtaken them. "Now that my stomach has been satisfied, I think there are other, ah, appetites that we should consider appeasing, don't you?" he murmured against the tingling skin of her palm.

At his words and the touch of his lips against her flesh, Morgana was instantly aware of an inescapable stinging heat cascading through her body; her breasts suddenly seemed heavy and aching, the nipples tightening, and where Royce's head lay cradled by her thighs, she was conscious of a throbbing, insistent hunger that burst into being. Her cheeks flushed, her fingers ceased their movements, and mesmerized by the hungry glitter in his golden eyes, she stammered breathlessly, "H-H-Here? Outs-s-side?"

Royce shifted slightly, and pressing his open mouth against her breast, he muttered, "Why *not* here? No one can see us from the house, we are totally alone, and Chambers will have made certain that we are not disturbed. . . ." His teeth closed gently around her peaking nipple, and through the fabric of her gown, Morgana felt the heat and moistness of his mouth, the gentle bite of his teeth, and she shuddered with desire.

They had not made love since the night before he had left for London, and Royce had spent most of this day in an agony of impatience, wanting emphatically to be alone with her, to kiss her demandingly and find solace in her slender body from the merciless, urgent demands of his flesh. He had come home from London nearly bursting with desire for her, but last night her brush with death had banked some of the fire of his passion, and sensing that it was comforting that she had needed most and not his urgent possession, he had made himself content with a few hungry kisses before she had eventually fallen asleep, cradled protectively next to his big body.

His voracity for her had grown all through the day, the knowledge that she was his wife intensifying the passion he felt for her, and feeling the tremor that shook her body as his teeth closed gently around her nipple, Royce finally allowed the fierce, aching passion that he had so carefully kept tightly reined all day to surge violently through his body. "I don't," he said thickly, urgently pulling her down to lie next to him, "think that I could control myself long enough for us to reach the house!" His lips brushing tantalizingly against hers, he added mockingly, "And just think how shocked Chambers would be if he opened the front door and found me having my wicked way with you right at his very feet!"

Morgana giggled at his words, and Royce's eyes narrowed. "Ah, you find my condition amusing, do you, wench? Well, let's just see if I can arouse an answering fire in you."

His kiss was devastatingly erotic, and blissfully Morgana gave herself up to his embrace, their location the last thing that was on her mind as the familiar tide of passion rolled over her. He kissed her deeply, his tongue plundering the warm confines of her mouth as if it had been months since they had last made love instead of mere days, and with his big body half lying on hers, she could feel the swollen hardness of him pressing conspicuously against her thigh, making her dizzyingly aware that his earlier comments had not been totally in jest.

Precisely how they came to be lying completely naked on a blanket beneath the dappled shade of an oak tree, Morgana never quite remembered. Vaguely she could recall Royce furiously removing his boots and jacket and her little, pointed-toe slippers, but when her gown and chemise disappeared, or who divested him of the remainder of his clothing, remained somewhat hazy. All she clearly remembered of that afternoon was the fierce sweetness of his lovemaking.

The patches of golden sunlight that filtered through the thick green foliage of the tree were warm where they touched her, but no warmer than the intoxicating heat of Royce's mouth as it moved from her lips to her breast, nor warmer than the sensual glide of his hand up her thigh. The wine, the warmth of the fading sunlight, were drugging, but no more drugging than the pull of Royce's mouth against her breast, no more drugging than the beat of her blood as his hands explored her pale, slender body. She was boneless beneath his skilled touch, melting in a welter of wanton sensations, her mouth aching for more of the fierce pressure of his, her nipples tight and hard, yearning for the feel of his lips and hands, and between her thighs, oh, there the lascivious, insidious demand for his touch, for his powerful possession, was the strongest. . . .

Willfully her fingers explored the wide expanse of his muscled chest with its whorls of tight, tawny curls, and a fis-

sion of delight shivered down her spine when he groaned as
she teased the stiffened nipples she found there. But her ex-
plorations did not stop at his chest; her brazen fingers continued to caress and skim across the warm, hard flesh of his
steel-muscled body, the long sweep of his back, the tightly
bunched mass of his buttocks, and she smiled dreamily when
her seeking fingers trailed low across his stomach and she
heard the harsh, swift intake of his breath. Of its own accord,
her hand slid lower until it encountered the rigid magnificence of his swollen organ, and sighing pleasurably, she
curled her fingers around the warm, solid width of him.

There was great pleasure to be had in stroking her husband
this way, in exploring his lean, tall body, in discovering the
things that gave him pleasure, but this fondling of him, this
intimate examination, only increased her own passionate
longings. Wordlessly she arched up against him, wanting his
touch, desperately wanting him to give her succor from the
hungry demands of her own flesh.

Royce did not deny her, his mouth compulsively reac-
quainting itself with the sweet curves and gentle slopes of her
slim body, his hands gliding with increasing urgency over her
flesh, inflaming her further, teasing her with the promise of
the shattering pleasure only he could give her. He kissed her
timelessly, his lips locked on hers, his tongue stabbing hotly
into her welcoming mouth, giving them both a heady prelude
of what he meant to do to her with his body. But he did not
content himself with mere kisses; his hands cupped and
kneaded her small, hard breasts, his thumb rubbing arous-
ingly across her throbbing nipples, increasing the warm,
aching yearning between her thighs.

Frantically she encouraged his erotic activities; the spas-
modic tightening of her fingers around his bulging shaft, the
helpless twisting of her body, and the soft moans of pleasure
she gave drove Royce onto greater excesses, his lips tenderly
ravaging her breasts, his hands trailing slowly down her

trembling body, to seek the silken flesh between her legs. With his wicked mouth hungrily pulling against her breasts and the insistent probing of his fingers at the very source of all her delirious yearnings, Morgana was nearly submerged in a turbulent sea of wanton delight.

Not immune to her blatantly seductive actions, Royce shuddered time and again beneath the sensual glide of her fingers along his swollen flesh, the exquisite torment of her stinging little bites at his ear and shoulders. His breathing ragged, knowing that if he did not take her soon, he would shame himself, he fought for control, wanting to prolong this sweet agony, wanting to increase her pleasure before their joining. With a mighty effort he twisted away from her all-too-arousing ministrations, and seeing the half-full bottle of wine lying above her head, a sinfully erotic vision suddenly danced before his eyes and he reached for the bottle.

A frankly carnal smile on his mouth, he glanced into her startled face and slowly poured the cool wine down the center of her slender body. Morgana gasped in surprise as the liquid touched her flesh, but Royce was mesmerized by the sight of the pale gold liquid sliding in sensual rivulets between her pink and white breasts, across her taut little stomach, down to the tight black curls at the juncture of her slim alabaster thighs.

Almost dazedly Royce tossed the empty bottle aside and hungrily began to trace the path the wine had followed with his warm, seeking mouth. Sipping the liquor from between her breasts, his lips straying now and then to her throbbing nipples, he muttered thickly, "Ambrosia! Pure nectar for the gods!"

There was something wildly titillating about the cool moistness of the wine followed by the heat and suction of Royce's mouth, and Morgana moaned, arching against the sweetness of his exploring lips, reaching out frantically to touch him. She was desperate for his possession, and with soft, incoherent sounds, she tried to tell him of her need, even as her arms tried to pull him to her.

Royce, too, was struggling against the tide of passion that threatened to overcome them, his body aching with the need to bury itself within her, but he was too powerfully addicted to the potent flavor of the wine sipped from her warm body to stop, and compulsively his searching mouth slid lower down across her stomach, to the black ringlets of hair at the juncture of her thighs. Shifting slightly, oblivious to the faint, shocked stiffening of her body, he slipped between her thighs, his hands sliding beneath her buttocks to lift her to him, his mouth and tongue hotly exploring the soft, wine-dampened flesh he found beneath the tight curls.

A piercing spasm of pure sensual pleasure arrowed up through Morgana's body at the first thrusting flick of Royce's tongue and she twisted violently upward, to her shameful astonishment, suddenly on fire for more of the decadent things he was doing to her. Her fingers clenched into the blanket as he continued to taste and probe between her legs with his knowing tongue, the most divinely erotic sensations splintering upward and through her entire body with increasing frequency and strength until Morgana was certain there could be no greater pleasure than this most sinfully intimate ravagement by her husband. She thrashed like an untamed creature beneath his hungry exploration, craving a release from the sharp, coiling need that seemed centered underneath his tongue as his hands gripped her buttocks tightly, controlling the helpless undulations of her body. Suddenly her entire body went rigid and a high, keening sound of utter joy was torn from her as sweet ecstasy exploded through her, wave after wave of intense pleasure crashing over her.

The exciting feel of her convulsing flesh beneath his tongue, the intoxicating sound of her release, was very nearly more than Royce could bear, and he fought to keep from spilling himself on the ground. It was only when the powerful spasms that racked her slender body stilled that he lifted his head and, sliding upward, pulled her into his arms, his hands caressing her, gently easing her descent to earth again.

Stunned, Morgana could only lie there in his arms, amazed at what she had experienced, hardly able to believe what he had done to her or the wonderful pleasure she had derived from such a wanton act. How long they lay there together, her head cradled against his shoulder as her body slowly returned to normal, she didn't know. It could have been a mere second or an hour, but suddenly, her thoughts still erotically hazy, she became aware of the rhythmic motion of his thumb as it rubbed her nipple, and more important, a quiver of renewed desire shot through her when she noticed the astonishing size of his swollen manhood against her hip.

"Royce?" she asked breathlessly, her breasts boldly peaking beneath his touch, her eyes cloudy with awakening passion.

He smiled, a lazy, possessive smile, and murmured, "I wondered when you would notice my predicament and decide to help, er, rid me of its embarrassing presence. . . ."

Already the willing victim of her body's reawakened demands, Morgana dazedly nodded her head and reached eagerly for him. He brushed her seeking fingers aside and groaned, muttering, "No, I don't think so—I am like a cannon that has been primed once too often. . . . Touch me and I'm afraid that we will both be disappointed—you, of course, more than me!"

The golden eyes glittering with all the suppressed passion he had within him, Royce pulled her to him and kissed her ravenously, his hands sliding over her body, swiftly bringing her once again to a point of pleading delight. Nearly out of control himself, he rolled onto his back, and guiding Morgana's eager body over him, he thrust upward violently, burying himself within her tight, warm sheath, impaling her with his bulging shaft.

Mindless with pleasure, filled with him, recklessly Morgana rode his arching body, her hips grinding down against him. It was a violent, hungry mating, both giving each other such fierce pleasure that when the raging storm of ecstasy hit them, Royce fairly exploded within her, shouting aloud his release, and Morgana, her body shaking from the force of her rapture, collapsed bonelessly against him, blissfully certain that one really could die of pleasure.

CHAPTER 28

L ost in the world that only lovers share, through the deepening purple twilight they slowly walked back to the house, their arms entwined, Morgana's dark head resting against Royce's shoulder. There was little sign of the wild passion they had shared such a short time ago, although a sharp eye would have noticed instantly that Royce's cravat was not as meticulously tied as it had been and that Morgana's curls were riotously tousled and that the spangled pink ribbon was mysteriously missing.

The sweet rapture that existed between them at this moment was a rare and splendid thing, and neither one of them was eager for the fears and anxieties that hovered just beyond conscious thought to intrude. Each was utterly enchanted by the other, and though the word "love" had not been spoken aloud between them, it would have been blatantly obvious to anyone who saw them that they were deeply, irrevocably, in love.

Perhaps the danger that threatened Morgana made these moments even more cherished, Royce didn't know; he only knew that he had never known or had never expected to know such fierce pleasure in the act of lovemaking, nor the depth of the warm contentment he experienced just having her near him. She was infinitely precious to him, but it never occurred to him to tell her so, it never dawned on him to say the words that would have banished the last lingering doubt in her mind, Instead, that night, as they lay in their marriage bed, he worshiped her again and again with his body, revealing with his hungry kisses and urgent possession all the love and tenderness that was within him.

Long after Morgana had fallen asleep in exhausted slumber, Royce lay awake, watching her as she slept in the golden flicker of the one remaining candle that was still lit, still not quite able to believe that he had been so fortunate, so very blessed, to have found her. It didn't matter who she was—there was a part of him who savagely wanted her to be just "Pip," with no ties to anyone, nothing to bind her to anyone but *him!* But as his loving gaze moved over those sweet features of hers, features that were stamped clearly with the look of the Devlin family, he knew with a hollow feeling in his chest that it would be impossible for her relationship to the Devlins to remain hidden forever.

Unwilling to speculate further about that particular problem, he lowered his eyes and appreciatively his glance strayed down the slender length of her body. The night was warm, and in her sleep, she had tossed the sheet aside, the rumpled white folds of linen ending bunched near her knees. She was lying on her side, facing him, and he frowned as his wandering gaze encountered the scar on her right buttock.

Reaching for the candle, he leaned forward, examining the sharp outlines of the scar against her pale skin. It was not, as he had noticed before, just an aimless network of scarring from an old burn; it had a definite design within its round shape. It was actually quite a large scar, about the size of an English penny, and his frown growing, Royce stared at the mark, his troubled gaze following the entwined initials HD, a rose above the letters, a pair of crossed sabers below. It looked, he thought with a curious feeling of disbelief, uncommonly like the crest of a coat of arms.

He studied the design for a long, long time, the certainty growing within him that it was indeed a crest that he was staring at, that someone, at some time in her young life, had, with calculated cruelty, branded Morgana. It was obviously an old scar, but why, he wondered, would someone go to such lengths? Mere viciousness? Or had someone wanted Morgana to be clearly identified by the crest? Again, why?

He had no trouble believing Stephen Devlin capable of such a cold-bloodedly barbaric act, but since the Earl had plainly abandoned Morgana at birth, why would he want to have her marked as his child? Her startling resemblance to the Devlin family should be proof enough! Royce grimaced. He didn't recognize the crest, although he was positive, now that he considered it, that he *had* seen it before—even so, he wasn't sure that it belonged to the Earl of St. Audries! But if it did, and Royce had a strong feeling that it did, then whose initials were inscribed within it? The D, he thought slowly, no doubt stood for Devlin, but the H? Certainly no one whom he had ever heard of within the immediate family had the initial H. Perhaps a distant relative? Was it possible that Morgana was *not* Stephen's daughter, but the offspring of some minor member of the family? But then, why the brand of the crest? Not just *any* member of the family was allowed to use it.

Morgana moved in her sleep, and half-waking, she smiled drowsily at him. Becoming aware of the candle in his hand and the fact that he was sitting upright in the bed, she murmured, "What are you doing? Is something wrong?"

Royce shook his head, and quick to reassure her, he said lightly, "Everything is fine; don't worry."

Becoming fully awake and puzzled by the candle, she frowned slightly and asked, "Are you looking for something?"

"*At* something might be more appropriate," he replied, smiling faintly. She smiled back at him, and realizing that now was as good a time as any to satisfy himself about the scar, he asked carefully, "I was examining that scar on your right hip. . . . When did you get it?"

Leaning up on her elbow, she squinted at the scar. "I don't know," she answered, mystified. "I've always had it—it's been there ever since I can remember." A small smile curved her mouth. "Mum said I came with it!"

Royce took a deep breath, not quite certain what to make of her words. "Came with it?" he repeated casually.

"I mean born with it, or whatever," she replied with a shrug.

Picking his way with caution, Royce put the candle down and asked seriously, "Didn't you ever look at it closely? It's not a birthmark."

Thoroughly confused, Morgana stared at him and then looked at the scar. "Royce," she explained patiently, "it's only a scar, and no, I haven't examined it. You forget that I haven't always had the luxury of a change of clothes, nor a bath—I slept in my clothes and wore the same garments for months on end." She flushed and muttered, "I've been naked more since I first met you than all the previous times of my life put together!"

A sensual smile suddenly appeared on his chiseled mouth. "And for *that* I am devotedly thankful!" But his light mood vanished almost immediately, and a frown between his eyebrows, he said, "Morgana, it isn't just a scar—I'm almost positive that it is a crest from a coat of arms. Are you sure that you don't remember anything about it? When you received it? Anything?"

Astonished, she glanced at the scar and then at his sober features. "A crest?" she asked doubtfully. "Why would I have a crest on my hip?" Her eyes widened and she swallowed painfully. "My father?" Her eyes widened even further as something else occurred to her. Her voice very low, she asked, "Do you think that it has anything to do with what happened last night?"

"I don't know," Royce answered levelly, "but I wouldn't be at all surprised. It identifies you without question." Honesty compelled him to add, "And it *could* be your father's crest. I don't recognize it, but I'm almost positive that I have seen it before."

Morgana sat up in bed, the linen sheet modestly covering her body. She had skirted around the issue of her father for weeks now, and it suddenly seemed the most important thing in the world to her to find out the truth—she had procrastinated long enough. Besides, what was there to fear? *He* couldn't hurt her! And pushing aside a cowardly desire to remain happily ignorant about the disdainful stranger who had fathered her, she demanded quickly before she could change her mind, "Tell me about him! Jane always claimed that my blood was blue. If, as you seem to believe, the scar is a crest, then that scar would seem to give credence to her statement." Her eyes locked on his, she questioned urgently, "Who is he? I want to know."

Reluctantly, and not even sure why he was so reluctant, Royce said baldly, "The Earl of St. Audries, Stephen Devlin."

If it was possible, her eyes grew even bigger, becoming almost round. "An Earl?" she repeated in a voice of disbelief. "Mother didn't make any bones about being a 'high-flyer'; I just never realized that she had flown quite that high!"

He could see little reason to keep the entire truth from her now that she had asked about her father, and taking a deep breath, he said, "It seems very likely—you bear an uncommon likeness to other members of the family; I noticed it immediately. The fact that you are a St. Audries cannot be denied." He frowned. "But the brand on your hip . . . Ever since I saw it the other night, I have been troubled by it—I just can't fathom a reason for it . . . especially if it does prove to be the St. Audries crest. Stephen made absolutely no provisions for you, and from your mother's unwillingness to tell you about him, it would appear that he didn't want to claim you, or she was so frightened of him that she *dare* not tell you, so what possible reason could there be for you to be branded in such a way? And if he was behind last night's attack on you, why? He's never intruded into your life before, so why would he want to kill you now?"

Morgana had no answers for him; in fact, it was as if a floodgate had burst open and she had dozens of questions about her father. Royce answered as many as he could, but since his interest in the St. Audries family had been minimal until very recently and his exchanges with the Earl had been hostile rather than friendly, beyond some very basic information, there was little he could tell her. He tried very hard not to let his personal dislike of the Earl creep into his voice, but the very neutrality of his tone gave him away. "You don't like him very much, do you?" she asked when he finished speaking.

Royce grimaced. "Let's just say that the Earl does not like Americans, and I, unfortunately, am not particularly impressed by either his wealth or his title . . . and I let him know it." She stared at him for a long time, and Royce wished fervently that he knew what was going on inside her head.

Morgana couldn't explain very well precisely what it was that she felt. A chaotic multitude of emotions was swirling wildly around in her brain as she sat there, the linen sheet clutched to her breast, her gaze seeing Royce, yet not seeing him. Certainly it was gratifying to find that one's father was a titled member of the aristocracy, a man of wealth and a member of a family whose name commanded respect . . . except Morgana had the distinct and unsettling conviction that while the *name* commanded respect, her father did not! It wasn't anything that Royce had said, it was more what he didn't say! Even taking into account the acknowledged animosity between them, there was a decided air of constraint about her husband when he spoke of her father, almost as if there were unpleasant things he didn't want her to learn about the Earl of St. Audries. . . .

She sighed. It didn't really matter to her—Stephen Devlin's entire contribution to her life had been merely the fact that Jane had once been his mistress, and Morgana couldn't say that she had any deep feeling about the man. She had been curious, it was true—who wouldn't be? But it wasn't as if she had cherished any *real* dreams of ever making his acquaintance or of insinuating herself into his life. That one glimpse she'd had of him the day she had picked Royce's pocket had definitely *not* encouraged her to seek him out—quite the reverse, she thought with a shudder, remembering the selfish arrogance of his chiseled features. How could a man like *that* be her father? And whether it was further curiosity, or just a reluctance to accept that supercilious, cold-eyed man as her father, or something else that prompted her next question, she didn't know. Her dark, curly head cocked to one side, she inquired softly, "You're positive that Stephen Devlin is my father? He doesn't have any other relatives who could have been Jane's protector instead?"

Royce slowly shook his tawny head. "Except for Stephen and Julian, there are no other Devlin men, and Stephen is the right age to have fathered you. Your half-brother, Julian, is only a few years older than you are, and there is no one else in the family that I know of." A queer expression suddenly crossed his face as he vaguely remembered a snatch of conversation with Zachary. "Wait! There was an older brother. . . . He held the title before Stephen. If I recall correctly, however, he died years ago—before you were even born—so I'm afraid that eliminates him."

Deciding that she was really being rather greedy not to be satisfied with a "bleeding lord" for a father, when poor Ben hadn't even a clue as to who his father was, she smiled and murmured, "It's not important—knowing Jane, he could have turned out to be a highwayman with a pocket full of blunt just as easily, and so I shall be content to claim an Earl for my father." She grinned at him. "Just think, I am not quite the little nobody you thought I was—except for the fact that I was born on the wrong side of the blanket, I'm damn near a bloody *lady!*"

Royce smiled back at her, but his thoughts were not wholly on her words. There was an uncomfortable niggle in the back of his brain that talking about the Earl's dead brother had roused into being. Hadn't Zachary mentioned something about the previous Earl's wife and infant daughter dying? Wasn't that how Stephen Devlin had come to inherit the fortune he was so quick to brag about? The infant who died would have inherited everything, except, of course, the title . . . but incredibly, *if* she had lived, it occurred to him, she would have looked very much like Morgana and have been about Morgana's age. . . . The most extraordinary suspicion suddenly sprang into full being within his brain. No! he told himself firmly. It couldn't be! Morgana was Stephen's illegitimate daughter! There was no other explanation. He was just letting his imagination run wild with him to think otherwise!

Yet long after Morgana had gone back to sleep, he lay there awake, seriously considering the unthinkable. If he believed that Stephen was blackhearted enough to murder his brother's infant daughter, possibly even her mother, in order to get his hands on the fortune, which Royce did, then it wasn't such a far leap to consider that something may have gone very wrong with Stephen's despicable plan. . . . . *The one-eyed man!*

Giving up all pretense of sleep, Royce slipped from the bed and, dragging on his robe, began to prowl restlessly about the room. If Morgana really was the long-supposed-dead heiress, it would supply answers to so many baffling questions. Suppose Stephen *had* contacted the one-eyed man to dispose of the child, and suppose, for his own reasons, the one-eyed man had not done so. Instead, Royce thought slowly, he could have placed the child in the care of someone he could trust . . . Jane Fowler, who had raised the child as her own. Precisely what the one-eyed man hoped to gain by this, Royce couldn't quite understand, but if his surmise was correct, it would help explain why the one-eyed man wanted her back so desperately—if for no other reason than to keep Stephen from discovering that he had betrayed him all those years ago!

And if Stephen had done as Royce was beginning to suspect with increasing conviction; if Morgana Fowler was really the *Lady* Morgana Devlin, heiress to a great fortune, then it gave Stephen Devlin a powerful motive for death. . . . It would explain why, after all these years, the Earl was suddenly very interested in her, why he had been nosing about the estate asking John Bullard questions about the young lady staying here . . . and why someone had tried to poison her last night.

It was a vile and exceedingly ugly scenario that was unfolding in Royce's brain, but as the minutes passed and he continued to consider it, he became even more convinced that he had stumbled onto at least part of the truth. He wandered over to where Morgana slept, her features bathed in the golden light of the candle that he had replaced on the table near the bed.

Was his little pickpocket an heiress to a great fortune? Instead of being a "bloody lady," as she had laughingly called herself, was she, in fact, a lady of fortune? The legitimate daughter of an Earl? It mattered little to him. It had been the little pickpocket who had utterly captivated him, who had all-unknowingly stolen his heart—he loved *her,* and antecedents be damned! He may have looked originally for a bride of birth and fortune, but that was before he had fallen in love with Morgana, and in his heart, he didn't want her to be anything but "Pip." He most definitely didn't want anyone else to be able to lay claim to her emotions or loyalties—he loved her, she was *his wife,* and that was all that truly mattered to Royce as he stared down into her lovely face.

But suppose she *was* that infant daughter who reportedly died years ago? he questioned grimly. What then? Was he selfish enough to want to keep her heritage from her? He didn't think so. If there was even a remote chance that she was indeed the supposedly dead heiress, then the truth had to be discovered and proven.

Unconsciously playing with his signet ring, he continued to pace, his thoughts veering furiously between complete incredulity at what he suspected and grim conviction. If she was Morgana Devlin, it neatly explained everything—the one-eyed man's obsession for her . . . Stephen's sudden interest and the murder attempt. He could think of no other solution that fitted all the pieces of the puzzle so well. Frowning, he stopped abruptly in the center of the room, staring down at his signet ring . . . the ring he had promised to send to Ben as proof that a message came from him. . . .

If the scar on her hip proved to be the crest of the St. Audries family . . . could it be that the brand served the same purpose as his ring? Proof of identity? His heart beating with painful strokes, he gazed blindly at the ring on his finger. Was the brand on her hip inflicted not as an act of cruelty, but as a desperate means to identify her?

"Royce?" Morgana called softly, interrupting his fantastically flying thoughts. "What is it? Can't you sleep?"

Wrenching his mind away from the path it seemed determined to follow, with an effort he focused on Morgana and discovered her half sitting, her clear gray eyes fixed curiously on him. "I'm sorry," he said apologetically. "Did my pacing wake you?"

"No, not your pacing—it was *you* I missed!" she answered with a faint blush on her cheeks.

His gaze riveted by the sight of one impudent nipple peeking out over the linen sheet, his dark thoughts vanished in an instant, to be replaced almost immediately by a sudden hunger for her. Walking over to the bed, he shrugged out of his robe, and an eager glint in the depths of his golden eyes, he murmured, "What a demanding little wench you are . . . and how fortunate for me!"

Morgana hadn't meant her comment precisely *that* way, but at the first touch of his mouth against hers, she decided blissfully that she was the fortunate one to have such a passionate lover for her husband. They made love unhurriedly, savoring each other's bodies, exploring and teasing until each could bear the sweet torment of the other's touch no longer, and frantically joining together to find a shatteringly exquisite assuagement from the passions that drove them.

With Royce's head resting against her breast, one muscled thigh thrown over her hips, Morgana listened to his even breathing, wondering why, now that he was finally asleep, she was wide awake. Of course, she told herself prosaically, it wasn't every day that she got married . . . nor every day that she discovered her father's identity. . . .

It was strange how the news that her father was an Earl affected her. She wasn't precisely elated, but she was relieved that he hadn't turned out to be some wealthy scoundrel who just happened to have had Jane in keeping at the time she was conceived . . . except—and this was what probably was keeping her awake—she had the definite impression that the Earl *was* a wealthy scoundrel! Royce hadn't wanted to tell her about him, and though he had chosen his words with care, the fact that her husband disliked her father a great deal had been unmistakable.

It bothered her, too, that until tonight, Royce had never introduced the subject of her father. She pulled a face. Well, she would have to take the blame for some of that—she certainly hadn't been exactly eager to talk about him either!

She had come a long way from St. Giles in a remarkably short period of time, but even though she had grown used to wearing silks and satins and to having servants wait upon her every whim, the *essential* Morgana hadn't changed—there was still more than a little of St.-Giles-raised Pip within her, and Pip was uneasy. In the world she had inhabited since birth, everyone's motives were suspect, *no one* did anything without expecting to gain from it, and anything that seemed too good to be true usually was!

It was incredible that she was married to the man who lay

sleeping by her side; incredible that he had bought this house for her; that he was willing to expend so much time and money on a little pickpocket and her brothers . . . except, it turned out, she wasn't *just* a little pickpocket—she was the daughter of an Earl! Granted it was the illegitimate daughter, but she found it curious and just a bit suspicious that Royce had never made any mention of that interesting fact until *after* they were married. He hadn't even mentioned her father until last night, just prior to asking—no, *telling*—her that she was going to marry him, even having conveniently gone so far as to obtain a special license. . . .

Feeling decidedly guilty and just a little mean-spirited to be entertaining such perfidious and disloyal thoughts about the man she loved, a man who had shown her nothing but kindness, she stirred restlessly. It was all nonsense! There was nothing the least bit suspicious about what he had done! Morgana told herself fiercely. Instead of lying here trying to make something ugly and underhanded out of his actions, she should be down on her knees thanking God that such a wonderful man had wanted to marry her!

But why? asked Pip coolly. He never said a word about love, and if he didn't love her, then why had he wanted to marry her? There were any number of wellborn, *respectable* young ladies for him to choose from—why you?

I don't know! Morgana answered hotly. There are probably lots of reasons—he just hasn't mentioned them yet. I love him, and that's all that matters!

Perhaps, Pip replied cynically, but I would give a great deal to know why his curiosity about that scar never came out until after you were married and why he never mentioned that your father was an Earl until after he had you safely bound to him by marriage.

It was a stupid argument, and her fists clenched tightly, deliberately Morgana shut out Pip's taunting questions. It was mere coincidence that they had discussed the scar and had talked for the first time about her father tonight. Mere coincidence—there was absolutely *nothing* sinister about it!

Hating herself for even considering any nefarious motive for Royce's actions, she snuggled closer to him, as if the warmth of his big body could drive away the chill that Pip's questions had aroused within her. It didn't *matter!* she repeated savagely to herself. She loved him!

Royce felt her move against him and gave up all pretense of sleep, the wild speculations about Morgana's past having come back to bedevil him the moment he had surfaced from the dreamy ecstasy of their lovemaking. Pulling her to him, he asked quietly, "Can't you sleep either?"

She shook her head, but before she could answer him, they both stiffened at the sound of a furtive rap on the door to the sitting room that separated her bedroom from his. The fitful light from the guttering candle threw Royce's features into sharp relief as he motioned Morgana to be still; with a quick, supple movement, he sprang from the bed and, jerking on his robe, stopped just long enough to grasp the pistol he kept beneath the pillow before stealthily leaving the bedroom. Her eyes huge in her small face, Morgana sat up, her heart beating at a frantic pace.

"Royce, are you awake?" came Zachary's hushed tones from the other side of the door as he quietly rapped again.

Instantly relaxing, Royce called over his shoulder to Morgana, "It is only Zachary."

Knowing that something significant must have occurred to have Zachary knocking on their door at this time of night, Morgana swiftly found her night robe and, hurriedly wrapping it around her naked body, followed Royce into the sitting room. She found not only Zachary with Royce, but her brother as well, and from the tense expressions on the two younger men's faces, she knew that she had not been wrong in her surmise.

"What is it?" she asked anxiously as she walked farther into the room, tying the belt of her robe about her slender waist.

Zachary spoke first, an apologetic look on his face. "I'm sorry to disturb you, but I saw the light under the door and thought that you might still be awake."

"It doesn't matter," Royce replied easily. "You must have thought it important or you would have waited until morning. What happened?"

"Well, we did as you requested. We drove into Tunbridge Wells and we wandered about—stopped at a few gaming establishments and one or two other places. We met quite a few people from London, and I introduced Jack to them, and then we both babbled like excited old maids about your wedding to Morgana today." Zachary grinned. "As you can imagine, everyone was rather astonished."

An answering grin curved Royce's mouth. "No doubt," he replied dryly. "But did you see any of Wetherly's house party in town?"

Zachary nodded his dark head. "I'm coming to that. We finally ended up at a public ball being held in one of the pump rooms in town, and it was there that we managed to track down Wetherly's party. We saw all of them—Wetherly, Stafford, Atwater, Newell . . ." He hesitated and then added carefully, "Even the Earl and his Countess were in attendance, as well as the widow Cresswell and Julia Summerfield and some others."

Royce could feel the tenseness that suddenly emanated from the two young men, and unconsciously he reached for Morgana, pulling her protectively to his side. "And?" he asked harshly. "What happened?"

Jack and Zachary exchanged glances and then Jack cleared his throat uneasily and muttered, "We had been enjoying ourselves, almost forgetting that there was another reason than merely passing a pleasant evening on the town for us to be where we were. Zachary had been introducing me to everyone, and as you said, I fitted right in—everything was going along very smoothly and we had made certain that everyone who crossed our path knew about the fact that you had married Morgana today." He took a deep breath. "We were in the pump room and had circled it several times, visiting and speaking with several people, when we came upon the Wetherly party, and I heard *his* voice!"

"His voice?" Royce repeated, puzzled.

"The one-eyed man's!" Zachary burst out excitedly. "Jack recognized it right off! The one-eyed man is one of Wetherly's guests!"

"You're certain?" Royce demanded swiftly, but not exactly surprised.

"I could not mistake it!" Jack answered stiffly. "He was *there,* and while we did not notice anyone leave the group, once we approached it, I never heard him speak again. He either kept quiet, having recognized me immediately and aware that I would know his voice, or he disguised it during the time we spent with the group. While Zachary performed introductions and made the announcement about your marriage today, I took the opportunity to unobtrusively examine each man carefully, looking for some clue that would reveal him to me." Jack shook his head disgustedly. "There was nothing about their faces that seemed familiar, and yet I know I heard his voice!"

Royce looked thoughtful. "I would say that your trip to Tunbridge Wells was even more productive than we could ever have imagined," he said eventually. Finding himself the target of three pairs of eyes in which astonishment was plainly revealed, he smiled faintly and elaborated, "You managed to spread the word of our marriage to Wetherly's entire party—no mean feat, considering we had no idea that they would all be attending that public ball. You've also, inadvertently it may be true, informed the one-eyed man of Morgana's changed status, but more importantly, we now know that he can only be one of a small group of guests staying at Wetherly's house." A dangerous expression on his handsome face, Royce drawled, "All we have to do is cut him out from the pack, and once we have him in our sights . . ."

"But can we?" Morgana asked sharply. "If Jack didn't recognize him and he continues to disguise his voice, how will you be able to discover which one of the gentlemen he is?"

"That's just it," Zachary interjected excitedly. "He can't keep his voice disguised all the time—someone who knows how he talks normally is bound to ask him what is wrong. All we need to look for is someone of Wetherly's party claiming to have a sore throat!"

"I hope it's that easy, but I doubt that it will be," Royce said dampeningly. "He's a clever bastard, and I think the most that we can assume is that Jack's appearance tonight gave him a hell of a shock!" An unpleasant smile suddenly curled Royce's lips. "And of course, the news of Morgana's marriage to me can't have pleased him either. I would suspect that at the moment, our one-eyed man is very nearly beside himself with rage. . . ."

CHAPTER 29

Royce was correct on both counts—seeing Jane's oldest brat, looking every inch a gentleman, strolling confidently across the crowded ballroom with Zachary Seymour *had* indeed been a hell of a shock for the one-eyed man! He'd barely been able to swiftly conceal the stunning jolt that the sight of Jacko had given him before he was beset with the terrifying knowledge that if Jane's brat had not already recognized the sound of his voice, as soon as he opened his mouth, Jacko was certain to identify him.

In the flurry of introductions, it had been easy enough to disguise his voice beneath a cough and a muttered greeting, but prolonged conversation anywhere in the vicinity of Jacko was fraught with danger, and he kept his mouth shut afterward. But how he had kept from exploding with rage when Zachary casually dropped the news that Manchester had married Morgana, he was never certain. He was aware that a muscle had bunched furiously in his cheek and that his hands had closed into impotent fists, but again, conscious of the situation, he had savagely brought himself instantly under control.

Years of hiding his real emotions behind a polite mask came to his aid, and he had forced a smile to his lips as he had listened to the cries of astonishment that had met Zachary's announcement. Heart pounding murderously in his chest, nearly breathless with the black rage that scalded through him, he had behaved faultlessly, his smile holding just the right amount of amusement at the various jocular comments made by his friends, his polite expression conveying just the exact hint of curiosity about the sudden match.

He had been so caught up in effectively concealing his own raging agitation that he could not even take malicious pleasure in the swiftly hidden expressions of appalled consternation and stark rage that had flickered across the faces of the Earl and Countess of St. Audries when Zachary had tossed out his explosive bit of news about the marriage. For once, the invincibility of the one-eyed man had utterly deserted him and he had been as helpless as any of his many victims, forced to stand there in a crowd of people and smile and act as if his world were not in immediate danger of crashing down about him, caught so totally off guard, first by Jacko's presence and then by the monstrous enormity of Zachary's announcement, that he almost couldn't comprehend it.

A febrile glitter in the black eyes, he sat silent in the coach during the ride back to Wetherly's home, and in desperate need to come to grips with this terrible calamity, he retired immediately to his room. Alone at last, he was able to let all his fury show.

Morgana married to Manchester! Fairly grinding his teeth with fury, he stormed around the room, his face twisted with hate and violent rage. Why had he never considered such a shattering event? How had all his glorious plans come to this unbelievable state of utter disarray? With a vicious movement, he sent an elegant chair crashing against the wall. *Manchester!* he thought malevolently. It always came back to that damned American!

He took a deep breath, his nostrils flaring whitely from the force of the rage that continued to roil within him as he tried to gain some semblance of mastery over his nearly maniacal emotions. But it was not just rage and fury that warred in his breast; for the first time in years, he was conscious of a faint feeling of alarm, and he cursed the day that he had ever laid eyes on Jane's children.

It was still almost inconceivable to him that Jacko had actually been there tonight at the assembly room, that if he had not spied him first, his days of hiding behind the disguise of the one-eyed man would have been over. It wasn't so much the loss of his disguise that worried him as it was the fact that Jacko would have known his real identity, and that knowledge would have given Jacko power over *him!* The one-eyed man could vanish forever without a trace, as had been his intention once he had married Morgana, but he . . . he could not afford to find himself in the position of being blackmailed for the rest of his life by Jacko! And if Jacko plumbed his identity . . . Manchester would learn the truth and he would be destroyed.

Slumping down in a chair, he buried his head in his hands. Had he ever envisioned this dangerous situation arising when he had first hit upon the scheme of killing the original one-eyed man and taking his identity? A bitter laugh broke from him. Oh, no! At twenty-one years of age, just up from the country, burning to make his fame and fortune, he had been so cocksure, so arrogantly confident that there was nothing that he could not accomplish if he set his cunning mind to it.

Having lived all his life, until then, buried in a corner of rustic simplicity in the north of England, he had been dazzled by London. As the local squire's youngest son, he had grown up being treated as a person to be fawned upon and pandered to by the local inhabitants, but in London . . . His eyes glittered angrily. In London he had been considered nothing more than a bucolic bumpkin by the haughty members of the ton, a ludicrous, unsophisticated figure to be tittered about or, in some cases, snubbed, and of course, when it was learned that a certain high-flyer being kept by Lord Bailey was actually his half sister, it had not increased his stature within the rarefied society that he so yearned to join.

His father had been, by country standards, a comfortably established man, but in London the squire's position and fortune had been considered paltry—a mere nothing—and as for *him* as the youngest son . . . Jane bluntly explained all of this to him when he had first called on her after arriving in London. She had invited him to stay with her at her elegant little house off Half Moon Street, a move that had been, as he was to learn to his cost, a disastrous mistake for someone intending to breech the inner ranks of the ton. Wealthy and aristocratic men might share Jane's bed, but that did not open any doors to her brother—quite the contrary! But he'd had no money, having come expressly to London to seek his fortune after a final violent falling out with his father and brother, and seeing the fine things his sister had acquired in such a short time, he was positive that he would be able to do even better—after all, he was a *man!*

Things had not worked out as he had envisioned, and he had found himself compelled to live on his sister's bounty, which infuriated him and made him resentful and envious of his amoral half sister. He had been livid when she had so stupidly gotten pregnant with Jacko, and as her belly increased, so did her latest protector's visits decrease, and more important to him, so did the aristocrat's generosity. And as the money dried up, his resentment and frustration had grown so much that he could hardly bear to be in the same room with Jane and her monstrously swelling belly.

Lifting his head from between his hands, he stared blankly around the attractive confines of his room in Wetherly's house. A cynical smile tugged at his mouth. It certainly was a far cry from the dingy, sordid little tavern where he had been sitting nursing his rage against Jane and fate with a pint of bitters, and had first caught sight of the one-eyed man. He hadn't paid much attention to the one-eyed man's furtive movements as the old man had sidled across the dimly lit interior and had eventually taken a small table in the darkest corner of the room. A small table that providentially just happened to be right behind where he had been sitting, cursing Jane and the stupidity of her actions.

In the beginning he had hardly been aware of the low murmur of voices behind him, but then gradually the import of what was being said impinged upon his consciousness and he began to listen carefully. He couldn't believe what he was hearing—the well-dressed gentleman who had joined the one-eyed man was actually arranging a murder. It was apparent from their conversation that the one-eyed man carried out this sort of business on a regular basis, and the money that the gentleman was willing to pay for this one act was a small fortune!

The notion of taking over the one-eyed man's identity, and

consequently his wealthy patrons, didn't occur to him that night—Jane sold a few pieces of jewelry the next day and they had enough money to live on for a while. But over the following weeks, with nothing better to do, he began to frequent the tavern where he had seen the one-eyed man, and when the fellow reappeared, he began to cunningly follow him, to stealthily ferret out all the man's secrets. By the time a year and a half had passed, he knew all there was to know about the one-eyed man, and the idea of killing him and becoming the one-eyed man himself had by then been in his mind for several months. And so one black night, well acquainted with his habits by now, he laid an ambush for the one-eyed man and coolly and efficiently murdered him and disposed of the body by weighing it down and tossing it in the Thames River. He didn't care whether it was discovered eventually or not—a few weeks in the river and the corpse would be unrecognizable.

And so, over twenty-five years ago, the squire's poor youngest son became the one-eyed man! It had been ludicrously easy to slip into the one-eyed man's shoes, so effortlessly simple to take the money that poured from the hands of those wealthy members of society who had dared snub him, but now who desperately needed his atrocious services. He didn't tell Jane in the beginning what he had done—she had recovered her figure and had, by the time Jacko was three months old, snared a new protector.

With the money from his first act as the one-eyed man— the murder of a rich old aunt, for an impatient and impecunious nephew —he found himself his own lodgings and put as much distance between himself and Jane as he could. He lived quietly and unobtrusively for several months, perfecting and honing the dual role he intended to play, and as his fortune grew and he became more familiar with the mores and manners of London society, he cautiously began to cultivate those members whose acquaintance would do him the most good.

He never mentioned his family, and since his first abortive foray into polite society had been exceedingly brief and shallow, by his twenty-sixth birthday, he was well established on the London scene, and no one ever connected his elegant form and charming manners with the brash, green boy who had arrived in London years before . . . or the one-eyed man.

His seamless intrusion into polite society opened up all sorts of opportunities for the one-eyed man, and he was quick to seize them, capitalizing on his dual roles, continuing to amass his fortune. He discovered he had a marvelously criminal mind, and in time, he expanded his range to include all manner of criminal activities, far beyond the scope of the original one-eyed man. As his fortune had grown, he had deliberately not kept in touch with Jane and had almost forgotten about her until he had passed her one evening at Covent Garden and she had approached him archly, teasing him about how fine he had become these days. Fortunately, he had been alone, and hoping that anyone who saw them together would leap to the conclusion that she had been soliciting him, he hustled her away so that they could talk privately.

Ben had been born by this time, and Jane was finding it harder to attract the attention of the wealthy young aristocrats as she had in the beginning. She still was living in the house near Half Moon Street, but with two children now, life was becoming more difficult for her.

Rising to his feet, he walked over and poured himself a large glass of whiskey. It was those stupid brats of hers! he thought viciously, not for the first time. Who in the hell wanted a mistress with a pair of mewling bastards hanging at her skirts! He'd said as much to her at the time, but she had shrugged and asked him for some money. He'd given it to her and he had ordered her to keep her mouth shut about any relationship between them—he didn't *ever* again want her to approach him as she had in Covent Garden! If I'd been wise, he admitted grimly, I'd have throttled her and the brats that night—at least then I wouldn't have had to endure tonight's nerve-shattering scene!

Precisely how Jane had become privy to his dual role, he didn't remember. No doubt, he thought with a grimace, he'd gotten drunk one night and had wanted to brag about his exploits to someone—he had been younger then, not as careful as he was now. Once she knew about the one-eyed man, though, he had made it a practice to visit her only in that disguise. He had wanted her to forget that she ever had a brother, and never appearing *as her brother* seemed as good a way as any to accomplish it. His secret had been safe with Jane—she had nothing to gain and everything to lose by making things difficult for him, and she'd been eager to receive the gold that he occasionally tossed her way.

He'd been anxious about Jane knowing about the one-eyed man, but over the years he had taken great pains to keep his public life totally separate from hers, and she had never known the full extent of either his fortune and his growing stature within polite society. A cruel smile curved his mouth. Stupid, silly slut! She had never even been suspicious and had believed right up until the day she died that he had lived in nearly as desperate straits as she and her children. He had never feared Jacko and Ben plumbing his disguise—they had been far too young to remember him as Jane's younger brother, and they had grown up believing that he was simply the one-eyed man. Even if Jane had risked mentioning that he was her brother, they still wouldn't have been likely to recognize him garbed in his fine clothes if they had passed him on the street.

No, he thought viciously, it isn't my face that will give me away, but my *voice!* His face darkened with rage and he poured himself another glass of whiskey.

Years ago, while he had realized immediately the necessity

of muffling his voice when dealing with his various victims if he wanted to continue to move freely among them, it had never occurred to him to do the same thing when in the company of Jane and the others. A stupid, *stupid* mistake!

Of course, he realized that Jacko recognizing his voice was the least of his worries—Morgana's marriage to Manchester had smashed the plans that he had nurtured for so many years, and unless he acted immediately, there would be no way that he could salvage anything from the ruins.

His mind working at a furious rate, he stared off into space, trying to decide how he was going to recover from this most recent catastrophic turn of events. Time had become of paramount importance—if he was to salvage any of his plans, he *had* to get Morgana away from Manchester instantly! Once she was introduced to society as Manchester's wife . . . His face twisted savagely. That wasn't going to happen—when she made her first appearance to the members of the ton, it would be as *his* wife!

So how to get her away from Manchester? A scowl wrinkling his brow, he reviewed Zachary and Jacko's comments. The two young men had clearly indicated that the marriage between Morgana and Manchester had been a love match, and if that was the case, then Morgana would no doubt do anything in her power to save the life of her very new husband. . . .

A note, he thought slowly, a very explicit note delivered to her in the morning, should bring her running to him. . . .

Very well, that took care of one problem, and a second note delivered to Manchester several hours *after* they had left for his own country estate should bring the distraught husband following quickly behind. . . .

A gleeful expression suffused his features. Yes! Yes! It was a splendid plan! First thing in the morning, he would inform Wetherly that he would be leaving for his home in Hastings, just a few hours ride from Tunbridge Wells, and since he had deliberately not committed himself for the full length of the house party, no one would think it strange if he departed ahead of time. He would be waiting for Morgana near Lime Tree Cottage, and once she was safely under his control, he would drive immediately to Hastings and make some very lethal preparations for her husband's arrival. Disposing of Manchester's body would be relatively easy—his home overlooked the sea, and it would be simple enough to make certain that when Royce Manchester's corpse sank into its icy depths, his body would never be recovered—Royce Manchester would simply disappear forever!

Almost chortling with delight at his own brilliance, he very nearly convinced himself that he had been scheming to arrange this entire sequence of events. It would be so perfect! Royce's new wife, a little nobody whom no one had ever met or heard of and who had bewitched the foolish American, would mysteriously run away, and the poor, half-demented Manchester, unwilling to believe that she had deserted him, would frantically follow her . . . and would never be seen again! Oh, but it was diabolically clever! A plan so very worthy of him!

Pouring himself another glass of whiskey, this time after taking time to admire the clarity of the amber liquid, a smug smile on his mouth, he sat down and contentedly sipped his drink. With Manchester dead and Morgana in his possession, he could arrange for a tragic accident to happen to Jacko—he wasn't about to run the risk of facing another incident like tonight's. And as for Ben . . . He smiled. Newgate was *such* a dangerous place—who knew what could happen to a young man so unfortunate as to be incarcerated there? Sometimes people even *died* in Newgate.

Of course, he didn't expect Morgana to tamely fall in with his plans. She needn't know anything, and although she was bound to suspect that he had something to do with the sudden demise of all the men in her life, he was confident that after a few months of his most assiduous and, if necessary, brutal care, she would be quite amenable to forgetting all about Manchester and would be willing, nay, eager, to marry him. A quiet wedding, a leisurely honeymoon in Europe, and then this winter, at the height of the season, he would appear on the London scene with his bride at his side, the missing and long-thought-dead Devlin heiress! No longer would those haughty peers look down their aristocratic noses at him—he would be one of them, lifted to those highest circles of society by the blue blood of his lovely bride.

He spent several more pleasurable moments dwelling on the bright future that was going to be his before his thoughts turned to the Earl and Countess of Devlin. But even thinking about Stephen and Lucinda and the fact that they already knew Morgana was alive didn't dampen his gleeful mood. In a matter of hours, Morgana would be safely beyond their reach and would remain so until he was ready to put the final phase of his plan in action.

A short distance down the hall from where he sat happily contemplating the success that would soon be his, Stephen and Lucinda were in Stephen's room, and there was nothing particularly happy about either one of them. Stephen was clearly shattered by the news that not only was Morgana still alive, but she was married to Royce Manchester! Lucinda, her hazel eyes snapping with rage, was furious about the stunning turn of events, perhaps most of all for having let herself believe that Stephen's plan would work. But while Stephen could only envision their eventual exposure and disgrace, Lucinda was not about ready to let that happen!

Stephen was sitting despondently in a chair, oblivious to Lucinda's rantings as she stormed about the room, his mind dwelling painfully on the stark ruin that stared them in the face. There was no way out. His scheme to murder Morgana had obviously failed, and he dared not seek out Clara to discover what had gone wrong. And nothing, he thought with weary despair, could have gone *more* wrong than to have Morgana married to Royce Manchester! He was ruined! If only, he mused bitterly, I had not been so squeamish and had disposed of the child myself! But he had not, and now he was going to pay for his lack of fortitude. Aware of the horrible scandal that would eventually break over their heads, he felt a shudder of hopelessness rack his body. Stephen could not even bear to think of the stares and whispers, the icy condemnation, that would follow him, and he winced when he considered that more than likely, he would end out his days in prison for what he had done. No. He would kill himself before he would suffer such an ignoble fate!

Lucinda suddenly stopped her wild pacing and glared at her silent husband. "Have you even heard a word of what I've been saying?" she demanded angrily.

Stephen looked at her, feeling strangely detached from everything. "No," he answered quietly. "But it doesn't matter anymore. We will be destroyed once Manchester introduces her to society—I suggest that in the meantime, you make whatever plans you feel are necessary for you and Julian."

Lucinda stared at him, and her lip curled contemptuously. "I suppose you're simply going to give up? Hide your head and hope that everything will just go away? Well, it won't, my addlepated, bird-witted coxcomb! We have to *do* something!"

His mind already made up about what he would do, her insults rolled smoothly off his back, and with an odd calmness, he replied, "No, not we—*you* have to do something. Leave me out of it."

Lucinda took a deep, furious breath. "All right!" she hissed. "I will take care of it—just as I have taken care of things in the past." She sailed from the room, leaving Stephen to stare indifferently at the door that slammed shut behind her.

Nearly vibrating with fury, Lucinda raged around her own room as she considered the quickest and easiest method by which to get rid of Morgana. She would have to do it herself, she thought savagely, she dared not involve anyone else, and this time Hester's brat *would* die! Nothing was going to prevent Julian from inheriting what was rightfully his! *Nothing!*

Events seemed surprisingly normal the next morning at Lime Tree Cottage, considering all that had happened over the past few days, and after breakfast, declining Royce's warm invitation to come for a drive with him, Morgana left him with Jack and Zachary and sought a few moments of quiet walking through the glorious garden at the rear of the house. For a bride of less than twenty-four hours, she was strangely pensive, and while marrying Royce resolved quite a few conflicts within her, she was increasingly troubled about the reasons for their hasty marriage. She didn't doubt that he enjoyed making love to her, and she wasn't so foolish not to realize that he had some measure of affection for her— but she couldn't help wondering about his motives for marrying a young woman of her station and circumstance, *especially* since he had never mentioned one word of love! Had the scar on her hip played any part in his reasons for marrying her? Was there something more that he wasn't telling her? Sighing, she pushed away her unprofitable thoughts and tried to focus on something more pleasant.

It can't be denied either that the attempt on her life preyed on her mind, and the fact that Jack had recognized the one-eyed man's voice last night hadn't helped to still the persistent fear that she would wake up soon and discover herself firmly in the power of the one-eyed man. Just knowing that he was here in the area frightened her, and coupled with the knowledge that someone wanted her dead, it was no wonder that she was not precisely the glowing bride one would expect.

Royce and the other two men left a short while later to drive into Tunbridge Wells to assess the results of last night's doings, and she was walking alone in the garden when Chambers approached her, a slight frown on his face. "Madam, this just arrived for you," he murmured uncertainly. "John Bullard said a groom from the local stables delivered it to him and insisted that it be taken to you immediately. Said it was a matter of life and death!" His eyes troubled, he handed her a plain white envelope.

A feeling of premonition slid icily down her spine, but not willing for Chambers to see her agitation, she smiled serenely and, after taking the envelope, waved him on his way. Selecting a stone seat embraced by a bevy of spicily scented flowers, she sat down and, with trembling fingers, opened the envelope and took out the single sheet of paper.

Her gaze immediately fell to the signature, and her breath caught sharply in her throat at the sight of a crude drawing of a skull with one eye blacked out. *The one-eyed man!* Numbly she read the curtly worded note, hardly able, at first, to take in the terrible things it promised if she did not meet him near the small bridge just a half mile from the gatekeeper's cottage at five o'clock this evening. The one-eyed man swore to kill Royce, and Morgana never doubted that unless she met his demands, Royce would be a dead man! Her initial reaction was to confide in Royce, but before she had taken even one step toward the house, she remembered that Royce and the others had driven to Tunbridge Wells, and in that same split second she realized sickly that telling Royce was the *last* thing she could do. If Royce knew of the threats against him, he would prevent her from meeting the one-eyed man. . . .

Morgana knew the one-eyed man did not make idle threats and that if she wanted Royce to live, she had no choice but to meet him as he had demanded. She didn't come to that decision lightly, but when she had exhausted every avenue of escape that she could possibly think of, it all came down to this: Did she dare risk Royce's life? There was one and only one answer to that terrible question, and fatalistically she knew that nothing would stop her from waiting at that bridge at five o'clock this evening. Every nerve in her body rebelled against that idea, but with a dull sort of apathy, she accepted that it was her fate that in order to save the man she loved most in the world, she would have to return to the person she hated most in the world.

She had always suspected that this time with Royce was only a dreamlike interlude, that it would have to end someday. Deep inside of herself she'd known that, known that the joys and sweet memories of these wonderful weeks would have to last her forever. If she felt any surprise, it was only that the one-eyed man had waited this long before ripping her world asunder.

It wasn't until she was sitting at her dressing table, the note lying folded in the center of the table, thinking desperately of some lie to tell Royce that would insure she would be gone before he came looking for her, that it occurred to her that there was a way out she had not considered. *She* could kill the one-eyed man! It was worth a try, and if she failed . . . She swallowed with difficulty. If she failed, it wouldn't matter anyway—her life would be over whether the one-eyed man killed her in a rage for daring to strike at him, or kept her alive and separated her from Royce.

Her decision made, she immediately began to consider how she was going to accomplish the act. A knife was the weapon with which she was most proficient, and it would be the easiest weapon to conceal on her body, and not willing to think upon it further, she went in search of one particular lethal instrument. The cottage had come equipped with a weapons collection, artfully displayed in a small room near the billiard room, and entering that room a few minutes later, she wandered about, checking all the various deadly instruments to be found there. It didn't take her very long to find precisely what she was looking for—a nicely balanced dagger from the seventeenth century. The slim, deadly weapon fit her hand nicely, and with a fierce smile of satisfaction, she slipped the dagger inside the small reticule she had brought with her in which to hide it.

If Royce and any of the others noticed that she seemed oddly subdued when they returned from town shortly after noon that day, no one commented on it, and when she mentioned having a headache just before four o'clock that afternoon and stated that she wanted to lie down quietly for a few hours, no one was very surprised. A concerned expression on his handsome features, Royce escorted her to the stairs. "Would you like me to keep you company, sweetheart?" he asked softly.

Realizing miserably that this could be the last time that she ever saw him, she felt a lump swell up painfully in her throat, and her eyes misted. Hungrily she stared at him, memorizing the sweep of his long black lashes, the intense brilliance of those amber gold eyes, and the chiseled planes of his beloved face. Helplessly she reached out to brush back an unruly lock of tawny hair, and her voice unnaturally husky from the emotions she was concealing, she muttered, "No. Just let me lie down quietly until it is time to dress for dinner." She forced a smile to her lips and managed to say lightly, "And if you disturb me before then, I shall be quite cross with you."

He grinned. "Very well, my dear. You have my word on it— I shall let no one, including me, into your room until then."

It was what she wanted to hear and yet she lingered, not able to tear herself away from him. Royce was watching her intently, almost as if he knew that something was very wrong, and aware that it would be fatal to arouse his suspicions, she turned and was on the point of going upstairs when there was the sound of approaching horses. Curious, she stood there, one foot on the bottom stair, Royce still by her side, as Chambers appeared and walked sedately across the wide hall to answer the knock on the door.

After a brief moment of low conversation, Chambers said over his shoulder as he ushered two gentlemen into the wide hallway, "Sir, it is your cousin come to visit from London."

The two fashionably attired men were strangers to Morgana, but she had barely noticed the older man before her disbelieving gaze fell upon the classically sculpted features of the tall, young, dark-haired man standing just behind him. A small, shocked gasp escaped from her as she stared mesmerized into features that bore an amazing resemblance to her own! Clutching the banister as if it were the only thing that kept her standing, she watched as his gray eyes met hers and his face reflected the astonished consternation that she knew was on her own face. Her voice rusty and thick, she demanded, "Who *are* you?"

Like a man in a daze, he took two steps toward her and said almost numbly, "I am Julian Devlin. Who are *you?*"

CHAPTER 30

Royce had known that Morgana was going to come face-to-face with either Julian or Stephen eventually—he just hadn't expected it to be under these circumstances, and he cursed himself roundly for not having foreseen just such an awkward incident as the one that was rapidly unfolding in his foyer. Unlike the other occupants of the spacious hallway, he recovered himself immediately and, with magnificent aplomb, murmured, "I think that I can answer both of your questions—Morgana, I'd like to introduce you to a gentleman I believe is your half brother, Julian Devlin. Julian, this is my wife, Morgana Manchester."

George, who had been as transfixed as the others, visibly started at Royce's words, and fumbling for his quizzing glass, quickly positioned it and stared intently at Morgana. "Apparent she's a Devlin," George finally stated, "but she ain't Julian's sister, even on the wrong side of the blanket, and if she *was* Morgana, she'd be his cousin, not his sister, but she ain't Morgana—Morgana Devlin died at birth! Fact!"

In utter bewilderment, everyone stared at George. "What the devil are you talking about?" Royce demanded sharply, one arm curved protectively around Morgana's slim shoulders.

George glanced at the fascinated expression on Chambers's face and said meaningfully, "Think we should retire to some place less public."

Zachary and Jack, drawn by their voices, stepped into the hall at that moment, and Zachary, his gaze darting from one face to the other, took in the situation instantly. Ignoring Jack's astonished gulp when he caught sight of Julian, Zachary swiftly crossed to Julian's side and, grasping his nerveless hand, pumped it vigorously up and down and exclaimed heartily, "Julian! By heaven, this is a pleasant surprise! Come into the salon and let me introduce you to a new friend of mine, Jack Fowler, Morgana's brother."

Silently blessing his cousin for his tact, Royce said smoothly, "Of course! Let us all adjourn to the salon, where we may be more comfortable." Gently urging a dazed Morgana along with him, he efficiently herded everyone toward the salon, stopping only long enough to say to Chambers "Please bring us a tray of refreshments—whiskey preferably!"

Numbly Morgana let Royce guide her to a chair in the salon and sinking down on it, she was unable to tear her gaze away from Julian Devlin's so very familiar face. Julian was having the same difficulty and the two of them were oblivious to everyone else, each one hardly able to believe in the stunning similarity of their features. Their resemblance to each other was even more remarkable since they were both of the same age and they could very well have been twins except for the differences that existed between Morgana's feminine features and Julian's definitely masculine ones.

There was an uncomfortable silence in the room, Royce closely watching Morgana, George absently twirling his quizzing glass as he stared off into space, Zachary's and

Jack's eyes moving from first Morgana's face and then to Julian's while those two continued to look at each other in incredulous disbelief. Chambers's entrance, with a tray loaded with several different kinds of refreshments, a few moments late momentarily introduced an air of normalcy and there was a flurry of movement and sporadic conversation while everyone was served.

Upon the butler's departure, silence would have fallen again had not Royce, a glass of whiskey in his hand, said bluntly, "And now George, would you mind explaining your very odd statements earlier."

"Nothing very odd about 'em!" George retorted smartly, "Told you Morgana Devlin died. . . ." he thought a bit and then continued, "nineteen years ago this spring. Everyone knew it! Why I even had a wager with Newell about whether Andrew's get would be a boy or girl! Remember it distinctly! Remember I won because the child was a girl—Morgana!"

George's words made even less sense than his previous ones, and shaking his head, Royce asked grimly, "Who the hell is Andrew, and what does he have to do with this situation?"

Julian roused himself slightly, and tearing his eyes away from Morgana's face, he said quietly, "I assume he is talking about Andrew Devlin, the sixth Earl of St. Audries; he was my uncle—my father inherited the title from him."

"Exactly!" George said happily. "Andrew Devlin, capital fellow! Liked 'im! Everybody did!"

"Are you telling me that Morgana is Andrew's byblow and not Stephen's?" Royce demanded with an edge to his voice.

"Already told you she ain't Morgana, but she couldn't be Stephen's, has to be Andrew's," George replied testily.

"How do you know that?"

George looked at Royce as if he were rather simpleminded and then, turning to Morgana, asked, "How old are you, gel?"

It never occurred to her to object to his right to question her, and she replied unhesitatingly, "Nineteen. I became nineteen this year, on the ninth of May."

At her answer, George's face paled, he took an agitated step backward, stared hard at her, and reaching for his quizzing glass, examined her even more closely from head to toe, almost as if she were some new form of life. Putting his quizzing glass down, he began to pace up and down the elegant room, his brow furrowed and his lips pursed. Obviously he was deep in thought, and everyone watched him, waiting with breathless expectancy for him to speak. Stopping suddenly in front of Morgana, he barked, "Your mother! What was her name?"

Morgana swallowed nervously and muttered, "Jane Fowler."

"High-flyer that had all the bucks atwitter twenty-five, thirty years ago? Striking gel—tall, bosomy creature with a head full of chestnut curls and china blue eyes?"

"Yes," Morgana answered reluctantly.

George reached again for his quizzing glass. "You don't have the look of her—you're a little slip of a thing, don't look at all like her! Not a bit."

Morgana bit her lip. "She always told me that I took after my father's side of the family."

George snorted. "Oh, you've the look of the Devlins, I'll grant you that, but there is something about the shape of your face and . . ." He looked a little uncomfortable, and clearing his throat, said gruffly, "Something about your small size and the slender build of you that reminds me of someone I met over twenty years ago in London." He glanced at Royce. "Remember it because she was the only female I ever felt the slightest inclination to marry. Remember a lot of things. Got an excellent memory. Remember things everyone has forgotten." When Royce would have impatiently interrupted him, George added hastily, "Thing is, I was only nineteen and she was already married. New bride in fact, on her honeymoon."

Royce was frowning. "And? What does all this have to do with my wife and her resemblance to the Devlins?"

George stood in the middle of the room, and it was apparent that he was grappling with a great problem. Finally, his expression extremely thoughtful, he said, "Think I should tell you a story."

Standing behind Morgana's chair, one hand resting possessively on her shoulder, Royce said grimly, "Tell your damn story, but get to the point of it."

George nodded and, with surprising succinctness, related a series of fascinating events, starting with Stephen Devlin's marriage to Lucinda and their subsequent, indefinite, removal to the continent, where Julian had been born. He touched briefly on Andrew Devlin's whirlwind courtship and marriage to the lovely little heiress of Bath and ended with an explanation of Andrew's death as well as those of his wife and infant daughter. His audience had listened raptly, their eyes locked in various degrees of astonishment and consternation on his face.

When he finished speaking, there was utter silence until Royce said slowly, "George, I've heard that tale before— perhaps not all of it, but Zachary mentioned something about it weeks ago in London. And while it is a very sad and affecting tale, will you please explain what the devil it has to do with Morgana!"

After taking a deep, fortifying sip of his wine, George replied evenly, "Well, there are still some things that I know that you don't, but one thing should be apparent from my story—Stephen can't have been her father; he was in Venice or some such place when she was conceived!" George thought a moment, then added fairly, "At least, he was supposed to be; didn't appear in England until Andrew had been dead for over a fortnight."

Royce was now staring very hard at George, a curious feeling of premonition stealing through his body.

Morgana had listened to the story so far in a state of curiosity, impatience, and growing bewilderment. What did these people, one of whom was named Andrew, have to do with her? She understood from George's exchange with Royce that it would seem that *Andrew* Devlin, not *Stephen* Devlin, was her father, which would explain his earlier statement about being Julian's cousin, and she was conscious of a curious feeling of relief that the icily arrogant man she had seen that day was her uncle and *not* her father! Andrew sounded much nicer! And it was comforting to know that he hadn't just abandoned her, that he had been dead by the time she was born—he might not even have known that Jane was pregnant when he died. Her voice soft with a mixture of wonder and pleasure, she said, "So Julian is my *cousin* and not my brother."

George nodded, but fixed a stern, considering gaze on her. "Is your name really Morgana . . . or did you just choose it to give yourself airs?"

Morgana stiffened furiously in her seat, her lovely eyes darkening with outrage. Her chin lifted haughtily, and through clenched teeth she got out, "It is *my* name! My mother gave it to me! And how dare you imply otherwise!"

George looked at her flushed, angry features a long time, and then, giving her a twisted smile, he bowed and said softly, "When you're angry, you resemble your mother to an astonishing degree." A tenderly reminiscent smile curved his mouth and he muttered, "She was a gentle soul, wanting to please everyone, but if you made her angry . . ." He shook himself as if brushing away a ghostly memory, and then, glancing back to Morgana, asked quietly, "You're certain of your birth date?"

Not the least mollified by anything he had said so far, the black curls fairly bristling with dislike, she snapped, "Yes! Just as I'm certain my name is Morgana, I know that I was born on May ninth, in the year 1796!"

"Interesting!" George said to the room at large, a peculiar expression crossing his usually amiable features. He glanced at Julian and, meeting Julian's intent gaze, muttered, "Don't think you're going to like what I'm going to imply next, and before you fly up into the boughs and decide to call me out, I'll tell you right now, I ain't meeting you—no matter how much you think I've insulted you!"

Looking across at Royce, George took a deep breath and said in a rush, "Think you should know something about that infant girl that died. . . ." He risked another wary glance at Julian before continuing reluctantly, "Everyone knew that the Devlins were poor as church mice. Oh, it's true St. Audries Hall was once a fine place, but that was before Andrew and Stephen's father had played ducks and drakes with the family fortune. Everyone knew that if Andrew married, it would have to be for money, and no one was very surprised that when he was finally leg-shackled, it was to an heiress." He hesitated, and appearing more and more uncomfortable, he went on doggedly, "When Andrew died, Stephen inherited the title and the little of the estate that was covered by the entail, but the *money* belonged to Hester . . . or her child if she died."

George cleared his throat nervously and took a sip of wine. "Everyone knew it—great many wagers in London about what Stephen was going to do if Hester and/or the child lived. Lot of speculation and rumor that spring about what was happening at St. Audries Hall. Everyone knew that the little widow was ill, that she hadn't wanted to live after Andrew was murdered, and no one was surprised when she died." Shooting an assessing glance at Julian's set features, he said bluntly, "People *were* surprised when the infant died. Lots of gossip about that! All sorts of ugly things were whispered— that Stephen had smothered the baby at birth, that Lucinda had drowned the infant. . . . Someone even said they had sold the baby to a band of gypsies as soon as Hester died. Lots of gossip."

Morgana stared at George in growing horror, her eyes huge

in her face, and she wondered if he was mad. She sent Julian an apologetic look, but it was obvious that Julian had reached the end of his forbearance.

His fists curled menacingly at his sides, he stood aggressively in front of George and demanded furiously, "Are you implying that my parents committed such a despicable act?"

Appearing not the least bit ruffled by Julian's actions, George met his angry gaze and said calmly, "Ain't implied anything yet—just repeated gossip! But before you work yourself into a rage, think you should know two very interesting things—the child that died was named Morgana, which isn't a very common name, and she was born on May ninth, 1796!"

Royce's hand involuntarily tightened on Morgana's shoulder at George's words, but she was not aware of his movement as she sat there stunned. Julian went white at his words, and he looked dazedly from Morgana's face to George's. His eyes dark with horror and disbelief, he demanded thickly, "Are you saying that she is my *legitimate* cousin? That my parents gave the baby to this Jane Fowler and then claimed that the infant had died?"

Reluctantly George nodded his head. "That's what *I* think!"

"That's *monstrous!*" Julian spat out explosively. "I know that my father is a cold man, but even he is not capable of such an atrocious deed!"

Pity in his gaze, George murmured gently, "Well, it could be a great coincidence—a young woman, clearly bearing the features of the Devlin family, same name as the dead infant, and having the same date of birth. But consider this—common knowledge that your father's pockets were let, everyone knew he wanted money, knew that half the reason he married your mother was because he thought she was going to inherit a fortune from some old aunt of hers!"

"That's a lie!" Julian shouted hotly. "A damned lie! I never thought I'd hear such ugly gossip from *you!*"

George shrugged. "Ain't a lie—everyone knew, knew your father was furious when the old tabby died and left everything to some distant cousin no one even knew existed. He and Lucinda were in London. Hadn't been married more than three weeks, and it was after that they left for the continent—he couldn't afford to live in England. Said so! Went around town snarling and grumbling about the unfairness of it all! Remember it!"

There was such simple, unvarnished honesty in George's face and tone that even Julian, outraged and infuriated though he was, had to give some credence to his words. His young features pale and set, he looked over at Royce and said with icy politeness, "If you will excuse me, I find that I must leave immediately. My father is staying at Martin Wetherly's home, which I understand is not very far away, and I must speak to him at once!" He threw George a challenging look. "I'm positive that he will be able to explain everything and that the *truth* bears no resemblance to the lies that have been spoken here this afternoon!"

Spinning on his heels, he stalked swiftly from the room.

Jack had not uttered a sound since he had first laid eyes on Julian Devlin, but now he asked simply, "Sir, do you honestly believe that Morgana really is this Morgana Devlin?"

George sent him a thoughtful glance, actually becoming aware of him for the first time. "One of Jane Fowler's get, ain't you?" he said finally. "You've got the look of her about you—something the young lady sitting over there doesn't! What's your name?"

Jack smiled crookedly. "Yes, Jane was my mother, and my name is Jacko . . . Jack."

George nodded and said politely, "Happy to meet you, Jack. Since no one has done the business, might as well introduce myself—I'm George Ponteby, a cousin of sorts to Royce." Having satisfied himself with the social niceties, George added, "And yes, I do believe that she is Morgana Devlin—young Julian didn't let me explain my most compelling reason for believing in her identity." He looked across the room, where Morgana sat like a frozen little statue. His voice soft, George muttered, "Said she looked like her mother when she was angry—I wasn't talking about Jane Fowler, I was talking about little Hester Devlin, Andrew's bride that I met and fell in love with twenty years ago."

Morgana's eyes flew to his, and George nodded. "It could be a coincidence, your name and birth date being the same as the legitimate child, and you could be a byblow of Andrews's . . . but Jane Fowler was never in Andrew's keeping, and *if* you were *their* child, I wouldn't see flashes of Hester in you."

Morgana took a deep, shuddering breath, her thoughts numb and bewildered. She didn't know *what* she felt. There was relief that Stephen wasn't her father, but she wasn't so certain that she was ready to relinquish Jane as her mother—Jane had raised her, and Jane had been the only mother she had ever known, but if Jane wasn't her mother . . . In a very small voice, she asked, "You mean Jack and Ben aren't my brothers?" Being an heiress, or even discovering that she was not the bastard child of some aristocrat, didn't seem as important as the bond she had shared with Jack and Ben ever since she could remember.

Dismay evident in his eyes, Jack swiftly crossed the room and knelt before her. Taking her hands in his, he said fiercely, "It doesn't matter if it turns out that Jane was not your mother—you'll always be my sister!" He gave her a twisted smile. "You may wear fine clothes these days and live in a fine house and answer to Morgana, but you're always going to be 'Pip' to me, and *nothing* will ever change that!" A thought occurred to him and he grinned at her. "Besides . . . nothing can be proven, so while it makes a fascinating tale, I'm afraid that you're just going to have to put up with me and Ben as your brothers—we won't let you disown us!"

"I wouldn't be so certain that there is not any proof," Royce said obliquely as he left his position behind her chair and walked over to the center of the room.

"What do you mean by that?" Morgana demanded, her heart twisting with sudden suspicion. "Do you know something that we don't?"

"Not exactly," Royce answered easily enough. Looking at George, he asked quietly, "Are you familiar with the coat of arms of the St. Audries family? Could you describe their crest?"

If George was puzzled by Royce's question, he gave no sign; he merely appeared thoughtful for a moment and then said, "Believe it's a pair of crossed sabers below and a rose above."

Morgana's breath caught painfully in her chest, and her eyes met Royce's. In bitter anguish she stared across the room at him, the painful certainty that he had known all along who she was coursing through her—why else had he married her? If he had known that she was the legitimate daughter of an Earl, heiress to a great fortune, it would explain everything! Dully she said, "I have a mark on my hip that depicts precisely those symbols . . . except that in the middle, there are the initials HD inscribed."

It was Zachary, standing riveted by the fireplace, who voiced the thought uppermost in everyone's mind. *"Hester Devlin!"*

"I'm afraid so," Royce replied carefully, puzzled by the expression in Morgana's eyes. She looked . . . disillusioned, as if he had failed her somehow. Watching her closely, his confusion growing as, all-unknowingly, he confirmed her worst fears, he muttered slowly, "When I first noticed the scar, I wondered if it wasn't a family crest, and I have to admit that it had already occurred to me, impossible though it seemed, that you might be the dead heiress. I didn't know then about the identical names and birth dates."

"Well, what are we going to do about it?" George asked dryly. "Going to cause a devil of a scandal!"

Morgana caught sight of the ormolu clock on the mantel, and her chest tightened painfully. It was after four-thirty! She had to leave *now* if she was to meet the one-eyed man! Her emotions shredded, her thoughts scrambled and irrational, she instantly rose to her feet. Whether she really was the legitimate daughter of an Earl, heiress to a fortune or not, wasn't very important to her at the moment—Royce's life was in danger, and that knowledge took precedence over everything else . . . even her pain at his conniving. She glanced at him, and her heart lurched as she met his golden-eyed stare. She loved him most dreadfully, and it hurt unbearably to think that he had married her simply because he believed that she was this supposedly dead Morgana Devlin, and therefore the inheritor of great wealth. But his duplicity didn't change her feelings, nor did it make unnecessary her coming meeting with the one-eyed man.

Frighteningly aware that the seconds were ticking away, she gathered up her skirts and said distractedly, "Excuse me, I want to be alone for a while. I have to think!"

When Royce would have escorted her from the room, she shook her black, curly head vehemently and, jerking her arm from his grasp, exclaimed sharply, "No! Don't you understand? I need to be *alone!*" With painful intensity, her gray eyes searched his. "I wondered why someone like you," she said at last, "with your wealth and well-connected background, wanted to marry me—a little nobody, a thieving pickpocket from one of the most notorious areas of London!" Her voice shook as she added, "Now I know." She gave a bitter little laugh. "I knew you didn't love me, but I hoped that you at least had *some* affection for me! It seems that I was wrong!"

Tears blinding her, deaf to Royce's anguished cry, she swept regally from the room. There was a painful silence in the wake of her departure, all three of the other gentlemen carefully avoiding looking at Royce's white, stricken features as he remained frozen in the center of the room, one arm outstretched as if to stop her.

"I *do* love her! More than anything else in the world!" Royce finally muttered in a fierce low tone, the expression in the golden eyes bleak and wounded. "I just never told *her* that I do!"

George walked over to him, and clasping him on the shoulder, he comforted gently, "Strange creatures, women. Give her time. Let her think about what has been said here this afternoon and she'll come to her senses. She's had a shock—we all have!"

Everyone *had* had a shock, but none had felt it as deeply as Julian Devlin. Even Morgana had been more forewarned than he—she at least had seen Stephen Devlin and knew of the startling resemblance, but Julian had been caught totally off guard. Even as his horses ate up the distance that separated Lime Tree Cottage from Wetherly's estate, Julian was still stunned, hardly able to believe what he had seen and heard. That Royce's bride was a Devlin was undeniable, but *Morgana* Devlin? He could not give credence to such an outlandish idea, and yet . . . and yet he could not entirely push the notion out of his mind.

Father will know, he thought grimly as his horses swept around the wide, circular driveway in front of Wetherly's house. Flipping his reins in the direction of the groom who had come running up at the sound of his arrival, Julian jumped down lithely and strode hurriedly up the broad steps to the door.

His knock on the door was answered by a butler in green and black livery. Upon identifying himself and requesting to see his father, Julian was politely invited into the house, and the butler explained that he believed Lord Devlin had last been seen in the master's study at the rear of the house. When the butler would have gone in search of Lord Devlin, Julian forestalled him with a charming smile and offered to find him himself if the butler would just be so kind as to give him directions to the study . . . and would he mind informing Lady Devlin that her son had come to call and where he would be? He would pay his respects to Mr. Wetherly once he had seen his parents.

The butler agreed, and a few seconds later, Julian was knocking on the door to Wetherly's study. He was hoping to see his father alone, and his hopes were rewarded when, upon being told to enter, he walked into the study and discovered the elegant room empty except for Stephen.

The Earl was sitting behind a narrow desk, a handsome pair of dueling pistols lying in the opened case in front of him. If he was surprised to see Julian, he gave no sign, merely remarking nastily, "Oh dear! Never tell me that Wetherly was so stupid as to invite *you* to the same house party that I am attending? One of us will have to leave, and since I am already here, I suspect that it will have to be you." Insincerity dripping from every word, he added, "I do hope that it will not inconvenience you in any way."

Julian flushed, his fists clenching at his sides. He and Stephen had been at each other's throats ever since he could remember, and there were times that he actively hated his father, but swallowing back his temper, he said levelly, "Wetherly did not invite me—I came to see you on a matter of the utmost importance."

"Oh? A new horse you wish to purchase? Or some new opera dancer that you want to set up in a tidy little house?"

Stephen was being deliberately provoking, since Julian never came to him for anything so trivial. Actually, he came to him for nothing these days, and hadn't from the moment he had turned eighteen, when his mother had, miraculously as far as Julian was concerned, convinced his father to settle a sum of money on him. The amount had not been particularly generous, but it *did* enable him to live independently from his father, and since he and Stephen only fought whenever they were in each other's company, they were seldom in each other's company.

Swallowing back the hot words that rose in his throat, he stared grimly at his father and said bluntly, "I have just come from Royce Manchester's house, where I met his bride." He hesitated only a second before blurting out, "She claims that her name is Morgana, and I tell you she bears a striking resemblance to me!"

There had been a curious stillness about Stephen when Julian had first mentioned Royce's name, but now he seemed to settle back comfortably against the leather chair in which he sat, a hand almost caressing the smooth wood of the pistol grip of one of the pistols in front of him. It was obvious that the truth was going to come out very soon, and since he didn't plan on being around when the horrendous scandal broke, Stephen saw no reason to deny himself the pleasure of getting a little revenge, of devastating Julian. A malevolent gleam in the gray eyes as he stared at the tall young man before him, Stephen fairly purred, "Oh, is that so? Why should you be surprised? She is your sister, after all."

"What? *My* sister?" Julian ejaculated involuntarily. Despite the blessed relief that flooded his body upon hearing Stephen claim her as his child, Julian persisted doggedly, "George Ponteby claims that you cannot be her father—that she is your brother's child."

Enjoying himself now, Stephen smiled with open malice. "But she is Andrew's child . . . his *legitimate* child." At Julian's look of utter horror, he continued pleasantly, "You see, after Hester died, your mother and I had to get rid of the brat if we wanted to enjoy the . . . ah, *elegancies* of life. Unfortunately the one-eyed man"—he glanced kindly at Julian's aghast features—"the gentleman hired to dispose of the child, seems to have double-crossed us."

Reeling from the brutal impact of Stephen's revelations, Julian stared dumbly at him, hardly able to conceive that his father was admitting to these ugly things. He shook his head dazedly, and clinging desperately to Stephen's earlier statement, he asked helplessly, "But you said she is my sister— how can that be?"

There was a choked sound from the doorway, and both gentlemen looked in that direction in time to see Lucinda, her eyes blazing with fury, catapult into the room. "That's *enough!* Don't you dare say another word!" she hissed at Stephen as she came to stand by her son's side.

"But don't you think it's time he learned the truth, my dear?" Stephen drawled, clearly relishing the moment.

His jaw granite-hard, the broad shoulders squared and ready for a blow, Julian answered tautly, "Yes. Explain yourself!"

Stephen's eyes were full of hatred as he stared at Julian's white face and spat, "You want the truth? Very well, your father was my brother, Andrew, and your mother tried to pawn you off as mine!" He glanced coldly at Lucinda and said viciously, "But I've always known—right from the beginning!" Almost conversationally he added, "It's why I had the one-eyed man arrange Andrew's murder—that and a strong desire to inherit the title while I was young enough to enjoy it and before Andrew fathered any legitimate children on Hester. But unfortunately I delayed a trifle too long and Morgana was born. So you see, the heir is the bastard, and the bastard is the heiress! Amusing, yes?"

"*You* had him murdered!" Lucinda burst out furiously. "Why, I'll kill you for that!"

Only Julian's quick action prevented her from attacking Stephen, and grasping her wrists, he growled, "Stop it! Is what he is saying the truth?"

She was too angry to lie, and twisting wildly in his strong grip, she snapped, "Yes, it's true! But it doesn't matter—no one can prove anything!" She threw Stephen a look of loathing. "*He's* certainly not going to admit to being a cuckold!"

"Mother!" Julian said desperately. "What about Morgana? Is that true? Did you know about it?"

A sullen expression crossed her face. "Yes, I knew, but I told you—it doesn't make any difference, *nothing* can be proven!"

Lucinda had always underestimated the streak of honor

that ran deep within Julian, and a look of total horror on his face, he backed slowly away from her, staring at her as if he had never seen her before. "My God!" he burst out passionately. "What kind of people *are* you? How could you have lived all these years with your consciences, knowing what you had done?"

Revulsion twisting his young features, he flung out of the room, wanting to put as much distance as possible between himself and these monstrous creatures.

A spiteful smile on his lips, Stephen stared at Lucinda and murmured, "Oh, my! I do think that your precious son is rather disillusioned with you! He never suspected before what a conniving, immoral bitch you are, did he? Such an honorable young man, your son. I have always wondered how he grew up to be so very ethical and virtuous—he certainly never learned it from you!" Openly sneering, he added, "Pity he is so high-minded—you might otherwise have been able to ride out the storm of gossip and speculation that is about to explode upon us." He laughed bitterly. "I have no doubt that he will run immediately to Morgana and nobly bestow the family fortune on her."

Lucinda glared at him, her hazel eyes glittering with fury. "Shut up! You've babbled more than enough as it is! And keep your vicious tongue off Julian! I'll soothe his ruffled sensibilities later, but right now I want to hear more about how you arranged Andrew's death."

"Oh, that!" Stephen commented with a little laugh. "It was easy enough to do. Once I received Andrew's letter informing me of his impending marriage, I knew that I hadn't any time to waste, and since we moved around so often in those days, staying one step ahead of our creditors, if you will remember, you didn't think it strange when I suggested we leave Italy immediately and relocate in Belgium. Before we even left, I wrote to a place that I had heard whispered would see to it that the one-eyed man got a message, and I made arrangements to meet with him in Dover. Remember just after our arrival at that wretched little coastal town of De Panne, I decided to make a trip into France?" Lucinda nodded, her eyes narrowed and fixed intently on his face. "Well, from France it was simple enough to cross the channel, meet with the one-eyed man, and make all the arrangements for Andrew's murder." Idly Stephen picked up one of the pistols, admiring its excellent craftsmanship. "It was ticklish and I was traveling nearly day and night, but everything went as it was supposed to, and when we received word of dear Andrew's death shortly thereafter, I returned to England a grief-stricken brother with no one the wiser. Clever, wasn't it?"

An expression of mingled pain and rage in her gaze, Lucinda said numbly, "You killed him to inherit the title?"

Stephen smiled coldly. "That and because I didn't appreciate having his bastard foisted off on me!"

Consumed by fury, Lucinda leaned over the desk and struck him viciously with the open palm of her hand. "I *loved* him!" she spat fiercely.

"I know," Stephen said icily, something very ugly leaping to his eyes when she struck him. Softly he snarled, "It's one of the reasons why I had him killed."

Something snapped inside Lucinda, and in a blind rage, she lunged across the narrow desk for the pistol in his hand. Stephen had been so intent on his own enjoyment of the situation that her wild attack caught him by surprise, and in desperate clumsiness, he tried to ward off her attack and rise from his chair at the same time. Ordinarily Lucinda would not have stood a chance in a physical confrontation with Stephen, but black rage gave her a powerful advantage and she fairly ripped the weapon from his grasp before he even comprehended her intent. Dancing nimbly away from him, her breasts heaving under the delicate silk of her fashionable gown, Lucinda pointed the pistol at him and calmly pulled the trigger.

Her ears ringing from the explosive sound of the pistol firing, through the cloud of blue-gray smoke that drifted between them, Lucinda stared with satisfaction at the widening expanse of blood that suddenly bloomed on the pristine whiteness of Stephen's shirt. A set, pleased smile on her mouth, she watched the look of astonishment that spread across his face.

"You shot me!" he exclaimed stupidly, his movements awkward and uncoordinated as he tried to stand upright. He half staggered, half fell onto the desk, sending several objects flying to the floor, including the twin to the pistol that Lucinda held in her hand.

"I know," Lucinda said pleasantly. "And I *enjoyed* it, you bastard!" Bending her face next to his as he lay partially on the desk, she hissed, "Just as you enjoyed telling me about Andrew, but the last laugh is mine, dear husband. Your beloved Hester didn't die naturally—the one-eyed man, yes, the same filthy creature you hired to kill Andrew, obtained arsenic for me, and *I* faithfully fed it to your sweet, *sweet* Hester!" She gave a half-mad laugh. "Ironic, isn't it?"

His gaze fixed in horror upon her, Stephen slid slowly to the floor behind the desk. Savagely he clung to life, one thought in his mind as feverishly he struggled to grab the second pistol lying a scant distance away on the floor in front of him. He could feel his life draining out of him and the effort exhausted him, but a second later, he sighed as his groping fingers closed around the grip of the pistol.

Mere seconds had passed since he had slid behind the desk, and unaware that he had reached the second pistol, Lucinda came quickly around the corner of the desk to make certain that he was dead. A dreadful caricature of a smile curving his bloodless lips, Stephen rolled over and, taking swift, deadly aim, shot her in the heart.

Death for Lucinda was instantaneous, and without a sound,

she slumped to the floor. In malevolent satisfaction, his eyes already beginning to glaze over in death, Stephen stared at her corpse and died gasping, "Who has the last laugh now, sweet bitch?"

CHAPTER 31

About the time that Julian had fled from Stephen and Lucinda at Wetherly's house, Morgana was creeping out the servants' entrance at Lime Tree Cottage. Hidden in the small woven basket she carried over her arm was the reticule containing the dagger, and after slipping through one of the small archways in the stone wall that surrounded the house, she began to wander idly in the direction of the gatekeeper's cottage. Wearing a plain frock of pale blue muslin, a chip-straw hat upon her head, and the basket on her arm; she hoped fervently that anyone who saw her would make the assumption that she was merely out for a stroll, picking flowers to amuse herself.

Deliberately she kept her mind blank of the earlier events, concentrating grimly on the coming confrontation with the one-eyed man. *After* she had finished with him would be soon enough to consider all the diverse and painful ramifications of this afternoon's revelations. But despite her best intentions, a wayward, hurtful thought about Royce's motives for marrying her slipped through the guard she had placed on her emotions, and she was aware of a dull ache in her heart.

Approaching the gatekeeper's cottage a few minutes later,

she pasted a merry smile on her face, and walking sedately up to John Bullard, who happened to be standing outside the cottage, she cried gaily, "Good afternoon! A pleasant day for a stroll, don't you think?"

John looked slightly startled to see the mistress of the house wandering about by herself this far from the main grounds, and his blue eyes widened. "Yes, madam, it is!"

Nodding politely and acting as if it were perfectly normal for her to be strolling out onto the public road that wound around the edges of the yew-enclosed estate, she said airily, "It's such a lovely day, I think I'll walk a bit further."

A worried expression on his face, Bullard watched until her slender form disappeared around a bend in the road, and then he hurried to the door of the cottage. His two brothers looked up as he poked his head inside and muttered, "Something queer is going on—the mistress just breezed past me bold as brass, walking down the road. Maybe it is all right, but I'm going up to the house and let the master know. One of you had better come outside and keep your eyes open." With that, he took off at a sprint for the main house.

Morgana had known it was risky letting anyone see her leave the estate, but there simply had been no other choice—Royce had chosen Lime Tree Cottage precisely because there was only one way in, and that was guarded by the Bullard brothers. She suspected that one of the brothers would inform Royce of her actions, and the instant she had passed out of John's sight, her leisurely manner left her; lifting her skirts, she began to run along the side of the narrow road. The bridge came into view almost immediately, and with a sudden thump of her heart, she spied a fashionable phaeton with a pair of handsome gray horses hitched to it, stopped just this side of the bridge.

Instinctively her step slowed as she came closer and noticed that the phaeton was empty and that the horses were tied to a tree that grew near the edge of the road. One hand resting comfortingly on the reticule, which concealed the dagger, she glanced around for any sign of the driver. The rig and horses seemed to have been abandoned, and wondering if she had somehow misread the one-eyed man's note, she called out softly, "Hello? Is anyone here?"

There was no reply, and increasingly puzzled and apprehensive, she looked up and down the empty expanse of road and then glanced uncertainly at the wooded areas that abounded on either side of the road. The sound of a twig snapping to her left made her jump, and walking cautiously in that direction, she asked sharply, "Who is it? Who's there?"

Again there was no reply, and becoming just a trifle angry, convinced that the one-eyed man was playing games with her, she lifted her chin and stepped briskly from the road to march into the wooded undergrowth, saying exasperatedly, "I know that you are there! Come out and have done with this bit of nonsense!" She had hardly walked more than four yards from the road when she heard a furtive rustle behind her and started to whirl in that direction. But she was too late—the stunning blow caught her fully on the back of the head, brutally knocking her unconscious. With a small moan, she crumpled to the ground, her hat flying off and the reticule spilling from the basket.

Stepping over Morgana's unconscious form, the one-eyed man smiled with satisfaction at his handiwork and efficiently set about tying and gagging her. When he was done, he gathered up her hat, the basket, and reticule, and returning to the phaeton, he tossed them in and reached for a large rug from the floor. He looked carefully up and down the road as Morgana had done earlier. The road remained empty, and there was no sound of any approaching vehicle. Returning swiftly to Morgana, he lifted her in his arms and quickly carried her to the phaeton. Placing her on the floor, he threw the rug over her body, making certain that it hid her and the other items he had tossed in previously.

It took but a second to untie the horses, and springing up into the seat of the vehicle, he wheeled the animals about and set off down the road at a steady pace—no reason to arouse suspicion by racing away. Once they had left the vicinity of Lime Tree Cottage would be soon enough to increase his speed. If people passed him, they would think that there was nothing amiss—all they would see would be a well-dressed gentleman seated atop his fancy phaeton, expertly handling a pair of high-stepping grays. He smiled. Who would ever guess that beneath the rug at his feet lay the bound and gagged body of Royce Manchester's bride? His smile grew and he congratulated himself for having been so very clever about this entire situation! And as the miles sped by, his belief in his own infallibility grew.

If he had known, perhaps, of the conversation taking place a scant five minutes after he had so blithely driven away from that bridge, he would not have felt quite so sanguine. But then, he had no way of knowing of John Bullard's serious disposition toward his duties, or of Julian's traumatic confrontation with Stephen and Lucinda, nor ever dreamed that Julian would whistle a fortune down the wind for the sake of honor. He also had never really paid any attention to George Ponteby's formidable memory or known of the deep-rooted honor of little Mr. Spurling, Royce's valet, but when all those ingredients came together . . .

It was John Bullard who informed Royce that Morgana was *not,* as he believed, upstairs in her bedroom. If John had harbored any worries that he was overreacting to Morgana's unorthodox little stroll, these were immediately put to rest.

The polite smile on Royce's face vanished as he listened to John's words and his handsome features took on a grim cast, the golden eyes narrowing and hardening as the seconds passed. John had barely paused for breath before Royce demanded in a voice like the crack of a whiplash, "How long ago was this?"

"N-N-Not ten m-m-minutes, sir!" John stammered.

George strolled into the hallway just then in search of his

host, and taking one look at Royce's face, he hurried over to him and inquired anxiously, "What is it? What the deuce has occurred *now?*"

"Young Bullard here says that not ten minutes ago, he saw Morgana leaving the estate . . . taking a bloody walk!"

"No reason why she shouldn't," George said reasonably. "Fine afternoon. Had a shock. Might have decided to take a walk to clear her mind. Logical thing to do."

Royce threw him a glance of loathing, and leaving George and John to stare openmouthed after him, he suddenly sprinted up the stairs, taking them two at a time, disappearing when he reached the top.

He reappeared almost immediately, practically flying down the stairs in his haste, a crumpled sheet of paper between his fingers. The grimness of his expression had deepened and hardened, only now a flicker of fear could be glimpsed in the flashing golden eyes, and thrusting the paper into George's hand, he groaned bitterly, "The little fool has gone to meet the one-eyed man! She was to meet him at five o'clock, and it is already several minutes past the hour! There is not a moment to lose if I am to catch them!"

Panicked as he had never been before in his life, Royce bolted down the hallway to the weapons room and snatched up a pistol and some shot and then sped out of the house, racing to the stables, his only thought to reach Morgana before it was too late. Oblivious to the stable boys' astonished stares, he stopped only long enough to finish loading the pistol and jam it into the waistband of his breeches. He then grabbed a bridle and swiftly threw it over the head of the first horse he came to. Swinging lithely up onto the animal's bare back, Royce suddenly became aware of several of the stable staff watching him in amazement. Catching Matt's eye, he commanded, "Have those blacks of mine harnessed to the gig, and get it ready to go *immediately*—I may need them! Do it *now!*"

Putting his heels to the flanks of the horse, without another word, Royce galloped away from the stables at a tearing pace. Upon reaching the entrance to the estate, he paused a second at the gatekeeper's cottage to demand tautly, "Your mistress, has she returned?"

"No, sir!" Harry Bullard replied instantly, his usually open features tight with concern.

Royce cursed under his breath and urged his horse down the road in the direction of the bridge. He had not let himself think beyond getting to the place where Morgana was to have met the one-eyed man, but as his horse thundered to a snorting stop at the bridge, and he looked frantically up and down the deserted, empty road, he was conscious of a terrible fear gnawing at his very vitals. Leaping down from his mount, he wasted precious seconds searching for any signs that could give him a clue as to what may have happened here, or even in which direction he should begin to look for his wife, but he could discern nothing from the ground around him.

Unwilling to squander more time in the fruitless checking for evidence, Royce swiftly remounted his horse and rode hurriedly back to the gatekeeper's lodge. His expression bleak, pulling his horse to a rearing halt just inside the gateway, he asked desperately of Harry, "Have you seen anyone go by on this road recently?"

Glumly, Harry shook his head. "No, sir. There were a few farm carts and people walking along the road early this morning, and about two hours ago some local youths passed by riding a couple of plow horses, but other than the vehicle with your guests in it, there has been nothing."

Royce hadn't expected him to answer any differently—the one-eyed man wouldn't have left anything to chance. His heart feeling like ice in his chest, dispiritedly he guided his horse toward the house. What was he to do? He *had* to find her! Sweet, benighted little fool to risk her life this way! How dare she! Torn between anger and despair, he kicked his horse into a trot. The one-eyed man had to have made some mistake! He just had to find it!

The gig and horses he had ordered were standing ready for him at the front of the house, and as he reluctantly dismounted and handed the reins to Matt, who came running up immediately, he wondered if there was anything to be gained by further casting about for the one-eyed man's trail. Remaining idle, however, was out of the question, and he was on the point of going into the house to inform the others of his decision to continue searching for Morgana when the sound of a rapidly approaching vehicle had him spinning around, hope flaring wildly within his breast.

But it was only Julian Devlin, and Royce's heart sank at the sight of Julian's tense, white features. It was obvious from his strained expression that the young man was laboring under great distress, and praying that Julian's appearance had nothing to do with Morgana's disappearance, Royce walked briskly over to where Julian had jerked his horses to a standstill and said with outward calm, "I hadn't expected to see you again quite so soon."

Coming down to stand next to Royce, Julian took a deep breath and said in a rush, "I've spoken with my parents!" He stopped abruptly as the realization hit him that what he had said was not precisely true.

Julian swallowed painfully and started to speak again, but before he could say any more, the front door flew open and George, Zachary, and Jack came hurrying toward them. Their faces full of anxiety, they barely acknowledged Julian's presence as George demanded, "Did you find her?"

Royce shook his head and replied tautly, "I rode to the bridge where they were to meet, but no one was there, and there was no sign of anyone about. I looked for clues to give me some idea which direction he may have taken her, but there was nothing."

"Good Lord!" George ejaculated. "What are we going to do?"

Grimly Royce answered, "Go after them—if I have to scour the entire English countryside, I intend to find them. I was on the point of coming inside and telling you this when Julian arrived."

George sent Julian a speculative glance, noting his unnaturally pale complexion and the distraught cast to his face. Momentarily diverted from Morgana's disappearance, George asked almost gently, "Talked to your parents, have you?"

Julian nodded unhappily. "Yes, I did—I've just come from seeing them." Still half-stunned by what he had learned so cruelly, Julian sent George a bitter, twisted smile and muttered, "Only, there is something that you didn't know— Stephen Devlin is *not* my father!" Ignoring the shocked gasps from the others, he gave a harsh, angry laugh. "Morgana and I are actually brother and sister, not cousins, as you suspected—according to Stephen, I am Andrew's bastard, and my mother did not deny it! As for the rest of it . . ." His composure suddenly shattered and his young face contorted dreadfully as he blurted out, "It's *true!* Everything you said! They both admitted it to me!" It was painful to see him fight to gain control of himself, but after a second, his features rigidly composed once more, he drew in a shuddering breath and, glancing over at Royce, said levelly, "Your wife is the legitimate daughter of Andrew and Hester Devlin! In order to get their hands on the fortune she would inherit from her mother, Stephen and my mother made arrangements with a one-eyed man to dispose of her after Hester died, but the one-eyed man betrayed them and didn't kill her!"

"Which," Royce exclaimed savagely, "explains why he has been so determined to get his hands on her—he knows who she is and must have concocted some elaborate scheme to gain control of her fortune!"

Jack cleared his throat uneasily. "I don't think that it's, um, *just* to get his hands on her fortune that he has kidnapped her—me and Ben have known for a long time that he wanted her in his bed," Jack said with unvarnished truth.

"Jesus!" Royce muttered, his eyes shutting in anguish at the ugly picture of Morgana enduring the embrace of the one-eyed man. "Jack, I could have wished that you hadn't brought up that aspect of the situation. We *must* find her as soon as possible!"

Confusion evident, Julian asked uncertainly, "Has something happened since I've been gone? You said 'kidnapped.'"

Zachary and Jack instantly crowded up to Julian, and both began to talk at once, rapidly explaining between the pair of them the current, rather grim situation. Ironically, the news that his half sister had been snatched by the one-eyed man was perhaps the very thing that Julian needed to hear. The knowledge of her terrible predicament, the possibility that her very life might be in danger, pushed his own unhappy situation to the back of his mind. It also gave him something to do other than dwell on the horrendous shocks he had suffered this day, and with a zealot's gleam in his eyes, with desperate eagerness he turned to Royce and vowed, "I will help you in any way that I can! Where shall we begin?"

Bleakly Royce stared off at the horizon. "I don't know," he said finally, a hint of defeat in his voice. Giving himself an angry shake, deliberately closing his mind to the fear and degradation that Morgana might be suffering at this very moment, holding a tight rein on his own fears for her, he continued more confidently, "We know that whatever method he used to spirit her away, he did not come past the entrance to Lime Tree Cottage . . . which lets us know that he had to be going in the direction of Tunbridge Wells. . . ." His mouth tightened and he spat frustratedly, "Which tells us precisely *nothing!* He could have taken her anywhere!"

Pulling his watch from its pocket in his vest, he glanced down at it, his expression growing even grimmer. "It's almost the half hour. . . . If we tarry any longer here, we will have lost whatever advantage my learning so soon about her meeting with him will have given us."

They held a short, tense discussion of the best way to proceed. It was decided that Royce and George would leave immediately in the gig that Royce had ordered readied earlier; they would head toward Tunbridge Wells, inquiring after Morgana as they went, leaving messages or directions whenever possible; the others would follow after them just as soon as horses could be readied for them. Julian's horses were exhausted, having already traveled from London today, and it was agreed that some of their party should be mounted individually, in order to be able to cast farther afield and search in several different directions at the same time.

The fact that Jack had never been on a horse in his life, nor driven one, created a temporary setback until it was deemed that it might be wise to have a second, larger vehicle available if they needed it—they had no way of knowing when or in what condition they might find Morgana. The solution was simple—Zachary and Julian would be astride the fastest horses in the stables, and Jack would follow in the yellow-bodied barouche, ably driven by Royce's coachman.

Having disposed of their various methods of transportation, and conscious of the minutes relentlessly ticking away, with mounting impatience Royce growled, "Come along, George! Let us be off—and pray that we discover some hint of which direction he has taken her!"

"Wait!" George said abruptly, and when Royce threw him an irascible look, he added imperturbably, "Been thinking."

"Oh, Lord! Not *now!*" Royce pleaded irritably, certain that George was about to embark on another long-winded explanation.

George shot him a reproachful glance and held up the note from the one-eyed man, which he still had clutched in his hand. A slight frown furrowed his forehead. "Believe I've seen this handwriting before. . . ."

His eyes fixed on his cousin's face with painful intensity, Royce asked raggedly, "Are you certain?"

George nodded. "Told you—remember everything!"

Julian gave a half-bitter, half-rueful laugh. "I can attest to *that!*" he said with feeling. "He does remember everything, whether it is twenty-year-old gossip or the fact that some high-flycr had china bluc cycs!"

George jumped as if he had been shot. "That's it!" he exclaimed excitedly. "Knew there was something else!" He looked at the handwriting on the paper and nodded and muttered as if to himself. "Of course, should have recognized his scrawl—took cnough vowcls from him over the years!"

In a suspiciously mild voice, Royce asked, "Would you mind sharing your knowledge with us? *Soon?*"

Sending his cousin a quelling glance, George said calmly, "Almost forgot something interesting about Jane Fowler. . . . She was born on the wrong side of the blanket, but she came from good stock—her father was a country squire, raised her properly, but she kicked over the traces and ran away with her half sister's fiancé to London."

Jack nodded his head and corroborated George's statement. "Yes, that's true—Mother never hid her past from us."

George beamed approvingly at Jack, and Royce choked back a despairing groan. Afraid that his cousin was about to embark on a lengthy discussion about Jane Fowler and what she had done or not done twenty-five years earlier, painfully conscious of time slipping away, Royce muttered, "George, *please!* If you have any affection for me, get to the damn point of your story!"

Looking slightly offended, George said stiffly, "Thing is, about two years after she appeared in London, her brother, one of the squire's legitimate get, showed up in town. He was green as grass and didn't realize that having a sister who was

a member of the demimonde would put him beyond the pale."
A thoughtful expression on his face, George murmured admiringly, "Didn't take him long to learn, though, and he quickly distanced himself from her and that crowd. He was a likable youth—known him for years, but don't think that there are many people who even remember that his sister was Jane Fowler."

"His name, George!" Royce demanded tautly, holding on to his temper with the greatest of effort.

"Allan Rufus Newell," George said simply.

"Newell!" Zachary and Julian ejaculated simultaneously, staring in astonishment at George. "B-B-But you may meet him nearly everywhere!" Zachary continued in confusion.

"Of course! That's how he knew where we would be the day Morgana was ordered to pick my pocket!" Royce breathed thickly. "We know the one-eyed man wrote that note, and if George has identified the handwriting as Newell's . . . Allan Newell *is* the one-eyed man! Which also explains how Morgana ended up with Jane Fowler! Her brother, as the one-eyed man, brought her the infant to raise."

"But *why?*" Jack questioned in obvious bewilderment.

A fierce, dangerous smile curved Royce's mouth. "That's something I intend to find out, just as soon as I lay my hands on him!" He speared George with a menacing glance. "And now, cousin," he began in a silken tone that fooled no one, "where can we find our elusive Mr. Newell?"

Eyeing Royce uneasily, George muttered, "Believe he has a summer home on the coast, near Hastings. Don't know its precise location, but once we reach Hastings, positive we can get directions to it."

It seemed logical, and without further discussion, Royce hustled George to the waiting gig; a moment later, the horses leaping forward at Royce's urgings, they swept down the driveway. As the gatekeeper's cottage came into sight, Royce slowed slightly and would have driven on past if Harry and

John had not suddenly appeared at the entrance, waving their arms frantically.

Jerking his horses to a halt, in a tone that would have given a lesser man pause, Royce barked, "Yes, what is it?" His eyes narrowed as he caught sight of a bloodied and disheveled Tom Cooper and Mr. Spurling standing uncertainly at the side of the cottage.

Mr. Spurling, his usually immaculate clothes dusty and torn, his nose bloodied and his lip split, walked over to the gig. Meeting Royce's hard stare, he said in a voice trembling with indignation, "I know that you believed that I was the one who allowed the intruder into the house in London—but I am innocent of that crime!" He shot Tom Cooper a bitter look. "I was not the only one up that night afterwards, when I left to return to my room, I found *him* lurking about. He denied any knowledge of what had happened, but since I knew that *I* had not let the one-eyed man into the house, I immediately suspected that Tom Cooper was the culprit." Drawing his diminutive body up as tall as he could, he went on doggedly, "I have watched him closely these past weeks, and today my efforts were rewarded."

Tom Cooper, wiping his own bloody nose, although looking slightly less for wear than Mr. Spurling, growled, "I didn't do anything wrong. He's dicked in the nob!"

Mr. Spurling smiled in a superior manner and, reaching into his torn vest, brought out a slip of folded paper. "I think you will find the contents of this note most revealing, sir!" He handed it to Royce, then glanced disdainfully back at Tom Cooper and said quietly, "I followed him into town this afternoon, where he furtively met a gentleman who remained concealed in the shadows. I was hidden from them, but close enough to hear the man's instructions as he gave Tom the note—you were not to receive it until eight o'clock this evening. I, er, forced him to give it to me."

Swiftly Royce scanned the missive, instantly recognizing the handwriting as the same in the note to Morgana. It was obvious why Newell had not wanted the letter delivered until later—at eight it would still be light enough for Royce to leave for the meeting detailed within, but it would be well after dark before he could have possibly reached the destination stated by Newell. Darkness would have been Newell's ally, and the three-hour delay would have given the man all the time in the world to set a trap for Royce. Morgana was to be the bait, and Royce didn't doubt for a moment that Allan Newell, as the one-eyed man, had every intention of killing him. . . .

Royce lifted his head, his gaze resting a brief, lethal moment on Tom Cooper's face. "Tie him up," he ordered flatly. "And guard him well—I don't want him getting to my quarry before me!" Looking down at Edward Spurling, he apologized charmingly, "I regret having suspected you, and I want to thank you for what you have done today—you have exposed the spy within our household and you may very well have saved my life! We will talk further upon my return."

Tossing the note to George, Royce cracked his whip, and as the horses sprang forward, he snarled softly, "It seems that we have some advantages, after all—we know Newell is the one-eyed man, we have over a two-hour head start, and we won't have to waste time searching for the bastard—he's given us a bloody map to follow!"

CHAPTER 32

Morgana's head ached dreadfully, and as she gradually became aware of her surroundings, she was bewildered at first by the predicament in which she found herself. It took her several increasingly terrified seconds before she realized that she was bound and gagged and lying on the bottom of a vehicle that was traveling rapidly down the road. Something heavy and scratchy covered her, and she guessed that it was a blanket or a rug. Hazily those last few minutes as she had stepped from the road came back to her, and when the full, horrifying realization of her disastrous situation hit her, for one awful moment she thought that she would faint from utter fright. *The one-eyed man had captured her!*

She allowed herself only a moment of stark terror, and then, closing her eyes and offering up a fervent prayer to whatever gods looked over fools like her, she focused all her thoughts and energies on considering how to escape from this perilous situation. From the murky gloom within and the bright glitter of sunlight that danced at the edge of her covering, it was obvious that the sun was still up. She had no idea how long she had been unconscious, but from the degree of light, she suspected that it had been for more than an hour.

Ignoring her aching head, keeping at bay demoralizing thoughts of what her fate might be, she experimentally wiggled her fingers and hands, which were tied behind her back, but it was apparent almost immediately that her captor was taking no chances—her bonds were secure and tight . . . painfully so. Since the fact that she was conscious seemed to be the only advantage she had at the moment, she kept her movements to a minimum, not wanting to alert him that she had awakened. Cautiously she tested to see if the ropes on her ankles were as firmly fastened as those on her wrists. They were. Suppressing a despairing groan, she next tried to dislodge the gag from her mouth, but that, too, had been tied in such a manner that defied her attempts to remove it.

Angry frustration welled up inside her, and she cursed herself for having been tricked so easily—she should have known that he would have set some sort of trap, and gullible fool that she was, she had waltzed eagerly into it. Longingly she thought of the dagger that she had concealed in her reticule and wondered if he had discovered it or had even bothered to bring her things along with him. She suspected that he had— he wouldn't have wanted to leave her belongings where someone else would find them—and she could only hope that, at some point, she might be able to reach the dagger . . . *if* he hadn't found it!

Assessing her grim situation, she came to the dismal conclusion that things could not be much worse for her, but she took comfort from the knowledge that at least Royce's life was not in danger. . . . She swallowed nervously. At least she *hoped* that Royce's life was not in danger—the one-eyed man was not to be trusted, and there was a tiny niggle of fear that once he had her safely disposed of somewhere, he would return and kill Royce anyway. A shudder went through her slender body. Oh, God! Please, she begged silently, don't let him kill Royce!

It was horrible enough that her fate hung in the balance, terrifying enough that she might be forced to endure whatever pain and degradation the one-eyed man intended to inflict upon her, but to know that it had been for nothing . . . to know that while she suffered whatever ugly destiny the one-eyed man had planned for her, she was powerless to stop the brutal murder of the person she loved with all her valiant heart, was nearly unbearable.

Conscious of the fact that she was doing herself no good dwelling on such painful musings, she tried to concentrate on something else, anything else, but though she could blank it from her mind for a while, insidiously those torturous thoughts would return again and again. Unfortunately when she would try to switch her thoughts to something else, inevitably they would turn to the stunning meeting with Julian Devlin this afternoon and the unsettling discovery that a woman she had loved deeply and had always believed to be her mother might not have been related to her at all! But what had devastated her was the knowledge that there was also a distinct possibility that she was an heiress to a fortune and that her husband might very well have married her simply because he already knew these things and hoped to gain from them.

With the one-eyed man's threat against Royce's life uppermost in her thoughts, however, there had not been even a moment in which to seriously consider what effect George Ponteby's disclosures might have upon her life, and now, as she lay bound and gagged, the helpless prisoner of a man she loathed and feared, did not seem a particularly propitious time either! Her emotions in a frantic, restless turmoil, her head pounding furiously from the blow she had received, and the ache in her tightly bound arms increasing with every jolting mile that the vehicle traveled, she gave up, stoically enduring the physical discomforts, waiting almost defeatedly for whatever fate had in store for her.

The journey seemed interminable, but just when she was certain that she was going to have to plead with him to untie her arms, the motion of the vehicle changed and she sensed that they had reached their destination. Her heart began to bang with sharp, painful beats, and like a small, frightened animal, she froze as the daylight around the edges of her covering disappeared and the horses were pulled to a stop. From the sudden cessation of light, she guessed that they had driven inside a stable or a barn, and tensely she waited for what would happen next.

The vehicle swayed as he stepped down, and for the next few moments, she heard the sounds of the horses being unharnessed and put away. A door closed and she could hear his footsteps fading as he walked away. Her listlessness had vanished, and lifting her head, she listened alertly, her mind racing with wild schemes to affect her escape. Silence descended for several moments, and she wondered how long it would be before he returned. Time enough for her to flee? She was just on the point of struggling to a sitting position when she heard him approaching and she stiffened.

Walking directly up to the vehicle, he drawled hatefully,

"Still pretending to be unconscious, my dear? It won't do you any good—I have been aware of your wakefulness for quite some time."

Since the gag in her mouth effectively prevented any coherent speech, Morgana simply glowered in the direction of his voice and remained silent.

As if he could see her reaction, he laughed, and a second later, she was swooped up, rug and all, and the breath was knocked from her as she was tossed unceremoniously over his shoulder. He rummaged around for another moment and murmured, "Mustn't forget the lady's basket and hat."

Her heart gave a great leap at his words. Was the reticule still in her basket? The dagger still safely hidden? For the first time since she had awakened and discovered her terrible peril, hope sprang to her breast.

As they left the barn, he said mockingly, "I'm sorry for the delay, but you see, I had to 'become' the one-eyed man—until I have taken care of a few more little details, I'm afraid the eye patch and the rest of it are most necessary." He chuckled, and it was obvious that he was in high fettle, very pleased with himself. "If all goes well," he continued easily, "after tonight, the one-eyed man will be no more!"

If I can get my hands on the dagger, Morgana vowed grimly, he certainly won't be!

He carried her what seemed like a considerable distance, and the bobbing motion of her body as he walked did not help the throbbing in her head at all. From her position, she caught occasional glimpses of the ground and could see that they were not traveling on any particular path—the ground was sparsely covered with wild grasses and weeds, dotted now and then with scrubby brushes, and as they walked, the sound and scent of the sea grew stronger. From the ever-increasing roar of the waves and the salty mist that seemed to permeate her very clothing, she knew that they must be on a cliff right at the very edge of the sea.

Suddenly, from the corner of her eye, she caught a glimpse of weather-beaten boards and he swerved, as if going around a corner; a few feet later, he stopped abruptly. Pushing open a door, he walked inside a building. A second later, Morgana found herself flung down onto a hard wooden chair, the rug falling away from her, and for the first time, she was able to fully see her surroundings. She was seated, she discovered, in a small, open-beamed room, two salt-stained windows on either side of the door through which she had entered giving her her first sight of the turbulent, ever-changing sea. A stone fireplace, obviously used for cooking, from the utensils hanging nearby, was against one wall, some tall oak cupboards were on the opposite side, and another doorway in the fourth wall presumably led to sleeping quarters at the rear of the building. Two surprisingly handsome leather chairs were placed on either side of the fireplace; the only other furniture in the room was a heavy chest near the entrance door and a sturdy table with three wooden-back chairs around it, one of which Morgana occupied. The floor and walls were bare.

She had deliberately avoided looking at the one-eyed man, but once she had completed her survey of her surroundings, she looked up at him, contempt flickering openly across her lovely features. He was standing directly in front of her, appearing as he always did—clothed in black, the dark slouch hat pulled low, the patch covering his one eye—and when her gaze touched his face, he smiled. That smile sent a shiver down her spine, but she lifted her chin proudly, determined not to let him know how very frightened of him she was.

"Still the haughty little bitch, I see," he observed mockingly, and carelessly tossed her basket and hat upon the table. He reached out and caressed her cheek and murmured, "I'll soon break you of your defiant ways, my dear . . . and take pleasure in doing so!"

She jerked her face away from his touch, and it took everything she possessed not to look at the basket to see if her reticule was still there, and more important, the dagger. Glaring ferociously at him, through the gag she spat out a muffled curse.

Her reaction seemed to please him and he laughed. To her astonishment, he loosened the gag and said smoothly, "There is no longer any need for this—you may scream all you want, but there is no one who will hear you. Unfortunately, I'm afraid you will have to remain tied up until after I've taken care of that husband of yours."

Her eyes huge, she demanded fiercely, "What do you mean? You promised not to hurt him if I obeyed your command."

"Promised?" he repeated with a lift of his one brow. "Odd, I don't remember promising not to hurt him. I only recall that I threatened to kill him *immediately* if you didn't meet me—I didn't write a thing about not killing him later. . . ."

"You bastard!" she shouted, struggling to launch herself at him, but the ropes prevented her from doing more than falling off her chair.

An angry glitter in the black eye, he lifted up her twisting body and thrust her back down on the chair. "That's *enough!* If you are wise, you will keep a civil tongue in your mouth," he snarled, and struck her brutally across the face.

Her ears ringing from the force of his blow, she glumly concluded that there was nothing to be gained from further antagonizing him, and sullenly she asked, "What do you plan to do with me?"

He smiled. "Oh, nothing very terrible, my dear—once I've eliminated Manchester, you and I will wed and you will take your rightful place in society."

Morgana gaped at him. "Are you mad?" she asked harshly. "I would rather die than marry you!"

"But would you rather your *brothers* die . . . than you marry me?"

She paled. "Why are you doing this?" she asked despairingly. "What do you hope to gain?"

A finger caressed her cheek and she flinched. "I intend to gain the Lady Morgana Devlin for my bride, and a very wealthy, aristocratic bride you will make me, my dear. I've planned this for a very long time and I don't intend to be deterred now—not even if I have to kill a dozen people to gain my way. With you at my side, there will be no door closed to me—your fortune, combined with mine, will make me one of the richest men in England, and with you as my wife, I will have the social prominence and power that I have always wanted." He glanced kindly at her. "You will find me a generous husband—you will have whatever you wish, and I will only require your presence at my side . . . and your willing cooperation in my bed." His eye traveled boldly over her small bosom. "Your *very* willing cooperation," he muttered, and pulled her into his arms, hungrily pressing his mouth against hers.

She fought to escape his ravaging kiss, but he held her fast, cruelly forcing her lips apart, his thrusting tongue brutally violating her mouth. Nearly gagging from the feel and taste of him, she finally managed to twist her head aside. "Don't!" she pleaded softly, her head lowered and turned away from him.

He was breathing heavily, and to her horror, even between the layers of clothing that separated them, she could feel his rigid member pushing insistently against her. Oh, dear God! Not *this!*

With an effort, he set her from him and said thickly, "There will be time enough to enjoy each other after I have disposed of Manchester."

Her heart icy, she cried desperately, "You will never get away with it! And even if you do kill Royce, you have no proof that I am Morgana Devlin—your plan will come to naught!"

"No proof?" he repeated archly. "Oh, but you are wrong there, my dear—I have a great deal of proof! Would you like to see it?"

Her eyes searched his face. Slowly she nodded. "Yes, I would."

He walked over to the chest and, taking a key from his pocket, unlocked it. Opening the chest, he scrabbled about for a second and then lifted out a leather-bound book. Smiling, he walked back toward her. "I must tell you that this modest place is my own particular little hideaway. I come here when I want to be alone or to admire some of the more fascinating, er, mementos I keep here."

He held the book in front of her, and she saw that it was a Bible. "You don't recognize this book, but it is your mother's Bible," he said conversationally. "I took it from her the night she died—the night you were born." He flipped it open and showed her the writing on the page.

Bewilderedly she read the delicate, flowing script in the right-hand corner of the page before her. *Hester Devlin, Countess St. Audries, her book, July 1, 1795.* It gave Morgana a peculiar feeling to read those words, and yet, of themselves, they proved nothing.

"Just because you have her Bible doesn't prove that she is my mother!" she said sharply. "Jane was my mother!"

Clearly enjoying himself, he shook his head. "Oh, no, that's not true. Your uncle, Stephen Devlin, at that time only a mere younger brother to an Earl, arranged for me to take you away. . . . Of course, he wanted me to kill you and get rid of your body, but it amused me to give you to Jane. Believe me, Hester Devlin was your mother, and Andrew Devlin, the sixth Earl of St. Audries, was your father. You have some of the finest blood in England running in your veins."

Confusion evident in her expression, she inquired helplessly, "But why?"

"Why did Stephen want you dead? Or why didn't I kill you?"

"Both!"

Smiling complacently, he sat down in one of the wooden chairs at the table near her. "Rather than telling it to you piecemeal, it will be much easier if you just listen while I regale you with a most diverting little story about the past," he explained cheerfully.

In fascinated horror, Morgana listened to the ugly and twisted events that had taken place over twenty years ago, events that had shaped her life and brought her to this moment in time. He spared her nothing, telling her with relish every tiny detail, from Julian's conception to the night that her mother had died from Lucinda's final dose of poison. The most difficult part for Morgana was when he read aloud her mother's pitiful letter, which he had extracted with flourish from the spine of the Bible. Hester's fear came through clearly, as did the love she bore her child and the betrayal she was trying so desperately to avenge. Morgana felt tears trembling on her lashes, and frantically she blinked them away, not wanting him to realize how powerfully her mother's letter affected her. Pale and shaken, reeling from the sheer vindictiveness of Stephen's act of violence against her father, stunned to learn that Julian was actually her half brother and that his mother had murdered her mother, she could only stare at him, her features full of revulsion and loathing.

"Why didn't you kill me?" she forced herself to ask.

He looked thoughtful. "I don't really know," he admitted. "You were rather a sickly baby—probably the result of the arsenic—and for a while Jane feared that you would die. But you didn't, and I really can't say why I let you live. A whim, perhaps? A perverse sort of pleasure in knowing that as long as you lived, I could crush Stephen at any time?" He shrugged. "I didn't actually think of marrying you for quite a number of years, but then one day I looked at you and realized that you were growing up to be quite a fetching little baggage." He smiled meaningfully at her. "I had arranged to sell you to a nobleman who preferred *very* young virgins, but Jane would have none of it and so I had to change my plans. I considered merely making you my mistress, the idea of having the *Lady* Morgana Devlin in my bed and at my command appealing rather strongly to me, but then I carried that thought one step further—what if I *married* you and saw to it that the truth came out . . . ?" He chuckled. "Of course, not my part in it! The one-eyed man would be the villain, while I would simply be your loving husband—the man who accidentally uncovered the entire dastardly plot. I thought that after we were married, I would 'discover' your mother's Bible in an old trunk that had been Jane's. No one will be more surprised and outraged than myself to find out that my half sister, a woman who, because of her, ah . . . unsavory way of life, I had not heard of in years, was part of such a dastardly plot. Clever, don't you agree?"

She gazed wordlessly at him for a very long time, not quite trusting herself to speak, fearful that no matter what he did to her, she would not be able to keep from hurling herself at him in a savage fury and, despite her bonds, not cease her wild attempts to inflict grievous injury on him until he had beaten her unconscious. Hatred welled up in her heart, and almost compulsively her eyes strayed to the basket sitting on the table *and the reticule lying within it!* Dizzying hope flooded through her slender body. If only he would leave for a while, provided the dagger was still inside the reticule, it would take her but a moment to free herself, and then . . . For a second she was mesmerized by the soul-satisfying picture of the one-eyed man lying dead at her feet, the dagger plunged through his black heart. But reality set in almost immediately and she realized sickly that unless fate smiled kindly upon her, she was doomed to suffer the fate he had planned for her.

Bitter regret washed over her and she was tormented by visions of everything *else* she could have done rather than embark on her own quest to kill the one-eyed man. I should have considered that I might fail and have left Royce a letter explaining everything. . . . Suddenly she stiffened. She hadn't left a note of her own, but as clearly as if she were standing in her bedchamber, she could see the one-eyed man's note lying crumpled on her dressing table, where she had left it in her haste to meet him.

Royce was certain to have found that note by now, and he would at least know what had happened to her . . . and perhaps try to find her? Hope once again rose within her, and in spite of knowing that it would be miraculous if Royce managed to discover where the one-eyed man had taken her, she clung comfortingly to the knowledge that Royce *might* at this very moment be following quickly behind them.

Not aware of any of the events that had taken place since her capture, she would not have believed that even as she sat staring helplessly at the one-eyed man, Royce was pulling his mercilessly driven horses to an exhausted stop at the very stable where the one-eyed man had unharnessed his own horses just half an hour ago.

Unlike the one-eyed man, who had not wanted to bring attention to himself and had been forced to travel at an unremarkable rate of speed, Royce hadn't given a damn who saw him madly racing down the road and he had not spared his horses, driving them at an unrelenting pace. George thought it the most terrifying ride of his life, and more than once, as Royce had approached a curve at breakneck speed, with never a check of the horses, he was quite positive that his life was over.

The foam-flecked horses, their heads hanging low in bone-deep exhaustion, remained motionless as Royce jumped down from the gig and made a quick inspection of the stable. Returning, he commented grimly, "He's been here. There is no sign of Morgana, but there is a vehicle inside and two horses, the sweat not yet completely dried on them, so we are not too far behind him." As he walked toward the gig, he pulled forth a folded slip of paper from his waistcoat.

Quickly perusing the instructions from the one-eyed man, Royce lifted his gaze, staring at the barren landscape around him, the scent and sound of the sea coming clearly to him.

"He states that there is a path which leads to the beach below the headlands and that once I've reached the shore, I should turn to the left and continue in that direction until I see the opening of a cave in the face of the promontory. He'll meet me there at eleven o'clock tonight."

"Never tell me you're going to do it!" George expostulated nervously. "It will be a trap! He means to kill you!"

A feral gleam in the golden eyes, Royce replied mockingly, "I know that, George, and I have no intention of walking blindly into his snare. Don't forget, if everything had gone according to his plan, I would just now be receiving these instructions—we are hours ahead of the schedule he set." He stood there frowning a moment. "He won't have Morgana in the cave—I'm certain of that—but more than likely he will have her somewhere nearby. . . ."

Before George's astonished gaze, Royce suddenly clambered gracefully up to the roof of the stable. Hands on his hips, feet planted apart as he balanced on the sloping roof, he stared off in the distance. "I see the path angling off to the right over there, but nothing else." He continued to rake the bleak landscape, hoping desperately to sight something that would give him a clue where next to look for Morgana. He had managed by sheer, obstinate tenacity to keep his fear for her under control during the wild, madcap dash to reach this destination, but as the minutes crept inexorably by, as the sunlight began gradually to lessen, he could feel his iron-hold grip slipping, and he was faced with the terrifying possibility that whatever luck he had possessed so far had vanished and that he might never see Morgana again.

Royce was almost dizzy from the suffocating fright and half-mad fury that erupted through him at that thought; his mouth tightened and the golden eyes narrowed. He was not beaten! He was going to find his wife; and when he found her, after he had shaken her senseless for scaring him this way, he was going to kiss her witless and let her hear from him in no uncertain terms precisely how very much he loved her! The one-eyed man was not going to win this time! Royce was on the point of turning away when something caught his eye, and his breath lodged painfully in his chest. Was that a rooftop near the edge of the cliff? Half-hidden by a slight rise in the land? From the ground it would have been invisible, but from his vantage point on top of the stable, Royce stared tensely at that irregular break in the landscape, passionately willing it to be what he was so frantically searching for. A shaft of the fading sunlight suddenly gilded the tiny weather vane that perched at the peak of the small building, and Royce let out a low, fierce, triumphant growl. It could merely be some fisherman's cottage, but instinct told him that he would find his wife there . . . and the one-eyed man!

Effortlessly leaping down from the roof, he hurried over to the gig, and checking the pistol he had brought with him, he said tersely to George, "There is a small cottage near the edge of the cliff—I suspect that Morgana will be found there . . . along with Newell. You remain here, and if I am not returned within the hour—drive as fast as these poor horses will take you to the nearest magistrate's and explain everything to him."

"Royce, be careful!" George replied urgently. "He is a killer and will stop at nothing to gain his aims."

Something dangerous and deadly moved in Royce's eyes. "He has my wife, George! I think that your fears should be for *him!*"

Without another word, Royce disappeared around the end of the stable.

Approaching the cottage was tricky because of the lack of cover, but using the slight undulations of the land itself and the few scrubby bushes that dotted the area, Royce gradually crept nearer. The falling twilight was to his advantage, and as he stealthily drew closer, he could see that there were no windows at the rear of the house, which allowed him to approach faster.

Careful to make no sound, the pistol held ready in one hand, he edged along the weather-beaten boards of the cottage, listening for any noise that would bolster his stubborn belief that Morgana was inside. *She had to be!* It was unthinkable that he had squandered precious time chasing after a will-o'-the-wisp notion. Unable to allow himself to consider even for a moment that the cottage might simply be a lonely fisherman's hut, he sidled cautiously around the corner of the building. The sight of the two windows and door facing the churning sea several feet below halted him abruptly, but dropping down to the ground, he inched forward until he was beneath one of the windows.

Like a balm and a benediction, the sound of Morgana's voice wafted to him, and involuntarily his eyes closed in a fervent, exultant prayer. He hadn't been aware of precisely how very fearful he had been until this moment, but hearing the familiar rise and fall of her voice, something inside him suddenly unclenched and he was conscious of a tremendous burden lifting.

The golden eyes glittering fiercely, his fingers tightened around the pistol, and Royce hoped for the sake of the one-eyed man that Morgana was unhurt, for if that blackhearted devil had harmed her . . . A primitive and unforgiving emotion welling up inside him, he began to creep forward.

Inside the cottage, totally oblivious to the danger just outside his doorway, the one-eyed man was preening himself before Morgana, boasting of his various successes. "Of course," he said smugly, "I've never been contacted by a member of the royal family, but just think if I had been—why, conceivably I could have been the uncrowned King of England!"

Despite the fact that her lovely features showed the strain of maintaining her flagging courage, Morgana's eyes flashed contemptuously and she declared spiritedly, "I don't care how clever you've been in the past—you're never going to get away with this! Royce is too smart to fall into your trap! He'll find me, and when he does, you'll rue the day you thought to best him!"

"Ah, do you think so, my sweet?" he drawled, standing very close to her, his black eye roving with increasing satisfaction over her slender form. Cupping her chin, he forced her head backward, and one thumb rubbing suggestively across her tight mouth, he murmured, "I wouldn't count on it! Just about now your soon-to-be-late husband should be receiving a message from me—one that gives him explicit instructions where to meet me!" He smiled when her eyes widened in angry alarm. "He should be arriving in oh, say, three hours, determined to wrest you from me! Of course," he continued lightly, "he won't be meeting me at this place! No, no, you'll remain here safely out of danger while I, er . . . dispose of him in a sea cave just below us. There are all sorts of hiding places within it, virtually made for someone like me to lie in wait for the unsuspecting. Not that Manchester will be unsuspecting—I believe that he has wit enough to surmise that I mean to kill him—but I am very familiar with the terrain of the cave, and he is not. Besides, he will be no match for someone of my cunning. Just think, my dear, before midnight you will be a widow!"

The one-eyed man had been so intent on impressing Morgana that he had not been paying attention to what was going on around him. The first intimation he had that there were going to have to be some drastic revisions within his plan was when the door to the cottage flew open and Royce drawled from the doorway, "I wouldn't be too sure of that, Newell! Before anyone leaves this place, one of us will die . . . and I have no intention of it being me!"

Morgana's heart nearly leapt from her breast at the sight of Royce standing arrogantly in the doorway, the pistol in his hand aimed unerringly at the heart of the one-eyed man. His cravat had been discarded and his white shirt was opened as far as the V of his embroidered waistcoat, the formfitting russet jacket revealing his powerful shoulders and arms, the buckskin breeches clinging faithfully to the hard muscle and sinew of his strong thighs, and fairly radiating from him was an air of something wild and dangerous. He looked magnificent, the thick, tawny hair falling in windswept locks about his head, the handsome face taut and full of vitality, and beneath the heavy black brows, the golden eyes . . . the golden eyes gleaming with a tiger's savage intensity.

Loving him passionately as she did, unutterably joyful that he had come and yet swamped with fear for his life, Morgana could not take her eyes off him. Instinctively she surged upward from her chair, intent on reaching him, but the one-eyed man moved with the speed of a striking snake, jerking her upright and holding her slender, blue-gowned body in front of him like a shield. From out of nowhere a pistol appeared in his hand, and leveling it at Royce, he smiled.

"And now what do you intend to do, Manchester?" the one-eyed man asked with a smirk, apparently not at all disturbed by this unexpected occurrence. "Your weapon is no good to you . . . unless, of course, you want to risk hitting her instead of me."

Thoughtfully Royce considered his prey, noting carefully that Morgana's much smaller body did not provide quite the amount of protection that Newell assumed it did. Never taking his eyes off Newell's face, apparently oblivious to the pistol aimed at him, Royce said coolly, "Actually, she isn't such a good shield for you, Newell—you don't want her dead any more than I do!" At Newell's start, Royce continued easily, "I haven't quite figured out precisely what you plan to do, but I'm convinced that my wife is at the heart of it, and without her, your schemes will come to naught. So I don't think you're really willing to risk her life."

Ignoring the bulk of Royce's words and honing in on the part that interested him most, the one-eyed man remarked, "That's twice you've called me 'Newell.' Why?"

"Did you think that we wouldn't put it all together?" Royce asked lightly. "I won't go into great detail how we concluded that you are Allan Newell, but suffice it to say that George Ponteby has a remarkable memory . . . and he remembered that Jane Fowler, *supposedly* my wife's mother, was your half sister. We've already concluded that Morgana is the legitimate daughter of the sixth Earl of St. Audries and his wife, Hester, but Jane Fowler was the link to you—once George identified her as your sister, everything else fell into place."

The one-eyed man's face contorted with rage, and the arm that held Morgana captive in front of him tightened painfully across her throat, making her wince. "You can't prove anything!" he snarled.

"I don't have to," Royce replied indifferently. "There are four or five of us who know, and all it will take is a word dropped here and there for the news to spread like wildfire amongst the ton that Allan Newell is actually the feared and hated one-eyed man! In less than a week the scandalmongers will have ruined you. Bow Street will be quite interested in you, too, I suspect. Give it up! Let Morgana and me go now and you will have just enough time to escape with your ill-gotten gains to the continent. . . . Otherwise, I will kill you where you stand."

Newell's fury-ravaged face gave no clue to the stunning jolt Royce's words had given him. His dreams, his world, were on the verge of shattering before him. With a craftiness born of desperation, he considered how to wrest victory out of what appeared to be crushing defeat. The solution was right there before him—he would simply have to find out who else knew the truth and kill them. He had already planned to kill Royce, Jacko, and Ben; what were a few more? Confidence flooding through him, he could now scoff at Royce's offer to let him escape. Why should he give up everything he had dreamed and planned for when it was just within grasp? As for Royce killing him where he stood—the idea was ludicrous! *He* held all the cards! Not Manchester!

An ugly smile on his mouth, his fingers tightening menacingly around the trigger of his pistol, Newell stated contemptuously, "It is you who is far more likely to be killed where you stand! Throw down your pistol at once!"

Royce had given him all the chances he was going to, and taking the measure of his man, he decided that time was running out for all of them. He dare not prolong this confrontation if he didn't want to be shot down before Morgana's very eyes. And as for obeying Newell's command, there was no question of *that!* If he were foolish enough to do so, Morgana would be a widow before his pistol hit the floor! He had never doubted his own skill, and despite the terrifying risks involved, there was really only one choice for him to make. . . .

Royce glanced for the first time at Morgana, noting her pale, frightened features, the lovely gray eyes dark and wide with fear as she gazed at him. Incredibly he smiled at her and murmured softly, "Don't look so worried, sweetheart—I won't let anything harm you, and I didn't come harrying after you to let him win in the end."

Morgana felt a bubble of hysterical laughter rise up within her at his words, but before a sound escaped her, without hesitation, Royce fired the pistol directly at Newell's head!

The small room was rent by the explosion of Royce's pistol, and in the stunned second that followed his action, Morgana was appallingly certain he'd shot her. Hardly conscious of the slackening hold of the one-eyed man, through the drifts of blue smoke that had billowed from the pistol, she stared in dazed disbelief at Royce as he slowly lowered his arm. It was only then that she became aware that she was unharmed and noticed the white creases near Royce's mouth and the look of taut concentration upon his face.

The thump of the one-eyed man's body hitting the floor made her jump and look down. Blankly, almost uncomprehendingly, she stared at the man lying dead on the floor by her feet. His black hat had fallen off, revealing a fine head of dark hair, and in the middle of his forehead . . . the neat round hole made by the bullet from Royce's pistol. She swayed dizzily from reaction and then she was swept up in Royce's embrace as he crushed her next to him and pressed urgent little kisses into her black, curly hair. They stood there a long time, locked together, Royce's voice in her ear whispering the words she had once longed to hear, but she was numb. She could feel nothing; it was as if all her emotions were encased in ice. Even after Royce had removed her bonds and they prepared to leave, she was only conscious of a great emptiness inside her.

From the doorway, with her mother's Bible, Hester's desperate letter inside it, clasped tightly in her hand, Morgana glanced back at the body of the one-eyed man lying sprawled on the floor. A little crack appeared in the ice that surrounded her. Hester would be glad, she thought fiercely, and then, turning away, she walked outside into the twilight with Royce.

EPILOGUE

Sunlight and Shadows

Come live with me, and be my love,
And we will some new pleasure prove
Of golden sands, and crystal brooks,
With silken lines, and silver hooks.

JOHN DONNE, "The Bait"

The Devlin family cemetery was enclosed by a low, ivy-covered stone wall and had been laid out on a small, tree-dotted hill about a half mile from St. Audries Hall. The scent of roses and honeysuckle wafted on the warm air, and a soft breeze rustled the green leaves of the oak trees that dappled the area with patches of shade. It was a tranquil place, especially so this late August afternoon as Morgana slowly wandered among the marble headstones and edifices that marked the graves of her ancestors.

She was wearing a gown of rose-striped muslin and carried a chip-straw hat adorned with a cherry-colored ribbon in one hand, and in the other, a basket filled with tall, spiky gladiolus, sweetly scented lavender, and spicy Stock, her mother's Bible with the fateful letter inside it lying underneath the flowers. This was not her first trip to the cemetery—she had come here often during the past weeks, sometimes to do nothing more than to sit at her parents' graves, bitterly mourning the senselessness of their deaths, other times simply to think, trying to make coherent decisions about her future . . . and Royce's. . . .

Today was no different, and after sadly laying the flowers she had brought with her upon her parents' graves, her muslin skirts billowing out on the ground around her, she had settled herself beneath a nearby oak tree. Lifting up the Bible, she took out her mother's letter and slowly read it once more, a tear trickling down her face. There was so much love in those desperate words of Hester's, and yet as long as the letter existed . . . Her face pensive, she stared sightlessly out into space wondering if she had made the right decisions. So much had happened, she thought somberly, since she and

Royce had walked away from the one-eyed man's cottage over a fortnight ago. . . .

They had not spoken as they had quickly returned to the stable, where George waited in a growing fever of alarm and impatience. His relief on seeing them had been almost comical, and if Morgana had not been so devastated by all she had learned, she might have been amused. But that terrible numbness had not abated, and even the arrival of Zachary and Julian, on horses almost as exhausted as Royce's, had done little to disturb her state of mind. Royce had swiftly explained to the others what had transpired, and it was decided that the wisest course was to leave immediately—Newell's body was certain to be discovered eventually, and there was no need for any of them to be involved in it. The one-eyed man had lived surrounded by mystery—let his death in an isolated cottage near the surging, restless sea be the same.

Jack's arrival with the barouche moments later was greeted with relief, and after a brief discussion, it was concluded that finding an inn or tavern to stay at for the night was the most practical course.

It was not until they were all comfortably situated in the private dining room of a cozy inn, not five miles away, that Morgana felt the first real thaw in the iciness that surrounded her. The conversation, at first, had naturally been about the one-eyed man's death and identity, but eventually it had turned to what Julian had learned from Stephen and Lucinda.

Seeing the pain and bewilderment on Julian's face as he had haltingly spoken of that ugly meeting with Stephen and Lucinda, Morgana felt something move within her. Watching his expressive features as he smiled encouragingly at her and did his best to make it clear that he bore *her* no ill will for his sudden change in fortune, she could feel some of the ice around her heart start to melt. That this handsome, charming young man was her brother, a brother she had never known existed, still astounded her, and yet she found herself powerfully drawn to him. After a fashion, he had suffered as dreadfully as she had, and yet he was still gallantly attempting to act as if he had not gone, in a matter of hours, from being the heir to an Earldom, slated someday to inherit a handsome estate and a magnificent fortune, to being the penniless bastard son of a man long dead, and her soft heart bled for him. He had been an innocent victim too, and it seemed wickedly cruel that he should have to endure the violent and sweeping transformation that would take place once the truth was known.

Frowning, she stared down at the remains on her plate, a startling thought occurring to her. The title would not have come to her under any circumstances, and as for the fortune . . .

Her heart twisted painfully, and from beneath her lashes she sent a sadly considering look at Royce, who sat by her side. He was a wealthy man, a *very* wealthy man, possessed of more riches than she had ever dreamed of or would ever require. . . . But suppose he *had* married her with the hopes of laying hands on the Devlin family fortune . . . ? She took in a deep, shuddering breath. There was one way, she admitted uneasily, to find out! Did she dare? Was she willing to risk everything?

Until now she had only been marginally aware of the conversation going on around her, but gradually it dawned on her that there was one vital piece of the vicious story that no one yet knew—that Lucinda had murdered Hester! With the one-eyed man dead, that left only herself and Julian's mother who knew the truth, and looking again at Julian's strained features, she swore fiercely to herself that no one would ever learn of it from *her!* Certainly not Julian—he had suffered enough!

Conversation lapsed when the inn's servants came in and cleared the remains of their dinner, and it was not until they were again alone and scattered now throughout the room that the talk immediately returned to the events of the day. The air of icy detachment that had blurred much of the evening for her had vanished, and Morgana was very conscious of Royce standing by her chair, his hand resting on her shoulder. Since they had left the cottage, he had thrown her several puzzled looks and he watched her closely, observing her every movement, assessing every nuance in her voice, and carefully examining every expression that crossed her face. What does he expect? she wondered bitterly. That now I know I am a lady, I shall suddenly put on disdainful airs and haughty manners?

She glanced up at him, and the warm look in the depths of those brilliant golden eyes made her remember all the passionate, wondrous words that he had poured into her ear as he had held her after the one-eyed man had died. Had he meant them? Did he really love her? Painfully she searched his face, and something in it must have, for the present at least, reassured her, because almost instantly she was aware of a lessening of the suspicion and confusion in her heart.

She looked away from Royce as Julian said dully, "Today has been horrible, but I actually dread more the scandal that is going to break over us once the truth becomes known!" He gave himself a shake, and stiffening his shoulders, he said, "I shall have to leave London, of course." He glanced over at Morgana. "I don't want to cause you any embarrassment, but if you do not mind, I would like to stay at St. Audries Hall for a few weeks until I can decide how I am to make my living." His beautiful mouth trembled for a moment before he declared gruffly, "I will not be a burden on you and will not make any demands, but I hope you will bear with me until I can find some form of employment." He smiled with a bitter ruefulness. "It will be difficult—all I have been trained for is to be the next Earl of St. Audries, but perhaps I can become an estate agent or the like."

His valiant attempt to lightly dismiss what was a terrible calamity for him tore at Morgana's heart, and her resolve instantly crystallized. Unaware that she was going to do it, she suddenly leaped to her feet and exclaimed passionately, "*No! I will not have it!*" Crossing swiftly to stand in front of him, she clutched his arms and stared intently up into the face that so resembled her own. Her voice shaking with emotion, with vehement intensity she said, "I grew up in the most abject poverty imaginable, believing myself to be a bastard child. It was a wretched existence—even in St. Giles, bastards are not highly considered." The gray eyes black with the violence of what she was feeling, with the strength born of her convictions, she shook him and vowed fiercely, "I would never condemn you or anyone to that form of degradation. *Never!*"

Raking the room with a fiery glance, she said thickly, "What we learned today goes no farther! No one else but ourselves ever need know the truth."

Into the startled silence that had fallen at her stunning pronouncement, George murmured, "I've been thinking much the same myself. All family here. Keep it amongst ourselves. There is no need to make a scandal." He looked kindly at Morgana and declared warmly, "Glad Royce married you! Got a good head on you, gel. Can't inherit the title. Royce is nearly as wealthy as Croesus, don't need money. Think it an excellent idea."

"Oh, do you!" Royce said with wrathful amusement, laughter dancing in the depths of his golden eyes. Preoccupied though he had been by Morgana's remoteness, he had been thinking along the same lines. Deliberately interjecting a lighter note into the proceedings, a mocking smile curving his mouth, he murmured teasingly, "You know, George, while I agree with most of what you have said, I do think you should at least let me decide if I want to whistle my wife's fortune down the wind that way."

Morgana froze, Royce's careless words confirming her worst fears. It *had* been her fortune that he wanted! Tautly she said, "I want Julian to have everything!"

At the odd note in her voice, Royce looked at her thoughtfully. Not liking the wild expression in her eyes, he said quietly, "Very well, my dear, but I think for the time being, we should all simply agree that today's events go no farther than ourselves. We can decide how to dispose of your mother's money at a later date."

"What about Stephen Devlin?" Zachary asked suddenly. "He is not likely to sit mutely by and let you strip him of everything."

Royce's face hardened. "I think that when he is confronted with the news that we have proof of what he did to Morgana, he will be quite amenable to whatever we decide. He's admitted to Julian that he arranged for Andrew's death, but I doubt if we can find proof of that, and distasteful though it may be, our wisest course may be to let sleeping dogs lie." He glanced over at Julian, who appeared positively stupefied at this latest unexpected turn of events, and said slowly, "If I understood the facts correctly, St. Audries Hall itself was part of the entail, and so we could not take it from him anyway—even though some of Hester's fortune was used to maintain it. Am I correct?" Dazedly Julian nodded. Smiling gently at him, Royce said lightly, "I see no reason, however, why Stephen and Lucinda should be allowed to live so richly on money that they have no right to, indeed, money that they bought with blood!" A frown marred his forehead. "Unfortunately," he added, "unless we are willing for the truth to come out, there is no way that we can have Stephen and Lucinda punished for either Stephen's part in Andrew's death or for what they both did to Morgana."

Never taking her eyes off of him, Morgana asked intently, "But what do you suggest we do? I do not want either one of them to profit any more than they have from their despicable acts." Her little face suddenly contorted with the violence of her emotions. "May God forgive me, but I wish them *dead!*"

Thinking it best to ignore her outburst, Royce commented smoothly, "Since Stephen will not be in any position to argue with us, I think he will agree to immediately turn over St. Audries Hall and all of its lands, as well as control of what remains of Hester's fortune, to Julian. For this, he and Lucinda will be allowed to live in the dower house on the small stipend that Julian will settle on them."

George nodded his head sagely. "Fairer than they deserve. Like to see 'em both hang!"

There was an embarrassed little silence, all carefully averting their gazes from Julian's face. They all might agree that Stephen and Lucinda deserved to hang, but they were also very conscious of the fact that Lucinda, unfortunately, as George muttered under his breath to Royce, *was* Julian's mother!

The next morning, when they returned to Lime Tree Cottage, to be greeted with the stunning news of the deaths of Stephen and Lucinda, Morgana was very glad of the decisions that had been made the previous night. The unexpected deaths of the Earl and his wife had very nearly shattered Julian, and she didn't like to think what he might have done if he had not known that he did not have to face the humiliation of the world knowing the dastardly acts committed by Stephen and Lucinda.

Their deaths created a painful dilemma for Julian and Morgana, but they finally agreed that in keeping with the decision not to reveal the truth, Stephen and Lucinda would have to be buried in the Devlin family cemetery. But *not,* Morgana had stated vehemently, anywhere near her parents! It revolted her to even think of them sharing the same soil, and consequently the seventh Earl of St. Audries and his Countess had been buried in the farthest corner of the cemetery, with only a small, plain marker to designate the remote spot.

Even now, over a fortnight since they had been buried, Morgana could not bring herself to look in the direction of the still bare earth that marked their graves. She had not mourned their deaths; to her shame, she had experienced again the same fierce satisfaction that had flooded through her when she had stared down at the body of the one-eyed man. They had deserved to die!

Sighing, she deliberately dragged her thoughts away from that fruitless direction and plucked a blade of grass. Such a lot had happened these past weeks. The hurried, immediate removal to St. Audries Hall. The funeral. Ben's release from Newgate. The departure of Ben, Jack, and Zachary for America on the very day of Ben's release.

It had been decided that Jack and Ben would stay with Zachary at his plantation near Baton Rouge until Royce and she joined them in the fall, when they would make further plans about their future. . . . But what about *my* future? she nearly wailed aloud. Everyone else was more than satisfied with the way things had turned out—her brothers were safely in America, hovering on the threshold of a new life; Julian was the Earl of St. Audries, his home and fortune secure; and Royce . . .

What *was* Royce thinking and feeling these days? she wondered miserably. She knew she was partially to blame for the chasm between them, her suspicion of his motives making her stiff and wary around him. But he, too, had changed over these past weeks—gone was the teasing, arrogant lover, the man who had captured her heart, and in his place, there was this unfailingly polite creature who quietly anticipated her wishes and silently watched her every move. With the lover, she might have been able to voice the fears in her heart, but this . . . this *stranger* that Royce had become made it impossible for her to reveal the uncertainties that racked her.

Reluctantly she admitted that he didn't act like a man who had married to gain wealth—not by so much as a look had he indicated that her total rejection of her rightful place and fortune had bothered him. If anything, she thought almost angrily, he had seemed inordinately pleased by her decision, and certainly no one could have asked for a kinder, more considerate husband than Royce. Look at all he had done for her and Ben and Jack. He had showered her with gifts and had risked his life to save her from the one-eyed man. It had even been his suggestion that they delay their departure from England rather than sailing with the others, so that she could become better acquainted with Julian.

Guilt smote her, and the terrible suspicion that she had misjudged him, which had occurred uncomfortably to her more than once these past weeks, suddenly flitted through her mind. She moved uneasily. Could he have really meant all those sweet words that he had poured into her ear? But if he had meant them, why was he acting so aloof? she asked herself despairingly. A blush stained her cheeks. He hadn't even visited her bed. Was that the act of a man in love?

As if her thoughts had conjured him up, she spied Royce's tall form walking toward her, and her heart raced in her chest. He looked heartbreakingly handsome as he came nearer, the breeze attractively riffling the tawny hair, his elegant coat and breeches revealing the splendid body they clothed. He carried a rolled-up piece of paper in his hand, and walking up to her, he said lightly, "I've been looking for you and I thought that I might find you here. May I join you?"

Almost shyly she nodded, and he promptly joined her on the ground, lounging negligently at her feet, one hand propping up his head as he lay on his side. There was a curious expression in the golden eyes, and as he stared at her, Morgana became increasingly nervous. Rushing into speech, she stammered, "D-D-Did you want t-t-to see me about anything s-s-special?"

He regarded her for a long, tension-mounting moment and then said quietly, "As a matter of fact, yes. Julian and I have worked out a settlement for you that we both believe is fair."

"A-A-A settlem-m-ment?" she asked stupidly. "What do you mean?"

Royce smiled wryly. "Your brother is a very honorable young man—his conscience has been bedeviling him and he has been having difficulty simply accepting your generous renunciation." He sent her a level look and continued carefully, "I've explained to him that I am a very rich man and that you will never want for anything, but that did not seem to satisfy him, and after some discussion, we compromised."

Her eyes locked painfully on his face, in a small voice she asked, "What sort of compromise?"

Silently he handed her the paper he had brought with him. He gave her a moment to unroll it, and then in that same careful tone he said, "A woman should have some sort of independence from her husband—especially in a case like ours." At her confused expression, he added dryly, "I am very rich— and since you have given away what is rightfully yours . . . you have nothing." Something flickered in the golden eyes, and his voice hardened. "I would not like to think that you suffer my presence because the alternative is being penniless and forced to go back to your old way of life. . . . To prevent that, Julian and I have decided that he shall settle a sum of money on you—money that you will be able to call your own, money that would enable you to live apart from me if that is your desire."

Astonishment held her motionless—she might have doubts about his motives, but she loved him passionately, and the notion of leaving him, of not being able to see him every day, had never occurred to her. *She loved him!* She would never leave him . . . but perhaps he wanted her to leave him? Dazedly her gaze dropped to the paper he had handed her and she quickly scanned it. Her face white, she lifted her head, and looking miserably at him, she stammered, "T-T-Ten th-th-thousand pounds a year! It is too much! I cannot accept it!"

Royce's mouth tightened. "Don't be a little fool! Compared to the whole of your mother's fortune, what Julian is giving you is a paltry sum! Take it!"

A bitter laugh shook her, any lingering hope that she had misjudged him shattered. A gust of anger swept through her, and throwing the paper in his face, she leaped to her feet. "Is that why you married me?" she demanded half-hysterically, half-furiously. "To get your hands on my mother's money?"

The expression on his face frightened her, and as he surged upright, instinctively she took a step backward. His hands caught her shoulders and he shook her impatiently. "You little fool!" he snarled. "Is that why you have been acting as skittish as a cat with kittens lately? Because you think I *knew?* And married you with my eye on Hester's fortune?" Almost with revulsion, he thrust her away from him. Keeping his hands tightly clenched at his sides, as if he did not trust himself not to do her a violence, he swore vehemently. "Good God! How wrong could I have been?" Shooting her a glance filled with dislike, he snapped, "And to think that I have been handling you with kid gloves because I didn't want to rush you into making decisions that weren't really what you wanted!" Advancing menacingly on her, the glitter in the golden eyes making her tremble, he snarled softly, "Well, the hell with *that!*"

Jerking her into his arms, he kissed her ravenously, like a man with a great hunger to assuage, and it was only when he felt her arms steal around his neck and her lips part for him that his mouth gentled. Clasping her to him, he rained half-tender, half-violent kisses on her mouth and throat, muttering fiercely, "You aggravating little baggage! How *dare* you think me a fortune hunter! I'm in love with you, you silly wench! I've been in love with you since that morning I came downstairs and found you gambling in the kitchen with Zachary and his friends." Tearing his caressing mouth from the base of her throat, he pushed her away slightly and shook her soundly. *"I love you!* And it was because I love you that I married you!" He kissed her again, almost savagely, and added thickly, "I know I rushed you into marriage and I've been trying these past weeks to give you time to think things through . . . to let you decide, now that you know your past, what you want to do. But I'm sorry, sweetheart, I'm afraid that as far as you are concerned, all my noble intentions have vanished—I love you too much to ever let you go!" His expression softened at the stunned look in her eyes. "Didn't you ever guess? Do you think that a man in my position acts as I did if he is not under some powerful compulsion?" His gaze darkened. "I have never been so fearful as I was when I realized that the one-eyed man had you—Morgana, I thought I would die of terror until I held you in my arms again!" He shook her again. "You *must* believe me!"

It was the culmination of every sweet dream, and her heart beating with thick, painful strokes, she stared at him almost fearfully, hardly daring to think that he could truly love her. Steadily he returned her stare, the warm glints in those topaz eyes telling her the most wondrous things imaginable. Bitter remorse fought with wild ecstasy as she gazed up at those beloved features, and suddenly she *did* believe! Oh, dear God, she had wronged him frightfully! But he *loved* her!

Trying to excuse herself, she wailed helplessly, "But you could have married anyone! Yet you chose me—a penniless thief with no pretensions to family or fortune—and when it came out that I was really the Lady Morgana Devlin, what else could I think?"

Catching her up in a violent embrace, he kissed her passionately, and Morgana responded ardently, her slender frame straining against him. Blissful moments later, he put her from him and said huskily, "You could have thought the truth—that I took one look at the sweetest little face I have ever seen and fell violently in love with you!"

"Oh, Royce!" she breathed ecstatically, a dazzling smile on her lovely face. "I love you, too!"

"And I should hope so!" he retorted with brutal candor, a mocking light in the dancing golden eyes. "After all that I have gone through to get you! You have cost me a fortune!

Loving me until the day I die is the least that I shall expect from you!"

"Oh, I will! I will!" she cried earnestly, and happily kissed his chin and jaw. "Till then and beyond!"

Her black curly head resting under his chin, their arms around each other, they stood there together for a long time, speaking the words that all lovers yearn to hear and cherish forever. It wasn't until they were gathering up her things, preparing to walk back to the house, that Julian's settlement came up again.

"Did you really mean what you said about wanting me to have this? So I will be independent of you?" she asked uncertainly.

He sent her a look. "Not too independent, I trust!" he teased gently. Tipping her face upward, he dropped a kiss on her nose and then said more seriously, "Julian is a young man with a great deal of pride. He very nearly lost everything that he had believed was his, and it is only through your generosity that he was able to retain it. There is nothing that you cannot ask of him that he will not do, but for *his* sake, take this money—it may mean little to you, but to him, it is of paramount importance."

An arrested expression on her features, she slowly nodded. "I hadn't thought of it that way."

Arm in arm, instinctively they strolled over to her parents' grave, the slowly fading sunlight gilding the weeping angels who stood with their wings outstretched over the graves. Reverently Morgana traced in the cool marble the dates of Andrew's and Hester's deaths. A tear trembled on her lashes. "They had such a short time together. . . ."

"But they had love, my dear, as we do," Royce said gently. Watching her face intently, he asked quietly, "Will you mind leaving all this? America is very different. We have no titles there."

Her eyes shimmering beneath their veil of tears, she shook her head. "I only want to be your wife," she replied simply, which earned her a very satisfying kiss from her husband. Honesty, however, compelled her to add, "If I had grown up here as Julian did, I might feel a pang at leaving, but St. Audries Hall, beautiful as it is, has no meaning to me." She glanced down at her mother's Bible, which she carried in her hand. "This . . . this means everything to me—it was hers, and I will cherish it forever!"

An odd look in his eyes, Royce asked quietly, "And the letter? What do you intend to do with it?"

She searched his face intently. Very slowly she asked, "Are you quite, quite certain that you are happy with the way things are? That you are not sorry that I did not claim Hester's fortune?"

"Quite certain!" Royce growled, and dragged her into his arms to kiss her nearly witless. When at last he raised his lips from her love-swollen mouth, he muttered fiercely, "You are all the fortune I will ever want!"

A blinding happiness transformed her face, and stepping a little away from him, she handed him the Bible and extracted her mother's letter. Holding it between her hands, she said mournfully, "I would like to keep it—next to her Bible, it is the only thing of hers that I have—but as long as it exists, there is the danger that someday the truth would come out . . . and Julian and whatever family he may have would be devastated by it—perhaps not in our lifetime, but who knows what the future may hold?"

Gently Royce said, "I'd hoped that you would feel that way, but I didn't want to ask it of you."

She nodded and, smiling through her tears, tore the letter into tiny pieces. With Royce's arm around her shoulders, they watched as the breeze scattered the fluttering pieces in all directions. It was done. Hester's letter had served its purpose. Perhaps not quite the way Hester had wanted, but in the only way that Morgana could see would do the least harm to the innocent. The one-eyed man was dead. Stephen and Lucinda were dead. Andrew's son, Julian, was the new Earl, and as for her . . .

She glanced at Royce, and at the look of love he sent her, her heart soared. They would be leaving the Old World, sailing soon to the New World, where the love they shared would only grow brighter and stronger with every passing day, and with a joyful little laugh, she kissed Royce's chin and was instantly enfolded in his powerful embrace. They started to walk away when something made her look back at her parents' grave and her breath caught sharply in her throat. It was a trick of light, she told herself softly, a trick of light that for one fleeting instant made the angel on her mother's grave appear to be smiling. . . .

If you enjoyed WHISPER TO ME OF LOVE,
don't miss Shirlee Busbee's

PASSION BECOMES HER

Available for the first time
as a Zebra mass-market paperback,
on sale in June 2012.

From his place of concealment near the Marquis of Ormsby's palatial London town house in Grosvenor Square, Asher Cordell watched the comings and goings of the multitude of handsome carriages that thronged the road in front of the brilliantly lit house. Any member of the ton still in town at the end of June, and fortunate enough to receive an invitation to Lord Ormsby's annual masked ball, was here tonight. Instituted over two decades ago, in time the Ormsby Masked Ball had come to signal the end of the Season, and after tonight most of the gentry would scatter far and wide across the breadth of England to spend the remainder of the summer at their country estates.

By London standards the hour was still early, approaching midnight, and Asher decided that he had wasted enough time determining that everything was going precisely as it should. Tonight's task wasn't difficult. It was a simple robbery—child's play for him. He'd already done two dry runs and could, he felt confident, find his way over the rear wall, through the spacious gardens, and into Lord Ormsby's library blindfolded. The previous evening, during the final practice run, standing in the middle of Ormsby's darkened library, he'd fleetingly considered stealing the famous Ormsby diamond necklace then and there, but decided against it. Changing plans on whim, he'd discovered, could cause fatal complications.

In the shadows of his hiding place, Asher grimaced. Christ. Could it ever! Last spring's events at Sherbrook Hall had certainly proven that fact and he wondered if the outcome would have been different if he'd held to his original plan. He sighed. Probably not. Collard had been up to no good and there was no telling how it would have ended. Bad enough that Collard had murdered that unpleasant wretch Whitley.

Bad enough that he'd shot and killed Collard, even if it had been to save his own neck.

He shook off the memory and concentrated on the task before him. This would be his last theft, he reminded himself; the last time he took such risks. After tonight, he would retire to Kent and spend his days overseeing his own holdings, becoming finally the respectable, wealthy gentleman farmer everyone already thought he was.

Eager to put the past behind him, he was on the point of slipping around to the back of the house when he recognized the latest vehicle to halt before Lord Ormsby's doors. The coach was not in the first stare of fashion and was pulled by four rather unimpressive bay horses, but the moment the vehicle lumbered into position, as if royalty had arrived, the milling contingent of meticulously groomed gentlemen lingering on the steps leaped to attention.

Asher grinned. Who would have ever guessed that eighteen-year-old Thalia Kirkwood would take London by storm? Odes, poems praising her fair beauty were forever being written about her these past few months. Thanks to her, flower stalls all across London did a bustling business, the scented, colorful blossoms purchased by eager swains finding their way to the modest house just off Cavendish Square that her father, the retiring Mr. Kirkwood, had taken for the Season. It was rumored that at least one duel had been fought over the fair Thalia and gossip claimed that since May her father had turned down offers from at least a half dozen lovesick, imminently suitable gentlemen—a few with the prospect of a title in the offing. To the dismay and long faces of many young bucks tonight, the current betting in the gentlemen's clubs was that before the family returned to Kent at the end of the week, Thalia's engagement to the Earl of Caswell would be announced.

It might be a masked ball, but there was little effort at disguise and there was no mistaking Thalia's tall, voluptuous form as she regally mounted the steps to the house, the upswept silvery fair hair gleaming in the torchlight. Her velvet cloak was sapphire blue, a perfect foil for her blond beauty, the color deepening, he knew, the icy blue of her brilliant eyes. The gentlemen swarmed around her, like bees to a fragrant bud, the servants bowing and scraping as they opened the heavy front doors.

Almost lost in the pandemonium surrounding Thalia's progress was the descent from the coach of her widowed older sister, Juliana. Though her husband had been dead for four years, it still gave Asher a start to think of Juliana as a widow. His lips twitched as he watched her gather up the folds of her pale green gown. He'd always considered her, at twenty-eight, only five years younger than himself, in much the same light as he did his two younger sisters, and thinking of Juliana even being *married* had been a challenge for him. He shook his head. Damn shame her husband, the younger son of a baronet with extensive lands in Hampshire, had died of lung congestion only three years into the marriage. There had been no children, but Juliana had been well provided for and shortly after her husband's death she had purchased a charming estate not five miles down the road from the home she had grown up in. With their mother long dead, upon Juliana's return to Kent, she had fallen back into her previous role of surrogate mother to Thalia. Since Mr. Kirkwood abhorred the constant round of soirees and balls so necessary for a young lady's successful Season, Juliana stepped into the role of chaperone for her younger sister's London Season. The notion of Juliana being anyone's chaperone was pure folly as far as Asher was concerned, recalling some of her youthful escapades. He decided that if anyone needed a chaperone, it was the elder sister, not the youngest.

Eyes narrowed, he watched as Juliana, a pair of elegant gentlemen on either side of her, followed her sister up the steps. Her cloak was in a soft shade of lavender and, as tall as Thalia, she carried herself with much the same grace as her younger sister. There was a glimpse of sable hair as Juliana passed by the torches on either side of the door and then she was gone.

Annoyed for allowing Thalia and Juliana's arrival to distract him, Asher shook himself and focused on the task at hand. After a last look around the area, he worked his way to the alley that ran behind the handsome homes that faced the square. His dark clothing making him nearly invisible, like a shadow he flowed along the wall at the rear of the houses. Arriving at the section of the wall he wanted, he made a careful survey and, seeing nothing to alarm him, he swung up and over the stone wall and silently dropped down onto the other side. Several feet beyond the place where he stood was the tradesmen and servants' entrance to the house and in the faint light of the small flickering torch above the doorway, he saw that the area was deserted.

Excellent, he thought, as he did a slow scan of the grounds. It was unlikely there would be any trysts by the staff tonight—from past experience he knew that every servant, even those hired just for tonight, would be far too busy seeing to the needs of the aristocratic guests to have any time for dallying.

He easily found the doors to the library and within two minutes of having breached the rear walls was standing inside Lord Ormsby's library. He stood motionless a moment, his gaze moving slowly around the room. A faint sliver of light showing beneath the door that opened onto one of the hallways of the interior of the house broke the utter blackness. Dark shapes loomed up here and there but, already familiar with the layout, he quickly crossed the room to where Ormsby's ornate desk sat in front of a pair of long windows.

He'd discovered Ormsby's hiding place the first night he'd broken into the house, although "broken in" and didn't quite describe simply pushing open the door to the library and strolling inside. He'd also learned during his observations of the routine of the Ormsby household, except for the front door and the gates at the rear of the building, that there was nothing to halt anyone with thievery in mind. The house was a sitting goose, ripe for plucking. He grinned. Which made his job so much easier. Sliding out the bottom drawer on the right side of the desk, his skillful fingers made short work of finding and opening the secret drawer. Something resembling a sneer crossed his lean features. Did Ormsby really think that a clever thief wouldn't discover the drawer and its contents?

Asher needed no light to find the famed Ormsby diamond necklace; the size of the diamonds and the heavy weight of the necklace told him the minute he touched it. He'd never actually seen the real necklace; in fact, except for the occasions the current marquis had shown it off to his various acquaintances, it had not been seen in public for nearly fifty years, not since Ormsby's mother had died. But Asher had once seen the necklace in the portrait of Lady Mary, wife of the first Marquis of Ormsby, which hung in the grand gallery at Ormsby Place.

Though he'd made note of the necklace—after all, it was rather famous—he hadn't thought to steal it . . . at the time. Like a dutiful guest he had studied the painting, his keen eye making note of the size and brilliance of the stones even in a mere portrait. No, he hadn't thought to steal it then and he wouldn't be here tonight taking it from the secret drawer and carefully slipping it into the specially sewn pocket of his jacket, if Ormsby hadn't . . .

His mouth tightened. He didn't as a rule steal from people he knew, nor was he inclined to hold grudges, especially against neighbors, even vain, arrogant, obnoxious neighbors, but in Ormsby's case he was willing to make an exception. Bastard shouldn't have shot my grandmother's favorite old dog, he thought grimly.

Petty to steal a priceless family heirloom because of the death of a dog? Asher shrugged. Perhaps. But it would be a long time before he forgot his grandmother's grief-stricken features when the body of her elderly spaniel, her companion and friend of many years, was dumped at her feet by one of the Ormsby grooms.

With all the arrogance of his master, the groom had said, "Milord sends his apologies. He saw the beast on the road and thinking it was the dog that has been killing the hens lately, shot him before he realized it was your old Captain."

Standing beside his grandmother, Asher's hands had clenched into fists and he fought back the urge to seek out and throttle Lord Ormsby for his cruelty to an old woman. In his heart he knew that the killing of Captain had been deliberate—not two days previously, to the marquis's open fury, his grandmother had turned down Ormsby's latest offer to buy several hundred acres of her land that adjoined his estate. Ormsby had simply killed the dog in petty retaliation. Another example, Asher thought tightly, of Ormsby striking out when displeased and to those weaker than himself.

When the groom rode away, Asher had helped his grandmother into the house. He had then quietly made arrangements for Captain to be buried near her favorite rosebush, a place the old woman and the old dog often sat for hours enjoying the garden and the soft play of light over the trees and shrubs. Watching the dirt fall into the dog's grave, he swore that Ormsby would pay *something* for his grandmother's sorrow. The great lord of the district wasn't going to walk away unscathed this time.

It had taken Asher a while to come up with an appropriate plan to ensure that Ormsby felt, perhaps for the first time in his arrogant life, the pain of loss that he often inflicted upon the common folk of the neighborhood. Killing him was out of the question—even Asher wasn't prepared to kill a man over a dog and an old woman's grief—but there had to be a way to pierce that smug composure. . . . He smiled in the darkness. The idea, when it came to him, had been perfect: Ormsby loved nothing more than himself and his possessions, so what better way to make him suffer, than to steal his most famous possession, the Ormsby diamond necklace?

What the devil he was going to do with the damned thing now that it rested in his pocket escaped him. He didn't need the money and selling it was out of the question. The necklace was too famous and the hue and cry once its theft was discovered would make it unlikely that any of his usual contacts would touch it. He could break it up into individual diamonds and have those reset if the whim took him, but he balked at the idea of such wanton destruction. If the portrait was anything to go by, it was a beautiful and uniquely designed piece of jewelry and he had an inherent dislike of destroying something so lovely. His lips twisted. Unless he wished to have his neck stretched on the gallows or face deportation to some godforsaken continent on the other side of the world, he'd have to hide the necklace somewhere it would never be discovered.

Asher slid the drawer shut. He'd bury the bloody thing in the ground if need be and plant a rosebush over it; for him it was enough to know that Ormsby's pride would have suffered a grievous wound. Bastard. Shouldn't have shot my grandmother's dog.

The opening of the door rooted him to the spot. He caught the merest glimpse of a woman's form in the light from the hallway before she shut the door behind her.

Without a moment's hesitation, he took a half dozen quick steps backward and melted into the heavy velvet folds of the drapes that hung at the sides of one of the long windows of the library. His back pressed hard against the wall next to the window where the drapes were gathered, he reached for the small pistol he carried inside his vest, but decided against it and his hand fell by his side. Escaping unseen was his plan and that didn't include firing his pistol; using the pistol would be his last resort. His thoughts scrambling, he listened intently as the female intruder walked swiftly in his direction. Had she seen him? No. He'd been too careful and he knew that no one had seen him slipping into the library. When she opened the door? No. He'd been on the other side of the room, concealed in the darkness well beyond the brief flash of light that had heralded her entrance; she could not have seen him. So why was she here? There was something furtive about her movements and he noted the fact that she had made no attempt to light a candle. What was she up to? Something occurred to him and he closed his eyes in a silent prayer. Please. Not a lovers' rendezvous.

A moment later, there was a faint ray of light beneath the curtains and, peeking through the drapes, Asher saw that his intruder had lit a tiny candle. Her back was to him and he stared bemused as she hurriedly explored the desk, obviously looking for something. He leaned his head back against the wall. Someone else thinking to steal the Ormsby necklace?

Intrigued, Asher watched as she hastily fumbled through first one drawer, then another. Under other circumstances he might have been amused at the situation, but with the Ormsby necklace burning like a fire red brand against his thigh, he rather wished that if she wanted the blasted necklace, she'd beaten him to it. For a second he wondered what would happen if he stepped from the drapes and gifted her with the necklace. Except as a way to inflict some humility in Ormsby, the necklace meant nothing to him. He considered the idea. No. The silly wench would probably scream at the sight of him and all hell would break loose.

Resigned to waiting for the woman to leave, he had just leaned his head back against the windowpane, when he heard her gasp. He jerked forward to see the cause of her alarm. The door was opening again.

As he had done, she flitted backward to hide amongst the drapes. Instinct more than design had Asher catching her around the waist and pulling her snugly against him at the same instant his other hand clamped over her mouth. Into her ear he hissed, "I mean you no harm—and for God's sake, don't scream or struggle."

The slight form in his arms stiffened and a curt nod was his answer, but Asher kept his arm locked tightly around her and his hand firmly over her mouth. Women were simply too damned unpredictable.

The latest arrival stood for a long moment in the doorway, the light from the large candelabrum he carried flooding the room with a soft glow.

"Hiding, my dear?" drawled the new arrival. When only silence met his words, he added impatiently, "Come now, I know that you are here. Did you really think that I wouldn't see you slip away? That I wasn't expecting you to try something?"

Asher's teeth ground together at the first sound of that rich, mellow voice. *Ormsby!* Bloody hell! If Ormsby discovered him here in the library, he'd have to shoot the bastard, after all. As for the woman . . . Christ! Could this last, simple job get any more complicated?

Loosening his grip on the woman's waist and praying that she wasn't going to cause him trouble the moment he removed his arm, he started again to reach for his pistol. The sound of another male voice froze his actions.

"Ormsby! I say, old fellow, what are you doing wandering around back here? Aren't you supposed to be dancing with the fair Thalia soon?"

Asher nearly groaned aloud. Killing Ormsby was one thing, but a second man as well? His only choice was the tall window behind him and he hoped to God that he sustained no real injury from leaping through it. But if he survived the window and if he could reach the back wall and disappear into the darkness . . . A faint, reckless grin flashed across his face. He might salvage tonight after all.

"Ah, thank you, Kingsley," drawled Ormsby, "for reminding me. I forgot."

"Forgot!" exclaimed Kingsley. "Forget a dance with the loveliest chit to grace London in decades? My dear man, you alarm me."

His voice bored, Ormsby replied, "I think you forget that I have watched her grow up. Remember if you will that the Kirkwoods are my neighbors. I am well acquainted with the family."

"That reminds me of something, been meaning to ask you for weeks—how the deuce could you let such a pretty piece slip through your fingers? I would have thought you'd have sewn her up before she ever stepped foot in London." Kingsley chuckled. "Losing your touch, old fellow? Her engagement to young Caswell will be announced any day now."

"Really? I wouldn't place my final wager just yet, if I were you."

"You know something the rest of us don't?"

"There is, my friend, if you will recall, many a slip between the cup and the lip. Miss Kirkwood is not yet Caswell's bride."

"You mean to snatch her out from underneath his nose?" Kingsley gasped. "The gossip says that it is a love match— even someone of your wealth and title can't compete with love. So how do you propose to change the tide?"

Ormsby laughed, although there was little humor in it. "I play my cards close to my vest but I would warn you not to buy a betrothal gift for the pair just yet," he said. "Now come along, let us rejoin my guests. I have left them too long."

Asher watched as the light retreated and Ormsby ushered Kingsley toward the door. But Kingsley seemed in no hurry. "But why did you leave in the first place? Ain't like you to wander off."

An ugly edge to his voice, Ormsby said, "I had my reasons. Believe me I had my reasons."

"Yes, but—"

The door shut and from inside the library there was only the faint murmur of voices as the two men moved down the hall.

Deciding not to wait around to see who else would pay the library a visit, the door had hardly shut before Asher shoved the young woman out from behind the drapes and began urging her toward the French doors that opened onto the gardens. He didn't have a precise plan; his one thought was to escape the grounds as fast as he could. The woman was a problem. He couldn't just let her go. Or could he?

He considered the idea. She'd certainly been quiet as a rock while Ormsby had been in the library. Clearly she hadn't wanted to be discovered either. He didn't know her reasons for sneaking into the library or for going through Ormsby's papers, but he knew one thing: she'd been up to no good. And if she'd been up to no good, then she had ample reason not to raise the alarm. Dare he risk it?

His hand still over her mouth and gripping her arm firmly, he pulled her outside. Pushing her ahead of him, they walked through the gardens, Asher not stopping until the back wall loomed up before them and the faint light from the torch over the servants' entrance pierced the darkness. He still hadn't made up his mind what to do, but taking everything into account, especially the fact that she had made no attempt to escape from him, it was possible that she might actually keep her mouth shut and not raise the alarm.

He glanced at the wall, still considering. Even if she screamed, he'd be up, over and away before anyone reached this deserted part of the grounds.

His lips pressed against her ear, he asked, "If I let you go, do you swear not to scream?"

She nodded vigorously and against his better judgment, he removed his hand. The moment his hand dropped, she spun around to face him and breathed, *"Asher?"*

His heart stopped. Christ! *Juliana.*

Hands on her hips, she demanded, "Asher Cordell, what were you doing in Lord Ormsby's library? I nearly died when you grabbed me."

"I think the question should be," he said quickly, "what were *you* doing there?"

"That is none of your business!" she answered sharply. "I am an invited guest to Lord Ormsby's home—you are not."

"And how do you know that? I am quite respectable—Eton, respectable family and all that. He could have invited me."

Juliana snorted. "Don't try to bamboozle me! He can't abide you and you know it."

"I know," Asher said mournfully. "His dislike is a terrible

burden for me." He looked hopeful. "Do you think there is something I could do to make him think better of me?"

She strangled back a laugh. "No! At this late stage there is nothing you could do to change his mind," she said bluntly. Shaking an admonishing finger at him, she added, "Perhaps if you hadn't turned the pigs loose in his newly planted field or hadn't stolen his best bull and put the animal with Squire Ripley's heifers he wouldn't think you so ripe for the gallows." She sent him a severe glance. "And we won't even talk about the disgraceful way you act around him. Asher, you actually yawned in his face at the Woodruffs' ball in January! What were you thinking?"

"That he's a bore?" When she narrowed her eyes at him, he added hastily, "Juliana, I was thirteen when I turned the pigs loose, and you know it was an accident—how could I know the gate would shatter when that old sow charged it?"

She sniffed.

"And I wasn't much older when the incident with the bull occurred." He grinned reminiscently. Juliana merely stared at him. "All right, I confess," he said, "I was a holy terror but you must admit that squire's calves the next year were some of the finest raised in the district."

"The squire may think you a fine fellow, but that act certainly did not endear you to Ormsby in the least," she muttered. Puzzled, she studied him in the dim light. "Why do you go out of your way to annoy him?"

Asher shrugged. "Mayhap if he showed a little consideration of others I wouldn't be so inclined to treat him so, ah, impolitely." The necklace searing his thigh, very aware of the passing time and the chance of discovery, he added, "And enjoyable though this little interlude has been, don't you think you ought to rejoin the guests?"

"After you tell me what you were doing skulking about in Ormsby's library," she said firmly.

Despite the tension coiling in his body, Asher leaned negligently against a small tree near the wall. Smiling at her, he said, "Of course. Right after you tell me why you were there."

She threw him a fulminating look. "You are the most infuriating, insufferable creature I have ever known in my life!"

He straightened up from his languid pose and bowed deeply before her. Smiling impudently at her, he murmured, "One does so try to please."

Her bosom swelled with indignation. "I've a good mind to tell Ormsby that you were in his library!" she threatened, knowing full well she'd face wild lions before she'd betray Asher—even if he was the most insolent and maddening man she'd ever met.

Amusement fled and an expression she had never seen before flashed in his eyes. In all the years she had known him, which had been nearly all her life, Asher had charmed her, shocked her, irritated her and infuriated her beyond reason but he'd never made her feel frightened before. Unconsciously she stepped backward and nervously measured the distance to the house.

Cursing himself, Asher wiped his expression clear of all sign of the violence that he feared had become an integral part of him. Forcing a smile, he flicked a gentle finger along her cheek. "Let us cry *pax,* Juliana, and go our separate ways and keep our secrets. Agreed?"

He didn't like it that she flinched when he touched her, but he kept the same easy smile on his lips and resumed his casual pose against the tree while he waited for her answer.

In the shadowy light, she sent him a searching look, then nodded. Without another word, she turned on her heels and marched back to the library's French doors.

Asher followed a few steps behind her. As she stepped into the library she glanced back at him. Her thoughts jumbled, she tried to think of something to say, but nothing came to mind.

She almost jumped out of her skin when he touched her on the shoulder. "Run along," he said softly. "I'll wait here until I know you're in the hallway."

Annoyed, but unable to think of anything else to do, Juliana did just that. Cautiously opening the door to the main hallway, she peeked out and, seeing it deserted, stepped quickly into the hall. Shutting the library door behind her, she hurried toward the ballroom.

Asher waited until he was certain she wasn't coming back and then walked across the room. At the desk, it took him only a moment to find and reopen the secret drawer and replace the Ormsby necklace. It was a bitter moment. He'd planned this for weeks and now it was all for naught. But he had no choice—Juliana knew he had been here and when the outcry, and there would surely be one, over the theft of the necklace arose, she would know that he had stolen it. Easing into the garden, he grimaced. And she was such an honest little thing, most likely she'd feel honor bound to tell Ormsby of his presence in the library or nag him to death until he returned the thing. Easier to return it now and wait for a better time.

Despite the outcome, Asher was lighthearted as he scaled the back wall and disappeared into the darkness. He was a great planner. And there would be another opportunity.

Arriving at his rooms near Fitzroy Square, he began to pack. He'd come to town this time without a valet and had traveled light. All of his belongings fit into the one valise and, buckling it shut, he looked around to see if he'd forgotten anything. He hadn't.

Tomorrow would find him riding back to Kent and the people he held dear. He'd had some reservations that he could settle down to the uneventful life of a gentleman farmer, but tonight's events insured that there would still be a little excitement to be gleaned. The Ormsby necklace was still out there and sooner or later he'd find a way to snatch it right from under Ormsby's nose. And Juliana . . . what the devil had she been searching for? He grinned. Finding out her secret might make life very interesting indeed. . . .